I0731927

Silver and the Stone

An Epic Tale of War, Betrayal, and Redemption

The Stonemaster Series Omnibus

by

Gene Herington

Cover art by Phil Dannels

Map by Josiah Yarbrough

Thank you, Lina, for all of your support.

Table of Contents

Refuge Ending	1
The Stonemaster Ascendant	37
The Gambit	115
The War for the Shield	229

THE EMERALD REFUGE
THE SHIELD
OF
ATHESIENE
TARSUN'S MARKET
THE SPEAKING
BOULDER

Refuge Ending

Pencheval listened to the scout tell of what he had seen and almost sighed. Of course his latest contract had left him with goblins. Anything less would have been too much like luck.

He already knew he would find trouble of the kind that would convince Knight Superior Rennoute to hire a Silver Lion mercenary such as himself. The knight meant to know what had befallen a patrol that had not returned from the far side of his sizeable valley, the Emerald Refuge, and he wasn't expecting a herd of sheep. One did not pay a hundred gold crowns otherwise, especially to someone that annoyed knights as much as Silver Lion adepts. Yet Pencheval had been Rennoute's only option aside from sending the patrol alone, as a problem with the draft-horse sized dragons everyone knew as drakes elsewhere in the valley left him with no knights to spare.

The mercenary had taken the job quite eagerly. He had come to this little corner of the kingdom to avoid any trouble and avail himself of the Emerald Refuge's famed serenity, but after a fortnight, serenity had become dull and left him pacing. A job was just the thing to take his mind away from the boredom caused by trying to take his mind away from his troubles, but he wished it had not been one with goblins.

Pencheval's first thought upon receiving the contract was that banditry was involved but he dismissed the notion. True, bandits laying low would cause a patrol to disappear so they could remain hidden, but they avoided this place as they would a plague. The Emerald Refuge was a sanctuary for the Temple of Athesiene, and it produced wine, bread, and prayers. There was too little to steal for too much risk, as running afoul of Athesiene's famously lethal knights was far too certain a death.

Trolls raiding livestock from the mountains or drakes hunting the same were also more than capable of killing an entire patrol, but doing so hardly fit what Pencheval knew about them. Trolls would only have killed what they meant to eat and cared little for any attack that couldn't hurt them, and drakes only hunted humans for food if nothing else was available. Either was more than a match for common soldiers, but lacked the drive to keep killing after they had the meat they wanted. Any soldier in retreat would have had plenty of time to flee as the creatures were distracted by their meals.

He would have preferred any of the previous possibilities to the goblins seen by the scout. Goblin tools and weapons were made of little but knapped stone, plant fiber cord, and the odd forked stick, so the mundane iron tools the humans here possessed would be a treasure to them. The spears and shields of a human patrol would have been a veritable fortune. If they outnumbered them no less than five to one, they would have slaughtered them wholesale for what they wore and carried.

It also meant the place would never be rid of them, as goblins were notorious survivors, possessed an abundance of low cunning, and they bred like rabbits. Once a clan of them had taken up a home in the mountains, uprooting them was nigh impossible. They protected their caves with traps and ambushes, taking advantage of the darkness that did not hinder their sight. Failing that, they would run, find a new home, and breed themselves anew, only to begin raiding once more. From the scout's report, a raiding band was in the process of stripping a farmstead bare, which meant they were gathering supplies for such a clan.

"Any thoughts, Lion?" The lieutenant of the patrol seemed genuinely curious, and Pencheval noticed none of the antipathy the knights had towards his guild, the Silver Lions. As he had spent his apprenticeship fighting goblins and any other number of mountain hazards keeping the trade route in Stonewall Pass open, he had more than a few tactics to spare in dealing with them.

"An ambush, but I'll need the archers."

"That can be arranged." The lieutenant nodded his agreement as Pencheval outlined a plan, and gave orders to his men to implement it.

***

Pencheval crested the hill the scout had used along the only dirt road leading into the farm and overlooked the place by himself. It stood in a small rolling field surrounded by craggy rocks, copses of trees, and chest-high scrub, just as the scout had described it. A wheat field was visible behind a cobblestone cottage roofed with thatch, and a sod-covered root cellar stood only as much above ground as the wooden fencing of the barnyard behind it. It might have been a peaceful place once, but goblins swarmed over it now.

The prowling gray raiders were literally ripping it apart for anything they found of worth, tearing planks out of the barn and the door from the cottage. Three of them manhandled an anvil bolted to a thick stump from a work shed, half-rolling and half-carrying it as they cursed its weight and each other. An overburdened thief staggered after them, iron tools poking through the burlap sack it had slung over its shoulder. Two more goblins tried to determine what the sacks they had taken from the farmhouse contained, only to choke on clouds of flour when they cut them open.

Next to a gap that had been torn in the fence, a group of goblins were butchering animals and cooking the meat over a bonfire. The donkey and chickens were easy enough to identify, but it wasn't until Pencheval noticed the pieces of clothing that he realized they were cooking the humans as well. He presumed the family had met its fate in the pile of corpses, but a survivor struggled vainly to free himself from the ropes binding his wrists to a post before the flint axe of the butcher reduced him to rations. He appeared to be a friar wearing only sandals and a battered hooded robe, once white but now crusted with mud and gore.

A goblin struggled up from the root cellar, scrambling to keep vegetables from spilling from a bulging, overfilled sack. It caught sight of Pencheval as it chased down a wayward turnip, pointed, and shouted in its shrill language at the top of its lungs. Every goblin within earshot stopped what it was doing and took up arms, screaming a warning in turn and pouring onto the road in front of the farmstead from the barnyard, the wheat field and the buildings. Many pointed at the single human and laughed, believing Pencheval an unlucky fool who had stumbled across his doom for lack of care.

He estimated there were roughly fifty of them massing in the road, what he remembered to be the size of a typical goblin raiding party. They wielded everything from rusted steel weapons to flint knives in their disturbingly long fingers. Several held spears that appeared to have been stolen from patrols like the one he accompanied now, staves shorn to accommodate the goblins' smaller stature, the tallest of which did not even stand as high as Pencheval's chest. Some shouted taunts and curses in their tongue as they massed while others bared pointed teeth and snarled.

Pencheval could not have cared less. He had killed hundreds of them while he had been an apprentice and he saw nothing exceptional about the lot before him now. His plan to deal with them was in place, and they would break as quickly as always once their leader was foolish enough to reveal itself and be cut down for its trouble. For now, though, they were due for a thinning. Pencheval slapped the visor down on his bascinet and drew his sword.

A goblin wearing an upturned copper teakettle for a helmet, bone-reinforced rawhide tunic, and wielding a steel short sword, pushed its way to the front of the mob and leered. Stockier than the others, it stepped in front of the eager mob, thrust its sword in Pencheval's direction and screamed. Pencheval recognized it as the leader and smiled wickedly. He had seen them dozens of times before, and this one was positioning itself to get the shiniest objects for its own before those around it made them disappear.

Pencheval was wearing enough armor to keep all of their eyes on him. The chainmail, gauntlet rivets, and sollerets were enough to get their attention, but the Argentsteel sword was what Pencheval believed they wanted most. The silvery gnomish alloy caught the light like polished jewelry and left them visibly entranced. As expected, once the goblins were confident their numbers could overwhelm him and that the potential gain was worth the risk, they charged down the road towards him and away from any hope of cover.

When they were between the farmstead and his hill, Pencheval willed his sword to burn with a Pitfire spell. It ignited with a roar, tentacles of flame writhing towards the goblins as though grasping for something to burn, and began to stink of sulfur and pitch. Wails and shrieks punctuated the pops and crackles of the flame any time the blade moved, and the goblin charge stumbled to a halt at the sight of the eldritch thing. The leader excoriated, punched and slapped those around it to get the charge back underway, but to no avail.

"Now!" Pencheval yelled the signal to the brush and trees far to the goblins' flank as they were in the open and stalled where he wanted them.

At his signal, archers that had moved quietly into hiding there as the goblins' attention was diverted revealed themselves and fired. A dozen goblins fell in the first volley, and another half dozen in the second, before they recovered from the shock of the ambush and scattered. The leader, suddenly finding itself surrounded by corpses, turned and ran for the cottage to escape.

"Oh no you don't," Pencheval muttered to himself and charged straight at it. As the Pitfire spell had served its purpose, he quit willing the blade to burn and instead willed his magic to make his charge as fast as that of a galloping horse. The goblin leader turned at the noise of his footsteps just in time to see the slash that struck it dead.

At the death of their leader, most of the goblins panicked and ran. Others stopped long enough to grab what spoils they could before scrambling towards the hills. Some few looked as though they still meant to fight, and Pencheval concentrated on them rather than those in retreat.

He charged and killed the butcher next to the barnyard, which had not yet tried to run and still held the bloody flint axe it had been using to cut meat. A chop split the head of another. One tried to skewer him from a hiding place in the wheat field, and he sheared away the spear tip before finishing it with a thrust. A fourth tried to jump Pencheval from behind with a fraying rope garrote, only to have the pommel of his sword smash its beak-like nose and slam it to the ground. Pencheval willed more strength to himself and stomped its skull, pulping it instantly. Searching for more enemies not in retreat, he realized he was on the farmstead killing goblins alone.

"Waiting for them to die of old age?" Pencheval shouted towards the borders of the farm where the patrol had executed its ambush. "Get to it!"

Archers and spearmen broke up into small teams and descended upon the scattering goblins. One group freed the prisoner lashed to the fence, while others cornered stragglers and those whose greed had gotten the better of their senses, slaying them as they tried to snatch one last treasure before escaping. Archers picked off those in full retreat and any others presenting a clear target.

Pencheval cautiously entered the farmhouse to clear it of goblins. It was completely ransacked, aside from a stretch of blood leading through the door towards the makeshift butcher's block. A hatch to the basement was removed, iron fixtures were half-torn from the walls, and jaggedly cut leather hinges remained where the doors once hung.

The Silver Lion followed the bloody trail through the side door and over to the pile of bodies next to where the prisoner had been tethered. The friar, now free, was rubbing his wrists and staring sadly at the remains of the family who once lived here. Upon regaining his composure, he began chanting rites over the dead. Wholly disinterested in the service, Pencheval searched for goblin corpses to determine their clan colors.

He found one with an arrow through the chest, slouched against the well. It had tied two strips of cloth around its right arm, gray over red. Pencheval recognized them as clan colors, but found it to be an unusual combination. In Stonewall Pass, the goblins generally chose only one color or trinket to distinguish themselves. Neither they nor any other goblins he had seen since wore colors in this manner.

"You. You're a Silver Lion." The friar prisoner pointed at him. "Does the Knight Superior know about the goblins? How many of your guild did you bring?"

"No. And none. Only the soldiers of Athesiene accompany me."

"None?" The friar rubbed his wrists again. "Then why are you here, if not for the goblins? And who are you?"

"I'm called Pencheval. Take up what you have, friar. We need to go."

"Go? What of the dead?"

"What of them?" Pencheval wondered if the daft wretch was unhappy to be alive. Was he not eager to leave the place where he nearly met his fate?

"What of them?" the friar asked indignantly. "Has your work left you so hardened you would deny last rites to the innocent? Are you in some rush to leave them to rot?"

"Knight Superior Rennoute wanted to know why his patrol did not return," Pencheval replied impassively. "I mean to tell him and avoid any more goblins. That's my rush."

"You mean to...wait. Pencheval. Pencheval the Silver Lion..." The friar's face went pale. "Skies above, you're the Hopeslayer."

Pencheval grumbled at being recognized as the Hopeslayer. It was a name he had traveled to this valley to avoid for a time, and even here it followed him. It had been two years since he had killed the badly misnamed bandit called the Hope of Terris Lyn, which earned him the title and left him with new troubles. Now the people of Terris Lyn thought of him as a monster, and the butcher he had killed had become a martyr to the common folk, blighted fools that they were.

He did not care what the common folk thought of him, but their misbegotten opinions were still a problem. Every so often, one of them would make a nuisance of themselves and attempt to avenge the Hope, resulting in their broken bones, missing teeth, and yet another explanation to the nearest guardsman. For a year after the bandit's death, the Thieves' Guild had tried to make an example of Pencheval for killing one of their more proficient members. The Silver Lion had left anyone they sent in far worse shape, usually face down in the nearest ditch.

"The Hopeslayer?" A nearby soldier scratched his head. "Heard tell you preferred killing bandits. Why are you here?"

"I'm enjoying the view." Pencheval stood up from examining the goblin. "Now we need to be off. If the goblins return they'll come in greater numbers."

"What of the other patrol?" The soldier was flustered. "Will we not search for them?"

"Not unless you mean to join them as meat in the hills," Pencheval replied. "A goblin clan has made their lair up there, and we alone are not sufficient to root them out. Likely they number a thousand or more."

"They were easy enough to kill here," the soldier countered. "Ambushed and slaughtered the lot of them, we did. If they're all that soft we'll be dealing with them soon enough."

"Don't let the raiding party fool you," Pencheval advised. "On their own terms, goblins are lethal, and they'll be on their own terms in the hills and mountains. Absent more force, we should return to the castle. At the very least the Knight Superior needs to know they've come."

***

Pencheval looked across the wheat field to the mountains, wondering which of them held the clan of goblins that was about to plague the valley. The survivors of the raiding party he and the patrol had scattered with relative ease were only running to one place with news of their defeat, and that was home. Depending on their chieftain, the clan would either lay low or retaliate if they had the numbers. Given that the last patrol had disappeared, he believed it would be the latter.

He was less certain of his enemies than the soldier who had dismissed them out of hand. Some clans had specialists in one thing or another and so might this one, even if no such sorts accompanied a mob of common raiders. The Silver Lion grimaced at the thought, remembering his apprenticeship fighting goblins in Stonewall Pass. The soldiers there had learned about one such clan's penchant for poisons the hard way when far too many of them died from it, and learning about this clan would mean deaths as well.

The Temple of Athesiene had never once reported trouble with goblins in the valley or they, like Lord Mallinus of Stonewall Pass, would beg constantly for warriors from any mercenaries they could find. A clan of goblins was an endless source of trouble, as the three clans at Stonewall Pass abundantly demonstrated during Pencheval's time there. If the goblins had raiders stripping homesteads of anything and everything, that sort of trouble was coming to the valley. The peace of the Emerald Refuge renowned across the Kingdom of Lerrisaine was about to collapse into a war of endless skirmishes.

Given this, the Temple of Athesiene would be yet another source of coin, and he was not glad of it. Peace was not in such quantity in Lerrisaine that he would see it lost, however well the violence paid Silver Lions like himself. Fighting was already abundant enough to make him wealthy, and he found no need for more of it. The trouble was that violence always seemed to happen on its own time whether he found need of it or not.

Despite it all, the friar had to insist on conducting a burial at the farmstead, so they were still there and not putting distance between themselves and trouble. Last rites made for great sentiments, unless a goblin clan of unknown strength, aggression and ability threatened from the mountains not so far distant. If they were killing patrols that strayed too close to their caves, they could not be that distant, which made it likely they could react before the patrol reached safety.

It was not a thought he enjoyed. The sun was setting at his back, and once it was down, the darkness would give the goblins an advantage. He could see in the dark with a Clearsight charm, but the soldiers and friar could not, while the goblins saw perfectly well without light of any sort. They would be in their element and they had used it to their advantage in the past. At the very least, goblin scouts could come and go with no trouble or risk to themselves, shadowing the patrol to relay their location or picking off stragglers given the opportunity.

"Why are you here?" The friar the patrol had freed from the goblins walked towards him, still moving stiffly from the bruises. His wrists were raw from where he had been bound to the fence while he waited his turn at the butcher's block. Graying hair and beard were matted and dirty.

"The Knight Superior offered me work reinforcing the patrol. I took it."

"Except he never does that because he has no more love for your guild than any other knight," the friar replied. "For as long as I can remember, he and his knights dealt with all the trouble themselves or with the help of their soldiers. You're the first Silver Lion I've seen in the Emerald Refuge, well, ever."

"He found himself in need of other aid."

"Perhaps that is true, but were I to guess, you didn't come here for contracts. You came to retreat from your troubles, unless there was some other Silver Lion staring off into the distance at the Shield of Athesiene this past fortnight."

Pencheval's eyes narrowed, but the friar only smiled kindly and shook his head in response. "I've traveled around this kingdom and several others spreading the word of the Lord on High, and I've seen enough to know when someone is questioning his life."

"Give it a rest, friar. I don't want a sermon."

"No. You're here for respite, not words. Not yet." The friar stood next to him and stared into the mountains. "What up there causes you such interest?"

"The clan of the goblins we drove off," Pencheval said, happy the subject had changed. "They are up there somewhere, teeming among the rocks and caves. It was likely they who killed the other patrol, and if they're as bad as those in Stonewall Pass they'll bedevil you for years to come."

"It's been years since anyone here has even heard of goblins, and they've come before." The friar gritted his teeth from the pain as he sat, breathing easier once he leaned back on his hands. "They can be undone, or at least frightened into sense."

"Perhaps, but that's a discussion for behind the walls of Tarsun's Market or the castle. We should have left before sunset."

"I have duties to the faithful of Athesiene," the friar insisted. "Duties which have no exceptions for safety or convenience."

"The goblins nearly butchered you for meat with the rest today, friar." Pencheval wondered if he had lost all sense. "Are you so eager to risk them again?"

"For the sake of my vows, yes. You may remember those in my temple take those sorts of things." The friar smiled and was met by a stony gaze. "My name is Dominik, by the way. Not that we common folk seem to interest you much in the tales they tell of you. Not enough coin on offer?"

Pencheval's nostrils flared and he bared his teeth. "I know well enough what the common folk offer, old man. I've received enough of it for a lifetime."

***

The Stonemaster, goblin Chief of Chieftains, was annoyed and perplexed. His decision to kill the small band of humans who came too close to discovering his horde had been all but forced. The white clad human warriors, which the scouts took to calling the Snow Clan, discovered a few things too many. Allowing them to tell their clan chief about the horde would have disrupted the plan, and so they had to die. The Snow Clan humans who controlled the valley would know about the horde when he used it on them and not before. The Chief of Chieftains wanted the advantage of surprise, horde or not, even if he could only use it once.

The deaths were necessary but also made it likely that the Snow Clan would want to know what had happened. What the Chief of Chieftains was not expecting was that they would send an even stronger group of humans and investigate with force instead of stealth. If they had been goblins, they would have sent scouts, determined what manner of enemy they faced, and either evaded or retaliated as their force permitted. Much to the Stonemaster's chagrin, the humans chose retaliation and had the strength for it, or at least that was the tale the stragglers told as they slowly trickled back to the horde's caves after their defeat.

He was not annoyed that the survivors ran as the others died because the information they brought was more than worth the lives lost. There were always more goblins, and a wise Chief of Chieftains did not punish his eyes and ears for seeing and hearing what needed to be known. He was annoyed because the Snow Clan chieftain was strong and aggressive, and perplexed at the presence of the human enforcer that did not seem to be one of its minions.

This human with its silvery big knife wasn't wearing the white of the Snow Clan humans. It wore black and grey with shiny metal on its arms, legs and head, and had a picture of something the survivor believed to be a mountain lion on its shirt. When the Stonemaster had asked for a description of its clan symbol, the bedraggled raider posed one leg in front of the other with hands and arms held forward in a twin claw stroke, mouth opened with his head to the side. The Chief of Chieftains recognized the pose and remembered that the mountain lion picture it described was a popular design among the human clans.

He guessed this new human was an enforcer because it had the shiniest big knife the informant had ever seen, and it took point in breaking the raiding party. But if it was an enforcer, where was its mob of humans? Why was it not commanding the others? That made it deadly, but not an enforcer.

Was it some sort of specialist from another clan, this 'gray lion' clan? The Chief of Chieftains had fought clans with Berserkers but even they were not as fell as this human was described to be. How did the Snow Clan gain its help? Did they give it many of the shiny yellow discs the humans seemed to love so much? Or was the Snow Clan Chieftain like the Chief of Chieftains, uniting other human clans beneath its own?

If it was uniting human clans it needed to be stopped now. There would be no rooting them from the mountain-castle they had built at the other side of the valley if they had their own horde. From what the Stonemaster had heard of its size from his scouts, it would cost his horde many lives to take it as it was. So it was time for the Gray Lion Clan to discover that an alliance with the Snow Clan was an exceedingly poor choice by sending its specialist back to them in a sack.

"The time is now, Chief of Chieftains." The Stonemaster looked towards his council, made up of chieftains and shamans from the clans which had united under him. It was the Shadowcreed Chieftain who had spoken, giving his advice from the discussion of what now to do with the horde. The Stonemaster gave the Shadowcreed Chieftain his undivided attention in response, and his advisor cringed.

The Stonemaster knew why. Lesser chieftains killed those who disagreed with them or gave them bad news, only to be slaughtered in turn by what they did not or would not hear. The fact that he was not so foolish was why he was a superior Chief of Chieftains. He did not keep council to hear only what he wished, and would have executed anyone who could only tell him of his greatness. He already knew of his own greatness. What he wanted was valuable advice, and they had better provide it.

"Why?" The Stonemaster leaned back into his bone throne and listened. If the Shadowcreed's chieftain had something to say besides an expression of impatience and bloodlust, the Chief of Chieftains meant to hear it.

"The patrol they sent was stronger, Chief of Chieftains." The hood-clad goblin regained his composure and stood. "If they return, they will tell their clan chief of us, and it will send many more. If they do not return, it will still send many more. Perhaps all of the Snow Clan will come. There will be no more half measures from them."

It was an irritating but valid point, the Stonemaster mused, and it wasn't like the Shadowcreed to rush headlong into a fight. Theirs was the way of stealth, ambush and trickery. If the Shadowcreed

Chieftain believed it was time for war, it was because the Snow Clan Chieftain had amply demonstrated its aggression to him.

"What do you suggest?"

"We go with the horde. This fight has begun." This time it was the towering Bloodmoon Chieftain who spoke. His clan had the strongest of the goblins and included Berserkers, and were the most eager for war. They survived by being so fearsome that other clans would not attack them, and so deadly they could kill anything else that would.

"There are not enough of us for the Snow Clan's mountain-castle," the Stonemaster said. He did not intend to attack until they had the numbers, because a wise Chief of Chieftains also knew discretion. The 'pride' the humans suffered was not shared by the goblins and they did not rush to their deaths over that human failing. It was another blessing of their god, the Fiend Under The Mountain, that this was so. "If we fight them now they'll kill us."

"But all in the valley is not the mountain-castle," the Bloodmoon Chieftain countered. "What of those other things? Like the farm-places, but more of them?"

"The humans call those 'towns.'" The Chief of Chieftains gave the suggestion some thought. Despite Bloodmoon's insatiable and occasionally irrational desire for conflict, the town was indeed another target entirely.

"Yes, the town. Crush the town. Take one victory first, then send speakers into the mountains. Other clans may not come for the mere promise of victory, but after an actual victory they will come. Clan upon clan will come once you have proved yourself a conquering Hordemaker, and then you will have numbers."

"Will the Snow Clan endure such an insult?" The Allspeaker, a shaman with the gift of speaking in any tongue he wished, added his usual caution to the discussion. "Crush the town, and the Snow Clan will come as well."

"Yes, they will." The Bloodmoon Chieftain laughed. "Let them come away from their mountain-castle. Let them come to face us where they have no high cliff-walls and giant cave-towers to shield their lack of numbers."

"Let them come and see who owns the night," the Shadowcreed Chieftain proclaimed. "Human eyes are cursed by their gods. They need sun or fire to see. After dark, they will be in the open on our terms. Do they dare?"

The Chief of Chieftains weighed the words of his council and found this plan suited him. It worked either way. If they took the town, the Snow Clan would have to act. If they came to the goblins, their numbers could be thinned before an attack on the mountain-castle. If they did not? Well, some of the humans in the town might know of the secrets of building caves. The human who had traded him his staff and that strange red liquid in the shiny bottle had called it 'masonry.' This masonry might be useful, and perhaps the 'smithing' that worked certain rocks into the shiny weapons and tools they found.

"How soon can we move?"

"Tomorrow night, we will be ready." The Bloodmoon Chieftain seemed eager.

"One other matter, Chief of Chieftains." The Allspeaker looked to the mouth of the cave. A thick stitching of bear hides to prevent things the Stonemaster did not wish seen or heard from escaping was draped over it. "The horde is speaking of the Gray Lion human in hushed tones. I have already heard them say it wields a demon in its big knife and can run like the wind. A survivor swears it crushed a skull with a single stomp of its foot and slew others with but a swing of its weapon. This will spark hesitation."

"Kill them," the Bloodmoon Chieftain suggested. "They will be silent then."

"It's too late. You can kill the speakers but not the tales." The Stonemaster narrowed his eyes. "We need the death of the Gray Lion clan human and those who accompany him. All of them. Brutally."

"Send my Berserkers," Bloodmoon suggested, smiling viciously. "All that will be left of them are their bones in our necklaces and kill-poles for the Snow Clan. When they return and chant over their victory, shiny big knife in hand, it will banish the fear."

"A good plan, but they are not fast enough to catch them." A strangely misshapen goblin, hunched to one side due to a growth of bone and spikes protruding from his left shoulder, leaned heavily on his walking stick as he limped forth. He was the Chieftain of the Beastwarper Clan, which had learned the secrets of growing and bending even the forms of trolls to their will. He was less a cripple for his works than their recipient, for despite his bent stature, the things he brewed had made him stronger and more cunning. Only the small size of the Beastwarper Clan had led them to join with the Stonemaster at all in the hopes of gaining the safety and success of greater numbers. "Send the Bonestrippers. No more than four will be necessary, and the humans will die."

"Send my Shadows as well," the Shadowcreed Chieftain added. "They can ride along and douse the fires at night. Then the Bonestrippers will slaughter the humans as they stagger about in the dark. There will be no survivors."

The Stonemaster smiled. Bonestrippers feared nothing, least of all fire, and would not stop until they were either dead or full. Darkness would not hinder them any more than his goblins and, most importantly, they killed with the sort of ferocity that could restore spirit to his horde. Yes, this would be the way the humans would die.

This Gray Lion Clan specialist with its burning, shiny big knife was about to learn that fear was a game two could play and that the Chief of Chieftains was far better at it. He just hoped the Bonestrippers wouldn't live up to their names too much. It wouldn't do to leave so little of the human that there was nothing for the killpole they would post on the spot it fell. A messy example slaying was far more effective in scaring away trouble than 'never seen again' and besides, the Stonemaster just had to have its shiny big knife for himself. Not only would this restore morale, but his treasures had been thinned in exchange for the staff and red liquid. While the trade had been well worth it, the Stonemaster meant to be wealthy again.

"Send them, Beastwarper. Send them and the Shadows too. Return with the shiny big knife of the Gray Lion Clan human as proof. There will be work enough for the Berserkers in the town."

Bloodmoon laughed. "We will pile human corpses into hills!"

"No," the Chief of Chieftains ordered. "Kill until they stop resisting and capture the rest. There are things I want them to tell me."

The Shadowcreed Chieftain patted the braided leather whip on his hip. "We'll be happy to make them talk. And beg. And scream."

"Go now, and rally the horde. We move soon."

The assembled council bowed and left, and the Stonemaster examined his staff yet again. It was carved from some sort of strange gray stone that had the grain of wood, the upper third thinning like the neck of a bottle before flaring outward again. An obsidian idol of some crouching winged creature the Stonemaster did not recognize capped it, fastened to the shaft in some manner he could not determine. The whole of it was half again taller than he was and top heavy, but not so unwieldy he couldn't do more than pose with it.

When the human who had offered it to him wanted four of his shiniest treasures in trade, he had nearly struck the greedy fool dead. Seeing that same human use the staff to double the size of his cave had changed his mind. It allowed its wielder to command the very stone beneath their feet and the strange red liquid he drank gave him the power to use it. Together, they fueled his rise as the Stonemaster, Chief of Chieftains and Hordemaker. Rivals had died away as the stone killed them at his will, and all others now followed him out of fear and a near religious awe. To them, he was the coming of a great warlord and blessed by the Fiend Under The Mountain.

With the staff, he would get everything he ever wanted: power, treasures, and the first true goblin clan-home. Why had the human traded it to him, even going so far as to speak the goblin tongue to approach him? Perhaps it had the sense to recognize greatness when it saw it and wanted to earn favor. The trade had proven so favorable that afterwards the Stonemaster had let it leave in peace. If it could find these sorts of treasures, what else might it trade when he was master of the whole valley and the mountains around it? It was worth letting it live to see.

***

Pencheval sat next to his campfire at the clearing the patrol had chosen for the night, oiling his sword and examining it to ensure it was still battle-worthy. As he expected, the fight against the goblin raiders had not so much as nicked the hand and a half blade. Gnomish Argentsteel was prized for its durability against harsh use, such as strikes powered by a Silver Lion willing himself strength, and could far better withstand the application of magic like Pitfire than ordinary steel. It was why his guild issued blades of this sort to their apprentices upon their proving themselves more than aspirants. It was also a mark of status as a Silver Lion, and he had to endure no small number of gadflies and minor courtiers attempting to acquire it.

He stopped polishing the blade and the disc-shaped counterweight on its pommel and shook his head. The friar had asked him why he was here, and apparently it was to be nothing more than he had been for the past few years. Why was he here, if all he meant to do was accept contracts again? He had traveled to this valley to stop being a wandering mercenary champion for a time and take advantage of the serenity, only to become a mercenary champion again.

Pencheval sighed and glanced at his right palm. The marking the glyphsmith had given him glimmered in the light of the campfire as though woven from strands of silver thread. No burns or cuts accompanied the manner of its placement, a process like branding that put it just under the skin. In fact, it did not appear as though it had ever been anything more than part of his hand. According to the glyphsmith, this allowed him to direct magic into his sword or anything else he touched, though he was warned few things could endure it.

He would wear that glyph for life now, as the work of the glyphsmith could not be undone save for death. At the time, it was nothing that concerned him. Not being condemned to the life of a dock hand or a death in the slums of Mudslight were all that mattered. That, and his newfound vocation had hardly led him to ruin.

He could do mercenary work well, and it had been both a good living and the instrument of his triumph over the Hope of Terris Lyn. The notoriety of being a Silver Lion scared most of the trouble away and boosted his price. He'd taken bounties and contracts as he pleased and had the wealthy buy his preference for their work with gifts of finery and luxuries. It was a life many attempted to attain during

Drillmaster Tagrine's assessment of the hundred or so aspirants vying alongside Pencheval for Silver Lion apprenticeships, only to fall away like dead leaves from an autumn tree when it proved too much to endure.

Becoming a Silver Lion was what he needed when he chose it years ago, but nothing he wanted now. What he wanted was the life he might have had before the Hope of Terris Lyn changed it, and he cursed himself for wanting a fairy tale. His family was gone and the close knit village in Terris Lyn where he was raised turned out to be as much a lie as the 'Hope' was, so there was no going back.

He broke from his thoughts when he felt the ground shake beneath his feet. Irregular vibrations like the footsteps of a band of giants grew closer. Soon he could hear them as well as feel the ground shiver. Large feet squelched into wet earth, nails grated on rocks, or small creatures gave frightened squeaks as they fled from something thumping through the dark. The soldiers and pickets were already seeking out the source of the approaching commotion with torches in hand as others nocked bows or armed themselves with shields and spears. Pencheval stood ready with his sword and then cursed himself for not anticipating what happened next.

He heard the crack of pottery and a splash behind him, and the orange glow of a campfire simply ceased to be. Another crack, and the smell of reeking fluid now accompanied the growing darkness. He turned to see three crude clay containers fly towards the remaining campfires, and in the distance the torches of pickets suddenly ceased to burn. More cracks and splashes, and the entire camp was left with little more than starlight. Soldiers with unadjusted eyes cursed as they staggered around in the dark.

"Goblins!" Pencheval willed his eyes to see. The Clearsight charm turned blackness into a picture of confusion cast in grays. Men fumbled and staggered in the darkness, cursing their circumstances or fumbling for light. Moving to take advantage of the circumstances, a dozen hooded goblins bore down on them as fast as they could without making noise.

"Behind you!" Pencheval tried to warn the soldiers but it was no use. They couldn't see in front of them, much less behind them, and several turned only to panic at what they could not find.

The first soldier the goblins reached fell from a cudgel cracked across the back of his knees as another goblin jumped on his back and garroted him. The second was tackled to the ground by two goblins before a third pounced on him, yanked up his head, and slashed his throat with a stone knife. All of the goblins wore some sort of dark hooded tunic which suggested to Pencheval that they were members of the same clan, but not the one from the farmstead. The screams of the dying and the shrill goblin tongue sent the whole camp reeling into chaos.

Pencheval cursed himself for a fool and charged the goblins picking off soldiers from the rear. Of course they were going to lead with a Firebane attack at night, especially if there was a distraction provided from another direction. They had only done this dozens of times at Stonewall Pass during his apprenticeship there. Now all he could do was react and try to prevent more deaths.

Those attacking were prowling three other soldiers for a kill when they saw Pencheval charging towards them. Several of them recoiled as they realized he could see and fled. Before scampering off, one of them leered at him and pointed up the hill towards the noise of the thundering footsteps. Pencheval followed its finger and stopped cold.

Four monstrous creatures lumbered towards the encampment, walking on their feet and the knuckles of their massive claws. Pencheval thought they might have been trolls at first but then realized they were far worse. They had too many bony plates growing over their arms and chest, and their toad-like mouths lolled open in brute stupidity wide enough for him to see the rows of serrated, triangular teeth. Each was twice as tall as he was and had what appeared to be a makeshift coverture of bone and wicker on its back, shaped like something a nest of wasps would build from mud. Each was also blindfolded with a leather covering, connected by cords or thongs through a window to whatever was inside the coverture. Other leather thongs wrapped the base of their horns, and when pulled caused the beast to turn its head less by force than conditioning. When the head turned, the beast turned as well, and their concealed riders kept them advancing in a crude line that way.

"Trolls on the field!" The warning was the best one Pencheval knew to give under the circumstances and was better than letting the creatures completely surprise the soldiers. He backed away and readied himself for a charge, remembering the counters he knew. Soldiers did what they could, but in this light they would only be able to see shadows and hear the threat coming from indistinct shapes in the dark.

The advance didn't stop as the riders spoke to one another in the shrill goblin tongue. After a few moments, each rider pointed his mount in the direction of one part of the camp or another and then pulled away the blindfold. The once brutish but docile creatures saw something they wanted in front of them, roared, and charged.

"Athesiene save..." Soldiers broke into screams as the beasts hit them hard. Pencheval saw one tear into confused ranks and smash soldiers through the air before snatching one and biting him in half. Spearmen thrust at indistinct shapes and archers fired at sounds, eyes still adjusting, attacking whatever they thought they could. Hastily formed shield walls broke under the onslaught of oversized claws, and Pencheval could not lend any of them aid because one of the things was charging straight for him.

His eyes narrowed as he remembered the words of Drillmaster Tagrine from his aspirant and apprentice days at the Silver Lion's drill field. *It's why they hire us, grunt.* They were the mercenaries of first choice to well-coined interests because they were able to defeat beasts like these. When one of the others made the mistake of complaining that training for this was insane, the Drillmaster had roared this particular revelation to him half a finger's length from his face, followed by the order to slap his visor down, put his guard up, and get to it. At least the swinging log they had been dodging to train did not have claws.

The countermove Drillmaster Tagrine had taught them for moments like this had been handy. It involved a spell that vastly accelerated its user but wore hard on the bones and muscles, and thus was parceled out by the moments. The move was to slip around the charge and then counterstrike, easily managed with a short burst of speed. Pencheval had used that move in real combat a dozen times before on trolls, and saw no reason it would fail on whatever this beast was.

When the monster was three of its strides from him, mouth open in a roar and arms raised to strike downward, Pencheval stopped willing his eyes to see and instead willed himself speed. It reduced the threatening charge to something almost comically slow, and he took the opportunity to sidestep the beast, let it pass, and then strike down against the back of its knee. The blow missed just high and bit instead into the meat of the thigh, causing the charging monster to stagger forward and catch its balance with its claws.

Pencheval cursed his aim and the beast's hide, which had proven tough enough to resist his blow even without the bony plates to improve it. Whatever it was, it was worse than a troll. Trolls had thick hides, but they were at least penetrable, and only attacked when they were hungry. These things were tougher and so vicious the goblins had to keep them blindfolded to tame their rage.

Pencheval could hear the muffled curses of the goblin rider, gray and visible as the Clearsight charm took hold once again. It ripped on cables and let the blindfold fall in an attempt to control its mount, likely realizing that its target was now behind it. The beast growled its protests and reached up towards the rider to retaliate, but the bony plates and thick hide of its arms restricted its wrath. Its claws pawed thin air in a futile attempt to maul its tormentor, leaving them both momentarily distracted.

Pencheval realized the coverture placement was more deliberate than he originally thought. It not only allowed the goblin to see but kept the beast from getting to the rider if the unfortunate goblin lost control, and he found it a good position to usurp. Once again dropping his Clearsight to will himself speed, he sidestepped behind the beast and spit the goblin rider on his sword. Pencheval cast it off of his blade before shattering the bone coverture and climbing to where it once was.

The beast kept pawing as it had with the goblin in an attempt to throw or crush the struggling newcomer, but Pencheval ducked and crouched within the space the coverture had been to remain out of its reach. Moments later, he found a soft spot between the head and neck, grabbed a horn, and hilted his sword into it. The roaring monster threw him before crashing to the ground dead.

Pencheval landed on his back in a briar, stars dancing before his eyes. He realized his sword wasn't in his hand, groaned, and rose to sit. He could still hear growls and screams in the distance, and whether he liked it or not, the fight was hardly done. Visor down and guard up, he thought to himself, and tried to summon his Clearsight once again.

***

Grizzik could not believe what he had just seen.

The idiot rider of that Bonestripper had one target. One. He was supposed to kill the Gray Lion Clan specialist, a task for which a Bonestripper should have proven more than adequate. The raging beast was enough to rip through a dozen humans, as the one he was riding had done when it wasn't eating them. Yet this one specialist had sidestepped it as though it was a clumsy newborn fawn and killed both it and its rider.

The Stonemaster was patient about any number of strange things, but to return and tell him the Bonestrippers had not been enough to kill the Gray Lion Clan human was certain death. He would command the very stone on which Grizzik would be standing to punish him. That was a fate he meant to avoid, especially now that the Gray Lion Clan human was hurt and unarmed.

Its continued existence would be easy enough to fix, and the only delay was the need to finish ripping through the humans in front of him. The handful of spearmen Grizzik fought thrust and slashed at his mount, and it was all he could do not to laugh at them. Given the thick and bony hide of the Bonestripper, they could as soon stab a boulder to death.

The beast shuddered and heaved, spraying the humans before it with the meat-stripped bones that were once their former companions. They cringed but desperately tried to stay together and fight. One last claw knocked them all flat, and Grizzik dropped the blinders so he could steer towards his new target. Time to finish the job he was sent to do, and earn favor with the Stonemaster when he returned with the human's shiny big knife.

***

Pencheval staggered to his feet, briars cracking as he broke free of their hold, and tried to find his sword through the stars flitting across his vision. He could hear the screams and roars punctuated by the crash of gigantic blows and the curses of goblins or soldiers. In his distraction, he almost missed the shadow of a hilt sticking from the bulk of a huge lump near him, and he stumbled over to rip it free.

He had just torn his sword from the body when he heard the thunder of something huge charging his way. He was still flailing and blundering about, so it was no surprise to him that a goblin seeing his condition would try to take advantage. Weak as they appeared to be to the greener soldiers at Stonewall Pass and himself at one time, the goblins always seemed to know how to pick their moments.

He put the blade in guard and found enough will and magic for the countermove, only to hear the footsteps slow as a huge shadow lumbered into view and then stopped just out of his reach. If the goblin on its back had witnessed the defeat of its fellow, Pencheval concluded, it had hoped to reach him before he was armed. Unable to do so, it slowed to caution because it wasn't eager to meet the same fate. The Silver Lion thanked the gods for its hesitation and willed his eyes to see once again.

Night hesitantly flickered to gray as he all but forced a Clearsight charm into being and the beast came into full view. He still thought it looked like a troll or might have been one once. Hulking, brutish, and placidly stupid with the leather folds around its eyes, yet now armored with bony plates and jutting horn on its shoulders, knees and chest. This one was leaning forward on its knuckles now, and the goblin snarled from above its shoulders.

Pencheval advanced. When he was close enough to attempt a strike, he saw one of the leather thongs draping from the coverture tighten as it was pulled. A gigantic claw arm swatted at him in response, and he countered the move by willing himself swiftness and dodging as he had been drilled. As the claw sailed over him, he maneuvered for a blow against the beast's ribs and thrust.

The sword chipped bony plates but did little else. The monster recoiled and lashed out blindly again, backhanding the spot where it thought its attacker was. Pencheval dodged beneath it and struck for the stomach, and again was unable to open a wound or draw blood. Despite it all, the goblin chose to remain in control and would not remove the blinders.

The increasingly frustrated mercenary gritted his teeth, fought through the pain of his rough landing, and managed to will himself enough speed to slip halfway around the monster. The goblin reined the beast to face him. The sharp turn left the monster on all fours and so close to Pencheval he could hear it sniffing the air. Trusting its nose, the monster lunged forward and snapped at him, missing only because of another limb-taxing burst of speed.

Pencheval stepped, dodged, and struck again to be rewarded by the same futility. He could not be strong, fast, and capable of sight all at once, and only his speed was saving him. So he would strike without effect, dodge the clumsy counterstrike, only to strike and be thwarted again by a stubbornly tough hide. The monster would tentatively claw after a blow, grasp blindly at a promising sound, snap at scents, and snarl or roar as Pencheval ducked it over and over.

For the moment, he couldn't kill the beast but it could not kill him either. He heard its rider cursing at the stalemate yet refuse to change tactics, which he believed was due to its fear. It wanted this done, but it also didn't want to die like the last one. The problem was that this would successfully wear him down if it continued.

The magic kept him alive but he could not sustain it indefinitely. He knew this fight would end him and the patrol if he did nothing else, especially as the sounds of beasts and screams in all directions suggested the goblins were gaining the upper hand. Despite his worsening circumstances, he resisted the urge to simply start hacking away at his enemy, knowing full well that giving in to panic would get him killed. He knew he needed a better plan, and the sounds of the beasts behind him inspired one.

The idea would play hell on his reserves of magic, but there was nothing for it if he was to turn this fight at all. The adept gritted his teeth, sheathed his sword, and ran as though in retreat. He heard the blinders slip from the beast he had just appeared to flee, goblin throwing caution to the wind to gain ground on a frustrating opponent it believed had broken.

When Pencheval saw another hulking shadow in front of him, he willed himself speed once again. As he taxed his protesting muscles the world around him slowed, and he hoped he had made the observation that these creatures were unmanageable without their blinders correctly. Committed to the action regardless, he charged straight into the beast he meant to target with the other raging down upon him.

The second rider noticed him and reacted far too slowly as Pencheval grabbed anything on its mount he could use to pull himself upwards, tore the leather blinders from its eyes, and vaulted over the coverture to the ground behind it. Two beasts with blinders gone now faced each other, and the first charged headlong into the second with a roar and a crash. The other responded with an onslaught of claws, and they tore into one another like starving wolves fighting over meat. Covertures shattered, pulping the goblin riders almost instantly in the fray, and the two distracted monsters ignored everything but each other.

Pencheval stumbled away from their fury and willed himself to see, but blackness bled away to gray slowly now. He could feel the cool sensation beneath his skin that meant his reserves of power were nearly spent. His magic had enhanced his strength and speed well enough, but the Clearsight spell would be all he could manage for a time.

It had happened to him in fighting before. What little he understood of how it worked was that magic was everywhere, but could only be collected so fast and in so much of a quantity without harming him. The power to do that was one of the things the gnomish glyphsmith imbued upon all Silver Lion apprentices that had proven ready, and he had been trained to use it along with the others by his other instructor, Spellkeeper Arthier.

It was that power that made Silver Lions more than a match for beasts of this sort when common soldiers and champions were not. He would recover it in time, but it would take more time than he had if the last beast's rider decided it would press. When he saw the lumbering monster head off into the darkness he realized to his relief that it would not. Pencheval could only guess the rider had been spooked at seeing one dead and two redirected by a single human and chose to escape. Much to his chagrin though, the goblins had already done most of the work they had come to accomplish.

Pencheval caught sight of the friar, who was desperately trying to pull an injured archer out of the way of the two slowing but still dangerous creatures venting fury on one another. Another soldier was in the distance on his knees, laughing away his sanity. A third clutched at his side and groaned on his back. All others had fled or were dead, fallen among the broken weapons, shattered shields, and cold firepits of their encampment. Many had been reduced to bones cracked and stripped by the monstrous digestion of their assailants. Forty men plus himself reduced to five in one attack, and the unmounted goblins were still at large.

The battered Lion weighed his options. He could leave them right now and no one would know, and his guild wouldn't care either way. The tenets of the Silver Lions only said that he would meet whatever contracts he took and stand by the other *guilden*, which they were not. He knew what had killed his patrol and the one before, and could report on it alone, thus fulfilling his contract with the Knight Superior.

It was the move any other number of mercenaries would have made and he felt absolutely filthy even thinking about it.

No, he had no use for the common folk. No, he had no patience for the fact the friar and the now-dead Lieutenant had delayed their departure from the farmstead for a night over a burial, giving these creatures plenty of time to catch and butcher them. No, his aching limbs, stiffening muscles, and near-death experiences in this fight had not left him particularly inclined to suffer fools. Regardless, he refused to desert.

It was an echo from the Pencheval he once was, listening to his father describe what it meant to be an honorable man. Deserting those who had been your allies in good faith was one of those things that was not done because it was low and craven. Rescuing them now when goblins might still be about was not the thing a mercenary would do, but it was the thing he would do.

He knew the hooded goblins were still out there though he couldn't see them with his weakened Clearsight charm. They were likely waiting for the Bonestrippers to flay each other before moving on them, and he imagined they were hiding among the endless possibilities of cover the rugged terrain provided. Keeping alert for them and picking his way among the bodies, Pencheval walked over to the wounded soldier, who started at the sound of his footsteps and weakly brandished a dagger his way.

"Stay...back," he groaned. "Goblin..."

"I'm not a goblin, but they are yet about," Pencheval answered. "Sheathe your blade."

"How do you...see...?"

"It's why they hire us." Pencheval lifted the soldier from the ground and threw him over his shoulder. He would reunite them all with the friar and then get them to leave, even if he had to beat the old man to persuade him not to die.

***

Taarag Stagskull sighed and shook his head in disbelief as he watched the last Bonestripper rider flee from a single beaten human. What manner of safety did the fool think he would find back at the horde after a failure like this? He and the others had been given everything and yet were defeated.

The ambush Taarag had led on the humans had worked well enough for his liking. The moments of distraction provided by the Bonestrippers were more than sufficient for a surprise attack. The clay jars of Firebane had left the humans blind and confused, little more than prey for the incoming riders. They should have finished what he started with ease, and yet they had not.

Granted, they had inflicted a satisfying amount of carnage, but it was not a massacre as the Stonemaster wanted. It should have been a massacre and would have been but for the Gray Lion Clan human. Taarag wondered how its clan had learned to be that strong. To defeat three Bonestrippers alone? It was hardly in top form now and limping away, but limping away with its life and a victory any Berserker would boast about for a year.

Returning with that news to the Stonemaster as that rider fleeing for the hills meant to do would be madness. The Chief of Chieftains had just lost three Bonestrippers. In exchange, he still lacked the prize he wanted taken and the enemy's death he most desired. It was an explanation he wasn't going to accept, and the retreating dolt would face all the wrath the Stonemaster could command from the rock beneath his feet.

The rider would not end well but Taarag saw it more as an opportunity. His party of goblin Shadows against the whole group of humans would have been suicide even after leading with a Firebane attack. Against two bruised and battered humans, two more so injured they could barely walk, and a last reduced to madness? That was far, far more advantageous.

Favor with the Stonemaster was there for the taking, and he could pluck it like so many ripe berries if he could motivate the goblins beneath him. At the moment, that was not looking certain. Despite the change in circumstances, he saw the others cringing. If it continued, their chance would pass as they cowered in the comforting darkness, and he knew why.

"The Bonestrippers have done their work," Taarag whispered to his unsettled band. "The humans are nothing now. Time to kill them."

"The Gray Lion Clan human lives." The enforcer realized the tremulous whisper likely summed up the feelings of the lot. One human, one stupid human, had left them paralyzed with fear. It would not do.

Taarag punched the speaker to the ground and bared his teeth. "It is so worn it can barely stand. Its companions are few and weak. And if we fail, the Stonemaster will hear of it, even if we don't tell him. Think you have a better chance against the Chief of Chieftains?" One by one, the cringing goblins shook their heads. Taarag gave them one more growl, and they reluctantly prepared their weapons.

"Good. We follow them until they drop, then ambush them. When all are dead, put the Gray Lion Clan's strange shirt on a killpole and take the shiny big knife. We will do this before dawn." The enforcer glared over the group of them, seeking more reluctance in need of punishment, but found none.

"The Gray Lion Clan human will die tonight."

***

"Come and watch the stars, my love."

It was always in the darker times, weak and weary, or bloodied after a fight that memories of Cecelia would echo in Pencheval's thoughts. That particular invitation had come on a spring night, when they were both in a hayloft wearing little more than straw and well away from prying eyes. She was snuggling into his shoulder and he was wishing the dawn would never come. On that night undisturbed in his memories she was still his betrothed and there had been nothing more to do but pull her to him.

Her memory was bittersweet even after all the years that had passed. He remembered peasant dresses flowing, brown curls bouncing, spontaneous smiles, and backwards glances at him when she danced ahead to enjoy the day. She had been his everything since they had met as children, and she still was. It was the time before Pencheval the farmer's son, content with his lot and happy as her betrothed, had her taken from him and became the Hopeslayer. It was the time before the Hope of Terris Lyn had set his own doom into motion by being the reason for the loss.

It was also a remembrance for another day. As Drillmaster Tagrine had told him, when it was time for battle, it was not time for distraction. He had beaten or tricked the beasts that had attacked him, but with the other goblins at large, he realized he wasn't remotely out of danger yet. Neither he nor the survivors would be until they were someplace safe, and the nearest town was Tarsun's Market at the center of the valley. It was no Shield of Athesiene, but it was garrisoned, walled, and the destination of a forced march he had to explain to a group of battered survivors who didn't want to hear it.

Friar Dominik was binding wounds as the soldier with the shattered mind curled up in a ball, rocking back and forth and muttering incoherently to himself. Pencheval shed light on the work with the one torch he could scavenge and kept watch with the Clearsight charm. A gray picture from outside the torch's glow blurred and bled into the colors it did reveal as the boundaries of its light ebbed and flowed. The charm was useful in that it didn't blind its user in the presence of light, and the effect had left apprentice Pencheval fascinated the first few times he had used it. As a journeyman, it was no longer anything but an advantage.

The Silver Lion could not see any goblins to the limit of his vision but he meant to be ready for them. Unless he misjudged them, they were still out there somewhere even if they weren't attacking. The contest between their fear of those who had beaten their monsters and their fear of failing their clan chief would keep them passive until it was decided, and he didn't believe the outcome would work to his advantage. If their chieftain could command such beasts, he believed the goblins would find attacking weakened, wounded humans far preferable to its wrath.

"Be swift, friar," Pencheval ordered. "We have to go."

"Go? These men can barely walk." The friar quit binding wounds and scowled. "The battle is done. Let them rest."

"It is not," Pencheval replied. "The monsters are gone, but the goblins that doused all the flames are still out there, along with who knows how many others. Either we get to someplace safe or we will likely die. That means we march for Tarsun's Market. Now."

"Now just a–"

"Enough!" Pencheval's bark echoed off the rocks. "We've done it your way once, friar, and here we are. There is no time for mourning or rites. Night is a boon to goblins and if any catch up with us, they will put it to use again. We. Must. Go." Pencheval pointed his torch at the mountains. "Or if you prefer, that's the goblins' home, if you'd like to save them the trouble of coming to you and me your endless mewling."

Dominik's eyes narrowed. "So you mean to save us? Are you the hero now?"

"Heroes are lies and fables," Pencheval retorted. "What you need is a Lion, and you have one."

"He's right." The soldier whose ribs the friar had been wrapping slowly stood. "We have to move. If they come with more of those monsters..."

"Or even just more goblins." The injured archer Pencheval guessed was the man the friar had been aiding from the field limped forward. He had suffered some cuts and a sprained ankle but nothing serious enough to keep him down. "Tarsun's Market will take us 'til dawn to reach in our state, but it's safe."

"Tend to him." Pencheval pointed to the soldier still muttering on the ground. "I'll take point. friar, can you fight?"

Dominik grimaced, but he took up his staff. "I've cracked a few skulls in my day."

"Take up the rear." Pencheval searched about for trouble again, but saw nothing to the limits of his magically enhanced vision. He was not reassured in the slightest.

Sword in one hand and torch in the other, Pencheval led the way to a source of lights in the distance he took for the town, followed by the two soldiers half dragging and half coaxing their mad companion along. He would have preferred Dominik had not taken the rear, but the soldiers were in less shape to fight than the friar and he was the only one armored well enough to take point.

The mercenary liked their chances if the goblins took too long to try something. Even now, he felt the subtle warmth beneath his skin as he absorbed magic, and he would have a stock of it again in an hour or so. Whether or not it would take an hour for the goblins to muster their courage and mount an ambush would make all the difference.

***

Pencheval suspected the goblins were coming, but the hours passed with no sign of them. His first guess was that they meant to wait until he and the survivors fled themselves ragged and then ambush them. To his chagrin, he surmised that any observers would have plenty of reason to believe that would happen.

For the past several hours, their march was nothing like that of hale men. The wounded had to be attended as Pencheval gritted his teeth and wondered when trouble would come. He was just as weary as the others, and had stumbled and cringed from the pain left by repeated uses of magic to give himself strength and speed. To make their travels tenser still, the panic and lunacy of the now-mad soldier Pencheval had pulled from the battlefield had to be quelled frequently, and none of this was hidden from anyone or anything.

In his moments of wishful thinking, he hoped that the goblins had been spooked by the deaths of their beasts and fled. He realized his fortunes were not that good when he crested a hill, and between him and the torchlight from Tarsun's Market was a spear-wielding goblin in a buck skull mask and a hooded tunic. A number of its fellows were with it, and looked as though they meant to hit them head-on.

"Goblins," he groaned as a warning to those behind him.

The weary Lion dropped the torch, slapped down his visor and raised his sword, bewildered by the tactic. The goblins had the numbers and were less worn and wounded, but in his experience they never used a frontal assault without an overwhelming swarm or in reaction to an attack they could not flee. He stayed on guard until he realized they weren't charging and that there were fewer of them than he remembered seeing during the Firebane attack.

"Beware! Behind you."

"Not the monsters." The soldier who had been driven mad shook loose from his two wounded companions and ran. "Not the monsters!"

The terrified man bolted past Friar Dominik, and his wounded companions could do little more than try and call him back. The friar looked as though he didn't know whether to chase him or defend the other two, a question Pencheval watched the goblins answer for him. The soldier ran straight into a half dozen hooded assailants that were sneaking up on the friar from the rear, and they were all too happy to attack the runner first. Pencheval heard a crack and a scream as a goblin smashed a club across his knees, and three more piled onto him as he fell. Surrounded now, he had no time to mourn.

Pencheval narrowed his eyes and willed his sword to burn, fighting off the urge to stop as his head swam from fatigue. Once again, the wail and grasping tentacles of flame from the Pitfire spell gave the goblins pause, and few showed any inclination to charge him. He took his sword in both hands, tried to stand ready against the goblins in front of him, and then faltered.

His enemies had waited too long to attack him and his reserves of magic had been renewed, but the strain of the march and the night had affected him. With the stumble came a loss in concentration from his already taxed will, and the illusion of his possessed weapon sputtered and extinguished. He heard a goblin scream in its tongue, followed by the patter of footsteps as they rushed in to kill him.

Pencheval could not use enough magic to scare them away but even without it, he was still an expert swordsman. Drillmaster Tagrine and hard experience during his apprenticeship had ensured it. The first three goblins to reach him died as fast as they arrived, but the fourth sidestepped a downward chop and stabbed at Pencheval's thigh. The chainmail leggings prevented the stone dagger from piercing, but the force of the thick and stubby blade bruised and staggered him.

A second took the opportunity to jump on Pencheval's sword arm and try to stab the blade out of his hands with a flint knife. The primitive blade stuck and then broke in the studded gauntlet, vambrace, and chainmail. Pencheval willed himself what strength he could, and despite the stabbing pain it left in his arm, used it to throw the goblin to the ground. It hit hard and didn't budge again.

He realized his first assailant was no longer at his feet when a frayed garrote slipped around the chainmail protecting his neck. The weight of something on his back pulled it taut and nearly yanked him to the ground. He slipped his hand between the rope and his armor, but could do little else but try and not be strangled.

He could see the goblin in the buck skull mask point and caper. Every other one of its companions charged and pounced on any gaps they saw. The first to reach him was kicked unconscious to the ground, but another managed to grab for a knee and force Pencheval to kneel. Yet another went for the sword to pry it away as a fourth attempted to pull Pencheval's hand from the garrote so its fellow could choke him.

The Silver Lion had to will himself strength just to keep from being overwhelmed. Muscles protested but grew stronger, leaving him in a brief stalemate with those that had swarmed him. They could not overwhelm him, but he could not break free, and he knew he would lose when the masked goblin with the spear walked forward to skewer him.

Just before it charged, spear aimed at Pencheval's gut, a loud wooden crack preceded the loosening of the garrote on his throat, and he felt a weight on his back lift as it thumped to the ground. Pencheval mentally thanked Friar Dominik for his help as he twisted, shielding himself against the spear thrust with the goblin on his left arm. The masked attacker cursed as its fellow caught the strike with its back. Pencheval took the moment of respite and his newly freed hand to bring his fist up and then down like a hammer on the head of the goblin tearing and stabbing at his sword, knocking it senseless in one shot. The one at his legs found itself suddenly alone and fled screaming.

He was free but staggering, stars dancing before his eyes, muscles protesting from the ache of a long march and repeated calls upon magically enhanced strength. The clipping of his legs left his knees and shins in pain and he no longer had the concentration to do more than will himself Clearsight. It was not much, but he believed it was enough.

His opponent came into clear gray view, and he thanked his luck for the fact he saw no more assailants accompanying it. It had pulled its spear from the back of its companion and prepared to face him. It cursed in its tongue and circled slowly, not eager to meet the same fate as its minions.

He still heard the soldiers and Dominik fighting behind him. Goblins screamed instead of humans, the shouts and repeated smacks of wood on bone suggesting they were getting the worst of the fight. He was glad they would suffer no more deaths tonight and returned to the next thing he meant to end.

Pencheval gritted his teeth, ignored his various miseries, and stepped forward quickly to thrust. The goblin sidestepped the attack and responded with a swift strike at his guts. The spear beat his guard but was turned by the brigandine tunic, merely tearing a chunk from his tabard instead. The goblin cursed in its shrill tongue and jumped back into guard, quickly thrusting for the legs. This time Pencheval struck for the spear, but the goblin pulled it back in time to prevent him from breaking it.

The two of them circled before the goblin struck again, aiming for his legs once more. Pencheval countered with a parry followed by a lunging thrust that found its mark. The hooded goblin in the buck skull mask dropped to its knees, and he finished it with a chop to the head.

He turned to join the fight behind him and saw the few remaining goblins fleeing at the death of their leader. Both soldiers, wielding bloody daggers, nodded their gratitude to him. Beaten, bloody, and wholly uncowed, the friar leaned on his staff and gasped for air.

"You're welcome, warrior," Dominik said when he finally found his breath again. He smiled at Pencheval and, despite himself, the weary mercenary gave him a wry grin.

"Not bad, old man. Not bad at all."

***

The weary group limped towards the gates of Tarsun's Market at dawn, finding comfort in the sight of its cobblestone walls. The brilliant sliver of the sun just cresting over the mountains at their back cast long shadows across the rocks and fields, and Pencheval breathed easier. After a night of near death experiences and far too many slain, he was grateful that safety and sleep were just within reach.

A guard standing at the top of a wooden tower behind the walls challenged Pencheval and he answered, pointing out the soldiers and the friar as his companions. Shouts and orders were exchanged, and the gate swung open, much to the Silver Lion's relief. A group wearing the white tabards of Athesiene's temple approached, quickly recognized their own, and offered assistance to everyone.

Pencheval received curious glances and the occasional horrified look, but he had grown accustomed to that. No one ever hired Silver Lion mercenaries except in response to something horrible and present, because only the king had the clout and coin to garrison them in peacetime. So not only were they seeing him as a herald of trouble, but he and his companions looked as though they had met it already, courtesy of the goblins and their beasts.

Everyone was escorted to the barracks and offered the services of a healer, an offer all accepted but Pencheval. He quickly accepted the offer of a bed though, and fell asleep almost instantly upon hitting the thin layer of straw. He'd slept on worse, and after the night he had just left behind him it didn't take him long to find sleep.

When he finally woke, the sun was setting and shadows were long. Muscles stiff and stomach growling, he made his way to a local tavern and quickly bought what they had ready. The simple but surprisingly hearty stew the tavern girl gave him and ale suited him well enough.

Pencheval shook his head. He had wanted a change from the dull moments of reflection in the town beneath the Shield of Athesiene, but this was not what he had in mind. He supposed the worst of it was over and he had served his contract, but far too many had died for his liking. The reason for being of knights and Silver Lion adepts was to deal with monsters that common soldiers could not, and Rennoute had likely hired him to accompany the patrol as a contingency against them. Whether or not he met such beasts under unusual circumstances should not have resulted in so many slain, but there was nothing he could do about it now aside from regretting it at his leisure over a meal.

He could not undo it, as much as he wished he could. There was nothing for it now but to rest, heal, and then leave to deliver the news to the Knight Superior that he had discovered the cause of the deaths. Not merely a clan of goblins, but a powerful clan of goblins had taken up a home in the mountains just bordering the valley. They would not have managed to react to the patrol's attack on their raiding party in under a day had they been any farther away. He guessed that would mean half the distance between Tarsun's Market and the eastern edge of the valley would forever be unsafe. Any who ventured there would find themselves robbed and butchered by the goblins picking at the fraying edges of the Emerald Refuge's borders.

The thought left Pencheval genuinely depressed. Violence was already plentiful enough for him. It was respite he found to be in short supply, and he was not so eager to lose what few peaceful places there were for the coin fighting brought him. Unless the Temple of Athesiene could rid themselves of the goblins with more efficacy than the Lord of Stonewall Pass they would plague the valley indefinitely, endless skirmishes draining lives and morale.

"Mind if I sit?"

Pencheval looked up at the battered friar. Bandaged and still weak, he leaned on his staff and moved as though his muscles were screaming. The weary mercenary gestured to a crude wooden chair across from him, feeling some sympathy for him over the shared pain of a forced march and a desperate fight. The friar winced as he sat but greeted resting on the hard wood as though it was strewn with padding and cushions.

"Was what we have just endured a sample of your occupation, Lion?" The friar seemed aghast at the thought.

"No. This is what happens when monsters catch you on their own terms." Pencheval took another drink from his pint of ale. "Were it a typical contract, the beasts would be known and posted by the local bounty master. I would have gone after it with a tracker and killed it as much on my own terms as I could while those who would be slain in the fight stayed far away. This is not how I meant to serve this contract, even if it is met."

He motioned for a tavern girl with a wooden pitcher, who walked over and refilled his cup. "Get him stew and ale."

The friar raised one hand in disagreement. "I will be fine, Lion."

"You've marched and fought hard, friar," Pencheval insisted. "You need to eat."

"It'll be bread crust for me unless you mean to pay. I'm sworn to poverty."

Pencheval fished a silver coin out of his pouch and left it on the table. The friar's eyes grew at the sight as the tavern girl took it and left.

"That's a bit much," the friar protested. "I couldn't ask..."

"It's small coin for a Silver Lion." Pencheval gave him a wry grin. "Those who need us pay well, and many need us."

"Small coin or not, it surprises. I would not expect charity from a man some say executed a hero for naught more than a foppish baron's gold."

Pencheval frowned and his eyes narrowed. "You know nothing of that, so presume nothing."

"I agree," Dominik replied to Pencheval's surprise. "So tell me, how did a man who would drag any survivors he could out of a massacre and guard them all night until they reached safety come to be known as a black hearted mercenary? Why would someone who speaks and acts with such contempt for the common folk care what happened to a common friar and a few common soldiers? We did nothing but slow you down and further risk your life."

"It matters little now."

"It matters to two soldiers and a friar." Dominik smiled gratefully at the tavern girl when she set a bowl of stew and a tankard of ale in front of him. "It matters to you or you would not have done it."

"Do you mean to batter me senseless with wisdom even as your stomach growls? Still your tongue and eat."

Dominik smiled and took his advice, happily shoveling stew into his mouth. A few moments later, he washed it down with the ale and wiped himself clean on his sleeve.

"Why come here if you were not seeking wisdom? None come here but for respite or guidance. No one sent for you, or I would have heard Rennoute's subordinates howling over it from across the valley. Were I to guess, I would say your life is wearing hard upon you, likely because the man you feel you must be is nothing like the man you actually are."

"Friar..."

"Cease your growling and quit pretending all you are is a mercenary and a war hound." Dominik's calm focus caught Pencheval off guard. "I am sworn to provide succor to any who need it. Despite my first impressions, you are someone in need. So unless you mean to spend another fortnight waiting for counsel from the clouds that will never spare it, let me help you face your demons, whatever they may be. They impede the good in you, and they will snap at your heels wherever you go until you defeat them."

Pencheval sighed and slumped back into his chair. "You did save my life, so I will indulge you. Ask me what you will. Once."

"What manner of quarrel did you have with the Hope of Terris Lyn, if you did not capture and kill him for a bounty in gold?"

"He murdered my betrothed and father for sport while I watched bleeding to death. I would have been dead along with them, had his companion done a better job of killing me. For fear he would attempt it again upon learning of my survival, I was forced to flee my home in Terris Lyn and lose myself among the multitude at the capital. It just happened that avenging all these offenses came with gold, so I took it."

"This cannot be. I passed through Terris Lyn many times. The people sang songs about the Hope, celebrated his victories... the man gave them charity! He tormented the baron and was not as you describe."

"Yes, he did torment the baron, but that did not make him a hero as I discovered. The so-called Hope of Terris Lyn was not the hope everyone thought him to be. He was simply an opposite to a noble no one could stand." Pencheval half-emptied the ale in his tankard. "But your reaction is commonplace. No one else believed me either, and few believe me still."

"And that is the reason for your contempt towards the common folk?"

"You've had enough questions for one day." Pencheval finished his ale and stood. "Enjoy your meal. Tasks yet await me."

Pencheval supposed the friar was trying to be helpful and reluctantly conceded he was right. Staring at the sky had done nothing for him. He doubted Dominik could do anything for him either, despite the friar's willingness to try.

No, the common folk in Terris Lyn had not believed him, either immediately after the murders or after the death of the Hope at his hands years later. People he had known for his whole life, childhood friends and kindly neighbors, would not hear what their 'Hope' had done and stoned him out of a square for even speaking of it. Their neighbor and friend, Pencheval, who had been a part of their tight-knit village for years, told them who their Hope truly was, and they chose to believe that revelation was slander woven out of whole cloth.

That was before he became a Silver Lion. Now all they could do was resent him in silence as Pencheval the friend, peasant and neighbor gave way to Pencheval the journeyman adept, mercenary and war hound. He had and could return to his childhood home in Terris Lyn without fear of reprisals owing to his skills and power, but it would never be home to him again. For all intents and purposes to him now, it was just another ink marking on a map.

Sick of the old memories and eager to do something else, he double-checked at the barracks to ensure that the local guards had sent word of his news to the Knight Superior. Goblins were not things anyone would care to meet by surprise and his client had to know of them. Whatever had kept them away to this point scared them no longer, and he was happy to hear that the soldiers had dispatched someone by horse while he was sleeping.

He returned to the tavern and rented a private room for the night, grateful he had survived the completion of this contract and planning for the next day. He would have a brigandine tunic to mend tomorrow and armor to get to the smith, but he could do that and recover within the safety of the walls and well away from goblins. His work was done, as miserably as it had ended, and he meant to put this behind him.

***

"Kill him."

The beaten and tied goblin on his knees before the Chief of Chieftains screamed as a single spike of stone blasted from the ground and impaled him. Rumbling as it grew, it raised the prisoner high enough into the air that the whole horde could see it done. The goblin victim twitched and choked, and the Stonemaster believed the crows would peck his eyes out before the time his dying was over.

The Chief of Chieftains inwardly cursed the fool. He had been the last of the Bonestripper riders sent after the humans, and had come back alone after fleeing the fight. He had gibbered excuses about the incompetence of his fellows and the need to save the Bonestripper from death at the hands of the mighty Gray Lion Clan human, excuses which the Stonemaster had not accepted. Four Bonestrippers and a patrol of the Shadowcreed Chieftain's stealthy Shadows should have been enough to slay them all, but more importantly, such an improbable defeat would be seen by his horde as a bad omen. He needed to not merely punish the fool that had failed him, but to single out a scapegoat and quell talk of ill tidings.

The rider had served nicely in both regards. His death, paired with a display of commanding the stone, would leave the horde obedient again. Though the horde thought otherwise, his commands to the rock were an act meant only for their consumption. The Stonemaster knew it was the work of his staff, and that the staff did as it was *willed* rather than told.

It was a bit of deceit that distracted the vast majority of goblins away from the true source of his power, and made it appear as though his word alone caused the rocks to obey. To all but a few of the shaman who knew better, his staff was just his favorite treasure, and those who knew otherwise were too scared of him to set that secret free. That meant the goblins believed he alone had the power of the Stonemaster, which left them in awe and discouraged thieves and rivals.

Some of the goblins in the horde cringed at the execution and others laughed, enjoying it as though it was so much entertainment. They were assembled now, watching the Stonemaster from ledges, cave entrances, or the gully below him as he stood on what they all called the Speaking Boulder. The Stonemaster's voice carried far and wide when he stood there, and the chattering and distraction dissipated as he motioned for silence. Tens of thousands stopped speaking as though commanded, gazing up at him expectantly.

"This fool was unworthy." The goblin warlord pointed to the twitching and impaled Bonestripper rider. "His incompetence alone is the reason the Gray Lion Clan human yet lives. Now we put this weakling behind us, and take from this valley as we will."

Murmurs and discontent came from all around him. Those enforcers he could see looked as though they would start beating compliance and belief into the horde, but that was not what was needed to unite them. Coercion alone would not be enough.

"Listen to me! I am the Stonemaster, Chief of Chieftains! I have been blessed by the Fiend Under The Mountains, our god! He has given me command over the stone and, against this, the Gray Lion Clan or any other will perish!" The tepid response was more like cheering now. The demonstrations of the staff's power meant he could propagandize that way and be believed, but he had more work to do.

"And not just me." The Stonemaster paused and let the moment of silence build tension in the assembled. "Who will stand against this power and us all? Who will stand against the horde? One puny human of the Gray Lion Clan? The Snow Clan humans huddling in fear in their mountain-castle across the valley? Those whose eyes were cursed by their gods so that they cannot see without flame or sun? No!"

The Berserkers began chanting. A hundred huge goblins daubed in red mud and wearing the pelts of black bears thrust their axes and maces into the air in time. Following in their lead, the horde began to chant the name of the Chief of Chieftains. He nearly let the moment overwhelm him but restrained the urge to bask in the adulation. He had not changed their mood just yet.

"We are the horde! This valley is ours, and we will thunder down the slopes as an avalanche. The Snow Clan and Gray Lion Clan will cower before us, toil for us, and beg for their lives! Neither they nor any other will ever threaten our survival!"

The chanting rang in earnest now. It was a sound like the screeching of a storm of insects, or a gigantic flock of birds. It echoed off the mountain walls, and the Stonemaster threw his arms wide as he reveled in it.

"Our new clan-home awaits!" The chanting turned to cheering, and those goblins nearest him began frothing from the desire to pour forth onto the humans.

"Bring my chair. We go forth now!"

Goblins whipped the harnessed rams to drag his litter forth. It was a giant wheeled construct of bones and wood carrying his elk-horn topped throne. Less a cart than a pulled platform with a canopy, goblins led the beasts of burden from the ground rather than a rider's seat. The Stonemaster took his place upon it and smiled.

His force was not merely strong, but overwhelming. Two score Bonestrippers, a hundred Berserkers, the stealthy and hooded Shadows, shamans, and pawns without number were the avalanche he had called them. He was pleased with himself for having forged such a horde. It would not be stopped, and the Gray Lion Clan human would be no more a match for them than anything else.

The Stonemaster Ascendant

Howe was certain he would ride his horse into the ground. The chestnut mare gleamed in sweat and its labored breathing sounded like a bellows. He had been unable to sit for an hour now, and his legs were stiff and sore as he half stood from the saddle. Still, it was better than death at the hands of the goblins.

He had never seen so many of them in one place. It was as though they had come from every mountain in the northern range. Thousands upon thousands of them. A cacophony like a gigantic swarm of insects or a flock of birds had drawn him to investigate, and what he found had left him fleeing since. To have half a horde of goblins notice you at once, and several riding those...monsters? He couldn't wheel his horse fast enough to escape.

Tarsun's Market was in sight now. The stone walls and heavy wooden gates were a comfort and he was glad he would be behind them soon. He briefly wondered if they would be enough, but for the time being he would be glad to take whatever safety they might offer against such a gathering of goblins.

"Open the gate!" He reared his mount to stop quickly just shy of the wooden doors. The panting horse stood still and bowed its head. "Lord on High protect me, let me in!"

The gates creaked open too slowly for his liking, and he bolted through them as fast as his exhausted mount could manage.

"What flee you, scout?" A soldier in a gambeson and the white tabard of Athesiene's temple took the reins as another offered him a skin of water.

"Goblins," he proclaimed before drinking deeply. "A horde of goblins."

"Horde?" The soldier holding the reins swallowed hard. "Knew about some raiders and their beasts, but nothing about a whole horde."

"No, it was a horde. A multitude as great as a swarm of locusts. A bone throne on a litter...Athesiene save us."

Howe returned the skin to the soldier that had offered it to him and took stock of his surroundings. His fellow soldiers were nervous and taking the news as well as he expected. Several townsfolk had gathered at his arrival, chattering amongst themselves over his frightful state until they heard the news. Some blanched in disbelief as others appeared ready to run or faint. Only one person didn't seem to mind.

From the doorway of the nearby tavern, a tall warrior in a chainmail hauberk, trousers, and armored boots stood with a pint tankard as though he could not be bothered to depart from his ale over such meager tidings as the news of a goblin horde. He wore a battered black tabard lined in gray and bearing the crest of a gray lion rampant. Howe gasped as he realized the man wore the tabard of a Silver Lion adept, but the warrior just shook his head, sighed, and returned to whatever he had been doing inside.

***

Pencheval plopped down at a table in the tavern's common room and put his face in his palm. Was it not enough that he had fought his way through a night long forced march not three days ago with the few survivors of a goblin ambush? An ambush by goblins riding beasts so fell they slaughtered men several at a time when they weren't feasting on them, bearing hides so thick he could barely cleave them? Now it wasn't just the raiding party he previously met or even goblins on their monsters, but an entire horde of them.

He found no cause to doubt the report of the scout. The man had been genuinely terrified, and one did not ride a horse into the ground over a raiding party. Nothing Pencheval saw of the soldiers of Athesiene led him to believe they were anything less than professional or prone to panic over slight circumstances. If anything, their sense of piety and purpose kept them strong when others would have fled. It was a mixed blessing demonstrated by the valor of the patrol Pencheval had accompanied. Given the choice to withdraw or fight to save their fellows, they chose death over discretion against an impossible foe.

No safety in Tarsun's Market then. Against even an entire clan of goblins the walls might suffice, but not against the tide of the horde that would crash against them. There were no great towers to aid in enfilading fire on the corners and no emplacements of siege machines atop them. Eventually, the goblins would overwhelm them with numbers because the lack of force and obstruction meant they could not be slain quickly enough to prevent it. If the beasts they rode could be brought to bear against the gates, stout as their rough timbers were, they would not even have to climb the walls. The monsters need only crash through and begin the slaughter in earnest.

That was not the first danger though. He also didn't want to be here when the townsfolk started reacting to the news. He had been foolish enough to try to warn such folk against dangers once, and the memories of the stoning he received for it always reminded him of his folly. The people of Terris Lyn didn't want to hear that their precious Hope was a murderer and worse, even from one they had known for years.

Pencheval had no intention of repeating that mistake here. These common folk weren't any better than his 'neighbors' and 'friends' in

Terris Lyn. He found absolutely no reason to believe their reaction would be any more measured, and he really couldn't care less about them. So why then stay? No one who mattered would care. His guild only required that his fellow *guilden* be supported or their patron the king on command, and none of them were here.

It was time to find Friar Dominik and go. He was worth the effort unlike the rest. A few nights ago, a timely blow from his quarterstaff had saved the mercenary from a goblin attempting to garrote him. Now that trouble was brewing it was time to return the favor and aid him in retaining his life.

Only The Shield of Athesiene had walls and towers both high and stout enough to resist the onslaught of a horde of goblins. The castle also garrisoned the bulk of the valley's forces, and likely possessed a priest or several that could wield their god's power to tremendous effect. He would see them both there safely and in all haste.

The serving girl refilled his tankard when he beckoned her over. He put a silver piece on the table in payment.

"Where do the friars stay here?"

The girl cocked her head quizzically at him. "Why?"

"I need to speak with my companion. I arrived with him and two soldiers a few days ago. Pressing matters."

"Generally they stay at the temple," she replied. "Or at the house of someone offering hospitality. Many here are charitable to them."

This place wasn't Terris Lyn then, Pencheval mused. Or at least, wasn't yet to the point the common folk would reveal themselves as the animals they actually were. He saw no point in giving them the opportunity.

"My thanks." Pencheval rose slowly, muscles still protesting with dull aching reminders of a tense and deadly night, and took his leave of the tavern.

***

For a moment, the town of Tarsun's Market reminded Pencheval of home before he banished the nostalgia as the remembrance of a fool. Despite the walls and cramped spacing of the wood frame and thatch buildings, it did have the rustic charm of the life he once thought he had. He shook off the sentiment. Believing in the life that had actually not been was to believe in the deception that nearly saw him dead.

He could hear the peal of the smith's hammer ringing in the distance through the bustle and noise of the peasantry. Some carried baskets of vegetables on their way to work, tools and other implements of the trades hanging from straps or belts. Others pulled carts or led animals. However, the general to-do about town had been replaced by a nervous buzz, and the conversations seemed strained or hushed. The news of the horde was spreading quickly and it was time to go.

He had paid no mind to the place at all until now. For the past two days he had ignored everything except his own fatigue. Two days of waking on his straw cot well after dawn, groaning because his stiff and sore muscles would not let him move without spasms of pain or a dull ache. After what it had taken him to get to Tarsun's Market, he supposed he was fortunate his troubles had only amounted to stiffness and bruises.

Rest and magic to aid recovery had left him almost well enough to travel, and more than well enough to stalk towards the temple of Athesiene in search of Friar Dominik. The place was easy enough to find. It was the largest building in town besides the tower house of its lord, and despite lacking the size of the great edifice at the capital, spires still rose from its four corners. Stained glass windows above the door depicted the revelation of the Lord on High at Mount Torin to Saint Marion, she as chaste and awed by the sight as the verses he learned in temple told. As per every other window he had seen, the Lord on High radiated light in beams of white and a brilliant red, the same color of the red peak appearing on the white tabards of Athesiene's soldiers.

Pencheval strode through the open double doors, drawing glances from a few surprised faces as his metal plated boots echoed from the floor. A priest attending the dais and pulpit at the far side turned to determine why the sounds of armor rang from the stones, and stopped what he was doing to greet him.

"I welcome you to the Temple of Athesiene, Bringer of Light to the Darkness and Lord on High." The father put his hands inside the sleeves of his robes. "May I help you, Lion?"

"I am seeking Friar Dominik. Middle aged man, gray hair and beard. Quarterstaff. Arrived with me two days ago at dawn after surviving goblins."

The priest kept his composure but still appeared unsettled to Pencheval. The mercenary didn't much care, even if he was the cause of it. The other options always tended to be things like apathy, hostility, or a desire to beat him for his coins and leave him in a ditch. Becoming a Silver Lion had changed all of that and he saw no reason to abandon their approach now.

"He is resting. He has not moved quickly since arriving."

"Where?" The incoming horde cared little if Dominik was weary or not, and Pencheval didn't want either of them here to see their indifference firsthand.

"The garden." The priest pointed towards a closed door on a side wall.

"I'll see myself out."

The door opened into a small but verdant space tucked between four walls near the center of the temple but open to the sky. A small fountain half-filled with water lilies burbled gently in its midst as a drizzle of water poured from the stone pitcher of a cherub's statue. Thick stone vases with plants sat among the corner gardens, paths set with flat stones winding between them. Pencheval saw Friar Dominik resting on a bench against a wall, relaxing to the sound of the fountain.

The steel-shod footsteps brought that to an end when the friar and everyone else there watched the mercenary stride directly to the bench where he sat. Dominik, who had previously been smiling in the calm, looked as though he wondered what manner of trouble was waiting to greet him. He sighed and recovered his composure.

"Good day, Pencheval. You do not seem contemplative but the garden is free to all."

"We need to go. Now." Pencheval anticipated slow travel due to Dominik's still weakened condition and meant to get a head start on the horde.

"Go? To what purpose, Lion? I can recover well enough here."

"You can recover well enough at The Shield of Athesiene once I escort you to it. Goblins come. A horde of them, and against so many the walls and forces here will not suffice."

"You mean just leave? Now that we are needed?" Dominik stood to confront him, but put his hand on his back as he rose. He slowly stretched himself upright, groaning at the effort. "What would possess me to do such a callous thing?"

"Good sense." Was one brush with goblins not enough to convince him, Pencheval wondered. The last time he had stopped for niceties the patrol that had rescued him was all but massacred.

"More like poor character." Dominik scowled. "If a horde comes this town will need my help and yours. After such a display of heroism as it took to escort me and two soldiers here safely you would again show such darkness?"

"I would remain breathing and see you do the same." He would also see the friar avoid the reaction when the horde was all that remained on the minds of the townsfolk. Panic was coming, followed by the residents showing their true vicious natures as they had in Terris Lyn.

"Then lend your sword and skills to the cause, for I will not leave this place so long as I may render aid." Dominik sat back on the bench. "If you think you may somehow manage it in the absence of coin."

Pencheval snorted and suppressed the urge to throw the wandering holy man over his shoulder. Naïve fool. Why should he not haul him away? Even after three near death experiences at the hands of goblins just to reach Tarsun's Market he would still not believe the fiends were the threat Pencheval claimed them to be. If made to leave, he could be foolish at his leisure behind the stouter walls of the castle without risking death.

So why not? Because the guards would try to stop him and the daft friar would resist. It was the same reason he didn't haul off anyone else but those with bounties on their heads. Frustrated by his circumstances, the mercenary turned and left without comment.

***

"Chief of Chieftains, we are spotted."

The Stonemaster, goblin Chief of Chieftains and master of the vast horde tending to invasion preparations around him, grumbled and rapped his talons in irritation against his staff. Did the rabble before him truly find cause to disturb his council meeting by announcing the obvious? Were the partitions of stitched hides circling his throne platform not sufficient to suggest that the Chief of Chieftains did not want his deliberations disrupted?

The human on its mount had crested the hill, taken one good look at the multitude, and fled as fast as its beast's legs could carry it. Of course it was because it had spotted them. The horde was as hard to miss as a storm front in a clear sky and far more threatening.

A single scout did not concern the goblin warlord. What the humans of the Snow Clan would do when they heard the scout's news concerned him. He had hoped to cover more ground before they discovered the horde. Despite their inferior numbers, the Snow Clan could still be plenty of trouble if warned far enough in advance. The human clan in their white shirts had better weapons, the protection of the town, and the mountain-castle at the other end of the valley.

"They will send their own horde," the shaman called the Allspeaker advised, showing the same excess of caution the Stonemaster always expected of him. "They will mean to stop us here."

"They will cross the valley to reach us? Night falls, and they are undone." The towering Bloodmoon Clan chieftain looked as though he was eager for the fight, as he always did. His Berserkers grew impatient for warfare, a reward the Stonemaster had promised them for joining the horde. It would not go well between him and the Bloodmoon if they found that promise unfulfilled.

"It is not war that should concern you, Chief of Chieftains. What if the humans flee to their mountain-castle?" The question came from the Beastwarper Clan chieftain, who leaned on his staff as ever. A growth of bone and spikes grew from his left shoulder like lichens from a tree, bending him and weighing him down. He never sat or walked as the others because of it. "They are fewer and can travel more quickly than us. If you mean to enslave them, their fear is also your frustration."

Despite his irritation at this newfound problem, the Stonemaster was glad to have the cunning Beastwarper Chieftain on his council. As usual, he had a valid point, and one more pertinent than what to do with a single human scout. His was the mind that had discovered the way to warp trolls into Bonestrippers, a useful and dangerous beast, and then break them to riders.

The Stonemaster meant to capture as many humans as he could in the town, and make them tell of their secrets. How did they find, make, and shape things of metal? How did they build things with the evenly similar stones that stuck together? How did they create the fields of strangely rowed plants from which they fed? He wouldn't know if they fled to their mountain-castle and remained beyond his reach.

"Run down the human and its beast," the rabble who interrupted the meeting suggested. His words were met with a glare by the Stonemaster, who wished to speak to his council and not his pawns.

"Go. Now."

"Yes, Chief of Chieftains." The goblin cringed and scurried away.

"Though the rabble speaks out of turn, something must be done," the Beastwarper Chieftain advised. "Our numbers are known."

"Or perhaps not so known." The Stonemaster sat back on his throne and scratched his head. "They know we are numerous. They need to believe we are too numerous."

"Chief of Chieftains, we do not understand." The Shadowcreed Chieftain cocked his head to one side. His clan of goblins were the best of the horde's spies and scouts, and practiced stealth and ambush to a degree of mastery few other goblins could attain. "What do you wish?"

"We know the land in the valley?"

"Yes, Chief of Chieftains. Our scouts have learned it carefully as per your command." The Shadowmoon Chieftain still seemed puzzled.

"These humans live around the town in all directions?"

"Sparsely, Chief of Chieftains, but they are there."

"Then now that they know we are many, we will make them believe we are everywhere." The Chief of Chieftains stood from his throne and stepped forward to gesture to the council beneath its platform. "Bloodmoon, send Berserkers north of the town. Shadowcreed, send Shadows to the south. Beastwarper's Bonestrippers will ride to the west of it. Each of you terrorize the rabble humans of the Snow Clan. Leave enough of them alive to tell tales of you assailing them from all directions. Make them believe the town is their only haven.

We will herd them there like so many goats and then snap the trap shut."

The Bloodmoon Chieftain laughed thunderously. The Chief of Chieftains heard a squeak and the clatter of dropped wicker as the booming noise startled a goblin on the other side of the partitions. "Yes! It will be done."

All in his council smiled except for the Allspeaker, who was ever hesitant about conflict. It was why the Stonemaster kept him there. The shaman valued caution over war, and counterbalanced the others who meant to curry favor by aiding the Stonemaster's conquest. That, and his capacity to speak in any tongue he wished was critical in the Hordemaker's plans to learn from his new slaves.

"Patience, Allspeaker. Your chance for favor comes once the humans are ours."

"Yes, Chief of Chieftains. But what of the other humans? If the Snow Clan Chieftain in the mountain-castle reacts too soon, this plan will fail."

"If the Snow Clan Chieftain comes out of its mountain-castle, its plan will fail," Bloodmoon countered. "But for their mighty mountain, we could defeat them now. We are more than enough to slaughter them on open ground."

***

Pencheval sat on the bench he had occupied at the tavern not an hour before, drinking ale, and racking his mind for answers he could not find. His reappearance drew curious glances from the tavern girl, but she was perfectly happy to pour him yet another wooden mug of the local stout without comment. He idly took another sip and tried to find a solution to his troubles.

To his frustration, no possible answers presented themselves. Instead, he merely wondered why he had returned here instead of continuing to argue. Would the danger cease if he plied himself with enough ale? Would Dominik grow sense of his own accord? He found neither to be likely and yet lacked any approach save force that would solve it.

Two soldiers bearing the tabards of Athesiene's temple walked into the tavern and over to him the second they realized he was there. Pencheval mentally checked to see if his sword was within easy reach. Satisfied of its placement, he calmly set his mug on the table in front of him, leaving his hand visible to appear non-threatening.

"Silver Lion, you are summoned to the presence of Knight-Brother Galot."

Pencheval assessed the speaker. He was a burly and slightly balding fellow equipped with a gambeson, a shield, and a spear. His companion was a lanky soldier bearing the same kit but more nervous.

Both were regular infantry spearmen of Athesiene's temple, Pencheval concluded. They were just doing what they were ordered and one of them was less than thrilled with the idea of confronting a Silver Lion. So far the tone was businesslike, but their message was stated as a command.

"Who is Knight-Brother Galot?"

"The lord of Tarsun's Market. He wishes to speak with you, and you will come."

That one was definitely a command, and the thought of beating both of them senseless briefly crossed his mind before he dismissed it completely. While the soldiers were no match for him, it wouldn't do to offend the lord of this town. He had yet to persuade Dominik to evacuate and he did not mean to be forcibly evicted over a senseless fight before he could do so. Such petty violence would also offend his client the Knight Superior and embarrass his guild. Neither would take that offense lightly.

He rose from the table. "Lead on."

Pencheval wondered if he had stumbled into some sort of strange place where knights actively sought out the aid of Silver Lions. His guild and the various knighthoods were on notoriously unfriendly terms, which Pencheval saw as a caste in decline disliking their far more effective replacements. At times the only reason they did not decide their difficulties by force of arms was the command of the royal house. Granted, in the face of a horde the lord would need every sword he could get, so the mercenary was hardly surprised. Merely having it happen twice in a fortnight was unusual to say the least.

The burly soldier motioned him to follow and the other took up position behind him as they left. It was not a polite escort to a contract offer then. The Knight-Brother disliked his presence for some reason. Pencheval concluded it was the usual knightly disgruntlement with his guild and remained wholly unfazed.

The soldiers led him past the townsfolk to a tall but less than imposing tower house across the main square from the temple. A stone tower four stories in height, which he estimated from the arrow slits, rose to an oddly out of place exposed beam house constituting the top two floors and flaring off from the main building. He could see trapdoors for shooting or dropping rocks and was unimpressed. Like the rest of the fortifications here, it was ample for common troubles but would not withstand a horde.

Polite but all business, the soldier in front walked through the gardens to the iron-banded door and hammered on it. It took two more tries and an irritated call to hurry up before someone opened a small viewing hatch in the door.

"Soldier?" The voice was nasally and irritated.

"We are here with the Lion."

"Bring him forthwith." The door opened, and a wizened but richly dressed man motioned for the soldiers to lead Pencheval inside. He dismissed them with a wave of his hand and scowled at the mercenary.

"Follow me to Galot."

The steward led Pencheval to the second floor with a desk and various furnishings, none of which suggested a living space. Sitting behind the desk was a middle-aged knight in a fluted breastplate reading over parchments. He rubbed his forehead in strain and did not immediately acknowledge the entrance. His salt and pepper hair looked mussed enough to suggest that his duties weighed upon him.

"The Silver Lion you commanded appear, Your Grace."

Galot took a deep breath and stopped reading. "Leave us."

The steward bowed and left the two of them alone. Galot threw the parchment in his hand to the desk and sat upright. Pencheval was unimpressed by the attempt to intimidate him.

"What mean you by even being here, Lion?" The knight scowled at him. "I have a horde bearing down on this town, and the first thing you do upon hearing of it is to inform anyone within earshot that we lack both the force and fortification to stop them."

"I gave one of your friars that assessment, Your Grace. Because you do."

"How nice of you to bless us with your wisdom," Galot snapped but did not reach for his weapon. "The fact you might cause a panic didn't occur to you?"

"Not especially, Your Grace." Pencheval wasn't worried about anyone but Dominik, and nothing the knight had said or done thus far changed that. "But I will repeat my assessment to you. Walled and garrisoned as this town may be, it is not enough to stop a horde."

"What do you suggest I do then, mercenary?" Galot replied derisively, "What great insights can you give me? I am in need of answers, and am stuck with none but you to provide them at this moment."

"Your Grace should evacuate to The Shield of Athesiene. No other place in the valley of the Emerald Refuge will stand against so many."

"Evacuate? The whole town just up and go?" Galot crossed his arms. "I should take the whole population and lead them outside the walls where some portion of that locust swarm of goblins may feed upon them as they see fit?" Galot clenched his jaws. "Think you might suggest something other than madness? I am sworn to protect this place and its people, not lead them to slaughter."

"You will lead no one to slaughter, Your Grace. Slaughter is coming here." Pencheval restrained his temper and his reply was matter-of-fact. "Do as I intend, and don't be here when it arrives."

"And why should I should put stock in your martial counsel? The patrol you were meant to safeguard from beasts didn't make it back, so you'll excuse me if I find your opinions less than convincing." This time Galot gazed at Pencheval calmly, and the increasingly irritated mercenary swallowed the urge to snarl his next words.

"If Your Grace believes he would fare better against those beasts than I, the horde will test your mettle soon enough." Pencheval flexed his fists. "Your armor is tempting enough that the goblins will seek you out."

They would indeed. Goblins favored shiny spoils, though the knight's power might be enough to save him. Might, if he had the time to call upon it, which Pencheval doubted. From what he remembered, the knights of Athesiene learned to invoke the power of their god during their time as squires. It made them nigh invulnerable, but it took so long to bring to bear it could not be done but before a battle.

Willing magic as Silver Lion adepts like himself could do was not as powerful. However, it could be done while in battle and took less than a heartbeat's time to grant benefit when it was all the time they had to spare. Speed was the Silver Lion's advantage and the one he found more practical than invocation. The ability to kill an opponent before they could finish a more potent spell had led more than one of them to victory and the retention of their lives.

"But for your contract with the Knight Superior, I would have you thrown from town." The word Pencheval believed he would have liked to use was 'whipped' but even here, they knew Lions and their guild were not ones to cross. "As it is, I will command you not to spread rumors and panic again. This place and its soldiers will protect these people, and if you don't care to believe it you will depart. Soon."

"Happily, Your Grace." The Lion meant to leave as soon as he could convince Dominik to join him. All this place would offer anyone was false hope. If the fool knight wanted to learn that the hard way, so be it.

"You may go, mercenary. Don't give me cause to summon you again."

"Your Grace." Pencheval gave a perfunctory bow and left without additional remark. He was done sparring with the suicidal and meant not to join them.

***

Pencheval strode across the market square, pushing past people as he made his way back to the temple from Galot's tower home. One grumbling tradesman turned with the idea to be irritated after a nudge knocked his tools to the stones, only to see the Silver Lion adept and scurry away instead. Their discomfiture kept them out of his way, though for all his menace he did not want to do anything but leave the town with Dominik.

Pencheval didn't care if the friar had taken a Vow of Poverty, Service, or Idiocy, he meant to save him. None of the town's defenses particularly impressed him and it was better to be safe than slain. If Knight-Brother Galot wanted to deny there was a problem and take his chances, he could do so without risking the two of them.

The double doors stood open, but when he clomped through the arches and towards the pulpit he was met with the forced cold civility of those who did not want him there. They kept their composure from their faith or good natures but their displeasure was clear to him. One senior sister, who sat with several girls in the pews, turned and openly scowled. None of this made the slightest bit of difference to Pencheval, so long as they told him what he wanted to know.

The agitated mercenary approached the priest at the altar and was met with a look of suppressed annoyance. "Where is Friar Dominik?"

"Is that all you have to say for yourself then?" The sister that had been scowling at him rose from her pew and all but rushed him. She leaned forward into his face and put her hands on her hips. He found the effect almost comical, as she was a head and a half shorter than he was. "The last time you were here, you told everyone within earshot the walls wouldn't protect them from the incoming horde. I've been trying to console my girls since, the poor dears."

"And this should bother me?" Pencheval was not concerned with her until he looked twice. It was easy enough to do as she scolded him. Something about her did seem familiar.

"Oh, why would it bother you then? Big mercenary like you not accustomed to showing human decency? More important things to do have you?"

"Give it a..." Pencheval still could not shake the feeling he had seen her before, but he didn't know where. Middle aged, dressed in the robes of a senior sister of Athesiene and annoyingly indignant? He had not been to the town of Tarsun's Market before and knew none of its residents prior to arriving a few days ago. Why then did she appear so familiar?

"Give it a what, you mailed knave? Have you suddenly lost the use of your tongue? I ought to switch you for your callousness, you brutish clanking lout!"

Her exhortations didn't faze him. He had taken worse from his drillmaster and hardened to it, and anything else paled in comparison. The raging of trolls barely impressed him, let alone a senior sister's shouting. It was simply that he thought he knew her...and then he remembered that he did.

"Nan?" She was familiar to him because she was someone he had known from long ago. But why was she here? *How* was she here?

The sister blinked twice at the sound of her name and examined him quizzically. She squinted at him and frowned. "Sister Nan. Do I know you, Silver Lion?"

"You are Nan, of Terris Lyn?" He did recognize her as Nan, years older than the last time they had met. He had been a boy when he realized she had simply disappeared from the barony. He had been left to wonder what had happened to her, but never found the answer.

He was disappointed she didn't recognize him but did not wonder why. He was no longer the lanky peasant lad happily tending to chores and grateful for gifts of berries. The Hope of Terris Lyn and his time as a Silver Lion had seen to that. "I am Pencheval. I know much has changed."

"Pencheval?" She peered closer, and then her eyes grew wide in recognition. "Not that Pencheval." She drew in breath and put her hand over her chest. "Lord on High bless you, lad. It is you."

"How did you get...why are you here?" Pencheval could barely find his tongue. He had thought Nan dead and lost forever.

"How are *you* here?" Nan looked him over, more in shock than anything else. "And how are you a Silver Lion? The lad I knew has changed."

"It's a long story, Nan. Some things happened in..." He did not want to tell the story of his loss at the hands of The Hope of Terris Lyn to her, as remembering it was painful enough.

"How is your father? Cecelia?" She grimaced. "You didn't leave them behind to chase the mad dream of becoming a Silver Lion, did you? What worth is a Lion's notoriety over family?"

"They're...gone." Pencheval swallowed hard.

Nan frowned. "Was it the Hope?"

The sister's question caught him off guard. She knew about the Hope of Terris Lyn? What he actually was? "It was. But I avenged them."

"Avenged? Wait. *You're* the Silver Lion they call the Hopeslayer because you're the one that killed him." Nan put her hands over her mouth, and then to his surprise, hugged him. The girls she had been tending, intent on their conversation, whispered to each other and giggled.

"Bless you Pencheval, for dealing with that monster." Barely able to restrain tears, the now Sister Nan let him go and turned away. "It is not a caring thing to say, but thank you. I have to...go."

Pencheval could only watch dumbstruck as Nan shuffled her charges from their prayers and towards the exit, hushing any who tried to ask her what the matter with him concerned. He could only guess that the reason she had disappeared was the same as his. She too had suffered a life-destroying visit from the Hope of Terris Lyn, a visit that made her eager to see him dead.

She knew. One person knew, and in that moment two years of telling himself he did not care what anyone else thought of the deed was illuminated as the lie it was. Nan's understanding of what he had actually done made all the difference to him. Were the common folk all not struck stupid then? This small vindication left him more uncertain about that than anything else. Unable to find purpose beyond attempting to sort through his confusion, he glanced briefly around the room at the newly quizzical faces and left without another word.

***

Dennick peeked hesitantly through the cracked door of his barn, a cudgel in one hand, a worn and flickering lantern in the other squeaking gently as he leaned to see. The sounds of distress from his cow had alerted him to something wrong. When those sounds suddenly stopped, he was sure it wasn't because it had fallen asleep. Someone had opened the door, which meant no animals were the cause of the distress.

The faint light showed him that his cow was still there, as was his horse, and they were both dead. Someone had slit their throats and left them to bleed out where they fell but left no trace otherwise. There were no footprints in the dust and nothing else was disturbed. He swallowed hard and shined his light across the barn at the pigs, and saw them nervously pacing their pen but alive. Confused and seriously considering retreat, he stepped inside and raised the lantern to check the lofts for intruders. He suddenly heard the squealing of pigs and the wet smacks of blows.

He snapped his lantern back to the swine and shuddered. Jagged stone blades stuck from their eyes, but the attacker was not visible. In fact, whoever had done it had not left a trace at all. Whoever or whatever it was had entered the pen, killed the pigs, and disappeared before he reacted. Feeling like a mouse at the mercy of a cat, he backed out of the barn, nervously jutting his cudgel in the direction of the slightest noise.

"Stay away from me," he stammered. "I'm armed!"

There was just enough light from the quarter moon to see a figure duck behind the tool shed. It was too short and strangely gaunt to be a human. It was possibly hooded, and it didn't appear to be in a hurry. Dennick tried to withdraw to his farmhouse, only to hear the clatter of someone or something rifling through his possessions inside. Out in the open and still unable to see his tormenters, he wildly jerked around in circles until the glow of his lantern landed on them.

They simply seemed to appear from nowhere. A half dozen of the hooded fiends looked back at him, feral gleams in their eyes picking them out from the rest of the night. He backed up, bumped into the edge of something, and nearly tumbled over it into the well. When he recovered, something whispered into his ear in a tongue that sounded like the buzz of a gigantic insect. He turned to see the last of his assailants leaning forward like a gargoyle from the well's conical roof, merely half a cubit from his head.

Denneck screamed, turned, and ran for Tarsun's Market, cursing the day he chose to live out in the valley alone.

***

Vhax Shadowseeker smiled from his perch atop the wood-cover of the strange stone ring that led to water. What wasn't to like about this night? Toy with a human until he pushed its fear to the breaking point and watch it run screaming? It was an absolute delight carrying out this command of the Stonemaster. If they terrorized two or three more of the humans' living places like this, the Shadowcreed's duties would be both amusing and successfully completed.

"What now?" One of the goblins near him sheathed his dagger and waited for instructions.

"The scouts say the next one is a short distance from here," Vhax answered. "We make more scared humans as we were told."

The order was met with laughter, and as one they prowled through the darkness to their next target.

***

Landings after a Bonestripper pounce were never pleasant, but the sense of exhilaration Ghin got from them were the best moments of his life.

Momentarily airborne on a gigantic Bonestripper, the sounds of terror as it descended on prey and the rending of flesh and bone? It was a moment of power most goblins would never experience. The fact the target was one of the human's hoofed animals made no difference. It was the moment of flight and not the target that made Ghin grateful to the Fiend Under The Mountain for his talent in directing one of these beasts.

Granted, killing opponents instead of hoofed animals was more satisfying, but those were not his instructions now. He was to terrify humans, and a ravenous Bonestripper feasting on their animals was just the thing to do it. The mere presence of the hulking, ape-like beast with a toad-like maw full of sharp teeth should be enough, but it would not do to leave the task to chance. The Stonemaster had punished the last rider to fail him with impalement before the entire horde. Ghin refused to meet the same fate over carelessness.

The several humans that were once in the cart, two large ones and a smaller one he thought might be a pup, had tried to flee the second they saw him. The panic of their hoofed animal prevented it. So they scrambled from their cart and fled on foot when they realized their beast would not pull them away. The biggest one of them kept looking backwards to see if Ghin was on their heels, but it needn't have bothered.

The rider had their fear and that's all he wanted. They would run until they dropped towards the place the Stonemaster wished them to go. They should thank their god, Ghin mused, since Bonestrippers were usually sent to inflict annihilation on opponents and not merely fear.

Were they a family? Probably, but Ghin couldn't tell them apart. He'd heard rumors that the human females were the lumpy ones, but didn't much care. He already knew enough to defeat them and that was all that mattered.

***

The goblin Berserker Maggax smashed his axe into the chest of the human he just killed before ripping its ribcage open. He could hear the horrified shock of another human staggering away from the carnage in fright, only to be backhanded to the ground by the unimpressed Berserker taking advantage of its distraction. Another of the underwhelmed goblin's companions saw two more humans fleeing, shook his head in disgust, and let them go.

In the tradition of the Bloodmoon Clan, Maggax tore out the dead human's heart. As those fleeing glanced over their shoulders to see if they were being pursued, he leered at them and bit into it. Horrified as they were by the sight, he did not consider it worthwhile at all. They were the puny human rabble of the Snow Clan and wholly unworthy of a Berserker's axe. Yet the kill that finished the fights always demanded a heart, and he kept to the ways of his clan.

The Stonemaster wanted scared humans, but making them was an unappealing task. There were no worthy battles against these lowest of humans in the Snow Clan. He couldn't kill them all as the Stonemaster forbade it, but he consoled himself with the knowledge that the efforts here would help bring the real fight to come. This annoyance helped herd the humans towards their town, and taking them there would be a battle over which he could boast.

"What a waste." One of the Berserkers Maggax had led here spat in frustration. "It would be harder butchering goats."

"Or stomping on snow rabbits." The one who had thrown the backhand pulled his unconscious human victim from the ground and held it in front of him like a ragdoll, disappointment apparent. He easily dwarfed the human dangling by its neck in his off hand. "Could they not send the rabble for this?"

"We do as we're told," Maggax growled. "The real fight comes soon. For now, scare the humans towards their town."

"Easy enough." Another Berserker thrust a tall pole into the ground. The head of one of the humans topped it, and a leather thong of ears and eyes draped over its crossbar. "We'll leave our usual gifts. The Snow Clan rabble will see them and run where we wish them to go."

***

It was just before dawn, or so Pencheval believed when he heard it in the distance. It buzzed and chirped like a drone of insects or a flock of birds, but suggested a far more malicious source. It was a distant but ongoing sound, an undercurrent to the rustle of his straw bed or the creak of the floorboards. Soft but sinister.

It brought tidings of the carnage to come and should have made deciding easy. He should have found Dominik and left by now but Nan's presence changed that plan. Nan's presence changed everything. If she was here, she needed rescue as much as the friar did or death at the claws of the goblins would find her as well. Yet she wouldn't leave her charges any more than Dominik would, which left him with twice as much trouble, as there was no forcing either of them to go.

Reason warring with his confusion over what to do next had kept him up most of the night. He couldn't leave but it was insane to stay. He had already lost Nan once, and the fact she recognized his deed against the Hope of Terris Lyn for what it really was made him doubly unwilling to depart without her. Except they had to depart or they would be dead.

If they stayed to fight the horde, he would lose her again along with his life. If he gave in to his better sense and abandoned this town while he could, he could still battle the horde at The Shield of Athesiene. It was a castle of no mean size and endurance held by a far greater force. However, the thought of deserting them to certain death made him nauseous with disgust even if he intended to do it for sound reasons. For the first time in a long while, he was genuinely conflicted.

His thoughts changed when he heard the wooden smack of a shutter or door beneath his window. He almost returned to his musing when it was followed by a snarl and a curse that bore a more than passing resemblance to the click and screech of the goblin tongue. Wishing he merely imagined it but expecting otherwise, he threw on a shirt, strapped his sword belt over his trousers, and slowly opened the door of his room to keep the hinges from squealing.

He picked his way down the hall towards the stairs descending to the first floor common room and glimpsed a flickering light from below. He descended the stair to a landing and found the innkeeper in a nightshirt and cap holding a lantern and a club. He appeared to be inching towards a door or opening out of Pencheval's view, and every so often the mercenary could hear the clink of pots and other cooking implements.

"Stand fast, innkeep," Pencheval whispered.

The proprietor started at the mercenary, wide paunch jiggling, and pointed towards the kitchen door.

"Animals in the kitchen," he whispered. "Likely dogs in the larder."

Pencheval heard the clatter of metal and another muffled curse. "No, they're goblins. Leave them to me."

"G-goblins? What do they want?"

"The metal, most likely. They can't make their own." Pencheval beckoned for the innkeeper to stay where he was and slowly slid his sword from its sheath. He inched towards the kitchen hoping to remain quiet, only to step on a creaky floorboard. All noise on the other side of the door suddenly ceased.

"Blighted luck." Pencheval willed his magic to give him sight, and the shadows not chased away by the single lantern resolved themselves into a picture in gray. The door to the kitchen was on the right wall opposite the bar. Pencheval was not worried that the goblins might use it, as they lacked the knowledge of how the latch worked. What did concern him was an ambush on the other side of the door, or them leaving the way they entered and disappearing into the shadows. He did not want them at large in the town, and was more than a little curious as to how they entered it.

As that creak had ruined any chance at stealth there was nothing for it but the direct approach. The mercenary rushed forth, grabbed the door's handle, and tore it open. He allowed his vision to darken as he instead willed his magic to grant him speed, and everything in his sight slowed to an almost humorous parody of its former self.

The goblins had not left. One crouched in a window's frame as though departing with an iron pot and a tea kettle. Another lurked under a large table covered with vegetables. That goblin slowly lunged upwards to stab him with a knapped knife. Pencheval thrust his sword downward, taking the goblin through the chest.

The goblin in the window accelerated and leapt away as Pencheval's quick burst of magically enhanced speed faded and ceased to affect his perception. It bolted as fast as a rabbit harried by a hound the second it hit the dirt and disappeared between the buildings across the street. The annoyed mercenary frowned and wiped his blade clean on the dead goblin's rags and hides.

"Filthy beggars."

The sound of boots on wood brought him back to the common room. The innkeeper was there in his now disheveled night shirt, gasping, distraught with the effort of running and exerted to the point of leaning on his knees. Three soldiers of Athesiene's temple wielding spears and shields accompanied him and briefly snapped into guard upon the mercenary's entry. Pencheval calmly sheathed his sword, gave half-hearted consideration to less provocative ways of telling them what happened, and then chose not to bother with sugar coating his remarks.

"The goblins have found a way through the walls." Just as I suggested they could to your master, he thought to himself. "You might want to inform Knight-Brother Galot."

It was certainly worth asking them to do it, particularly if Dominik and Nan would not go on his word alone. Galot might not listen to him but he would believe his own eyes when he saw a dead goblin. Would the knight finally gain some sense and evacuate the town to the better defenses of the castle? Surely all would leave on the lord's word, including those the Lion meant to save.

And what would he do if Galot chose to remain despite evidence? He was back to trying to convince Nan and Dominik to leave with him, a task that frustrated him to no end. Time grew short and they adamantly refused to evade the incoming horde. Perhaps this would be enough to at least weaken their resolve in that regard.

***

"What do you know of the Silver Lion called Pencheval, friar?"

Friar Dominik rose from his prayers in the quiet alcove and turned towards the voice to find a senior sister awaiting his response. It wasn't the first time someone had asked him about the Silver Lion adept. He found it unusual only in that the sister knew the mercenary's name.

Everyone knew the black garbed bounty hunter was here, but most of the time the folk would ask only if he meant to capture someone and who it might be. Others wondered why the Lion was allowed to stay if he had no business. Pencheval was as out of place as a wolf in a flock of sheep and almost as unwelcome.

No one until now cared anything else about him. No one except for one very upset senior sister whose confrontation and surprising reconciliation with the Lion had been a topic of conversation recently. Dominik was glad she asked, as he was curious why their encounter ended the way it did.

"You must be Sister Nan. As I recall, you are having about the same manner of luck as I am with our resident mercenary." Dominik took up his staff and leaned on it. "He is callous, bears a contempt for the common folk, and shows the same unnerving aptitude for violence as the rest of his guild. Yet for some odd reason, he pulled me and two soldiers from the jaws of death when fleeing alone might have been far safer for him."

"He saved you?"

"Aye, though he has grown callous again. Except for his clumsy attempts at persuading me to depart with him to the castle, no life here concerns him save his own." Dominik scratched his head. "Clearly he desires to change his path, or he would not be here. Yet the darkness ebbs and flows within him like the tide, revealing then drowning in turn the glimmers of goodness he yet retains. If I may ask sister, how came you to know him?"

"I've known him since long before he wore the black tabard, friar." She sat down on a bench and leaned back against the wall. "In truth, I never expected to see him as a Silver Lion, though I fear I know which darkness put him on that path."

"Which darkness, sister?"

"The misbegotten Hope of Terris Lyn." Nan grimaced, and Friar Dominik presumed it was at the thought of the Hope.

"Yours is the second time an opinion of him did not match what I hear on my travels." Dominik sat down next to Nan. "If this Hope of Terris Lyn was truly such a blight, why is he sung and hailed as a martyred hero?"

"Because he was no mean rogue, friar. Until the day he crossed my path, even I believed him the hero. I have never seen nor wished to see again any such capacity for manipulation and deceit as I saw in him."

"This man has deceived his way into legend?"

"It was less hard than you might expect, given his circumstances," she answered. "Those in Terris Lyn were desperate for a hero, so for his own ends he gave them the illusion of one. The baron there was a grasping fop, pretender to the society and refinement of the capital. His taxation and apathy to the suffering of the folk gave the Hope of Terris Lyn all the opening he needed to play that role to perfection."

Dominik remembered the evening after their arrival in Tarsun's Market when Pencheval had said much the same thing. He had been incredulous and unwilling to believe him. He was not so eager to dismiss the report after hearing it from a senior sister of Athesiene.

"The Hope lived as any other rogue, only quietly, taking what he wished in secret or in the guise of acting for the common folk. It's what he did the night he...disillusioned me." Nan bowed her head. "When I told the people of Terris Lyn what wickedness he had wrought upon me, the lies he had woven ensured no one would hear any of it. They were so desperate to cling to some hope of salvation from the baron they would believe nothing but what he would have them believe. He was a hero to them, and any words to the contrary were slander and treated as such."

"So you left and came here." Dominik found no cause to torment the sister by asking for further explanation of the Hope's crimes, as the rogue's assault and worse against her was clear enough to him now. "You believe the Hope of Terris Lyn did this to Pencheval?"

"Pencheval would not have told me of him if the Hope had not been involved. He would still believe him the hero as do all the rest." Nan swallowed and regained her composure.

"I remember his father and that girl Cecelia." Nan clenched her jaw. "They were adorable together and rarely parted. If the Hope of Terris Lyn killed them he tore out the better part of that boy's soul. If the town reacted to his accusations the same way they reacted to mine, it would explain his contempt for the common folk. Given the tabard he now wears and the callousness I hear from him, I fear he found his answers in much darker places than I found mine."

"You believe his guild is a path to darkness, yet you were grateful that he avenged you on the Hope. Would he have been strong enough to end the villain had he not become a Silver Lion? His vocation does not condemn him."

Nan frowned. "You misunderstand. It is not his proficiency with a blade or what he did to the Hope of Terris Lyn that concerns me. That beast earned anything he suffered at Pencheval's hand. It's what the Hope of Terris Lyn still does to him."

"He is slain two years now, sister. What can that rogue do to the Lion?"

"You've seen him, friar. Laboring under the misconceptions brought about by the Hope, he sees naught but potential betrayal in everyone he meets, unmoved by any evidence it may not be so. It ends any possibility of kinship or community and that is no small curse. The beast torments him from the grave and the Lion does not see it."

Dominik nodded. "There is cause to believe it. It was his brutality that earned him the name of the Hopeslayer. Should it continue, he will wander, and then die unmourned."

"Continue?"

"From what I gather in the tales that cannot be dismissed as exaggeration, Pencheval made the whole barony watch the Hope die. The rogue almost managed to escape his execution when the Silver Lion succeeded where the noose failed. The lad made it a spectacle, crushing the hopes of all those that saw it, and crushing them again as they watched him leave with a fortune in gold for his efforts."

"Striking down an evil, but harming the manipulated as well because he believed them all the same. Indiscriminate vengeance and nothing beyond it."

"Except his misconceptions," Dominik added. "'Heroes are lies and fables' was what he said to me when I asked him if he was going to be one a few days ago. Now I know from whom he gained that grim bit of cynicism."

"The Hope of Terris Lyn was a monster. He cloaked himself in spun tales and fancy clothing, but he was a monster still, sure as any troll, drake, or goblin. And his claws are still in Pencheval."

Dominik stood. "If you have found a path away from the Hope's darkness into the light, you are more capable of providing him guidance than I am. He surely needs it."

The echo of heavy boot steps clomped quickly down the nave and drew a sigh from the friar. "That would be him now, sister, trying to save me again. He will draw Galot's ire should he continue."

"Leave the matter to me, friar. I left him behind once. Not again."

Dominik waited for Nan to stand and leave before following her. His attempts to get through to whatever matters tormented the Silver Lion had not succeeded. It was his hope that she would do better. Together, they might put a halt to this and in the process convince the Lion not to desert a town full of innocents.

Upon entering the main hall, however, they saw Knight-Brother Galot and not Pencheval speaking with the father. He could not hear what they were saying but the priest seemed aghast. After a quick exchange, the clergyman rushed away and called for anyone within earshot to attend him.

"Your Grace?" Friar Dominik looked at the scene, confused and suddenly worried.

Galot turned to him and Nan. "We will need your assistance soon, friar. Sister. This morning survivors came in from the west gate, some run half to death. They tell tales of goblin attacks north, west, and south of here."

"Outriders from the horde, Your Grace?"

"Outriders from the rest of the horde we thought was only east of us, friar. We are surrounded, so pray that your Silver Lion companion was wrong about our chances. There is no direction to flee, and fighting is all we can do now."

Dominik felt cold sweat form on his brow, but refused to shirk his vows. "What do you need of me, Your Grace?"

"If you have any sway over the Silver Lion, we will need his sword. Disgusting as the thought may be, we are all in this now. Persuade him to aid us."

***

Pencheval knew goblins were dangerous. He had spent years fighting them in Stonewall Pass and nearly died at their hands less than a fortnight ago. For all their lack of stature or advancement in little beyond raiding, recent experience alone had again proved that goblins were not creatures with which anyone should trifle. And yet, had anyone up until now told him their sound alone would be enough to wreak havoc, he would have called them mad.

He remembered the chatter of the raiding party when he first discovered goblins in the Emerald Refuge. The talk was shrill but did not outlast the fight. Listening to it for days on end was another matter entirely. The maddening and endless insect-like background noise growing ever louder left him on edge along with everyone around him.

He stood just outside the door of the tavern on an otherwise pleasant spring morning wondering what fresh trouble he would find today, and found no shortage of signs it would happen. A woman in a house across the street opened the shutters of a window, quickly watered the plants in the sill, and slammed the ill-fitting covers shut again. Farmers or craftsmen pulled hats around their ears as they rushed to their destinations. Others brushed past him to get into the tavern and snapped orders for ale to the proprietor grinding his teeth behind the bar.

A carpenter bumped into a farmer carrying vegetables, which knocked them to the ground and immediately provoked a fight. Two guardsmen barked orders to stop, which were ignored by the shouting combatants. Too frazzled to step between them or pull them away from one another, they clubbed both participants unconscious.

Plenty of the usual trouble then, Pencheval mused. He had seen variations on these themes for two days now and had no hope that it would improve. Everyone was snapping at everyone else and his most recent problem was having to wait on more ale as his competition for it tried to drown the cacophony ever in the wind.

If the horde was grinding down resistance just approaching the town, what would they do when they arrived? He wished he could have convinced Nan and Dominik to flee to The Shield of Athesiene before all of this, but they would not go, and he refused to leave without them. He had only just found Nan again and would not desert Dominik after the friar had saved his life, even as some corners of his mind cursed him as a fool for remaining.

"What have you brought down on us?"

The owner of the voice could be heard from the street intersecting the one in front of the tavern to his right, along with the sound of an angry crowd. Pencheval almost dismissed it as someone else's problem, more of that trouble he intended to avoid, but he recognized the man who replied.

"Wh-what have I brought? I'm a scout!" Scout Howe was terrified. He heard guards bark orders followed by the sounds of a scuffle, and Howe yelled for help once again. The crowd cheered and the guards went silent, which led Pencheval to believe that the encounter had not ended well.

It was a mob meaning to exact retribution for the presence of the horde, at least in their own addled minds. It was a madness that had nothing to do with him. He told himself he should try to save Nan and Dominik before such trouble came for them. This lot were just common folk, the same sort as in Terris Lyn that didn't deserve the efforts he had spent on them to this point. So why could he not just ignore it? He could not put his finger on the reason he chose to stand and act regardless.

Pencheval ran towards the noise and shoved his way through a crowd of bystanders to reach it. Complaints and would-be assailants melted away at the sight of his tabard until he finally arrived at the source of the trouble. A dozen villagers with various improvised weapons stood around a bound Scout Howe, and a man built like a smith and wearing a soot-stained leather apron pulled him to his feet. A rope tied into a noose dangled from the nearest lamp post. Some of the crowd cheered, others looked worried, but most stood by while it happened.

Pencheval used his magic to give power to his voice and stopped the whole scene with the Lion's Roar spell. The amplified, leonine shout shocked the bystanders to silence. Howe started, and every member of the would-be mob turned to face the interruption of their previous mischief. A weasel of a man with a club pointed at him, his face twisted into unfocused rage and madness.

"And *you*," he said with accusation in his voice. "Harbinger of death! Herald of the Black Archer, whose arrows struck down many soldiers not a fortnight ago!"

"*Bringer* of death," Pencheval replied sternly, "and herald of your pain and suffering if you don't heed me. Unhand him and end this, or have it ended."

"You come to our town." The mob's speaker stepped forth. "You bring your goblin demons with you." He jabbed the tip of his club into Pencheval's chest, shaking in rage. "And then you think to *command* me?"

"Wrong answer." Pencheval grabbed his weapon hand and twisted it away until he broke the wrist. When his accuser screamed, he struck him with a punch that broke his jaw, sent teeth and blood flying, and left him unconscious. He dangled limply from the weapon arm Pencheval still held, and the unimpressed Lion dropped him to the street without ceremony.

"Which of you is next?" He turned to the others, his gaze stern. He saw no one in the crowd of bystanders do more than recoil and heard nothing but shock and tears from them.

The compatriots of the weasel looked hesitant, though one or two seemed lost enough to the goblin induced lunacy to try something else. Pencheval took stock and saw nothing that particularly concerned him aside from their numbers. They were scared, poorly armed, and barely trained peasants with farm implements and clubs.

Cursing the inaction of the others, the smith threw Scout Howe to the ground and stalked towards Pencheval. Pencheval let him get within arm's reach before rapping the fingers of his left hand on his sword hilt. When the smith glanced at the movement, the mercenary took advantage of the distraction and tore off the brute's ear. The shock left the huge man screaming and clutching the side of his head, blood flowing from underneath his hand and down the side of his neck.

The Silver Lion waited until he was satisfied that the horror had dissuaded the others. When he found the looks of shock numerous enough for his liking, he followed up with a punch to the ribs and another to the face. The final blow knocked the brute onto his back. He ceased to move but for the trickles of blood where his ear once was. After several tense moments, some of the others cautiously backed away while the rest broke and fled.

"This farce is over," Pencheval roared at the remaining bystanders. "Be gone!"

Did they really mean to stand by? The Silver Lion caught himself and was incredulous he would credit them with resolve. Of course they did. They were common folk. Howe was their scout, but they had done nothing to save him because they were capable of no better. He had seen nothing else from their sort since Terris Lyn.

At least they gave him plenty of berth after that display. Satisfied that they would be no trouble, he pulled a knife from the belt of the now unconscious and shattered lynching leader and walked over to Scout Howe.

"What are you doing?" The panicked soldier tried to squirm away from him.

"Saving your life." Pencheval cut him loose of his bonds. "Can you walk?"

"Yes, but the guardsmen are badly beaten." Howe pointed towards a stairwell descending into the basement of a home. Two men wearing the white tabards of Athesiene's soldiers groaned where the lynch mob had thrown them. They lacked their weapons and appeared unable to leave on their own due to injuries rather than binding.

He helped one of them to their feet and supported him while he walked. "Grab the other one. It's going to be a rough trip to the barracks."

"Why did you save me?" Howe seemed perplexed, which didn't surprise Pencheval in the slightest. Silver Lions were known for their brutal efficacy and not their charity.

"Never look a gift horse in the mouth, scout."

Pencheval didn't really want to tell him why. It was because once, a long time ago, he had been at the mercy of a mob made up of townsfolk he mistakenly thought he knew. He simply could not bear to stand by and let it happen to someone else.

***

"What have you seen, Shadow?"

The Stonemaster sat on his throne with his council in attendance, eagerly awaiting the news this particular Shadow had for him. This specialist had been sent to spy upon the humans in their own town, a task which could not have been completed by the rabble. The Shadows alone possessed that skill in stealth and prided themselves upon it. Given the look on his face and the fact he returned, the warlord expected good news.

"I went to the town as commanded, Chief of Chieftains. Discovered another weapon against the humans."

"What other weapon?" The Stonemaster leaned forward and listened. He saw nothing on the Shadow, save his hooded tunic, and hints of the various blades concealed in what most would mistake for the rags he wore. Yet the underlings dared not lie to him. He had made more than enough examples for them to be very clear about the consequences of that.

"The horde can be heard from the town, Chief of Chieftains. The noise strains the humans so much they turn on one another. Two went so mad the Gray Lion had to crush them."

"You mean the chatter?" No one in a goblin clan thought anything of the noise because it was ever present. Goblins in the horde spoke day and night as they did in their clan-homes or anywhere else they gathered. The lowest of goblin rabble could disregard it at will and even sleep through it.

Yet this mere noise disturbed the humans? Disturbed them enough that it drove them to attack their own? That was an unexpected blessing and would make them much easier to defeat.

"Well done."

"One last thing, Chief of Chieftains." The Shadow looked downward and scratched the back of his head, hesitating. "Two of the rabble were caught trying to steal human treasures. One of them was killed and the other fled. The humans know we can enter their town."

The Stonemaster snarled. "Spread the word! There will be looting enough once the town is captured and no sooner. Do you know if the humans found our entry point?"

"Our entry point is everywhere, Chief of Chieftains. Their cliff-walls are so rough they barely slowed my travel at all. I climbed them easily to scout there."

The Bloodmoon Chieftain laughed. "The humans believe themselves safer than they actually are."

"And so it will remain. Tell the horde of my prohibition and give the Snow Clan no cause to consider the walls. Let them seek hidden entrances in vain." The warlord forgot his irritation, sat back on his throne, and steepled his hands. "No need to rush our preparations if even our sounds help defeat the Snow Clan. Let them hear us coming. It should be amusing to see what it has done to them once we arrive."

***

Pencheval sat on a bench outside of his usual tavern, cursing the shortage of space that kept him out of the common room. Strained and shouting townsfolk had filled it until there was only space to stand. They harried the proprietor for ale that grew increasingly short in supply.

Those who weren't making preparations, or flooding the temple for prayers and sermons, used the tavern as an escape. Yet there was no real respite from the blighted screeching, that ever-present reminder in the conversations, the meals, and what now passed for sleep that death approached. At least now those same people gave him a wide berth.

Those few that noticed him at all as they tried to flee the noise rushed away, keeping their distance out of fear. His display at the lynching he prevented had made him even less popular with the townsfolk, and he was no more inclined to care than ever. He was just happy a tenuous but lasting order had been restored, brought about by the example Galot made when he hanged the two lynch mob members the Lion rendered too unconscious to scatter. Even now they dangled from their nooses in the square as the knight had not seen fit to remove them. Pencheval did not hold Galot in high regard, but the fact he wouldn't tolerate a descent into mob rule redounded to his credit.

The guardsmen noticed him as well but reacted differently from the others. Every so often one of them would pass on patrol and nod respectfully at him. His intervention in the lynching had left the garrison grateful to him, something he did not quite know how to take.

"May I join you, Pencheval?"

Pencheval looked up at the voice of Nan. Unlike the frightened or hurried people passing him for the past hour, the senior sister was unusually calm and smiling at him. He was happy to see her once more, and gestured to the opposite side of the bench.

"You are welcome here, though I know not how much trouble keeping my company may cause you."

"The people here don't attack the sisters or anyone else who has taken orders." Nan pulled her robes forward and sat down.

"Why not? They were eager enough to attack that scout I saved not a day ago. It's why I wanted to leave here with you and Dominik." Pencheval snorted. "This was inevitable. Now the trouble's closer still and safety less certain."

"You could have gone." Nan smiled at him, but Pencheval only grumbled and crossed his arms.

"I owe the friar. But for a well-timed stroke of his quarterstaff I would have been spit on a goblin spear like a haunch of meat. Now we might not even live through the madness of the townsfolk before the goblins have another go at it."

"Not all is Terris Lyn, Pencheval."

"Is it not?" Pencheval's expression softened. "I understand why you had to leave now, Nan. I was stoned out of a square when I told my 'neighbors' the Hope had murdered my father and my betrothed. They would have killed me but for the fact the constable arranged a hasty departure to the capital with a caravan to save my life."

"They were manipulated, Pencheval. They needed hope against the baron and that fiend was all too eager to deceive them."

"And you are so forgiving? What were we that they would believe a lie over us? Were we not there for them in their darkest hours? Did they not know us for years before all of this? We were, and they discarded us for a myth."

"It was desperation and naught more," Nan insisted. "You remember the baron. Did we not also need someone, anyone to help us believe we might be rid of him at long last?"

The Lion did remember the baron, though not because he wished to do so. For as long as he had lived in Terris Lyn, the grasping fop was one of the troubles he had learned to avoid. The noble pretended to manners he did not possess, dressed in anything a silver-tongued merchant told him was fashionable, and powdered himself so excessively he appeared as a festival clown with a beauty mark. It would have been comic but for the toll his self-indulgence took on Pencheval and everyone else there.

One of the Lion's old friends made the mistake of laughing at his appearance and earned twenty lashes on the spot for the transgression. At other times, the noble would attempt to impress someone he thought might improve his station, and wring additional coin or labor from his subjects for a feast or spectacle. The only saving grace was that the pretender did not travel through his own lands, claiming to hate the sight of the filthy peasants in a ridiculous parody of a courtly lisp.

The fact he had taken gold from the baron for the capture and death of the Hope of Terris Lyn was merely a means to two ends, his own enrichment and his vengeance. The looks of defeat, the tears, and the barely restrained anguish on the faces of his former 'friends' and 'neighbors' were the least they owed him after their betrayals. To stone a man for telling the truth about the murder of his betrothed and family? Nan's choice to pity them was not a decision he shared.

"It was not just them," Pencheval said, ignoring the question. "Once I made it to the capital, I was forced to eke out an existence in a place you go when you have nowhere else. It was so mean even the guardsmen there would not travel through it. The rogues owned it, and would as soon kill you for the boots on your feet as greet you. I was robbed and beaten more times than I could count before I learned to fight back."

"Nor did that account for the callous taskmasters, the shiftless, the liars, and the uncharitable who could not stoop to give so much as a greeting to a lowly dockhand as myself," the mercenary continued. "More people who could not be told from those in Terris Lyn."

"Then why save any of them? I've spoken to Dominik and know what you did for the survivors of that massacre not a fortnight ago. He believes you seek a reprieve from the darkness and so do I. If you were utterly certain of what you've just told me you would not have come here seeking answers."

"I found my answer six years ago, sister." Pencheval tugged on his tabard with two fingers. "One of their recruiters happened by after a particularly nasty brawl. He told me the Guild of the Silver Lion always needed strong warriors, and that if I could earn my apprenticeship I would know neither poverty nor disrespect again. And he spoke the truth."

"At what cost to you, Pencheval?"

"At what cost? For what they taught and gave me, the fifth of my bounties and contracts I owe them is a pittance."

"That is not what I meant."

"What mean you, then? That I finally see the common folk for what they are and treat them accordingly?"

"There are the good and the bad, Pencheval, but you assume the worst in everyone. I have lived here nigh on a decade. These are good people, only scared. See through to what is and paint not the world with the colors of Terris Lyn."

"About a dozen of those 'good people' tried to hang a scout for doing his duty. Most of his neighbors stood by to watch and he would have dangled but for me. He lives because of my disregard for the rabble and willingness to terrify them." Pencheval put his hands on his knees. "Your compassion is appreciated but it will get you killed, Nan. Fear and pain are all the common folk understand, and they are tongues I speak fluently."

"If the darkness is all you see in those around you, the Hope of Terris Lyn torments you still."

"Torments me still? That beast is dead." Pencheval was no longer in the mood for riddles. "Two years ago I avenged us both on him. I planted my boot on his head and ran him through as he squealed for his life on the gallows he meant to escape. I left with a bounty in gold to the despair of those who rejected us both over loyalty to a lie. They could do nothing but watch me depart. He is beaten and all of Terris Lyn laid low."

"The man is dead, Pencheval," Nan explained, voice softening, "but his shadow remains cast over you. He has brought despair to your life through the misconceptions he has inflicted on you, and you do not even know it."

"He opened my eyes to what really is," Pencheval replied. "I am glad you found a life here, Nan, but there is so much filth elsewhere in Lerrisaine my guild was founded to deal with it. We grow heavy with coin laying waste to the vermin."

"And I defeated his shadow first, Pencheval. I could do nothing about the man as you did, but neither do I struggle with the burdens on my soul." Nan stood and laid a hand on his shoulder. "Will you believe a demon lies masked behind the face of everyone you meet, seeing only enemies just waiting for their moment to turn on you? What sort of life could you hope to have then?"

"A well-paid one."

Nan frowned at him. "I believe none of it. Yours are not the actions of a black-hearted mercenary. Bluster as you wish, but there are glimmers of light yet in you, light you don't know how to reach or merely refuse to bury."

Pencheval gave her a wry grin. "You are as insufferable as the friar. Have you not seen enough to be convinced this place is a graveyard waiting to be filled? It will be, either by the goblins or the madness of its residents. Let me escort you to The Shield of Athesiene, where a proper force may yet muster and deal with this."

“We are going nowhere, and neither are you, unless you mean to break through the goblins all around us,” she answered. “Galot has assessed the horde and found it worse than we feared. We are surrounded, and we need your help.”

Surrounded? Pencheval inwardly cursed himself for not dragging Nan and Dominik out of the western gate and all the way to The Shield of Athesiene in irons if need be. He could have apologized to them in safety had he chosen coarseness over persuasion, but now he feared his inaction would see the three of them slain.

***

Pencheval hammered the heavy knocker on the door of Knight-Brother Galot’s tower home for the fourth time. The place became his destination immediately upon hearing Nan’s news that they were surrounded. Given that, he found it pathetic that he could walk up to the front door unchallenged.

It was the sort of fortification that kept him insisting they should go to the castle at the western end of the valley. The wooden fence did little more than keep wandering animals from feasting on the vegetable gardens around the base of the tower, and the gates on each of the streets latched shut with no more than a glorified wrought iron hook. There stood no barricades, no sentries on the roof, and no obstructions to an invading force at all. It may have been practical as a defended home but far less than ideal against a horde of goblins.

The irritated Lion had not been impressed the first time he saw it. After days of endless goblin screeching in the distance, he demoted that estimation to the illusion of security occupied by a suicidal knight. Yet Nan had needed his help and if the reports were true, he was as in this now as the town. So why would they ask for him and then not answer the door?

Just as Pencheval gave serious thought to roaring at the occupants, Galot’s steward ripped open a small viewing window above the knocker and wrinkled his nose in disgust.

“Unless you have business Lion, depart.”

“One of your sisters said you needed my help, so here I am,” the mercenary retorted. “Escort me to the Knight-Brother and let me ask what he wishes.”

“Ah, that.” The window closed and Pencheval heard the clank and squeaks of an iron bolt pulling back. The door creaked open, and the wizened caretaker of the place looked at him as though he was some sort of bug.

“Follow me up the stairs. Try to mind your manners this time.”

“Walk.”

“Hmph.” The steward beckoned, and Pencheval followed him until they reached the office on the floor above.

The Knight-Brother stood over a table covered with maps and missives, speaking with two of his officers. No one appeared happy about the discussion, which was no surprise to him. He found the prospect of being drowned in a sea of goblins unpalatable himself.

"We still hear naught but from the east, Your Grace," one of them told the Knight-Brother. "Could they not be outriders?"

"Unusual to find them around the other side of the town if so," Galot replied. "And so far that they waylaid travelers an hour west."

"Perhaps we are but threatened from three sides."

"We could not evacuate before and certainly cannot now," Galot insisted. "We make our stand here for it is all we can do to protect this place and its people. How does the muster proceed?"

"Any who can take up arms have received them or found their own, Your Grace. Drilling proceeds slowly due to the accursed racket sapping morale and affecting discipline. Even so, we can field a thousand under arms of combined militia and regulars."

Galot rubbed his forehead with three fingers and waved them away. "Resume your work. You may go."

"Yes, Your Grace." The two officers saluted and passed by the steward and Pencheval as they left.

"The Silver Lion, Your Grace. In regards to your request for aid."

"Thank you, steward. You may go."

"Yes, Your Grace." The steward bowed and departed.

Galot leaned forward onto the map table, fingers tapping nervously as Pencheval waited for him to speak. If he was bluffing about being surrounded, he was doing as convincing a job of it as Pencheval had ever seen. The strain was evident on his face, and after a deep breath the grim knight spoke.

"I take it either Sister Nan or Friar Dominik has informed you of our circumstances."

"I know what they were told, Your Grace. How do you conclude that we are surrounded?"

"Survivors of attacks fled here from all directions. All speak of the same enemy." Galot looked at the mercenary. "What know you of goblins? You have seen much of them?"

"Yes, Your Grace," Pencheval answered. "Raiders and thieves, or they were at Stonewall Pass. Preferred tactics are ambushes, misdirection, and waylaying easy targets in the night far away from soldiers. They would hit caravans in broad daylight if they had numbers enough to drown them in a flood of warriors, but those times were rare."

"What manner of siege craft do they possess?"

"If they even know of siege craft, I saw no sign of it." Pencheval would have found the concept absurd but for the muffled sound of an approaching horde and the madness it caused in all those around him.

"At no time during my residence in the place did they attack the castle there. They traveled in mobs of no more than a hundred, intent on a task or an ambush. Precious little suggests they have the patience or discipline to wait out the months of a siege."

"Which means once they arrive, they will attack." Galot rubbed his forehead.

"Through whatever hidden means the goblin thief I killed days ago used, among others."

"Likely the well," Galot postulated. "We checked the rest. Three other paths beneath the town bypass the gates, but they are still blocked by walls or obstructions."

"Be very certain," Pencheval warned him. "Goblins are deadly if they surprise."

Galot nodded and leafed through the papers on the table. He gestured for Pencheval to stand at the other side. "Your history with them is helpful, but what know you of the goblins in this valley?" He lifted a page and skimmed it before showing it to the mercenary. "Survivors report great beasts. These goblins used them as mounts?"

"Yes." Pencheval joined him at the table but did not glance at the report. "They rode four of them against us. We fought them off and killed three of them, but at great loss of life. I do not know how many more they retain."

"Do you know what they were?"

Pencheval shook his head. "I have seen nothing like them. They are brutish and ravenous creatures with thick hides. What little I discovered is that the goblins command the monsters from a covered spot they cannot reach if angered. They are kept blindfolded, for they will attack anything before them that they see, including others of their kind." Both of these facts had saved him not too long ago. What it had taken to slay them was burned into his memory.

The Knight-Brother paused for a time and then met Pencheval's gaze. "I have no illusions of how the Guild of the Silver Lion and the various knighthoods see one another. Our relations are strained at best, but is negotiating your services even necessary at this point? We will never be true allies, but you need to unite with us to save yourself as well."

"I am not fool enough to argue for coin in the shadow of a mutual enemy," Pencheval said without irritation or malice. He was a Silver Lion and of course the Knight-Brother would think he would seek payment. Under less dire circumstances, he would have asked for a small fortune in gold and likely received it. Now unification was his only chance at living through this. It was not the time to barter.

"I command the forces here," Galot said. "Will you obey?"

"Yes."

"Do you require anything from us?"

"For a siege, I will need a heater shield." Against trolls and other great beasts, shields were worthless. Any beast he had fought could crush or tear one away in a single blow and break the arm holding it. Dodging was the only real defense against monsters and shields hindered that. A shield would also keep him from swinging a sword with both hands when nothing less would cut through a toughened hide, so he did not carry one.

Sieges, however, were another matter entirely. They were fought against enemies using weapons a shield would turn, and they were invaluable against arrows. While he had not yet seen goblins using archery or even slingers, those in this valley had already surprised him once. Even if they did not use arrows, it would serve him against the knives and spears they might well bring to bear on him.

"Anything else?"

"Do you know if reinforcement comes from The Shield of Athesiene?" Pencheval hoped for good news but did not expect it.

"We received a response from the pigeon I sent them." Galot tapped the table. "They believe they can muster enough of a force to break through in a month, and then march here in two or three days. They will not send aid before then for fear of losing their might piecemeal to the horde."

"So we hold out, or we die." Pencheval was not convinced the fighting would last that long, and it didn't reassure him. It would be decided one way or the other long before the arrival of reinforcements, and the odds did not favor Tarsun's Market.

***

"Does everyone understand their place in the fight for the town?"

The Stonemaster stood on a rise with his council, looking towards the small shape of the human town in the distance. Strangely square cliff-walls surrounded it. He believed the humans had built them rather than merely settling where they found them, for he had never seen cliffs so short or oddly shaped in the mountains of his clan's home or that of any other clan.

He knew they could do that. The human that had traded him his staff had called the required skill 'masonry.' It was a skill he meant to learn. If the goblins could ever come to build their own towns and mountain-castles, he would not command a clan of goblins or even a horde of goblins. He could have ten hordes of goblins, or even a hundred, for their numbers could spread at will. Territory he could not even imagine would be his, and the goblins within them would call him Master of All Clan-Homes!

He shook his ambitions from his thoughts. He did not own the town yet, and his meeting with his council was to make sure nothing went wrong in taking it. Any fool chieftain could bluster and rage about what would happen if his underlings failed him, but he was no fool. It was best to avert problems with good sense rather than punish after failures a little checking would prevent.

Such forethought was why he was a superior Chief of Chieftains, Hordemaker, and soon to be goblin legend. That and many other advantages over lesser goblins meant he was not just another in a long line of the short-lived deluded aspiring to a greatness they would never attain. Executions may be amusing to the horde, but failure was not, and neither was losing to the petty mob of humans in the distance.

"Yes, Chief of Chieftains." The Beastwarper Chieftain leaned on his staff. "The rabble climb the walls and overwhelm the Snow Clan humans. My Bonestrippers stay to the flanks, and attack any humans riding their strange hoofed beasts at us."

"As that happens, we will take advantage of the distraction to vanquish their light," the Shadowcreed Chieftain confirmed, smiling at the thought of the ambush he would inflict. "My Shadows have already entered and left the town with no fool human the wiser. Much they can do with a diversion like this."

"And when the Snow Clan rabble is overrun, my Berserkers will kill their under-chieftain and the Gray Lion, and finish any Snow Clan warriors that continue to fight." The Bloodmoon Chieftain almost appeared disappointed to the Stonemaster. The warlord knew it was because he would not be among those doing the killing. The under-chieftain and Gray Lion were prizes his Berserkers would boast about for months. "It will break the Snow Clan and leave them groveling for mercy at our feet."

"Slay as few of their rabble as possible," the Stonemaster commanded them. "There is much for the Allspeaker to do once this place is ours."

The Allspeaker stood silently behind the other members of the council, looking worried and nervous as he nodded his understanding. His lack of enthusiasm did not bother the Stonemaster. The underling knew his place, and that was enough, for his talent would be useful not in the battle but in what came after it.

The Fiend Under The Mountain had gifted that shaman with the ability to speak in any tongue he wished. He was the only goblin in the horde that could communicate with the Snow Clan humans by any means other than pain or death, a necessity for the Chief of Chieftains to learn their secrets. Much of the treasure that would be found in the town, namely the knowledge, would not be possible to take without him.

"Preparations are ready. We attack tomorrow night." The Stonemaster looked at the lit town once again. The thought of the conquest to come sent a thrill through him. The horde's first victory and his next step towards greatness was so very, very close.

***

With the crackle of breaking wooden beams and a crash, the last of the homes on the eastern wall fell. The owner put his head in his hands but did not complain. The buildings were ordered removed to make way for archers and the catapults oxen pulled down the main street. With word that the horde could be seen and not merely heard in the distance, no one was eager to leave the eastern defenses wanting.

Pencheval could guess why Galot had waited as long as he could to clear away the buildings. In the absence of an imminent threat, the tensions caused by destroying homes and livelihoods after the endless goblin cacophony would have triggered a riot. If the goblins were to be thrown back at all, it would only be if the town was not turning on itself.

People all but shouted at one another to be heard over the noise now. Soldiers communicated by pointing and gesturing rather than speaking when they could. Anyone that did not need to be in the streets sheltered indoors. Pencheval adjusted the visor on his helmet again and was glad he wore it even if the goblins were not upon them yet. The bascinet and arming cap dulled the shrillness.

A trickle of townsfolk had taken their chances and fled west for the castle in the previous days, and no one had heard word of them since. Though no goblin hordes could be seen from the north, west, or south, no one was eager to leave the town to search for them. Goblin mobs fifty strong patrolled outside of bowshot even if their hordes did not appear. Every so often a pair of the troll-like beasts would lumber by, goblin riders safely ensconced in the wicker covertures on their backs, and they alone were enough to leave everyone assuming the worst.

Pencheval thought of Nan, the only thing about this whole mess that kept him from being numb to it. She was the first familiar face from Terris Lyn he had been happy to see since the deaths of his fiancée Cecelia and his father. How would he save the last connection he had to a different life? How would he live through the goblin attack, and did it much matter? He could not say it did but for his reunion with Nan. Yes, without her he would have left sooner with Dominik in tow, and perhaps avoided all of this, but he would still be back to where he was before.

Back to the nothing where he wandered only to wander, meeting the contracts of those for whom he cared little. Back to paying his fifth to the guild with the coin from those contracts, only to start it all over again. Two years of that had gained him wealth and a fearsome reputation, but nothing beyond it and nothing he wanted. What he wanted was a simple but joyful life with Cecelia, a dream he could never attain again.

The choice of being dead but reunited with Cecelia or a storied but empty life balanced quite evenly on his scales up to this point. But for Nan and Dominik, the possibility of meeting his fate at the claws of a goblin horde would have been no more to him than one outcome among several. He would not have known his preference before, but they were two people he did not wish slain. It was a feeling of worthy purpose he had not known for years.

He shook off his reverie and returned to the inn to check his gear one last time. He could reflect on his life and remember Cecelia later. Helping Nan and Dominik meant there were goblins to face here, and it would soon be time to join Galot on the wall and start killing.

***

The Stonemaster surveyed the cliff-walls of the human town as his horde waited around him. The Snow Clan warriors of the humans stood atop it, torches in hand, straining to see in the dark. He smiled at their clumsiness. This was why he waited until night to advance.

He could have reached the town during the daytime, but restrained his ambitions and did not rush his horde forward once the prize came into view. Foolish haste was the mark of the inferior. By waiting, goblin eyes had the advantage over those of the humans, and the light cast by their fires could be avoided until the attack.

Only one of them appeared to have no difficulty surveying the goblins in return. It was a tall human in a shiny steel suit wearing a black, sleeveless shirt. Unlike the others, it stood looking directly at him as though the night was no hindrance to it at all. Though he could only see bits of gray from its clan markings at this distance, the warlord knew which human this was from the tales his goblins told of it.

This was the human they had taken to calling the Gray Lion. The butcher of Bonestrippers. The human in black and metal that left his horde in whispers for fear of summoning it. To hear them whimper of it, it could command a burning demon in its shiny long knife and possessed the might of a Berserker. Its presence would be a problem but nothing his horde could not overwhelm with numbers.

He stood next to another human in the shiniest metal clothing the horde's master had ever seen. One of the under-chieftains of the Snow Clan chieftain, still in its mountain-castle? Of course it would keep the best place for itself and leave this place to the underlings. Yet what manner of wealth must its master possess if even the under-chieftain could wear such shiny treasures? The warlord's mouth watered at the thought, and of what he would take once they defeated the Snow Clan.

"Organize the horde, but keep out of the light," the Stonemaster ordered to a goblin messenger he kept near his throne platform for that purpose. "The humans know we are here but struggle to see."

"Yes, Chief of Chieftains." The messenger ran off to spread the word.

"Will your voice carry from here, Allspeaker?"

The shaman cringed next to the throne at the sight of the human warriors. "Yes, Chief of Chieftains, but the others must be still."

"It will be so when I command it." The warlord took a moment to enjoy the fact he wielded enough power to command such a host to silence. "And have the other shamans ready their magic. If they do not submit, we go over the cliff-wall."

***

It was not a scene Pencheval ever thought he would see.

Until now goblin hordes were dusty things of history, campfire tales told by the master during his apprenticeship at Stonewall Pass. Great swarms of goblins would sweep through the human kingdoms before humans had a proper understanding of arms and before the rise of mages. It had been much harder to repel them then, and they had been considered disasters akin to famine, drought, or a plague of locusts. Seeing this now, he could understand why, and wished they had remained historical.

A Clearsight charm showed him that there were far more of them than attacked him previously and far more than even a clan. The magic enabled his sight to cut through the night and show the host to him in shades of gray. A score of the same beast riders that had cut down his patrol stood reined on the flanks, and between them were thousands of goblins. Most appeared to be the rank and file, primitives the size of children armed with stone weapons and whatever they could steal.

Others were the specialists Pencheval knew some goblin clans possessed. A brutish lot of goblins, taller than the rest by head and shoulders, wore the skins of black bears and wielded heavy weapons in both hands. Others wearing sleeveless hooded tunics seemed to appear and disappear between their fellows. Those with staves topped with feathers, skulls, and teeth like the shamans and still others that might be chieftains gathered around a great litter of wood and bone. Upon it was seated a goblin Pencheval assumed to be the master.

The warlord leaned back on a throne of twisted wood and bone topped with an ornamental skull perched within the arc of a pair of elk horns. It held a staff that bore no decoration aside from the figure of some crouching winged beast atop it, and it was half again as tall as its wielder. The smirking goblin wore a large silver plate strapped to its chest, an animal hide adorned with teeth draped around its collar, and a hide kilt dangling feathers and uncut gems from a thick studded belt. It calmly met his gaze, appearing wholly unconcerned that one of the humans could see it.

The horde appeared to be waiting, either to organize itself for a charge or to simply finish arriving. He was certain they would attack at some point, for the preparations he saw could be for nothing else. Many bore large wicker shields that would keep them alive for a time, even if they did not look sturdy enough to last the fight. Others wore hide cloaks and many had ropes, and despite the lack of towers or siege engines he was still nervous. Among the goblin talents of which he knew was that they could climb sheer faces and surfaces where humans could find no purchase. What little they had might well be enough.

"What say you, Lion?" Knight-Brother Galot gazed out into the darkness but only knew what his ears told him.

"It is a sizeable horde, Your Grace. Their leader sits in the throne there." Pencheval pointed directly at the warlord, but knew the others would be unable to see it. "There are no siege engines and the goblins seem prepared for arrows, but their shields are little more than wicker. I believe they will attack tonight."

The knight turned to his Captain. "Make ready the archers and catapults. All arrows are to be aflame."

"Yes, Your Grace." The Captain barked orders down to his men, and the soldiers scrambled to obey.

"Anything else, Lion?"

"The beasts that I mentioned to you before, those that killed most of the patrol I accompanied before we drove them away, currently guard the flanks. I don't know if they are strong enough to tear out the gate or if they are even meant to, but you should prepare regardless. They are certainly strong enough to kill cavalry."

Another order sent a soldier to the gatehouse. Moments later, Pencheval heard the portcullis drop, but the sound didn't make him feel any more secure. Instead, it seemed an almost trivial thing to do.

***

"Silence the horde."

Messengers flew in all directions with the instructions of the Stonemaster, and at his word thousands of goblins grew still. The Chief of Chieftains could see those humans on the wall grow nervous, running their fingers around the neck-holes of their shirts or pawing at weapons. Only the Gray Lion Clan warrior looked as though it was just waiting, and continued to stare right at him.

The Stonemaster leered back at it in response. So his clan had learned the secrets of something any goblin pup could do at birth? It was only noteworthy in that it made the troublesome wretch easy to identify.

The bemused warlord chuckled and sat back on his throne. Let this supposed nightmare of might and metal look. Let it take stock of the doom before it. He would give the human plenty to see soon enough.

"Speak now, and tell them my will," the warlord commanded the Allspeaker.

***

Pencheval knew something was coming. The insectoid screeching had grown increasingly still until nothing remained but an eerie silence, broken only by an errant growl from one of the beasts on the flanks. After days of listening to the endless cacophony grow louder and more harrowing, the silence was not the relief he expected it would be.

Then the voice came. He willed magic into his eyes once again, and felt them grow warmer from the Clearsight charm as the picture in gray beyond the range of the torchlight resolved itself anew. It allowed him to see the goblin with the shaman's staff speaking from just in front of the throne.

To his surprise, it was a tongue he understood, unusually loud and marked by a strange accent that suggested a bird or insect. "Humans of the Snow Clan. You will submit. Make way for us to enter and you will come to no harm. Resist, and we will attack your town and punish you."

"Snow Clan?" One of the soldiers scratched his head in confusion.

"Sounds like they think we're a clan like they are," Pencheval guessed.

Galot's eyes narrowed. "And did that jackanapes just order us to surrender?"

"I believe so, Your Grace," Pencheval replied. He was not eager to take it up on the offer.

"How far away is it?"

"One hundred and fifty paces, Your Grace, by my estimation."

The knight turned to the catapults below. "Artillerist, are any catapults set to throw to a range of one hundred and fifty paces?"

"Aye, Your Grace." A portly sergeant with a coarse beard and a metal cap cupped his hands around his mouth so he could be heard from the ground. "Two engines loaded with boulders if it please you."

"The goblins have demanded our surrender. Send them our reply."

"Aye, Your Grace. You heard his lordship. Loose!"

Pencheval heard the creak and whoosh of two catapult arms and the thud of counterweights striking wood. The artillerist barked orders, and the crews scrambled to reload with the knock and rattle of winched chains.

***

The Chief of Chieftains looked up at the boulders arcing towards his horde and sighed. It was not the response he was expecting even in defiance. At worst he thought they would shout something the Allspeaker would translate either as a threat of death or a refusal to submit. But he never expected to see great rocks flying across the sky.

He found the attempt to intimidate the humans with the goblins' numbers worthwhile, if only on the off chance it would keep from weakening the might of his horde here. The mountain-castle would require far more goblins than he had now, and a submission by the Snow Clan would have avoided the work of rebuilding their numbers before adding to them. Yet it seemed the under-chieftain was as aggressive as its master and able to inflict death accordingly. If this human would respond to a demand of submission with shaman tricks, this would be a hard fight.

"How do they make the boulders fly?" The goblins around the warlord cringed and nearly broke at the sight, but the Chief of Chieftains only smiled. Lesser warlords in weaker positions would flinch, but the Stonemaster was not one of them. That was why he was the Chief of Chieftains and not rabble. No one else would have recognized the opportunity to boost the morale of his underlings.

The Stonemaster stood up, thrust his staff in the direction of the two boulders, and bared his teeth. "You will not harm us!"

As the horde watched, the boulders crumbled to rubble, rubble ground into pebbles, and the pebbles reduced to powder. As the stones disintegrated, their shapes grew less distinct until they were mere spheres of dust trailing tails. When they finally struck the ground, it was with a puff rather than a crash, throwing dust in all directions and flattening a few goblins beneath them. Moments later, a goblin that had been hit sat up from the blow, blinked twice, and laughed hysterically at his good fortune. The horde watched in awe as the goblins beneath the dust dug themselves free and shook off what was once a flying rock.

"Mere rocks will not harm us!" The Stonemaster threw his arms wide. "I am the Stonemaster! I speak and the very stone obeys me! I can lead you to victory! Send forth the vines and scale the walls, we will crush the humans now!"

"Death to the Snow Clan!" The Bloodmoon Chieftain's battle cry rang out and the Berserkers howled and raged, clashing weapons together and calling down curses upon the humans.

Goblins chittered excitedly. The Bonestrippers at the flanks growled and snorted in agitation. From out of the mob next to their places by the throne, several of the shamans pointed staves at the ground, and a massed tangle of vines slithered its way from their feet towards the walls.

The Stonemaster smiled as his pawns put his plan into action. When those vines reached the cliff-walls even a lame goat would be able to climb them, and it would be more than enough for his goblins to swarm the defenders.

***

Pencheval's satisfaction slowly descended into dismay as the two large boulders flew towards the goblin horde and disintegrated, landing as little more than billowing clouds of dust. The pose of the warlord made what was responsible for their transformation very, very clear. That was not the work of a mere shaman, or at least he had never seen a goblin shaman wield that much power.

"Mage on the field! The stones did not fall."

"Lord on High protect us." A soldier next to Pencheval clasped his hands together and prayed under his breath.

"Go to the other side of the gatehouse, Lion. Now!" Pencheval watched Galot draw his sword and kneel, resting the point of the blade in the stone. The mercenary scrambled to his post as a crescendo of shouting rose from the horde. He saw several somethings slither into the torchlight towards the walls.

"Athesiene, Lord on High," Galot prayed. "You who bring light to the darkness and redeemer of the lost. I pray you, grant this humble servant the strength to defend Your faithful and Your works. Make me Your instrument!"

Pencheval turned at the door of the gatehouse out of curiosity, but saw nothing he expected of such an invocation. No light from the heavens, no stroke of thunder, nor a burst of trumpets. Instead, a brilliant white light illuminated the joints and edges of Galot's armor and clothing. His sword flickered with a few bright specks, then gleamed with a white light, and then burned like a beacon. Soldiers cheered as Galot raised his weapon to rally them, but Pencheval only resumed his haste.

"Cease your gawking!" The determined Lion roared at the soldiers glancing around him to see Galot as he exited the gatehouse. He grabbed one by the collar and turned him to face the horde. "There lies your enemy. They have come a long way to die and not a one of you will disappoint them!" Pencheval slapped down his visor, drew his sword, and took his place on the battlements.

He remembered the patrol and considered his options for magic. Should he use it to grant himself strength? That was useful against great beasts but overkill for goblins, and would leave his muscles screaming long before the fight's end. Pitfire spell? A small group of goblins was superstitious enough to freeze or flee when his sword became a burning demon, but a horde in the presence of their warlord would not. For a flood of goblins, he decided on the spell that let him take advantage of his most abundant resource to fight them: the goblins themselves.

For that, he found the Waymaker spell ideal. It was cast upon his sword, so it would not tax his muscles. As its name suggested, it made way through tight groups by hurling anything it hit backwards, knocking down shield walls and spearmen. If a goblin so much as touched the point the spell would send it flying over the wall, while its companions below saw what awaited them should they reach the top. Goblin morale was touchy at best, and repeated demonstrations of a spectacular death ahead were just the thing to break them.

Heralded by battle shouts and screams, a tide of goblins emerged from the night into the glow of the torches. They held wicker shields or other crude protections over their heads as they loped towards the wall. Under any other circumstances, their less than ferocious charge would have seemed comical to him but their numbers were almost unthinkable. The front stretched as wide as the whole length of the eastern wall and emerged unceasingly from the darkness.

Pencheval gritted his teeth. They would be fighting all night to even slow them down, and that was assuming they were not utterly overrun.

"Archers! Loose!" Galot's command echoed from the other side of the gatehouse. His amplified voice echoed over the sound of the horde. Pencheval heard the twang of several score of longbows in response. A rain of burning arrows descended on the attackers, struck goblins dead, and ignited wicker. Eddies formed in the charge as goblins sidestepped those extinguishing shields in the dirt or scattered away from the fires on newly made corpses.

Pencheval heard slithering and glanced down. Several ropy, loosely stranded growths struck the walls and fanned out from the base, unraveling themselves into distinct vines as they climbed the stones. The strands anchored themselves at irregular intervals, leaving loops and toughened leaves that goblin-sized attackers could easily grasp or use as footholds. The Silver Lion frowned. The goblins may have been without siege towers or engines, but they had not come unprepared.

"Catapults! Fire!"

Pencheval heard the heavy throw as six burning projectiles arced into the air. They all overshot the charging goblins, but a Clearsight charm allowed him to see them strike the rest of the horde. The splash and glow of their impact revealed goblins alight as others scampered away in terror. He was briefly relieved that the mage did not seem to have the power to stop burning casks of pitch. Yet the solid hits barely made a dent in the numbers.

The first of the goblins made it to the wall, dropped their shields, and started to climb. To Pencheval's dismay, they were not slowed in the least by the ascent. They scaled the wall as fast as they ran and the soldiers next to him started at the sight of it.

He smacked the shield with his sword blade twice to refocus them. "Give them nothing but defeat!"

"Glory to the Lord on High!" A nearby sergeant pointed at the wall, and soldiers dropped rocks from piles they had prepared in advance. Goblins screamed as they were hit and Pencheval could hear them fall. He knew they would crest the battlements when soldiers stopped dropping rocks and reached for weapons.

Clawed hands appeared at irregular intervals along the battlements. Goblins appeared with bared teeth, leapt on or over the edge, and drew weapons. Several appeared near him and the first one took a spear to the chest. He willed the Waymaker spell into his sword, and felt the glyph in his right hand grow warm. He thrust at a goblin reaching for a dagger at its belt and hit cleanly.

The impact did not pierce it, but the force of the spell sent it flying backwards into the night. It twisted and somersaulted until it crashed onto a shield, dying and killing the one beneath it. Goblins scattered or simply ran over both victims, but the flood continued.

Soldiers cheered, and another rain of burning arrows flew at Galot's call. He heard the artillerists command their crews, and the jingle and rumble of chain-wound winches pulling weighted catapult arms back into firing positions. Pencheval allowed himself some small hope and struck the next goblin cresting the wall dead. This fight had only just begun, but at least it was well begun.

***

The Stonemaster refused to flinch as the great globs of burning stench splashed into the horde around him. Showing fear now would break the goblins' will and cause them to scatter. One did not lead a horde of even this size into battle and retain it if one fled at the first sign of adversity, so he suppressed any apprehension and stood tall.

The warlord saw two more swarms of burning sticks fly into the sky from the human town. Unwilling to risk being slain by one, he yanked the nearest shield bearer in front of him by the collar as he stepped back under his throne's awning. The burning swarm smacked the bones of his litter and the shield of the goblin, but did not strike anyone dead. The warlord's unwitting protection plucked two of them from his shield when he was released, and dumped a gourd of water on it to extinguish a few smoking embers that remained.

The Stonemaster was not particularly worried yet. Reducing the flying rocks to dust gave heart to the horde with wondrous effect, and he had not wasted their zeal by hesitating. Now the rabble needed to overwhelm the humans on the wall. It was a stalemate so far, but the attack was by no means spent. There were goblins enough and only two humans caused him to worry.

The Gray Lion warrior was as difficult to kill as the survivors' tales made it out to be. Every so often its shiny big knife would send a goblin flying in a way that was not possible without shaman tricks. As for the Snow Clan under-chieftain, it glowed with the light of the sun and incinerated any goblins that climbed too close to it. They would have to be stopped, and at the moment he did not know if even the swarm of rabble would be enough to do it.

It was a sentiment he kept to himself.

***

Pencheval felt relief that the past half hour of fighting had found his assessment of the town's defenses incorrect. Yes, the goblins could climb the walls, but they still had to crest the battlements. It was there they stopped to draw their weapons, and that moment of hesitation left no few of them slain.

He had wondered in the moments before the hit if the soldiers had been ground down by the incessant screech and chatter in the days prior to the attack. They had run themselves ragged making preparations, quickly mustering new recruits, and keeping order in the town. He received his answer in the initial hit, and he was well satisfied.

The soldiers were frazzled, frustrated, and taking it out on their tormentors. They gave battle cries to their god and no quarter to their enemies. They stabbed or clubbed wounded goblins where they fell. They struck blows with obvious rage and frustration, and dropped rocks on heads with relish. Farther down the wall, a sergeant poured boiling water over the climbers with sadistic glee. The goblins had inflicted their tortures and the defenders now meant to give it back.

It was a sentiment Pencheval wholeheartedly shared. These were the fiends that had harried him across a forced march with a handful of survivors after they massacred his patrol. They had tormented him and the town with their screeching, a sound that had driven those around him nigh to madness and left him looking over his shoulder for townsfolk that would attack him next. He had long ago had enough of it.

He smashed one goblin's teeth with the edge of his shield and sent another flying over the wall with a Waymaker spell. He now enjoyed every strike that left a goblin dead. No, he would not be driven out by this filth again and he meant for them to know it before they died.

"Death to them all!" The Lion's sword stroke sheared a goblin in two from the collarbone to the ribs.

"Glory to the Lord on High!" A spearman ran another goblin through and pushed its companion from the battlements with his shield.

Pencheval took a deep breath and went back to it. There was no more time for battle cries. Now was the time to start killing in earnest.

***

This wasn't happening.

The Stonemaster watched in horror as the humans of the Snow Clan thwarted him. There were so many goblins the warlord could not see the ground between himself and the cliff-walls, and yet they were not enough. Goblins swarmed up the sides along vines and stones, and yet the humans, with their farcically low numbers, threw them back. He could see the glowing form of the under-chieftain leading the Snow Clan to a successful resistance while the roars of the black-garbed thorn in his side punctuated the strikes of its shiny big knife.

Another glob of the burning, sticky stench flew through the sky and splashed down near him, leaving burning splotches along his throne's canopy. Several goblins near the Stonemaster scrambled away from the flames and the horde started to panic at the absence of victory. At every splash of the stench or fall of burning sticks more and more of them fled away in all directions.

The Bloodmoon Chieftain glared at the walls, increasingly angry at restraining his retaliation to it. The gigantic warrior looked as though he was trying to decide if now would be a good time to usurp the Stonemaster's title of Chief of Chieftains and throw his clan into the fight. The nervous warlord knew his Berserkers would fall into line behind him whatever he chose.

Desperate for a solution, the Chief of Chieftains looked to his staff. The human that had traded it to him had said it would occasionally get tired and need rest if all of its magic was expended. He was never willing to let it get to that point for fear his rivals might take that time to challenge him, but a failure here would see him dead whether he had the staff or not. Leading a horde to defeat had killed no few aspirants to the title of Chief of Chieftains, and he would be no different.

Terrified of losing and infuriated by his circumstances, the Stonemaster stepped forth from his canopy and put the staff before him. No, this night would not be his end, for he was no mere pretender. Lesser Chiefs of Chieftains would merely curse their minions for failure, while those who truly deserved the title would take the initiative and fight to make their own wills manifest.

He poured his will into the staff with a vengeance, leering as he felt the stone beneath him rumble and pound in response. Shamans, rabble, and council alike backed away as the ground beneath their feet shook and churned. They scattered when geysers of cobblestone and broken rock erupted in a circle around him. The furious horde's master raged at the cliff-walls and commanded his staff to give him every drop of magic it had left.

"You are mine. All of you!"

***

Pencheval reassured himself that the defense was going well. The goblins were still throwing themselves at the eastern wall, but the soldiers matched their efforts with sufficient resistance. Numbers alone were not strategy, and they showed no signs of trying to use them in any way but brute force. There were no towers, no siege engines, nor even an attempt to wrap north and south from the eastern wall to stretch the defenders thin.

The Silver Lion smiled. Should the goblins continue this way, they would be nursing a horrific defeat by morning. Past that, it would be merely a matter of mop up as he and Athesiene's temple advanced to eliminate those that had not fled.

His good spirits soured to dismay when *it* rumbled into being.

The whole battle seemed to come to a halt as the ground shook beneath the wall. His first instinct was to cast a Clearsight charm in order to find the source. He saw the warlord surrounded by columns of rock just before they poured inwards like crashing waves. The ground and stone flowed as though they had become some strange liquid until it congealed into a shape, growing limbs ending in jagged, sturdy talons. No head formed, but the relief of a crouching gargoyle molded into being on the moss-covered slab of a torso. The thing towered over everything near it and was at least thrice as tall as himself.

Pencheval heard the newly formed rock-being scream in a bass parody of the goblin tongue as it thundered towards him. Goblins scrambled to get out of the way before being trampled, some less successfully than others. Soldiers shivered, cursed, or simply broke once it came into the light, and for the first time in the fight the Silver Lion genuinely feared defeat.

***

"Idiots! Fools and incompetents! Can you not swarm?"

The Stonemaster charged through the rabble towards the walls, feeling powerful but slightly disoriented as the goblins beneath him scrambled out of the way. He felt as though he was striding across the field on a pair of stout tree trunks and stood even higher than the Bonestrippers on his flanks. Stone encased him entirely and he saw by no means he could understand. Yet he was less concerned with the mysteries of his stone construct than what he would destroy with it.

His two prime targets were the Gray Lion and the under-chieftain. True, the under-chieftain was the leader, but the black-garbed human in metal was a dark legend among the horde. Goblins still whispered of its might when they thought the Chief of Chieftains could not hear them, and would not cease their nervous chatter about it. Only its death would end those tales for good and rekindle his conquest of the valley. Since his minions were failing him, he would have to slay it himself.

The warlord willed the stone construct empowering him to attack the Gray Lion on the cliff-wall and it rushed forward to do his bidding. It stomped several goblins flat and caused the rest to part before him, which did not concern him in the least. He intended to execute some of them for failure anyway, more so if they could not even take this simple place without his direct intervention. There was no time like the present to do it.

When he reached the cliff-walls the stone construct thrust its talons into the cobblestone and lifted him upwards. Rock clattered away and goblins scaling the walls either shimmied to the side or fell. The wall was not even twice as tall as the construct and it scaled the distance in mere heartbeats. One human warrior did find the courage to empty a cauldron of burning water on him as he ascended but it merely splashed harmlessly from the stone. The form protected him; he felt nothing at all.

Battlements clattered to the ground as the stone construct crested the wall and stood. Snow Clan warriors scattered and two were crushed underfoot as it stomped towards its target. The Gray Lion discarded its shield and took its shiny big knife in both hands. It yelled something at him and put up its guard.

The Stonemaster chuckled and willed the stone construct to kill it. A gigantic claw crashed into the cliff-wall where its target once was, missing as the human dodged with inexplicable speed. It stood next to the arm, making a gesture with two of its fingers, palm facing towards it, that the frustrated Chief of Chieftains took for a taunt.

The warlord willed the stone construct to attack again, only this time he imagined it swiping towards the strangely jagged top of the cliff-walls to pin his prey. This time, the human dodged not to the side that had been denied it but inward with the same impossible speed. Too close for a claw stroke, the Stonemaster willed it stomped, and a taloned foot crashed down where the warrior once stood. Unable to find his opponent, the frustrated Chief of Chieftains turned only to see the human standing behind him, and heard it laugh through its shiny head covering.

Infuriated, the Stonemaster willed the construct to attack with both claws to deny the human any space to dodge. Both claws crashed down, and to his frustration he watched the Gray Lion evade them in a way that could not be explained as anything but a shaman trick. He recovered to try again, but the stone beneath his feet shifted and crumbled away. The blows his stone construct threw did not land against the human, but destroyed enough of the cliff-wall that it could no longer hold. It slid away beneath him like a rock slide, and he fell to crash onto a strange thing of wood and darkened metal below.

***

"And stay down!"

Pencheval had not expected anything like this from a goblin, not even the warlord. He knew it was capable of more than a shaman's practical but primitive magic, but not this. Still, he had fought too many monsters to simply give in to fear, and remained perfectly capable of planning under pressure after years of experience and training.

He knew the warlord was drawing on some sort of magic and initially expected to taunt it into expending it all. It was a tactic commonly referred to by his fellow *guilden* as a burn fight. That plan had been the first thing to die the instant he saw one of its blows smite the wall. It had the strength to tear the ground out from under its own feet, and when it kept attacking he settled on that plan as far less risky.

Whatever else it was, it was enraged at him, and that rage made the gambit successful. The magic-wielding warlord had plowed through its own horde to ultimately expend its powers tearing the wall out from under its own feet. It had defeated itself in its haste to kill him, but much to his chagrin the mage landed on one of the catapults when it fell.

It did not move for so long that the soldiers cheered, and the stalling and cringing goblins appeared ready to break. Despite the moment of apparent victory he was not reassured. If the warlord could no longer wield magic, then why was its construct still intact? Had it encased itself in a stone coffin in its rush to defeat him? He realized the answer when it stirred, rose, and tore into the wall with both claws.

***

Foolish, the Stonemaster mused as the stone construct rose from the rubble at last. Impulsive and foolish. He knew better than to let his temper run away with him, and yet this one human enraged him like no other. This one Gray Lion killed three Bonestrippers. It killed the Shadows. It fought his horde and defeated his plans time and time again. Now, the fearsome and infuriating thing had tricked him into thrashing himself from the cliff-walls. Had he not been inside the stone construct the staff made for him, he would have died from it.

The Gray Lion was a problem he could not defeat alone. But he was not alone, and there was nothing here a horde of goblins could not overcome. He also now knew that his stone construct could destroy the cliff-walls, such as the one under the feet of the dark warrior with the shiny big knife. He would have grinned wickedly at it, but settled for watching it scramble as he willed the construct to tear it down. Two claws shoveled into the oddly set stones time and again, throwing them to the ground as the Snow Clan above and beside him screamed in fear.

He tore until he punched through to the horde on the other side. The collapse bounced harmlessly from his construct and dropped human warriors into the rubble. Goblins scrambled to escape or swarmed humans that had the misfortune of surviving the fall.

The warlord chortled as he saw the Gray Lion scramble to escape the rockslide, unable to do anything else. The others tried to cling to the rocks but could not. The bass laughter of the Chief of Chieftains boomed from the chest of the stone construct as he enjoyed their ongoing defeat. None of these humans demonstrated a capacity to climb greater than a goblin pup, and it was their undoing now.

He ripped and shoveled as the humans around him stabbed and beat the stone construct in vain or simply fled in fear, tearing until the hole in the cliff wall would pass a score of goblins abreast. With such a gap in the defenses and no more need to climb, his horde could flood the city as fast as they could enter, and all due to his inherent superiority. No lesser goblin could have drawn an epiphany from a fall and then turned the tide of a battle with it.

He basked in the power rush. The goblins obeyed him and the humans fled or attacked him in vain. His command over the stone made him the master of a horde, and someday, many others. He turned on the humans underfoot, which stumbled and staggered away upon gaining his attention, and reveled in their fear until a glow in the distance interrupted him.

The Gray Lion had escaped but the task was not yet done. He could see the Snow Clan under-chieftain descend from the other side of the cave in the middle of the cliff-wall, and was reminded it could also wield a shaman's power. He would have to deal with it himself and leave the rest to the horde.

The goblins standing on the other side of the breach stood shocked and stalled at the warlord's rampage. Some were half-buried in falling stones and the rest were not eager to pass through the gap. He willed his stone construct to face them.

"Do I have to do everything for you fools? Take the town!"

They could deal with the human rabble now, or they had better. He had done too much hand holding as it was and another problem came his way. The glowing human under-chieftain waded through the press towards him, inspiring its warriors as it passed. They cheered and rallied with renewed vigor, something that could not be allowed to stand.

He had seen the under-chieftain burn the goblins climbing the cliff walls. Would it also do that to his stone body? It was not something he cared to test.

He examined the human contrivance upon which he landed. It was a conglomeration of wood and metal with a purpose that eluded him. Yet the wrecked thing still had something he could use, a square tree trunk topped with a huge metal bowl. A snip of a claw freed it from the wreckage, and he willed his stone construct to grasp it so he could use it to smash his target. If something was to burn in order to kill the under-chieftain, it wouldn't be him.

The rabble poured through, over, and around the lines of defenders, and the under-chieftain slashed his weapon through several of them as it made its way forward. The slash burned its targets into skeletons and ash. The Stonemaster willed his construct to raise its new weapon and charge, and it thundered forward obediently. Yes, the metal bowl thing could do the work, and he would not stand idly and wait to suffer the same fate.

The human leader raised its shield to defend. The Stonemaster laughed at the futile gesture as the improvised mace descended, expecting it to flatten the human like a beetle. Instead, the metal bowl struck something in thin air before it even reached the under-chieftain. The point of impact glowed with an ivory light and rippled away from the blow as from a stone dropped into a lake. The enraged goblin warlord tried to force the bowl through whatever shaman trick the human used to protect itself, but he could not penetrate it.

The metal bowl glowed red from the heat of the under-chieftain's magic and the tree trunk to which it was attached blackened, sparks and cinders forming along its surface. He pulled it back when orange coals began to appear and raised it to strike again. The under-chieftain did not await the blow passively, but responded by charging at the legs of his stone construct. He ordered it to kick the human, and felt a surge of satisfaction when the stone foot appeared to travel unhindered.

Again, the blow struck the strange glowing something in thin air before reaching the under-chieftain, and once again ripples of bright light appeared where a dead human should have been. It retaliated with its burning big knife. The blow sheared through a third of the stone leg, igniting the moss and vegetation caught between the crevasses. An orange something like thick water or blood dribbled down where stone had once been before congealing back into rock. The Stonemaster loudly cursed the fact that the Snow Clan chieftain did not promote weaklings as under-chieftains and staggered back.

Weakling or no weakling, he would not be beaten here. Greatness awaited him, and no glowing shaman under-chieftain, no Gray Lion Clan specialist, and no incompetent rabble would stop him. There was no stopping him.

***

Pencheval grabbed a soldier frantically spinning his arms for balance at the edge of the crumbling wall and pulled him to safety. He tossed him through the open door of the gatehouse, and took a moment to regain his composure. He had never been on a wall so quickly and utterly sapped, magic or not. Most of the soldiers on it had not escaped the assault of the goblin warlord and had either fallen to their deaths or into the claws of the goblins below.

"What? How did you? How did it..." The soldier sat up, looked through the expanse of nothingness that was once part of the town's defenses and shuddered.

"I know not, but I will stop it." Pencheval inwardly cursed the fact the battle still raged and stood. "Shut and barricade the door."

Several goblins crawled up from the ground and looked into the gatehouse, saw Pencheval, and began to shove each other to go first. The mercenary took advantage of their distraction to slam the heavy door in their faces. He leaned against it to keep the attackers from forcing their way inside.

"Bar the door!"

The soldier scrambled to his feet and obeyed, dropping a heavy wooden bar propped up against the wall into the door's brackets. They heard no hammering to get through it, and Pencheval concluded that it was because the goblins still feared him.

"What do we do? They've broken through!"

"You fight!" Pencheval pointed to the opposite door. "Go join your brothers on the other wall and kill goblins!"

The soldier stood tall and straightened his tabard as he regained his sense of purpose. "Aye, and right gladly. Glory to the Lord on High!" The soldier took up a spear from a rack and ran through the other door, killing another of the seemingly endless horde as it tried to vault the battlements.

Pencheval heard something strike a barrier with the gong of metal and saw an undulating light gleam from the ground below, followed by the sound of searing wood. Galot's invocation was repelling the goblin warlord and his power still held, which meant this fight was not yet over. If he aided the Knight-Brother, they might yet decapitate this snake.

The goblins at the door had hesitated. They knew and feared him for what he had done up to this point. If he joined Galot and defeated the warlord, he would be the bane of their master as well. Would the goblins flee if their leader fell? Could he strike down the will of an entire horde to fight?

Finding that this was the only idea he had left now that they had breached the wall, Pencheval rushed out the door and threw himself back into the fray. He hoped he could punch through to Galot in time to aid him against the warlord. It was either that or a fight through the streets and certain defeat. The wall had been the only thing to rob the goblins of their advantage of numbers. Now that they had breached it, the defenders could not hold it or the town.

***

Why couldn't that Fiend-forsaken under-chieftain die like a normal human?

Its durability frustrated the Stonemaster. One blow after another bounced from the power of its shaman trick like drops of rain. It could not avoid them like the Gray Lion but it had no need to do so. Furthermore, he could not do this all night even with the breach and the Snow Clan's warriors tied up with the rabble.

The human's power had blackened his stone construct in several places and the crumbling left arm was all but ready to fall away. Even if the construct did endure whatever shaman trick burned his goblins, it would not last once the magic of the staff was expended. He would be unprotected against the human's power if it outlived his attacks. The Stonemaster despaired for a way to break the shield, and looked to the melee around him for answers.

Stones? No, the strange force stopped them. Wood? No, it would burn that as it did his improvised weapon with the metal bowl. Flame? Nothing that burned was within reach. Then in a burst of inspiration, he remembered what it would not burn.

The under-chieftain had fought on the wall shoulder-to-shoulder with its warriors. Its minions were not hurt by this shaman trick. They did not burn if they were too close. So he willed his construct to snatch one of them from the fight swirling around him and throw it directly at his opponent.

The human connected with its master, knocking it to the ground but not harming it. The Stonemaster followed up with the downward smash of his improvised club. The under-chieftain raised its shield in time, and the strange force blocked it again. Yet the light was not as bright as before and the blow came to within an arm's length of it, much closer than before.

He snatched another Snow Clan warrior and threw it. The screaming human stunned the under-chieftain, but the left arm that lifted it crumbled away. The construct then shivered and shifted with the sound of falling gravel, dropping to one knee as a leg gave way. The warlord suppressed his panic and acted.

He willed it to lash out once more, and the bowl again struck the under-chieftain's glowing protection, slamming to a halt barely a hand's length from its target. Again, and the club all but touched the human's shield before he saw one of the talons on the construct's remaining claw fall away. Desperate as he saw his staff's magic failing, he hissed and willed his crumbling construct to strike again.

He saw the human's shield of light ripple weakly, then flicker. He continued to push and the shaman trick disappeared. The metal bowl pressed into the shield and crushed it against the under-chieftain. Triumphant, he tried to raise his improvised club one last time, but the talons fell away. All that remained was an arm-shaped clump of rock dribbling dirt and moss as it disintegrated.

He took the chance that it was enough, raised the stump, and smashed it down onto the under-chieftain. The last thing he saw before he found himself in a collapsing pile of rubble was the success of the blow. The weight of it alone collapsed the human's shiny metal shirt as it spit blood.

When he heard his horde tear into the human leader, he smiled.

***

Halfway down the stair Pencheval watched the goblin warlord crumble too late. The last blow it struck before falling into a pile of stone left Galot mortally wounded, invocation expended, and raising one hand weakly before the goblins swarmed him. He disappeared into the press as though in a flood.

"Athesiene save us..." Pencheval could see the soldier next to him shiver as he lost his resolve.

"Back to the wall," the disheartened mercenary said quietly, uncertain of what to do now beyond basic tactics.

"Lord on High protect us. Lord on High protect–"

Pencheval grabbed the soldier by the collar. "Back to the wall! Get to higher ground!"

The Lion tried to take his own advice and drag the soldier along with him, but he felt a knife stab the plate and leather of his armored boots. He glanced down to find the goblin that did it and the scores behind it swarming the walls and the stairs to get him. Another jumped from above to garrote the soldier next to him. He took one step towards the beleaguered man to assist only to find himself too beset to do more than fight his own assailants.

The tide of goblins attacked with no order or strategy beyond overwhelming numbers. They poured over the archers and artillerists on the ground and up the wall as far as he could see. Goblins climbed both up and down the stairs to reach him or clawed at his feet from the edges. One jumped from above to land on his back, and he threw it before it could wrap a rope around his neck.

He could hear nothing through the cacophony from the soldiers above him but knew they could not be faring well. He took his sword in both hands and reaped anything before him, barely keeping pace with the flood of replacements. He willed a Waymaker spell into his sword and struck the goblin before him with a thrust. The force of the spell sent it tumbling up and backwards, knocking several of its companions to the ground long enough for the harried Lion to kill them. Another spell to the rear kept his back clear long enough for him to wade to the top of the wall.

The white-clad defenders were no less harried, but lacking his access to magic, fell quickly to goblin numbers. A pocket of spearmen tried to form a circular shield wall. As he watched, goblins jumped on their shields and spears to overburden them, and then stabbed them to death as their defenses fell from the weight. A sergeant with a heavy mace brained the goblin in front of him, only to have another crack a cudgel across the back of his knees. Four goblins hacked him to death when he struck the ground.

He could not even approach the soldiers to assist. The goblins could not fell him, but he could do nothing else but keep them at bay. Every few steps forward he would be buffeted from the press or forced to dislodge a goblin from his arms or back. They attacked with garrotes, knives, cudgels, or anything they had stolen, swarming him and everything else.

He had no purpose now but to escape, but to where? Down into the cauldron of goblins beneath him, along with their warlord? No. Along the top of the wall and then...where? West. He smashed a skull with the pommel of his sword and mowed his way towards the northern wall. West to The Shield of Athesiene, a formidable fortification with a proper force. He sheared through two goblins jumping at him at once. West, where he should have gone before all of this. He would have cursed himself, but could not spare even a moment for it.

He glimpsed to the west into the town. The third of Tarsun's Market closest to the eastern wall was still lit, but beyond it was darkness. It reminded Pencheval of the Firebane attack the goblins had used on the patrol to douse all light in preparation for a massacre. While the bulk of the horde had attacked the eastern wall, other goblins had taken advantage of the distraction and hit the whole town from behind. Whatever else they had done, they blackened it to their advantage along the way.

The temple still glowed with inner lights but was surrounded by darkness. With no resistance the goblins would not be long in taking it. Dominik and Nan were there, and this time, they would join him in escaping, even if he had to wring submission from them first. He could just barely see the stair midway down the northern wall, and it was his next destination if he meant to reach them.

If, Pencheval mused. If he could fight through a swarm, and then through an unknown host concealed by night, he could reach the temple. Despite his resolve to persevere and escape, he did not find that anything akin to certain.

***

The Stonemaster brushed the last of the stone construct from his shoulders, unhappy it was gone but well satisfied with how it was spent. With it, he had turned the tide of battle to his favor and slain the human under-chieftain of the Snow Clan, succeeding where other goblins had failed. He surveyed his circumstances from the pile of stones, dirt, and moss that remained of his once-powerful form and leered in satisfaction.

Goblins poured through the breach he had torn in the cliff-walls. Snow Clan warriors flailed about vainly before falling to the tide of the horde. Even the Gray Lion warrior could not stand before them. It staggered and flailed with its shiny big knife in a vain attempt to save itself.

Several goblins dropped to their knees at the foot of the rubble on which he stood, threw their arms wide, and proclaimed his glory. He basked in their unabashed awe. Why should they not acknowledge his greatness? His might should provoke displays of worship. With such a Chief of Chieftains as himself there could be naught but victory.

"You are truly blessed by the Fiend Under The Mountain!" One of the goblins paying him homage bowed until his hands touched the ground. "He has granted you a great victory!"

Perhaps he had, the warlord thought. And perhaps it would bring him more awe and adulation to claim he actually was Blessed by the Fiend. Perhaps the horde would obey him more readily if they thought that was true and be less eager to challenge him. The staff certainly gave him the magic to sell that claim, particularly since the vast majority of them did not understand it.

"Find the Bloodmoon Chieftain," he commanded, regretting that the worship would end. "Tell him to send the Berserkers after the Gray Lion warrior and all remaining resistance."

"Yes, Chief of Chieftains." The rabble scrambled to obey.

"Take it all!" Yes, Blessed by the Fiend did have a nice ring to it. Perhaps even Prophet of the Fiend. However, his new title was a consideration for after the battle. For now, it was simply satisfying enough to watch his plans bear fruit.

***

Pencheval did not know how long he had fought to turn the corner and gain purchase on the northern wall. He knew only that it was still night time and that the onslaught of goblins had not ceased. They rushed up both sides of the wall on which he stood. They paced ahead of him on the ground to scale the wall before him and double back. They tried to take him from behind only to be flipped and thrown time and again. He yet stood but their numbers took their toll on him.

Each was the size of a child but they were legion. Few struck him more than once but together they were a hailstorm of blows. They beat the plates from his armored boots as his shins absorbed clubs meant to break his legs or trip him. Stabs and slashes by knapped stone blades tore links away from his chainmail and carved away pieces of his brigandine and tabard.

The harried Lion was in no better shape than his gear. His muscles ached from repeated summons of magically enhanced strength. The sword glyph in his right hand burned as he blasted one goblin after another into the crowds with Waymaker spells that never seemed to be enough. Chest heaving for air, Pencheval hacked and staggered forward, more pushed and slammed on his chosen path than anything else.

Another goblin attempted to garrote him, but he grabbed it and tossed it over the wall. More work with his sword cut enough of a path to reach the corner. Pencheval turned and used a Clearsight charm to show him his assailants down the darkened northern wall in shades of bone, ash, and dried blood. They were still so numerous and densely packed he could not see the stones beneath their feet, and no other humans along his path lived.

His eyes burned and his arms felt weak. Was this his end, drowned in a sea of goblins? He could feel his heart sink until he found the thing within him that he first discovered in the slums of the capital. It was the ferocity of a war hound that first emerged when a group of muggers had tried to take his only coin and leave him dead in a ditch. It was not a noble hound, but a gaunt, ragged, and ravenous thing that would kill or worse for what little it had. It was the thing that saved him that day and it renewed his spirit now.

The battered mercenary refused to die without a fight and knew exactly what manner of fight it would be. If the goblin numbers gave them courage, then it was time to remind them of their fear. He roared and charged, meaning to renew their trepidation with as much shock and horror as he could inflict.

The first goblin he reached staggered away screaming as it tried to hold its guts in with one hand, victim of a slash across the midriff. Pencheval grabbed a handful of another goblin's face and the pathetic beast started to howl. The mercenary felt warmth in his arm as his magic gave him strength and tore. His would-be assailant jumped up and down with both hands over the bleeding ruin as he threw the gore to the ground. The endless horde did not cease, but he could see some of them hesitate.

The sword rose and fell. A stomp so thoroughly crushed a goblin foot the fiend hopped away shrieking, leaving a blood trail in its wake. He bisected an enforcer trying to rally the now-stalling goblins and flicked the pieces apart with the tip of his blade so they could see what fate awaited them if they obeyed.

Limbs flew. Pommel strikes reduced skulls to pulp. He tore eyes and ears from goblin faces, and their former owners wailed from it. One goblin after another died horribly or struck the ground crippled. He left a string of the grievously injured mewling and screaming in his wake, and slowly the shock took its toll.

Fewer and fewer goblins attacked him as he continued to lay waste. By the time he was halfway to the northern stair, they preferred to keep their distance or climb to the ground below to evade him entirely. Once he killed or maimed so many he stood at the stair's top landing, every goblin he could see flinched and backed away from his sword's point as he held them at bay with it.

Keeping his blade pointed towards the goblins, Pencheval picked his way down the stair. He scanned quickly in all directions to see if any other goblins meant him harm. Every time he laid eyes on his now reluctant attackers, they would cringe, try to slink away, or hiss. Some few retained a desire to curry favor with their warlord and looked ready to spring upon him from above, but reconsidered when they caught the Lion's attention. After scrambling back from a jump, those goblins would spit words at him he took for epithets.

Halfway down the stair, the horde on the wall dispersed, and a single goblin waved farewell to him with a leer on its face. He was grateful goblins were survivors and thieves rather than warriors but wondered what new trouble awaited him. He did not believe they were allowing him to withdraw this easily even after what he had done to them. They had simply decided whatever waited in the darkened streets below could deal with him now, and believed that it actually could.

***

Pencheval trudged to the bottom of the stair and cast a Clearsight charm to take stock of his circumstances. His eyes saw into the darkness and showed him a very different sort of trouble. The streets and buildings seemed deserted, but the lack of obvious enemies did nothing to reassure him. He knew they were above him and could hear them not so far distant.

He was sure the darkness was goblin work, but even with the Clearsight charm he saw nothing. Where were the people? If they were hiding, it was from something that was not the horde as a whole. That suggested that whatever had doused all the lights was still out there, waiting to take advantage of the darkness. Perhaps it was that hooded clan of goblins that had attacked his patrol those nights back, the one with a penchant for stealth. He had not seen them until they wished to be seen, and by then they were attempting to kill him.

He glimpsed through an alley into the town square to where he did hear and see goblins. They were not killing the humans as much as capturing them and herding them to a heavily guarded area in the open. Other goblins looted and overwhelmed the town with little resistance.

He wondered why they had not taken it all by now. They surely had the numbers, but had not yet brought them to bear. Were the efforts to capture humans blunting the offensive? Were they distracted by an abundance of things they wanted? Was that why this part of town was pitch black and yet seemingly devoid of them? Whatever it was, he did not believe it would last.

He was in the element of the goblins now. Darkness was where they did their worst work, and he realized it when he scanned the rooftops and found a hooded goblin staring back at him that he had not noticed even a moment before. What was even more disturbing was that it wasn't making any attempt to remain unseen. In the past, the only reason a goblin ever showed itself was as a distraction for an ambush, but then why do so much to douse all the light? Near total darkness meant that they need not do anything but waylay near-blind humans as they found them.

"Szzhast," Pencheval thought he heard as the goblin on the roof spoke. It pulled a piece of cloth from under its tunic and waved it at him. It even walked towards a dim patch of light so he could take better stock of it. Pencheval recognized it as the same sort of white robe worn by the sisters in town. The goblin leered and beckoned him towards the square.

It knew about Nan. How had its clan uncovered that bit of knowledge? It would have had to notice him, and then Nan, in broad daylight while spying on them inside the town. He did not even wish to contemplate how it possessed stealth and spy craft of that caliber.

It knew this fact, unhindered by the language barrier, and suggested that the goblins held her captive in the square.

"Szzhast." The goblin pulled a knife and tore into the garment with it. "Szzhast tzzik."

No, they weren't suggesting she was in that direction. They were suggesting that they had her and would kill her if he did not go in that direction. It was an obvious trap but his only option if true. All that was left was to save her and Dominik before the goblins completely swarmed the town. The thought of deserting them left him so disgusted he refused to consider it.

He was so intent on rescuing his companions that he didn't hear the footsteps behind him until they came in a rush. He turned sharply and caught a brief glimpse of the largest goblin he had ever seen before it defeated his guard and smashed his faceplate into his helmet with the haft of a weapon.

***

The goblin Berserker Tzak Fangripper roared triumphantly as the Gray Lion staggered back, flailing blindly before it with its shiny big knife now that he had smashed the eye-holes of its metal mask shut. He knew that their shiny masks bent instead of broke when they were struck, and occasionally that left them helpless. He disliked the Shadows, but agreed that there was value in knowing about your prey. That bit of knowledge had aided him here.

The Shadow distracting the warrior on top of the human's cave had insisted on an ambush. Defeating the strong in single combat made for better boasts, but the Stonemaster made it exceedingly clear that he *would* cooperate with the Shadowcreed to slay the Gray Lion. This one warrior human had killed three Bonestrippers and cut its way through the rabble on the cliff-walls in feats of might that rivaled even Berserkers like himself. When the rest of the horde spoke of this human, they did so in hushed whispers for fear of calling it forth.

He wished he could have fought that human in its prime, but one did not survive a goblin horde in their prime. The human was as described, but battered now. The strange metal skin it wore was rent in many places, and the square scaly hide atop of it was in no better shape. Its shirt was so torn that he could barely recognize the Gray Lion symbol that served as its lan markings through the flapping tears and triangles of cloth. Yet the fact it had made it to him at all spoke much about its strength.

He had no doubt as to the outcome of this fight. He had slain trolls, the great bat-lizards whose teeth he wore around his neck, and rival clans' warriors by the score. That was why the Bloodmoon Chieftain had chosen him for the glory of killing the Gray Lion. Many of the mighty had fallen before him, but this specialist would be a particularly glorious kill.

A glorious but staggering, winded, and injured kill. The disappointed Berserker feared he would only be an executioner until the human reached up and tore the mask away from its shiny hat with one hand so it could again see. Tzak smiled. This human was far from finished, and he almost drooled at the thought of eating its heart after a real fight.

***

Pencheval felt his head snap backwards and knew his visor had been crumpled when he could no longer see. He slashed his sword wildly in front of him to buy a few moments' time as he magically enhanced his strength. He tore the dented armor from his bascinet, snapping the hinge, and threw it aside. The dazed mercenary shook off the blow, cursing the fact he had just allowed it, and blinked in disbelief at the sight of his opponent.

It was the biggest, most brutish goblin he had ever seen in his life, nearly as tall as he was and at least as muscled as a blacksmith. It smiled wickedly and raised its guard, wielding a vicious steel battle axe in one hand and a sturdy stone mace in the other. The goblin wore a bearskin cloak and a necklace of drake fangs around its neck, along with a kilt of crudely stitched hides.

Of course he would be faced with a goblin mean enough to kill one or more drakes by itself, the Lion thought sarcastically. Why would this night go any better for him now? The goblins on the wall had let him enter the darkness unhindered for a reason, and he feared he may have found it.

He heard the goblin on the roof scream, and the one in front of him snarled back. It beckoned him to do something with its weapons, which he found oddly out of character. Pencheval wondered if it was trying to distract him from an ambush, but when he stood there long enough to expend its patience, it clashed its weapons together and charged.

It attacked him with a dual downward strike. Pencheval parried, and only his magically enhanced strength kept the brute from ripping his sword from his hands through sheer force alone. The goblin laughed as it continued to press, openly chortling because he had not been found wanting. The confused Lion had never met a goblin that looked forward to a fight and pushed it away. His opponent expertly recovered into a guard, appearing eager for more.

It never did to underestimate goblins, Pencheval reminded himself, and circled his opponent to prevent the one on the roof from being at his back.

***

Tzak kept up his guard and turned to face the human as it circled, grateful to the Fiend Under The Mountain that his opponent could still fight and use its shaman tricks. The last exchange had been thrilling. The human retained its weapon despite the power of his blow and even managed to push him away. This might yet be a good fight.

He fumed at the Shadow on the roof. He did not need his opinion about why he should have jumped the human after blinding it. The Stonemaster had given the task of killing it to the Bloodmoon Clan, as well he should have, and Tzak would kill it his way.

If the Chief of Chieftains had wanted the Shadows to get themselves slaughtered like they did when they failed to kill the Gray Lion before, he would have commanded it so. The Shadow had no room for speech and its advice on how to fight was little more than an irritation. Besides, this promised to be a battle for the boasting and he meant to savor it.

Tzak bid the Gray Lion to try again with the motion of his axe, and to his great satisfaction the human obliged him. It moved like a jackrabbit to flank him, and he responded to the unusual burst of speed by shoulder slamming it off balance. He assaulted and pushed it until it slammed against the wood wall of one of the strange caves in this place and pinned the arm holding the big shiny knife with his mace. He followed up with an axe aimed at the junction between its neck and collarbone. Instead of a kill, the human pulled the blow to one side with its hand on his wrist.

It attempted to disarm him, but he kept it from taking his weapon by strength alone. After two more futile attempts to twist his axe out of his hand, it smashed its head and shiny hat into his face. The Berserker staggered and felt the human push him away. He stumbled backwards and saw the Gray Lion step forward to clear the wood wall and allow itself room to swing.

The human was stronger, faster, and bigger than most he had seen this night. Was its clan like that of the Bloodmoon, blessed with the secrets of making bigger and stronger humans? Had this one earned the right to become one through glory like all the Berserkers of the Bloodmoon Clan? It certainly fought like it, and that blow to the face once again reminded Tzak that he faced a truly worthy foe.

"What are you doing? Quit toying with the Gray Lion specialist and slay it before it slays you!"

"I don't tell you how to sneak, Shadow. Don't tell me how to fight!" Annoyed as he was, Tzak was forced to agree. Blood dripped from his forehead and stars danced before his eyes, which could leave him vulnerable. He would not join the army of the Fiend Under The Mountain by dying from a preventable failure. This fight had been satisfying, but it was time to obey the Stonemaster and kill the Gray Lion. Its death would give him glory and the pole draped with the trophies he carved from it would not post itself.

***

What in the name of the Lord on High was this thing?

Pencheval appraised his opponent, which was again shouting back at the hooded goblin on the roof after what sounded like a complaint, and inwardly cursed. It had met him strength for strength and speed for speed, even with the aid of his magic. Furthermore, none of the moves that had served him in the past proved effective against it now.

The helmeted head butt did little more than cause the thing to stagger. The same attack had killed any number of lesser enemies with bared heads or even leather helmets. It had even retained its weapon through sheer strength alone when the same attempt to disarm had broken the bones of those he fought in the past. This goblin, this thing, whatever it was, just took it all in stride and appeared to want more.

After voicing its complaints to the goblin on the roof, the brute resumed its attack with an onslaught. There was no finesse in the hail of blows it threw at him, only a desire to overwhelm a battered enemy. Pencheval staggered, parried, and dodged away, fatigue forcing errors that nearly killed him. He cursed the fact that it had accurately assessed his condition when the battle axe hooked around his blade and tore it from his hands.

Disarmed and short of options, Pencheval commanded his magic to grant him speed and charged. His opponent moved more quickly to his perception than most but still could not prevent him from rushing within its guard. The Lion tackled it at chest level and landed on top of it after successfully slamming it to the ground. It was the only move of which he could conceive after losing his sword. If nothing else, robbing it of the ability to use its mace and axe would buy him a moment's respite.

Pencheval grunted on impact. Tackling the goblin had felt like running headlong into a stone wall. It did drop its weapons, but only so it could try to strangle him, something the chain guard around his neck prevented. When it realized that guard hindered its counterattack, it grasped a handful of it and tore it free from several of the rivets fastening it to his bascinet. Worst of all, the brutal thing looked ecstatic about the turn of events, and not the slightest bit concerned about an inferior position.

***

Tzak was elated. Not since he had slain the great bat-lizard for its fangs had he enjoyed this sort of fight. Again, he had thought he would be nothing more than an executioner, but to his great delight, he was wrong. The tackle was a move the Berserker found a considered counter after the human lost its weapon. This human could use its shiny big knife and fight without it as well.

It wasn't the first time he found himself in this position, and knew what to do to escape it. He tried to wrap his hands around the human's neck to strangle it, but the strange metal skin got in his way. He did not know what manner of beast he would have to skin to get his own, but at least it tore away with one hand, flapping and dangling at a single rip and exposing the neck beneath.

Tzak clenched the metal with one hand and pulled the Gray Lion close enough to reach its throat with the other. The human pinned its forearm just beneath Tzak's neck and pushed to dislodge him. Tzak kept hold regardless, successfully preventing the Gray Lion's escape, and grabbed its throat. A blur in his vision as its forearm disappeared momentarily stopped him from crushing its windpipe, and he realized the mistake too late. He felt one pain in his ribcage and another across his throat, and then all he could do was choke on his own blood.

***

Pencheval mentally thanked an old friend from his apprentice days for the trick that had saved him. His fellow apprentice Gantillion was a rogue, a rake, and an annoyance. He was also at home in a fight, and his advice had been well worth it to take.

"Grouch," he advised, using the nickname he had given Pencheval, "keep a couple of daggers under that overblown shirt we all have to wear. They might save you someday." He had been right and that was exactly what that dagger had done.

The ragged Lion breathed a sigh of relief. The goblin nearly had him when its hand wrapped around his neck, and he found no cause to believe that if he had hesitated to stab it he would still be alive. If it had succeeded in clamping down for more than a moment or two it might have crushed his windpipe and strangled him. As it was, he had to fight his own rising panic to grant himself speed and put a dagger first into its ribs and then across its throat.

The brutish goblin choked but still pawed at him weakly. Pencheval pulled its hand away and pinned it. Unwilling to leave its death to chance, he finished it with yet another thrust between the ribs and staggered to his feet to get the measure of what troubles yet awaited him.

A multitude of goblins had gathered on the rooftops and in the windows of buildings on this street to witness the fight. At the fall of the brutish goblin, some of them cringed, others gaped in astonishment, and still others disappeared in haste. The hooded goblin with the sister's robe screamed at them, only to be hit in the chest by a thrown battle axe from the ground below. At that the goblins fled in earnest, and Pencheval, thankful for his aim and the throwing quality of his opponent's weapon, sheathed his blades and leaned on his knees to suck in one deep breath after another.

To proclaim their territory and threaten trespassers, goblins posted poles draped with the teeth, eyes, and ears of their victims. Pencheval and the other apprentices found the entrance to one of their cave lairs littered with such totems after the Lord of Stonewall Pass hired the Lions to destroy it. Hoping he could make that work for him, Pencheval tore the necklace of drake's teeth from the brutish goblin and tied them around his belt.

He saw someone on the roof of the temple wave at him with a torch and beckon him to the side opposite the square. The Lion saw it as proof that the goblins had not overrun the temple before he could reach it. There would be no counterattack after the fall of the wall, but if there were survivors there might yet be enough troops to break through and escape with Nan and Dominik.

Pencheval trudged onward, worming between the thin alleys and keeping buildings between himself and the too-near swarm of goblins in the square. There was real hope he might escape this invasion and he meant to remain alive and free from capture. If he succeeded in reaching the temple he might still save his companions.

***

"It did *what*?"

The Stonemaster listened to the ill tidings of the rabble before him in the great stone field at the middle of town, surrounded by a bodyguard of warriors. In spite of the news, he enjoyed the fear of the cowering humans they captured and herded. It was the only bright spot in what should have been a rout by now.

The success at the eastern wall had left much of his horde believing the fight had already ended in their favor. The rabble and warriors nearest to him obeyed his commands and continued to herd and capture humans, but the horde as a whole no longer acted with a single purpose. Those yet outside the cliff-walls were content to be stalled by their numbers and reluctant to risk their lives now that this was all but done.

Reports by his messengers about the breach said the movement was akin to a herd of a hundred goats trying to pass through a gap large enough for only one. Those that were making haste did so only to disappear into the town for loot, and fights over those prizes were more than the enforcers could bring to heel. The goblin warlord found it infuriating and absurd. Given their advantage, they should have defeated the whole human clan-home by now. Yet they had not even made it halfway to the western wall, a place darkened by the

Shadowcreed to the goblins' advantage, because the greatest resistance to the horde was itself.

He glanced at his staff, the treasure that gave him power over the stone. He would not be able to awe any of them into submission with it until it had sufficiently rested. All he could do now was save face and not show weakness by pretending all of this proceeded as he desired. He had promised them victory and loot; why not allow everyone to believe he was simply keeping his word? It was a good plan and it would have been enough, except for the news the messenger brought about the Gray Lion.

"The Gray Lion defeated Tzak Fangripper, Chief of Chieftains. He has failed you."

The annoyed warlord was unimpressed by the goblin cringing before him. It was typical of the rabble to blame the failures on the slain and then exaggerate the threat. He did not bother to ask any more because he did not care to hear any more excuses. It was all but certain the next thing the fool would do was wail about demons in the human's shiny big knife.

The Stonemaster frowned and watched the messenger respond by holding up his hands in fear, but did no more. He expected nothing better because rabble were rabble. If they were good for more than dying in a fight and menial labor they would have shown it by the time they stopped being pups.

"Where is the Gray Lion now?"

"We saw it limping towards the great cave with the colored shiny pictures, Chief of Chieftains. It stays within the part of the town we have not yet overrun." The rabble pointed towards the largest of the human caves next to the stone field in which the Chief of Chieftains stood. It was an impressive thing decorated by the humans with strange pictures pieced together from flat and colored stones.

The Stonemaster cursed himself for not following his instincts when the Bloodmoon Chieftain had proclaimed that Tzak could defeat the Gray Lion alone. At the time, the Berserker certainly seemed equal to the task. The giant possessed a stolen metal axe he had forcibly taken from its last owner and wore a necklace of great bat-lizard teeth around his neck. He swore he would chant over the death of the Gray Lion before sunrise and carried proof that he had slain fell enemies in the past. It was enough for the warlord to allow him his methods aside from a command to cooperate with the Shadowcreed.

Now in hindsight he knew otherwise. He should have told the Bloodmoon Chieftain to send half a dozen. Yet the Berserkers' master had to do it his way, and he was not one to treat like a common pawn. Now they would have to rip the Gray Lion from one of the human caves, which would sap even more strength from his horde as it had done on the walls. This time the Stonemaster resolved to do it his way, the way it should have been done before.

According to the Shadowcreed, the last of the holdouts cowered in the same great cave to which the Gray Lion fled. He was happy that at least he could take care of them all at once. There would be no more foolery and no more single warriors.

"You!" The Stonemaster pointed to a group of rabble, who looked down in deference. "Bring the others to me. We mass to attack the great cave."

"How many others, Chief of Chieftains?"

"All of them!" He knew all would not obey but only required enough to defeat the last of the Snow Clan and finally kill that blighted Gray Lion.

He would mass superior numbers and overwhelm his enemies in proper fashion. It was the goblin way and it would prevail. Champions and single combat were for foolish humans, and he refused to disregard his better judgment again.

***

Pencheval half-staggered to an open-frame house and leaned against a rough corner beam. The weary Lion resisted the temptation to relax and catch his breath. He could not tell how many goblins watched and found his weakness to their liking. The trophy of drake's teeth dangling from his belt might aid him, but he still refused to encourage any opportunistic ambushes by appearing spent.

He continued to worm his way through the alleys and back paths to the rear of the temple. The shrill cacophony reminded him that far too many goblins gathered in the square not two hundred paces from him. They were a squabbling and disorganized horde, but a horde nonetheless, and nothing he cared to tempt.

The streets and homes remained eerily absent of humans. Every so often he would see a body, struck from some blind direction by a knife, but nothing else. Few torches burned, no humans begged or screamed, and little could be heard above the noise of the horde. Pencheval wondered if the townsfolk simply hid, or departed for a place to take shelter when darkness descended on them.

Every so often a goblin or several would peer from a window to discover what fool walked into their clutches. When they did, he stood upright and did his best to appear hale. They would leer until they beheld the leather thong of drake's teeth hanging from his belt and slink back into the darkness, incredulous and terrified. After watching several groups of goblins think twice, the Silver Lion was almost grateful he was forced to fight the brutish one. Their recognition of its trophy, and what manner of might it took to steal it, kept them from attacking him out of fear.

It bought him enough of a reprieve to reach the temple. The figure on the roof beckoned downwards to a heavy wooden door with the torch before disappearing inside an attic entrance the mercenary could not discern from the ground. Pencheval rushed to it and pushed only to find it would not budge. He put his shoulder to it and felt the slight shift of something heavy on the other side.

He cursed under his breath. Of course it was barricaded. No one inside the temple with any sense would have left it otherwise. Yet he wasn't happy with the sensible right at this moment. The damn goblins were within earshot, and if another one of the brutish ones came his way while he was waiting...

Movement. Pencheval saw into the darkness with the Clearsight charm he had not allowed to fade since his fight with the brute. He saw a short hooded figure disappear between the buildings across the street. He had seen none of them on the way here, and therefore believed the glimpse was deliberate. Was it trying to distract or unnerve him? That meant others were close.

He heard the scraping of something heavy moving across stone behind the door when several other hooded goblins appeared in windows and on rooftops. Even with the Clearsight charm he had not seen them climb or approach. He put his sword into guard and scanned left and right down the street to find nothing charging or sneaking up on him. When he again glanced towards the hooded goblins, their numbers had increased. No cursing, no noise, just a growing mob appraising him as though he was their next meal.

Pencheval swallowed hard and banged on the door. "Now would be good!"

He gritted his teeth as dozens of new goblins appeared. They were not the hooded ones, and they hissed and spat words he believed were curses as they gathered the courage to charge him. Despite the necklace of drake's teeth that had frightened the goblins before, they realized their numbers gave them the advantage against one mauled human and leered at him as though he was a wounded animal ripe for a kill.

"Open the door!" Pencheval backed into the opening the second he heard the squeak of hinges and saw a dim arc of light under his feet.

One of the hooded goblins screamed an order in its tongue as he escaped and the newly formed mob across the street charged. He dropped his sword, slammed the door shut, and scrambled to lock it with its wrought iron bolts.

"Move, Lion!" A pair of battered soldiers put their backs into sliding a heavy cabinet back across the door, and Pencheval aided them. It grated into place and muffled the screams of goblins as they tried to beat their way into the temple. He repeatedly heard the smack of something heavy on the timbers but the entrance held for now.

"Good thing I spotted you on the wall, Lion." Scout Howe stood before the mercenary, still holding the lit torch Pencheval assumed was he saw at the roof of the temple. "Not that you were hard to miss. Quite the feat of arms, that."

"How did you find me after I descended from the wall?" Pencheval leaned on his knees and caught his breath.

"Saw a big pack of goblins looking at something. Assumed it was you. Turns out I was right."

"Glad you're good at your job, scout."

"Never look a gift horse in the mouth, Lion," Howe replied, and smiled.

Pencheval gave him a wry grin. Nan may have had a point after all. They weren't all as those from Terris Lyn.

***

"What do we do now?"

Pencheval wondered the exact same thing as he strode through the smell of dust and around the pulpit. The sisters and clergy tended the wounded, and far too few soldiers were there defending them or escaping the rout. The pews nearest the front door had been ripped from the floor and stacked against it, seeming to him an all too flimsy barrier against the screeching horde outside. The crowds turned when he clomped into the nave, and to his relief, Nan and Dominik were among them.

"Pencheval? What happened to you?" Nan put her hands over her mouth and the rest of the room gaped at him. He did not wonder why. The ripped chain guard around his helmet still dangled and jingled in time to his footsteps, and everything he wore was either rent, torn, or gore-splattered.

He was grateful that at least his Argentsteel hand and a half sword remained intact. The gnomish alloy had proven true yet again. Despite hours of fighting and channeling enough magic to melt any ordinary weapon ten times over, the blade did not have so much as a nick upon it. Yet it was so drowned in goblins' blood no inch of it glimmered in the light.

"The damnable goblin warlord is a mage," Pencheval answered. "The blighted monster tore through the wall. I couldn't stop it...we must regroup."

"Regroup? Where?" Scout Howe shrugged and waited expectantly. "Where is it safe to regroup?"

"The Shield of Athesiene," Pencheval offered. The few soldiers present looked at him as though he was mad, though the clergy merely seemed unconvinced.

"We are surrounded, Lion," Howe reminded him.

"Are we? Then why did they not attack all four walls? Perhaps those reports of goblins were just outriders. At the very worst, there are fewer of them between us and the castle than those that come from the east."

"Even were it true, why did the town go dark but for goblins from the west?"

"Not goblins from the west. The hooded clan from the horde. They are hidden but they are few. We take our chances to the western gate, and then–"

"And then the beasts they used to protect their flanks run us down and eat us? They patrol the walls!"

"Do you all mean to wait here and die?" Pencheval's voice cracked as he tried to control his irritation. "They will come and they will kill us."

"Or throw us with the others in the square," Nan stated calmly. "They are not putting everyone to the sword. And what of the wounded?"

Those injured on the pews hale enough to be aware of the conversation gave Pencheval their full attention after the question. The Lion tried to answer but the words caught in his throat. For the first time in years, he could not find enough callous disregard to state the unvarnished truth, much less in the matter-of-fact way he would have done not even a month ago.

Those who could not leave would fall into the hands of the goblins and could expect no more mercy than anyone else. Possibly less, as they would serve no other purpose to them but food, the same fate any of their captives might meet at any time. Either they left those who could not travel here to die, or they threw their lives away in a vain attempt to defend them and everyone died.

He clenched his teeth. What good was keeping the truth from them? It would kill them whether he spoke it or not. He clenched his jaw and cursed his own weakness, but could not meet Nan's gaze or answer the question.

"Then I cannot go, Pencheval." Nan spoke softly, which did nothing to reassure the battered Lion.

"There is nothing here but death." He spoke in an exaggerated calm that belied the fact he could barely retain his wits. "We must make for the gate."

"You can escape the town beneath the temple," Nan answered, "but you will do so without me."

"Madness," Dominik said. "The only way out through the catacombs and caverns was sealed with stone and mortar years ago. How would we escape?"

"With this." Pencheval sheathed his sword and pulled the gauntlet from his right hand, revealing the silver glyph in his palm to the assembled. Angry red irritation from hard use outlined the gnomish symbol. "It wouldn't be the first time I've had to break through a wall."

"If the exit is to the west, a forest is not far," Howe offered. "It stretches nigh halfway from here to the castle."

"Whatever we mean to do, decide it now!" A soldier watching through the windows into the square swiftly backed away, only just dodging a spray of shattered stained glass.

The rough and chipped claws of a goblin mob tore at the iron frame that once held the glass, but the grates kept them at bay. The mercenary feared it would not be for long, because he could hear the scrape and scrabbling of dozens of them climbing the walls and tearing at the roof in an attempt to force entry. If there were this many, Pencheval believed it was at the behest of their master, which would make this the battle to end the town's last resistance.

"We should have listened to you, Lion." Nan smiled at him. "Now all the hope we have is at the castle, and you must join it there, or we are well and truly lost."

"If you believe it so, listen to me now." He felt some hope rise that he might persuade her to go. "Muster with me at The Shield of Athesiene. They will need all the help they can get."

"I cannot go. These people will be the prisoners of goblins and I will not desert them to it."

Pencheval shuddered in one last attempt to retain his temper and failed utterly.

"Addlewits! Mule stubborn fools!" Pencheval's magic reacted to his emotions and amplified his voice. His frustration thundered across the room. Friar Dominik started and the crowd recoiled. "Have you lost all command of sense? Death claws at the walls!"

"We tend the faithful of the Lord on High, Pencheval," Nan replied evenly. "I have greater responsibilities than my own life."

"This town is lost! If the goblins catch you, they will kill you if you are fortunate. Kill and then butcher you if you are not."

"The Lord on High protects, Pencheval."

"No! We are leaving!"

Pencheval reached forward to drag her along, no longer interested in persuasion or diplomacy. He had suffered days of despair knowing this would happen. He watched it approach without any way to get anyone to believe him. He fought his way across the top of the wall after the defenders fell, and beat the brutish goblin in the town only by the skin of his teeth. None of it was so he could turn his back on Nan and see her lost when escape was within reach.

He felt nothing beyond a desire to rescue her and could not restrain it any longer in his weakened state. He could not see her lost to another nightmare worse than the Hope of Terris Lyn. Not ever again.

He was within a half-dozen paces when he saw her hands rise, followed by a crack like thunder and a bright flash of light. A blast of heat hit him as though from opening the door of an oven and slammed him to the ground. Stars danced before his eyes and his ears rang in a loud tone that gave no hint of ever subsiding.

When he regained enough of his sense a few heartbeats later, he saw the blurry view of a ceiling and Nan standing calmly above him.

"I knew you would find yourself again, Pencheval. The hard-working, faithful Pencheval that would do anything to help his own. The Pencheval that realizes not all other people are demons in disguise. You do remember, or you wouldn't be here trying to save us."

"Nan–"

"You must go. There is nothing you can do now but flee or die. Go to The Shield of Athesiene and join forces with the Knight Superior. Together you may end this horde."

"I will not. Abandon..." Pencheval staggered to his knees and reached towards Nan, who easily evaded his grasp. There was a scrape of iron on stone from behind her as the frames for the stained glass shifted and gave under the goblin attack.

"That, Pencheval, is the real you," Nan replied. "Time and tragedy have led you to forget it, but it yet remains. And for the same reason you would not desert me, I must stay and help my own."

A loud metallic crash on stone turned Pencheval's gaze to the windows, where a frame had fallen free and goblins swarmed inward. They crawled along the walls clinging like insects, landed on the ground, and then hissed. Pencheval realized they were waiting for their companions and massing instead of attacking him one at a time.

"Leave now," Nan insisted. "Take the friar and others with you."

"You cannot stay Lion," Howe added. "They will kill you. The brute and the stone monster of their master proved it. They mean your death for certain, and there will be no capture for you or us."

Pencheval glanced at Nan and then back at the goblins.

"I will not be moved any more than the last time." Nan met Pencheval's eyes and raised her hands again. He saw the white light of a spell form between them and realized she had been the one to smite him.

Unable to find another ounce of ferocity within himself, he backed away and towards the place where Howe and Friar Dominik beckoned him. It was the most miserable decision he had ever made in his life. After all he had inflicted and all he had endured to save her, he could do naught but flee and barely that.

He backed through the door to the narrow stone stair and down, sword ready to keep his enemies at bay. Nan watched him go as she was surrounded by goblins, seemingly confused by her refusal to acknowledge them or cower before their weapons. They did not kill her, but he knew nothing more of her fate as he descended out of view.

***

Pencheval slammed the door at the foot of the stair, then barred it. He heard the beating and shrill curses of goblins in their tongue on the other side. Using his magic to grant himself strength, he tore a nearby statue from the floor and jammed it diagonally against the wood. Momentarily safe behind the blocked door with those few he could save, the frustrated mercenary leaned on both hands against a wall.

"No!" He slammed one fist against the stone and bowed his head. Not since he laid on the floor of his family's cottage seven years ago, bleeding and unable to move as the Hope of Terris Lyn and his henchmen murdered Cecelia and his father had he felt this helpless.

"Pencheval, you couldn't..."

The Silver Lion stood up from the wall and held up one finger to stop Friar Dominik from speaking.

"So help me holy man, if you tell me you mean to return to that carnage up the stair I will beat you senseless."

"No. I mean to help you attain whatever purpose the Lord on High has for you." The old man leaned on his staff. "I know not why you came to this place just as all this began, but you are here for some reason Athesiene has not revealed to us. Nothing else can explain your presence in all of this."

"Purpose of Athesiene?" Pencheval spat. "This is a rout, not purpose."

"Purpose or no, we still have to live through this," Howe interjected, glancing nervously at the door. "If we mean to escape, we should depart in haste."

Pencheval motioned for them to lead the way and sank into despair. Escape? That's what he might have done from a cage. This was humiliating defeat. And to abandon Nan? What was spellcraft to him? He'd shrugged off worse and should have been dragging the naïve and stubborn sister along with him, by her neck if need be.

His eyes burned and nausea threatened at the thought of just scurrying away as she was captured. He had not failed this badly as an apprentice. Yet what more could he do given the circumstances? She would not go and he had neither the time nor strength to make her depart otherwise.

Friar Dominik wound them through tight tunnels too short for him to traverse without hunching. They crawled through the dark with only a spattering of torches, reminded of what this failure would bring by the bones resting in the niches along the walls. The wet chill left the Lion feeling like a worm, reduced to fleeing by a horde of primitive goblins.

He questioned all he had done before it had come to this. What more could he have done? What more should he have done? Dragged them away sooner? Wrung sense into Knight-Brother Galot by way of his neck? Found some means to persuade them that their fortifications, forces, and magic were lacking against such a horde as this? Persisted until they realized these shortfalls were not present at The Shield of Athesiene?

He leaned against a wall, the cold, moist stone soothing the irritation of the glyph in his palm, and clenched his teeth. What more could he have done? Nothing that mattered now. What more he could do was to unite with the force mustering at the castle. Once amassed, they could put the goblins to the sword, spear, and arrow. Burn them to ashes with the power of a whole order of Athesiene's knights. Cut them down in retreat and slay their wounded. Reduce their warlord to a groveling ruin before impaling it with a pike and mounting it in the square to die very, very slowly for all of this.

His growing fury and magically enhanced strength made short work of the wall when they finally arrived at it. He beat it down with a shoulder until the mortar cracked and the bricks shifted, allowing them to clear it away by hand until the opening was large enough to pass. A Clearsight charm allowed him to find the cave entrance and a small patrol of goblins nearby helping themselves to water from a stream.

Not enough to be another horde, he told himself. Had they been tricked into thinking that Tarsun's Market was their only safe haven for the purpose of their capture? If so, the goblin warlord on the bone throne was more cunning than he had originally surmised. The possibility infuriated him enough to charge the patrol without waiting for the others. He was not yet done with the goblins, and he intended to send them that message before he left.

***

The Stonemaster stood on the western cliff-wall accompanied by his council, arms open wide as he exalted in the adulation of the goblins below him. The Bloodmoon Chieftain chanted victory rites. The Shadowcreed Chieftain leered from underneath his black hood. The Beastwarper Chieftain leaned on his staff as though contemplating some secret he had discovered in the town beneath him. All basked in the victory except the Allspeaker, who paced nervously at the thought of yet another threat.

The first rays of dawn gleamed from a tiny sliver of the sun still tucked behind the mountains, stealing the goblin advantage but not robbing the warlord of his prize. The town and a real victory were his. The horde owned this place and everything in it, including the Snow Clan humans. Best of all, messengers reported that word of the Gray Lion fleeing like a wolf cub with its tail between its legs stifled talk of its terrifying invincibility.

He could see the captured humans huddled in fear in the field of stone where he left them under guard. A few Snow Clan warriors were prisoners with them, but most of the rest were slain. While the battle yet raged, they were as unwilling to quit as the Bloodmoon Clan, but far less able to do anything about it. The Berserkers had made short work of the scattered resistance as fast as they found it.

It was not all perfect. He had lost more goblins than he expected. The Gray Lion had wrought horrible damage by itself before being forced to flee. In addition to the dead, it left a surfeit of crippled and wounded goblins that would have to be slain now that they were more of a drain than they were worth. It was the goblin way, but being forced to kill so many might rekindle the fear the dark human warrior caused his horde.

He would also need better tactics in the future. He would have lost the town but for his direct intervention. Perhaps he should lead with the stone construct at the mountain-castle when they went to take it. Perhaps he should do many other things he did not yet know to do. For the moment, however, he was ascendant.

"Victory!" The Bloodmoon Chieftain roared. The goblins standing on the rooftops cheered and capered at the pronouncement. One fell through a soft spot in the shingles and disappeared, a misfortune that provoked laughter from his fellows before the celebration resumed.

"Victory." The elated warlord basked in the glow, but soon his mind began to weigh what came next. "What of the Gray Lion?"

"We were finally able to break into the tunnels beneath the great cave, Chief of Chieftains," the Shadowcreed Chieftain answered. "It broke through some stones into another cave and ran into a group of rabble."

"It is slain then? Bring forth its shiny big knife." The Stonemaster was hopeful, but feared he already knew the answer.

"We cannot, Chief of Chieftains. The Gray Lion slaughtered the rabble and nailed their enforcer to a tree with his own spear."

"It is not defeated yet," the Bloodmoon Chieftain said with something that sounded too much like respect for the Stonemaster's liking. He was not happy about the failure of his Berserker, but that was a conversation for another day.

"You believe it goes to the mountain-castle then?"

"Yes, and a pity. That one should have been born to the Bloodmoon Clan. Its fury will find no place among the humans."

"It has fled, and for the time being that is enough." The Stonemaster was almost surprised by the relief he felt from that fact. "Now it is time to tell other clans of our success. Send the speakers you suggested before the horde set out."

"Yes, Chief of Chieftains. They will come."

"How many more clans can we find?"

"Six that we can reach," the Shadowmoon Chieftain informed him. "They will tell us of more if they are persuaded to join the horde."

"Shadowcreed, have your Shadows scout the valley and keep watch on the humans. If any of the Snow Clan mean mischief here, or from the mountain-castle, I would know of it."

"Yes, Chief of Chieftains." The Shadowcreed Chieftain descended into the town to carry out the command and seemed to disappear into the throngs of rabble.

"Beastwarper, keep your Bonestrippers outside the walls. We have captured many humans and I don't want them killed in a rampage."

"Yes, Chief of Chieftains, but they will need to eat in time."

"Use them to punish the humans that disobey us," the Stonemaster ordered, "should any stop submitting."

The warlord turned to the Allspeaker to find the shaman muttering to himself.

"Allspeaker, your time is now. Find humans that look useful, and demand their knowledge. Take Berserkers with you to help persuade them to speak."

"Yes, Chief of Chieftains." The Allspeaker seemed relieved that he would be given a guard. The Stonemaster was not surprised. The shaman was always nervous about his own safety.

No matter. The shaman could believe doom lurked around every corner if it suited him, but the Chief of Chieftains would not. The warlord meant to enjoy his moment, but then it was time to get back to work. Victory was thrilling, but plans were better, and much still needed to be done. Half the valley was not all of the valley, and so it was not enough.

***

"My chieftain, we found a strange human."

The Beastwarper Chieftain turned from his examination of the great cave where the Gray Lion had taken shelter before it fled. Despite the damage, he still found it an impressive thing. He tried to discern the significance of the place but could not fathom it. Perhaps the humans had built it for their chieftain? Perhaps their gods? The colorful images he had heard once decorated it might have shown him, had they not been ripped away in the fight to capture the humans and kill the Gray Lion.

The goblin that had spoken was one of the rabble and wore the dark green armband of his clan beneath the gray band of the horde. A dozen more were with him, and they all guarded a single human with bound hands. It was one of the humans he believed was female. It wore a red-trimmed robe colored the white of the Snow Clan.

Was the robe ceremonial? What did it denote? Could the human that wore it tell him about the great cave? If it lived here, it would know something. For now, it was time to determine why the rabble found this one strange.

"Speak." The Beastwarper Chieftain leaned on his staff and listened, happy that his first mysteries came the dawn after victory.

"We broke into the large cave where the Gray Lion fled." The goblin pointed towards the big cave the Beastwarper Chieftain contemplated. "While we were forcing entry, this shaman attacked the Gray Lion. The trick it used was enough to smash it to the ground. We thought it was dead, but it rose again, and fled after being threatened." The goblin looked confused. "What does it mean?"

"Did this human attack you as well?"

"No, my chieftain. It submitted quietly after the Gray Lion was gone."

The Beastwarper Chieftain smiled. Dissention in the Snow Clan? Did some humans not like the orders of the Snow Clan Chieftain and mean to kill the Gray Lion? Goblin clans would do this if united by someone less fearsome than the Stonemaster and his council. It suggested that the Snow Clan Chieftain was not as strong in maintaining order among its clan, which was a good sign.

Still, it was a shaman. Perhaps all the Snow Clan shamans dressed this way, and it was good to know. They were not the sorts you wanted surprising you because they could kill so quickly. If they could be identified by their clothes it made finding them simpler. Caution told him he should have it slain this instant, but if it had attacked the Gray Lion, it might be a possible ally.

He decided that the benefit outweighed the risk. No, it would not do to kill this one. If it hated the Gray Lion, it might tell him what it knew about the lethal specialist and its clan in the hopes of slaying it. If nothing else, the humans knew shaman tricks the Beastwarper Clan did not and it would be made to share them.

"Do you know anything else?"

"It tried to head towards the humans in the stone field, my chieftain. It might have used magic on us had we not bound it after we pulled it away."

"It was seeking other humans. Take it back to the others and let it find them. When it does, we will know who to threaten to loosen its tongue. I will ask it many things when the Allspeaker is with me."

"Yes, my chieftain."

"Keep four warriors on it at all times. I do not want it slain or escaping."

"As you say, my chieftain." The goblins pulled the human away by the leash attached to its hands. The human looked back at the Beastwarper Chieftain too calmly for his comfort and then turned to be led towards the other humans.

If it was a shaman, perhaps it was smart as well, he mused. Good. It would know much more that way. And it would learn quickly that it would be wise to tell him everything.

Its answers to his questions would be among the real treasure in this place. Not the cloth, the shaped wood, or even the metal interested him as much. The knowledge of the humans had far more value. If he could take it and learn it, the goblins could become more than small clans of hunter-gatherers squabbling amongst themselves. The fact the Stonemaster was enlightened enough to know this made the curious chieftain smile. He had chosen well when he chose to join the horde.

The Gambit

"Lord on High be praised!"

Pencheval silently agreed with Friar Dominik's sentiment as the castle finally revealed itself in the distance. It was a welcome sight after just escaping a horde. The handful of ragged survivors with him cheered their arrival.

A single massive keep rose towards the sky draped in the white and red banners of Athesiene's temple. Stout stone buildings and round towers stood in its shadow atop a steep hill ringed by a parapet. At every change of direction in the irregular outer walls rose another powerful, flat-topped tower, and around the base of those walls stood its town. It was a grand fortification; a place to repel the largest of armies and their siege machines.

Yet it was no longer as peaceful as it was when the Silver Lion mercenary left it to serve his contract not even a month ago. He could see hundreds in the fields digging, little wisps of dirt flying from tiny earthworks in the distance. In the trenches closest to the town, wooden stakes protruded from artificial hills and redoubts. The trenches were not placed to protect troops, but to make a forward advance impossible in a straight line. They were nothing more than obstacles for a vast horde of goblins to cross, while archers and artillerists punished them from the battlements and towers.

A great beacon blazed atop the high keep. It was a spectacular column of fire inside some manner of brazier, and it burned nearly a quarter as high as the structure beneath it. It had not been lit when he originally arrived, and he thought it nothing more than another sign that they prepared for the horde.

This was the place to defeat the goblins. It was the seat of Athesiene's order of knights, several of its stronger priests, and the base of thousands of troops. It was where that town should have fled instead of standing their ground. Instead, only he and a few others escaped the goblins' latest depredations after it fell.

Pencheval could hear Friar Dominik pray and give thanks to his god. He had been Pencheval's companion ever since the mercenary helped a patrol rescue him from a goblin raiding party a month ago. Between the raiding party and the escape from town, he had so much life-saving luck it was likely responsible for his piety.

"Why does that beacon burn atop the keep?" Pencheval pointed to the towering flame.

"His lordship does that to summon all his knights," the friar answered, seeming a little annoyed that Pencheval had interrupted his prayer. "He'll need them all against that horde."

Pencheval nodded agreement and for once, looked forward to aiding knights for more than coin. He disliked the goblin wretches before he arrived in the valley, and now he utterly despised them. Their massacre of a patrol during a contract, followed by fleeing their entire horde, left him wanting to return the punishment. Nor was it any small matter to him that they forced him to desert someone in Tarsun's Market he had wished to rescue.

"It's time to make the Knight Superior's acquaintance again."

***

Pencheval supposed it wasn't the first time heads turned at his entrance.

Outriders met the small group well before they arrived and led them through the earthworks towards the town. At the gate, a small crowd craned their necks to see why there was such a fuss and were shocked by the reason. As they winded through the town towards a fortified encampment, two women screamed, one dumbstruck farmer let his cart's handles slip through his fingers, and the ring of a smith's hammer stopped as he gawked at the ragged Lion.

Pencheval did not wonder why. He had fought through a sizeable part of the goblin horde just to make it this far and it showed. He held his dented bascinet under one arm, and his torn chainmail neck guard jangled in time to his step. Nothing remained of his visor but a snapped piece of wire dangling from a twisted hinge. A shredded black tabard covered ravaged brigandine and chainmail, and what might have once been armored boots bore one last dented plate and torn rivets. All of it was splattered in the gore of the many he had slain in the process of escaping.

He ignored these small scenes of horrified common folk and followed the soldiers between two lines of tents. He had business with the Knight Superior, and his appearance did not much concern him. He had survived in large part because of a decision he could barely stomach, and he meant to redeem it by helping the temple retake their town and eradicate the horde.

Knight Superior Rennoute stood at a table with several of his order, three officers, and a map. The lord of the valley was as the Lion remembered him. He bore graying, shoulder-length hair and a close-cropped beard. A fluted breastplate was the only armor he wore over the red and white robes of a Knight-Brother. If not for a gold medallion denoting his rank and his ceremonial sword, he would simply have appeared as an older member of his Order. When Rennoute finally took note of the survivors, he did not flinch at the sight of the weary Lion. Instead, he motioned to those around him.

Soldiers appeared and offered assistance, which many of his companions accepted. Pencheval waved away one who offered to escort him to a tent or a healer. To his surprise, Friar Dominik did the same and continued to follow him as he approached the valley's lord. Soldiers and knights parted but kept their eyes on him as he took a place at the table and nodded respectfully to Rennoute.

"Your Grace, Tarsun's Market has fallen."

"So our scouts have informed us, Lion," Rennoute replied. "Our thanks for escorting what survivors you could."

"I can help you reclaim it," Pencheval continued. He could see the distaste for his offer from the knights present, but Rennoute remained impassive.

"You are welcome to rest and repair in the town beneath the castle," Rennoute said. "For your efforts, a suit of drakeskin armor will be yours to replace the ruin you now wear."

"Thank you, Your Grace. I will be ready to march in half a fort–"

"And then you will leave."

Pencheval was dumbstruck. Leave? Did this fool not want for swords? What manner of enemy did he think he faced? And whose help did he think he dismissed? Any lord of Lerrisaine in Rennoute's place would be begging for Pencheval to stay.

"Your Grace, could we perhaps reconsider?" Friar Dominik spoke, which left Rennoute momentarily surprised.

"No. If the mercenary means to make himself helpful, he can tell the captain all he knows of the goblin horde." Rennoute waved one hand at Pencheval. "You may go. Feel free to make use of the town, if you wish."

Exhausted, devoid of ideas, and dismissed by the local lord, Pencheval turned and walked away, followed by the friar. This was not something he expected. He knew rescuing Nan and avenging himself on the goblin horde would be challenging, but not like this.

***

The Stonemaster, goblin Chief of Chieftains and Hordemaker, gazed out over the human town he had conquered and put his face in his palm.

The once-human town bustled with the activity of goblins and was his first step in taking the whole of the human Snow Clan's valley. He had effectively cut their lands in half, and victory had been sweet. Three days ago, he stood on their western cliff-wall and soared high on his feeling of success. Now he had to rule it, which was another matter entirely; all the petty day-to-day conflicts of a clan were magnified substantially in a horde.

He looked out of a hole in the side of the human tall cave and watched a group of goblins fight over spoils. It was a scene that played out all over the town, which the horde less occupied than covered. He could see his forces in every open space, many atop the human living places, and others slept on the cliff-walls after improvising shelters. The town was so filled with goblins going about their business that movement around it regularly ceased. The jamming of motion to a stop resulted in more fights as enforcers restored order.

It was bad but not catastrophic. Close quarter living was their way, for the clans congregated in their caves. But the humans? They could not bear the numbers and did not take being kept together in their large cave well. He had been forced to store them there when it should have been his cave by right, but it was the only structure large enough to protect them from the horde.

Their treatment of the humans bordered on outright defiance. What part of 'capture the humans' did they not understand? The Berserkers killed their last pockets of resistance as they were commanded, yet when the horde fell to looting after breaching the wall, they treated far too many humans as free range meat. Now there were not enough of them to fill their own great cave, when they once filled the town.

Those humans made noises at their god and struggled to remain sane. That place was the best protection from the horde, but it was by no means sufficient to isolate them from its chatter. The noise was nothing to the goblins, but it was a weapon against the humans who went mad at the sound. Now they were immersed in it. Would it break them all?

They reacted badly when he ordered their wounded slain because they were worthless. When the Allspeaker, a shaman that could speak any tongue he wished, warned that they would suffer the same if they were no longer useful, he was greeted with shock and not submission. Intimidation was not what it used to be.

And now that they had this place, the council chieftains took their own paths. The Shadowcreed Chieftain disappeared into the press of the horde for hours on end. The Beastwarper Chieftain obsessed over a single human shaman, constantly appropriating the Allspeaker to talk with it and any other human he thought might know something of interest. He would soon have to remind them both who was Chief of Chieftains here.

At least Bloodmoon had sent speakers into the mountains to find other clans and bolster the horde. The horde had suffered many dead or wounded, a plurality of which were inflicted by a single human specialist of the Gray Lion Clan. Though he would never admit it, the Chief of Chieftains had nightmares about that unyielding human and its shiny big knife. In the worst of the visions, he would turn and it would suddenly be there, ending his ambitions with a laugh and a downward stroke.

The escape of the Gray Lion Clan human was the worst problem they had faced. His horde still talked of it in whispers as though fearing the most evil of spirits, and it had become a dark thing looming over the whole effort. If anything would keep them from moving, that human alone could do it, and that meant it had to die; brutally, painfully, and publicly.

The Chief of Chieftains heard the curses and grunts of the rabble struggling to haul his bone throne from the ground to this room. Goblins pushed and lifted, and the throne scraped into position. All of its bearers stopped to catch their breath, and one fell to the floor, gasping.

"You there."

"Yes, Chief of..." The goblin rabble wheezed. "Chief of Chieftains."

"Find others and bring ten humans from the great cave here. It is time to break them."

The goblin moved to speak and only wheezed for his effort. The Stonemaster waved him away and it stumbled towards the stairs to obey. The warlord could not be bothered by his minion's exhaustion. The humans had been one of the prizes he meant to take once he conquered this place. It was time to render them useful.

***

Nan looked around at the animal's pen the goblins had created in the temple's nave and despaired.

Three days ago, goblins had bound her hands and took her before their leader. The thing bore a cluster of bone spikes upon its left shoulder that reminded her of the lichens on a tree and gave orders to those that brought her. It took them an hour to reach its place on the western wall in the morning through the press, and an hour to return her to the temple after it made its will known to them. In that short span of time, the vast swarm had torn its interior to pieces.

The wounded she had remained behind to tend were gone. There had been no chance to bargain or negotiate for their aid. Bloodstains covered the bare stone where they and the pews once were. The blighted horde had also stripped the wooden fixtures from the nave and the pulpit with horrid speed, leaving only scraps and the ragged remains of seats where stubborn bolts refused to yield. When she first saw what they had done, the horror left her momentarily unable to stand.

Now the room bore crude barriers and simple shelters the goblins made, yet they less guarded them than swarmed all the spaces along the perimeter around them. The blighted things could climb like insects and perched on the statues and fixtures they had not utterly destroyed or looted. No less than several dozens of them kept guard or watched them at all times, and the sound...

The sound of the horde at a distance was misery. Within the horde, it was nigh insufferable, and the walls did little to muffle it. The screech and click of the goblins outside occasionally changed but never ended.

It had been a grand place three days ago, and she did not recognize it now. Nan could reach no other conclusion than that it was an animal's pen, and possibly a slaughterhouse as well. The survivors were so few they did not even fill the floor.

Is this what Pencheval feared when he fought his way across the horde to save her? In some of her darker moments, she wished she had accepted his help when he offered it. In the rest, she prayed to the Lord on High for the strength to attend her responsibilities. Keeping to them felt as though she tried to bail the water from a sinking boat with a thimble.

A hard knock on the door, enough to be heard over the endless screech, caused Nan and many of the other townsfolk to start. One of the guards at the door peeked through a crack, gasped, and gesticulated to its fellows. Several of them pulled the heavy double doors open at its insistence with the squeal of protesting hinges. Nan did not know what to think of the display but knew it would be bad.

A group of four entered. The one in the lead limped forward and appraised her, eyes gleaming with a sinister intelligence – it was the one she met when the town fell. Its growth of bone clearly weighed it to the left side, and it leaned heavily on its staff for support.

Next to it was something that looked like a witch doctor or druid. It dressed in strange rags and hides marked with primitive shapes and bore a staff topped with a ram's skull. That one seemed more worried than curious, and kept closest to the two brutish guards.

They flanked the pair and wore bearskin cloaks. Unusually massive, they towered over the other goblins and townsfolk, and seemed just a hair's breadth away from a rampage. Each of them bore two weapons; one was stone and wood bound together with leather, and the others were steel axes inlaid with primitive symbols etched by primitive means.

As the group approached, the four goblins that always guarded her nodded respectfully at them. She noted they wore a dark green armband that matched the clothing of the lame goblin. She wondered if it was their leader. What else could it be?

The goblin leaning on its staff turned to the witch doctor and said something. In response, it quickly glanced to both sides, anticipating a threat, and spoke.

"The Beastwarper Chieftain has questions, human. You will answer."

Nan started in surprise. A goblin spoke their tongue? It was the first to do so. "I am Nan, senior sister in the Temple of Athesiene. And you are?"

The goblin bearing the ram's head staff spoke to the other, which replied.

"The Beastwarper Chieftain. Names are for those too low for titles. Tell me of the Gray Lion Clan human. We know you know of it."

"Gray Lion...I don't understand."

The two murmured to each other. "The one you blasted with shaman tricks as we broke into this great cave. Big human. Shiny big knife. Black shirt bearing the symbol of the Gray Lion Clan."

"Pencheval?" Nan spoke before she could restrain herself. This brought an excited burst of speech from the witch doctor, which was met by more from the deformed one.

"Penn Cheval. Its name is Penn Cheval. Good." The one that appeared to be in command adjusted itself against the staff and carried on the conversation with the assistance of the witch doctor.

"We, too, wish this Penn Cheval dead. We know how difficult it is to kill. Tell us more of its clan and together we will slay it."

"Want him dead?" She was not eager to tell it much more of Pencheval, and saw the opportunity to be less than forthright with this bit of miscomprehension.

Yes, she had attacked Pencheval. The Silver Lion tried to pull her away from her duties in a heartwarming, but misguided, attempt to save her life. If the goblins didn't know this, it might be useful.

Nan nodded. "I, too, wish him dead and agree. He is a Silver Lion. It is his guild."

"Guild?" The witch doctor chirped the word with an undertone of clicks. "Clan?"

"No. Guild."

"Annoying humans. Why so many words for a clan? Can you not call a single thing just one thing?" The witch doctor appeared annoyed at having to translate that, but was quickly glared back into submission by the other. "How many of the Silver Lion Clan are here?"

"I only saw Pencheval."

"Why is it here?"

"His guild fights for coin. He is no different."

"The shiny gold discs. If we give it many shiny gold discs, will it fight the Snow Clan for us?"

"No, but if the Knight Superior offers more coin, more of them will come."

"Come from where?"

"The south. There are many more like Pencheval."

She thought the witch doctor might faint from fear. After a few moments of silence, the other one poked him, and he quickly babbled a translation. The two brutes smiled as though eager at the news, but the eyes of the lame goblin narrowed.

"How many more?"

"It is said between one and two hundred like him, and they train others every other year."

"Does the Snow Clan Chieftain have enough shiny discs to make others come?"

"I fear it may be so." Nan feigned frustration as best as she could. "I could not kill one of them. What hope have I against a hundred like Pencheval?"

This time the fear was evident on both of them. Whatever Pencheval had done to them in his escape had made a lasting impression. Could she dissuade the goblins from the occupation of Tarsun's Market this way? She found it worth a try; she hadn't heard of any other ideas.

"A hundred like Penn Cheval. Good to know. You will continue to answer truthfully." The warped goblin leaning on its staff bared its teeth and the witch doctor continued to translate. "For you to do otherwise would be unfortunate. My guards grow bored in the absence of violence, and punishing humans would be entertainment for them. Humans such as these."

The goblin pointed to a man on the floor in the fetal position. She recognized him as Wot, a hardworking if nervous cobbler. The fall of the town to the horde had been more than he could bear. She raised her hands in defense.

"Keep your shaman tricks to yourself. We are too many to defeat." This time, the witch doctor spoke without translating the leader, pointing around to the dozens of goblins keeping watch with its staff. "Obey or be punished. Cause trouble, and be slain. Cooperate, and the Silver Lion Clan human dies as we both wish. You decide."

As if to punctuate the point, the translator waved one of the brutes forward. It lunged forth and grabbed her by the throat, lifted her from the ground, and pulled her towards its face. She looked into the unflinching eyes of the thing and saw nothing but fury and bloodlust. It roared and screeched a series of sounds that suggested it was only a moment away from rending her limb from limb.

"Decide now." She struggled to breathe as the room grew darker and panic threatened to overwhelm her.

"Coop...er...ate." She saw no choice in the matter, but that just meant the game was to lie more convincingly. She had to keep their attention, or these things would simply threaten someone else and hurt those in her care.

She didn't know if she could manage it. Deception under interrogation was not something with which she was familiar. Then again, the goblins did not seem to know humans all that well. Could they read through her lies if only one of them could even speak their tongue? Could they realize she was stalling?

"Wise." The witch doctor said something to the brute holding her throat. It put her down and resumed its place as she gasped for breath. "The horde slays all. We will kill our mutual enemies in the Silver Lion Clan."

She rubbed her throat and smiled as well as she was able. The leader goblin smiled back, turned, and left with its retinue. She plopped down on the floor in relief and suppressed the urge for flight.

Intrigue? This was to be a battle of intrigue with the goblins? It could not be any harder than learning the magic of a sister from the temple, or at least she hoped not. She was not about to tell them what they needed to take the Emerald Refuge from the Knight Superior, but an error would likely get her killed along with those for whom she cared.

***

Friar Dominik swallowed hard at the closed door of Rennoute's study, drawing an odd glance from the spearman guarding it. He reminded himself that despite his purpose, he was not in danger. The lord of the Emerald Refuge was not a cruel or capricious man; he was just in error about needing the help of the Silver Lion.

And one friar would take it upon himself to correct a Knight Superior? That was well beyond his station and it felt like a weight on his shoulders. Friars did not advocate military decisions to the knights of Athesiene, much less the lord of their Order. Yet, this was necessary – and more importantly, urgent.

Feeling much like a fish out of water, Dominik cleared his throat and smiled nervously at the guard.

"I would like to see the Knight Superior," Dominik requested. "At once, if he is available."

"I will make the request of his lordship," the guard responded in a businesslike manner. "Wait here."

The soldier entered the study and closed the door. Dominik heard muted and indistinct voices from the other side. He mumbled to himself, considering what to say and how to say it, only to jump when the door opened again.

"He will see you," the soldier informed him. Dominik nodded his thanks and entered.

Rennoute looked up from behind his desk to acknowledge Dominik but did not rise. Dominik approached him, adjusted himself nervously, and nodded respectfully.

"Thank you for seeing me, Your Grace. If you could spare a moment, I wish to speak with you about the Silver Lion."

"He will be tended, friar," Rennoute reassured him. "Silver Lion or not, I will turn no one of his valor away when they need succor."

"Of course not, Your Grace. I would not suggest you would do such a thing. Except..."

"Except?" The Knight Superior waited patiently for the friar to continue. Dominik felt cold sweat form on his forehead.

"Would it perhaps not be wiser to accept his offer to assist you? Surely his sword would be useful in the face of a goblin horde. I have seen them. Their host is vast."

"His sword is not the issue," Rennoute said. "I would not have hired him to help search for a patrol gone missing a month ago were his skills in doubt. His guild is known for keeping its contracts fastidiously, and he has done more than was agreed."

"Then why not accept his aid, Your Grace? Do you lack the coin?"

"Because he is a Silver Lion, friar."

"Because he is a...do we judge men by their tabards now?" Dominik felt his nervousness slip away as the purpose of his temple filled him with resolve. When did they simply dismiss someone by their associations? Had the Lord on High not redeemed truly darkened souls?

"I know the temple's work, friar. So do those above us both. They so believe in it that they founded a knight's order and maintain a small army to ensure the faithful such as yourself are defended while engaging in it. The Silver Lions do not share that measure of belief."

"This Silver Lion fought in the battle to retain Tarsun's Market, Your Grace. He survived and overcame things that would kill most men."

"And again, you mistake aptitude for purpose." The Knight Superior steepled his fingers. "Do you know what the Silver Lions are?"

"A guild of mercenary warriors trained in magic, Your Grace. Many seek their services, for they are capable against beasts and threats most cannot overcome."

"No. That is what they do."

"I don't understand, Your Grace."

"Silver Lion adepts are powerful mercenaries, true. But they are war hounds without conscience or conviction."

Friar Dominik soured at the comparison of Pencheval to a dog but kept the disgust from his face.

"Their guild goes forth and recruits the dispossessed, the vicious, the desperate, and the ruthless once every two years. A group of a hundred of these rogues are tested to their limits in a trial six fortnights in length to determine which of the aspirants will become apprentices. Many flee its rigors and others suffer great harm. It is a process only the truly determined succeed in completing, and the successful rarely number more than a score. The adepts call it 'The Six' and it is not fondly remembered."

"Do we also not determine the worth of those who say they mean to join us, Your Grace?"

"Not by measuring their ruthless determination and inhumanity," Rennoute answered. "Their apprentices are indoctrinated very simply. Don't fail their contracts, don't embarrass their guild, and don't anger their patron, the king. In the absence of any moral compass beyond that pittance, the training to make them increasingly ferocious and skillful is enhanced by some gnomish process no one else can duplicate. This grants them their magic and links it to a will uncommitted to a higher purpose."

"After serving years as an apprentice, those who have taken it to heart and still remain become journeymen, much like the one that accompanied you. At that rank, they have captured, suppressed, or slain hundreds with no more consideration than whether or not the contract paid well. Their only restraint is a fear of crossing their guild or the king."

Rennoute rapped his fingers together. "I do not need anyone of this sort. If we are fortunate, we will be outnumbered by a mere ten to one, and that is a place only for those made resolute by the Lord on High. You do not overcome such odds unless you believe and trust that those around you do as well."

"Your Grace misjudges this one."

"I do not," Rennoute countered. "Whatever feats of arms he has used to save you do not define him. I will not begrudge you an attempt to find the light in his darkness, as is our way with any who come to us for aid in good faith. Neither will I rely on what little good you may have uncovered in him to be sufficient resolve against a goblin horde."

"I beg Your Grace to reconsider. He knows one of the sisters in Tarsun's Market and almost died trying to rescue her. He will aid you for the chance to try again."

"He has a mercenary's principles, and even were I willing, I lack the coin to retain him for a protracted campaign. The goblins in Tarsun's Market will require one now. It will be the work of years and endless skirmishes to reduce their numbers before laying siege. If we do anything less, they will overrun us on open ground."

"You will not face them here, Your Grace?"

"Do you suppose they will grant us favorable ground by the asking, friar?"

Dominik noticed the note of irritation in Rennoute's voice and bit his tongue. "My apologies, Your Grace. You are lord here."

"It would be a blessing from the Lord on High if this could end another way, but there is nothing to be done. If the goblin warlord was clever enough to capture a town, it is clever enough not to walk to its death. You may go."

The last three words were in the tone of a command, and Dominik bowed before leaving. "Your Grace."

***

How many taverns had this been?

Pencheval sat in a corner of the common room, alone at a table, nursing yet another mug of stout. The idleness did not sit well with him, nor the fact he all but felt the innkeeper's glare on the back of his neck. The man had only barely concealed the distaste for his presence, and those few in the common room with him kept their distance.

He knew he had to act but did not know what to do. He believed he would begin his quest to rescue Nan by allying with the knights of Athesiene's Order. The thought was nauseating and for anyone less than Nan, he would not have even considered it. Fighting alongside knights? And to be rejected out of hand by them when he would aid them for no expense? What manner of madness had he found here?

For one, it was the madness of his 'no expense' offer to them. Offering his aid for free might change the Knight Superior's mind, but it would also violate one of his guild's least flexible tenants. Drillmaster Tagrine had translated the florid language of the guild charter with his usual bombast; Silver Lions always get paid, and the guild always gets a fifth. To do otherwise was to invite their wrath, and their wrath was not a thing to countenance.

But Nan was worth the risk. She had been worth the risk when he tried to rip her from the claws of a goblin horde. As the only other person who knew of the Hope of Terris Lyn's true nature, she had restored something in him he did not realize was lost. He would be damned, excoriated, and punished by his guild before he simply abandoned her to her fate.

"I hardly recognized you, Lion." Pencheval glanced up from his mug and found Friar Dominik examining him.

"The tabard needs some work," Pencheval grumbled. The tabard was rags and would take no small amount of stitching to come close to being whole again. As it was, he wore a newly purchased laced shirt because his old one was fit only for bandage stock. The cloth shoes felt far too light on his feet while his armored boots were under repair, along with his chainmail and helmet. His vambraces, brigandine, and leather gloves were lost as scrap, but he did find his new pair of elbow length gauntlets to his liking.

"I should say so," the friar replied, and sat down. Pencheval waved over a server, who brought him a mug and ale.

"What do you know of the Knight Superior, friar? I will need his aid and he surely needs mine. Can he be persuaded?"

"I tried not long ago and know he will not accept your help, despite my efforts."

"Bah." Pencheval frowned. "The stubborn wretch will not hear of a Lion's help? Does he have spare legions in his cupboards?"

"Mind your tongue, Lion," the friar warned nervously. "The Knight Superior is lord here."

"Oh yes, the knighthoods. The temple's order and the precious chevlers in their fiefs. Why do you suppose, given they currently exist, that a guild duplicating their place in the scheme of things can boast the patronage of the king?"

Dominik leaned forward and whispered. "Pencheval, this line of speech will bring you ill fortune."

"Oh, I cannot complain to their faces. The king would not have them know that their time is past, after all, but I can grumble about them in the corner of a tavern."

"Past? How can you think this? Did you not see the power of Knight-Brother Galot on the wall?"

"No doubting the valor of Galot, friar. Some of the knights can fight. Some of the chevlers are actually worth their titles. Some. Sometimes. And even those that are may or may not help you for reasons you cannot predict.

"That is why there are Silver Lions, friar. We are certainty. There is no wondering if such-and-so a knight can fight or if they are nothing more than a pompous ass in a colorful costume. Nor will we duel each other to the death over ridiculous and incomprehensible points of honor. Perhaps the temple's order will find that something is worth their time, and perhaps they won't. With Silver Lions, things are far more certain."

Pencheval drained his mug and slammed it to the table. "I am a journeyman adept, friar. All journeyman Silver Lion adepts can fight like me. If you want my help, you offer me a contract and coin. If I like your offer, your contract is served. Period. End of the tale. No haughty noble sensibilities to tolerate or secret codes to decipher. We solve problems for a reward, and when we say we are warriors, it is true to the last one of us."

"Lion–"

"Am I annoying you?" Pencheval turned to glare at the innkeeper, whose mug cleaning had grown increasingly noisome as the conversation progressed. The aggravated proprietor shrank from the mercenary's gaze and returned to his chores.

Friar Dominik frowned. "Word will spread now."

"They will only know what is obvious," Pencheval snapped. "And if any mean to make more of it than words, they know where to find me."

"No doubting your skill at arms," the friar offered, "but how will this help you persuade anyone? If you mean to rescue Sister Nan, that is what you must do now, and a tongue set free to vent your opinions will not aid you."

Pencheval opened his mouth to speak only to find he lacked the disposition for more words. Persuade a knight? It was true. Disgusting to the point of needing stronger drink, but true. He murmured something, put his mug to his lips, and remembered it was empty when he threw back his head and tasted nothing but air.

Blighted luck, he mused. He found no more cause to believe he would persuade the Knight Superior any more than he had Galot. If such were the case, it would end in disaster as it did in Tarsun's Market, and Nan would be lost to him for good.

***

"What did the human say?"

The Allspeaker restrained the urge to hiss at the question. He had not been in this human clan-home more than ten days, and he could barely stomach hearing it again. As the only goblin in the entire horde that could speak the human tongue, he had been the center of attention of far too many parties and unsure of what to do about it.

Nothing, the shaman guessed. He had heard it so often it echoed in his dreams, and he could do nothing. Those that asked it of him were either one of the council chieftains, or at this moment, the Stonemaster himself, and they could not be dismissed.

He gave his warlord a submissive look. "The human says something called a catapult makes the rocks fly, Chief of Chieftains."

"Does it know how?"

The Allspeaker examined it and did not believe it could be so. The terrified human before him seemed scrawny and garbed in patched clothes. The Snow Clan warriors wore white and strangely puffy shirts that stretched to their knees. It was rabble, or he believed it to be.

"The Chief of Chieftains wants to know how this catapult makes the rocks fly."

"I...I don't know! I swear! The soldiers use those things!" It glanced at one of the Berserkers guarding the council and held up its hands to ward off their wrath.

"The human says it does not know because their warriors use them."

"Fiend-forsaken Snow Clan rabble," the Stonemaster grumbled. "Does it know anything useful?"

The Allspeaker turned back to the cowering human and was grateful he was not in its position. The Stonemaster meant to steal their knowledge and break the humans to his rule. If he was that human, he would prove he was useful and acquiesce with all haste.

"What do you do for the Snow Clan? If you have value, speak immediately."

"The Snow Clan? Value? What do I do?" The human shrugged. "What is a Snow Clan?"

"What do you do?" The Allspeaker gestured to the Berserker on his right. The gigantic brute grabbed the human by its shirt, slammed its face to the floor, and twisted its arm to a painful angle.

"You will answer!"

The human screamed and squirmed in the Berserker's grip. "I work for the stock master in the warehouse! I move what he asks me to!"

"The human says he moves things in something called a warehouse, Chief of Chieftains."

"Menial labor. It's rabble." The Chief of Chieftains gestured to the Berserker, who executed the human by grasping a handful of its hair and slamming it face first into the stone. Its squirming ceased immediately. "Bring forth the next one."

The Berserker, bored with his work, carried and then threw the body from the hole in the wall. The Allspeaker heard the corpse land. Those who would drag it to the butchers chittered below. The last six humans wailed at its death and cowered. There had been ten of them this morning, but the first four had been found wanting by the Stonemaster and met the fate of that rabble.

The Allspeaker rubbed his chin at the survivors. He did not know why they hesitated in paying homage to his warlord; any goblin would have been pragmatic enough about their circumstances to submit long before this. He honestly wished they would, because until they did, he would hear the same question over and over again.

What did the human say? Enough to get it killed. The Allspeaker did not find this a particularly good use of the humans, as they did not have an infinite supply of them. But it was the Chief of Chieftain's will, and he would not question it. If nothing else, it was better them than him.

Perhaps the one in the strangely colorful clothing that felt like soft moss might know something. It had better. The floor grew slippery with human blood from wrong answers.

***

"What do you mean, you won't stitch it?"

Pencheval stood in what passed for a small tailor's shop at the Shield of Athesiene. A box overflowing with yarns, thread, and draped with cloth dominated one lone wooden counter near the wall opposite the door and was organized in no fashion he could readily determine. A large window allowed the entry of light and a meager breeze to cool the place. Aside from those and a pair of wardrobes he could see nothing that suggested he would care to buy clothing here.

The proprietor was an aging crone rocking back and forth in a well-worn chair incongruously placed in the middle of the floor. The floorboards beneath it creaked and all but threatened to break. She had glanced up from her knitting at his entrance long enough to determine she didn't like what she saw.

"It's rags." She snorted at the half-folded and half-balled tabard in Pencheval's fist. "You need a replacement, not a seamstress."

"Only my guild issues them, and they're nowhere near here. What do you recommend?"

"Go to your guild and get a new one. You leaving will make everyone happy."

Pencheval gritted his teeth. "Did I mention I can pay well?"

"You did, and I care almost as much as you did when I told you that everyone would be happier if you left."

"Do you at least have thread?" Pencheval checked his temper. This was insufferable, but he had no choice but to bear it. Word had indeed spread as Dominik warned him, and the townsfolk were now less than cooperative.

"Aye." She didn't look up at him.

"Fine. I'll take a ball of it in black."

"Do we look like we do fancy dyes here, Lion? You get two choices. White or off-white."

"Two choices." Pencheval breathed deeply to keep from cursing. Bad enough he would have to stitch his own tabard back to a semblance of order, but with thread the wrong color, as well?

"Two. You *can* count, can't you?"

"Off-white it is, then."

"Good decision." In too long a time he procured a quantity of the stuff and a needle along with it, and both seemed far too dainty for his hands. His sewing was the envy of no one and tended to leave him with poked fingers. Far from ideal, but would serve well enough to restore his tabard to something he could recognize.

It would also become something the goblins could recognize once again. They flinched from fear at the sight of it during the battle of Tarsun's Market. They recognized it, and him, well enough that many would not cross or attack him.

It was a good start, but then what? Rennoute would not let him attempt a rescue. He had no plan beyond restoring his gear, nor could Dominik find any other course of action. Perhaps another of the survivors could help him? Scout Howe had escaped along with him and might know something. Pencheval had saved his life, and he might be more amenable than the other townsfolk.

***

"Show mercy! I'll tell you everything!"

The Allspeaker heard the words and believed them. Nothing with any sense cared to be struck by a Berserker, particularly one wearing the gore of the three humans he had previously killed with his bare hands. The question was whether or not it had anything of worth to say.

Its appearance seemed promising. The cringing thing was dressed in good clothing and appeared to be one of the higher status sort. Well equipped, sure, but it did not seem accustomed to easy living. Was it one of the enforcers? That particular combination of traits suggested it.

"What did the human say, shaman?" The Chief of Chieftains stared down as it begged on its knees, appearing intrigued.

"It says it will tell us everything, Chief of Chieftains. I think that means it submitted."

The Allspeaker was surprised that it took this long. The Chief of Chieftains arranged this place specifically to sort and break the humans. Each human was dragged to the spot where the others had been executed, and the dried blood was left on the floor by design. It was forbidden for them to stand without permission, but only cringe at the bone throne of the Stonemaster and the Berserker that would execute it. Outside of the hole in the wall, one could easily hear the sound of goblin butchers rendering human remains into food even above the chatter of the horde. Why any of this was lost on the troll-stupid humans until now was a mystery to him.

"What are you doing?" One of the humans in the group sounded aghast.

"Be silent, human. We did not speak to you."

"You can't do this!" The human lunged forward at its fellow only to have the Berserker intercept it and slap it senseless in one blow. The move stunned the one begging for its life into silence. The Berserker sneered at it after saving it from the attack and returned to the Allspeaker's side.

"Do not listen to the other humans. You have chosen wisely." The Allspeaker did his best to appear non-threatening. They had a submission, and now they only needed persuasion. He hoped the Stonemaster would agree.

"Right. Whatever you say." The human straightened his garb and stood upright. The Berserker glowered at him but the Allspeaker shook his head – there was no point in punishing the cooperative.

"What do you know?"

"Plenty. Ask what you want to know, and I'll tell you. You're the boss."

"What did it say, shaman?"

"It says it will talk, Chief of Chieftains, and wishes to know what you want to know."

"Tell me about the Silver Lion." The Allspeaker translated for his warlord, and the human cleared its throat.

"They're a bunch of bounty hunters and mercenaries, you see. Most of them stay in the capital, but every so often some of them go out into the countryside looking to kill monsters and bandits for coin. That one we saw here was the first I've ever seen this far north."

"Will it take our coin?"

"Can't really say. If you tried to kill him, he won't listen long enough to hear your offer. Word has it the Silver Lions are a rough lot."

"Word?"

"Yes, word. I know people who know things." The human swallowed hard and smiled nervously.

"Is that all?"

"No, no, no!" The human stammered the words in what the Allspeaker assumed was an attempt to justify retaining its life. "I can explain things, and also know the people around town. You just keep me safe and I'll point you in the right direction."

The Allspeaker translated, and the Chief of Chieftains waved a messenger forward. "Put a gray band on the human and keep it protected at all times. Store it away from the other humans. It is ours now."

"Yes, Chief of Chieftains." The messenger scrambled down to the floor below.

The warlord gestured at the human. "Tell it that it will be rewarded if it proves useful, Allspeaker."

"The Stonemaster, Chief of Chieftains and Hordemaker is pleased with you, human. Continue to be useful, and you will be rewarded."

"Right then." The human smiled, only to look confused as goblins with spears and knives emerged from the ground floor and surrounded it.

"What's all this?"

"They are your protection." The Allspeaker saw the reaction of the other humans to its submission and was glad the guards were so numerous. They had not yet broken to the new rule and might be dangerous to the new asset.

“Hold out your arm.” The human did as instructed, and a goblin tied a gray band around it.

The Allspeaker was happy the butchery had stopped, if only until this human proved useless. Until now, all he could do was watch as the Chief of Chieftains wasted potential knowledge the despairing shaman might never have the chance to access again. He silently enjoyed the moment, for good news was always in short supply.

They had another human now, but it had only confirmed what the human shaman had told him about this Penn Cheval; Silver Lions fought for the shiny gold discs. The one they had battled was not unique, and it would not fight for the goblins. Good to know, but it did not reveal any new way to defeat the worst of the horde’s enemies.

***

Pencheval clomped up the board and dirt path leading to a rugged fortress outside of the Shield of Athesiene. Four walls of lumber sharpened to points stood on a flattened and artificial hill. A few timber towers lashed together with rope rose above the defenses and archers kept watch from behind plank nests atop them. It had not been here when he originally arrived a month ago.

“State your business, Lion.” One of the guards at the gate held out a hand to stop him.

“Seeking a scout by the name of Howe. He returned here with me from Tarsun’s Market.”

“Aye. If they don’t have him in the field again, he’s here.” The guard waved him along. “Got no orders about keeping you out any more than anyone else, so you can pass. Just don’t cause no trouble.”

Inside were neat rows of canvas pup tents, only large enough to hold two. Many were empty and held nothing but a pair of bundled bedrolls. A few soldiers sat around a campfire over which hung an iron pot, and they only stopped long enough to determine that he was not trouble before returning to their conversation. Somewhere in the distance was the grate and hiss of a grinding wheel against the edge of a blade mixed with the hammering of a smith.

Howe was easy to find. He sat on an upturned log outside of the tent he currently shared with no one. He attended to sharpening a sturdy oak leaf dagger, and tested the edge with his thumb every few strokes. When he saw Pencheval, he sheathed it and smiled.

“Lion?” Howe appraised the mercenary. “I take it your repairs required some improvisation?”

Pencheval resisted the urge to punch him. Yes, that was one way to describe his tabard. Another was the agony of his repeatedly poked thumbs. The irregular stitches closed gaping holes and torn strips to less than a professional degree. Instead of a mark of his notoriety, it seemed a shredded black shirt bearing a barely recognizable lion rampant, poked through and laced with a strange ivory light. He hadn't even attempted to mend the ragged hem fraying and tossing about his knees.

"It does not bear consideration, scout." Pencheval ignored the blisters the ordeal had gifted his fingers. "What news have you regarding the Knight Superior's plan to defeat the horde?"

"Everything says he's massing." Howe gestured to the empty tents. "They set the soldiers here to dig earthworks the second they knew of the horde. This camp went up in a few days and rumor has it, others may rise. His lordship intends a campaign, which means it could be years dealing with the goblins."

"Years?" Nan did not have years. Nan was surrounded by a horde of goblins that only temporarily found use in keeping the people of Tarsun's Market alive. They could afford to do that in the warmer seasons, but what happened come winter? A lot of hungry mouths surrounded a lot of human meat they found all too edible, especially if there was nothing else.

"Years." Howe sighed. "Autumn will be gone by then, if she isn't already dead."

"Autumn?"

"My horse. The invasion forced me to leave her behind in Tarsun's Market. Too many damn goblins, and the little blighters eat everything. Could be she's dead already."

"And Nan."

"Aye." Howe leaned forward on his knees. "You know that sister didn't leave you a choice but to go without her, right? You did all you could have done."

"Perhaps." Pencheval appreciated the thought but did not agree with him.

No, he had not done all he could do. He didn't return here so he could be evicted from the Emerald Refuge and forced to abandon her again. It was not apparent how he could rescue her yet, but he meant to find a way. He had to find a way.

His conviction almost surprised him. He was not accustomed to noble purpose after years as a Silver Lion mercenary. This was not about a trade disposing of Lerrisaine's filth for coin. It was not about guild strictures, haggling over contracts, or enjoying and occasionally regretting his reputation. This was about saving an old friend who had shared a particular suffering with him. Just one singular thing to accomplish for no more reason than it was the right thing to do.

"What now, Pencheval? The Knight Superior commands you depart soon."

"That may have to wait," Pencheval replied without thinking. He didn't know how he would manage it yet, but he would not leave; he could not turn his back on this.

***

"Sister, will it ever stop?"

Nan looked down at the boy holding his ears and put her hand gently on his shoulder. "Yes, child, it will. Once the Knight Superior comes and defeats the goblins."

She already knew of what he spoke because he suffered from the same thing they all did. The interminable noise from the goblins outside, even dulled by the walls, drove them all to their wit's end. The endless sound, like a flock of birds or giant insects, grated on the nerves like no other.

One member of her four personal guards listened to them talking, chittered something, and returned to keeping watch. Its purpose seemed less to keep her prisoner than to keep her from harm, and to keep her from causing any. If they were minions of that 'Beastwarper Chieftain,' it meant they were here by its pleasure alone.

It had wanted to speak with her and did with the aid of the strange witch doctor. Was it a shaman of some sort, or had it just learned enough to know the human tongue? She could not say.

Ironically, her guards were the friendly ones. Not all of the goblins in the temple were particularly concerned with their well-being. One particularly nasty villain perched on a statue above the nave narrowed its eyes at her, which it did every time she spoke to one of the townsfolk. When it was once again satisfied that she wasn't brewing a revolt, it returned to scanning the others.

Yesterday, Willem had cracked at the sound outside. His suffering did not impress that particular goblin. It screamed at him once, and then chittered to others on the floor. They fell upon him until he died for being insufficiently obedient in his madness.

Nan had known him since he was still learning to walk. She had tried to intervene and woke up on the floor a time later to a pounding headache. She could only guess that one of her 'bodyguards' struck her to prevent her magic without killing her.

She could see that the little she tried to do would make no difference over time. Every morning the goblins came to take ten of them somewhere, and those they took never returned. It was only this morning that this did not occur. Yet even if it had stopped, they would kill someone for doing more than suffering in silence. Eventually, they would be the death of everyone, and she felt helpless to prevent it.

The door into the temple squealed open again, and the deformed Beastwarper Chieftain entered with the witch doctor and several guards. Two of the huge brutish ones accompanied him. It approached her to the cadence of clicks from its staff and Nan waved the boy away to go somewhere safe. He scurried from her without question, gazing nervously at the approaching forms.

The Beastwarper Chieftain spoke and the witch doctor goblin translated once more.

"The Beastwarper Chieftain says we have found another human that confirms your tale about the Silver Lion, Penn Cheval. You were wise not to lie to us. Continue speaking the truth and you will be rewarded."

Nan suppressed the urge to gasp. Another human? Did one of the townsfolk break under torture, or worse, choose to collaborate? This complicated her attempt to stall for time.

"Of course I would not lie to you. The Silver Lion is our mutual enemy."

The witch doctor reiterated this to the Beastwarper Chieftain, who smiled wickedly in response before replying.

"It will die. None stand before the horde forever. Yet the new human will continue to confirm your information."

Nan did not need a translator to know what that meant. It was a veiled threat. If she lied too egregiously, this new person would confirm it. What would happen then? One of the brutes killed more townsfolk? Perhaps that boy she just consoled? How would she stall now?

What did the collaborator know? What didn't that person know? If they were like most in the valley, they didn't know how to read. Could she stall the horde with books? Why would they care?

"I know something that might help," Nan blurted, hoping to keep this fiendish intelligence from learning more of the temple or Pencheval. If she could distract them with the less destructive knowledge in the books, perhaps she would divert it from questions that would put the Knight Superior's forces at risk.

"What would that be?" The Beastwarper Chieftain seemed genuinely curious as the witch doctor translated for it.

"They are called books. Let me show them to you."

***

"I fail to see what was so nebulous about the command of the Knight Superior, knave."

Pencheval finished his mouthful of stew and found the door into the tavern darkened with one of Rennoute's knights. The serving girl altered her path to avoid him, and all sound behind the bar stopped. The rest of the occupants grew quiet and cringed when he glanced at them. For Pencheval, it was just another knight.

He was unconcerned about his circumstances in the short term. His dagger was within easy reach and with just a thought, he could speed himself to such a degree it would end the knight before his hand reached his hilt. The magic granted to him by gnomish work was not as powerful as the invocations of Athesiene's knights, but neither was it as slow. He lacked the power of their god, but summoning the magics he could perform took less than a moment, and with little more than the expenditure of will.

The knight could not match that burst of superhuman speed without magic of his own, but he hoped it would not come to that. It would save him in the event of a fight, but it would make everyone else at the castle hostile very quickly.

After a few moments of what he supposed was meant to be an intimidating silence, he put his spoon in his stew and met the knight's glare with unflinching eyes.

"What is your problem?" Pencheval refused to show weakness. Most of the people he had dealt with in the past, either in negotiations or in conflict, reacted to that as a wolf might a wounded fawn. If nothing else, he would certainly not be cowed by a knight.

"The soldiers report some reluctance on your part to go. Perhaps you should think before you speak."

Howe reported him? No, he had saved Howe from a mob and nothing he had seen since led him to believe the scout was an ingrate. However, any other number of soldiers might have heard him, and not knowing him from anyone else, quickly told their superiors of potential trouble.

"Why? Is there someone here that should frighten me?"

The knight scowled and flexed the grip on his sword arm. Pencheval did not flinch.

"First and last polite warning, and only for the valor you have shown at Tarsun's Market. We are in a state of war with the goblins. You will do as the Knight Superior commands and not cause circumstances to become more dire. As much leeway as the king allows your guild, you do not get to decide whether or not to obey a command to leave by a liege lord."

The annoyed mercenary gritted his teeth. That was absolutely true. The king's patronage meant a noble could not force a Silver Lion to stay or serve bounties without payment. If they wanted him gone, however, they could demand he go and treat him as any other miscreant if he refused.

True, but a fact that changed nothing. He stayed to rescue Nan, or the goblins would take her and everyone else in Tarsun's Market.

"I'll take it under advisement."

"Suit yourself, mercenary." Barely restraining his temper, the knight turned and strode away. Pencheval didn't mind the exit, for he had infuriated many opponents during all of this – that knight was just one more among too many.

Yes, he did make a lot of people angry. He was about to dismiss it as another day in the life when he remembered he made one particular goblin warlord extraordinarily angry. Perhaps it was time to propose that this would be useful to the Knight Superior.

***

What had happened here?

The Stonemaster stood at the eastern cliff-wall of the human town and looked at the wood and straw scrap littering the area. The horde had not done this in the attack. He surmised that it was the remains of the human caves after they were pulled to the ground.

So they *could* be destroyed with some ease; it was good to know. The humans knew how to build their own thatch and wood caves larger than a hut, but they were far more fragile than real caves. Perhaps the human under-chieftain he killed had them ripped to the ground.

Was it to put the marvelous rock throwing things in place behind the cliff-walls? He stood at one now with his newfound human minion as it tried to make the weapon work with the help of the Allspeaker. Why else would it be? It had wanted to defend with them and the thatch caves were in the way. Facing a horde, the human under-chieftain made the same decision the Stonemaster would have made in its place. Best to fight for your lives and rebuild your caves later if you didn't think you could flee.

Five of these things stood more or less intact. His minions occasionally walked out on the one long timber with the metal bowl and fell as the constructs wobbled from the weight. He had destroyed the sixth in the battle to take the town in order to gain the thing he used to slay the human under-chieftain. Its long timber and bowl was a blackened ruin left where it lay.

They did not take all the space along the cliff-wall, and that was where the horde had met the human archers between them. The Fiend-forsaken things had wreaked havoc on his horde until he broke through the wall and let them meet their unobstructed numbers. They had ended the archers and reduced the bodies to food with a speed only managed by a tide of ravenous goblins. Perhaps half of them even made it as far as the butchers.

"Chief of Chieftains, the human says the round thing with branches attaches to the arm and pulls it down so you can put more rocks in the bowl."

"Pulls it down how?" The Stonemaster heard the Allspeaker translate his question. The human approached the device, only to be stopped by a guard full of wary goblins.

The curious warlord waved them back. “Let it through.”

The Stonemaster saw the human grab two of the branches of a large tree trunk and try to turn it. He saw the arm start to move in the proper direction and the bowl lower. The human was not enough to do it alone, but the principle was clear to him now.

“You four, turn that as the human did.” The rabble to whom he pointed did so, and he saw the arm descend. The human said something when the bowl reached the ground.

“What did it say, Allspeaker?”

“It said something should lock it into place until you are ready to let the arm go again, Chief of Chieftains. It does not know what but guesses that it is something called a ‘latch’ attached to another of those branch things.”

“No wonder most humans do not know how to use this catapult. It is a complicated thing.”

“Yes, Chief of Chieftains.” The Allspeaker agreed with him less energetically than usual. Bags darkened the shaman’s eyes and he leaned heavily on his staff.

If he had been rabble, his exhaustion would have been his problem alone. As the only shaman that could speak the human tongue, he was another matter entirely. These tasks that ran him ragged would have to stop for a time.

“When this is done, rest. I need you ready to speak to more humans.”

“Many thanks, Chief of Chieftains.”

A loud thump interrupted the conversation as the arm rose violently into the air. The several goblins turning the branches complained and pointed at each other in blame for it. The warlord heard the human speak again, and the Allspeaker translated it without request.

“The human says that was not the proper lever to keep the arm in place, Chief of Chieftains, and that it will keep looking.”

“Keep going until you know enough to make it throw rocks.” The Chief of Chieftains wanted these big weapons. They would be useful in taking the mountain-castle at the western end of the valley, if he could find a way to use them – or rather when, for he refused to quit until he did.

This human was proving useful.

***

The Beastwarper Chieftain was skeptical at first, but the more thought he gave these books, the more the concept suited him.

The human shaman had led him to a place with wooden walls running parallel to one another across the stone; these walls contained the books. The horde had left the place in disarray, as with much they touched, and that gave his human great distress. After reminding it that it was wasting his patience, it took the first book it saw from the ground, showed him the insides, and explained its function.

Books contained knowledge drawn in symbolic form. Each had a leather cover binding a stack of something the human called pages, on which they drew their symbols. Symbols in sequences made words which told of knowledge, and occasionally there were pictures. The books outlived the speaker and the knowledge they contained could then be recovered by anyone who could read the same symbols.

From what he gathered, this was a precious few. The shaman was one of those that could. So not only could books store knowledge, but only a select few could access it. Such a capacity for restriction left the power knowledge gave in the hands of only those that could read it. He found the thought intoxicating.

He could create books and then restrict this skill of reading to only the chosen. The readers would have the power and the rabble would not, which helped guarantee their positions. The knowledge would exist in a manner far more portable than cave walls and easier to control than oral traditions. For whatever reason, the human had given him everything he could possibly want.

The work ahead was considerable but obvious; the goblins would need their own symbols. Either that, or steal the humans' symbols and put them to use. The human shaman could teach him. No, the human shaman *would* teach him, or it would suffer.

He had hoped to find the human secrets of stone and steel, but this? This was the collection and storage of all knowledge! The knowledge of warping beasts as he did, or warping goblins as the Bloodmoon shamans did with their Berserkers. The ways of stealth the Shadowcreed used? Poisons? Weapons? Magic? Communing with their god, the Fiend Under The Mountain? All could be coded in books with symbols to be taught time and again.

This not only empowered goblins, but it reduced their risk. Once goblins could create books, there would be no need of invasions. The proper humans could simply be taken, their knowledge forced from them, and then encoded in books. Knowledge enough for goblins to build their own clan-homes or metal treasures. With enough books, would there be any limit to what they might know? The thought of their potential excited the chieftain to no end.

"You!" The member of his bodyguard to whom he pointed bowed in response. "Find the Allspeaker and bring him to me." Could the Allspeaker read these symbols already? If he could, the goblins had already won.

"The Stonemaster sent word, my chieftain. The Chief of Chieftains commands him to rest after he is done with the human rock-throwing thing. It could be some time before we may summon him again."

"Fiend-forsaken luck." The Allspeaker was pulled between himself and the Stonemaster. Of course it was going to drain him, yet around him in this place of books and wood walls was everything the goblins needed. The turning point of goblinkind, right here in an innocuous thing of leather and thin skins.

This was victory and the Stonemaster needed to know. There was too much risk in attacking the mountain-castle now when all the reward any of them could ever want was right here for the taking. In the short term, this could possibly save his life.

Or perhaps he should keep this to himself? This was power after all, despite the risk if the Chief of Chieftains remained ignorant of it. He lifted a book from the ground and contemplated it. He had a decision to make.

***

Pencheval turned his head to the open window as the first glimmers of dawn finally became the morning. He had been awake long enough to watch the light slowly grow brighter and the motes dance in its beams. For an hour he had listened to his personal demons tell him that what he intended would only result in his death; that Nan was lost the second she refused his help and it served her right.

This morning was a half-fortnight after he offered his sword and was instead told to depart. It was the last day they would allow him to stay in town, and nothing changed his belief that the Knight Superior would see him leave one way or the other. All that remained was to go to the smith for his drakeskin armor and repaired gear. After that, the Pencheval he had been not even a year ago would have cut his losses and obeyed, for all he considered law in Lerrisaine would have it so.

His conscience would not hear of it now. It nagged at him to rebel against it all. Nan might already be dead, but she would certainly be dead by spring if he did not act. The newly emboldened voice had been a whisper only just loud enough to remind him of honor a month ago. In Tarsun's Market, it had led him to save Howe from a mob and Nan from a horde. Now it spoke confidently and made no secret of the torment it would give him if he abandoned her.

Yes, he was a Silver Lion and no coin was to be found in this. Their way had been his way and his certainty for a long while, but not now. Despite all the problems it had solved for him, was it the way he should have followed all this time? All he knew this morning was that he had to rescue Nan, and that certainty was the thing he meant to follow. He dressed himself, strapped on his sword belt, and descended to the common room to find what awaited him.

Friar Dominik sat there on a bench, waiting for something. In addition to robes, he wore a large shoulder bag Pencheval had not seen him carry before. He suspected it was because he had never traveled with Dominik on any trip that was planned in advance. The last two times they escaped goblins under less than ideal circumstances.

The mercenary descended the stairs, drawing the friar's attention, and he stood in recognition. There were a few other guests in the room and the only other glance he received was from the innkeeper. The man tended to the cleanliness of the bar, smiling at the sight of the Lion's apparent departure.

"Friar?" Pencheval found it odd he would be there.

"Good morrow, Lion." The friar did not sound convinced of that. If anything, he could hear the defeat in his voice.

"Do you mean to travel somewhere?"

"With you. The Knight Superior and his order are aware that your armor is complete and that you mean to receive it this morning. They will not tolerate your presence long thereafter."

So the friar simply reiterated the obvious. "Dominik, there may yet be a way–"

"There is naught you can do. The Knight Superior will not have your help and is suspicious of you now. They have enough force to make you go if you do not voluntarily leave."

He could hear the resignation in the friar's voice and knew why. Supposedly, he had been brought to the valley for some higher purpose, or so Dominik had told him. Not long after arriving at the Shield of Athesiene, the Knight Superior tore that sense of higher purpose from him. He would also ruin Pencheval's chance to save Nan if the mercenary's one last attempt at persuasion failed.

"Friar, it would be best if you did not find yourself in the middle of what happens next."

"No, Lion. I said I would accompany you to whatever the Lord on High meant for you. I just thought it would be here."

Pencheval considered knocking him senseless. It was better for the friar to be unconscious than on the wrong side of a wrathful lord. The townsfolk would see nothing more than the animal they believed he was, and Dominik would appear only as a victim. This sort of thinking left him queasy, so he simply walked towards the exit and allowed him to follow.

"My thanks." Pencheval meant it for the time he had saved his life and for the sentiment he expressed now. Perhaps Dominik was right. Perhaps he had some higher purpose. Perhaps today was the day he died in his attempt to achieve it. He would know before dusk.

The journey through the dirt streets was filled with the glances of people all too happy to see him leave or die. Any greetings by the townsfolk were more in mockery than goodwill. They seemed to think he would be humbled, or at least gone, before much longer. When he reached the smith, he saw why.

The Knight Superior stood in the street by the forge with ten of his order in full armor and what Pencheval estimated at a hundred spearmen. They filled it as far as he could see. The Knight Superior kept his eyes on him but showed nothing but a calm resolve. Pencheval felt the butterflies in his stomach, reminded himself of his goal, and advanced.

He stopped ten paces from the force. "Your Grace."

"Silver Lion," the Knight Superior stated in a calm tone, "your deeds have been worthy and your armor awaits. We are grateful for the assistance you have provided us beyond your contract."

It seemed far too perfunctory a speech to Pencheval. Knights stood calmly with their footing ready for battle and the soldiers were a thicket of spears. It was not a force he could hope to match even in his former gear, and certainly not in a ragged tabard and a sword belt. If nothing else, he would join his late father and fiancée Cecelia in high fashion.

"You still need my help, Your Grace."

"We do not." The Knight Superior's eyes narrowed. "This I have made plain and I will repeat myself no longer. Take what we have promised you and go."

Pencheval had spent days trying to find the words that might persuade him. He had since given up as he had never found talent or use for the silver tongues of diplomats. What he could do was be himself, and it was why he tried to warn the friar away from this.

"Then let me make my meaning plain," Pencheval replied without flinching. "I mean to rescue Nan from that horde of ravenous vermin, and naught save death will prevent it."

"Do you think we are so arrayed as decoration? We are not your honor guard." A knight reached for his hilt. "You have been commanded to go. The law says you will go or you will meet your death."

"It's all but certain," Pencheval replied. "You have the force to defeat me and the rank to order it done. The king's law says I must obey. The guild's law says I must obey. I have nothing to gain but the wrath of too many forces that can and will punish my refusal." Pencheval flicked the tip of his thumb across his bottom lip. "The answer is still no."

"Your Grace, the Silver Lion is merely–"

"Silence, friar!" The Knight Superior stared daggers into Dominik, and the friar obeyed him immediately.

Rennoute turned his glare on Pencheval. "Speak and pray I do not find your words wanting."

"I can shorten this war, Your Grace."

"And by what means do you think you may accomplish that?"

"The only place in the valley that could meet and defeat a goblin horde is here. I alone provoke enough wrath in their warlord to goad it into attacking."

"Madness," the knight who had reached for his weapon replied. "Delusions of grandeur to think this horde holds you in such high enmity."

"By now you know the goblins have stopped at Tarsun's Market," Pencheval continued, ignoring the scorn. "For what other reason would their warlord do this than to mass? I know firsthand of its cunning. It tricked the whole town into remaining exactly where it wanted them to be and then took it all. It will not come here before it thinks it is ready."

"And?"

"That horde must feed," Pencheval answered. "If your campaign takes years, there will be nothing left of the Emerald Refuge. Goblins consume everything. They took the farms apart and slaughtered the people for rations. It makes no difference if they meant to capture the townsfolk or not. If they winter in Tarsun's Market, all there are lost."

"I'm sure no thought of the coin for such a contract ever crossed your mind." The knight that continued to threaten him tensed his grip around the hilt of his sword. Pencheval heard Dominik whimper.

"If this was bartering for coin, what manner of fool would I be?" Pencheval gestured to the force behind Rennoute. "I have bargained contracts for years. Never have I done so with anyone who did not want me present. And death pays poorly."

"Spare me your knavery." Shutters along the houses closed and peasants scrambled from the streets.

"No knavery, Your Grace. No games. I have neither the talent nor the temperament for them."

Pencheval spoke directly to Rennoute. "I can do what I say, Your Grace. Unlike your knights I have hurt or thwarted that warlord at every opportunity. It became a great stone being at Tarsun's Market to attack me personally. It sent brutish champions to see me dead. None of yours provoke such hatred in it. They may in time, but time is not something you have in abundance if you mean to save this place."

"So now you tell fanciful tales to demonstrate how you have so much more valor than us?" The knight at Rennoute's side drew his sword halfway from its scabbard before Rennoute stopped him with a gesture.

"Do you still doubt my sincerity? What have I to gain with any of this beyond what I say? I am risking death and the wrath of my masters to serve you free of contract. The worst that could happen is that I die slaying your enemies. If there is even a chance of success to mitigate this disaster, will you not take it?"

"If your offer is sincere," Rennoute replied, vexation apparent on his face. "Or is this display of conviction so that perhaps, in retrospect, I would pay you a fortune for your help when all is done? Yet if it be true, here are your terms and you will get none other."

"If you truly mean to pursue the rescue of our sister you quest as the others beside me have done. I grant you your armor and one volunteer. You will go forth into the valley with no more than what two horses can carry and you either succeed in your efforts or die trying. There is no coin offered for this and it is not negotiable. Either accept or deny this instant and naught more."

"I agree to Your Grace's terms." Pencheval had attained what he wished and didn't hesitate. This drew more than one look of surprise and grudging respect from the knight willing to kill him for his master.

"One last thing. If my scouts find you are using the goblin horde as an opportunity to pillage, rape, or abuse my goodwill in any regard, several of my order will return your ashes to the capital in a chamber pot."

"Your Grace."

"Take your armor and find who will aid you in this. You depart at dawn tomorrow."

"Yes, Your Grace."

***

Pencheval watched the Knight Superior depart with his force, took one deep breath, and exhaled loudly. Friar Dominik muttered prayers under his breath and thanked the Lord on High for His mercy. Pencheval took a moment to agree before ducking under an awning and into the open forge of the smith.

The dumbstruck artisan slowly pointed to an armor stand and Pencheval examined his work. The scaled and sculpted drake leather armor pieces fit nicely over the clean and repaired chainmail byrnie. Pencheval stripped his tabard and donned it over shirt and trousers right there in the shop.

Newly relinked chain slid over clothing and he welcomed the weight of it. The lack of armor had left him feeling near naked and unnaturally light. He did not see his damaged bascinet, but the barbute that replaced it would suffice. There was no visor, but the eyes and face were exposed by no more than large slits. They made it easy to see or breathe, but not so much they tempted blows as a soft target. He admired it for a moment, then set it aside for the drakeskin.

The smith had boiled and shaped pieces from the hide of a Northern Sundiver. The miniature dragons were ravenous predators of livestock and named after their preferred attack of descending upon prey with the sun at their backs. What they lacked in size they reclaimed in speed, ferocity, and an uncanny aim with the balls of sticky fire they spat.

He remembered their coloration of gray with spectacular red patterns. Whatever the smith had used to harden these pieces left the gray a near blackness and the red darkened to tones of brick. It felt far lighter and less flexible than his brigandine, but he recalled that it was prized for its remarkable strength.

He emerged from the shop with his helm under his arm to find the half-panicked friar and two knights of Athesiene's order awaiting him. Their presence did not bother him. He had what he needed now and meant to return the hell the goblins had inflicted on them all.

"Dominik?"

Dominik shivered, leaning on his staff, but the knights simply awaited him calmly.

"Lord on High be praised, Lion," Dominik blurted. "And well you should do so now, for He has saved you this day."

"I have not but started yet," Pencheval replied, drawing one bitter chuckle from a knight.

"I should get back to my bed, I think," Dominik said to no one in particular, and shivered. "We have much to do come the morrow."

"No, friar. This I must do with another. It will require the sort of effort I put into serving contracts, and you would not endure."

"I would not–"

"He chooses his own second, friar," one of the knights interrupted. "We go to seek that person with him now. If it is not you, then it is not."

Pencheval couldn't tell if the friar was disappointed or relieved. Whichever it was, he did not appear ready to argue.

"Athesiene's light guide you to victory over the horde, Pencheval. May whatever you intend succeed." The friar stumbled away, leaning heavily on his staff.

"Your second?"

"One of your scouts, if he agrees. I know where to find him."

***

All activity in the wooden fortress stopped as Pencheval passed, and he resisted the urge to smirk. The two knights walking behind him were not a common sight as an honor guard to common folk, even if those folk were as unusual as Silver Lion mercenaries. Howe glanced up from his work to determine what caused the distraction and watched agape as Pencheval approached.

"Lion?" He leaned to one side to get a better look at the knights in full armor and then checked Pencheval's wrists before scratching his head. “The lack of irons is perplexing. What are they doing here with you if it’s not to take you into custody?”

“I’ve spoken with the Knight Superior. He’s agreed to let me to stay and aid in routing the goblins. His terms were quite rigid.”

“Spoken?” Howe glanced at the knights again. “Rumors fly about how that conversation went. Whatever terms you were offered, you were lucky it wasn’t a rough death.”

“I have a plan, and I need your help to execute it.”

“Well, it couldn’t be worse than your discussion with his lordship. What do you mean to do?”

“Go and annoy the goblin warlord into attacking the castle.”

“Of course.” Howe put his face in his palm. “Clearly you find amusement in such things as throwing rocks at hornet’s nests and tempting the gallows.”

“This is not a jest, Howe,” Pencheval countered with all seriousness. “Goblins consume everything. If the campaign proceeds as Rennoute currently plans, the goblins will winter in Tarsun’s Market, and everyone there will be gone come spring. A raiding party of fifty strips homesteads bare. A horde is infinitely worse.”

“I know. I’ve seen it too.” Howe stood and crossed his arms. “So what do you need from me?”

“You know the valley and where the goblins might go for supplies. I need them to know I’ve returned to begin the warlord’s annoyance in earnest. If this gambit succeeds, it will shorten this war and do it on Rennoute’s terms. Otherwise, you will battle the vermin for years to come as they lay waste to everything in the Emerald Refuge.”

“How many others do you have for this?”

“None,” Pencheval replied, hoping it would not discourage the skeptical scout. “I only get one volunteer. That’s why they’re here. It’s the way Rennoute wants it done.”

“You are well and truly mental, Lion.”

“You saw how I was forced to leave, Howe. How we were all forced to go. Will you do nothing when you have a chance to give some of that back?”

“No, and I’m well and truly mental for it, too.” Howe offered Pencheval his hand. “I’ll help you in this. Lord on High have mercy on us both for our foolishness.”

Pencheval shook his hand and gave him a wry grin. “Tomorrow at dawn, then. We’ll get horses.” His history with the beasts suggested the monsters always ate them first, but this was not a plan for those who could not flee quickly.

“I’ll be finding my own ere we’re done, but yes, theirs will do for a time.”

***

"The Berserkers spar amongst themselves more frequently, Chief of Chieftains. Their thirst for war grows keen."

The Stonemaster snarled and all that calmed his mood was the whoosh and thump of the human rock throwing thing. Its goblin handlers could now use it well enough to throw on command. They tested it on human furniture, laughing as yet another chair arced through the sky until it disappeared beneath the line of the cliff-wall. The knowledge of how to use these weapons would make taking the mountain-castle easier, if the horde remained together that long.

The Allspeaker did not flinch or seem to have more energy than it took to stand at his display. He awaited the warlord with drooping, bloodshot eyes and slouched from the exertion of constant translation. Both he and Beastwarper made use of that power, and the moments of respite he recently granted his exhausted minion were not nearly sufficient.

It would not do to run the shaman into the ground. He could keep the humans contained without speaking to them but nothing more. He certainly could not take their knowledge from them without the shaman's talent for speech.

"What does the Beastwarper Chieftain ask of you?" Does it bode as much trouble as the restless Bloodmoon? He feared he knew the answer already.

"He speaks only to a single human shaman, Chief of Chieftains. He asks it of magic and knowledge, and it told him of their source. He obsesses over that source now."

"What source?"

"He did not say. I do know that since it told him of something called books, he puts great stock in strange stiff leather things with many thin skins between them. The skins are covered with symbols, such as the ones we paint on cave walls. He seems to think they contain some sort of power."

"What power?" Power of the sort he had not bothered to mention to the Chief of Chieftains. Then again, if it was real power, he would not. Certainly the Chief of Chieftains would have kept such knowledge to himself were the circumstances reversed. Should Beastwarper succeed, would he then use it to gain leadership of the horde?

"I will assess that matter personally. You will tell me the instant you see him gain any new magic or power."

"Yes, Chief of Chieftains." The Allspeaker bowed his head in obedience.

The Shadowcreed and their chieftain might be trouble as well, but he was not concerned about them yet. That master of stealth came and went, watched, and schemed, but showed no interest in usurpation. His Shadows were an assassination risk, but leading the horde? It was true Shadowcreed had his own plans as any clan chieftain would, but they were plans the burdens of rule would disrupt.

Perhaps they schemed against him and perhaps they did not. Either way, it never hurt to plan for the inevitable. Success bred rivals; it had always been thus among the goblins and always would be. When it concerned someone of his singular greatness? He expected rivals by the score.

***

Pencheval did not remember the last time he rode a horse. Though he had the coin enough to buy and maintain one, he found traveling on foot or by caravan much more predictable. Horses bucked and fled at the sight of creatures like trolls that found them all too edible. They also made approaching camps of brigands without drawing attention near impossible, and those were two things he would not tolerate.

It was far different this time. This matter would require speed, because the goblins would know of his presence by design. He needed a mount whether he liked it or not, but took consolation from the fact a knight was forced to hand him the reins by order of his lord. He wore the look of a man who had just swallowed a rotten egg, and Pencheval suppressed the urge to laugh in his face.

He rode away from the Shield of Athesiene accompanied by Scout Howe, who seemed happier to wave back at the soldiers cheering him than the mercenary did. It was because he knew no one waved at him for any other reason than that they were happy to see him leave. He could not care less about their disdain.

Nan was his concern. He could not rescue her unless he acted and damn what anyone else thought of him. The Knight Superior had given him sanction to act, and their confrontation inspired the approach he meant to use on the goblin warlord.

He had cost the Knight Superior face when he resisted him and put him in a hard position. Yes, the lord of the Emerald Refuge could have had him killed on the spot, but that would have cost him men and future trouble with the Lion's guild. So he laid down the law that day and gave him one option, retaining face when Pencheval accepted. Somewhere in the back of his mind, Rennoute knew he had no better options. He might even have listened to quieter reason but for Pencheval's lack of diplomacy.

The mercenary chuckled. He was not capable of quieter reason after years in the Guild of the Silver Lion. The sorts he confronted during his work understood only strength and hard negotiation. Developing those had served him well, but they demanded the bulk of his efforts to gain. Subtle diplomacy was for those far more capable of it than he was.

"So, what's the plan?" Howe stopped waving at the soldiers. "We're certainly not taking Tarsun's Market as we are."

"No. The object is to goad the goblin warlord into moving against the castle before it is ready."

Howe shook his head. "And how do you believe that will end for us?"

"Just fine, if we make it back to the castle before they do."

"Your optimism is the sunshine in my day," Howe replied sarcastically. "So where do we start? How will we do this?"

"A Silver Lion their warlord grew wrathful enough to attack personally, me, keeps thwarting it until it is so affronted, it can do nothing but act."

"Like the Knight Superior that almost had you executed on the street yesterday?"

"Exactly."

"You were supposed to deny that, Lion. Confirming it's the basis of your plan does not reassure me of your sanity."

Under any other circumstances, Pencheval would have conceded the point to Howe and agreed, but these were not any other circumstances. Nan needed aid and he could not provide it until they smashed the horde. He was uncertain of many things as a result of his stay in the valley but convinced of this.

That conviction had kept him strong in the street against Rennoute. It kept him strong during the fight at Tarsun's Market as he reaped through a horde that should have felled him. Now, it kept him strong with this plan. It was a source of strength he had not tapped since he resolved to become a Lion and avenge himself and his fallen upon the Hope of Terris Lyn.

Unlike that conviction, there was no hatred here. Yes, he believed the goblins had to die, but his first purpose was Nan. It was one more glimpse of something like humanity through the fraying garb of his current life.

"If this was not a thing I thought must be done, I would not be risking myself for it. Recklessness in mercenary work makes for ill fortune."

Howe nodded tentatively. "That explanation will do for now. But if we do not speak the goblin tongue, how will we provoke their warlord?"

"By announcing our presence with something the goblins use themselves. We merely need to find some goblins to begin."

"Well, something large is moving over yonder." Howe pointed in the distance, but Pencheval spotted nothing. "Big and lumbering.

Might be similar to those monsters moving around the walls before the horde hit Tarsun's Market. Can't tell how many at this distance."

"As good a place as any to start." Pencheval was glad of Howe's presence now. If the scout's eyes were this keen, he would find enough goblins to commence the humiliation of that stone-clad warlord in earnest.

***

"Begging pardon of Your Grace, but are you certain this is wise?"

Rennoute did not fault the knight for questioning the wisdom of allowing the Silver Lion to quest. He had done so himself at least twice after dismissing the force he brought with him to the smith's forge. He had since dismissed all doubt.

The Lion's general disposition, for all of its faults, was not the issue. The well-being of the Emerald Refuge was the issue. Whether he cared for the Lion or not, he needed all the help he could muster. It would be worth all the trouble the mercenary's presence had caused if his mad scheme bore fruit.

"You wonder if the Silver Lion will go forth and wreak mischief despite my warnings?"

"Yes, Your Grace. What would stop him? If he meant harm, the scout he chose could not prevent it or escape him to warn us."

"Your suspicion is warranted, but that was no Silver Lion in the street this morning."

"Your Grace?"

"He had his reward. He could have taken it and departed in peace. Had he still been the mercenary we thought him to be, he would have done so."

He would in fact be halfway to the capital by now, Rennoute mused. Drakeskin armor was an uncommonly stout and valuable gift. If nothing else, he could have sold it for a small fortune. If this Silver Lion had only been a Silver Lion any longer, he would not have risked himself against Rennoute's force. Here there was only risk and no profit. Anywhere else, many others would be elated for his aid and pay handsomely for it.

Yet this Pencheval had not stood resolute and calmly defied his soldiers and knights for coin. He had accepted Rennoute's conditions without hesitation and failed to flinch at the threat of death. What had the Lion told him but the truth? This Nan, who Dominik had informed him was one of the sisters in Tarsun's Market, meant more to him than his own life. In all his years and no small number of reports about the nature of the Silver Lions, he had never known any of them to do such a thing.

"You believe the friar, Your Grace? That the Lord on High has a higher purpose for that mercenary?"

"It would not be the first time he has answered prayers in mysterious ways, brother. This morn alone showed too much strangeness to dismiss that conclusion now."

***

The Shadowcreed Chieftain found the narrow space between some of the human thatch caves useful things. The shadows did not hinder goblin sight, but the places were too cramped to occupy for long. Their emptiness was a rare luxury in this human town, where the horde could be heard everywhere and every other conceivable place burst to overflowing with the rabble.

"My chieftain."

The Shadow, who by any other perception would seem to have appeared out of nowhere, spoke to announce his presence. It was disguised as another clan's enforcer, forgoing its hooded tunic to blend into the throngs. The garb marked its accomplishment but also made them obvious to everyone else. When he meant for them to spy on the council, it was not good to be noticed.

"Speak."

"The Stonemaster grows suspicious of the Beastwarper Chieftain. Rumor has it Beastwarper is wringing secrets of magic from his human prisoner."

The Shadowcreed Chieftain suspected trouble but this confirmed it. He had merely thought the Bloodmoon would cause it first. Their giant chieftain only joined the horde for war and waited for it to begin anew. His Berserkers sparred more frequently since arriving and bullied rabble unfortunate enough to be within reach when their frustrations peaked.

"What is the source of this magic in the rumors?"

"The Allspeaker spoke to the Chief of Chieftains yesterday. He says Beastwarper obsesses over the human things of stiff leather binding many thin skins between them. They contain pictures and symbols he has not yet deciphered. He did not mention this to the Stonemaster, and this makes our warlord wonder if a coup is in the offing."

The Shadowcreed Chieftain nodded sagely. In every tale he ever heard of hordes, the warlord changed at least once. Usually this resulted in the dissolution of the force as the new Chief of Chieftains could not rally those the old one did. It had not happened yet, but was ever a possibility.

The usurper simply wouldn't be him. The Chief of Chieftains of any horde had to do too much and was entirely too visible. He did not want any rank higher than a council chieftain and did not expect it even if the Stonemaster attained his great new clan-home.

His fortunes awaited in the shadows beneath that rule. Many things were forbidden and others mandatory for the rabble. To the goblin that could aid with these, much power and wealth was possible. So while his clan were merely scouts and assassins for the horde at this moment in time, they would be far more should the Stonemaster succeed.

He would see to it personally, unless the horde disintegrated for infighting.

"Anything else?"

"The rock throwing things are a fascination to the horde. Other human weapons are in short supply and great demand. Their knives are not to be missed." The Shadow patted a human dagger in its strange leather holder on his belt. The chieftain chuckled because he already had two of his own.

"Continue to watch the Stonemaster. Should he begin to fail, notify me at once."

"Yes, my chieftain." The Shadow bowed and rejoined the throngs just outside of this cramped place.

This venture of the horde was not yet undone and it didn't concern Shadowcreed that this might change. He knew exactly what his clan would do in the event it came to a sudden and chaotic end. He knew before he even joined the horde for it was what his clan had done as far back as the tales of them told.

The Shadowcreed would disappear if all else failed. No more than an hour after the horde descended into dissolution, his entire clan would be gone with all the valuables they could carry. Those in the field knew what the signs of that would be and would disappear just as quickly. They would unite again someplace far from where the Stonemaster originally found them, enjoy the spoils, and start anew. There were other goblin leaders who wanted things they did not or could not have, and a few words in the right ear would lead the Shadowcreed to their next rich pickings.

He just hoped it wasn't over yet.

***

Howe noticed them first, but Pencheval heard them shortly thereafter.

The screech and click in the distance gave away the goblins long before the pair stumbled upon them. They stopped at the sound, and could hear the snap of beams and the horrified last cries of animals before a wet smack silenced them for good. Howe bowed his head.

"Farmstead up ahead. Hope those folk made it to the castle."

"Any approach where we can't be seen?"

"Just from the trees." Howe thumbed to the left side of the road where the forest stood, but not so thick as to be impassible.

They left the horses hitched to branches and Pencheval let Howe lead the way. They stopped shortly before reaching the tree line with a clear view of the pillaging. Pencheval only noted thirty or so goblins, but the lack of their usual numbers had not hindered their enthusiasm for the task.

Two goblins piled fence beams while a third bundled them for portaging four at a time. Another goblin carved a limb from of a freshly slain mule and roasted it skin and all over a bonfire. Several stuffed bags with vegetables and fought over iron farm tools, earning some of them punches as their enforcer took them all. They tore into the stocks greedily and bagged anything they did not eat.

How many times had this happened since the horde arrived? Were there fewer than the usual fifty or so because the volume of foraging parties across the valley spread them thin? Was it simply a hedge against losing too many at one time in the event of discovery by the temple's forces? It was possible, as this lot were closer to the castle than Tarsun's Market. Whatever the reason, they were an opportune target and would make an excellent start.

"What now?" Howe whispered the question.

"We get them to investigate the wood for that one random human they saw." Pencheval slowly unsheathed his Argentsteel blade and stayed within the forest growth.

"I'm guessing that one random human isn't you."

"You need do nothing but get their attention," Pencheval assured him. "After that, I'll take point. Shoot any throwing spears and daggers."

"Or slingers."

"I have yet to see one."

"They have them," Howe assured him. "One rude blighter I met a while back had the nerve to sling a stone at my horse. It died."

"We're about to send it some company."

"I certainly hope so." Howe stepped from out of the tree line, pulled his bowstring back to his chin, and let loose. One in a group arguing over something dropped from the arrow in its chest. The others scattered at the shot, and a stocky goblin Pencheval took for the enforcer pointed at Howe and shrieked instructions. He feigned panic as a dozen goblins charged him and fled past the scrub concealing the waiting Lion.

Pencheval smiled. The goblins had nearly slain him twice, but not this time. There would be no more surprises from them and no more fighting defensively in the hopes he would last an hour longer. These goblins would know fear, and he would spend all summer giving their warlord frustration and misery if that was what it took to make it move.

The goblins realized Pencheval's presence too late when a downward slash executed his first target in a surprise attack. Another half dozen fell before panic overwhelmed them, and only three lived to flee past the tree line. Satisfied with his entrance, the Lion charged towards the farmstead and willed his magic to grant him speed. He covered the distance to the rest of the raiders as rapidly as a galloping horse and waded straight into the fight.

He kept on offensive as goblins scattered. When too many congealed into a mob that might overwhelm him, he used the Waymaker spell to send goblins flying into their fellows. Every time he heard the hiss of an arrow, a goblin would fall from a roof or drop from behind a corner. He and Howe routed the raiding party in short order, and only a few survivors fled with a mere fraction of what they came to steal.

"And tell your master I'm not done with you yet!"

One last goblin with a bulging sack fell forward with an arrow in its back. Pencheval waved at Howe to cease, and he emerged from the trees as the few survivors scattered into the distance. Howe put one hand up to his eyes to watch them go. He let out a long whistle before joining the Lion at the farmstead.

"Right good to give some of that back," Howe told him. "Yet it seems precious few."

"They saw me well enough, and escaped with very little for their losses. Our goading has only just begun."

"As you say. Now what?"

"If we wish to be understood by the goblins, we do as they do." Pencheval struck the head from the nearest goblin corpse. "We post a pole here. It's basically a warning not to come here again on pain of death. Their lairs in Stonewall Pass bore dozens of them."

"I'll leave it to you, Lion." Howe did not appear as though he found the idea palatable.

Pencheval didn't blame him, but that did not change his plan. The goblin warlord needed more of a reason to move than stay. Perhaps it would take the threats as an affront to its power and its pride would lead it to rashness.

***

Nan crouched next to an old man groaning on the floor and wet his forehead for the third time. It was most certainly a fever. Proximity in a large building did nothing unpleasant to the health of the goblins, but the humans showed the first signs of disease. She smiled consolingly at him and kept her trepidations to herself.

The warped goblin Beastwarper Chieftain was sufficiently distracted by the books not to threaten any more of her charges. It obsessed over them surrounded by its guard. The witch doctor would ask her questions, and the bodyguard of the chieftain kept close watch. It kept them well away from the others.

Yet what were the consequences of this bit of desperation? Could the goblins actually learn to make their own books? How much more dangerous would they become if they did? The little nightmares were nasty enough with their low cunning and impossible numbers. What would happen if they could gain the knowledge granted by reading?

It was less of a concern than whether or not she and the rest of the townsfolk would live through the summer. She didn't know, and she was sick of not knowing. The constant presence of the goblins and the uncertainty were agony.

The endless cacophony kept her nerves on edge. The sound tore into the spirits of the townsfolk and she constantly kept the hood of her robe upon her head in a futile attempt to dampen it. Others had tied shirts around their ears or abused hats to destruction to ward away the screeching.

The guards were ever testy. The one nasty leader ordered three more executions from its favorite perch on the statue for revolts and escape attempts only it perceived. Only her ever-present contingent of four guards kept its attention at bay, but they were no better. They did little to hinder her so long as she appeared docile but also acted to keep her that way.

The Beastwarper Chieftain never sent advance word for their meetings. It generally arrived in the morning and monopolized her until her voice grew hoarse from reading. If the goblins meant to keep them terrified, dispirited, and unable to think, she did not know what they would do differently.

The double doors of the temple cracked open and Nan suppressed the urge to groan. She had already read to the Beastwarper Chieftain today. What did it want now? She rose to meet its entrance and saw something she did not expect instead.

Guards and watches bowed their heads in respect as a new leader entered. It wore a hide around its neck and shoulders decorated with fangs. A thick belt with metal studs adorned with uncut red stones, feathers, and teeth clasped over a hide kilt. Leather thongs strapped a silver plate that might once have been a platter to its chest, and it bore a staff half again as tall as it was. It was a plain thing that changed thickness like a long and impossibly thin vase, only flaring at the top to seat a crouching winged statue of black with ruby eyes. No goblin in the room looked directly at it unbidden, and she guessed it was at the very least another chieftain.

The witch doctor accompanied it, along with twenty guards and a rogue of a human with oil-slicked hair and a ponytail. The villain looked at the humans in the temple and smirked, apparently happy he was not among them. He was the other human the Beastwarper Chieftain had mentioned, and his new master had placed him in its entourage. For what reason had they come? She knew when the witch doctor pointed directly at her.

The bodyguard around the staff-bearing goblin advanced and kept her at bay with pointed weapons. She put up her hands to calm them and tried not to make any sudden moves. Her guard of four goblins parted in response and treated this new leader in the same manner as the others.

"There's a good girl," the rogue told her. "You want to make nice with this one, you do."

"And you are?"

The goblin with the staff snarled at her and chittered in its tongue.

"The Stonemaster, Chief of Chieftains, Hordemaker and Chosen of the Fiend commands you not to speak until he demands answers of you," the witch doctor translated.

Nan nodded, uncertain of her circumstances.

"Good." The shaman pointed at her again. "What do you know of this human?"

"That one? She's a sister of the temple." The rogue answered without coercion or hesitation. Nan frowned at his complicity. So he was a collaborator.

"What are they?"

"They tend this place and do nice things for the folk. Soup, prayers, and all."

The witch doctor translated this for the Stonemaster, who looked at her quizzically and said something.

"The Stonemaster wishes to know why it would attack the Silver Lion."

"So it was her then? Ha! That was a right foolish thing to do." The rogue looked her up and down. "Knew one of them had done it, but didn't know it was her. She seemed right friendly with him before you arrived and without violence, no less."

The witch doctor translated again, and the Stonemaster glared at Nan. It spoke in its tongue, its voice a menacing buzz.

"The Chief of Chieftains demands to know why you attacked the Silver Lion warrior if you were previously allied with it."

Nan swallowed hard. Why had it come? It wanted to know if she had lied to the goblins this whole time, which she had. What should she do now? She tried to assemble a plausible answer but the words would not come. Its glare never faltered, and when she stuttered for too long, it barked a word and rapped its staff against the floor.

The flagstones beneath her feet shook and then *slithered*. It was as though it had become dozens of gigantic gray serpents writhing through and into the ground. She staggered under the force and tried to restrain the fear that this goblin had summoned demons from within the earth to kill her. Half the room under the prisoners churned and she felt helpless to save the weeping and groaning townsfolk.

"You should answer him, love," the rogue said, looking a little less than pleased with the display himself.

"I got sick of him!" Nan blurted it out, frustration very real from her circumstances and nerves laid raw, granting it more force than she expected. "He disrupted everything! Where he went trouble followed! Then he tried to force me from the others! So I struck him down, and despite what you had done, it was still not enough to kill him!"

The rogue blinked twice and the witch doctor translated. The goblin with the staff turned to the rogue and spoke.

"The Chief of Chieftains wishes to know if you believe this sister, human."

"Can't rightly find fault with her, boss," the rogue confirmed after a moment's consideration. "Lions are always more needed than wanted and they don't make no one happy. I certainly wasn't happy about his presence here. Could be she did take the chance to kill him when she thought she could. Dipping in the till, were we?" The collaborator sneered at her. "Temple don't like that and they can pay for Lions."

"How dare you..." Nan stepped forward and was quickly met by a plethora of sharp objects from the goblin bodyguard.

The one they had called the Stonemaster said something to the witch doctor and turned to go. Its bodyguard and the collaborator fell into a group around and behind it.

"The Stonemaster is satisfied with your answers for now, human. Pray to your gods he remains so."

Nan found herself more relieved than she expected from the goblins' departure. She sniffed as the double doors finally closed, and found to her surprise she was crying. She knew her duties would become hard in their presence, but even with her faith, they were almost more than she could bear.

***

Pencheval wiped the gore from his sword and contemplated the turning millstone inside the partially stripped water mill. The grate of the stone, the sound of the stream, and the odd squeaks of the water wheel kept a strangely regular time. Half of the flour bags within the stores were gone, and one spilled where he had slain the goblin trying to steal it.

He had not found the former occupants in the remains, and he hoped they had fled. His eyes narrowed on second consideration. Tarsun's Market was far closer than the castle. If the mill's owner ran there, they had fallen from the frying pan into the fire.

Could they or any of the humans there still be alive? The goblins may wish to capture them, but there was truly no telling if they had the discipline to keep prisoners for any length of time. He had never found more of humans than their bones when he helped clear a lair at Stonewall Pass, and that was a clan of a mere thousand. In a horde of thousands, how long would they last when so many hungered?

"Hasn't been that long since we left, Lion, but I see naught of changes yet."

Pencheval grimaced and put away his sword, wishing Howe wouldn't remind him of the obvious. "We should have started tales by now."

"Tales for certain, but this is nothing more than slow attrition. If you mean to provoke something before the winter, we'll have to hit them somewhere else. Or somehow."

Pencheval rapped the hilt of his sword with his fingers nervously. "Yes, we will. That means going after their brutes and monsters."

"Their brutes and...I had to open my mouth." Howe pulled another of his arrows from a goblin. Pencheval was glad he agreed to help him. The scout's archery was dangerously precise and he had a knack for noticing which goblins were most in need of his attention at any given time. "Well, if we're going to throw rocks at a hornet's nest, we may as well commit."

"They will come," Pencheval assured him. "If I cause enough trouble, that warlord will want me dead."

"Assuming you succeed, we have one other problem. To pursue you to the castle, it will have to think you've returned there, yes?"

"I already know what to do about that."

"I hope it involves sending a pigeon with an insult to its mother from far, far away."

Pencheval gave Howe a sideways glance and said nothing more. To manage that, the warlord would have to see which direction he went after he confronted it. That would require a display at the western wall of Tarsun's Market and ready horses. It might work, if he could get there, and if they didn't decide to throw a few battalions at him after he made himself such a ready target. They feared him, but it would only go so far before their numbers gave them courage they did not individually possess.

The Lion saw no point in troubling Howe with that conclusion yet.

***

"What do you mean, the Gray Lion has grown scales?"

The Stonemaster sat on his bone throne and glared down at the survivor of a foraging party he caught spreading tales of Penn Cheval's return. After the usual hysterics about the Silver Lion's strength and ferocity, the fool had started making hand gestures like the gnashing of a great bat-lizard's teeth to emphasize his description. The survivor's frenetic babbling in front of the council kept him wondering why he had not executed the fool yet.

Of course Penn Cheval had not grown scales, but the truth was no improvement. Either it had found a great bat-lizard and stolen its hide, or it was rewarded with such a hide because the Snow Clan could kill and skin one. Neither of those explanations would be comfort to a horde primarily composed of superstitious rabble. Whether they believed this Silver Lion had grown scales, taken them by force, or earned them as a reward, these rumors would cause mass desertions.

"It has grown impatient," the Bloodmoon Chieftain offered, smiling. "I had hoped this would be the case. Send my Berserkers, and we will kill it."

The Stonemaster expected dissent, but to his chagrin, he received none. Beastwarper nodded his agreement silently, and Shadowcreed did not respond at all; even they had enough of this Penn Cheval, having lost Bonestrippers and Shadows to it. It did not bode well when most of his council let an opportunity to earn favor pass.

It annoyed him, but a solution to Penn Cheval was still on offer. The survivor had not mentioned humans accompanied it aside from an archer of some sort. So not only was it nearly alone, it was out in the open where the Bloodmoon craved combat.

"Send them in pairs." One Berserker was all but a match for the human warrior and its shiny big knife. Two would doom Penn Cheval and the bow-wielder. "I want the Silver Lion and its companion dead."

"It will be done." Bloodmoon smiled wickedly and departed the council. No few of his Berserkers would be happy with his commands tonight.

"Be gone," the Stonemaster snarled at the goblin survivor, and it happily scrambled from the council chamber.

"Now to the next problem. Summon my human." A messenger scurried off to obey. There was one other matter to deal with this evening, and it may not end well for several of the assembled.

"It has proven useful then?" Shadowcreed seemed genuinely curious. He had not needed the Allspeaker for his work and had not understood anything he heard from the humans.

"Yes. It was most helpful when it grew enough sense to submit."

"What do you want it to tell you now?"

"Whether or not we should be rid of the Beastwarper's pet."

The Beastwarper Chieftain rose and leaned on his staff. “That one knows magic and has told me of something that could change goblins forever. It would be wise not to discard it.”

“Yes, I know it knows magic. I also know it is telling you of these books, which you neglected to mention to me until now.”

“I have not yet learned to make them, Chief of Chieftains.”

The warlord was sure that was not the reason for his silence. Yes, perhaps these ‘books’ were important. Perhaps that shaman taught Beastwarper something the human under the Stonemaster’s control could duplicate. If so, he would have the shaman killed and not have to worry if these books would be brought to his attention again only when they were used to usurp him.

Shadowcreed changed his position to make for a quick exit and chose to remain out of this conversation. The nature of this issue was not lost on him, but then little ever was.

“I will ask my human, regardless.”

The familiar sound of that human’s complaints accompanied its entrance as the messenger he sent and its bodyguard herded it into the council. When it saw the Stonemaster, it straightened its shirt and said something that sounded friendly.

“The human greets you, Chief of Chieftains,” the Allspeaker translated. “It would like to know your commands.”

“Tell it to wait for now.” The Allspeaker spoke to the human, who simply shrugged and crossed its arms.

The Stonemaster glared at the Beastwarper Chieftain. “Now you will tell me of these books.”

“Books are the way humans capture and store knowledge far greater than an oral tradition or the pictures we draw in the caves, Chief of Chieftains,” Beastwarper explained. “If we learn to make our own, we would not need to conquer the humans to build our own great clan-homes. We could take them as we need them, force them to tell of what they know, and then put it in the books. They last far longer than any one goblin and could teach knowledge to those who can decipher their symbols with a skill called reading.”

“Speak this to the human,” the Stonemaster ordered his shaman, who seemed interested in these things himself. “I want to know if it knows of these books.”

The Allspeaker translated in the human tongue. Their speech seemed such a dull and soft thing to the warlord. There were no clicks or screeches, and no sense of the energy that thousands of goblins generated when whole clans spoke together. When the Allspeaker completed his words, the human answered, scratching its head and then shaking it.

"This human knows of books, Chief of Chieftains, but cannot decipher them. He says they are the things priests and learned humans use and cannot read them for you."

"What of this knowledge?"

"It can't say." The Allspeaker shrugged. "Yet if these things contain power, wouldn't the stronger humans want to keep it from the rabble?"

"Exactly." Beastwarper offered his concurrence quickly.

In truth, their words contained a great deal of sense. The human shaman knew magic, and this one didn't. Were these books the reason why? Furthermore, the human that had traded him the staff did not speak to him of books because it might not have known of them, or it might not have wanted him to know of them. That spoke of another treasure besides what this human could tell him.

So Beastwarper had not been wasting his time or that of the Allspeaker. His human shaman did have worth despite the danger of keeping it alive. The warlord's better judgment said he should have it slain out of caution regardless, but would any human that could read books be any less dangerous? It mattered not so long as he was not the one taking the risk.

The Stonemaster leaned back into his throne. "The human may go."

The Allspeaker translated as the goblin bodyguard herded it away, and it left after a quick nod in his direction.

"Do you know how to create and decipher the contents of these books?"

"The humans have their own symbols. They do not appear to be pictures of anything we know. Given time, I can make the shaman explain them to us, but I will need the Allspeaker."

"No more than half a day of his time will you take from this point," the Stonemaster commanded. "I need him to use this other human. Determine how these books work, then learn to make your own without him."

"Yes, Chief of Chieftains." Beastwarper did not seem elated by this, but the Stonemaster could not care less. The Allspeaker was his minion first and foremost, and foremost his to command. He had his own purposes for him and did not need him drained. As it was, Beastwarper should be grateful he was not roasting over a bonfire for failing to disclose this discovery when he found it.

The others had better remember who commanded this horde and why there was a horde in the first place. It was his greatness and his alone that had forged it and brought it this far. He would not play second to anyone else's ambitions.

***

The Bloodmoon Chieftain snorted and spat at the display he witnessed in the council. Pathetic! How was it that only he, and he alone, would take a chance at glory when the Stonemaster offered it? Were Shadowcreed and Beastwarper reduced to mewling pups from an excess of caution?

Penn Cheval from the Silver Lion Clan had returned at last, picking at the edges of the horde. It could not be for any reason other than to have the survivors announce its presence. Warriors as Penn Cheval did not concern themselves with rabble beyond slapping them out of its way. It had already defeated one Berserker after battling its way through enough of the horde to kill a hundred humans, and he knew it could do worse. What else could its attacks be but a challenge?

"My warriors, cease and hear me!"

Two dozen Berserkers stopped tending their weapons, training, and bullying lesser goblins to listen. Many of them seemed eager for his words as they gathered to him. These were the worthy, those who had earned the right to take the shaman's brew, endure the Time of Pain and Hunger, and grow into Berserkers. They would be more than enough, and the glory of killing this Penn Cheval would be the Bloodmoon Clan's alone.

"Yes, my chieftain?"

"The Gray Lion warrior returns. We know from one of the humans that its clan is called the Silver Lion Clan, and it is called Penn Cheval. One of you will have the glory of killing it."

Wicked grins and eager roars greeted this news. No, the Bloodmoon were not weak or afraid. Even the Beastwarper Chieftain, who was so eager to send his monsters after this human before, would have no part of it now. No matter. When they kill it, the Stonemaster's favor would see the Bloodmoon made first among the council, exactly as it should be.

"Where is it now?"

"It is wandering the valley slaying foragers for stories," the chieftain explained. "It was last seen with one companion and two of the human riding beasts half a day northwest of here."

"We can seek it out, my chieftain, but the beasts will make it hard to catch."

"That should not be a problem," Bloodmoon reassured them. "It is not killing foraging parties and allowing some few to escape out of carelessness. It wants us to know it is here because it wants war."

"It will get war. Then I will take its shiny big knife for my own."

"When you wake, that dream will end, and you will see it is mine." The two Berserkers that spoke shoved one another, but did not break into a brawl.

"Enough! We will tarry no longer. The opportunity to take our rightful place in the horde has come. Go forth in pairs and find the human and its companion. Slay them both and return with the shiny big knife as proof."

"Immediately, my chieftain."

"And beware of the Snow Clan. They mass at their mountain-castle now, but they may skirmish with the horde in greater numbers. Only deal with the Silver Lion."

"As you say, my chieftain."

"Depart, and do not return with failure."

A chorus of roars followed by the chants to the Fiend Under The Mountain rose from the group as they shoved, argued, and finally paired up to depart. Two by two, they left their enclave towards the wood wall at the west of town, and the Bloodmoon Chieftain longed to join them.

Usurping the former chieftain had given him power, but far less battle; others did the fighting for him now. It was a thing to make him wistful at times. Opportunities to fight were few and his might made for short work of most enemies. Even the great bat-lizards could do little more than provide momentary diversions.

He considered killing this Penn Cheval personally. It was a deed that might well make him the Chief of Chieftains of this horde. Every goblin knew of the human warrior, whispered in fear over it, or boasted it would be the one to kill and rob it when they knew it was nowhere within earshot. Yes, perhaps it would be time to take matters into his own hands.

The council was not as eager to follow the Stonemaster, or Beastwarper and Shadowcreed would once again have competed for the warlord's favor. After a mere month or so in this place, that spoke of a weak hand. If this continued and the opportunity presented itself, it was time to usurp yet another title. The Bloodmoon were the chosen warriors of the Fiend Under The Mountain, and it was long overdue for them to be revered as such.

***

"Saint Marion's Revelation, what is that?"

Pencheval held his hand over his eyes to block out the afternoon sun and scanned in the same direction that had Howe so dismayed. He saw nothing beyond a few hints of movement. Perhaps something had walked behind a copse of trees or a hill?

"I see naught."

"It is distant, for certain, but too much to be nothing." Howe scrambled up a knoll and dropped prone, still intent on whatever he had seen. "They probably can't see us from here, but I'm taking no chances."

Pencheval scratched his head but joined the anxious Howe. He pointed in the distance and again, Pencheval saw next to nothing. A flash of motion here and there. Perhaps a herd of something running towards Tarsun's Market? No, not a herd. A herd would not be running towards the town.

"Goblins?"

"They don't move like they have four legs."

"How many?"

"At a guess? Seven, eight hundred."

It wasn't a raiding party then, Pencheval concluded. While the goblins liked to do a thorough job of pillaging, there were never more than fifty or so raiders at a time and never somewhere they could be so easily discovered.

"What say you, Lion?"

"I fear the goblin warlord draws others to its banner," Pencheval responded and grimaced. The fight for the town had taken some toll on the horde, but it massed anew.

"It's telling all its folk about the grand things it's done," Howe agreed. "They've come to get in on the looting."

"And bringing their skills with them," Pencheval added. "Each clan differs from the others. We'll only discover the method of their mischief at the cost of lives."

"And you're more concerned with lives then? Will your own guild recognize you when you return?"

Pencheval momentarily gave thought to snarling a response, but remembered the observation was closer to the truth than it had once been. He was concerned with a life in that town. Nan was still there, if she was still alive, as the goblins bolstered their numbers. That meant more hungry fiends surrounding a supply of human meat they would be perfectly happy to consume.

"It only adds to the urgency of our task, Howe."

"I hope you have a plan in that regard, Lion. Summer is here, and there is no sign of a goblin advance on the castle. Numbers will only make a final battle worse."

Pencheval silently agreed. Killing foraging parties alone was not goading their master. In a perverse way, his work thus far may only have increased the risk to the townsfolk in Tarsun's Market. The goblins would eat one way or the other. Removing distant sources of sustenance would only make those sources before them more tempting.

To truly affront the goblin warlord would require something far worse. That meant robbing it of minions it was loathe to lose. The brutes and beasts were likely valuable things and it would not wait as someone killed them one or two at a time. Perhaps thinking its valuable forces would be nibbled to death would be enough.

***

"Chief of Chieftains, the human numbers dwindle."

Generally, the Allspeaker did not enjoy giving the Chief of Chieftains bad news, though that warlord was better about realizing its worth than most. This was something that bore mentioning, however, despite his misgivings.

Failing to do so as all the humans died could be hazardous to his health. Two powerful chieftains, one of which commanded a horde and the stone beneath his feet, desired their knowledge. Should they not have access to it for whatever reason, many things would go wrong.

"We have slain a few to break the rest, Allspeaker. It is our way."

"Yes, Chief of Chieftains, but they do not have our numbers." The nervous shaman had the attention of the entire council now, and he did not enjoy it. "Some in the big cave had to be slain for going mad. Our sound was useful in the battle but proves bad for their keeping."

"It keeps them in terror and their fear keeps them meek," the Bloodmoon Chieftain countered.

"If they go mad, mighty chieftain, they tell us nothing."

"The shaman has a point," Beastwarper agreed. "You cannot steal the secrets of a human with broken sense."

"You have a solution?"

"Yes, Chief of Chieftains. We know of the passages under the great cave. One cannot hear the horde down there. Let the humans stay there half the time. Perhaps they will last longer that way."

"And perhaps they will have time to plan revolt or escape beneath the ground," Shadowcreed argued. "The corridors are tight with few hiding places. It is a place to dwell but not to keep watch."

"Can they escape the way Penn Cheval did?" The Stonemaster was keenly aware of the manner in which the Silver Lion human had escaped the fall of the town and had been touchy about it for days after.

"No, Chief of Chieftains," Shadowcreed answered hastily. "We have sealed its way out. No other humans showed strength enough to break through stone as the Silver Lion warrior did. There were no other flat stone cave walls when we searched the passageways. Human bones, but no walls."

"We can see there and they cannot," Beastwarper reminded the Stonemaster. "Keep guards with them and give them little light. They will not rise up against us, for we own the darkness."

"Make the arrangements, Allspeaker," the Stonemaster commanded. "I have not learned enough from them to discard them yet."

"Yes, Chief of Chieftains." The Allspeaker felt a great relief as the council reached the desired conclusion without his help. He had convinced his warlord not to squander this great resource of humans. Now he hoped he might learn enough from them to make all this risk worthwhile.

***

"Is this everyone?"

The Viperfang Chieftain waited as his speaker announced him to the council and was not impressed by the numbers. True, the assembled host stretched across all of the living places in the humans' former clan-home, but it seemed incomplete. It was sizeable, but not such a horde as his towering companion and messenger had boasted.

"Yes." The giant next to him was a Berserker of the Bloodmoon Clan, and its words had convinced him to come. If one of them sang the praises of a horde, it was a horde for the ages, or so he thought at the time. They did no one's bidding as slaves, and he had believed the warrior when he said loot and conquest were on offer for his clan. The fact they had already won a victory was enough to finally persuade him.

Yet this was the horde that impressed them? What he saw was an initial disappointment. It fell short of expectations, but he was here now. While lacking numbers, it was a gathering of goblins that could be made better with enough poisons. That craft of the Viperfang had slain even trolls and the great bat-lizards. It also made short work of humans, and so would the horde once his clan supplied them with it.

"What is the title of the Chief of Chieftains here?"

"The Stonemaster," the brute answered. It had become more taciturn since its initial boasts and chanting on arrival at his clan.

"And the humans you said you made prisoners?"

"We keep them in the large cave." The Berserker pointed. "You do not kill them without the permission of the Stonemaster."

"Very well." That edict seemed a little odd. Why keep the food alive once you had and needed it? Perhaps this Stonemaster was using the humans to find treasures for him. Admittedly, they always seemed to have a few and made the best things to steal. Aside from that and being edible, the perplexed chieftain could find no other uses for them.

The warlord on the bone throne waved the giant next to him forward. "We are summoned now. Follow me."

The Viperfang Chieftain shrugged and entered a council circle, which he found as wanting as the horde. The Bloodmoon Chieftain was as impressive a sight as his clan, but only three others? One lame goblin with a growth of spiky bone jutting from one shoulder leaned heavily on a staff to stand to the right hand of the throne. On the left, one and only one shaman waited with a staff topped by a ram's skull.

A single individual in a sleeveless, hooded black tunic waited back in the shadows. His only true affectation was a leather whip with sharp bone woven into the braid. Word was that he was chieftain of the Shadowcreed Clan, a host of dangerously stealthy opportunists.

"Welcome to the lands of the Snow Clan." The warlord on the throne rose in greeting.

"Mighty Stonemaster, I am the Viperfang Chieftain. I have heard of your power and your victory."

"You were wise to listen to the messenger I sent. Follow me, and you will share in the human treasures and lands. We will take everything from them, and I will make you a war chieftain in command of many more than you brought."

"War chieftain?" Did this one not know his council wanted for leaders?

The Stonemaster frowned. "Several hundred you have brought. Two thousand you will have to command if you agree."

Two thousand? It was not a place on the council; it was, however, thrice what his entire clan could bring to bear on any enemy. Even as a war chieftain beneath the council, his power would grow. Besides, one of the current members of that council might suddenly die of a strange and untraceable condition to clear the way for him.

"We will join you, Chief of Chieftains."

"You have chosen well. Wear my band of grey above your own as the others of the horde do. When you are banded, choose a human weapon for your own as a sign of your rank. You are a war chieftain now."

"As you say, Chief of Chieftains."

One of the Stonemaster's messengers tied a gray band around his arm, and Viperfang departed to return to his own clan. They had been made to wait just outside the town, which was the only thing about this horde that had impressed him so far. Any Chief of Chieftains with sense would confirm potential arrivals before giving them the run of their territories. In that much at least this Stonemaster did not disappoint. If only the rest had been as fruitful.

***

Nan could not think of any other time she was grateful to be in the catacombs beneath the temple. It had been so long since she had heard anything like the silence they offered. The damp chill and few lanterns flickering far from her in the passageways were hardly comfort, but they offered the luxury of the goblins' absence.

She could hear some few goblins beyond the darkness, so far away their speech echoed as distant sounds relieved of their sharper edges. After the horde, the few times they spoke seemed absolutely placid. Most of the townsfolk she could see had already fallen asleep, curled up against the walls and each other, strain from the endless noise no longer evident on their faces.

Would this respite come to nothing? She half wondered if the goblins put them here so the cold would keep them fresher until the end. It had been at least a month since the town had fallen to them, and she had seen too many die.

First they killed the wounded, just as Pencheval predicted. Then they killed those that went mad. The warlord killed those brought before him that it didn't find useful, or so the only few to return had told her. Only they and the collaborator had survived such a visit.

She still did not believe in Pencheval's path, but she understood it now. She had stalled for what little she was worth as those around her died and it seemed for naught. Circumstances beyond her control ended the lives she wanted most to preserve, and she was beyond sick of the helplessness. Fury crept around the edges of her despair and defeat that she had not felt since Terris Lyn. Pencheval had reached his limits long ago and chose to become a Silver Lion; now she had reached hers.

She was as desperate and in need as Pencheval had once been. It had lead him to the wrong answer to end his suffering. He had the power to slay the darkness, true, but she remembered the glyph in his palm. He would never be the same after what the Silver Lions had done to him, but did it matter?

She frowned. Yes, it mattered. He had his might but nearly lost himself. Was her hour so dark she wanted the Lord on High to make her like a Silver Lion? Aside from Pencheval, they fought for little more than coin and the commands of the king.

No. She wanted the Lord on High to give her the power to save His faithful. She did not care how it ended, so long as He did. She was grateful for the healing spells and the ability to defend herself against ruffians, but her little magic was nothing she could use on a horde.

She had one means by which she might act, and it had perils of its own. The Lord on High granted magic to some, but its every use was a moment when Athesiene judged the intent of His faithful. Some would have it stripped when their purposes were judged unworthy. Others lived lives of faithful service and wielded His power until their dying day. In rare instances, He changed the magic of those He allowed to wield it to provide in their hours of need.

The temple preached what the Lord on High might grant from The Histories in many services she attended. The saints of old, like Aaron, asked for wisdom. Marion, to whom the Lord on High first revealed Himself, asked for power to spread His word. They both discarded all greed, ambition, or power lust, and gave themselves over completely to the faith.

Would Athesiene grace her with power to save a handful of faithful in a remote valley? To be even a fraction of what those saints had been might be enough. It was a nigh impossible proposition, but the only recourse she saw.

It was not the path she thought she would ever embrace, but it was a path regardless. Stall the goblins. Attend to the townsfolk. Embrace the faith. In the absence of any other hope, it was either that or slow death at the claws of the horde.

***

"The blighters pour into the valley like a plague of rats."

Howe pointed off into the distance from the copse of trees in which Pencheval and he hid, and the frustrated Lion frowned. This was the fourth mob of goblins Howe had spotted as they circumvented Tarsun's Market. The scout estimated the groups at hundreds strong, so how many were they between them? A thousand more to join the horde? Two thousand?

Too many. The warlord would be stronger than ever and ready at least to winter in Tarsun's Market, secure in its position. The temple had made no headway well into summer and faced the prospect of lean seasons. They could not grow food, could not raise livestock, and could not last forever.

Pencheval rapped a tree with his fingertips. "Will the knights not thin their numbers?"

"If they can catch them before they get to the town, certainly. But no two groups of goblins leave the mountains from the same place. Assuming a scout found them just as they entered the valley, they could not return, report, and have the knights ride out to meet them before they joined the safety of numbers in Tarsun's Market."

"Then we continue as we were."

"Find one of their monsters. Can we not do that and say we did?"

"Nothing less will draw attention to us now." Pencheval shared Howe's lack of enthusiasm, but the warlord retained the sense to wait and mass. He had not sufficiently infuriated it and would not until he had heaped truly intolerable losses on its head. The beasts seemed to be the most powerful of its minions and it surely did not have them in vast numbers.

At the very least, it would disrupt the horde. They already feared him. If he killed their most powerful at will, how would that affect the way they viewed their master? Could he provoke defections and discord?

"We'll need a better plan than 'Oops, giant monster!' I heard tales of that surprise attack on the patrol. That would end our budding careers as aspiring bards' tales right quick."

"Preparation and an ambush. If they patrol, we can determine their route and act accordingly."

"I know a camp that might aid in that, if the goblins haven't stripped it first."

"Lead on."

***

What was this Penn Cheval?

The Viperfang Chieftain had set forth to take stock of his new forces and one name kept emerging in terrified whispers. Penn Cheval. The Gray Lion Clan warrior. He had never heard the kind of fright this beast provoked before, and he had seen goblins shiver at the thought of avalanches and great bat-lizards.

When he asked about it, his minions told him tales of a human that bore a demon in its shiny big knife, could run like the wind, and fought like a Berserker. It killed by the dozens when it wasn't merely content to leave goblins crippled and screaming, which it had done during the battle to take this human town. A battle it *lost*.

A human. *One* human held this much terror over an entire horde of goblins? There were thousands among the horde, and it swelled from the clans traveling to it from the mountains. They had stealth, great beasts, and mighty warriors, but still feared one human.

How did a Hordemaker allow one human, fell as it might be, to do this to a horde? The goblins here should hold their warlord in more fear and awe than this human. At the very least, the Chief of Chieftains should be making examples and demanding no more talk of it. If he had not yet acted, it was another mark against him.

An admittedly impressive bone throne and a tall staff did not make a Chief of Chieftains. Perhaps it was time to take his title and his chair. It was just a matter of being certain the risk was justified by more than a passing chance of success.

***

"It's here?"

Pencheval saw nothing but a thick copse of evergreens beside the deer path along which they led the horses. The trees had become increasingly dense as they travelled, shorter growth giving way to taller trees with high branches. Howe lashed his horse to a sapling and motioned for Pencheval to do the same.

"It is here, Lion. Its former occupants will be at the Shield of Athesiene, but it is here."

"Hope this amounts to something."

Howe ducked and wove through the branches as the irritated Lion followed, crunching the spongy carpet of fallen needles. Every so often, a loose twig would slap him in the helmet or face, leaving the smell of pine and sticky bits of sap behind. He grumbled and bore it all.

They emerged into a small clearing with a campsite. It contained a single canvas pup tent, large river stones ringing a fire pit, and a small contingent of cook pots. Pine cones and leaf litter partially covered cold ashes and collected around the edges of the tent. Howe prodded both bedrolls with the end of his bow, and a snake bolted from beneath them and slithered away. It did not appear anyone, including the goblins, had been here in some time.

"A hidden place to rest is good, but not what we need." Pencheval was underwhelmed.

"That as well, but it might have...there." Howe walked over to a shaded nook underneath a half-fallen tree. After removing a few dead branches that appeared as any other forest litter, he exposed a large trunk.

"Good, they didn't find it." Howe opened the lid, looked down towards the contents, and waved Pencheval over to join him. "These gems might help."

The curious mercenary examined the trunk and smiled. It contained a pair of rugged steel bear traps, jaws large enough to catch a fully grown man in the thigh. Both sat closed and oiled in the bottom, their anchors and chains coiled neatly along with them. They weren't enough to kill one of the goblins' monsters, but they might be enough to separate them if he had to fight more than one.

"Outstanding."

"Not all the threats here need a knight's attention," Howe explained. "Rangers keep the animals at bay, and they keep their tools in camps like this one."

"All we need now is an ambush spot."

"If the monsters still patrol the town's perimeter, I know a good one with poor footing and too steep a hill for such mindless beasts. The only shortcoming is that it's not far beyond sight of the walls. They will know they're under attack if they keep any kind of watch."

"Unfortunate, but necessary." It was also possibly useful, but the Lion saw no cause to alarm Howe with that opinion.

"We go forth, then. It's a half a day's journey from–" Howe raised his head and nocked an arrow in his bow. Pencheval reached for the hilt of his sword and scanned around him. He neither saw nor heard a thing.

"What?"

"The animals grow silent and twigs snapped. Something is trying to be quiet that has little use for stealth."

Pencheval didn't question Howe. His perception had proven unerring so far. But were they goblins? No. The ones with the hoods were dangerously stealthy. Highwaymen and brigands, perhaps.

A huge paw of a hand snapped a branch out of the way and answered his question. Its owner strode into the campsite and smiled wickedly, brandishing a flanged steel mace in one hand. It was one of the brutish goblins as he had faced in single combat not long ago in Tarsun's Market. Its companion cleared its own way through the branches by pushing them aside with two heavy stone axes.

Howe let an arrow fly, and it hummed into the chest of the one with the axes. The brute reacted as though it had been stung by a bee, yelled something at Howe in its tongue, and charged him. Its companion did the same to Pencheval, and he had no time to wonder how they came to be here.

***

Magur was annoyed that the humans could move so quickly on their riding beasts but happy they had them. The animals had given away their general location and their talking had done the rest. He had followed the noise to find the Silver Lion Clan human, still wearing its clan shirt despite the damage it had endured. Magur did not blame it. He was proud to call himself Bloodmoon for all knew of their might. If the rest of the Silver Lion Clan was as strong as this one, being part of it would be an honor.

Beneath it, Penn Cheval wore the hide of a great bat-lizard proudly. Some human craftsman had made impressive work of it. Surely the scales were a gift, as the human had not worn this before. To kill as many of the Snow Clan's enemies as this Penn Cheval? No chieftain with sense would have left such an ally unrewarded. The Snow Clan Chieftain must have given him the riding beasts and the rabble with the bow, too.

Yet now was not the time to reflect on Penn Cheval's changes. Glory awaited because Drox had chosen the weakling human with the bow. His temper would deny him the proper kill today.

The Berserker charged forward with the mace but left his off-hand free. He remembered the tales of the fight this human had with Tzak. It had beaten him with hidden weapons because both of his hands were too busy to defend. That was not a mistake he meant to repeat. First remove the small knife, then kill the human.

***

Pencheval cursed the charge of both of the brutish goblins as he put his sword into guard. He was far more ready to deal with them than when he all but staggered from exhaustion in Tarsun's Market, but that was not his primary concern. Howe had his own brute to face, and his arrows did little more to them than draw curses.

Pencheval realized Howe was no match for them. He only had a bow and a dagger; they would not be remotely enough to stop his opponent. Either he drew the attention of both brutes, or he would have to bury Howe after this fight ended.

The Berserker that charged him struck with its mace and Pencheval parried. The force nearly tore the sword from his grip as one like it had in Tarsun's Market. Unlike Tarsun's Market, he had magic to spare and had not battled half a night before this fight. He willed a Waymaker spell into his blade to repel the goblin and its superhuman strength.

The spell popped, and the brute staggered backwards a step or two. Unfazed, it regained its balance and pressed. This time, Pencheval sidestepped and snapped his sword's pommel into the side of its skull. It staggered and dropped its guard, but a scream from Howe prevented Pencheval from shearing away its head.

He involuntarily glanced and found the other brute standing over the scout with an axe raised to strike. Pencheval grimaced, willed himself speed, and switched his grip on the sword. As the world slowed to a crawl, he snatched his dagger from the small of his back and threw it. It struck the bear's hide cloak of the axe wielder just under the right arm where the ribs would be and did not fully penetrate. It was enough to stall a killing blow to Howe, and that was all Pencheval saw before the warrior in front of him planted a fist into his helmet.

Pencheval felt the blow through the steel and quilted arming cap. He staggered backwards as consciousness threatened to flee him just as he gained the attention of both goblins. The one Howe shot pulled the dagger from its cloak and snapped the arrows in its chest. The other yelled what sounded like curses or complaints as it advanced.

***

"Tend to your own human!"

Magur gave serious thought to ending Drox on the spot. One little knife in the side kept him from finishing the human rabble? Did his temper turn his purpose so easily? If the fool lived through this, he would have to cure him of that shortcoming with the mace.

"I can punish them both. Stay out of my way!"

"Stay out of *my* way!" This was intolerable, but at least one good thing had happened. To save the bow-wielding rabble from Drox, the human had thrown away its hidden knife. If it only had the one, it had lost its advantage.

The human shook its head to regain its sense and resumed guard. The Silver Lion Clan warrior did not disappoint, and Drox may serve a purpose yet. They could both kill it, and then he would have the shiny big knife. That would involve executing Drox, which he found to his liking after enduring his temper. This far from the horde, he could simply blame his irate companion's death on Penn Cheval.

"If you mean to do this, at least try to keep up with the fighting." Magur stepped into another blow, and Drox struck from beside him.

"Do I look like a pup to you?" Both stone axes flew towards the human, and then there was nothing for it but to beat him to the kill.

Despite being unwelcome, Drox had turned the fight in their favor. The human had saved its rabble companion but struggled to defend against the two of them. It wielded its shiny big knife like an expert and dodged killing strokes with the shaman trick that gave it bursts of speed, but its movements smacked of a growing desperation.

It was a shame the Silver Lion Clan warrior could not be slain in single combat, but at least this was enough to defeat it. When the human was forced to defend against the hail of blows from the axes, it opened itself to a strike with the haft of the mace. Another blow sent it tumbling onto its back.

Magur cursed as Drox shouldered him out of the way, raised both axes to strike the killing blow, and caught an arrow with the back of his neck. He choked, dropping his weapons, and stumbled about trying to fight the inevitable. Magur gave him nothing more than a bitter snort. It served the idiot right.

This was why you finished your enemies when they were at your mercy. It prevented reversals of fortune like this and the spoiling of opportune circumstances. Now, with the perfect chance to slay the fallen Penn Cheval, he had to kill the rabble with the bow instead. The fool human knew how to use it and he could not leave it to its own devices any longer.

Magur rushed the other human, which dropped the bow and scrambled from his charge. The annoyed Berserker stomped it, snapping it cleanly near the middle, and strode forth to brain the wretch. It should not have been this way. He slapped rabble like this from his path on the way to slay real enemies, yet dying like Drox was out of the question.

He was within the mace's reach when he heard a roar like a mountain lion and discovered the newly rearmed Penn Cheval raging towards him. The moment's distraction earned him a knife in the back. He turned to backhand the rabble wielding it senseless before putting his mace into guard to meet the Silver Lion. The knife left a prickling sensation high on his right shoulder blade but did nothing to slow him.

***

Pencheval admired Howe's courage but wished he had fled from the brute rather than stab it. The scout, like many of Athesiene's soldiers, had shown more resolve than sense. The mercenary deliberately dramatized his charge with a Lion's Roar to draw the thing off of him. Howe took the wrong hint and struck for a killing blow instead of escaping, and he hoped that slap didn't break the scout's neck.

The goblin believed his show of raging forth, sword raised over his head, and stood so as to slip it and counterattack. When it moved to take advantage of his 'uncontrolled charge' Pencheval adjusted and removed its weapon arm below the elbow before finishing it with a thrust. Unlike its companion, the brute died before it hit the ground.

"Howe." Pencheval moved to help the fallen scout and to his relief found he still breathed.

The Silver Lion threw him over his shoulders and put him next to the campfire. They weren't going anywhere now. Time to hide the horses and gather firewood, for this place would be home until Howe could move again.

***

Pencheval wiped the sweat from his forehead with the back of one arm and drank from a waterskin next to the fire ring. An afternoon spent burying the two brutes was more trouble than they deserved, but it was better than bears or wolves catching the scent of easy meat. He had enough troubles with the goblins without inviting more of it.

Howe laid unconscious on a bedroll inside the canvas tent. At least he was still alive. Either of those things could have killed him with their bare hands, much less their weapons, and the fact they had not was no small amount of luck.

They won that skirmish, but the results of this gambit so far had not justified risking his life or Howe's. The horde at Tarsun's Market still massed as the warlord bolstered its numbers. Nan's fate was uncertain and it was misery. Was she still alive, or would this accomplish nothing more than to bring about vengeance for her?

He breathed deeply and reassured himself. Many things were uncertain, but this was not a fool's errand. If he succeeded, the warlord would lead his as yet insufficient horde to ruin in a fit of wrath. That cleared the way to Nan and shortened an entire war. His success was the only chance the valley had for a swift return to serenity, and that Nan had to live.

He stopped ruminating when he heard the scout groan, prop himself up on his elbows, and squint in pain.

"What...where am I?"

"In the hunter's camp with the bear traps," Pencheval answered. "One of the goblin brutes struck you. Be at ease, we are not leaving tonight."

"More welcome words were never spoken," Howe groaned, easing himself back down on the bedroll. "I take it we won."

"Yes." Pencheval took another drink from his skin.

"Don't be too enthused." Howe felt along his face winced when he touched the welt the brute gave him. "Really, don't be too enthused. I have a splitting headache."

"This skirmish is won, but we have more to do."

"My pounding head to the contrary, I'm not dead yet." Howe sat up. "What now?"

"We continue as we have. If we fail, many more will die than must to end this horde."

Pencheval took another drink from the waterskin and offered it to Howe. The scout refused it by holding up his hand.

"Time enough for that come the morning." Howe groaned and laid down again. "Call me when it's my watch."

"Rest." Pencheval shook his head and then idly watched the campfire crackle before him.

This matter with the goblin brutes had changed nothing. This would be done when Nan was safe and no sooner. That meant destroying the horde and leaving its warlord beaten, broken, and begging for its life right before it died.

For what it had caused, it would die.

***

Nan sat in the library and waited to be addressed as the Beastwarper Chieftain and its translator examined yet another book. It flipped through the pages to see the pictures and puzzle at the symbols. For the third day now it did not first command her to start reading – at least it was not looking over her shoulder as its minion told her to read the same lines time and again.

She rubbed her eyes in exhaustion and took the moment to silently pray to the Lord on High. She had served Him and His faithful by remaining in this goblin-infested nightmare when rescue had been at hand. Some sense of entitlement crept into her thoughts and she banished it from her mind. It was not her place to question or demand rewards of Athesiene. She asked only for the power to save those few remaining from the goblins.

"His. To. Reee."

Nan started at the sound of another goblin voice. It was not the witch doctor, which spoke to her in accented but perfect words. She saw the chieftain dragging the tip of one clawed finger along a sentence and heard it chitter at its minion. The witch doctor shrugged and pointed to Nan, saying something that sounded like a suggestion.

"Read!"

The warped goblin jabbed a claw into the book, and Nan suppressed her dismay long enough to see where it pointed. She looked at the word and gasped. It was as the goblin said it was: history.

"His. To. Ree!"

"The Beastwarper Chieftain wishes to know if these symbols mean the word he has spoken. Answer, or die."

"Yes. Yes." She stammered the confirmation.

She watched a wicked grin spread across its face as the witch doctor translated her words. It had learned enough to grasp the concept of the written word. The tome was a history, and if it knew that much, how many other words had it grasped? It would not steal the wisdom in the more florid and sophisticated tomes yet, but it knew the basics now, and in little more than a month.

The tome shut with an echoing boom. "Book."

The witch doctor said something to the lame chieftain and it hissed at him in response. Unconcerned with the chieftain's reaction, the minion turned and left. Whatever had happened was not something her tormenter could prevent. Perhaps the one with the silver plate on its chest and staff had ordered it? This 'Stonemaster?'

The snarling goblin chieftain waved her from the room. "Go."

Had this chieftain learned the other's talent? Perhaps and perhaps not. Yet even without the other's gift of tongues, it could very well listen to its minion translate. It was also smart enough to learn the words over time. She nodded and left its presence, horrified that she may have given the goblins something that would make them far worse.

There was no time for regret now. She needed to tend the children and Wot would be on the brink of madness again in the nave. She had stalled as well as she could and now only one possibility remained. Serve the Lord on High and His faithful, and hope her patron found her worthy. Do what she had done for the past ten years and walk this path to its end.

***

"Saint Marion's revelation, I hate that sound."

Pencheval remained crouched in the undergrowth just inside the tree line and silently agreed with Howe. They were not half a mile away from Tarsun's Market and the unceasing sound of the horde. The screech and click reminded him of a bitter defeat and a purpose only half-completed.

He had saved Dominik and a few others that night. Nan had adamantly refused to go to the point of using spell craft to prevent her separation from those she meant to help. Those that had returned with him knew they were beaten and meant, perhaps, to fight another day.

"We will silence it yet. But for now, we need the goblin beasts."

"They patrol the outside of the walls still. You can see their trail from here."

"Where?" Pencheval did not see anything in the plains around Tarsun's Market at first glance beyond the rugged patches of stone and dirt.

"They are there," the scout huffed. "And they are close to that place I mentioned for an ambush."

"Can we get there without being seen?"

"We can stay in the woods but–Shhh! Conceal yourself!"

Howe's hiss of a whisper led Pencheval to duck within the cover of the foliage as the thump of footsteps from two large creatures slowly rose above the horde's chatter. Pencheval shook his head at Howe's acute perception and was once again glad he had chosen him. He remembered the sound from the attack on his patrol in the spring and was not fondly reminded of that outcome.

A pair of the creatures bearing bone and wicker covertures on their backs trod parallel to the tree line. Both were blindfolded, and in broad daylight he could see the leather thongs attached to their horns and various parts of their faces. They alternately slackened and tensed, and when they did the creatures turned or changed their pace.

They moved as he remembered from the patrol, walking on their hind legs and the knuckles of their oversized claws. Their gaits left their covertures halfway between the horizontal and vertical, which gave the goblins plenty of space to view what was before them over their horned heads.

Regular growls and grumbles revealed the rows of triangular, serrated teeth in a mouth large enough to swallow a man whole. Hides bore bone plates which Pencheval remembered had repelled his sword strokes well. Their attack at night had made them fearsome, but that was not corrected by seeing them in broad daylight.

As the beasts drew closer, Pencheval coiled back into the brush and wished he had chosen to fall prone as Howe did. When they were within sixty paces of them, the one closest to the tree line stopped, turned in both directions, and sniffed at the air. The goblin atop it looked out from the coverture and scanned to determine what caused its curiosity. Its companion realized it had stopped and turned as well. Pencheval saw it emerge and speak, but could not hear the words over the din.

Could they smell them from there? Pencheval had not believed it was possible. Yet there it was, sniffing the air like a bloodhound, and bringing them to the attention of the goblins. If he or Howe moved, the goblins were close enough to detect them, and he heard Howe suppress a whimper to remain still and silent.

He checked his breathing and could hear his heartbeat pounding in his ears. If those two found them and charged, it would be seen by anything with eyes on the walls of Tarsun's Market. While he couldn't make out distinct shapes, he could see that those walls were manned by far too many goblins.

For too long a time the mounted goblins searched the tree line as their monsters sniffed the air. It lasted until the goblins relented, reined their mounts away from their distractions, and resumed their patrol. The tension flowed from him and he realized he had been grinding his teeth. Howe audibly expelled his breath.

"Can we complete this ambush with haste?" Howe half-whimpered the question, and Pencheval found he was no more happy about the circumstances than the scout.

"We can indeed. In fact, we will complete it before sunset."

"Wh-what?"

"Goblin eyes can see in darkness. Hiding in the woods at night this close to the town favors them by hindering us and us alone. So we must come and go in daylight. How far is this place you mentioned from here?"

"Not an hour's travel, even hiding in the wood."

"Take us there. Time is not our ally."

***

He's mental, Howe thought to himself as he watched Tarsun's Market from the opposing side of a small hill. He's parted ways with the last of his sense. Was their near discovery not enough of an adventure today?

His nerves were far from calmed, but at least the Lion had been wise enough to agree to this place for an ambush. A small path curved between two hills to a stone bridge. The squat cobblestone construction crossed a muddy stream to the only dirt road through a swampy field. It ran between the two halves of that field, little more than several dry islands connected by dirt piled higher than the muck around it. Years of foot and horse travel had worn it into a single path.

The two bear traps from the camp laid set and ready at the hill side of the bridge, and the rest was a trap in and of itself. Anything as large as one of the goblin creatures would sink into the mud like a knight mounted on a horse in steel barding. The Lion had smiled when he saw it and now both of them laid on a hill as they awaited those beasts again.

Pencheval had saved him from a mob, but little he heard about him up to that point could explain it. Yes, he had warned that friar friend of his that the horde would take the town and that they should up and leave before its arrival. He made no such offer to anyone else save this Nan, which did nothing to dissuade Howe of Silver Lion notoriety.

So who was this Pencheval now? Why did he have such regard for this sister? Perhaps she had found the light in his darkness as was the wont of the clergy here. Maybe he knew her before he was a Lion. Whatever it was had brought out someone who would gamble his life on a long shot.

While he had no great love for where that long shot took him today, it was a long shot he preferred to the alternative. The only other plan had been Rennoute's plan to mass and campaign for years. They might fight skirmishes as they massed, but the reinforcements would arrive just in time to winter with the rest of the troops.

Pencheval's idea to goad the goblins into the certain death a siege on the Shield of Athesiene could inflict was a good one, on the off chance they could make it happen. It would save thousands of lives and shorten this conflict to little more than an aggressively bad memory. Too many had died already and a campaign promised far more of it. If there was a chance, why not take it?

A pair of thumping footsteps approached after a two-hour wait. No more time for boredom then. It was likely another day in the life of a Silver Lion, but he did not look forward to it in the slightest. He hoped this mercenary knew what he was doing, because if he died, Howe would join him shortly thereafter.

"They come, Lion."

Pencheval, who had been resting on his back to make sure none approached them through the wood unnoticed, lifted his sword and rose to a crouch. "Get their attention and depart swiftly. Have the horses ready."

"You need not tell me twice." Howe wiped his forehead nervously, stood, and waved his arms. One of the large beasts sniffed in his direction before a slight motion set it into a run. It roared in the distance and charged, followed by the other.

"Lord on High be with you, Lion." Howe scrambled down the hill and towards the horses on the other side of the swampy fields. Pencheval accompanied him as far as the opposite side of the bridge from the traps and waited with his weapon in hand. It was time for the Lion to execute his part of this plan and for the scout to be far, far away from it.

***

"Fiend's breath, we're guarding the grass."

"Be silent! Do you mean to bring trouble from the boss?"

"Trouble?" Tik wasn't worried about the enforcers. They didn't care if the rabble grumbled so long as they did their job. "What is there to guard? The rocks and grass are where they were before. Same as yesterday. Same as tomorrow. Same until the humans either come here or we go to the mountain-castle."

"What's that about then?"

Tik only just heard the roaring over the noise of the horde. He put his hand over his eyes to find it, and his eyes landed on the source immediately. One of the Bonestrippers had seen something and barreled toward a pair of small hills. He could not tell if anything was there, but the rider had seen it and allowed his mount to chase it.

"Can't tell what it's charging," Tik replied. "Maybe it's a Snow Clan scout?"

"What else would it be? Their riders don't let them run wild."

Tik laughed. "Fool don't know how to keep its head down."

So it wouldn't be a dull day guarding the fields after all. Given the Bonestrippers, it wouldn't be interesting for long, but it did break the tedium. Besides, one dead human was one less human trying to kill him.

***

Pencheval was glad he could order the battlefield to his choosing when the first of the goblins' monsters thundered over the hill. He saw the leather thongs on its face tense, and it changed course to charge him across the bridge. It missed the traps with both arms, but hit one squarely with a giant foot. To his chagrin, it was so ineffectual the monster didn't even notice it was there until the anchor chain pulled taut and snapped.

It stopped despite the curses of its rider. Unharmed but confused, it poked the steel teeth with a claw as though trying to determine what nuisance nibbled on its leg. The trap caused it no injury; it bit hard but drew no blood. Several of the teeth that had caught bone plates even bent from the force of the pull.

Pencheval wished it had done more but was satisfied enough with this. The beast ignored him utterly as it poked and pried at the bear trap. He willed himself speed and charged, reminding himself of where to hit from the time he had slain one before; soft spot in the neck, just behind the horns. Hilt a sword there and they died.

Then, ever so slowed by his perception, another thundered over the knoll, saw them both, and did something Pencheval hoped never to see again. Instead of crashing into its companion, it leapt over it. It appeared as though it would just clear his target, but if he continued his charge he would be caught by its landing. Not eager to meet the flying creature head on, he leapt over the left side of the bridge, away from its arc and towards the shore.

The world accelerated again as his magically enhanced speed faded. The slowly descending monster roared as one foot crashed through the opposite side of the bridge. It sent cobblestones flying before landing on all fours in the mire. The commotion startled the other from the bear trap, and it swung its head towards the crash and put its back to Pencheval. The mercenary wished he could take advantage of its distraction or the other's poor footing but was forced to toss his sword away to keep from landing on it. When he hit the muddy bank, his feet sank halfway to his knees and threatened immobility.

Pencheval cursed his luck. The plan was always the first thing to die when the enemy was met and this ambush was no exception. He willed himself strength to pull his legs free from the mud and his feet slowly rose with a wet sucking sound. He stumbled over to his sword, snatched it from the ground, and turned just in time to see the goblin on the trapped beast pull two thongs of leather pinned with bone thorns to the corners of its mount's mouth.

The beast let out a roar so loud he could see Howe cover his ears in the distance. The sound was deafening even through the helmet and arming cap. Was it an attack? No, he and Howe still stood and were none the worse for it.

It was an alarm. Could the goblins hear it from the walls of Tarsun's Market? He could not divine why this would *not* be the case. That damnable noise was loud enough to wake the dead. Best to be done with this and quickly.

***

What became of the Bonestrippers?

Tix stood between two of the rocks in the strangely irregular cliff-wall, straining to see something that suggested the beasts had slain a human or several, yet they simply seemed to disappear after going over the hills.

"Where are they?" Dozens had joined him at the edge, and he grasped at the stones to keep from being pushed to his death. They were as eager for a break in the doldrum as he was and meant to make the most of it. It was not every day a Bonestripper attacked a target.

A shrieking roar broke through the background noise of the horde so clearly he did not know what to make of it. It didn't sound like a death scream. So if it had slain nothing and nothing had slain it, why did it happen?

"What was that?"

Several of the Beastwarper Clan started at the noise and shouted down the walls and to the ground below.

"It's an alarm! Trouble comes!"

"What manner of trouble?" Tix swallowed hard. He had seen nothing. If the enforcer thought he missed something he should have caught, he would likely die for it. "I see nothing!"

"Something is there! The riders do not signal without cause! But what would be so much trouble such a small hill could hide...Gray Lion Clan! Warn our chieftain!"

Warnings and fear flew over rooftops, through the streets, and along the walls like so many bees. Penn Cheval. The Gray Lion Clan. The Bonestrippers battle with the dark human. It is here.

***

There was no more time for anything but haste.

After sounding its alarm, the beast on the bridge resumed its dumb attempts to prod and pick the trap from its feet. Pencheval charged to take advantage of its renewed distraction. He closed half the distance before the goblin on its back pulled the blindfold from its eyes in fright. The moment it saw him it snapped onto the knuckles of its giant paws and lunged forward with a roar.

The Lion waited until it raised a claw to strike before willing his magic to grant him speed. The beast seemed stuck in a monstrous pose, right claw slowly descending as Pencheval slipped the blow towards its now exposed side. He clasped his blade in a half-sword guard and jammed the point through two exposed ribs. The beast's slow attack changed to a cringe of pain. It dropped to all fours, blood dripping from its mouth as it gurgled for breath.

Its legs thrashed as its stuck rider tried to free itself and bolt. Pencheval snatched the half-emerged goblin by the rags, slammed it to the ground, and ran it through. The next blow shattered the coverture to give Pencheval the room he needed to land the finishing stroke. One more sword thrust just behind the horn, and this one would be ready for the harvesting.

A roar and the wet sounds of something large forcing its way through deep mud turned the mercenary from that task. The other beast, mud streaked and furious, splashed across the stream with the curses of its rider. Muddy clouds billowed to life in the water where it passed. Pencheval reluctantly moved away from his prize so he could see them both. The one before him was on lower and less stable ground, but it was still fresh, and its rider might not make the same mistakes the other did.

***

The Stonemaster heard the buzz through the town long before the messenger arrived. The tone had changed from the business of the day to an undercurrent of fear. Penn Cheval. The Gray Lion Clan is killing Bonestrippers.

One gasping rabble messenger with a club scurried to Beastwarper and bowed. It wore the dark green band of his clan. "Alarm, my chieftain. Bonestrippers are fighting. Everyone says it's the Gray Lion Clan warrior!"

"Do we have better information than 'everyone says' or will you leave me with speculation?" Beastwarper's eyes narrowed and the rabble before him cringed.

"Do I look unimportant to you?" The Stonemaster all but yelled the words and immediately became the center of attention.

"Forgive me, Chief of Chieftains. A battle rages and the Bonestrippers sounded an alarm. They only do that for good cause."

"It's Penn Cheval, or one of the humans like the under-chieftain of the Snow Clan that ruled this town before us." It was not hard to guess. No other humans could give the Bonestrippers enough trouble to provoke an alarm. "Send something to finish it."

"Chief of Chieftains, too many Bonestrippers in one place–"

"That was not a request!" The Stonemaster leaned forward in his bone throne and bared his teeth.

The warlord gave serious thought to making an example for this impertinence. He was the master here. He did not ask favors and he was not to be ignored. "Send. More. Now!"

"Yes, Chief of Chieftains. Send messengers to the walls. Signal the other Bonestrippers and send them onward."

"Immediately, my chieftain!" The messenger, horrified at being in the middle of this spat, scrambled from the council area to obey.

At least Bloodmoon had a legitimate excuse, even if he watched all of this with a bemused look on his face. Most of his Berserkers were already in the valley hunting Penn Cheval. Perhaps they would join the fight if they could reach it in time.

***

"No, please no. What are they doing?"

All Nan knew was that something happened beyond the windows so many of the goblins crowded now. Something changed in the chatter outside, and it had changed the mood of the guards in the temple. Those four the Beastwarper Chieftain placed on her seemed worried by it.

"What are you doing?" Wot yelled at the goblins along the walls, pulling stringy knots of gray hair down around his ears in yet another futile attempt to dampen the noise. "Answer me!"

The boss of the room had shoved two guards away from the windows to more intently listen to the noise outside. After Wot's outburst, it snapped its pair of evil, beady eyes on him before screaming at him. If its history held, it was the one and only warning Wot would receive before it ordered one of the others to kill him.

"Wot, it is not our concern," Nan told him, putting one hand gently on his shoulder. "Please sit down."

"What are they keeping from us?"

"Nothing, old friend. Now rest."

She asked the Lord on High for His mercy and Wot slowly grew docile as her magic granted him serenity. He returned to sitting on the floor and rocked back and forth on his knees. Nan felt helpless to do more, and she could bear it no longer.

She gave thought to blasting the goblin boss with the same spell she used on Pencheval, but restrained herself. Assuming one of the guards on her did not knock her senseless again, all she would accomplish was to die; they would surely kill her for her one futile act of rebellion. There was no saving her charges then, and no serving the Lord on High.

What then? Sooner or later she would not be able to stop one of the townsfolk from going mad only to watch that boss command their death for it. Nor did the horde ever cease. The goblins chattered day or night and slept like cats, only in naps, and never at the same time.

She glared at the boss in the room from under her hood, being careful not to make eye contact. Could it not give them a moment's respite? No. It *would* give them a moment's respite.

The thought struck her like an epiphany and she willed as much magic to her as she could without moving. Why don't you rest, little goblin? Why don't you rest *forever*?

She watched as the spell she willed into the goblin boss took effect. A dumbstruck look replaced its endless scanning of the room and its limbs went slack. It remained perched near the window, suspended in its stupor, for only a moment longer. Then it slowly tipped backwards and crashed to the floor. It landed head first on the stones and did not rise.

Her four goblin guards started and chittered, pointing at the calamity. They did not move to restrain or harm her, and she made no sign that she had anything to do with its death. Goblins checked the boss for signs of what caused its fall and seemed all the more disturbed at the lack of any.

Nan did her best to appear defeated and silently prayed to the Lord on High for forgiveness. She willed the rise of magic again to determine His judgment and found it not only intact but growing. She smiled and thanked Athesiene for His blessing.

The epiphany and the spell were His work. How else could it have been exactly what she needed when she needed it? It struck down the goblins and left them unable to divine the source of their trouble. So long as she took pains to conceal her part in it, she could defend her charges and none of their captors would be the wiser.

Let the goblins scream and panic. They would do much more of it soon. If this was the will of Athesiene, they would come to know sleep as a curse before much longer. She would see to it and gladly.

***

The beast that churned its way up from the mire lumbered to a halt on the dry road just before the bridge. It stopped with a long, low growl as Pencheval watched its reins pull taut. This rider was not as eager to meet him as the last one.

Pencheval gritted his teeth. While this one felt no immediate cause to attack him, it stood astride the only path to the horses. If it remained where it was, he would have to fight it to reach them. During that time, whatever its companion's alarm summoned rushed towards them. There was no other dry path to take, a fact the stymied Lion did not believe was lost on the rider.

Pencheval advanced with a half-sword grip on his weapon to try and slip around the reluctant goblin and its mount. A leather strap whipped against its face and the beast lunged forward. Pencheval willed himself a burst of magically enhanced speed to dodge backwards to where he started. The beast snapped its jaws closed where he once stood before its rider reined it back onto the road.

He frowned at it. The goblins did not have much going for them, but the blighters excelled at self-preservation. It knew all it had to do was stall and enough goblins to overwhelm him might arrive to assist. Worse still, more of these beasts may have answered the call.

A gurgle and groan escaped from the monster with the punctured lung, and it slumped to the ground. Would taking what he wanted from it goad the other from his path? He walked to the body and struck a horn from its head, and it did not so much as grunt. He kept his eyes on the one before him as he crouched down to take it, but the other rider did nothing more than curse.

He jammed the horn in his belt so he could keep both hands for his sword. It was half as long as his blade's sheath and jabbed at his tabard but remained in place. Pencheval was careful of his footing as he sidled to the other horn, and when the beast at the road did not react, struck it from his kill.

The downed monster slammed the side of its head into him in a final burst of wrath. He felt as though struck by a maul and flailed his arms and legs as he flew over the stream and into the muck. He shook his head to clear his senses in time to see a shadow blocking the sun.

The other Bonestripper had pounced to take advantage of the moment. Huge and brutish arms extended for the long jump, and its toad-like maw opened wide enough to bite him in two. He willed himself an excess of speed in his panic, burning too many reserves of magic, and the world around him slowed to near still life.

A sharp pain jabbed in his ribs as he scurried away. His hands clawed him backwards through cold mud, leaving splashes of it hanging in midair as the hulking beast descended more slowly than a drifting feather. He gritted his teeth and scrambled for safety despite his pain. Whatever that last burst of wrath had inflicted on him could not be attended until he escaped this.

He was halfway to the bank of the dry road when his speed departed, and the beast missed by a mere sword's length. Instead, it again fell face-first into the mire and sank deeply from the force of its landing. Feet disappeared to the knee and claws sank to the elbows as jaws snapped where he once laid. Giant limbs struggled against the grip of the mire and the monster roared, spraying mud through its teeth.

The creature thrashed to get free with no success. Pencheval could hear the screech of the goblin on its back as it cursed its circumstances. It could do nothing as the beast threw it about inside its coverture more violently than the bucking of an unbroken horse.

He stood to collect his sword and another sharp jab in the ribs greeted his effort. He groaned as he felt for his one horn and found it. The other laid out of reach, and he left it for whatever the alarm would bring. His injury complicated an already dire set of circumstances, and he limped towards Howe as quickly as the shooting pains in his side would let him.

***

Howe dodged another set of descending hooves from his agitated mount. For all that was holy, could these blighted beasts cease raging long enough for him to calm the horses? Even at a hundred paces, the goblins' monsters spooked them to near panic. The distressed sapling to which they were lashed pulled and bent from their exertions, but not so much it broke or tore from the earth. Yet.

He didn't know how much longer that would last. Whatever else, at least that mad Lion had what he wanted. One beast dead, another in the mire unable to move, and a horn for whatever manner of gruesome taunt he meant to display to the horde's warlord. It had cost him though.

The mud-splattered warrior limped down the dry path towards him. He would have leapt on a horse to get him before reinforcements arrived, but couldn't calm them enough to get into the saddle. If they were this panicked now, they certainly wouldn't run towards their fears even with blinders.

May the Lord on High be with Pencheval, Howe silently prayed, for the Lion needed His intervention.

***

Pencheval sheathed his sword and grunted from the spike of pain. That rotten beast had just enough left to complicate his escape. The other had jumped right into its own frustration and raged now, but only because it tried to feast on him. Between the two of them, he was grateful he could still put one foot in front of the other.

The injured warrior attempted to jog, but the pain forced him back into a limp. He felt his breath rasp and tasted blood, and the irony of it left him bitter. A beast he had slain by puncturing its lung might well avenge itself by doing the same to him.

Preventing that meant using magic, which he was reluctant to do for healing. While it could kill pain and restore him to fighting condition, the price was an agonizing recovery. But what choice did he have?

No goblins had yet come, but nothing about them was ever so easy as an alarm going unheeded. It was more likely that a unicorn would suddenly appear and fly Howe and himself to safety on a rainbow. No, it was more a question of how many hundreds of them would answer and how many more beasts they would bring. He willed his magic to kill his pain knowing he would spend days regretting it.

He felt the first irregular vibrations in the ground beneath his feet and that justified its use. Every few heartbeats they grew stronger. The bursts were too few for a horde of goblins and the roars in the distance confirmed it. It seemed the warlord had no faith that the horde might reach him in time, so it sent more beasts. He loped forward into a jog, unwilling to wait for the stampede he felt beneath the road.

He saw Howe point just as he heard two roars from behind him no farther away than the hills. He heard one of them splash and slurp into the mud, and the spring and clank of the remaining bear trap catch another.

He glimpsed behind him. One creature had fallen headlong into the mire. It fought and raged at the grasping muck but made little headway. The other had completely torn the last bear trap from its anchor and only just crossed the bridge. It poked dumbly at the strange thing on the end of its claw as its reins flexed and whipped in vain to get it moving.

No time to stop, Pencheval admonished himself. One burst of luck was not an escape. He continued to push himself towards the horses, which Howe held by the reins. Every so often he would move to calm one, and for the moment they seemed cooperative. Once again, he was grateful for Howe's help. Without him, their mounts might have bolted, and they would be on foot against the goblins' beasts.

"Make haste!" The barely audible Howe beckoned him furiously.

***

For one brief and involuntary moment, Howe felt the urge to jump on a horse and run it into the ground to escape, all else be damned. Three beasts and their riders? How many more did the goblins have, and how many more charged here to meet them?

Yes, this ambush site had been ideal for them. They fell into the mire and remained trapped there as he expected. Yet at some indeterminate point, the one on the dry road treating the bear trap snapped to its arm like a delicate bracelet would rip it free. Absent distraction, it would charge them and the horses would be beyond calming. It was all he could do to control them now.

There was no time to tarry, and yet he did. The Lion limping towards him after this mad plan came to fruition had saved him from a lynching. If the mercenary could maintain his pace, he might make it this far before any more of those beasts arrived. There would be plenty of hard riding then, but no sooner.

A horse pulled at the reins nervously and he suppressed agreement with its sentiment. No, we won't leave yet. There was more to this than his own fear and he would not abandon his own.

***

Twenty more paces to the horses. Pencheval gasped and forced himself to continue. Twenty more paces and the mess was behind him. All that remained of the mire was a few tangles of browned grasses growing on its edges and a snake bolting under a bush.

It was close enough to risk more magic. He willed himself the speed of a galloping horse and closed. Every step felt as though gravel ground against his ribs but he did not stop. In a few heartbeats, he grasped the horn of his saddle to catch his breath and cough.

Howe's eyes bulged from the fear. "Bloody hell, Lion. Can you ride?"

"I will," Pencheval insisted. "We are only safe..." Pencheval coughed and spit blood. He willed more magic into his side and again, the pain subsided. "We are only safe when this is behind us."

"Now would be a good time for that!" Howe pointed down the field to another of the goblin creatures. It stood on solid ground and still searched, but its rider had possessed the sense to go around the mire instead of through it. Pencheval spat. Of course some of the goblins would know the terrain. Little about them was ever easy.

"Into the trees before they see–"

The warp and cracking of steel pins preceded the roar from the monster on the road across the mire. It tossed away the half of the bear trap dangling in its grip and lumbered forward on all fours at the bidding of its rider. The sound caught the attention of the one in the field, which charged to join its companion.

"Now what?" Howe's voice cracked from the fear on the last word.

"We outrun them!" Pencheval mounted his horse and gritted his teeth.

Howe leapt into his saddle. "Best plan I've heard all day!"

Howe shouted and whipped the reins of his horse. Pencheval did the same, feeling every hoof beat as a blow to his chest. The thumps and roars of the beasts behind him would either end with the creatures left in their dust or with them as meat.

Hooves struck dirt, and every nervous whinny or snort left Pencheval wondering if it would buck him. Every so often, a goblin's monster would growl or roar, and the bellows of their breathing seemed entirely too close. He heard one claw whoosh through air, and he slapped the reins in response. His horse pushed itself until he thought it would fall.

Down a hill and across a stream left one beast in pursuit and the sound of something large slurping vast quantities of water. The curses of its goblin rider fell far behind him. A short time thereafter, the breath of the other wheezed instead of bellowed and it thumped to a stop.

Neither Pencheval nor Howe reined their horse until they could hear and see nothing. By that time, the shadows grew long and they were at the edge of another wood. Sweat slicked both mounts and exertion left them drooping.

Howe dismounted and put his hand on his back. Pencheval more pulled himself from the saddle than dismounted. When his foot touched the ground, the pain in his chest staggered him.

"Damnable goblins..." Pencheval gurgled. The last thing he saw before the world went dark was Howe running towards him.

***

The Stonemaster glared over the wall at the one Bonestripper stumbling back to the town. Its shoulders drooped from exhaustion, and it stopped to shake the clods of mud from its hide before dropping prone and crossing its arms to rest. All that might and fury amounted to nothing more than a half a dozen of the Beastwarper's most powerful defeated by a stretch of muddy ground and Penn Cheval. The scouts he sent confirmed it long before this.

He glared off into the distance and bared his teeth. This was not possible. One human should not have done this, even Penn Cheval. This level of idiocy left him seriously considering the execution of the Beastwarper Chieftain. Yet had it been idiocy or something else? Had Beastwarper done this to undermine his position?

The lame but clever chieftain had certainly given these books a great deal of time and not mentioned the outcome to him. One victory, and members of his council made plays for his horde, his title, and his power as if they had any hope of replacing him. His greatness alone created and maintained this horde. It was his and only his!

He saw one goblin messenger tentatively lift a hand to get his attention out of the corner of one eye, think twice about it, and resume cringing.

"Speak." The word sounded like the buzz of a hornet's nest.

"Great, uh, Chief of Chieftains. The Viperfang Chieftain approaches for an audience." The messenger was clearly not happy delivering the news, but the Viperfang Chieftain approaching him on the wall showed no such fear. Several of the new arrivals and war chieftains he had made accompanied him. Their weapons were in hand and threatening.

"Tell me, great Chief of Chieftains, how one human causes you such distress?" The Viperfang Chieftain bared his teeth. "We have come a long way for victory, and yet one human makes a mockery of you."

"Best you remember who is master here and quickly."

"I know it is not you. One human, however powerful, could not do this to a true leader. My clan did not come this far to submit to a weakling. I also know that you must speak for the stone to obey, so I will not grant you last words before you die."

You did not know enough then, the Stonemaster mused.

The cobblestones beneath the feet of the war chieftains burst upwards into blossoms of slender spikes. Before any of them could react, they impaled their feet, groins, and guts. Weapons clattered to the ground or dropped to nestle between the long and slender thorns. A single droplet of blood rolled down the point that had pierced the Viperfang Chieftain's skull. The Stonemaster watched as death froze their faces into horrified looks.

He heard the local drop in chatter and surveyed his audience. Goblins on the rooftops and near them on the wall recoiled at his work. Good. He meant to discourage future attempts at his title and it was just the reaction he needed.

"This is what happens when you forget who is master, as they did!" The infuriated warlord motioned towards his impaled victims. "I am the Stonemaster, Chief of Chieftains, and Blessed by the Fiend. *I* command this horde and you are not fit to even countenance replacing me! Now back to work, all of you, and think on what will happen if you try to overthrow me!"

The Stonemaster heard a whimper and found the messenger on his knees, half in shock. He was pressed against the oddly irregular wall between him and the Viperfang Chieftain.

"Leave them there until I say to remove them." Satisfied that his authority was intact, the Chief of Chieftains walked back towards his tower cave as though nothing had happened. As far as he was concerned, nothing *had* happened. The coup attempt ended the only possible way it could because his greatness could not be denied by a group of pretenders.

The council was a whole other matter. How many of them meant to take his bone throne for their own? Beastwarper at the very least would bear more scrutiny. Giving the Bonestrippers' master the run of that human shaman had made him duplicitous. If their knowledge was advantageous enough for that to happen, the Stonemaster would treat with the humans alone and keep them all for himself.

***

"Please Pencheval, my father will be looking for me."

Cecelia was no more eager to leave his company than he was to let her go, and she smiled at him despite her protest. Her eyes sparkled as she slid her hands from his shoulders. The copper wedding band she had accepted from him gleamed in the light, and he could barely contain his joy.

"Let me walk you home. Your father should know."

"And he will, as soon as I explain it to him." Cecelia put her hands on his chest and laid her head between them. Her hair smelled faintly of her sweat and fresh spring air. "You were not his first choice."

"And I would choose no one else."

His new fiancée stood on her toes to kiss him. "Nor would I. Now let me go so I can convince him. We'll see each other again soon."

Pencheval's eyes snapped open and he gasped. He felt a thin bedroll beneath him and saw a few stars in the night sky. A quarter moon and a small crackling light he assumed to be a campfire were the only illumination.

"Lion?" He heard Howe's voice but could not see him.

Pencheval sat up on his elbows and groaned. The sharp pain in his ribs had returned along with the sensation that he had tried to salve it with a mace. The magic had done its work to keep him alive, but now exacted its payment from him.

"I am well enough, scout." He put his hand on his ribs. "Dreams and nothing more."

"You should be grateful you're alive. Your ribs are broken and you're right lucky they didn't shred your insides."

The Lion reluctantly agreed with the scout's assessment. Given his mad plan, he was lucky he had not been slain fortnights ago. As it was, the goblin beasts almost brought that plan, and him, to an end.

Less demanding healing magic would restore him to fighting condition in a fortnight instead of four. It was not as punishing as the spell he used during his emergency and would not leave him wishing he could avoid it. This time it was not avoidable, because time was not on their side. The fighting seasons grew shorter and the forces wintering in place more likely. If he meant to avert that, he found no alternative to being in top form before attempting the insane.

He had gathered all he needed to prepare; he had slain brutes, disrupted foraging, and killed a goblin beast within sight of the town's walls. It would irritate the horde's master but was not singular enough to infuriate it. For that, he would have to cap a summer of insults and injuries with a display of temerity at the town's western wall.

He meant to use one of the goblins' poles to demonstrate he had so little regard for the warlord and its horde that he would draw a line in the dirt within sight of them. It was a line he counted on that warlord to cross. When it did, the best case was that he and Howe would flee a vast host of angry goblins on horseback. The worst case was that enough goblins remained outside the walls to surround them and end this gambit, along with both of their lives.

It was nothing resembling sensible, but he saw no alternative to this he would accept. If he did something, failure was possible. If he did nothing, failure was certain.

The Knight Superior still massed troops and nothing close to a sufficient number of them would arrive to begin an offense before winter. Absent Pencheval's success, Rennoute's campaign of years would commence in the spring after the horde wintered in place. Whether the goblins meant to keep the humans of the town prisoners or not, a ravenous horde would have access to a meat source they would happily consume in an otherwise lean season. There would be no humans at all to save should that occur.

With Cecelia, he could do nothing. Had he the power of a journeyman adept then, the Hope of Terris Lyn and his henchmen would have been dead before their mischief began. He would have taken the rogue's head to the baron's bountymaster, made himself wealthy with the baron's gold, then departed that miserable place with his fiancée and father in tow.

He had that power now. He was not yet a champion or master, but his might was considerable regardless. He did not even consider fleeing or doing naught. He had been forced to do nothing by a knife wound once when he and his were threatened, and inaction did not suit him any longer.

"When I am healed, I will deliver my last affront to the warlord of this horde. It might be best if–"

"You're still mental, Lion. First you're daft enough to think of this plan, and then you're daft enough to think I won't see it through with you." Howe took a flask from under his cloak and drank a long swig from it. When he was done, he visibly gritted his teeth. "It may take more whisky, but I'm in this to the end."

"In that case, we will need another pole made with the trophies we've collected. Something large enough to be seen from a distance. We must insult their warlord far enough from the walls to flee when it reacts."

"I'll attend to it." Howe took another drink from his flask. "Mock the horde's warlord at the town's walls? Why not? It's been a strange summer. May as well end on a mad note, too."

***

Nan dabbed the sweat from the forehead of her fevered patient and despaired at the task before her. Between the meager food, the endless strain, and the close quarters, too many were ill. Coughs and groans accompanied the general distress as the months of captivity took their toll on everyone's health. At least the goblins were merely callous to the suffering they created and did not interfere.

Half a fortnight had passed since the odd incident with the goblins peering through the windows. Since then, they had been less stern than nervous. Guards kept their distance from the humans, and those that could perched well away from them on the various fixtures about the nave. The four the Beastwarper Chieftain kept on her were not happy about their task and shuffled nervously. Every night for the past few days, a half a dozen of their kin would fall asleep, never to awake again.

This morning had been the first time the goblins had not robbed their fallen of possessions. They tossed them out through the double doors intact, chittering in near panic at those outside. It all suggested they thought they were afflicted by a plague. Their reaction was as she hoped.

For days she had cursed those that slept to never wake as they herded her and the townsfolk to the catacombs every night. She knew the goblins would not run from her or fear her. She was an old woman in sister's robes and nothing like, say, a Silver Lion. But the power the Lord on High granted her was easily mistaken for disease, particularly since the townsfolk periodically fell ill.

The fact they remained meant they still feared their master more than the thought of plague. It tested her patience now that she had the power to return the torments she and the others had endured. The thought of striking one down blatantly crossed her mind, tempted her, and fell silent as she repressed it once again. That way would end in her death and correct the mistaken assumptions of the goblins.

She resolved to continue as she was. The mere work of days brought them to this. If she but persisted, they would eventually believe the plague had come for them. Humans would flee plague and descend into irrationality when afflicted by it. What would the goblins do when they finally feared it more than their warlord?

She hoped it was enough to save the town.

***

The Shadowcreed Chieftain kept track of what was needful to know, and heard a new word whispered in the corners with dread. Plague. It was but a rumor yet, and he had certainly seen no signs of mass illness. Humans fell ill, but they tended to be less hardy about such things as diseases. That was not the horde's concern.

A goblin plague was another matter entirely. This one was rumored to cause sleep. One goblin in the human great cave had suddenly grown tired and fell to its death from a perch. For days afterwards, a few of the goblins that went to sleep in the great cave each night never woke again. It threatened desertion and trouble.

Perhaps it was the shaman? He had sent the Shadows to inquire, but none of the goblins noticed the human using shaman tricks. There were no bursts of light and sound as that one had used on Penn Cheval, no dancing about with staves, and no entreaties to its gods as loud as its voice would carry. If the Beastwarper's human had anything to do with the endless sleep, it made no sign of it.

Perhaps their god had seen fit to intervene on their behalf. If that was the case, a hasty exit was in order. He would rather cross the Stonemaster than a god, but first he would confirm the presence of that god beyond doubt. So long as this new sleeping plague was nothing more than a rumor, it was not cause enough to desert.

Nine new clans had joined them thus far this summer, and the horde was now stronger than it was when it began. Since the Stonemaster forcefully demonstrated who was master in the coup attempt a few days ago, there had been no more challenges to his authority. Food was still available and Penn Cheval had not reappeared since its attack on the Bonestrippers. A handful of goblins worried about plague did not outweigh these yet.

Still, it was always good to know about the possibility of trouble. Plagues were something they should outrun. No one had ever hidden from such a thing.

***

"What is the meaning of this?"

The Stonemaster's inquiry brought an immediate halt to the argument outside the great cave. Goblins gathered around the entrance stopped screaming at those within. A pile of goblin corpses lay just outside the wood wall, and no one was eager to touch them. In fact, those within the great cave seemed near panic.

"Chief of Chieftains, it is a plague!" The nearest rabble to him bowed and avoided looking him in the eyes. "The bodies bear the disease. They sleep, and never wake!"

So the rumors of panic over a sleeping plague were true. Did it actually exist? No. One of the humans was poisoning food while the guards slept or the last human shaman cursed them. Since goblins were far more wary of treachery than the humans, his guess was that the shaman had tricks it had not mentioned to anyone. Poisoners were easy to catch.

"Do the humans get the plague?"

"No, Chief of Chieftains."

"Then force two of the stronger looking ones to move the bodies, idiot. Do it now!"

"Yes, Chief of Chieftains!" The rabble scrambled to obey and the frustrated warlord sighed. Did he have to solve everything? If the vast bulk of his horde was rabble, apparently so. They would believe any superstitious blather over more likely possibilities. He strode towards the door and the crowd parted before him.

"Chief of Chieftains! We cannot remain in the great cave! The plague kills us in our sleep!"

"Are any ill before they sleep?"

"They don't seem so, Chief of Chieftains, but–"

"Don't sleep in the great cave then. Only the guards watching the humans remain. The others may sleep elsewhere."

"Thank you, Chief of Chieftains!" The goblins at the door spread the news. Some goblins within cheered and those he could see through the door showed great relief.

The Stonemaster shook his head and departed, annoyed with the rabble. At least this issue had been mitigated, and a few days were all he needed to test his suspicions. If the goblins stopped falling, it was because the one that targeted them no longer had safe choices to kill. The enforcer he left on the perch had been the only waking goblin to get this 'sleeping plague' since it began. If what he believed was true, that was because the human inflicting this particular curse chose a safer way to use it.

Seven days this continued. In a few more, if the manner of this 'plague' changed, the shaman would reveal itself to be the problem and die for it. It had already been a thorn in his side since it had told Beastwarper about the books. Being the only other possible cause of this would make it far more trouble than it was worth.

***

Pencheval woke to the staccato chirps of a bird on a nearby branch.

It was the first time he enjoyed or even noticed such a sound since he arrived. It was a small thing, but comforting in the face of what he intended to do next. He rose from his bedroll and the pain in his ribs that was once all too present was little more than stiffness.

He stood and stretched, turning from side to side. The motions confirmed he was limber and caused him no anguish. He felt hale enough to fight again after a fortnight of lingering agony and long watches.

Howe sat next to the ring of stones containing the ashes of their last campfire. He seemed to stare off at some great point in the distance as he ate and washed it down with the contents of a waterskin.

"Howe?"

"Care for breakfast?" Pencheval saw the strain on his face. "Our last meal consists of jerky, cheese, and water."

"You can still go, Howe. I will not hold it against you if you leave me to this gamble alone. 'Twas my plan after all."

"I agreed to join you, and the knights don't much care for cowardice. I'm as committed to this as you now."

"We will prevail."

"Your words to the Lord on High's ears, Lion." Howe corked his waterskin and dug a flask out from under his cloak. "We'll know in half a day's travel. Some of it will be in the open along the road to town."

Pencheval sat on a log near the ashes and dug out a handful of jerky. It wasn't much like a last meal to him. He believed he would know for certain if it was one by the afternoon.

***

"Speak."

"Great Chief of Chieftains, since you allowed us to rest outside the great cave, no one else fell to the sleeping plague."

The rabble seemed elated and in awe of him. As well he should, the warlord mused. He was as far above them as goblins were above beetles. Yet basking in his worship had not been the point of bringing him before the council.

The Beastwarper and Shadowcreed Chieftains seemed perplexed, but Bloodmoon only yawned from boredom.

"No other signs of illness?"

"Only among the humans, Chief of Chieftains."

"That is all I wished to know. I will come to the great cave soon. Make sure the human shaman does not go to the caves below it."

"As you say, Chief of Chieftains."

"You may return there now."

The rabble guard departed backwards, bowing every few steps. The Stonemaster suppressed a smile. At least that one knew respect.

His council would be another matter, but that rabble still knew his place.

"You have determined something about this plague, Chief of Chieftains?" Shadowcreed seemed genuinely curious.

"It is a curse that is the work of the shaman. I will kill it shortly."

"Chief of Chieftains–"

"You have had enough time with that human, Beastwarper!" The Stonemaster inadvertently willed rage into his staff. An unfocused tremor shook the stone floor and walls of the council room in the tall cave. It surprised him and everyone assembled but the Bloodmoon Chieftain, who only reacted with a bass chuckle and a respectful nod. "It successfully tricked an entire cave full of rabble into believing a plague had come. That is a measure of cunning and power worthy of the Fiend! If it had succeeded it would have split the horde!"

"Its death is not required, Chief of Chieftains. Reveal your knowledge of this to it and kill several of its humans in retaliation. Threaten it with more if such curses come again. You can enforce your will and still keep the only human here that can read."

Shadowcreed glanced upwards at the ceiling in thought and finally shook his head. "No. The human can fake a plague. If it lives, it may find other trouble to cause. One of us could be the next to never wake."

"You have learned all of books from it you..."

He heard the change in the horde's chatter first. No words were discernable from the hole in the wall, but the undercurrent of shock and panic signaled something amiss. The other chieftains noticed it as well, and Shadowcreed whispered something to the rabble it used as a messenger.

"Yes," the Stonemaster interjected sourly, "find out what is happening and be swift about it."

Before the rabble could depart, a wheezing messenger scrambled into the council room.

"Chief of Chieftains, the Gray Lion Clan warrior..." It leaned on its knees and huffed.

"What about it? Speak!"

"It is here. At the western cliff-wall. With a kill pole!"

"How many of the Snow Clan are with it?" And how did a horde of humans go unnoticed by the scouts? He would roast them alive for this incompetence!

"Only one. What does it mean?"

"What?" The Stonemaster could not believe its temerity. Penn Cheval had wreaked havoc escaping the town during the invasion, but it was still forced to flee. What did it think had changed since the horde battered it to within an inch of its life? Who did it think it insulted?

"It has come to die is what it means," Bloodmoon rumbled, and departed the chambers without leave.

The Stonemaster's eyes narrowed but he did nothing. Now was not the time to cross another council chieftain, particularly that of the Bloodmoon. If he meant to send his Berserkers after Penn Cheval, he could very well do so.

No one else was eager to battle it any more.

***

Pencheval stood within a hundred paces of the western gate of Tarsun's Market and took stock of the town. Three months in goblin clutches had led it to ruin. Rutted trails wove in all directions through the fields. The endless traffic of goblins up and down the walls left broken stones and chipped mortar. The whole seemed like a web of desolation woven by some gigantic spider.

He held the pole Howe had lashed together for him in his left hand and displayed it to the assembled. The one long horn he took from the goblin's beast was the crossbar, and from it dangled the necklaces and weapons of the brutes. A drooping leather thong of desiccated goblin fingers hung behind them, and the whole was taller than him by two heads. He hoped it was enough to make his meaning plain.

The endless screech and click of the goblin horde overpowered all other noise from within the town. He could not determine what the ever-growing number of goblins along the walls said, but they had taken notice of him. He was encouraged by the fact none of them moved against him, or even so much as sounded a general alarm.

"Howe?"

"No need to worry yourself, Lion," Howe stammered. "If trouble's coming, you'll be the first to know." The scout's voice strained so badly it cracked. Pencheval questioned his own sanity but refused to flee his last real chance to save Nan.

Yet none of the goblins reacted but to gawk. The beasts he knew patrolled the walls did not attack. He warned them away, and they took him at his word when he suggested death would befall those who did not heed him. Had he really shaken the horde this much? What happened next was anyone's guess, but their warlord bore this insult every moment he stood here.

***

"One human. With a kill pole. Why is it not dead or dying?" The Stonemaster grumbled the question to no one in particular.

The rabble crowded the western cliff-wall, and they did not even throw taunts and curses at it. They just stood there and pointed. Did his enforcers lack any initiative? Did Bonestrippers not patrol the walls?

Did he have to do everything himself? Did he *want* to do everything himself? The Stonemaster's own trepidation disgusted him. Penn Cheval was but one human, and even he feared it?

No. He would not fear it. He would take charge and show it once and for all why he was a Chief of Chieftains, and it would soon be tortured to death. Without another word, he hurried towards the western cliff-wall with his staff wearing a scowl. This Penn Cheval's arrogance would cost it dearly.

***

The Bloodmoon Chieftain strode towards his warriors at their sparring place in disgust. He had departed the council because he refused to submit to the Stonemaster any longer. That a human, even one as mighty as Penn Cheval, dared approach a horde in their captured stronghold with a kill pole? He had quartered enemies alive for half of such an affront.

The fact the human would even think to insult the horde like this meant the Stonemaster's reign should come to an end. A warlord with a horde should command fear and despair. Such defiance meant the current Chief of Chieftains could not do that properly, and now was the time to usurp him.

But how to go about it? Killing the warlord immediately would do no good. The Bloodmoon Chieftain was mighty, but not yet impressive enough to tell a horde that he would make a better Chief of Chieftains than the Stonemaster. That would take a display unmatched by any of them, and the opportunity for that stood not far from the western cliff-wall.

Yes, the death of Penn Cheval would do nicely. If it meant to draw a line in the dirt, he would happily cross it before impaling it on its own kill pole and displaying it as the horde's favorite decoration. Penn Cheval had been tough to slay until now, but it would not stand against the most powerful thing the Bloodmoon Clan brought with them.

"My chieftain." A half a dozen Berserkers rose to meet him. Excellent. They would make appropriate war chieftains when this was done. In a horde this size, some few of the rabble might even learn enough of war and glory to become Berserkers themselves. It could happen under the right leadership. *His* leadership.

"A singular moment of glory has befallen us today, my warriors."

"We have heard the talk, my chieftain. Which of us will have the glory of defeating Penn Cheval?" The assembled awaited an answer eagerly. One licked his lips in anticipation and others grasped and clenched weapons.

"I will," he replied. "Bring me Rage. The Silver Lion Clan warrior has earned the kind of death it will inflict."

"Yes, my chieftain." They tried to suppress their shock, but it showed regardless.

At least they obeyed, which was more than could be said for the Stonemaster's powers of command. Pathetic, but of little consequence. He would take care of both matters today, and smiled at the thought of bearing his clan's greatest weapon. It was a thing to impress a horde into obedience, slay its worst enemy, and kill a weakling he had once thought to be a Chief of Chieftains.

***

Pencheval did not know if he should be flattered or frustrated by the goblin reaction to his presence. Did they mass on the wall or merely speculate on his reasons for confronting them this way? So far, whatever it was did not involve an attack.

He felt something like pride before reminding himself of why he was here. He meant to affront this horde's warlord with this display and it was not yet present. Sooner or later it would react, preferably to the point of attacking on a field that favored the temple, but only if it bore witness before something else reacted in its place.

Would something else react? Their master was not here and they did nothing. Did that mean the warlord lacked enough control over the horde to order an attack on the Shield of Athesiene? If that was out of the question, could he at least manage this force's dissolution? Failure now would mean the only hope of Nan's rescue was out of reach.

Pencheval noticed a disturbance in the goblins to the left of the gatehouse. He could not tell exactly what caused the others to cringe and move, but he noticed the glint of silver on its chest and that the staff it bore was half again as tall as it was. It was the warlord, berating the goblins around it, and growing angrier every moment they did not move. Despite its wrath, the multitude still chose not to attack.

Its grip was tenuous then. Pencheval chuckled. He knew he had wreaked havoc among the goblins but not this much. He willed power into his voice and gave the Lion's Roar. The leonine and magically amplified battle cry echoed from the stones over the horde's chatter, and they cringed from it.

Something from behind the horde answered with a roar of its own. It sounded as though one of the goblin beasts ran loose, and a number of goblins on the opposite side of the gatehouse scattered at something's approach. He saw a head emerge from the throngs; then shoulders, a chest and the glint of metal.

A gigantic brute of a goblin in a bearskin cloak waded through the assembled, slapping those too slow for its liking out of its path. Something reddish coated its skin. It wore a primitive necklace of bones, feathers, and something that glinted like uncut gems. When it reached the battlements, it put one hand on the stones and vaulted them.

As he watched, incredulous, the warrior goblin dropped the height of three stories and landed with no more difficulty than if it had merely jumped a small stream. It stood, pushed its cloak away from its weapon arm, and hefted an axe of some sort over its shoulder.

It was far too fine to be goblin made and seemed almost diminutive in its grip despite being as long as a footman's mace. A thick square hammer counterbalanced the blade on the opposite face, and deep shadows darkened the metalwork like an antique. The whole of it seemed forged from aged brass, but despite seeming ancient, the metal showed no signs of wear.

The weapon hummed and buzzed violently at irregular intervals. Every time it did, it made a sound like a snarling animal. Its owner listened to its fury intently and smiled as though enjoying it. After a few moments of indulgence, it grasped the thing with both hands and advanced on him.

Pencheval left his pole planted in the dirt and stepped forward into guard. Whatever it was and whatever it wielded, he could not run now, or this display was for naught. Either he defeated this champion of the horde, or his affront would amount to little more than laughingstock.

***

So this was Penn Cheval.

The Bloodmoon Chieftain once again regretted that this human had not been born to his clan. To create a kill pole and dare an entire horde to war? This was the stuff of a true Berserker. If it meant to impress its gods, it was doing well. If he had done this to a human horde, the Fiend would have made him a war chieftain in the afterlife.

It was almost as tall as he was and powerfully built. Its weapon and chain skin were in good repair, but the clan shirt that so many of the rabble had described before was only barely recognizable. It had taken some pains to repair it, or more likely made one of the Snow Clan rabble do it. The torn and frayed gray mountain lion suffered the toll of battles, but still rampaged proudly on its chest.

Some of its old armor was no more. It had replaced it with pieces of great bat-lizard hide. Had the Snow Clan Chieftain rewarded it with that? For slaying so many of its enemies, why would it not? It seemed strong and spoke of great deeds. Perhaps the Bloodmoon Clan should start wearing it, too. There was no such thing as seeming too fearsome.

The human warrior drove the end of its kill pole into the ground and took up its shiny big knife with both hands. Yes, it was strong. It did not hold its weapon tentatively, but it did not approach. Bloodmoon refused to mistake that for weakness. This one had slain Bonestrippers, Berserkers, and multitudes of the rabble. It awaited him only because it wished to fight where it stood.

He heard Rage snarl in his grip and nodded in agreement. Yes, it was time to stop admiring the human and strike it dead. The axe was ever impatient for blood when he removed it from its hides. Whatever spirit of battle had taken up residence in this weapon had that in common with the Bloodmoon. Perhaps that was why the Fiend saw fit to bring it into their keeping.

This human gave him an excuse to hear the axe snarl again. So few earned the right to die by it, and fortunately for him, Penn Cheval would not slay itself. He smiled at his impending glory. A horde of his own and a new weapon for his clan were only one battle away.

***

"Saint Marion's revelation, did that thing's father bed a troll?"

Pencheval gritted his teeth at Howe's curse but did not dare to take his eyes off of the approaching brute. He had fought a goblin like it twice before, but they seemed scrawny by comparison; *he* was scrawny by comparison. Worse still, when its weapon snarled and screeched, it smiled at its wrath and advanced.

So not only was this giant unafraid of him, it was perfectly happy to wield an ancient, and potentially unstable, magical weapon. For the first time in a long while, the Lion felt a sensation that bordered on panic. His opponent had started this fight by leaping from a height of three stories, was borderline mental, and wielded something that threatened to shatter explosively with every motion. Even the goblins' beasts, as fell as they were, scared him less than the total disregard this brute had for its own life.

Should he flee? No, though the butterflies in his stomach lessened when he thought of it. He had fought all summer to get this chance. If he fled, nothing would come of it, and Nan would be goblin rations by spring. The warlord could claim victory over him through the actions of its champion and he could spend the rest of his life knowing he might have saved Nan had he chosen courage over fear. He gritted his teeth and refused to flee.

He let it come to him, remembering that the warlord standing on the battlements had power over the stone. It had used that power in the battle to take Tarsun's Market. If it could use it against him at this range, it would have done so by now. He found no need to get closer either to the walls or the brute when he well knew he was beyond the warlord's grasp right where he stood.

The brute let one hand fall from its grip on the haft and held the axe at its side when it was within ten paces. When it was within five, it appraised him, smiled, and spread its arms in welcome.

"Penn Cheval!"

Pencheval started in shock. How did it know his name? And why did it greet him? In the time it took him to recover from his surprise and confusion, it covered the distance between them and slammed a kick straight into his guts.

It felt like a blow from a battering ram. He barely retained a grip on his sword as he hit the ground and skidded to a stop. The blow left him unable to breathe easily, and he willed his magic to dull the pain and restore him.

The sound of cheers and screams from the battlements rose and crashed upon him like a great wave. He sat up in time to see the brute pull his pole from the ground, look him in the eyes, and tap the axe blade against the shaft. The gentlest touch sheared cleanly through the sapling-thick post, dropping fist-sized chunks of wood to the ground one after another.

When it reached the crossbar, it dropped the trophies and made a show of grinding them into the dirt with its foot. Pencheval winced and staggered to his feet. He had dared the goblins to act against him, and of course this monster had to be the one to accept the challenge.

***

The Stonemaster watched the scene between the Silver Lion Clan warrior and Bloodmoon unfold. What Bloodmoon intended was obvious. He would have offered to kill Penn Cheval and asked permission were he not preparing to replace him. First, impress the horde by leaping from the battlements and killing their greatest fear; then, declare himself Chief of Chieftains after doing what no one else could.

The goblins all around him on the western cliff-wall cheered and made no secret of their enthusiasm as the brute sliced Penn Cheval's kill pole to pieces. They quit minding him at all. There was an excellent chance that this meant their loyalties were in flux, which was ever the goblin way. They would unite behind anyone who showed them better odds and discard their old chieftain if the offer was sufficiently persuasive. The death of the Silver Lion Clan warrior would be very persuasive.

All he could do now was hope Penn Cheval defeated Bloodmoon, which was a sentiment he kept to himself. A mob awaited him if he voiced it. He kept his face blank and his eyes on the spectacle.

He also remained wary of knives in the crowd. If the human did win and escape after so blatantly threatening him before his own horde, he would appear as weak as any other fallen Chief of Chieftains.

Loyalists and rebels would rise in the ensuing chaos. Retaining his life and his horde after that would become tenuous.

Tenuous, but given his singular greatness, realistically possible. Thus, it was still a better outcome than Bloodmoon prevailing in this fight. Should that gigantic warrior win, every goblin in the horde would find him preferable to its current leader. He weighed plans for escape and contingencies should that occur. Yes, it meant he would lose his horde, but tomorrow would be another day.

If he lived to see it.

***

The Bloodmoon Chieftain didn't remember humans being that springy.

He did not show his surprise at its resiliency as he tore down the human's kill pole and ground it under his heel as it watched. Showing anything but complete dominance would have made a poor display for the horde, and they were watching. No goblin here was indifferent to the fate of this human, known amongst them as the Gray Lion Clan warrior, the Demonbearer, or any number of epithets among those it had thwarted. This battle was the center of all attention, and he could not even hint that he might be wanting.

Yet that kick should have crushed its guts and possibly broken its back. It had done that to humans he faced in the past. One blow, and the rabble collected the human's treasures for him and dragged its body to the butchers. It should not have lived, much less retained its weapon and risen from the ground. How could it do this?

It was a shame he could not wrest the secret of its might from it. He already knew it had its own shaman tricks. One of them let it repel blows, at least to some degree. Perhaps it was the bat-lizard hide it wore.

No matter. Nothing yet had survived the wrath of Rage, and it snarled as he pumped it over his head with both hands in triumph. He heard the roar and screech of the horde and smiled. First the human, then the Stonemaster, and he would have a horde of his own – exactly as a Bloodmoon Chieftain should.

***

Pencheval was grateful that the brute was too busy preening for the goblin horde to rush into a finisher even though it made no sense to him. When it was time to fight, you fought, and celebrated after if such was your wont. Your opponent was beaten when he was in irons, unconscious, or dead; whichever your goal dictated.

Still, if it wanted to play to the crowd, that suited him just fine. He would put the time to good use recovering. His guts felt as if they might collapse, but despite the ache he could still rise and lift his sword. The stout drake scales he wore served their purpose and saved him from that thing's trick.

It had used his name to surprise him, and he let it. He gritted his teeth and refocused himself on the fight. If this thing surprised him one more time, it would slay him with that horrifically sharp axe. So how it knew what it did was not something he would consider until it died. Swing sword now, ask questions later.

Wincing, he put his sword back into guard, and considered spells as the brute twirled its axe and hammer combination. The Cudgel spell was all he could think to use. It removed all sharpness from his blade, but focused the force of the blow into something that would knock a normal man on his back. That was useful when subdual was the goal. In a pinch, it was also good for making it hard to retain weapons, such as the unstable, snarling thing the warrior held before him.

Seemingly happy that its display had satisfied the horde, the gigantic goblin grasped his weapon with both hands and charged. Pencheval willed himself speed in time to get out of the way. The axe descended with a roar, and seemed to snarl as it rose to parry the slash he meant to be the counterattack. His perception of time returned to normal as the towering goblin pushed him away. The aching Lion took the opportunity to second guess his tactics and resumed guard. To his chagrin, this brute could maintain the pace even when he used magic to defeat it.

The giant resumed its offensive, and Pencheval sought in vain for an advantage against the hail of blows. The axe audibly cut air as he dodged but his opponent never overextended or lost its balance. By goblin standards, it was the most skilled and astute warrior he had yet faced. It made no mistakes caused by anger or frustration, displayed next to no warning when it launched a strike, and gave no sign that it grew weary.

When one blow became a feint in an attempt to defeat his dodge, Pencheval was forced to parry, and willed the Cudgel spell into his blade on contact. The combined power of the spell and strike staggered him backwards. The snarling axe and hammer shrieked and squealed at an ear-splitting pitch that suggested it was going to explode. Gritting its teeth in pain, the goblin brute staggered and shook the shock out of its hands one after the other.

Pencheval's eyes narrowed. The spell had its intended effect. This goblin champion may be mighty, but how much could its hands and wrists take? The first spell might not render them feeble alone, but the fifth? The tenth? It was a plan against a foe that left his nerves more on edge than any other, including the warlord's stone construct. He could disarm and kill it so long as he made no more mistakes.

Best not to err again then.

***

Bloodmoon felt the ache fade from his fingers and gritted his teeth. He knew this Penn Cheval had a few shaman tricks. He did not know about that one. Perhaps there was a demon in its shiny big knife as there was a spirit of war in his axe. Perhaps the gifts it bestowed upon that knife always changed. Perhaps the human was a full-fledged shaman and a warrior, which was a dire thought, and it made the knife do what it needed.

The human had either dodged or parried. It only parried if it thought the blow was sufficiently weak, and then it would use the strange shaman trick that made Rage scream and his hands hurt. Would that happen enough to make him drop the axe? Not if he disarmed the human first.

If there was no shiny big knife between Rage and the human, nothing would save it from the carnage he meant to inflict upon it. Rage was sharp enough that it would cut through the human's great bat-lizard hide and its shiny chain skin. He smiled at the thought of severed limbs and standing over its corpse. The horde could see his display of superiority and perhaps the Stonemaster would be dead before he returned to town. The only question now was how to go about it.

***

Pencheval had enough of playing defense, and stepped forward to strike. The brute dodged the thrust with surprising speed and circled, smiling at the attack. Like the goblin brutes he had fought in the town and the forest camp, it was eager for a fight. Unlike those warriors, it was far more capable of winning one.

It counterattacked with two powerful blows. Pencheval dodged a chop he could not deflect and stepped backwards as the snarling weapon cleaved only air where his chest was a moment before. Then his opponent shifted its footing, changed its grip, and slid forward.

The pommel strike was too obvious, the Lion thought, and moved to counterattack. Yet the blow never happened. Instead, the thing suddenly shifted and grabbed his sword wrist in a steel grip. It twisted his weapon out of the way and slammed a knee just under Pencheval's chest. He doubled over, gasping for air, and heard a growl as something else struck him. The force sent him spinning from the ground.

Pencheval choked and wheezed as he breathed. The sky and ground tumbled into a mad swirl before he struck the earth. In one incongruous moment of lucidity, the Silver Lion realized why the pommel strike had seemed so obvious: that had been the idea.

***

Now this was a kill for the boasting.

The Bloodmoon Chieftain pumped his axe over his head and roared. He heard the horde cheer and the screech was intoxicating. This was how such a force was won and kept. Not with the fancy staff the Stonemaster believed he had successfully kept secret from him, and not by claiming you were Blessed by the Fiend. You built a tale of deeds no other goblin could match and they would follow you. This deed ended with him becoming a Chief of Chieftains, Wielder of Rage, and the Lionslayer!

He was almost sad the battle had to end. It had been skilled, but not skilled enough to see the feint. Then again, no one else ever expected someone so large to be skilled in reversals and trickery. He did not know why. The Fiend Under The Mountain gifted goblins with cunning and this was well known. He was no exception and never had been.

Yet was it defeated? Penn Cheval's breath rasped and it barely moved, but it did still move. He had robbed it of much breath, but thought he would have taken it all by now. That blow would have killed any other human outright, but it did not surprise him that Penn Cheval had survived it.

He smiled when he saw the prostrate human groan, spit out a mouthful of blood, and rise to its hand and knees. Where would he find an enemy like this again? Perhaps it might recover enough to resume the battle.

Tempting as he found that thought, he found it far less desirable than seizing power over the horde and glory for himself. No, he resolved the human would not rise this time, and stepped into an overhand chop that would end it for good.

***

"Get up, Lion!"

Pencheval thought it might have been Cecelia's voice. It was distant and muted as though hearing it through a pillow and he could not tell the gender. Was Cecelia here? No, that was pain in his chest and cold steel pressing against his face. He was still alive, and someone admonished him to rise.

Someone had hit him hard. What was it? Not the voice. It was the large goblin. It could hurt him with blows from bare limbs even through his armor. That knee had doubled him over despite the strong drakescale he wore and set him up for a killing stroke. The blow would have been sufficient to the task had he worn nothing but his old brigandine.

Barely able to breathe and unaware of his surroundings, he willed his magic to restore him. He had used it on his ribs before, but slowly. Doing so in haste, and using enough to salve all of this, was a desperate move. It would leave him wishing he was dead for days afterward, but was preferable to actually being dead. If the large goblin was still here, and there was no reason to believe it would flee if it had him like this, he needed to move now.

He felt warmth spread through his torso and the disquieting sensation of organs and bones shifting as the spell restored him. Darkness and stupor gave way to the realization he was face down on the ground. Some parts of his body were numb, but his head felt as though it was made of fibers slowly pulling apart. Not quite back to normal, but more than enough to put him back in the fight.

What was the goblin doing? He did not mean to wait for what was most likely a killing blow. He spit warm liquid out of his mouth, and realized it was blood as his sense of taste returned. Groaning, he rose to his hands and knees and heard the rush of feet towards him. The footsteps landed too heavily to be Howe's.

He reached down, pulled forth what magic he could, and willed himself speed. He looked up in time to see the brutish goblin above him raise an axe over its head. Wasting no more time on thought, he reached to the small of his back, snatched his dagger, and drove it through the side of the goblin's left knee.

The descending stroke halted as the brute staggered in slow motion, wearing a look of pain. His perception accelerated as the momentary burst of speed ended, and the roaring goblin grabbed its knee and hopped backwards. It limped away from him as he stumbled to his feet.

He had something else. Did he have something else? Yes, a sword. He searched and found the glint of silvery Argentsteel behind his agonized opponent. The blasted goblin either had the foresight to put itself between him and his weapon, or his luck was about the same it ever was.

The wounded Lion grumbled. Nothing for it then but to go through the blighter to get it. It certainly wasn't going to oblige him and return his dagger.

***

"Dung stain! May the Fiend chew your guts for all time!"

What was this Fiend-forsaken human? He had it defeated and it still counterattacked. Not just a counterattack, but a counterattack that may have crippled him. Pain shot through the angry chieftain's leg from the slightest motion, but he could not reach down to remove the cause. That would mean taking his eyes off of the now standing Penn Cheval, which seemed to have found something else it wanted behind him.

He did not need to turn to know what it was. It was the human's shiny big knife. If it no longer had its dagger and its shiny big knife was gone, it was unarmed. Under any other circumstances, he would chop and tear this human to pieces. With a knife through the knee, that wasn't going to happen just yet.

His weapon growled, and he smiled despite the pain. Yes, he still had Rage, and it still hungered. Let the human try to get to its shiny big knife. If it came to him, it would save him the newfound agony of going over to the impossibly fell warrior to kill it.

***

Pencheval took stock of the grimacing and enraged brute heavily favoring its left leg. The dagger bought him his life and some time, but not victory. He still had to defeat this thing, and now he had to do it unarmed. He snorted at the thought that using his fists against this monster was only the second worst idea he had today.

It was either that or keep hoping the goblins on the wall stayed there as his magic returned. He felt the first hints of a chill unrelated to the summer's day, a sign he had drained most of his reserves. Perhaps a few bursts of strength and speed remained until his powers were exhausted for a time, but little else.

No time for prudence then. The Lion stepped forward as though to punch. When the brute raised its axe to make him pay for the mistake, he threw a handful of dirt into its eyes. The grit struck and made it squint, but it attacked regardless with a wild swing. Pencheval dodged the snarling axe before counterattacking with a punch to the ribs.

It felt like striking a boulder and did not draw even a wince from his opponent. The madly swung axe growled as he dodged again and punched its gut. He shook his sore hand as the blow again did nothing. He felt his options slip away as the beast cleared its eyes of dirt, gritted its teeth, and raised an overhand chop to end him.

Pencheval willed all his remaining magic to grant him speed and forfeited all defense to strike first. The swift punch struck the goblin's throat and this time he felt its flesh give. The brute staggered, choked, and stumbled on its bad knee.

"And now you're mine!" Pencheval took hold of the axe haft with both hands and wrenched it repeatedly. Even as it choked, his opponent refused to relinquish its weapon until the struggle broke its wrist.

He felt the axe vibrate in his hands. Unwilling to hold the weapon any longer than necessary, he hefted it over his head and struck. The hammer side pulped its former wielder's skull with a sound like a roar and a wet smack.

The body fell to the ground, and Pencheval realized all he heard was the low and endless hum from the axe. The death of the horde's champion silenced everything on the wall. What had it been that its defeat would cause such shock? Whatever it was, it wouldn't last, and if he was to complete his task haste was in order.

What to do? He had already stolen their champion's weapon and killed it. With the intent to add insult to injury, he stripped the bear-skin cloak from his opponent and wrapped the axe in it. He could feel the hum calm to nothing inside the matted fur, and he tucked the new-found prize under his arm as he retrieved his dagger and sword.

A few shocked murmurs, but nothing changed. It was not enough of a push. What else could he do that they would understand? He only knew of one other thing.

He inhaled deeply and roared wicked, mocking laughter at the assembled. The slight bit of magic remaining at his disposal sent it echoing from the walls, and with that the horde went mad. Goblins lunged at the warlord, which yelled and rapped its staff to the ground. A moment later, blossoms of stone blades impaled everything within ten paces of it.

The screech and click rose as from the throngs he once heard cheering the words of the king. It started as a dull roar and grew into a sound that drowned out all others. Goblins attacked goblins as the warlord gestured wildly and yelled commands he could not hear. Beasts outside of the walls roared in reaction to the madness.

"Lion, you have done your worst and more. Time to be away!"

Pencheval agreed and reluctantly turned his back on the goblins rebelling against their warlord. He was satisfied with his work but that satisfaction would be fleeting. The price of burning that much magic to regain fighting form would be several days of crippling pain in another of Howe's hidden campsites. It had not hit him yet, but he had an hour at most before that changed. Fortunately, the coming pain was already well justified.

The last of his gambit cost the warlord so much face its horde turned on it. If it lived through this, it knew Pencheval had caused its suffering and where he went. If that was not enough to make it attack the castle, he knew of nothing more he could do.

***

The sudden silence was something Nan thought she would never hear above ground again.

The horde's chatter occasionally changed tenor and energy, but this silence flowed over it like a wave. Goblins heard something from their fellows and gazed in shock towards the west for a reason she did not understand. After listening intently to something she could not hear, the horde screeched and chittered anew.

This time, the sounds seemed confrontational and confused. Goblins in the temple looked at one another, nervously grasped weapons, and gathered into groups. Each group regarded the others suspiciously. Her four guards took notice and surrounded her.

The first dying screams came from outside the doors and confirmed what she suspected. The horde had turned on itself. Groups of guards glanced uncertainly around at each other, hesitated, and finally settled on plans of action.

Several stacked wood and scrap to reinforce the door. Another group massed and fell on an old woman with knives and clubs, beating her to death before ripping into the corpse and eating their fill. Frightened prisoners stumbled away from the scene and cringed.

The remaining goblins chattered with each other before drawing knives and turning their attention to her and the remaining townsfolk. Those at the door joined them, and she realized they were less attempting to protect themselves with a barricade than prevent intrusion while they feasted. One licked its lips, appraising her and her charges as its next meal. Nan rose indignantly and lifted her hands to cast.

One of her guards managed a short chirp of protest before all four of them slouched, as if utterly weary. One made it two steps before it collapsed into sleep, never to wake. She waved one hand in the direction of those feeding on the woman and all of them fell the same way.

"Do not take another step!" Nan motioned in the direction of the mob that formed to feed, and they recoiled briefly. Some backed away and others circled. Goblins chittered, hissed, and cursed at her in their tongue.

"Sister?" Wot gazed up at her from the floor, not understanding the meaning of the gestures.

Nan didn't know what to tell him. Yes, she had been the one to cause the goblin's sleep. That made her an assassin, but what was the alternative but to slowly die to the last of them? He didn't seem able to grasp what it was she had done and could do.

The power remained unabated after the goblins fell. In fact, she felt no limit to her reservoir of it at all. Athesiene wished His faithful rescued, and that was what she meant to do.

"The catacombs. We must get there!" Nan scanned the room nervously and saw far too many hungry fiends for her liking.

"But the goblins down there..."

"Or the horde gone mad here?" The last of the soldiers, an aging sergeant Nan remembered was called Alfried, gestured for the prisoners to gather. "Our chance to escape is upon us and we have naught for a choice but death. To the door!"

"How?"

Nan glanced towards the entrance to the passages below. There were as many goblins between them and it as were in the room before them. They hesitated at her display of power, but they would not merely let them pass

The soldier ripped a plank from an improvised goblin fence and grasped it with both hands. "Through them."

Those that could stand on their own followed his lead. Lean but willing, they pointed clubs, broken rocks, or fists in all directions. Goblins took courage from their numbers, and inched in towards them.

"Stay close!"

"This isn't happening." Wot curled up on the floor and rocked back and forth. "It's not, it's not..."

"Help the–"

Something leapt at Nan, and as a reflex, she willed the burst of sound and light that had stunned attackers so well in the past. Her newfound strength flowed into it, and it stopped the goblin in midair. Yet the merely incapacitating magic was not as it once was.

The thunderclap and blast scorched her leaping assailant to the bone and sent it flying backwards into the crowd. The burst burned the goblins within six paces to char and tore limbs and heads from bodies. A pile of debris amongst them became a storm of burning chunks and massive splinters. It struck near a score of goblins dead and more fell screaming, clutching at stumps or flailing on the floor from burns.

Townsfolk screamed and the statues shook from the force of the spell. The stench of burning flesh and the sounds of goblin agony nearly overwhelmed her. No one here bore love for the goblins, but the destruction provoked nausea and made her head swim. This could not be the purpose the Lord on High had for her, could it?

"Lord on High forgive me," Nan whispered in shock. Killing these creatures in their sleep was far less horrific.

"Lord on High be praised!" Alfried yelled from across the room. "They fear you now, sister. You can clear the way!"

Nan noticed the goblins scramble away from her mere attention. They would move for her and she could use that to free the townsfolk. It was a variation of the fear Pencheval caused and wielded against them, and the thought of doing so as well beggared her capacity for malice.

This could not be, but what was the alternative? She glanced back at where that woman had died, becoming food for the horde. One glance at the mob and a gesture sent a half a dozen more to sleep, and the goblins again ebbed from their path.

"Open the door and let us depart! Aid those who cannot walk!"

"No, no no no..." Wot bolted towards the double doors. "Not with the witch!"

He made it as far as the goblin line before they eagerly fell upon him. Clubs and knives rose and fell with sprays of blood. The sight of goblins carving gobs of meat out of him sent the rest of the townsfolk panicking towards the catacomb door.

"You will cease!"

Another thunderclap startled those fleeing from fright to a halt. The blast ignited all the goblins feasting on Wot and blew another storm of rocks and splinters into those behind them. The shock hit the double wooden doors, cracking them open as it crushed the barricade and heavy wooden bolt sealing them. The right door creaked and then fell from the wall, hinges undone by the burst, and revealed the melee in the square outside.

She saw all the goblins within twenty paces of the outer door stop fighting on the spot. One cocked its head quizzically at the sight of her, then all rushed for the newly blasted opening. They crowded the doorway as others climbed through open windows and crawled towards the floor.

"Go!" She heard the townsfolk scurry towards the catacombs. Shouts and distressed screams accompanied the frenzied departure. The chittering grew louder as the goblins outside scrambled against those within to attack and feed on those that fell. Nan heard screams as more townsfolk died, and she realized in horror that they were eating those trampled from the mass panic.

"Sister, hold them a little longer!" She heard the smack of wood and a goblin screech.

Hold them for what? The selfish townsfolk that trampled the helpless? Animals! How could this madness befall a place renowned for its serenity?

Three goblins that drew too close to her slumped and fell asleep. The rest backed away again in fright. The power had bought more time and still it did not seem enough.

She wondered how Pencheval performed the feats he did. She could hear the pounding of her heart in her ears and feel the butterflies in her stomach. Her arms felt too weak to hold a weapon even if she possessed one.

She backed towards the catacomb entrance with hands raised. Goblins inched forward but did not press. Easily a hundred of them stood at bay only for fear of what she had done, and what she might do. The fear mixed with their hunger and made them like the tides, flowing forward and ebbing as each feeling temporarily gained purchase over the other.

"How long?"

"Almost there!" A screech accompanied another wooden crack and a goblin hit the floor. Nan turned and willed all those near Alfried and the door to sleep. A third of her intended targets slumped and fell, giving the soldier a far wider berth.

"Lord on High bless you, sister!" The soldier gestured wildly at the dozen townsfolk remaining. "Go! Swiftly!"

Nan smiled wanly. He had already blessed her. She would save her charges at last with the power He had granted her, and she hoped with all her heart He would not grant her any more. Her service now felt like a mountain on her shoulders and too much like butchery to bear.

The goblins advanced as she fell back. Hunger and frustration overcame fear as they pressed forward. They meant to prevent the escape of the human meat and to feed upon it all.

Nan gritted her teeth for one last summoning of Athesiene's wrath. The thunder and white hot blast ignited five goblins that edged too close and felled a dozen more with burns so black they did not scream from pain. The spell found no scrap to throw but its power alone smote goblins to the floor and ripped their limbs asunder to twenty paces distance. She fought the urge to vomit from the smell of charred flesh.

"Please be enough. Please be enough..." She shuffled backwards until she felt a hand on her shoulder.

"It is done." The soldier smiled at her. "And I will not leave you behind. Go."

Nan stumbled through the door and shuffled down the stairs, only half aware of Alfried slamming the bolt into place. The sergeant scrambled down behind her and aided her to the bottom.

"Sister, we must block the goblins."

"Block...block the goblins?" Nan nodded slowly. "How?"

"Collapse the stair if you can. We will leave as the Lion did."

"The Lion. Pencheval?"

"Yes, he said he could force passage through a wall, remember? Whatever is there now, the goblins could not have replaced the masonry."

"Yes."

She looked up the stairs and heard goblins scratch and pound at the door. When she heard a plank break, she gestured towards the ceiling above the top landing and willed a burst to strike there. A single white hot blast flashed before the thunder blew out the door and collapsed the ceiling. Rock fell as dust billowed down the stairs. The rumble and musty smell did not seem entirely real to her.

After the collapse, she could not even hear the goblins above her, and only the light of a single torch let her see at all. She saw three other torches in sconces and gestured languidly. They burst into flame as the townsfolk gasped.

She straightened the hood on her head and sat. "I need some time..." Nan shivered from something other than the chill of the caves.

"Rest, sister." The soldier turned to the survivors. "You lot, pass a torch to the rear. We're not waiting here long."

Nan listened half-heartedly as she thought of what to do. The catacombs were not extensive and she heard no goblins chittering from within them now. An hour's travel would see them to the place she believed Pencheval had forced passage. And then? She could save her charges at last.

No. She could save these miserable vermin who had trampled the innocent in their haste to save their own lives. And after all she had done to keep them comforted and healthy, why would Wot call her a witch? She had suffered, endured, and played scribe to a goblin chieftain for this? She had become a slayer for them only to see them laid bare for what they truly were.

Of them all, only she and Alfried had tried to save lives and were not sworn to the darkness like witches or the filthy goblins. He alone proved worth her suffering and deserved her aid for his selflessness. The rest could accompany them only because they were now here.

Whatever else, the Lord on High did not find her wanting. The power she brought to bear did not suit her, but neither did it recede. It was well intact and ready for use again, though the thought of burning goblins and exploding wrath left her ill.

She wondered if she had become like Pencheval. She rose to this occasion, as awkward as her first battle had been, and now did not know her path any longer. She knew it was with the temple, but how would she be a sister like this? Was there no going back?

"Sister, we're ready when you are."

Alfried smiled kindly at her and offered her a hand, and the other townsfolk merely waited. Some were scared of their circumstances and others openly frightened of her. She reached up to the offered assistance and the soldier pulled her to her feet.

"Thank you."

He nodded an acknowledgement. "Time we were away, sister."

"If I never again see a goblin, it will be a blessing from above."

"Truer words were never spoken." Alfried motioned for Nan to lead the way, and she took a torch from him to do so.

***

The Shadowcreed Chieftain started from another blast of lightning and thunder from within the human great cave. The very cliff-walls of that place shivered from them. Yet the fools still rushed within? It did contain much livestock forbidden before the split in the horde, but there were easier ways to eat. Garroting one's enemies for what they possessed, for instance, was safer and had the additional benefit of reducing the number of one's rivals. It was also smarter than crossing a god.

The storm inside the cave could be the work of nothing but a god. It had probably caused the sleeping sickness as well. It had not simply been the human shaman as the Stonemaster claimed. The shaman's god may have made it the instrument, but those goblins died from its wrath alone.

So far that god had not noticed the Shadowcreed, and their chieftain saw no cause to change that. There was too much risk in tempting its wrath and no way to profit by it. He would happily cross the Stonemaster first.

"What do we do, my chieftain?"

The Shadow had not asked in a mocking tone; it genuinely wanted to know his will and was only just restraining fear. He and his companions had chosen to avoid the conflict and serve the clan by coming to him instead. He was grateful for their good sense. This venture had come to an end and word must spread.

"I will tell the Stonemaster we are loyal and mean to aid him. When night falls, steal all you can carry and depart to the meeting place we chose before we joined the horde."

"Yes, my chieftain."

"If you kill for loot, slay only the rebels. You are forbidden to attack those still loyal to the Stonemaster. It will keep our former Chief of Chieftains believing we still aid him. He does not need to know otherwise until we are far out of his grasp."

"As you say, my chieftain."

"I will depart tomorrow morning. Be gone by then or risk facing the Stonemaster's wrath alone. We will wait until the first snows for those in the valley. Ensure they know my will."

"It will be done, my chieftain." The Shadows dropped from the roof of the human cave and he did not hear them land. Excellent. With such stealth, they would have all the human goods they could want back in the mountains where they belonged. The Stonemaster would never be the wiser until it was far too late to stop them.

***

"Stand fast and state your...Lion?"

The wiry watchman calling down from the wooden tower along the road recognized them. Pencheval found that odd only in that his tone was something he rarely heard. Generally, he was addressed in fear or barely disguised contempt. This rang more of respect.

Howe reined his horse to a stop. "Scout Howe and the Silver Lion, Pencheval. We return to the Shield of Athesiene."

The watchman laughed. "Welcome back! It's a right merry bit of work you've done on the goblins."

"Thank you?" Howe scratched his head, but the soldier did not mean to send an alarm or return them in chains. Perhaps something had come of this summer.

"Any word? We've been evading goblins." Pencheval suppressed memories of the last four days. His magic had healed him enough to win, but its price had been so much agony he could barely drink water. This morning had been the first time since the fight with the goblin champion that even trying to stand did not result in spasms and shooting pain.

"As of two days ago, the goblins were still at each other's throats," the watchman replied. "Blighters are doing all the fighting for us. Lord on High willing, the horde might break from the discord!"

Pencheval was perfectly happy with that result. A dispersed horde of goblins cleared the way to Nan without a battle.

"Any news about the townsfolk? I am seeking a sister that was captured in the town."

"Aye. The ones that fled here before the horde struck Tarsun's Market are very happy about it. Beyond that, I know naught of survivors. His lordship might know more about a sister, and you'll get to ask him because he commanded you to report to him when you returned."

"We will be away then." The mercenary had not been able to do more than recover for days and wanted news. He hoped that Nan had not been slain in the chaos.

"Ride slowly. The temple in the capital sent five companies to reinforce us and they don't all know you. On the bright side, you won't have to worry about buying your own stout after the hell you gave those bastards!"

Riding slowly suited Pencheval. It was the first time in a while he had not fled in haste from goblins with forced marches or panicked rides. Now that the pain had left him, he was grateful his latest adventure had not battered him to within an inch of his life. These were rare luxuries in a valley once known for its peace.

He had returned with a victory and the temple seemed happy enough about it. Whether or not he had satisfied Rennoute remained to be seen, and he hoped the watchman's demeanor was indicative of good news. At least he retained the goblin champion's axe. The bearskin cloak bundle that held it remained lashed to a saddlebag, proof he had done much to make good on his affront. All that remained now was Nan.

He did not doubt the worth in attempting that gambit. It was the only way he knew to aid the stubborn sister. Yet if the horde had degenerated into rebellion against their warlord, had the chaos killed her instead?

Pencheval resisted the urge to spur his horse to find the answers. Rennoute would know more and perhaps he would be inclined to tell him of it. He merely had to enter the camp and castle the army's way, which meant doing as they said. His answers would have to wait a while longer.

***

The Stonemaster sat back in his bone throne, suppressed a sigh of relief, and took stock of his circumstances.

Five days of rebellion and madness ended as he predicted. Despite shifting fortunes and a few close calls, his inherent greatness had carried the day. He ruled as Chief of Chieftains once again. The horde cringed at his displeasure and even now scrambled to bury the dead and restore order in the town.

Yet the discord only happened in the first place because of that vile and unfathomably dangerous Silver Lion Clan warrior, Penn Cheval. Not only had it been brazen enough to display a kill pole against his advance and his primacy, but it had then enforced it by striking the Bloodmoon Chieftain dead. To the faces of the entire horde!

To improve on that feat, it stole Bloodmoon's weapon and laughed as it departed. It was symbolic but sufficient. Not only had its display cost him face, but the horde now feared the Silver Lion Clan human more than they did him. He was grateful the rest of its clan was said to be far south of the valley.

What it had inflicted alone was enough. He surveyed his council, and conspicuous by his absence was the Shadowcreed Chieftain. He had come to him at the first of the fighting and sworn he was loyal, and indeed messengers reported Shadows slaying the rebels throughout the first night. By the next morning, he had disappeared along with his entire clan, and they had taken a considerable amount of human weapons and treasures with them.

The Bloodmoon Speaker, as the new member of his council from that clan called himself, had led the Berserkers to his defense. The Speaker made no secret of the reason why. They meant to avenge themselves on Penn Cheval and recover their axe, and they well knew they would need the horde intact to do it. The price of their help was an attack on the mountain-castle, an attack for which the Speaker was openly impatient.

The Allspeaker stood next to his throne with the last remaining human in the town, the one that had submitted to the Stonemaster during his sorting and proven so helpful. It appeared unnerved by all the fighting but its bodyguard kept it well herded. The Stonemaster gave its discomfiture little thought. It should be grateful it chose the winning side in this, or it would be dying from impalement like those fools in the great cave.

Their failure and defiance of his commands called for nothing less. In their haste to feed on the humans, they had allowed many of them to escape on the first day of the revolt. The shaman the Beastwarper Chieftain said he controlled had been anything but contained, and the sound of its wrath thundered above even the horde. It slew dozens in broad daylight and he could do nothing about it.

Beastwarper waited patiently for his word, and the Stonemaster suspected he knew why he had remained. Circumstances strengthened his position considerably. He could not attack the mountain-castle without the warped leader's Bonestrippers, and he no longer had the time to wait due to the Bloodmoon. The clever chieftain knew he could ask what he would for his aid, and that would be knowledge from the human shamans they captured at the mountain-castle.

It was not all a loss. The Bloodmoon Chieftain had only chosen to fight the Silver Lion Clan warrior alone so he could gain enough glory to usurp rule over the horde. The death of that giant had rid him of a deadly rival. The Bloodmoon were brutes, but they were not a clan with which to trifle. He was relieved the rest of the clan was not party to their former leader's machinations.

"When do we move? The horde obeys you again." The Bloodmoon Speaker tensed one fist.

"When we have laid the plans to attack the mountain-castle. It is the largest clan-home of the humans here, and the best defended."

"Those may take time in the absence of the Shadowcreed," Beastwarper offered. "We will be back to using the rabble for scouts."

"Don't give me excuses, sniveling cripple. The humans must bleed."

"If you think the humans require no thought at all, go forth with your clan and use muscle alone." Beastwarper leered at the Bloodmoon Speaker. "Brute force will serve you as well against the stronghold of the Snow Clan as it did against Penn Cheval."

"Still the mockery in your tongue or I will do it for you, dung stain!"

"Enough!" The ground shook as the Stonemaster willed irritation into his staff. The argument ceased and goblins around the council meeting cringed. "Beastwarper is correct. First we plan, then we go. Swarming does not work on the humans as it should when their cliff-walls are in the way."

This was intolerable. He was reduced to using persuasion to quell the infighting of his own council when once they curried his favor. All of his humans had escaped except one. And the horde suffered so many losses from the revolts it all but erased the gains he made from massing clans over the summer.

The Silver Lion Clan warrior had much for which to answer. When the mountain-castle fell, Penn Cheval would know pain. Vast quantities of pain. That reason alone kept him determined to continue, and even taking the valley as a new clan-home paled in comparison.

He clenched his teeth and restrained his rage. No one inflicted anything like this upon him without retribution. Not the Bloodmoon Chieftain. Not Penn Cheval. Not a gaggle of incompetent and disobedient rabble. No one!

***

"The Silver Lion to see you, milord."

The other guard at the door to Rennoute's study looked upon Pencheval and Howe with undisguised awe. It was something Pencheval was unaccustomed to receiving. In the past he inspired fear, nervous respect, or contempt, but never awe. It was yet another benefit of his gambit against the goblins.

"You may enter, Lion. Scout." The guard who announced them stepped quickly out of his way. He passed as the soldier gave him a respectful nod, uncertain of what to do now.

"Your Grace. The watchman along the road said you wished to see us?"

"To put it mildly, warrior." Rennoute stood from behind his desk and walked towards them. "I would never believe such a thing as you two have accomplished possible, yet word of your deeds has not ceased among the army for days."

"We have heaped insult and injury upon the horde and its warlord, Your Grace. If it does not move, I know of nothing more to inflict upon it."

"You have, and I hold your quest fulfilled, Lion. Now there is another matter to discuss with you."

"Your Grace?"

"Whatever you did to goad the horde into a fool's errand threw them into disarray long enough for the last of the townsfolk to escape. Fifty-seven survivors arrived the day before you did. One of them was the last of the clergy in Tarsun's Market, a sister by the name of Nan."

Rennoute informed him of this in the even tone of voice one might use to break bad news to a friend. It was another thing he did not expect. He was relieved Nan lived but dreaded what word of her came next.

"By Your Grace's leave, I would like to see her."

"Friar Dominik is with her in the castle's chapel, Lion. We cannot let her leave for fear of her safety."

"Her safety? Does she need healing?"

Rennoute shook his head. "No more than the others. Food and rest. The concern is about the peasantry. Half of them think she is a witch now, and others swear she is Saint Marion reborn."

"She is no witch," Pencheval growled, "and I will stand champion to her against any such accusation."

"You and every knight in my order, Lion. The Lord on High has blessed her with power. She is a nascent Disciple, and when one of them rises it is always to turmoil. The Histories tell of our past Disciples, and they read like her tale in the present day."

"By all that's holy." Howe muttered the epithet before he could stop himself, but received no more than an amused chuckle from Rennoute.

Pencheval did not care to believe Athesiene had intervened on her behalf. If He had, He had taken His sweet time about it. So long as the temple did, however, they would keep Nan safe. Annoyed to no end by Friar Dominik, but safe.

"Again, I ask Your Grace's leave..."

"You may go, Lion. You will leave your weapons with the knight guarding her, but you may go. Mind your tongue and spare her your gruffness. She cannot endure your growling and will not be made to do so."

"Yes, Your Grace."

"Scout, remain here. There are many gaps in information about your adventures with the Lion, and you will fill them now."

"Yes, milord." Howe clapped Pencheval on the shoulder, and he nodded back before swiftly departing.

***

The chapel was a much smaller place than the temple in Tarsun's Market, but the silence was no less deep. Two rows of ten short wooden pews polished to a soft glow stretched to a dais and pulpit. Behind it hung the white banners of Athesiene bearing the red peak of The Lord on High. Small windows of stained glass depicting scenes and saints from The Histories blocked most of the incoming light in their deep stone sills. A few lanterns lit the place and it smelled faintly of incense.

The knight who had taken Pencheval's weapons watched him from the door but said nothing. Sitting on the front pew was a form cloaked in a rich red robe with the hood pulled over a bowed head. The woman he assumed was Nan did not react to his entry.

"Nan?" Pencheval kept his tone conversational and walked towards her. A narrow carpet muffled his boot steps, but his voice echoed through the silence.

"Dominik assured me you would return." Nan's voice sounded much older, weary, and spoke of the same patience she had before. "He says you set out to rescue me."

"I would not leave you there if there was aught I could do."

"There were days I wished I had left with you." Nan did not move. "I am almost ashamed to admit it."

"No one sane desires to be captive to goblins," Pencheval reassured her. "You feared, and yet you stayed because you believed your responsibilities were worth more than your life. What cause have you for shame?"

"That I did not do more. That I did too much. That I have returned to yet more madness."

Pencheval kept his steps light and sat down on the pew next to her. He gave her an arm's length of space.

"There is no such thing as perfect war, Nan. You do what you think you must. Decisions become choices between evils and lives end. It is the fault of the goblins this has happened and no one else, least of all you."

"The Lord on High agrees with you, I think." Nan looked up and turned to him. What he had first mistaken for the depredations of starvation and abuse showed instead a face that appeared five years *younger* than the one he had seen in Tarsun's Market; only her eyes showed fear and misery.

"Nan?"

"He granted me the power to save the last of them." Nan seemed to be on the verge of tears. "He drove the goblins mad and we escaped in the chaos. But they hungered and more died. Too many dead..."

"What more could you have possibly done?"

"If I had used the power sooner, could I have saved more of the worthy?"

"Worthy? I don't understand..."

"It is such might I fear to wield it, Pencheval. It blasts goblins asunder. The rocks they piled against the hole you made in the catacombs became dust with a gesture. Torches lit with a thought and it shook the walls of the temple. So much power they called me a witch..."

"The goblins deserved any fate you inflicted upon them. And a witch would not act as you did."

"Lion, your time nears its end." The knight called from the back of the chapel. "She will hear no more of you."

Nan chuckled and brushed away tears. "Some believe as you do, Pencheval. Including my armored nanny."

Pencheval gave her a smile he hoped was reassuring and rose. He did not understand all she had endured, but he refused to pester her on any point. The Knight Superior had spoken truly. She could only endure so much after her ordeal.

"I will not depart this valley yet, Nan. You will see me again."

"And I thank you. I will be here. After months among the goblins, I have come to value greatly the chapel's silence."

Pencheval collected his sword belt and left without comment, but only because he did not wish to show his wrath to Nan. No, he would not leave yet. There was a goblin warlord and a horde that had to suffer for what they had done to them both, and the havoc they inflicted on Howe and Dominik.

Let them come, he silently asked of the Lord on High. Please, let them come. If He wished them reaped, he would happily oblige.

***

"Chief of Chieftains, bat-lizards come!"

The Stonemaster knew there was fear in the horde, but did not immediately believe the news. An attack by great bat-lizards hunting goblins? They did not come into the valley, or had not since he had taken the town. Now they came in such numbers all the horde's chatter spoke of panic.

He wondered if the Fiend himself had chosen this moment to frustrate all his efforts. His power over stone would not strike them from the sky. They would not stay any longer than it took to snatch a few rabble, but after the revolt and the shaman tricks that human used to escape, they might very well be enough to shatter the horde.

He looked through one of the openings in the wall of his tall cave and scanned the skies where those beneath him pointed. The bat-lizards appeared only as specks, but even from this distance he could see their wings beat. Nigh a score of them, and they approached too quickly to be anything else.

They also flew in a strangely ordered fashion. Generally, the great bat-lizards attacked alone, took what they wanted, and then left. He had never seen so many at once and with...riders? Something was on each of their backs, and it wasn't a thing that was usually there.

"Come with me," the Stonemaster ordered his bodyguard. When they hesitated, he struck one to the ground with his staff.

"Come. With. Me!" The Stonemaster again resolved to punish Penn Cheval for costing him the awe that commanded near instant obedience.

"Yes, Chief of Chieftains." Accompanied by his bodyguard, the Stonemaster left his tall cave and strode towards the western wood wall. To his surprise, the wingbeats suggested the bat-lizards slowed and landed outside of the town's cliff-walls.

He could hear the panic become a buzz again as word spread. It was another clan! Yet from where did they come? The Stonemaster had never heard of a clan that could tame the great bat-lizards, and it would have been all anyone discussed had they known.

"Open the wood wall!" His stone body could deal with them if they proved hostile. His bodyguard would get the worst of it should that contingency arise, but that was not something they needed to know. It was time to determine why this clan was here, and he needed his cohort to impress.

The wood wall creaked open and a sight the Chief of Chieftains never thought he would see greeted him. A goblin in a strange head dress of bones and feathers sat atop a reined bat-lizard. The creature kept its wings half-folded against its body and did nothing to dislodge or attack its rider. Spectacular red patterns gleamed from duller gray scales and it let out a low growl as it rested.

Behind the leader were the rest of the riders and beside him was one of the Bloodmoon Clan's Berserkers. He was one of the messengers their former chieftain sent into the mountains to find clans for his cause. That one had indeed found a clan, and had brought back both an opportunity and a problem.

"Hail to you, mighty Stonemaster! I am Leth, Speaker for the Chieftain of the Skyfang Clan. He sends you greetings and an offer."

A Speaker? The Stonemaster almost snarled at him but held his tongue. With whom did this Skyfang Chieftain believe he dealt? He was the Stonemaster, Chief of Chieftains of a goblin horde! You came in person or not at all.

It was an affront, but given his circumstances one the Chief of Chieftains was forced to endure. To rebuff such a gift as this was beyond foolish. It was time to hear this one's offer and agree to it. Whether or not he meant to keep that agreement was not yet decided.

"Welcome to this place, Leth of the Skyfang. I will hear your chieftain's words."

"My chieftain offers you this force of great bat-lizards to take the mountain-castle and give you the valley. In return, you will grant the Skyfang landing and hunting privileges within your territories from the day you defeat the humans onward."

So he would have to renege later, he told himself. They could take from him forever for the work of one battle? That offer was miserable but this was not the time to alter it.

In the short term, it was too good to refuse. The horde along the cliff-walls gawked and pointed and he could hear their awe. If the bat-lizards gave dreams of victory back to his numbers and ended chatter about desertion, they were far more worth than trouble. Announcing their alliance to the horde would inspire it, and that was before putting the Skyfang's riders to more practical use.

The possibilities they offered against the Snow Clan were considerable. Burn the human thatch caves from above. Destroy their rock throwers so they could not rain stone and fire upon the horde. Keep them sleepless and in fear of another attack in the dark. Keep them cringing at the threats above them instead of fighting those below during the main assault. Terrorize their rabble and scatter their warriors. With such things available to him, the walls of their mountain-castle would do them no good.

"I accept." He only had to deceive them long enough, and the Speaker Leth nodded his understanding. Yes, by all means use the bat-lizards to defeat the Snow Clan. Perhaps we will take the knowledge of taming them from you afterwards. He could almost see the reaction of the Beastwarper Chieftain; it was certain he had heard this news by now.

"Dismount and join my council, Leth. We go with the horde before the next moon, and there is much we must tell you of your place against the Snow Clan."

He expected the humans celebrated the revolt Penn Cheval caused. Let them sleep soundly with the belief they had beaten him for a time longer. When he finally reached the mountain-castle with the horde, theirs would be a rude awakening.

The War for the Shield

One

"Of course I will do as you ask!"

Nan sighed and smiled at the awestruck Friar Dominik as he leaned forward in anticipation of her next words. It was a jarring change from what he had been in the now fallen town of Tarsun's Market, but she had changed since then as well. There, she had only been senior Sister Nan, a teacher of school-aged girls and leader of prayers. She was above him in the hierarchy of Athesiene's Temple, but still within some normalcy of life.

That was before the grand proclamation, when the castle's resident priest, Father Victor, determined she was a Disciple by whatever means the temple could. At that moment, she watched the order of the world as she knew it float away on the winds. The faithful like Dominik could barely contain their awe, and it rendered him completely unable to hold a normal conversation with her since.

"Friar, mind your voice." The knight currently guarding her and the castle's chapel may as well have been her wet nurse. His purpose was to keep her from harm and anything at all vexing. He scowled at the friar, who nodded nervously at the command and restrained his still evident enthusiasm for whatever divine words she was supposed to tell him next.

All of this from the title of 'Disciple.' It was a thing without rank and little precedence. Yes, previous Disciples were mentioned in The Histories. There, all their trials and tribulations were described in tidy and neatly numbered sentences that belied that title's weight. Yet reading about the travails of those that possessed it before was nothing like living it and precious little preparation.

She had pursued this as her only hope of escape from the horde, and to her chagrin the Lord on High found her worthy. She had saved what few survivors she could from the goblins and sent a number of their horde to their god, which she hoped devoured them screaming. And what remained? The safe silence of the castle's chapel and a dearth of people with whom she could calmly speak, or any of the once abundant mundane moments at all.

"My apologies. Disciple, what more would you know of the Lion?"

"Dominik, please continue our work with him. You remember it from Tarsun's Market?"

"Without fail, Disciple. But he has rid himself of many of his demons already. Was that the purpose of our trials with the horde?"

Another request for wisdom? Perhaps it was their purpose. Perhaps the horde catalyzed events Athesiene found needful. Perhaps if she gave him her opinion, factions of the temple would kill each other over disagreements with it. If so, she would be far from the first Disciple who found themselves in the middle of a war having done naught but pursue the work of the Lord on High.

"The Lord on High wants the horde gone, friar. That I can tell you for certain."

"We will attend to that, and gladly," the knight guarding the door interjected.

That she did know for certain. Athesiene had granted her the power, and it grew as she struck one goblin dead after another. So much power she felt like a dam holding back a great reservoir of it, without any more control over its volume and fury than to open flood gates she might never close again. Between that and the newfound need to watch her tongue, she could feel the weight of a mountain on her shoulders.

"Friar, perhaps we might continue this another time."

"Yes, Disciple. My apologies!" One more scowl from the knight sent the friar scurrying towards the door, gesturing nervously at them both. Nan let her shoulders slump and bowed her head.

"It was wise of the Disciple to say it was the Lord on High's will that the horde be slain. It will unite all at the castle against them." The knight gave her a respectful nod and then returned to his watch on the door.

Nan considered his response. Something she had said as little more than an observation might do that much? What might a moment's frustration or weariness do? She sat back on her pew and prayed to the Lord on High for wisdom and a moment's respite. She did not know if she would receive either.

***

Wingleader Jux understood his instructions but cared little for them.

The pens for their mounts stood outside of the human town occupied by a goblin horde. He could see a ragged hole in the eastern cliff-wall they boasted was made by their Chief of Chieftains during the battle, a warlord called the Stonemaster. It spoke of more power than the Skyfang Clan usually faced, an observation lost on the pompous lip-flapper his chieftain had sent as the leader of this envoy.

Goblins crowded the cliff-wall and hole to gawk at their bat-lizards as enforcers punished them for their distractions in vain. Base rabble, this lot. Little more than crawling bugs, unable to fly and unable to comprehend the majesty of his clan. So long as kept their distance from the pens, there would be no trouble and no sounds of screaming before the crunch and squish of bat-lizard jaws on meals within easy reach.

Why were they stooping to help the ground-bound goblins of this Stonemaster? So many of the ground-bound came to them for protection and offered nothing for it but pathetic tributes and their rabble in return. The Skyfang Clan already controlled more territory than any other clan; valleys and places in the deep mountains were already theirs. Yet the messenger of the mighty Bloodmoon Clan had intrigued his chieftain, so he sent the wingleader with Speaker Leth.

Perhaps the chieftain wanted southern territorial rights. It was easy enough to fly here, and he never tired of riding the bat-lizards. There was a rare wonder in flying over mountains no goblin could ever hope to climb, and soaring over the landscape brought a peace few others would ever know. Watching the mount beneath him make nigh imperceptible movements to glide through the skies, wind in his face and clouds passing around him, never lost its splendor.

Admittedly this Stonemaster had a horde and could conceivably hold such a territory. It was a rare enough thing to draw the notice of even the Skyfang. Yet this warlord was ground-bound, and all the ground-bound clans wanted the same thing: the secrets of taming great bat-lizards that only the Skyfang knew. The envy was palpable on every other goblin face he saw.

The warlord fighting the humans they called the Snow Clan agreed far too readily to hard terms. It was obvious treachery from someone too powerful to discount, yet Leth sat on his council now, too puffed with his own self-importance to see the danger. The chieftain said he was master on this journey, and they had struck a bargain upon landing which meant they would bring fire and fear to the humans. They would burn as all the others that had challenged the Skyfang or found themselves burdened with the misfortune of impeding his chieftain's ambitions.

The horde could not stop speaking of the target. They called it a mountain-castle, and it was the humans' strongest clan-home. Though the mountain-castle was stone, much of the area around it was wood and thatch that would burn. It made no sense to him. If they knew caves were better and could make their own, why build so many huts?

It made no difference. The Skyfang's part in this would be to precede the horde and burn obstacles. By the time the horde reached the place, the humans would fear the skies. No one the Skyfang had fought in the past could ever do more than beg for terms. The Snow Clan may be strong, but they, like the horde, were still ground-bound.

Their first attack would come tonight, and the three he would send needed their instructions. There was much to burn, but it would not all happen at once. Mounts must remain fresh, as well as the riders, and a long grind inflicted more suffering and despair. Strike and fly, over and over, until they burned the defenses of the Snow Clan to ashes and made their warriors meek with fright. Once the horde arrived and this 'Allspeaker' shaman made the Chief of Chieftains' will known to them, they would eagerly submit.

***

Pencheval raised his mug of stout to the soldier that bought it for him and the man returned the gesture. It was the fourth mug he did not have to buy for himself this evening, and he quietly kept his surprise at the admiration to himself. Yes, he had returned triumphant in a mad plan to provoke the horde to its destruction and left their enemies tearing at each other's throats. The fact he might have saved no few of them from death at the hands of the goblins kept the drinks flowing.

He knew it was fleeting. If the goblins meant to come, they would do it soon. So while today was drinks and the admiration of an army, tomorrow could see him hip deep in battle against the horde. Nor did he know what mischief they would manage in the meantime. Their sound alone drove the folk to madness, and there were plenty of them here.

"Worse ways to end a quest, Lion." Howe raised his mug to Pencheval and pulled a tavern girl closer to him. She laughed and strained against her corset, leaving Howe merry and Pencheval briefly wistful. He had something like that once, but nothing else ever compared after her death all those years ago.

Pencheval gave him a wan smile and drank deeply. Scout Howe had been the first unfortunate soul to warn of the horde and would have been lynched for it in Tarsun's Market but for the Lion's intervention. He returned the favor over the summer by saving Pencheval from one of the goblins' brutes during the fight to goad them into moving.

It seemed like forever since he simply sat in a tavern with a companion for the sole purpose of drinking the night to dawn. The closest he had come was with his fellow Silver Lion apprentices at Stonewall Pass, but the pain of his losses still drained the mirth from all endeavors. It earned him the appellation of 'Grouch' from one of those apprentices, a rogue called Gantillion, and the name neither vexed nor amused him.

Howe smiled, lifted his cup to his lips, and then paused as though he heard a threat through the bustle and clink of the tavern's common room. He turned towards the door and frowned. "That's never a good sound."

"What is never–" Pencheval rose and put his sword within easy reach. He had come to respect Howe's perception; as a scout the man had no equal. When he grasped the hilt, Howe shook his head.

"You won't need that, Lion. One galloping horse and a frantic soldier, not an enemy."

"Lord on High protect us! Watch!" The ragged voice from outside rang above the noise of the tavern and the hooves thundering against the dirt road. Chatter stopped as soldiers rose and bustled towards the door. Howe reluctantly released his now frowning tavern girl, and Pencheval narrowed his eyes.

"Hold there, scout, and report!" Someone outside stopped the horse, and the man astride it landed hard as he dismounted.

"The goblins..." Pencheval heard him gasp.

"What of them?"

"They have drakes!" He heard the scout cough and gasp. "The bastards ride them! Nigh a score of them, big as draft horses!"

"Someone get that poor blighter a drink, he's lost all his sense." A soldier, genuinely concerned, bought a mug of stout from the nearest serving girl and wove through the crowd.

"He's not mad," Pencheval offered. "They do have beasts. They're big and powerful, but they're not drakes." He had seen and fought such beasts, larger than trolls with mouths wide enough to swallow a man whole. He had not mistaken them for drakes, but that made them no less fell. Their lack of wings did little to slow their capacity for butchery.

The scout stumbled through the door. Dust covered whatever his sweat left unsoaked, and his eyes gleamed madly from panic. "No, I saw those, too. Great loping beasts with teeth and plates. But the gray lizards with red patterns were drakes!"

"Saint Marion's Revelation." Howe wiped his mouth and frowned.

"Something you forgot to tell us, you daft bastard?" a random soldier called to Howe from the crowd. "You stood at their walls and you didn't see the drakes?"

Howe's eyes bulged. "There weren't any there, I swear it!"

"We saw no drakes," Pencheval insisted. "If they'd had them then, they would have made their presence plain." Nor would he be standing here now, as the beasts need not have even landed to kill them both.

"And I tell you all, they have drakes! Those damn sun diver things, sure as the day is long."

Pencheval had no reason to disbelieve him. He had long ago learned never to underestimate goblins, but this was beyond the pale even for them. No clan he had ever encountered knew how to tame drakes, and now one joined the horde that had a score? Indeed, the goblins were coming, and if those that could fly remained unchecked, there would be nothing but ashes to meet the horde when it arrived.

***

"Why do we still not go?"

The Stonemaster, goblin Chief of Chieftains and twice a Hordemaker, repressed the urge to strike the Bloodmoon Speaker dead with his staff's stone magic. Every change in the horde's fortunes provoked that question from him. After losing their chieftain, the Bloodmoon Clan were obsessed with avenging him and themselves on the Silver Lion Clan warrior, Penn Cheval. They had to lay waste to the Snow Clan humans to do it, something they could not accomplish without the horde, and their patience with waiting was ever in short supply.

"Patience, mighty Speaker. The Skyfang will open the way for you. Give our great bat-lizards half a moon's time, and nothing will stand between your axes and the Snow Clan. Pain and punishment will be yours to inflict on the humans as you will."

Leth, the Speaker the Skyfang sent, was good with his words but also a smug worm. The headpiece of bones and feathers he wore made him appear more impressive than the warlord, a nigh intolerable arrogance on his part. Irritating, but if Leth could mollify the Bloodmoon, the Chief of Chieftains was perfectly content to let him do it.

"They are magnificent creatures," the Beastwarper Chieftain complimented in a tone the Stonemaster found a shade too insincere. He was master of the Bonestrippers, useful but dangerous monsters he warped from troll cubs using mixtures far beyond the warlord's comprehension. Those potions had left their mark on him, though. A growth of bone spikes resembling the lichens on a tree grew from his left shoulder, and forced his dependence on a staff to walk or even stand upright.

Beastwarper's fascination with the bat-lizards since their arrival was as obsessive as his previous fascination with a single human shaman before its escape. It had told him of books and to his credit, he had learned enough of their skill called writing to consider creating his own. Yet that shaman had caused an enormous amount of trouble, killing dozens in its escape, and likely provoking the desertion of the Shadowcreed Clan. He had been minutes from slaying it before the appearance of Penn Cheval at the western cliff-wall diverted him.

Beastwarper's obsession with the shaman had been costly. His obsession with the bat-lizards was another matter entirely. If he could learn to tame them, and possibly warp them? That was a thing that justified deaths and trouble. It would justify much, for this time Beastwarper would share that knowledge, or the warlord would relieve him of his bone spikes and his skin with a knife.

"They are the pride of the Skyfang, wise chieftain," Speaker Leth answered, nose involuntarily rising into the air. "With them, we command the skies, and we shall bring fire to the humans and their mountain-castle. Such is the will of our great chieftain, and so it shall be."

The Stonemaster suppressed a snarl. That preening, pompous goat's ass would pay for his arrogance someday. For now, that arrogance may yet be manipulated.

"They are glorious, but nothing that cannot be improved, Skyfang."

"Improved? Ridiculous." Leth made a show of indignation the Stonemaster saw as bluster to conceal he was knocked off balance.

"You have come to the horde for an alliance. Did you believe we could offer you nothing in return?" The Stonemaster sat back in his bone throne and smiled. "You may find your journey here more than worthwhile."

"Indeed." The Stonemaster could see Beastwarper suppress a smile as he fell into line with the plan. "I have created great beasts from mere trolls. What could I do with your bat-lizards? With your training and my arts, backed by a horde? Not merely bat-lizards. Cloudrippers. Fellwings. We could push far into human lands together."

"Territories such that it would take moons to fly from one end to the other." The Stonemaster saw Leth hesitate even as he licked his lips at the thought.

"But we would need to start with hatchlings," Beastwarper continued. "You can get them, can't you? No more than two, possibly three, and I could perfect that work upon them. Such beasts as you have never beheld for us all."

And while Beastwarper made them mighty creatures, both he and the Stonemaster would observe how to train them. After that, there would be no need of the Skyfang and their usurious bargains. The Stonemaster made a show of waiting patiently for an answer, but inside suppressed the urge to laugh himself senseless.

"This is..." Leth hesitated, and the Stonemaster almost snarled. Perhaps his chieftain denied him that much leeway to bargain. Or worse, perhaps the Skyfang Chieftain only sent this pompous simpleton because he knew nothing they might steal.

A leathery crack against air and a reptilian shriek interrupted the council. The thumps of wings grew as three bat-lizards and their riders rose above the eastern cliff-wall and into the sky. The horde chittered and screeched as the beasts flew over the town, slowly gaining speed until they needed only to beat their wings to maintain their glide. They disappeared over the western cliff-wall and into the distance towards the humans' mountain-castle.

The Stonemaster leered at the carnage he knew would follow. The Shadowcreed had been fools to desert. With this much force at his command, everything would belong to him soon.

Two

"What do you wield against drakes, Howe?"

Pencheval and Howe rushed towards the castle, leaving the tavern's warm glow behind them. If the drakes were coming, they would come in the night, when the goblins could see, but the temple's forces would be half blind. Darkness impeded nothing with goblin eyes, and they always took advantage of it. Pairing that advantage with the might of a drake required a counter at once.

"What do we wield," Howe started incredulously, "against a drake attack? They have never come to the Shield of Athesiene. How are we supposed to–"

"Enough!" Pencheval stopped abruptly. "Stay your panic and maintain your wits. Your knights have certainly dealt with drakes before, because they have fashioned their hides into armor. What do they do?"

"We use lures and drakebows. Do you think we merely smite them from the sky?"

"Drakebows?"

"Yes. A right mighty piece of work, but unwieldy. To kill a drake, you pin a cow to the ground and light a fire sprinkled with Drake's Lure next to it. When it burns blue, you find a good shooting spot and wait. The smell carries for hours, and if the drake's nose does as you wish, it takes advantage of your offering and leaves you with a shot." Howe spread his hands. "But the drake is on the ground eating. We do not shoot them from the air."

"And a longbow?"

"Assuming you can even hit one while it's flying, an arrow will do naught against it. All the beatings you took this summer, and you don't yet appreciate the hardiness of drake's hide? The smith did little more than mold the pieces and preserve them for you!"

Pencheval looked down at the drakescale breastplate visible beneath his tabard, a reward from the Knight Superior for his efforts during the battle to hold Tarsun's Market. Brick red patterns wove along dark gray scales, part of the back leather from a drake. It was easily as thick as his thumb was long and springy as steel, though it only weighed half as much.

It had saved his life against a mighty goblin champion at Tarsun's Market. Twice. He valued it highly now but realized that drakes all wore similar armor, if only because it was their own hides.

"And the priests?"

"Father Victor is blessed by the Lord on High, but his work strengthens armies and fortifications. He is also too old to leave the castle anymore, much less stand in battle."

"And the knights don't battle them?"

"If the drake is on the ground, yes. You've seen what they can do with Knight-Brother Galot, Athesiene grant him rest and peace. The Knight Superior can make them stronger still, but none can strike the beasts from the air. The knights are mighty against armies, but can no more fly than we can. Don't know what the Disciple can do, but I hope she's feeling generous."

"The Discip–Nan?" It took Pencheval a moment to realize Howe referred to Nan in a wholly different way now. It was as though the thought of bothering her for aid was like petitioning Athesiene in person. He may as well have spoken about two entirely different people.

"Yes, Lion. That was her name, I believe. If you have sway with her, perhaps you might convince her to help us? If the drakes defeat the army, they defeat her, too."

If he had sway with her? Pencheval was flabbergasted by his tone. It was the same Nan they knew from Tarsun's Market. The one that struck him with that blasted spell to keep him from rescuing her. The one that sat in the chapel recovering from the horror of imprisonment at the claws of the horde. Power or no power, favor of the Lord on High or not, she was still Nan. Why did Howe refer to her as though she was completely separate from all of this? His tone almost suggested he thought her separate from this world.

"I'll speak with her," Pencheval said as an offhand remark as they hastened towards the castle to report and prepare. Howe looked as relieved as Pencheval had ever seen him.

"You'll have everyone's gratitude if you succeed."

***

Drim enjoyed the rush of speed as the valley fell away behind him and his two riders. He could clearly see that behemoth called the mountain-castle at half the distance between it and the horde. It was all but inconceivable anyone could build their own mountain, and yet there it was, lit by the fires the humans needed to see in the darkness.

Wingleader Jux had been wise to order the attacks at night. The humans and their cursed eyes needed light to see, or so all the stories of humans said. This would be the first time he had ever fought any of them. The Fiend Under The Mountain had given goblins proper eyes that could tell night from day but saw just as well in darkness. They were enough for both them and the bat-lizards.

His orders were simple. Two smaller wooden clan-homes stood before the mountain-castle to shelter additional Snow Clan warriors. While the horde would surely overrun them when they attacked, they impeded movement as many other things would. Their task was to burn one of them to the ground and then return to the human town in the middle of the valley. It was not half an evening's work.

The great bat-lizards excelled at burning but were unable to do so more than two or three times an attack. Their fire was small but stubborn; it burned until it ran out of fuel, and its victims could do little about it. A day or two after being well fed and rested the bat-lizards' flames returned, and it took a Wingleader who knew the beasts to use them well in this way. Tonight Jux had done so, for the three of them were easily enough to destroy one human place of tall wooden walls and cloth huts without being an excessive force.

The structures appeared in the distance, and Drim decided on the one to the left. He would attack first, and then his two riders would follow in the order they had chosen. He could not command them verbally from his seat, but they could watch and then do.

He reined his bat-lizard and its head turned more by training than force. It had been reared to this since it hatched and knew of nothing other than goblins, which was the secret of rendering them obedient. He felt the bat-lizard tilt beneath him, and it beat its wings to climb when he rapped his heels on its back. The straps of the high-backed chair that kept him in place pulled tightly against one side as the beast banked and rose.

In the distance, a human watched and pointed from atop some sort of wooden watch post. He saw it pull something that looked like a bow and sneered. It could not hurt the bat-lizard with that weapon or even hit it. They were too strong, too fast, and soon the Snow Clan would realize, too fell.

First shots to the wood walls, the second to the cloth huts–let the humans try to fight the flames and know terror. He climbed and circled until the building dwindled, straps pulling and mount hissing from the effort, then slapped the reins into a dive.

A rush of wind hit his face as the descent pressed him back into the chair. He felt pinned by the speed as the humans' wooden warrior home grew quickly underneath him. Halfway to the ground, the bat-lizard roared and spit the ball of burning, sticky death it would deal on this attack, then avoided crashing by leveling off and banking steeply to the left. He again felt pinned and pulled, but the straps kept him seated, and he smiled at the screams he heard behind him. He would know how well he struck before the attack was at an end.

Twice as he made his wide circle in the sky he heard roars behind him. He saw the humans in their wooden huts scream as he passed over. It made little difference if they shot arrows at him or not; no one had so much as touched either himself or his mount in all the years he had done this. Behind him, the leathery wingbeats of his riders slapped the air.

He circled until he could see his target again. Black smoke rose from three orange glows within the wood walls. Two struck the walls themselves, and a third burned from within. It was a good start, and another run would see this task done.

He reared his mount to climb and it did so. Strong wings beat air until he rose to his desired height. Again, he felt pressed against the back of his chair as he dove, and the great bat-lizard roared as it spat yet another glob of flame at the humans. It coughed and grunted in pain several times, signs that it expended all its fire for tonight.

He flew over his target. A brief wafting of wood smoke and the acrid smell of bat-lizard flame reached his nostrils. Humans screamed and scrambled as those in the high watch places leapt from them to escape. Unfortunately, most of the field was churned dirt, as they had built up strange small hills around his target. That prevented a true conflagration, but what the humans threw on the Skyfang's work did nothing to slow it as it consumed its way from a few smoking tendrils to great black gouts of smoke and a crackling wildfire.

Task complete, he reined his mount towards the horde as he heard the roars of the mounts behind him. Six shots were enough to keep half a clan consumed in panic and futile efforts to forestall the inevitable. With so much wood in one place, all the humans would see was how easy it was for the Skyfang Clan to lay them low.

He gave his target one last backward glance and laughed. If Jux ordered two such strikes a night, there would be little between the horde and the mountain-castle but a smooth path strewn with ashes.

***

Pencheval snapped around inside the passage through the castle's barbican as a roar broke the silence. An orange streak of flame shot into the fortress on his right and sparked rising screams of panic. The sound of the beast and the fireball were unmistakable. It was a Northern Sundiver, just as the scout said, and he had arrived to warn of them only a few minutes early.

How old was his news? Days? The scout clearly pushed himself and his horse to breaking, but how much of time did he spend concealing himself from flying enemies? He certainly avoided riding the direct route along the roads to the castle.

The drakes suffered no such limitations. They could fly across what would be a day's travel on foot from Tarsun's Market as fast as sparrows, and feared nothing in the skies. The scout may have learned of them days ago, but they neither needed stealth nor suffered the limits of travel by foot or horseback.

"Saint Marion's revelation, that unlucky blighter must have just beaten them here. I must warn the Knight Superior and get to the walls!" Howe bolted towards the castle, leaving Pencheval in the tunnel under the barbican.

The mercenary willed his magic to give him sight through the darkness with a Clearsight charm after another ball of flame struck the fortress. Night turned to shades of gray, and the underbelly of a drake resolved itself, legs pulled against its sides as it banked away from the Shield of Athesiene. A second drake leveled after a dive, and the rider on its back was indistinct but apparent. Something like a saddle or a seat kept it there, but he could not clearly determine why.

"Drakes! To arms!" The voice in the distance accompanied soldiers running in all directions. Townsfolk panicked, and the whole became a huge muddle as they collided and hindered the forces.

Pencheval scrambled towards the town from the gate, unwilling to remain for fear of being trampled in a panic. An archer in the distance scanned the skies but could see nothing. Another pointed as a drake glided briefly into the lights on the edge of the town, banked, and accelerated too quickly to shoot. Townsfolk either rushed into their homes or towards the gate, and Pencheval scrambled from their paths.

Everywhere he glanced was another scene of chaos. A small knot of spearmen spoke to a hysterical woman holding an infant, pointing back to the homes in the town as she screamed at them. Soldiers scrambled from the towers in the fort, and he could only assume they tried to fight the blaze or escape it. Archers on the walls searched but fired at nothing for want of targets they could hit. If that damnable goblin warlord fielded its horde at this moment, it could not have asked for an enemy in more perfect disarray.

He again sought out the drakes, and the Clearsight charm rendered them visible. They circled to attack the fortress from another side, and first climbed before diving. One more roar, and a ball of fire again landed within the walls. The remaining two repeated the maneuver, one after the other, in something that resembled not so much an attack as a game of follow the leader.

What frightened him was the deadly simplicity of it all. A clan of goblins had trained drakes as mounts and could make them spit fire on command. They need not even need to speak to one another in the sky to do it; just agree on a plan, determine the order of attack, and then engage in it. If the leader did something, then so did the others. There was much at the Shield of Athesiene they could burn this way. Not all in one night, certainly, but they had more than one night.

Three more attacks landed before they flew away in the direction of Tarsun's Market. That much at least was obvious; the goblins would be based nowhere else.

Pencheval brought himself back to the now. The fortress was ablaze, and drake's flame was notoriously difficult to extinguish. If that caught the soldiers unawares, they would find themselves surrounded by an inferno before they could escape it.

He tried to push through the press to get to the fortress. Those not fleeing the flames ran towards it with buckets, shovels, or bare hands. They made little headway through the panicked and found themselves buffeted in return for their efforts. Pencheval was forced from the main road to a spot where he could only watch as the flames reduced the fortress to ruins and cinders.

Three drakes. One wooden fortress lost in less than an hour. A whole town brought to panic, and the army unable to react. The scout said he saw a score of drakes? If they could not stop them, and quickly, their attacks against the temple would end in flame and blood.

***

Nan snapped upright from her bed at the sound of panicked shouting and the thumps of booted feet passing her chambers in the castle. Goblins? She forced the memory of their endless cacophony from her mind, gritting her teeth at the endless screech and click.

She rose, put on her robe, and raised its hood. After months of the horde's endless chatter, she craved what little silence it could bring her. The sounds outside the door seemed a shade more muted, dampening to softened thumps and distant voices.

She cracked the door open to look into the hallway. A few torches lit the darkness, and the knight guarding the entrance to her chambers turned to her. They were the only two left in the hall.

"What news? Is something amiss?"

"Several soldiers rushed past on urgent business, Disciple. They did not stop to inform me of their purpose, but it is most likely to report an attack."

"Attack? The goblins come now?" Nan felt a burst of hatred for them, and again the sound of the horde rose in her mind. She shook her head to suppress it.

"I know not, but they will inform me if I am required. Until then, I was commanded to defend the Disciple, and that is what I mean to do."

Must he talk to her that way? The knights insisted on referring to her strictly as 'the Disciple' as though one might say 'the reliquary' or describe any other artifact. Was she now merely some holy thing to be displayed and paraded?

"Do they need aid? I can assist now." She could assist very well. If it meant smiting goblins, she would be more than happy to oblige.

"Again, I know not, but I will inform the Knight Superior of the Disciple's offer come the morrow. For now, please remain within the keep."

Nan sighed. Until she could speak to someone less inclined to think her every step was worthy of a written line in The Histories, little remained to be done. "Thank you, brother, and good night."

"Good night, Disciple." The knight resumed his watch, and Nan shut the door on the madness outside.

***

"You are summoned, Lion."

Pencheval turned his attention from the crackling ruins of the fortress half hidden by the last of the smoke. Neither he nor anyone else could do anything but let the flame have its feast, and naught remained but a blackened ruin. At least the earthworks stopped the conflagration from spreading, recently turned earth acting as a firebreak and denying the flames more fuel.

It was all he was able to do to remain out of the chaos, which had subsided enough since the attack to allow soldiers to move through the crowds once again. All he had done until then was pass the time waiting for dawn, wracking his mind for counters to the drakes. If Rennoute had sent for him, he was not the only one.

"Lead on, soldier." The one who had been sent to retrieve him carried a spear but left his shield slung over his back.

"Right then."

The trail led them to the gates of the castle, past panicked faces and soldiers strained to their limits. He could hear Friar Dominik preaching the words of his god and The Histories to a crowd, and many prayed and kneeled by the well where they gathered. Guards stood on the walls in good order, but Pencheval noticed their tension. They all faced an enemy they could not fight, or so they believed.

The messenger led him to a war room. A large table surrounded by knights and officers bore drawing and scrolls bearing what Pencheval assumed were quartermaster's reports and the valley's map. Rennoute spoke and asked questions of the gathered, listening as an officer told him of the damage. The fortress was a total loss and there was no cause to believe the goblins would hesitate to repeat that display on anything they wished.

"So now to the question at hand. What do we do against them?"

"We kill them, Your Grace." Pencheval strode up to the table and nodded respectfully. "We defeat them as any other enemy. They will burn nothing if they are dead."

"As any other enemy? I trust you have slain them in the past."

"No, but I know of them and how it is done."

An officer scowled at him. "You know how it is done. Such use have we for theory now." Pencheval noted that he was the only one who bore Rennoute's seal on his uniform tabard. Perhaps he was a general or the castellan.

"You have use of the obvious," Pencheval growled back. "Dead enemies win wars. You have one you must defeat with all haste. In the case of drakes, Howe has told me how you hunt them. He says you use Drake's Lure to get them to land. How much of it do you have?"

"Four barrels of Drake's Lure," a knight across from Pencheval answered calmly. "One hundred steel bolts and six drakebows."

"Howe spoke of those as well."

"A powerful crossbow. It is so mighty the bolts must be forged from steel lest they shatter." The knight shook his head. "It is also so unwieldy they cannot be used in a fight, even if the drakes were slow enough to hit while on wing."

"Furthermore, the night renders them useless," the same officer argued. "We have archers skilled in the weapon, but they can't see in the dark."

"Drake's Lure attracts drakes when burned. Put the bait within the glow of the flame, then shoot the drake once it begins to feed."

"Which all but guarantees the death of the archer."

"Unless you send a Lion with him to ensure that doesn't happen."

"I hear our first plan," Rennoute stated, ending the discussion. "Any others?"

"What of the Disciple, Your Grace?" the knight standing next to Rennoute offered. "She has offered us aid."

"We will protect the Disciple until all are ready," Rennoute replied. "I would expect nothing less of her than such courage as she shows now, but the people cannot accept her yet. The Disciple's appearance may provoke more discord."

"Some wonder why she has not yet appeared, Your Grace." A sister in robes as Nan wore when Pencheval first saw her in Tarsun's Market frowned. "Others believe that her appearance would be ill tidings, and that you hold her captive as a witch."

"Which proves the Knight Superior's point." Pencheval rapped the table. "I agree with Your Grace. Nan is not trained in warfare or the use of her newfound might. I can tell you from experience that uncontrolled magic is a hazard worse than drakes."

"You will show proper deference to the Disciple, Lion." The tone of the knight remained calm but suddenly grew deadly serious. "They are the greatest among us."

"I knew your Disciple when we were both merely peasants in Terris Lyn, Your Grace. I hold her in such high regard that I spent an entire summer trying to goad a horde of goblins away from her at risk to my own life. Yet if she wields the wrath of Athesiene, she must learn to use it carefully, for good intentions will not salve the deaths caused by inexperience."

It was something Pencheval knew firsthand. When the gnome that granted his power first seated him in the chair where he would receive it, he explained it as though it was just another topic like the weather. He asked about Pencheval's health, then told him to drink the potion that looked and tasted of liquid metal. After that, he hummed to himself as he put the glyph in Pencheval's palm, muttering something about 'tolerances' and 'within the limitations' after he finished. Just another day for the glyphsmith, but it changed the Lion's life forever.

He reported to a field large enough to race horses with several thick wooden training dummies and nine other apprentices, including his friend Gantillion. He first realized the magic had come when he slapped his hand idly against a bench in boredom and broke one of its planks with his now uncontrolled strength. Gant had not been blessed with such might, but shortly thereafter cut his wooden dinner plate in half *with his thumb* as his signature Sharpness spell manifested without bidding.

It was then he learned why there were ten small tents pitched in the field. One of the Spellkeeper's staff informed them in businesslike tones that they were confined to the tents until they could control their new powers. It took days of intensive training before Pencheval tentatively saw the world as something not made of glass and parchment again. And Nan said she reduced rocks to dust with but a gesture? She had not accidentally done it to someone in the castle yet, but it was best to keep her out of conflict until she could manifest more control.

"The Disciple is not as you are, Lion."

"Enough." The Knight Superior gave the command weight without yelling it. "We have a plan and a volunteer. Make the arrangements, Castellan Galter."

"Yes, Your Grace." The officer wearing Rennoute's seal appeared displeased but kept it to himself.

"When you are finished, Lion, get some sleep. If the goblins hold to their history, tomorrow night will not be restful."

"Yes, Your Grace." Pencheval was just as certain they would attack again. After this night's triumph, they would be certain enough of going unchallenged to return.

Three

"This begins well, Leth."

The Stonemaster sat back on his bone chair and smiled. The warlord had only imagined what the bat-lizards might do to this point. To hear of it firsthand and realize little of what he believed possible before was wishful thinking left him elated. One human warrior home burned, and the humans did not inflict so much as a scratch on the horde in return. It was as one-sided a victory against the Snow Clan as he dared dream was possible.

"Of course, great Stonemaster. You allied wisely when you agreed to my chieftain's offer."

The Stonemaster smiled and nodded in a way he hoped concealed his real intentions. Yes, he did agree to let the Skyfang aid him in gaining the mountain-castle. He meant to keep his end of that bargain somewhat more flexible.

"Tonight we fly again, and their other warrior home will fall." Leth spoke in solemn tones and puffed out his chest, and the Stonemaster noticed the Bloodmoon Speaker and the Beastwarper Chieftain restrain their annoyance with his pomposity. "I will order two flights a night, and we will lay waste to the Snow Clan."

The Stonemaster was momentarily tempted. Yes, two flights a night would do nightmarish things to the Snow Clan. It could also exhaust the bat-lizards when he most needed them during the attack. Nor would it do to have that black-garbed Penn Cheval die before he could inflict the slow and agonizing death it deserved upon it.

"I would ask that you wait until the main attack to do that."

"An unusual request, considering that would hasten your victory."

"He speaks truly," the Bloodmoon Speaker huffed. "Burn the humans. Take their lands and their mountain-castle. Then punish the Silver Lion Clan warrior."

"Unless it flees," the Stonemaster answered smoothly. "Yes, two flights a night would grind upon the humans. Grind upon them enough that perhaps all hope is lost, and they flee the valley with your clan's greatest treasure rather than face us. We all mean them suffering now, but will you inflict it if the humans are gone when you arrive?"

"What say you then, Chief of Chieftains?" The Bloodmoon Speaker bared his teeth briefly, but the Stonemaster realized he had his ear.

“Give them some measure of false hope,” he answered. “Send only one flight a night until we move. Let them believe our wrath has limits. Let them believe it until it is too late.”

“Our sound gives them madness and keeps them hiding behind their cliff-walls rather than fleeing us,” he continued. “Once they believe themselves trapped, send enough flame to burn them to ruins. Those that live will be ours for the taking, if only for fear of leaving their cliff-walls lest the horde slaughter them.”

“This plan has merit,” Beastwarper agreed. “We have scared the humans into remaining in place once before. Yet if we mean to do this, we must do it soon, else the humans flee before the bat-lizards while the horde’s noise is unknown to them.”

“The other warrior home burns, and we move,” the Stonemaster answered. “Other targets require destruction then, but not this night.”

“It will be done, Chief of Chieftains,” Leth answered. “I will inform my wingleader of his instructions.”

“And I will ready the Berserkers. Finally!” Leth departed and the Bloodmoon Speaker strode away. Beastwarper leaned heavily on his staff to rise, hindered by his disfigurement, but the Stonemaster bid him to come forth instead.

“Chief of Chieftains?”

The Stonemaster rose from his bone chair and walked towards him. Beastwarper seemed momentarily shocked by the gesture, only to resume the look of sinister intellect he wore in his dealings with everyone else. The warlord approached until he stood face to face with him, and Beastwarper waited, refusing to be intimidated by it.

“Let me make this matter plain, Beastwarper,” the Stonemaster stated in quieter tones. “Your work with the human shaman was costly, and the knowledge gained dubious. In the matter of the bat-lizards we very much agree. Learning to tame our own is worth the deaths it may cause. If you help me learn those secrets, I will grant you the weight of a Bonestripper in human treasures once the mountain-castle falls. Their shamans will be yours to question as you will.”

“My gratitude, Chief of Chieftains.”

“And if you cause another disaster as the thunder-wielding shaman in the great cave, I will have you roasted alive.”

A brief gleam of rage appeared in Beastwarper’s eyes before the unyielding warlord glared him back into submission. No, Beastwarper would not get such leeway as he did before. The Stonemaster refused to repeat the error of allowing that ever again.

"Leth is the key," Beastwarper suggested, twisting to avoid reacting to the threat.

"No, he is the fool. The voice of the chieftain that will tell us nothing if he is captured, for he knows nothing. His part in this is only pretty speech and prattling."

"Then his wingleader?"

"Most assuredly. He leads the riders and their bat-lizards. He would know much of them."

"If so, how do we corner one who can flee into the skies?"

"That matter will require thought. Until then, see what can be gained by observation."

"Yes, Chief of Chieftains."

"You may go."

Beastwarper strained to turn and shuffle away, the growth of bone on his left shoulder hindering him as it always did. The warlord watched him briefly and then returned to his chair. No mistakes this time, even at the risk of Beastwarper's irritation. The free hand had cost him with that one, and his greatness would see to it that no additional failures plagued him.

***

Wingleader Jux inspected his camp and wished for the extended cave-pens of the Skyfang's clan-home. They were large and twisting passages lit by flames to keep the bat-lizards warm. There, the beasts remained within the protection of stone, well fed on meat and prisoners, and would burst from their mountains in flight during exercise days and forays. So many magnificent bat-lizards served by all the clans that fell to their knees before his own.

Their place here sat in a field outside the cliff-walls of the horde, and his few riders surrounded their mounts with low sapling barriers. Such things did little more than show the boundaries to the uninitiated so they did not step within reach of their deaths. The bat-lizards themselves were not at risk from the elements or attack.

They remained in place by pinning a loop of rope around their necks to the ground before them. The adults never realized they had grown too strong to be held fast by it–a bit of training that had held bat-lizards in place long before Jux was born. If they were broken to the rope as hatchlings, it would pin them for life.

He and his riders were more of a concern. There was a limit to the preparations and provisions they could carry along with them, and they had to improvise the rest. It left them short of protection from both the elements and the horde, and other goblins were ever a source of rivals. The rabble gaped in awe at the beasts from the cliff-walls, but some few grew interested for more cause than their magnificence.

Speaker Leth emerged from the hole in the cliff-walls and strode towards him with a superior grin. Jux shook his head, imagining what new troubles would be heaped upon him. He kept his face blank and waited when Leth waved to gain his attention.

"Yes, Speaker."

"The Council has agreed upon a plan," Leth announced, putting far too much weight on the words.

"Tell me what we are to do."

"Only one flight tonight to destroy the other warrior home of the humans. There won't be two flights a night until the horde is close enough for them to hear."

"Speaker, if we don't burn the humans quickly, they will prepare. Some of the rabble here say they can hunt bat-lizards. Even this Silver Lion Clan human of which all here speak is said to wear their skin."

"The Stonemaster would not lead the humans to believe fleeing is their only choice," Leth countered. "One flight tonight. The worst we can inflict comes soon."

"I don't trust this Stonemaster, Speaker. He and the warped one, this Beastwarper Chieftain, take far too great an interest in our works."

"They are as awed as any other clans, and no more capable of learning our secrets."

"Respectfully, these are not as the others." Jux tried to keep his voice even. "This Stonemaster forged a horde. He's neither a weakling nor a fool. Until that Bloodmoon Clan warrior came, we knew nothing of him, and such assumptions are dangerous."

"We will aid them. Our chieftain commands it."

"Yes, Speaker." Jux saw no point in arguing. The Skyfang Chieftain made him leader, likely under the assumption they would deal with clans no different from the ones they knew. The facts at this place so far told a wholly different tale.

Something about the Stonemaster set him above all other possible rivals. Yes, he had forged a horde, which was a rare feat, but it was more than that. It was as if the Fiend Under The Mountain had blessed him with some manner of power they could not understand. If he had that much power, he had ambition to accompany it, and the arts of taming bat-lizards would serve such ambitions too nicely to overlook.

"One flight tonight. Be ready." Leth waved dismissively at Jux and strode towards the horde, seemingly convinced all matters were in hand. The wingleader kept his mouth shut and weighed his options if the worst happened.

Too many lost bat-lizards, and they fled. At the first sign of treachery, they fled. Those unable to flee would die to preserve the secrets of the Skyfang, for his chieftain would show no mercy to him if those left behind were the reason a clan of rivals with tame bat-lizards rose.

Admittedly, the bargain Leth struck with the Stonemaster would be ideal on the off chance the warlord made it in earnest. He found it more likely the Chief of Chieftains would simply seek to use them and then attempt to capture them if he could. There was always duplicity, but both the Stonemaster and the warped one seemed more capable of it. Allowing them to succeed was out of the question, no matter who he had to burn to prevent it.

***

"Please, we will protect you all!"

A scurrying rogue shouldered past Friar Dominik, nearly knocking him into the crying boy he led back to his mother. They were the fifth family he had to reunite in the press to enter the castle. No one was expecting anything like a drake attack, and the rain of fire sent the town herding into the barbican like panicked livestock.

Only the darkness and disorder kept this from happening during the attack. Now that it was well into morning, the crowds pressed in earnest. The troops were unable to stop them short of closing the gates or locking shields.

The Shield of Athesiene dwarfed the town at the base of its eastern wall, but the townsfolk would crowd it regardless. He was unsure that the stone walls would protect them from drakes, but the grand fortification gave all who saw it hope that it could protect them from anything. Even Dominik found its fall inconceivable as he laid eyes upon it.

Most struggled to pass the crowded gates, but a few had other ideas. One small family packed everything they could onto a single mule and made their way to the town's gate, disappearing between the low wooden wall and the burned remains of the fortress. Dominik guessed their destination was the pass; there was no other reason to leave the castle except to flee the valley. Their final fate was uncertain, as highwaymen would prey upon those appearing weak or helpless.

Another man sat on his porch with a large clay bottle and laughed ever more drunkenly at the throngs wailing before the gate. It was hardly a good response to the drakes, but perhaps a more reasoned one. If they came from the skies, there was nowhere to run, and that one meant to meet his end without sobriety.

"Please, friar, can the Disciple not save us?" An old woman clasped his robe weakly with both hands. "Where has she gone?"

"You mean the witch?" A portly man adjusted his belt. "She's imprisoned in the dungeons, as she ought to be. You want safety, get to the castle."

"Mind your tongue, you miserable knave!" A lean but determined man in a wide hat grabbed the portly one by the collar and slammed a right hook into his cheek. He staggered back, face dripping blood. "She's the reason I lived through capture at Tarsun's Market. On my life, she's a Disciple and no mistake!"

"Yeah? She ain't here to save you from me!" The portly man struck his attacker in the gut and was on him moments after he fell.

"Enough!" Dominik twirled his staff and let it whoosh through the air before cracking the large man across the shoulders and the other on the head for good measure. "The drakes weren't enough for you? End your bickering and strife!"

Dominik restrained the urge to crack the large heretic repeatedly until the blood from his scalp ran down his collar. A Disciple's rise was to turmoil, just as The Histories told. Some would recognize the truth, and others would require more convincing. The fact he already knew it did not in any way excuse him from the duties of his faith.

He would aid as many of the townsfolk as he could, and that might mean the use of a quarterstaff. However, it was not his place to punish the ignorance of those who realized the Disciple's glory more slowly than himself. Nor was it his place to shatter the bottle of that drunk whose laughter only intensified at the display, however satisfying that unworthy thought was.

The two combatants staggered to their feet, glancing first at one another and then at Dominik. Their shared look of thrashing the friar disappeared when several soldiers approached and stood beside him. They glared at the pair and pointed to the gate, and the two limped towards it holding hands over sore spots.

Dominik wondered what was happening within, aside from soldiers cursing the new residents. He had not seen Pencheval since last night. Perhaps he was trying to determine a strategy to deal with the drakes or hearing one from the Knight Superior. Otherwise, this was little more than shuffling the folk into a stouter cage that would more securely hold them as the drakes' fire fell.

***

"Pardon my cynicism, Lion, but the fact you sought me out means you must want to do something life threatening."

Pencheval found no fault with Howe's accuracy as he approached him on the wall. The scout stood there with his arms crossed, waiting for the Lion to explain his next absurdity to him. Around him, soldiers attended to tasks or looked down at the crowd flooding into the courtyard through the gate far below them.

The wall was easily thick enough to let six soldiers pass shoulder to shoulder, and small hatches were set at even intervals next to the machicolated battlements. Anyone stationed here would be able to drop rocks or pour burning liquids on forces scaling the walls without exposing themselves to arrows, which would only be half useful against goblins. The vermin could climb but were too feeble to use more than slings.

"Someone has to kill the drakes. I could use your help."

"It's been a while since I've had the misfortune of carrying a drakebow. I'd take the opportunity to complain bitterly, but their necessity was made abundantly clear last night." Howe cupped his hands around his mouth and called down the wall. "Sergeant, permission to go with the Lion and plan my imminent death hunting drakes?"

"Aye, and take your buffoon's tongue with ye!"

"Come with me, Lion, and let me show you the wonders of our back-breaking drakebow. Then you can tell me why you think shooting just one drake when they return will be useful."

Pencheval's eyebrows rose in surprise. Just one? He followed the scout to the armory, and when the soldier attending the equipment produced a drakebow and windlass, he understood why.

Howe strained to lift it with both hands when the armorer gave it to him. The sturdy wooden stock was nigh as long as the scout was tall. Its wrought iron stirrup was scuffed from use and the wide lathe was a thick recurve of steel. The half a dozen bolts that accompanied it resembled steel knitting needles with long tapering points. Howe was right; that beast would slow its wielder to a crawl.

He was also correct about the windlass. In a fight with multiple drakes, they would get one shot, and only one shot. Then, whether or not the bolt struck true, they would have to deal with the others, and that assumed any of the drakes fell for the trap when all had riders that could see it for what it was.

"Can you shoot only by the light of a campfire? It might be all you get."

"It's not my idea of perfect circumstances, but I can. Now on to the part where all of this is worth it."

"It's simple. Goblins value themselves over most else. They may do great things if they fear their leaders, but when the tides of battle change, they will see to their own lives. I believe we can make the drake riding clan of goblins do this despite their warlord and quit the field."

"By killing just one drake?"

"By demonstrating they can't attack us with impunity. This is the first clan of goblins I've ever seen that could tame drakes, and they surely value them. So what happens if we show them we can slay them? They'll fight if they think they're immune to reprisals, so they need to stop being immune to reprisals."

"A long shot, but better than meekly waiting to burn," Howe answered, tentatively nodding his head. "A drake trap takes a good vantage point for a shot, a goat or a cow for bait, a bonfire, and some Drake's Lure."

"And?"

"And then I wish for the good old days when drakes only hunted livestock without goblin riders possessing better wits."

"That means you aren't firing without concealment. Any goblin that sees you from the air will target you."

"Aye. A trap set near the fortress...no, a trap set at the open gate to town. Clear shot through the gate from inside the first buildings along that street. Goblins can see in the dark, but they still can't see through a roof."

"Keep your bow completely inside the window," Pencheval added, "else a goblin spots it from the air."

Howe sighed. "My options narrow by the moment. And what will you be doing in all of this?"

"I'm there if something goes wrong." It was not the way Pencheval would have preferred to slay a drake, but they narrowed his options as well. No common crossbow could harm them, and throwing a battle axe at them was no better. His magically enhanced speed *might* let him strike one in flight, but the blow would do little beyond getting the drake's attention.

"More of a plan than we had this summer, Lion. What know you of drakes?"

"From what I saw last night, a drake will roar before it spits fire," Pencheval explained. "They do that when they hunt to startle their prey immobile. The goblins couldn't train that out of them."

"Short warning, but still warning," Howe said. "Good. If a drake notices you, get behind something so it can't swoop down upon you. I've heard of others doing this with even trees or shrubs the beasts might easily breach. When they swoop they don't like obstacles whether they can break them or not."

"Going prone?"

"Never do it, according to one of the knights I served on a drake hunt. It won't go over you, but it will go out of its way to land on you and chew you to pieces."

"Good to not learn that the hard way. Do you have anything for the bolts?"

"For the bolts?" Howe cocked his head.

"Reaper's Ink, man." Pencheval's voice lowered to a whisper. The Guild of the Silver Lion recommended it as the poison of choice against drakes and other large beasts despite its vile reputation and tenuous legality. The doses cost two gold crowns each and one could kill themselves with it if they so much as scratched their skin with a treated arrowhead. "You're hunting drakes."

"Reaper's Ink? How do you even know about that stuff?" Howe recoiled. "I've killed a drake before. Let me deal with the bow and don't even think of Reaper's Ink within sight of a knight if you mean to keep your neck out of a noose."

"It's your shot, scout," Pencheval told him.

"And you?"

"The goblins provided the weapon I'll use should I have the misfortune of facing one of these things on the ground."

The axe he took from a goblin champion at Tarsun's Market not long ago made him nervous. Free of its hides, it would snarl and hum from magical instability, but it was sharp enough to cleave through a sapling with a mere touch. It would be ideal against the thick hide of a drake, if it did not explode in his hands first. If all else failed, nothing enjoyed being stabbed in the eyes with a dagger, and even a drake would flinch if it was forced to defend against one.

As his Argentsteel sword would be dead weight in this fight, he decided to leave it in his chambers. While excellent against smaller and more fragile opponents, it was of no more use against such toughness than any other sword. The blade simply lacked the concentration of force needed to punch through drake's hide, magically enhanced strength or not.

It smacked of something resembling a plan, and one he hoped would work. If they were unsuccessful in knocking this drake riding clan of goblins back on their heels even once, there was little hope for defeating both them and the horde.

Four

Pencheval searched the darkened sky to the east through an open window, knowing it was only a matter of time before the drakes appeared. A few stars still gleamed over the glow of the bonfire that dominated most of the view. He wondered when a star would go dark and then reappear as a goblin and its mount flew across it.

He and Scout Howe waited within a small hut, and he found the improvised hunting blind less than ideal. It was meager place with wooden walls and a thatch roof. The only thing in it that would not burn was the cobblestone fireplace. The former owners had a table and a large wooden bed for an entire family but little else. It was a drake-ready firetrap only awaiting their arrival, but it possessed the sole redeeming quality of an excellent vantage.

Howe had moved the two chairs at the table so he could reposition it. It now lined up with the window and served as a platform for his weapon. He stared along the loaded bolt, making minute adjustments to line it up with a cow pinned next to the bonfire. He would take the shot only if a drake took the bait, and it might if properly lured.

The theory was that Drake's Lure made the fire smell exactly like drake's flame. That and the livestock was usually enough to trick one into thinking it had stumbled onto an easy meal and land. That was when Howe would take his shot, hopefully either killing the drake or wounding it to the point Pencheval could finish it with the axe.

The grim Lion considered the options and concluded the matter was trouble in any case. They might shoot a drake tonight, or they might watch as the riders again succeeded because they prevented their mounts from landing. More than one might land, or the goblins might counter the trap by incinerating the town. Even if they succeeded in downing a drake, the others would know of the trouble and either retaliate, flee, or fall back to return with still more drakes. If they retaliated, the pair would have to retreat with all haste through roads that wove between highly flammable wood and thatch buildings.

"Any last words, mercenary?" Howe snapped his head back to take a shot from his flask, then sucked air through his teeth. "Best be profound while you can. The Black Archer may find his mark on both of us tonight."

"We will prevail. We've done it before."

"Aye, but the horde had no drakes then."

"That is only an advantage to them until those who brought them decide they've lost too many," he reassured. "How many do they ever lose against other goblins? It won't take all their deaths to make retreat seem their best course."

"Perhaps. And perhaps it will only take one drake's death for them to avenge it by sending them all. If there was any way around it, I'd rather be drinking."

Pencheval nodded. At least Howe realized he could do nothing but fight if he meant to save the valley. The knights and soldiers also certainly knew, but what of the townsfolk? Some of them already fled.

One spring in Tarsun's Market, it was what he meant to do himself. The horde was someone else's problem and he saw no reason to die to it. That was before he was reunited with Nan only to lose her again when that town fell. After what it had done to her, himself, and to those here he befriended, he refused to leave until their warlord died for its predations.

The pinned cow mooed and dropped its head to nibble on a weed in the road, oblivious to its purpose. That would change soon, but the drake would not let it suffer long.

"Time to watch and wait." Pencheval willed his magic to grant him vision with a Clearsight charm. Night disappeared into shades of gray, only showing the orange glow of firelight and browns of the dirt road into town where there was already light. The sky was empty of all but a few clouds, and nothing moved inside the now abandoned fortress standing across from its ruined twin.

"Good luck to you, Lion. If you see them coming, don't wait. That Drake's Lure will burn for a good long while."

"Speaking of which..." Three dark dots appeared in the distance, black against the gray of the Clearsight charm. The indistinct specks became clearer as they grew, alternating between slow wingbeats and glides. The flick of a long tail gave them away as more than birds.

"How many?" Howe placed the stock of the drakebow against his shoulder and took aim at the cow.

"Three, as before."

"Be swift!"

Pencheval snatched the bag of Drake's Lure and ran. Unburdened by his sword, he scrambled through the door and towards the flame. A few moments later, he upended the open bag over it. He recoiled with his forearm over his face as an acrid, burning stench replaced the pleasant smell of wood smoke. The once docile cow protested its pinning with plaintive wails.

Pencheval gave the animal a moment's pity before scrambling back towards the hut. He had announced the meal to a trio of drakes, and it could await them alone.

***

Bur closed his eyes for a moment, enjoying the feel of cool air and the sound of wingbeats beneath him. It was time for the Skyfang Clan to once again show the humans who was master, and he eagerly anticipated his part in making them watch another of their warrior homes burn. He would do this as the second of three in the line of attacks, behind only his Enforcer.

In the distance, he could see the tiny lights of the human's mountain-castle. While night did little to block his vision, he was grateful they made his target so much easier to find. Well lit was still far better than merely visible.

The valley floor swept beneath and behind him. One of the human paths made the trail easy to follow, and the mountain-castle grew in size as they approached. His bat-lizard's wings stopped flapping as it glided to spare its strength, and he reined it back as it pulled too far from their line.

When his Enforcer reined his bat-lizard to the north, Bur counted his heartbeats, and on the tenth one did the same. All he had to do was watch his leader and repeat what he did. An arc and turn brought him into line with the other human warrior home, and a...goat?

No, it was too big to be a goat, even obscured by a billowing fire. It did not make noises like a goat either, though he could hear its panic as he turned through the air to follow his leader. One startled sound he never heard before escaped it as the lead mount roared and spat flame at the other warrior home. As its light grew, he realized no Snow Clan warriors occupied it.

No matter. Neither an empty warrior home nor a strange not-goat could threaten him or his mount. He reined to fly in line with his Enforcer and rose, anticipating the dive. A moment later, the bat-lizard dropped, and he pressed against the seat as it dove into range.

He snapped his heels against his mount to command it to spit flame, and to his surprise it ignored him. Instead, it beat its wings to decelerate and land on the other side. Bur repeated the snap of his heels and slapped the reins, but his bat-lizard stubbornly refused to heed him.

Fiend-forsaken beast! What did it want on the ground so badly that it landed? It never disobeyed him before, and if his enforcer thought he could no longer command it, it would mean the whip or even his life.

He felt its claws touch the ground next to a smoking bonfire. It smelled exactly the same as bat-lizard flame, only in such quantity he nearly choked. His eyes watered as his mount charged through the fire at the creature on the other side. The flame did nothing to his beast, but he coughed from the clouds of smoke and fanned away the heat.

The bat-lizard's body and head twisted as it snapped forward. Its prey gave one last agonized cry before falling silent. One leg moved forward to pin it as the sounds of a rending carcass reached Bur's ears, followed by the slow, deliberate motions of a bat-lizard adjusting its food so it could swallow it whole. Bur felt something large pass through its gullet, and then heard it roar in agony before it scurried back through the remains of the flame.

He could feel it favor its right front leg as it moved. Still blinded and coughing from the smoke, Bur felt along leather straps and rubbery hide until his fingers touched on a short steel protrusion. A dart? An arrow? If it was, it had pierced so deeply little more than a thumb's length remained. Had the humans poisoned it?

If they had, it was hardly enough, as his mount roared and spat. The glob of flame struck something nearby, and then his bat-lizard limped forward to attack. It made it a half a dozen steps before it groaned, feet slipping from under it. Bur's eyes teared as the last of the smoke cleared from his vision, and he saw two humans scramble from a burning thatch hut. One took rags or hides from an axe that snarled in its hands, and the other held a strange bow fastened to a long piece of wood. It slowed the human down, but it still refused to drop the heavy thing.

The human with the axe wore bat-lizard skin over another shiny metal skin. Over it all it wore a dark shirt bearing the battered but recognizable symbol of a gray lion. Was it a human from another clan? The Snow Clan wore white shirts, but this one? Fiend's breath, was it this Penn Cheval the horde feared?

He saw the warrior wave the other one towards the mountain-castle and glance at the skies. A moment later it smiled wickedly, took up its axe in both hands, and charged him.

***

Outstanding.

Pencheval smiled at the results of Howe's shot. The scout had indeed taken care of the arrows, and whatever he applied rendered a charging drake into a fat, torpid cat. The swift but thrashing death caused by enough Reaper's Ink it was not, but it just laid there, unable to do anything but die.

He raised his axe and charged. Its companions would not reach it in time to save it, but he meant to avoid their wrath when they did return. The glob of flame from but one drake rapidly reduced their hunting blind of a cottage to a roasting pit, and left them scrambling for their lives. What would two more drakes do?

The beast noticed him and raised its head to bite too slowly. The descending blade sank to the shaft and cleaved the skull so easily it felt like slicing a melon. Perhaps that was the purpose of that axe before the goblins stumbled upon it crawling the depths. Perhaps it had once belonged to the dwarves of legend, now long gone from the world. Pencheval shook the thoughts from his mind and climbed over the corpse to the rider. Now was not the time to care about the origins of his weapon.

The goblin rider desperately pulled at the straps holding it fast to the chair. Before it could free itself, Pencheval sheared away most of its torso with a single swift stroke. He was grateful for the ease with which preparation had rendered this rider defeated until he heard another roar in the distance and the approach of wingbeats.

Pencheval willed himself sight, and the flying form of a drake resolved itself from darkness through the smoke and heat. It dove straight at him, and in the distance the other one followed behind it. He found no cause to believe they meant anything but his death.

"Howe, get to cover!" Pencheval turned towards the castle to flee and was grateful he did not see Howe out in the open.

He turned and ran, listened as the wingbeats grew louder, and remembered what he learned from the night before. First it roared, then it spat. Yet how well could it compensate for a moving target at this speed? He heard one particularly powerful thump of leathery wings, then the roar. The second the screech broke the silence he willed himself speed, snapped sharply to his right, and charged shoulder-first into a closed shop door.

The lock broke as a glow briefly lit the room before him, and a brief but intense heat fell on his back as the drake's flame passed by him. He heard it hiss when it hit the dirt road. A quick rush of wind from a giant wingbeat lapped at his tabard before he stumbled and fell to the floor, and he turned in time to see the last of a tail flicker and disappear.

His perception of time returned to normal as his magically enhanced speed faded, and he heard one drake fly away as the other roared. Once again he saw an orange glow briefly light the street through the door. He expected the thatch roof to crackle and smoke any moment, but the flame seemed to disappear into the distance. Disappear to where?

Anywhere in town would be deadly, he reminded himself. Most of it was flammable, and all of the rooftops were thatch. This place could easily burn to the castle walls, and if the drakes pinned the defenders, it would.

With both him and Howe still in it.

How many times could a drake spit flame in succession? Too many given his luck. He stumbled through the door as the axe snarled from its instability and scanned the skies for drakes. He saw them climb and turn, and then realized orange glowed from both sides of the street.

Buildings burned between them and the castle. The riders had not pinned them between the flames yet, but if they lingered that could well change. Then what? The goblins could harass them from the sky until the smoke or heat killed them or land to herd them into the flames. They had little to fear in either case. The riders could fly away from the danger while Pencheval and Howe could not.

"Howe!"

"Not dead yet, Lion!" Howe lumbered from the door of a cottage across the street, lugging the drakebow and nervously searching the skies for drakes. "But I don't think we've convinced them to flee!"

***

Enforcer Bryx snarled as his mount banked sharply to avoid the cliff-walls of the mountain-castle. Straps pulled tightly at his chest as the world flipped sideways. For some strange reason, the human he targeted successfully dodged into a big hut just as his bat-lizard spat. It avoided its short but painful death, leaving the glob of flame sputtering in the dirt and him to curse his luck.

It would die tonight. Wingleader Jux would take news of a bat-lizard's death badly, and if Bryx wished to avoid suffering for this disaster, he had best punish it. Fortunately, the places among which it hid were easily burned, as the hut Bur's mount set alight demonstrated beyond all doubt.

His bat-lizard coughed and wheezed. It would not spit flame again tonight. However, it could scatter burning thatch and wood, as the flames licking the tops of these huts would give it no pause. A rake of the claws would send burning wood and straw flying into other wood and straw, spreading enough destruction to bring those two humans the death by roasting they so richly deserved.

Bryx turned and flew, glancing back at the cliff-walls as he did. Hundreds of human warriors stood atop them. Some readied large things which appeared as giant bows mounted on many pieces of large wood. Could the ground-bound fools hit him in mid-flight?

He would not give them the chance. He could pitch and turn without making himself as easy a target as that fool Bur. They normally used the bat-lizards this way to cause rockslides, but it would work just as well on these piles of tinder. It was time to return this injury and make the humans suffer.

***

"Back to the castle!" Pencheval snatched the drakebow from Howe. It was easily twice as heavy as his Argentsteel sword, and he could feel its weight threaten to pry it loose from his fingers.

"How will that help?" Howe scrambled to maintain pace as Pencheval raced up the road towards the outer gate.

"Do you remember seeing a thatch rooftop on the keep?" Pencheval remembered seeing only stone in the towers and slate rooftops along the rest. The drake could fly about the walls and buildings, but they would find nothing to burn.

"Better than in the street!"

The barbican's gate remained open to allow them entry into the outer walls. Rennoute's castellan initially balked at the request to leave it unbarred, but Pencheval ended the discussion by asking him how a sealed gate would ward the castle from drakes. The castellan conceded its futility and left them this route to escape.

Pencheval snapped around at a roar and a crash behind him. Some bulk only half-visible in the night smashed into the burning roof of a cottage, shattering beams and spraying cinders across the street. Glowing embers landed on rooftops and wooden shingles, leaving dozens of small fires blooming among new fuel.

"Run, Lion!"

He spotted the other drake as it dove the same way. Claws raked over another burning rooftop just before them and sent more incendiary wreckage into those parts of the town still unravaged. Howe and Pencheval recoiled as the roof of the buildings opposite them ignited.

"Run or burn!" Pencheval charged between the igniting structures and heard Howe's footsteps behind him. The smell of wood smoke reached him as the crackle and roar of growing flames drowned out departing wingbeats. By the time they reached the barbican's gate, the orange glow lit the stones of the walls and the street beneath their feet, casting dark shadows ahead of them.

Pencheval willed his Clearsight charm to grant him sight in darkness. The drakes circling for another pass resolved themselves in shades of gray. He did not know what they meant to strike next, but their wrath at their companion's death was yet unsated.

***

Bryx reined his mount into a slow turn and kept to a lazy arc away from the human warriors on the cliff-walls. He meant to give the flames he scattered time to feed and grow, as he needed more than a few smoldering huts before he could repeat the attack. After the death of a bat-lizard, he refused to settle for mere irritation. Nor would Wingmaster Jux accept anything but real damage for it either, regardless of what he previously commanded.

The humans escaped into that peak with the biggest stone base. Perhaps there was a passage through it into the cliff-walls or into the caves under the mountain-castle. Bryx shrieked a curse but kept his distance.

Infuriating as the bat-lizard's death was, they could not fly any closer to the walls in pursuit. Risking impacts was pointless, and even a slowdown could be fatal as it gave the humans a real chance to strike back. He took some comfort from what the humans would lose to down just one bat-lizard. Perhaps they escaped, but the reprisals would not please the rest of their clan.

Bryx heard an additional set of wingbeats and found the last rider to his left. His spooked minion pointed furiously in the direction of the horde and then shrugged as if awaiting an answer. Bryx shook his fist at him and pointed for him to fall behind and follow. He was the enforcer here, and if that fool flew off and left him despite the command he would pay for it in pain once he landed.

He saw the rider grit his teeth but obey. Good. They would only be here for two more passes at most and he meant to make them count. One rake across another burning hut and then perhaps something on the cliff-walls would die for this outrage. A bat-lizard sending a Snow Clan enforcer or two screaming to their deaths would bring a spectacular end to this attack and disabuse the humans of the notion their mountain-castle could offer them any real safety.

The slow arc brought the human huts back into view. A healthy and slowly spreading orange glow accompanied the rising smoke and left so many wonderful options. It was just a matter of deciding on the proper target to scatter and all of their huts would burn.

***

Howe leaned on his knees within the narrow passage under the barbican, gasping for air. He looked at the burning town they only just escaped and shook his head.

"But for the grace of Athesiene, Lion, we would be roasted. Lord on High be praised."

"It's not done yet." Pencheval rolled his head until his neck popped.

"It's not...what?"

"Two drakes still fly. If we mean to discourage them, then the more we slay tonight, the better."

Howe gaped at Pencheval for a moment, then stood upright and shook his head. "No. Not even going to feign surprise. I should be accustomed to this by now after a summer tormenting an entire goblin horde with you."

"Just another day in the life." Pencheval offered Howe his drakebow, and the scout took it.

"Right then." Howe put the stirrup of the crossbow into the dirt and slipped his foot into it. He clapped a windlass from a shoulder bag onto the weapon, hooking the bowstring before cranking it with both hands.

"We'll need more bait to take another shot," Howe told the waiting mercenary. "Don't happen to have another cow under that tabard, do you?"

"No, I have something better."

"Do I even dare ask?" Pencheval heard the bowstring click into place.

"We have the warrior who slew their companion and its drake," Pencheval reminded him as the axe in his hands snarled. "Can you hit it if it's coming straight at me?"

"There was a time I thought you were mental, but clearly the word does not do you justice." Howe pulled a bolt from a quiver and nocked it into place. A whitish substance covered it from the point to halfway down the shaft, and Howe took care to avoid touching it.

"*If* I can see it coming, and *if* it slows down, and *if* the rider is content to not simply fly by and slam you from the battlements, I might be able to shoot it before it removes more than a limb or your head." Howe removed his foot from the stirrup and put the drakebow in a ready position. After the run he could only just hold it before him.

"The battlements?"

"Yes, Lion. If you mean to pursue this mad plan, the only place with enough of a view to offer bait and take this shot will be from the top of a tower. The barbican's roof is closest."

Pencheval frowned. It was a risky way to kill another drake. The roof offered no real cover and nowhere to run besides down. And while he had not considered it before, the drakes did have the option to simply throw their bulk at them without stopping, which made the risk even worse.

Yet there was no real alternative he could see. If he meant to inflict losses on the drake riders, the faster it happened, the sooner they broke and fled. Right now that meant using the only plan they had before the attackers returned to the horde. It was both lunacy and the best idea time and circumstances allowed him.

"To the tower it is then."

"Remember the tactics we discussed before this, Lion. You may need them."

***

Bryx held his breath as his bat-lizard soared through the smoke and clawed a spray of burning debris into another cluster of human dwellings. Unbearable heat quickly yielded to a rush of cooler wind and the thump of his mount beating its wings to regain speed. He reined it upwards and away from the cliff-walls, and again not so much as an arrow from the Snow Clan answered the attack.

Word among the horde was that humans fared poorly huddled together for long. When their town burned they would have nothing but the mountain-castle. The warriors there were strong, but if they had to deal with their rabble constantly underfoot? Bryx smiled at the thought of their dismay. It was not the worst he meant to inflict, but it would do for now.

A human warrior home and their town burned in one attack. That would justify the loss of a bat-lizard to Wingmaster Jux. Anything less and his response to the night's losses could well be fatal. But now the task was done, and he considered what he would say to explain this as he soared towards the horde.

Behind him, he heard a roaring bat-lizard before the rip and crash of another hut shattered to flinders. A quick glance confirmed the spread of flame along entire paths and the first flickers in the wooden huts nearest the face of the cliff-wall. The humans could not rush to extinguish the flames for fear of the skies, and in fact could do little to quell them even once they left. One more little stone in the mountain of suffering they would inflict upon the Snow Clan.

Another roar like a mountain lion attracted his attention to the top of one of the flat round peaks. There, a single human in armor and a dark shirt lifted its axe into the air and shook it at him. It dwindled into the distance as he put his back to the mountain-castle and the last rider pulled alongside him.

Bryx's companion glanced backwards to see what interested him so much, shook his head, and dragged his finger along his throat. Bryx agreed with him. Yes, it was a trap. The human meant to taunt him near the walls where the bulk of the Snow Clan force could swarm him with arrows and the large bows built on logs.

Yet it was the human that killed his rider and left him in such a tenuous position with the wingleader. Caution warred with vengeance until the mountain-castle was no more than a small collection of lights in the distance. A quick spike of fear at the wingleader's reaction decided the question. He motioned for his companion to return to the horde, reined his mount, and commanded it to climb.

Its breathing grew labored as it rose, and his incredulous minion obeyed. He flew a wide arc towards the mountains and back towards the mountain-castle. By now the human would believe him departed, but if it remained where it was, he would rudely disillusion it. He had no flame and approached the extent of his mount's endurance, but it had enough for one more ambush before he left.

The burning town was good. A burning town and a dead warrior was better. If that warrior also happened to be this Penn Cheval that so terrified the horde, one loss would be a pittance to pay for its defeat.

***

Pencheval lowered the axe he took from the goblin champion and, with the benefit of a Clearsight charm, watched the drake riders retreat. The weapon let out one last growl before subsiding into a ragged humming. He did not expect his hastily conceived trap to be perfect, but ignored? Hardly.

Perhaps they saw through it. They had to know after the fight on the ground that he was not simply offering himself up to be slaughtered. Perhaps, having achieved all they intended, they merely returned to the horde with news of the battle. They failed to kill him, but their damage still burned below.

Easily half of the town would be ruins and ashes by dawn–likely all of it. Those buildings farthest from the start of the arson yet blazed, while those which first burned were reduced to lazy wisps of smoke and glowing embers. Even with the charm allowing him sight through darkness, he saw nothing moving below. If any chose to remain in the town, they likely perished for their misjudgment.

"Precious little for what was lost." Pencheval bowed his head.

Howe joined him at the edge, and he heard the sound of the drakebow's stirrup scrape against the stone roof. "Saint Marion's revelation. This was the price for just one drake?"

"A goblin's sight and cunning paired with the power of a drake is a damnable combination. It may have been mere luck the one disregarded its rider for a meal."

"Then what do we do now?"

"We find another way and quickly. One loss may give them either pause or wrath. With goblins, it is never safe to assume their reaction will make it easy."

Howe clicked his bow's windlass onto its stock and delicately placed the treated bolt back in its quiver. The scout took great pains to avoid firing the weapon dry, and instead winched it back to unloaded after releasing the string from the trigger.

Pencheval took the opportunity to put his axe in a nearby bag. Its humming subsided as it was once again shielded from whatever caused its instability. He wiped the sweat from his brow with the back of his left forearm and gave one last look at the town.

"I don't suppose you've ever faced drakes at the castle before."

"No one's ever ridden drakes against us or anyone else we know," Howe replied. "I wish it had remained–" Howe snapped to the right and put his hand over his eyes. "Did you hear that?"

"Hear what?" Pencheval heard the soldiers beneath him talking and the crackle of flames in the distance.

"It sounded like–leathery flaps through air!" Howe pointed, and several of the soldiers shouted as Pencheval willed himself sight. Howe's uncanny perception noted the sound before anyone else, but only the Clearsight charm showed Pencheval a drake barreling towards them and far too near. By the time he realized he should tackle Howe out of its reach, it was close enough to count its teeth.

A flash of light briefly rendered night into day. He saw the shadow-black silhouette of a drake being thrown to one side like a leaf in a gale before a thunderclap knocked both him and Howe flat. He barely heard its pained roar over the ringing in his ears and saw nothing as it screeched and flapped wildly above him. Spots danced before his eyes, and he shook his head to try and regain his senses.

He thought he imagined the second flash only to again hear thunder. It was not as close or as powerful, but it was definitely not his imagination. The drake roared again, and the flapping of wings faded into the distance as it hurried away.

It was one of the clergy, and a powerful one. Whoever it was had saved them from the drake, albeit at the expense of feeling as though a god had struck him down. He found it a small price to pay. Had the drake actually hit him, it would have slammed him from the barbican and possibly slain him on the spot.

"Thunder...and lighting? What?" Howe moaned as he tried to move.

"Nan." After what she had told Pencheval when they reunited, she was the only one who could have done this. It was still not pleasant to endure that particular spell, but far preferable to suffering death at the claws of a horridly swift drake.

***

"Disciple, you are out in the open!"

Nan struggled to catch her breath and quell her fear of the keep's dizzying height. Though exhausted from the climb, the power she expended to launch the two unsuccessful attacks against that...thing...was as replenished as it was before. Whatever else, the Lord on High still found her worthy.

At least He did not judge her by her aim. Twice she struck at the drake to save Pencheval, and twice it evaded death only to shriek its irritation and fly away. She hoped it had quit the field. Had that archer with him not pointed she never would have cast in time. As it was, the first blast was more a reflex than a deliberate action. The drake flew so swiftly a second thought would have seen Pencheval slain.

She heard the hiss of a sword leaving its scabbard, and her bodyguard knight interposed himself between her and the last sighting of the drake with his shield raised to his face.

"Disciple, please return to the keep! We don't know for certain if the goblins have fled."

"If they haven't, my task is not yet done."

Pencheval slowly rose from the stones and shook off the spell. Both he and the archer still lived, and she quietly gave thanks to the Lord on High. She remembered using that spell on the goblins and scorching them to death if they were too close. Would she have done that to him had she missed? The thought of it left her heart in her throat from the panic.

Yet if she had not acted, the Lion would be dead. Not dazed, or recovering slowly, but dead. Smashed off the battlements by that horrid goblin and its overgrown lizard. The thought was cold consolation, and the fear she could have burned Pencheval to the bone barely subsided.

"If there is a place for you in this, Disciple, it will be within a battle plan. Right now, we are exposed on the keep's roof and goblin eyes see far better than ours at night. If they are still in the skies, we are known to them, but they will be invisible to us until it is too late."

Nan saw Pencheval stand completely upright, stretch his back, and then look directly at her. Surely they were no more than shadows to him? She realized he did notice her when he waved upwards and then helped his companion to his feet.

"How did he just do that?"

"One of the friars says the Lion knows a charm that grants him sight in darkness, Disciple. If he fought goblins in the past, it was likely one of the first he learned."

"Dominik?"

"I cannot say, Disciple. Now I beg of you, please quit the roof and return to the safety of the keep."

Nan surveyed the scene and reluctantly agreed with the knight. Pencheval and his companion were unharmed, but the soldiers cringed from the display. The sounds of terrified townsfolk reached even the roof, dulled as they were by the distance. Use of her newfound power could save lives, and yet still bore consequences she did not care to countenance. Her actions had tremendous weight, for better or worse. So far, it had been for both.

She looked down at the ladder leading back into the keep. Tonight she winded herself for a good cause. After months as a goblin prisoner helpless to do more than despair and obey, a second night of shrieking drakes was too much to passively bear. The keep's roof seemed a good vantage to end them, but saving Pencheval was as good a purpose for the climb if not a better one.

Perhaps next time, she would just go to the walls.

Five

Nan sat in the front pew of the castle's chapel, leaning against the arm rest for support. After last night's hard climb to the top of the keep, she was not eager to move from it. The polished but unpadded wood never seemed more comfortable, and the deep silence was the sweetest it had ever been since her retreat to it.

Had the use of Athesiene's power last night been a mistake? Her aches and fatigue insisted that it was. The screams and horror of those below all but confirmed it. Yet she was certain of her actions despite all else. That power had saved Pencheval, and moreover, it had given a goblin some measure of a long overdue comeuppance.

"Begging the pardon of the Disciple, but using the Lord on High's will so soon was unwise."

Unwise? Nan was horrified by the cool disconnect of the knight from their circumstances. Was he not on the roof of the keep with her, able to see the havoc inflicted by the drakes as well as herself? Could he very well not see who she saved?

She slowly rose to her feet, ignoring her protesting muscles. "And were you in my stead, what would you have done? I knew that Lion since before he could walk. Would you have me leave him to the goblins?"

"I humbly submit, Disciple, that perhaps such things do not inspire the troops or maintain order. Many more than two are at stake here."

"Horsefeathers! If anything is wrong, it is that I hide away in a chapel when the Lord on High's valley is at stake."

Nan put her hand over her chest. Did she just proclaim that? She did. On a second moment's consideration she agreed with it. She had all this power, so why would she not use it?

Uncertainty and the nigh unbearable weight of it all returned to her. Yes, the power was immense and Athesiene had not seen fit to relieve her of it. But would it be enough? She lit the skies with His fire and the drake outran it. Worse still, would it be so much she wrought only panic instead of victory?

The latch on the chapel door cracked open and the knight placed himself between her and the entrant. It would be touching but for the unreality of it all. Not long ago she was Sister Nan, schoolteacher and then prisoner. Now the entirety of Athesiene's monastic knightly order showed her deference and called her Disciple. The sudden shift still jarred her.

"Go no farther with weapons, Lion."

"I wear no weapons, knight." It was a familiar voice absent the notes of irritation and gruffness it once bore at Tarsun's Market.

Pencheval appeared none the worse for wear after his close call last night. He wore his tabard but no sword belt this morning. Why would he be without it?

"I would speak with Nan."

"The Disciple is weary. Unless you have a matter of import, leave."

"He stays, brother." Nan put her hands on her hips and tapped her foot. "You want to consider me a Disciple? Well, then, I'm a Disciple and I say he can speak with me."

"As you say." The knight resumed his post near the door and kept his sword within easy reach. "Do not harm the Disciple, or you answer to me with your life."

"I've fought to save your Disciple. Why would I harm her?" Pencheval smirked at the knight, but Nan glared at them both. Her armored bodyguard remained impassive, but Pencheval cleared his throat and squirmed awkwardly.

"And you! What manner of madness so infected you that you tried to kill three drakes by yourself?"

"No manner of madness, Nan. The forces here had a method of hunting drakes. We needed to know if we could use it or not on those ridden by the goblins. We could last night, and now they have one less drake and a wealth of doubt for their troubles."

"A wealth of doubt? What wealth of doubt? The town burned to ashes! I could see it from the keep, and you're lucky the horrid things flew close enough for me to strike at them!"

"Those who brought the drakes now know we can slay them," he replied. Nan was stunned that he could remain so calm about the events of last night. Perhaps it was because such things had been his life for so long. "Will they now doubt their alliances enough to leave? One drake may not be sufficient to discourage them, but how many more will they bear to lose?"

"Even if they flee to their home, the remaining goblins still have a horde."

"The horde alone, Disciple, will not be enough against the Shield of Athesiene," the knight at the door replied calmly. "The drakes make all the difference, and so he went. We manned the walls to give them pause and provided the Lion and scout a place to retreat."

"Is it all just...augh!" Nan threw her hands in the air. So much death and destruction met so calmly. She had only tolerated it in Tarsun's Market because she thought it was what the circumstances demanded to save her charges. But this?

"Nan?"

"What?" Nan scowled at Pencheval, who met her gaze calmly.

"Thank you for your aid. You likely saved us both."

Nan blinked twice and was struck by being reminded of the obvious. The Lord on High granted her power to stop the goblins. Not merely at Tarsun's Market, but in the whole valley of the Emerald Refuge. His works and faithful were threatened by the ravenous tide of them.

Her intervention last night saved two lives. Uncertainty or not, bearable or not, she no longer doubted that her place was to act. She was not the issue despite the treatment and awe of those around her suggesting otherwise, nor was her need for silence. Hers was the work of the Lord on High, and it was time to attend it.

"You are welcome, lad," she smiled. "But more remains to do."

The unending cacophony of the goblin horde returned as a memory, and she felt rubbed raw from even remembering its sound. She banished the thought as well as she could. She would not run as she was once forced to do from Terris Lyn. She would not hide from the goblins or her new path as a Disciple. She would act, as mad as it all felt, if only because Athesiene still seemed to find her worthy.

"It is time for you to leave, Lion."

"You worry too much," Pencheval said dismissively.

"Enough from you both! I've half a mind to switch you two." The knight seemed dumbstruck by the remark. Pencheval snorted and nodded a goodbye before striding towards the exit.

"I would be glad for your aid again, Nan. We are sorely in need of it."

***

The Stonemaster sat in council and suppressed the urge to laugh in the face of the rattled Leth. The Skyfang Speaker had arrived here so haughtily on his bat-lizard, convinced that the warlord would accept any offer he made without hesitation just from the sheer awe of the display. That was before last night, when three bat-lizards left for the mountain-castle and only two returned. Not a catastrophic loss, but it was clear he expected none at all.

Amusing as that was, victory called for more than indulging petty malice at Leth's expense. Despite the amusement the warlord found in the Speaker's half-convincing show of indignation, it would be a disaster if he reconsidered his options. If he chose to leave, the Stonemaster had ample opportunity to kill the Skyfang for reneging on the agreement before they took flight, but that would still deny him bat-lizards.

"This is intolerable! What shaman trick did the Snow Clan use to make a bat-lizard land, and why did you not tell us they could do this?"

"Because we didn't know." The Stonemaster kept his face blank because that statement was only half true. He knew the Snow Clan could kill bat-lizards, or they could not have given Penn Cheval the scales it now wore. How they accomplished that feat was just a mystery until now.

"Cease your wailing! Did you think the mountain-castle would fall without losses?" The Bloodmoon Speaker looked as though he would slap Leth senseless in true Bloodmoon fashion but thought twice about it.

"What is important now is that we learn from this and determine a better course of action," the Beastwarper Chieftain offered. "The humans have their tactics. All that remains to determine is what they did and what we will now do."

"What we will now do? They can make the bat-lizards land, which..."

"Renders them vulnerable?"

The Stonemaster blinked but kept his face expressionless. Beastwarper had drawn an obvious conclusion, but Leth appeared as someone who realized he should not have opened his mouth. The warlord found such caution wise. It was bad to damage the illusion of one's invincibility when on the ground with a horde.

Leth's discomfiture suggested the bat-lizards could be overpowered. If they were not loyal solely to the Skyfang, the Stonemaster potentially had a wealth of bat-lizards before him, ready for the taking. Or would, if he knew how to command them.

"Do they know how many humans attacked them?"

"The other riders said they only saw two outside of the mountain-castle's cliff-walls," Leth answered. "A large human with an axe wearing much armor, over which it wore a black shirt bearing the picture of a gray mountain lion. The other was shorter and wielded something they thought might be like a bow. Once they crossed through the cliff-wall into the confines of the mountain-castle, one of their shamans filled the skies with lightning and thunder."

"Penn Cheval and its rabble. And it dares wield Rage?" The Bloodmoon Speaker clenched his fists and all but shivered from fury. "It will pay for its temerity!"

"We may also know of that shaman," Beastwarper answered. "At least we can say what to do against it. If it tried to strike at you with thunder and lightning and failed, it is because you were too swift for it."

"Penn Cheval. That was the Silver Lion Clan warrior? You said he had a big shiny knife. And what of this shaman?" Leth glared at the Stonemaster accusingly, but the warlord merely gazed back and smiled.

"Do you search for excuses to leave us, Leth? One lost bat-lizard and the mighty Skyfang flee? You may wish to reconsider." The Stonemaster rapped his fingers along his staff. "You gain your privileges here only if you help us gain victory over the Snow Clan. If you leave before then, you return to your chieftain not merely empty-handed but with one fewer bat-lizard. What do you suppose he will do to you should that happen?"

The Stonemaster suppressed a smirk as Leth descended into uncertainty and badly concealed fear. That took care of the desertion possibility. Now it was time to deal with the Snow Clan and their strategy against the onslaught.

"Bring the two surviving riders before the council," the warlord commanded. "There is much we must ask them to determine the cause of this and how these tricks may be defeated."

"And swiftly, for we make our way to the mountain-castle tonight." The Bloodmoon Speaker smiled and glanced behind him towards the western wood-wall of the human town.

The Stonemaster knew what he watched. Hundreds of the rabble, guided by the Allspeaker and the warlord's last remaining human, pushed, pulled, and cajoled the large rock throwing things out into the fields where the horde massed. They knew enough of their use to throw rocks against the Snow Clan, and the thought of punishing the humans with their own weapons after the damage they inflicted on the horde sat well with him.

"Be not dismayed, Leth," Beastwarper reassured him. "With your bat-lizards and that which the horde can bring to bear, this is but a temporary setback. The humans will know punishment and they will know fear."

"And when at last they break, we will take everything from them."

***

Knight Superior Rennoute stopped momentarily in the barbican's tunnel at a single wail rising above the sounds of morning business. It came from the scorched ruin that remained of the town, one more sound of suffering added to his history of defending the faithful. He knew it would not be the last and resumed his walk to inspect the damage.

The smell of char and ashes accompanied the blackened ruins of the buildings. Scorched and unidentifiable debris splashed across the streets from where drakes struck the roof-tops, and only partial walls of stone still stood. In the distance, one final creak preceded the crash of timbers as the last of a roof gave way to the pull of the earth.

Vultures perched on the remains of walls, waddled along the ground, or flapped from one ruin to the next seeking meals. Every so often one of them fell on something it saw in the streets. Rennoute did not concern himself with the details; whatever could not escape the fire fed them now.

At the end of the street near the last of the town's former gate, the drake slain by the Lion almost seemed asleep. Its wings fell limp to the earth beside it, and its head laid flat as though resting on the ground. Only the bloody gash in its skull and dead rider showed otherwise. Three vultures fought over the goblin remains on its back, but two more contented themselves with its eyes. It seemed a small thing now compared to the damage around it.

He reminded himself that this was inevitable; the town would have burned regardless. Once the goblins were close enough, he would have ordered it done. It was cover from attack he could not afford, as the two temporary fortresses had been. Naught would remain but the earthworks left to slow and dismay an advancing horde as his forces punished them with arrows and trebuchets.

This, however, was a quest gone wrong. The Silver Lion meant to down a drake, and the goblins had wrought this as a result. With their chatter in the distance, razing the village would have been easily portrayed as a necessity. Now, it left sorrowful peasants with long hours to think upon their losses and what mischief they might consider in their despair.

"Your Grace!" A spearman keeping watch upon the various small scenes of misery noticed him and snapped to attention. The two others with him did the same.

"What news?"

"No return of the drakes this morning, Your Grace. The folk search their homes, but they leave each other alone. No looters or thieving so far."

"Big, scaly bastard!" One of the peasants charged from a side street with a charred timber, straight at the downed drake. Vultures squawked and flew from his path as he hammered it ineffectually. "Black Archer take all drakes and goblins!"

"Oy, you! Mind your temper in his grace's presence!"

The shivering wretch dropped his club and gave Rennoute his full attention. Soot stained his hands and clothing, and he likely wore all he now owned in this world. All this, for just one drake. They hunted these beasts whenever they chose to come to the Emerald Refuge for livestock, and never had they lost so much to kill one.

"What'll we do now?" The man trudged forward to meet him. Others searching through the remains of their lives, individually or in families, slowly approached the growing crowd and begged him for succor. They kept their distance due to the soldiers and the knights that accompanied him.

"Return to the courtyard with what you can," Rennoute commanded, careful not to let any lack of resolve slip into his voice. "This castle has withstood all who have come to take this valley from us. It is the Shield of Athesiene, and it is His will that it endures. You will be safe within."

"But the drakes, Your Grace..."

"They will fall, as that one did." Rennoute gestured to the prostrate drake, which once again attracted the attention of vultures. "We will rebuild once the horde falls, and it *will* fall."

Momentarily placated but only half convinced, the townsfolk shuffled back towards the gate. Rennoute remained stoic, despite the weight on his shoulders. The loss of the town was predictable, as early as it had come, and at least the Lion had something to show for his efforts insofar as what he paid for it.

He was less willing to overlook the fact that the Disciple had found it necessary to intervene on his behalf. She was the first in generations the Lord on High saw fit to reward with His grace, and he would not see her die because this mercenary found himself in more trouble than he could handle. That meant they needed tactics and a strategy against the drakes. Immediately.

"Soldier."

"Yes, Your Grace?"

"Find the Silver Lion and inform him that he is summoned to the war council chambers. He is not to tarry."

"Yes, Your Grace." The spearman snapped to attention and saluted before rushing off to obey.

***

Pencheval was ushered into a war council of grim faces, and he expected nothing else. The soldiers pounded on the door to his chambers this morning bearing a very direct summons from the Knight Superior. Rennoute lost most of the town outside the walls last night, and the narrowed eyes of the castellan made it clear some of the attendees had found a target for their blame.

"You summoned me, Your Grace?"

"Join us." The command was curt and hinted at suppressed irritation. Pencheval nodded and took a place standing around the table.

"In exchange for the death of a single drake and its rider, we lost the town. While it is all but certain the goblins would have burned or pillaged it regardless, it is a high price to pay for what little we inflicted, and we cannot make such exchanges again. We need better tactics against the drakes, and none will leave this place until we find them."

"We possess ballistae, Your Grace," the castellan offered. "We need not get so close as to use a drakebow. Get the drakes to stop from a distance, and we could slay them from the walls."

"Except those drakes have goblin riders," Pencheval countered. "They may not yet know what a ballista does, but they learn quickly when their lives are threatened. One hit, and you would immediately become targets."

"We could do the same with showers of arrows, Your Grace," a knight suggested. "The drakes may not be harmed by them, but the riders are far from immune. Robbed of the one controlling them, would the drakes then revert to more predictable form? Perhaps absent a rider they would become as any other tame beast."

Rennoute nodded. "Aught else?"

Pencheval frowned. "Surely you are as aware of what Nan did last night as I am, Your Grace."

"For which you should be grateful," the castellan said with barely concealed disdain. "Few can say they were saved by someone so blessed with the Lord on High's favor. Don't suggest it should lead to anything else."

"I concur. The Disciple is not ready for this struggle, Lion." Rennoute glared at him. "We do not ask of war from our clergy, least of all a Disciple, until they have trained in it for years. The power granted by the Lord on High beggars belief and requires a practiced hand to wield wisely."

"Yes, Your Grace, and up until last night I would have been the first to agree with you. Yet we don't have years. If you mean to do anything but flee this valley before the goblins come again, war is here, now, and it will not wait."

"The Emerald Refuge belongs to the temple and the Lord on High. We have defended it for generations and we will not cede it to goblin filth!"

"Then I respectfully suggest that Your Grace consider Nan, as she isn't content with remaining separate from this. The goblins have drakes and we want for ways to counter them. They won't stop until they are victorious, scattered, or dead."

"Preposterous!" A knight smacked the table with one hand. "We would risk a Disciple with what? A single battle's experience and a day or two of training? She will be slain for nothing when we can attend to this."

"Do you believe I suggest this lightly? I fought a summer to take her from harm's way, but we are short of options. We need all the might we can muster against enemies that can take wing, and hers is considerable."

"The Lord on High's might is considerable," the knight corrected him. "A might that could have left you as naught but a scorch mark on that tower. Five paces too close, and it may well have done so. The Disciple can unwittingly kill those that protect her, and it is for that reason we say she must first be trained."

"Father Victor will attend to what little we can tell the Disciple of her path, brother." The Knight Superior scowled. "As she refuses to remain passive, so the Lion's plan must be. The Disciple means to battle, and what little we can do for her, we will. No less than two of the knights accompany the Disciple outside of the keep at all times. We may be forced to risk her, but that does not mean we will be careless."

"Yes, Your Grace."

"By Your Grace's leave, I will do for her what I can," Pencheval offered.

The castellan seemed aghast. "A Disciple? Trained by a Silver Lion?"

"Just one old friend talking to another, Your Grace."

"The Disciple does not mind your company, Lion. So long as that remains true, speak to her if you wish."

"Thank you, Your Grace."

***

The Stonemaster sat on his chair perplexed.

Both of the surviving riders from last night's attack answered every question put to them. Their companion followed after the first to attack and the bat-lizard instead landed at a strange bonfire. It tore into some strange beast that was not a goat, and the humans shot it with a weapon none of them knew they had. Despite two useful bits of information, nothing they revealed left him any closer to a solution. The humans knew how to trick bat-lizards to the ground, but it only worked on one of them. That spoke only of an incompetent rider.

Yet how many such riders did the Skyfang bring, and could the Snow Clan inflict enough losses upon them to break them into fleeing to their clan-home? Worse still, might they accomplish the unthinkable and kill them all? Not if they stopped sending them until they found a way to avoid another death.

"The rider was foolish," Bloodmoon grumbled.

"Foolish nothing! Some magic in the flame beguiled the bat-lizard."

"So why did it not beguile the other two?" The Beastwarper Chieftain adjusted his grip on his staff. "Because it had already slain the beast used for bait, which was the real cause of it."

"Perhaps my human will know more." The Stonemaster waved a messenger forward. "Bring it forth."

"Yes, Chief of Chieftains." The messenger scrambled to obey.

"You have a human?" Leth cocked his head to one side. "Do you keep it as a prisoner?"

"No. It had the sense to submit before dying. The others were less cooperative."

In truth, the warlord kept it more as a keepsake than anything else. One human was a pittance compared to the number he possessed not long ago. One small but useful thing that made the final fate of their town slightly less than a complete loss. As it was now, that place a day behind them was little more than a ruin filled with the ghosts of its former Snow Clan occupants.

"Does it speak our tongue?" The Skyfang Speaker seemed impressed.

"No, but the Allspeaker speaks all tongues, and can tell us what it knows." At that observation, the shaman to the right of the Stonemaster's throne seemed excessively cautious again. At least it made him obedient, if occasionally annoying, the warlord thought. One did not need that much fear to live.

The crowd of goblin bodyguards preceding the human herded it into the council space. It lacked its former swagger, and the clothes it wore billowed and hung from a thinning frame where once they fit snugly. Perhaps the bat-lizards had unnerved it, or perhaps its handlers starved it. If so, he would kill them and feed the human their rations, for it was worth more than they were.

It said something, and its voice held a weary and ragged edge.

"The human greets you, Chief of Chieftains, and wishes to know what you want."

"Have it tell us about the mountain-castle. Explain that it is the large stone thing at the other end of the valley if it doesn't know what that means."

The Allspeaker interpreted the request to the human. It blinked twice in disbelief before answering.

"The human says that place is a castle and the home of their 'Knight Superior,' Chief of Chieftains," the Allspeaker explained. "I think that is the title of the Snow Clan Chieftain here. It says most of their warriors are there, and it has high cliff-walls. It avoids that place because it has most of the 'knights' and doesn't recommend attacking it."

"We don't want its thoughts on war," the Bloodmoon Speaker rumbled. "Does it know any ways past the cliff-walls?"

The Allspeaker reiterated the question, and the human gave him a short explanation.

"It says in the few instances it went there, it gave things to some of the warriors in exchange for them to ignore it," the Allspeaker answered. "The human called it 'silver.'"

More barter, the Stonemaster mused and shook his head. Instead of one thing for another, merely one thing for favorable treatment. No, the humans would not ignore them in exchange for loot.

"Does it know what the large creature that attracted the bat-lizard might have been or the blue flame?" The Skyfang Speaker scratched his head. "Give it the sounds the riders gave you."

"What? It was one of their goats." The Allspeaker snorted at the absurdity.

"Humor our guest, Allspeaker," the Stonemaster commanded.

"Yes, Chief of Chieftains." The Allspeaker translated, ending with the odd noise made by the creature in its panic. The human cocked its head and answered. The Allspeaker asked more of it, and it continued.

"The human thinks it was a cow, Chief of Chieftains. It says they are larger than goats and make a sound like I gave it. It doesn't know about the strange flame but does know the humans hunt bat-lizards. They called them 'drakes.'"

"These cows have enough meat to tempt a bat-lizard into landing." The Stonemaster rapped his fingers on the arm of his bone chair. His nails clicked on it.

"We have long since trained them to ignore goats on command, Chief of Chieftains," the Skyfang Speaker explained proudly. "What about this creature is so different?"

"Nothing, if they are all dead," Beastwarper offered.

"Even if we could do that without the Shadowcreed, it would make for a lean winter." Starving the horde was out of the question. Any humans they captured for knowledge at the mountain-castle would die before the spring if that happened.

"The humans don't threaten the bat-lizards and neither do goats, but these cows will. If you mean to capture that place, you need the Skyfang. To send them again without risking their mounts, their prey must die. I can make the thing that will do that."

"Make?"

"Bloodseekers, Chief of Chieftains. I have enough Deepglow for a swarm of them." The Allspeaker recoiled and Leth gasped.

"Deepglow? Fiend's breath, Beastwarper, you have that here?"

The Stonemaster knew he used it. No such beast as a Bonestripper could exist without the foul stuff. To even reach it, one descended as far under the mountains and towards the Fiend as they could stand to go. In its raw form, it glowed with a pale light like a full moon and collected in small puddles with no obvious source. Some thought it might be the Fiend's blood, and others the Fiend's wrath manifested in a liquid. So much as touching it with a finger would leave a goblin horribly warped, disfigured, or worse. It rarely granted anything as merciful as a swift death except in quantity.

Yet some few clans, through either madness or cunning, learned a way to use it productively. For the Bloodmoon, it warped goblins into Berserkers. For the Beastwarpers, trolls into Bonestrippers. For most, a mad shaman swore it would grant great power only to lead himself or another to disaster. But to discover more than one way to harness Deepglow? That spoke of the same reckless obsessiveness Beastwarper displayed with his human shaman in the town. He should be grateful he only suffered from one disfigurement.

"It is stored safely, Chief of Chieftains. But if you mean to rob humans of their bait, we must act now."

"What do these Bloodseekers do?"

"They kill livestock, Chief of Chieftains. They live only for a day, but in that time they slaughter much. We use them to punish enemies who are foolish enough to raid us or starve those too entrenched in their caves to risk attacking."

"Will they kill these cows?"

"I've seen them feed on anything with four legs they could catch. Even if they avoid the cows, if we take the other meat from the humans, they won't be so eager to waste it on bait."

"How long?"

"With enough bees or wasps, two days. Then the Skyfang can release them near the mountain-castle and return. Their hunger will do the rest."

"Begin, Beastwarper, but keep them from the horde's stock."

Deepglow. For anything less than taking the mountain-castle and punishing Penn Cheval, even considering that blighted stuff was out of the question. So long as the Beastwarper kept it far away from him, however, he would let that warped chieftain use it.

***

Pencheval stood atop the keep, overlooking the castle from a commanding view as he waited for the sun to set. Despite at first considering it a suicidal vantage when facing drakes, he quickly changed his mind. The beacon covering nigh half the roof was a massive brazier of thick and blackened iron. It sat on a solid stone foundation, and the space under it close to that foundation was all but drake proof. None of them could fly to reach anyone there without risking an impact, and the metal was nearly as thick as his fingers were long. Despite the lack of any other obstacles, aside from the two knights accompanying them, it was more than enough safety within easy reach.

He had struggled to find the words to ask Nan for her assistance, only to have her insist on joining them against the drakes the second she saw him. She had simply had enough of remaining passive against the horde. Perhaps it was some desire to repay her captivity by the goblins, or perhaps it was the sense of duty that had kept her by the wounded in Tarsun's Market even as the horde breached the walls.

Despite her willingness to help them, he wished it could be otherwise. He felt it beyond the pale to risk an old friend who spent months as a prisoner and was yet untrained in war. To field her now was nothing less than a necessity created by the drake attacks, and even so was unreasonable beyond even the rough standards of his own guild. They were not gentle in training their adepts, but they were thorough, and apprentices never went without guidance until they proved they could pass muster.

"When do you think they will return, Pencheval?"

"After dark, Nan. For now, we must wait." Pencheval stared off into the darkening sky, though there was enough light to see far from the top of the keep.

"Time enough to hope I don't kill any but the enemy."

"You won't, Nan," he reassured her.

Pencheval was genuinely sympathetic. His first experiences with real magic taught him respect for it quickly. Small as his spellcraft was, he knew it exacted a toll and could kill in careless hands. One misstep could leave him in a sea of pain or with a world of regret. Even after months of training and years of experience wielding it under strain, he never forgot its peril.

Nan had neither training nor experience in wielding a power the Knight Superior said beggared belief, and no more of a teacher than himself.

"Has anyone spoken to you of this power?"

"Father Victor visited me today. His quotes from The Histories left me with few clues. I know much of what the other Disciples did with their power, but little of the details."

"Focus on doing one thing at a time," Pencheval advised her. "The first mistake many of us made as apprentices was believing spellcraft could carry a day, and do as much as we wanted at once. We were quickly disillusioned of that."

"That has been my experience so far, despite the sheer might of it. Like trying to will a change in the course of a river or guiding an avalanche, but true." Nan frowned at him. "I can barely aim it. A wave of the hand, or a thought, and...too much."

"Nan, if you fear slaying your own, don't try to kill. You can support the army or hinder the enemy without risking loss of life."

"Even that may be too much to ask. All I do is made many times stronger." Nan shivered. "A small stunning charm I once used now blasts goblins to scorched corpses, and a sleeping spell sent part of a horde into terror fearing plague. If I bless or try to heal a soldier, will I slay them? Blast the walls if I mean to strengthen them?"

"Nan, you escaped Tarsun's Market without slaying your own. Believe that you can aid us." Pencheval put his hand on her shoulder.

"Athesiene believed in you enough to give you this. You can find a way."

Nan patted his hand before folding her arms across her chest. "Did you ever believe, in your wildest dreams, we would be this one day?"

"Before we knew of the Hope of Terris Lyn? No." Pencheval shook his head. "I thought I would be a farmer all my life and could not rid my thoughts of Cecelia. You were just the nice lady with the pies and berries."

"And muffins. I'm hurt you forgot them." Nan managed a chuckle. "Despite that fop of a baron, it was a good life once. Simpler."

"Another lie, like the Hope of Terris Lyn. We lived a minstrel's tale until the music finally came to an end." Pencheval brushed a wrinkle from his tabard. The ripped and battered fabric strained to remain whole. "We both found our places, though."

"Yes, though yours it not what you believe, Pencheval. You have become more than a Lion and are surely not the man I met in Tarsun's Market."

"Back to trying to save me from my wretched existence as a blackguard mercenary?" Pencheval gave her a wry grin. "It heartens me to see you return to form."

"Before this war is won, lad, I will turn you completely from the darkness. I've already found what passes for your humor."

Pencheval snorted. Perhaps she had. Perhaps he could also aid her in the end. Whatever else, they were certainly not where they began all those years ago, believing life began and ended in that pastoral deception called Terris Lyn.

***

Friar Dominik looked up at the sky from the courtyard and could not fathom how anyone would remain calm once the drakes returned. The space between the staggering height of the keep and the outer walls left him feeling as though he was in a gigantic trench awaiting claws and flame to descend upon him. He felt a continuous dread just standing there, and the folk who lost everything in the town had to live in it. It was why he had spent the last two nights attending to them.

Since the attacks began, the army of Athesiene was forced to take refuge solely in the castle. The soldiers filled all space inside it and on the walls, and left the townsfolk in the courtyard to make their way as they could. This was sufficient in a normal siege, but against the drakes they may as well be animals trapped in a pit.

He was not there alone. Several of the castle's sisters prayed with the townsfolk in their encampment or read from The Histories. A spearman sat with several around a campfire and told stories as others kept watch, their presence an implicit threat of retaliation for any mischief. The Knight Superior wanted no trouble from within, as he had enough with the goblins.

"What about the witch?"

Dominik heard it, or thought he heard it. He searched for the source, but all he saw were faces peering from tents or those who ignored him. One glance was met by someone who eyed him suspiciously before scratching the corner of his mouth and putting his head down. He was with two others who quit speaking and kept around their fire.

Dominik shook his head. Trouble, or simply himself imagining trouble? No. Given the rise of other Disciples in The Histories, it was very well trouble. Accusations of witchcraft were on the tamer end of what many Disciples faced before they were accepted as legitimate voices of the Lord on High, and he wished this once they might forego such superstitions and see the truth. The drakes were turmoil enough.

***

Pencheval rubbed his eyes and squinted to see the first rays of dawn breaking over the mountains in the distance. The knights next to him kept their vigil with less complaint, but Nan had since fallen asleep. He was glad it had been the sort of night that allowed it. The drakes did not attack and inflicted nothing more on them than boredom.

He wished it would last. The death of a drake may have knocked the goblins back on their heels, but nothing about them was ever easy. They might be frightened now, but if their warlord still meant to take this place, it contemplated nothing but its next move. The drakes would resume their terror when, and not if, they chose to attack once again.

"Athesiene granted us respite," a knight said. "Yet it is too much to hope that it lasts."

"It won't," Pencheval answered. "The horde only considers what to do next. This won't end until it is smashed."

"Perhaps that lull was for the best. The Disciple is yet unaccustomed to night watch."

Nan slept against a stack of burlap bags beneath the metal bowl of the beacon, nodding up and down as she breathed. Pencheval shook his head. Had she learned to sleep against anything while prisoner to the goblins? What other choice would they have given her? She was lucky to have survived that ordeal at all, something she would not have done unless she grew stronger.

"Nan?" Pencheval spoke softly and hoped her reaction did not draw on her newfound power.

She started awake and looked around. "What? Are they here?"

"No, Nan. They didn't attack last night."

"It's...dawn?" Nan watched the sun rise for a moment, then shielded her eyes with the hood of her robe. "Why did you let me sleep?"

"Naught was there requiring your aid," Pencheval replied.

"These watches are dull things." Nan slowly stood and brushed the wrinkles from her robes. "Yet the battles are dreadful things."

"That's the way of it. Boredom or shock. For now, we must all get some sleep and be ready. The goblins won't let us rest for long."

"What do you suppose they will do next?"

"If they stay true to form," Pencheval replied, "it will be something none of us saw coming."

Six

"Now is not the time!"

Dominik lifted his head from prayers at the braying of a mule. A mother and two children watched a struggling and increasingly frustrated man he assumed was the husband tugging at its reins. Did that lout mean to leave? If he did, he would be better served taking the advice of his protesting mount.

"Lord on High be with you. I will return shortly." The small crowd around him nodded, and Dominik rose to stop this bit of ruin before it began.

"Friend, where would you go with your family? Here you are already safe. Outside goblins lurk, and drakes rule the skies."

"Aye, and you can keep them!" The angry peasant with a short goatee seemed ready to switch his mule into action. His children pressed closer to their mother. "The goblins only want the castle. We're safer in Pennit's Hollow."

"That's eight days from here, and two through the pass. If they mean to catch you, they will. You're betting your lives that they either don't know you're going or don't care if you do."

"We're caught right here," the man answered. "They already have us 'cause the walls don't stop drakes. That Lion spoke truly in Tarsun's Market a while back when he said to flee. We'd be dead right now if I hadn't heeded him then, and you'll be dead if you don't heed him now!"

"I am heeding him," Dominik countered. "I heard his words in Tarsun's Market, for he told them to me first hand. Flee to the castle, where the horde could be met and defeated. He has kept to his own advice, and fights beside the Disciple to save us all. Do you think a Silver Lion doesn't know where to do battle?"

"He knows how to burn our town to the ground, right enough." A heavyset, bearded man with a bag over his shoulders strode over to the argument, frowning. "All I own now's in this bag, thanks be to the Hopeslayer. The only place to go now is the capital, and with the drakes gone, I'll be headin' there to start anew."

"You'll never make it!"

"Feeling's mutual, friar." The first man dropped the reins to his mule. It brayed in momentary victory. "Nothing's flying now and there's that Disciple here. Want to see how badly she lets the thunder and lightning go astray? I don't."

"Mind your tongue about the Disciple!"

"Keep that staff on the ground!"

Dominik snapped around at the spearman's command and realized he was no longer using his staff as a walking stick. He let it drop from his second hand and put it back in the dirt.

"Ye've done enough diligence with them, friar. No commands against anyone leaving by his grace or the castellan. They want to go, they get to go."

"Do you not see–"

"Back away, friar." The soldier motioned Dominik away from them as another family stepped forward to leave. One of them persuaded the mule to cooperate. "It's for them to decide and not you. Do we need to tell you again with the cat?"

One of the soldiers near the spearman patted a cat o' nine tails on his belt. Dominik was shocked but did as he was bid. He supposed they all must choose what to do, but they were panicked folk making bad decisions. Could they at least not attempt to calm them first?

No, because the castellan wanted order. That meant no one twirling a quarterstaff and no forcing malcontents to stay if they wanted to go. As that was likely also the will of the Knight Superior, there was nothing more to be done. Gritting his teeth, he watched the smallish group finally make its way to the barbican. They were all dead, and they would know it soon enough.

***

"Why are you whimpering over such an easy task?"

The Stonemaster would have asked Leth that question himself had keeping the Skyfang in his service not been such an issue. As it was, Leth took the abuse from the Bloodmoon Speaker only because no one with sense would gift the hulking warrior with an excuse. The scowling beast could surely intimidate but lacked understanding of subtler manipulation. Despite this, the essence of his complaint was correct.

A scout reported some of the humans were fleeing to the south. In the time it took him to return with the news, the humans could have made it to the mountain pass that was their only possible destination. If nothing was ever heard from them again, other humans might assume their success and flee before the horde could capture them. The Skyfang could deal with that matter but were reluctant to fly until the Bloodseekers did their worst to the Snow Clan.

"I wouldn't be careless with bat-lizards either," the Stonemaster said to grant Leth the possibility of retaining face. "Yet for three drakes, this task is little more than an execution. Send them after the humans fleeing through the pass. Leave enough alive to tell tales of your butchery, or none will remain in the mountain-castle. That means a lean winter for the horde and your riders."

"And the humans have other value. Think of the knowledge we could glean from them once we capture them. The Allspeaker can talk with those that are useful. We can offer them their lives for what they know, and you would have a full share in it."

The Stonemaster suppressed the urge to frown. Beastwarper was trying to persuade Leth with an argument the warped chieftain himself would accept, and in the process revealed too much. Yes, the humans' knowledge would be useful. However, it was unwise to remind the Skyfang that they were also a source of knowledge too good to ignore.

"This is risky." Leth rapped his fingers on his seat. "They have bait for the bat-lizards."

"They are rabble with livestock. Penn Cheval is still at the mountain-castle and none of the Snow Clan warriors accompany them. They are fleeing and nothing more than food for your beasts."

"Don't eat them all," Bloodmoon grumbled. "The horde needs food through the winter."

"I will see to it." Leth still seemed reluctant, but he left the council towards the pens of his clan's mounts without any additional complaint.

"His excess of caution grows more insufferable." The Bloodmoon Speaker crossed his arms. "But for the bat-lizards there would be no point to him."

"Something another success will correct," the Stonemaster added, looking towards the Beastwarper Chieftain. "How fare the Bloodseekers?"

"My clan collects what we need, Chief of Chieftains, but they are scattered. Yet no more than a day, and we will be ready."

"This cannot fail. The Skyfang are skittish enough after the loss of their bat-lizard. Annoying that someone with such power be so fearful to use it, but circumstances are as they are."

"So win this battle," Bloodmoon rumbled. "We need the sniveling rat, headpiece and all."

Beastwarper chuckled. "The Bloodseekers have never failed to wreak havoc on an enemy, Chief of Chieftains. The Snow Clan's supply of bait, and much of their will to fight, will be gone before much longer."

***

"Yes, I will announce you at once!"

Nan smiled and suppressed the urge to scream. Both the guards at the door to the Knight Superior's study seemed awed by her approach. What else would they do but respond to her request as though the Lord on High Himself made it? It might denote some newfound respect Athesiene's favor granted her, but it made for an endless series of jarring moments.

She almost wished they would treat her only as a senior sister from Tarsun's Market again. It made her inferior in rank to the Knight Superior, but it was familiar. Normal. Now, she was met with either awe or fear. Only Pencheval could still hold a sane conversation with her, and he gathered what strength and rest he could during daytime like everyone else who served upon the walls during the night.

The door to Rennoute's study swung open as quickly as the guard who announced her could manage it. "He will see you now, Disciple!"

"Thank you, soldier." She caught herself before she snapped an admonition to behave like all was as it used to be. There was no point to it. All was not as it used to be, and she was just another among that which was amiss.

The Knight Superior stood behind his desk, and it was as out of place as everything else. Knight Superiors did not rise for sisters or any of their other subjects, yet there he was. Did it foretell of another awkward conversation? She hoped not, because she needed his help now.

"Disciple. How may I aid you?"

"I would like to discuss my place against the horde, Your Grace," Nan requested.

Rennoute frowned at her. "I would ask that the Disciple refrain from participating in this war or any other until you are trained. However, I will do for the Disciple as I can."

"Pencheval spoke with me about supporting the troops, Your Grace. The drakes move too swiftly to smite and I fear harming those here accidentally. What can I do?"

"Make things easier for us or harder for the goblins in ways that do not require you to directly target either, Disciple."

"How, Your Grace?"

"Do not smite the drakes, Disciple. Hinder them. Hinder their riders. Make it hard to fly above us. Shield the skies so they cannot act against the troops. Slow them so our troops can act against them. Not all in war is simply striking an enemy dead."

Shield the skies? The magnitude of that request was nigh unthinkable, but did she have the power? It was ever present and vast beyond her ability to believe it, so perhaps she could.

"Can you suggest how, Your Grace?"

"Wielding a Disciple's power is beyond me," Rennoute replied. "Perhaps The Histories might aid you?"

"Thank you, Your Grace." Father Victor thought so, too, and they were both wrong. Yes, it told tales of the other Disciples, but none of them ever had to slay drakes. Worse still, only Dothea ever commented on her inspiration in using the power. Be aware of the little things around you, for they may teach you what you need to know.

"One last matter, Your Grace. Do you know what became of a sergeant that returned with me from Tarsun's Market? Alfried was his name."

"He returned to service, Disciple. Castellan Galter knows more of his specific post. However, news of your ascension to Disciple has sent both awe and fright through the troops. I do not recommend seeing him again until that changes."

Of course not. Why should anything else about this matter make it any more ordinary? Alfried had aided her in the escape from the goblins and kept her focused until she could return. He had been the only one there that proved worth all her suffering and change. And now he, too, was caught up in these future words written in The Histories about Disciple Nan.

Furthermore, no less than the Knight Superior told her this in the same deferential tones she used to speak to him. The whole conversation felt as two people believing they referred to someone of higher station. It was surreal to her, and yet she almost knew the answer to the next request before she made it.

"By Your Grace's leave, I would like to depart."

"The Disciple may come and go as she wishes. However, I must deal with the defense of the valley and would request that you not disturb me or the troops for unnecessary purposes."

"Thank you, Your Grace." Nan turned, and the door squealed as the guard rushed to open it for her.

Maddening. The soldiers were awestruck, and one of the few people she would have liked to see again was among them. He was possibly even terrified of her. Could Father Victor not have kept this matter of Disciples to himself until the danger had passed? Or perhaps, forever?

***

Wingleader Jux was grateful to feel the wind on his face and the rush of it past his ears once again. He lived for the moments he could fly upon a bat-lizard, even though he took the reins now to restore morale among his riders. One fallen bat-lizard was more of a loss than they had endured in some time. He had to show that loss was an oddity, and flying this menial execution personally was sure to do it.

Some of the humans meant to flee the valley through a pass south of the mountain-castle. Enough of them needed to die to convince the others that contemplating flight was madness. Kill a few and let the rest survive to kindle panic back at the mountain-castle. He and his other rider should be sufficient for this, and when they returned with news of their success, it would quell the excess of caution rising in the others.

He was not happy leaving Speaker Leth to his own devices. It was obvious to him that the Stonemaster had ambitions of gaining bat-lizards–more specifically, *their* bat-lizards. The warlord and the lame chieftain, this Beastwarper, played Leth like a drum and gained far too much from him. Was it within the pompous bug's power, all the Skyfang's secrets might be theirs already.

He would have to deal with it in time. Perhaps during the final battle when the horde was most sorely pressed. If the humans they scared into remaining at the mountain-castle believed themselves trapped and that only death awaited them in defeat they would fight like demons. This Silver Lion Clan warrior in particular, this Penn Cheval, was not something he cared to face. It made him grateful that he and the Skyfang would be in the air and untouchable when that battle came.

The group he saw below huddled around a campfire possessed no such mettle. There were no more than a dozen humans and a few of their livestock. No glints of metal, no chain skin, and none of the white shirts worn by the Snow Clan warriors. They were rabble, and their chieftain must have let them leave to dispose of malcontents or excess mouths to feed.

They would not be rid of them quite yet, Jux mused, and motioned for his companion to follow. The humans remained unaware of them, and they would hit them from the other side. Two raging bat-lizards killing livestock and tearing them to pieces for easier eating would be more than sufficient discouragement for those with a mind to flee the valley.

Jux reined his mount for a wide turn. Too swift, and the bat-lizard would screech in protest as it banked, warning the humans below. His companion did the same and again, no noise. At least he knew how to fly his bat-lizard, unlike the idiot that allowed his mount to be baited and then slain.

He smiled. There was no risk of baiting tonight. He felt the straps on his chair pull taut against him as his mount turned and placed him between the humans and escape from the valley. A big dirt path they had worn through the pass all but told their direction.

He reined his bat-lizard into a dive. The wind roared in his ears and the drop pushed his back into the chair. At one half the distance to the ground, he pulled the reins taut sharply. His mount roared as giant wings slapped at air. It jarred him when it landed within a few lengths of the campfire and utterly terrified the humans. They screamed as their livestock bucked and pulled at their tethers. Jux quickly chose a target and goaded his mount forward.

One crack of the wings powered its pounce as it landed on the nearest human and ripped with its claws. Shortly thereafter, he heard his minion land behind him and charge something to his left. One of the livestock brayed in terror before a snap of jaws silenced it for good. Three wet crunches preceded the sound of a bat-lizard orienting its food so it could swallow.

One human had the gall to charge with a spear bearing four tiny points. The bat-lizard he rode responded by slamming forward with its bulk, knocking the rabble senseless by sheer weight and then crushing its chest with a claw. Several other humans were so terrified they could not even flee. Some were smaller than the others and clinging to one on its knees.

Human pups, perhaps? What did it matter? Humans were livestock, pups or grown. They would all die sooner or later when the horde won, and now was as good a time as any to send them to their gods. Enough humans had already fled to deliver the news to the Snow Clan.

***

"What is this absurdity meant to do?"

The Stonemaster silently agreed with the Bloodmoon Speaker. At first glance, this *was* an absurdity. His council and Jux stood with the Beastwarper Chieftain near a domed wicker hut far from the horde. The hides and rags that covered every bit of it contained the muted buzz of angry bees within. Every so often, they could hear the panicked sounds of the goat from which they had taken blood for the Beastwarper's strange rituals. In short, all of his leadership stood in the middle of a field attending a hut full of bugs because what would happen next might spook the horde.

The Bloodmoon Speaker crossed his arms in annoyance and showed no fear at all. Leth scratched his head as Wingleader Jux stood next to him, worry obvious on his face. Since a half a dozen of his riders would have to carry the swarm once it was ready, his concern was far from misplaced.

Beastwarper ignored the lot of them, instead making preparations and muttering incomprehensibly as he laid out the tools and bowls he would need for the Bloodseekers. He had smeared most of the blood he took from the goat on the inside of a half dozen leather sacks. The Stonemaster surmised it was bait for his creations so they would go where he wanted them and not where they wished. They all backed away from the warped chieftain as he motioned two of his shamans to bring forth a heavy stone pot with a thick lid.

"This won't take long."

Beastwarper lifted a honeycomb and cracked it over a large wooden bowl. Golden streams dripped and drizzled, slowly spreading into a viscous puddle. The lame chieftain invoked the Fiend Under The Mountain for his aid as the last few drops fell. When nothing remained, he threw the empty shell aside and repeated the invocation six more times with additional pieces of honeycomb.

Once the bowl was half full, he took a small cup of the goat's blood and mixed it into the contents. Invocations fell to a low, ragged chanting as he stirred until all was evenly blended. It was the work of entirely too practiced a hand, and the Stonemaster was grateful the lame chieftain performed his rituals far from him. How deranged must he be to learn more than one use for Deepglow? Enough so that even after it crippled him he still wielded it.

"Open it now."

The two Beastwarper Clan shamans did as their chieftain bade them, and the Stonemaster was surprised to see how little of the pot was actual space. The Deepglow glowed from within a hole no bigger around than his fist. The rest was solid, roughhewn stone a hand's length thick. Mad as Beastwarper was, even he took no chances with the Deepglow.

The Stonemaster found it fascinating despite knowing how deadly it was. It glowed with the pale light of a full moon and lapped gently against the sides of the pot like water. Beastwarper waited until it was still, then dipped a long, thin bone shaved to a slender point into it. It rippled and shimmered as though haunted, and when the point emerged, a mere drop of it clung to the end like glowing dew.

Beastwarper delicately moved it over the bowl and with a single practiced flick dropped the tiny point of light into the mixture. It only just sank beneath the surface, slowly diffusing into the thick soup in which it landed. The chieftain motioned for the shamans to replace the lid, and he took the bowl back to the rock where he worked.

He returned the thin bone tool to a leather wrap and lifted another bone instrument engraved with symbols. He used it to mix the Deepglow with the rest and never ceased chanting until he was done. The final mixture was a dark and glittering amber, and he motioned for his shaman to take it after returning his tool to its wraps. The shaman carefully carried the bowl to the dome and placed it within. He tied a flap on its side shut before waving a few bees from himself and backing away.

Beastwarper tossed the bowl that held the goat's blood into one of the bags and handed it to Wingleader Jux. "We will know the Bloodseekers are ready when the goat is dead. Then, they will follow the scent of its blood to the bags. Once you have them, you and your riders take them immediately to the mountain-castle. If you value your lives, don't open the bags before you arrive, and don't remain once you have dropped them on the humans."

"I understand," Jux grumbled.

"Your vengeance comes soon," Beastwarper reassured him. "There is no punishment like Bloodseekers, and your wings will deliver it."

The Stonemaster took one step back as the buzz inside the dome changed to a startling degree. The droning grew deeper and more aggressive, and every so often something would smack against the cloth and leather so ferociously it threatened escape. The goat's bleating grew more panicked and then ceased as the buzzing drowned it out, and the frenzied pops against the sides multiplied until it sounded like torrential rain.

He was pleased with the results but not with the Beastwarper. Only enough Deepglow to create a small swarm of these Bloodseekers? He saw enough of the stuff to reduce a quarter of the horde to corpses or shrieking, disfigured nightmares. Perhaps he just meant to keep knowledge of his advantages to himself, which was the goblin way. Either that, or Beastwarper did not care to expend it all to serve him.

The fact Beastwarper again forgot who was master was an issue for another time. They had their weapon and the warlord meant to use it. "Take them and fly, Jux. Remind the Snow Clan that we are still here."

***

Pencheval stood on the roof of the keep, accompanying Nan and two knights as he watched for signs of drakes in the distance. They would return again. Two night's respite meant nothing, particularly if the two forms flying towards the pass the night before were not just his fears made manifest.

The damnable goblins always attacked at night, but never with anything that smacked as much of a siege as this. The interminable nights may not give the goblins pause, but it put the soldiers on edge and did nothing for his sense of ease. Adjusting to night's watch left his eyes burning and him aggravated as he learned to sleep during the day.

At least his living was more generous than for most in the castle. The Knight Superior set aside a room for his use on the upper floor of the hall attached to the keep, a small chamber that was previously a servant's quarters. Despite being only as long and wide as his straw bed, he considered it a boon, for the castle was so crowded by soldiers they slept anywhere they could find space.

The Clearsight charm that gave him sight in darkness showed him nothing on the horizon in the east. Roads, hills, and forests shaded in gray dwindled into the distance. In the skies, he saw only stars and a few ribbons of clouds illuminated by moonlight.

Perhaps the reason they did not yet return was because they already set other schemes into motion. The hooded goblin spies from Tarsun's Market had not yet come into play. If they identified Nan, they could kill her before anyone even knew of mischief. Perhaps they watched from inside the walls even now. He felt a chill down his spine as he continued his search for trouble.

"What do you mean to do when the drakes return, Nan?" Her pause did not reassure him.

"Hinder them," she replied tentatively. "By what means? May the Lord on High grant me guidance."

The Lion's eyes narrowed. If asking the Lord on High for wisdom was her plan, Nan needed to return to the keep. He wracked his mind for an answer instead. Nan would not go, just as in Tarsun's Market when she refused to abandon the wounded, and none had the will or means to make her do otherwise. Her courage did her credit, but it would get her killed if the drake riders' arrival was met only by her freezing in uncertainty.

"I've yet to see any bird or beast willingly fly through a storm's winds," Pencheval suggested.

"Wind?" Nan sounded thoughtful.

"Not merely wind. A storm. Make a gale above the soldiers to discourage the drakes from diving upon them. It might be enough to–"

Six diminutive forms emerged in the distance, flying in a loose grouping. Their wings were too large and tails too long to be birds. The respite was over.

"Sound the alarm. Goblins come!"

"Sound the alarm! Drakes come!" One of the knights called down to the soldiers on the walls near the keep. Pencheval saw word spread and heard bells ring from below.

"How many?"

"Six. Seems they mean to undo what relief they allowed us in one night."

"I will give them cause to regret it," Nan declared.

Above the keep, Pencheval heard the wind whistle and grow until it raged. The howling edges of the storm lapped at his tabard and sword, and a half-filled sack blew into the back of his legs. Banners swayed as one of the knights temporarily braced himself, and the smells of ash accompanied the fine gray tendrils lapping over the beacon. Soldiers looked up in horror and panicked screams rose from below.

"That is as much as I can create," she told him. The winds above disappeared into nothingness with disquieting swiftness, leaving those on the walls confused but relieved.

"When they come, I will tell you where they are and where I believe they mean to attack. Put the winds above those standing there and let them do the rest. If I warn you they are attacking the keep, retreat within. If there is no time, get beneath the beacon. It has held far more flame than any drake ever spat and it should protect you."

"How far?" Nan sounded determined but nervous.

"They're...stopping?" In the time they spoke, the drakes drew close enough for Pencheval to distinguish their shapes. Bodies tilted upward and wings beat furiously to slow them to a hover. Tails lashed and feet clawed at air as the riders reined them for no reason he could see, and then turned them away. One after another the goblins repeated this, and the confused mercenary scratched his head.

"They're retreating. Why are they retreating?"

"Perhaps the winds dissuaded them?" The knight suggesting this sounded less than convinced.

"How would they do that? The storm was too far away for them to hear and there was naught to see of it."

"And what has the attention of the soldiers?" One of the knights motioned towards the eastern wall.

Pencheval could not tell from the height, but soldiers warned one another and pointed into the distance. As he watched, several small clouds of tiny dark forms flew over the battlements and down towards the courtyard below. In moments, the panicked neighing and cries of agonized horses rang and echoed from the stones.

"They weren't attacking. They were delivering those! Get within the keep!"

Of course they would not attack where those that might defeat them waited. Nothing with goblins was ever that easy. Now he had to descend the keep to get to the fight, and that presumed they had sent something he could smite with a blade.

The spies in the hoods had been so much simpler.

***

Bees?

Scout Howe heard the buzz approaching from the distance, and it was the last thing he expected. The alarm was for drakes, and even in the starlight he could see them. The flash of motion in the pale light, the low growls, and the thump of wingbeats could not be anything else. Yet instead of a diving drake with an orange glow behind its jagged teeth, there came instead the low drone of bees.

A black cloud of bugs flew over the walls and down into the courtyard, dodging past the soldiers. They were not anything like the wasps or hornets that he knew. The buzz of the wings bore an eerie pitch like a minor chord, and short glimpses hinted at shapes he hoped he never saw again. Their rush towards the stables, followed by the sounds of dying horses, almost left him wishing for drakes he could shoot and escape.

"Lord on High protect us." The soldier next to him still held his bow, one arrow nocked but not pulled to his cheek.

"Why are you standin' around?" One burly sergeant pulled his cloak from his shoulders and half-wrapped it around his wrist. "They're killing the horses. Get to bloody work!"

"Yes, sergeant!" Howe took his cloak from his shoulders and scrambled to the courtyard below. Swatting bugs was the last thing he expected to do when he heard the alarm, but if they meant to save the horses that was what they had to do.

Goblins. If it was not their drakes it was their brutes. If not their brutes, it was their sheer numbers. Still not yet satisfied, they sent their hornets or whatever they were after the horses. Saint Marion's revelation, could they not come and attack in siege like any other damn army? At least that much he could endure and understand.

By the time they reached the stables no sound came from within but the infernal buzzing. The strange pitch of wings mixed with the wet sounds of a great many tiny things eating at once. Every so often one of them would strike a wall, cracking a wooden plank with a loud thump. His sergeant backed away, and other soldiers carrying torches or ready cloaks did the same.

Howe's eyes narrowed as he listened. The swarm's fury increased in volume and drowned out all other noises. None of the others appeared to realize what it meant, and even Howe could barely bring himself to believe it.

He shouted to make himself heard. "Sergeant, it's growing! We must back away!"

"It's what?"

A black cloud erupted through the thatch roof and several of the windows, swarming in all directions. One part of the swarm shot straight past the soldiers and descended on a pigsty. Pigs squealed and shrieked as the things covered all exposed skin from head to tail, and they lasted no more than a step before collapsing. Wet sounds accompanied the buzz as the writhing second skin feasted on them, and one lighted on Howe's arm long enough for him to see what it was.

Perhaps it had been a hornet once. Perhaps it had been a bee. But now it was nigh half as long as his thumb and horribly disfigured. Six legs, no two of which bent in exactly the same way, left it limping as it turned to depart. Its obsidian black wings glinted in the torchlight, and its jaws...

The four sharp mandibles did not move in any way Howe thought was natural, yet they made short work of the horses and pigs. The pained cries of the cattle and bleating of goats made their next targets clear. The swarm may not threaten the folk, but they ate the livestock alive, and that meant starvation.

A sergeant pointed at the sty. “Burn the pigs! Burn them now!”

Howe snapped back to the pigsty where a black carpet devoured half-eaten corpses. Meatless ribs grew in length as the carpet sank, exposing still more bones. One of the soldiers tossed a torch into the mess, striking one of the pigs and sending a number of the bugs crackling to their deaths before it bounced into the mud.

The swarm ascended from their repast and attacked. Howe found himself in the middle of a humming cloud, and he swatted anything that landed on him. Every time he struck one it felt like grasping a rose by its thorns, and the bites felt like small daggers. Blood spread on his tunic under the unrelenting mandibles. The soldiers in gambesons fared no better, and everything around him was terror and panic.

He felt a spike of fear as he found no way to live through this. No knife or bow could defeat this enemy.

***

An eerie droning outside of the keep grew louder as Pencheval rushed down the stairs. The sound did not quite overpower the screams, and he realized the swarm’s victims still lived. Howe and Dominik were threatened and it was not too late to save them.

If the goblins could do this all along, why wait until now? Perhaps it was too indiscriminate to release when the horde was at the walls of Tarsun’s Market, else they would have unleashed it after they arrived. That was why the drake riders released them and fled. If they remained they risked becoming targets.

What would defeat it? All he knew that might prevail was the Pitfire spell. It created a burning simulacrum of a demonic being around his sword, which excelled at spooking goblins in a pinch. More than an illusion, it was made of real fire, and lashed far enough outward from the blade to strike anything in the air. It would have to do.

When Pencheval finally reached the ground floor, he found a soldier desperately pressing against the exit door. A patter of wooden smacks that sounded of hail left the terrified guard glancing at the keyhole, fearful something might find a path through it and into the keep. The two arrowslits flanking the door were stuffed with burlap and cloth, and every so often something would smack them with enough force to make his head jerk at the sound.

“Move aside!”

The soldier gaped at the Lion, eyes bulging with fear. “Are you mad?”

Pencheval grabbed him by the collar. “You move, or I move you. Flee if you must, but do not impede me!”

"You want to die that badly, you daft bastard? I'll leave you to it!" The soldier scrambled up the stairs, and Pencheval heard another door slam shut above him.

The mercenary took a deep breath to calm himself. All on the other side of the door was screaming and an angry buzz. Wishing he had an enemy he could strike with a sword, he unbolted the door, flung it open, and fell blasted to the floor by a sudden gale.

The howling wind pelted him with...something. He dropped his weapon and struggled to stand, shielding his face from the storm and whatever it had swept up in its fury. Outside, the soldiers struggled to rise from the ground, and amongst them was a carpet of black.

He felt something sting just above one eyebrow, and plucked what appeared to be a strangely warped wasp's leg from it. The gale played havoc with the soldiers, but it crushed the insects flat or tore them to pieces. Black flecks flew through the air like thick snow.

It was the storm wind he suggested to Nan. It could have come from nowhere else. She had remembered his suggestion and used it on the soldiers from above to save them. A harsh salvation, but a salvation nonetheless.

The wind raged for long moments and then simply ceased, leaving the night as calm as it had been before it came. No clouds of bugs or buzzing remained in its wake, only their dead and scattered bodies. Pencheval staggered to the courtyard and grimaced. Some of the soldiers rose, brushing their tabards clean. Others laid where they fell, gambesons spotted with blood and rent with dozens of tiny tears where the things chewed their way to their targets.

"Saint Marion's...revelation." A man dressed in a tunic, trousers, and an archer's bracer rose up to his elbows and blinked. Blood smeared and speckled his face and clothing, and he seemed weak from its loss. Recognizing Scout Howe, Pencheval picked his way through the mess towards him. Mud and less benign things squished beneath his feet as he crossed the courtyard strewn with bugs.

"Don't I...know you from somewhere?"

"Aye, and you'll remember again in time." Pencheval lifted Howe and put him across his shoulders. "The threat has passed! We need healers!"

"This way!" One of the knights stood near the barbican. He was limned by the same light that shined from Knight-Brother Galot when he invoked the power of the Lord on High in Tarsun's Market. The glow struggled to emerge from a coating of gray dust. Pencheval realized the armor and robe were both blotched and spotted with hundreds of tiny smears of ash. If his power matched Galot's, he incinerated and wore the ashes of anything that tried to sting him.

Soldiers rushed to aid who they could and several of the sisters brought bandages. One of them gestured to Pencheval, and he followed her to an infirmary. How had the goblins done this? It made no difference, for they would not do it again once he had their warlord dangling from the point of his sword, squealing for its life like a stuck pig.

***

Friar Dominik stumbled out of the barbican's gate after it was opened at dawn. He was disgusted with wishing he could have simply slept through last night and left the castle's problems to someone else. Whatever wicked forces those goblins summoned sent a swarm to slaughter all of the livestock, and it did. It did not even spare the hounds.

At least two dozen soldiers died, and more were rushed to the infirmary in the hopes of saving them from bites and bleeding. It was why the Disciple called down the storm in the courtyard. The swarm could not be defeated any other way, and indeed it died as the winds tore it to pieces.

The townsfolk were first in fear of the swarm, and then after its departure, in fear of the Disciple. Some screamed that the gale destroyed their shelters, while others saw it for the blessing it was. The army only just brought the mob formed in the aftermath to heel this morning and had to whip more than one of them to pacify the rest.

He was not so foolish he saw the Disciple as a curse. But why did she wait until all the livestock were gone? Perhaps she knew something he did not. Perhaps it took that long for her to bring the Lord on High's power to bear. Father Victor claimed it was demanding to wield, and he saw no reason to question the venerable priest. He pressed the palm of his left hand to his forehead and tried to suppress the helpless rage.

The Disciple was a timely blessing, but rose to turmoil as The Histories told. Fools and ingrates among the townsfolk rioted. Soldiers moved to brutality on orders from the Knight Superior. An overcrowded castle slowly ground tempers to dust. How much longer would order remain?

It was so easy to read about it or hear it preached. He could just nod and understand the truth of it from the comfort of a temple. But to read of it, and how others overcame it, was nothing at all like living through it!

Something that sounded like a scream in the distance echoed from the stones. Dominik searched for it, exhaustion and lack of sleep rendering all he saw as less than real. He squinted towards a small figure running along the road from the pass, struggling to keep her feet. Staggering, exhausted, and mud-stained, she stumbled towards the Shield of Athesiene and fell.

"What?" Dominik put his hand over his eyes to check. He heard shouts from the walls as soldiers called to one another. He was still wondering if she was actually there when the clomp of boots passed him.

"Back inside, you!" One soldier pointed at the gate. "Can't you hear the goblins?"

"Goblins? Yes, of course."

Dominik stopped to listen and heard it for the first time. An undercurrent to the marching feet and the dull echoes of piteous screams. Something just beneath the breeze and the sounds of the archers stepping up to the battlements to provide cover for those soldiers as they left.

It was a sound like the endless buzz of insects or a flock of birds, only much darker. It rang with a malice he could very well place, for he had heard it once before in Tarsun's Market. It was the sound of a goblin horde.

The goblins were close enough to hear, and even more turmoil would follow. He wished he could remain in the relative peace of the burned town for a while longer. It had none of the castle's strife, but the only safety was within the fortification's walls, and he might find some sleep there if his troubles would let him.

Seven

The Beastwarper Chieftain limped along with the aid of a staff, wishing he could seek his answers with less exertion as he approached the pens of the Skyfang Clan. One rider caught a glimpse of him, then stopped watering a mount to chitter a warning to those riders along the double rows. Though the reaction served his intent to take stock of the Skyfang's defenses, his curiosity about the bat-lizards themselves quickly turned his purpose.

What manner of training or shaman trick could keep a bat-lizard within the confines of a stick ring? He knew the Skyfang had chopped those saplings after arrival, which meant they held no magic. Yet the bat-lizards remained in place and did not so much as tug at the ropes 'pinning' them to the ground. A casual jerk of their heads would dislodge the stakes to which they were tied, if nothing else.

The arrangement was ludicrous. Yet the one beast that gave him its attention did nothing more than appraise him lazily with one eye. It was as though it could not even think of escape.

Magic? No. This was training, and despite discovering how to subdue Bonestrippers into mounts, Beastwarper envied it. Capturing bat-lizards, much less training them, were feats his clan had never matched.

How did one even begin to do such a thing? They were ferocious and untouchable, either swooping down at his clan's goats, or snatching one of the rabble that found themselves too far from shelter. Until now, bat-lizards were gloriously beautiful and dizzying to contemplate, but never tame.

Never until the one that eyed him now. After determining Beastwarper was neither a threat nor a rider, the bat-lizard returned to rest. The chieftain could not keep his mind from it, even as he heard the rising alarm of guards. At least a Bonestripper's weight of reptilian perfection laid there awaiting command, spectacular red patterns weaving across gray scales. The possibilities of such a thing were mesmerizing...

"What do you want?"

Beastwarper snapped out of his reverie. Wingleader Jux glared at him, and he could see the other Skyfang approaching mounts or reaching for weapons. A half a dozen riders accompanied the Skyfang leader, annoyingly alert and prepared. The chieftain found no reason to antagonize him yet.

"Pardon my curiosity," Beastwarper spoke in a calm tone. "Beasts and what can be done with them are my life's work. To be so close to a bat-lizard was merely too tempting."

"What can be done with them? What you can do is keep your Deepglow far away from them!"

Jux hissed, but Beastwarper remained calm as he took stock of the area. Two riders moved within the stick pens and pulled the stakes pinning the rope collars of their bat-lizards to the ground. They kept them in hand as the creatures rose, intentions to unleash them obvious. They were trying to intimidate him.

Their actions suggested they need not even ride them in order to command them. It made sense. All this time, and not so much as one bat-lizard ever slipped its bonds? Not if they were able to control them this way. If pulling a stick from the ground was all a Skyfang rider need do to grant himself the aid of his mount, it would make capturing one of them difficult.

"Of course I would do no such a thing unpermitted." He almost flinched, believing the conciliatory words too unctuous. "Besides, acquiring Deepglow is no small matter, and I don't waste it."

"Good to know. Now be gone." Jux pointed back to the main body of the horde. "If you mean to negotiate with the Skyfang, speak to Leth."

"Very well." This time, Beastwarper almost balked at remaining civil. He was a chieftain! Under any other circumstances, such treatment would result in the offender becoming the next meal of a Bonestripper. In the case of the Skyfang, he had no choice in the matter but to bear it, but at least he had succeeded in learning what he wished to know.

If they were to overwhelm the Skyfang, they could not simply overrun the camp with rabble or try to catch a rider unawares. Several of them were always wary and they all kept within easy reach of their pens. He might perhaps offer something to one of them for knowledge, but what? How lean did a clan with its own bat-lizards live, and would they leave it to join another clan unable to fly?

He remembered admiring the bat-lizard not a few moments ago as he limped away with his guards. If he could learn to tame them, all his efforts would be worth their miseries. They were such magnificent things.

***

"No, the Lion will not be joining us this time, Galter. Nor will anything said here be mentioned to him."

"Yes, Your Grace." Castellan Galter walked over to the door of the war council chambers and put the bolt across it.

"Those who left for the pass did not return save for one survivor. The drake riders attacked them there, but were either too sloppy to kill them all or allowed survivors by intent. She knows more escaped the attack but not where they are."

"Little changes, Your Grace," a knight replied. "We did not intend to flee. That we cannot alters nothing."

"Little changes for us." The stalwart knight left him proud, but he knew his order would be the exception and not the rule. "This tale spread through the soldiers and townsfolk. They know there is no option for flight, and that will lead to fear and strife."

"Whatever blighted swarm the goblins summoned did their worst, Your Grace," the castellan continued. "We no longer have horses, which means we no longer have cavalry. Any animals inside the castle, which were all of them, are dead now. Though it means we no longer need to feed them, we can no longer eat them, either. We must ration at once."

"Proceed," Rennoute commanded. "Do you know if any traces of that swarm remain?"

"Nothing but corpses blasted to motes, Your Grace," the castellan reported. "The winds destroyed them all, but it also killed several of the soldiers."

"The swarm would have slain many more than it did had the Disciple not acted," Rennoute replied. "You do not mention this to her, and neither do your men. So far as any of you say, the swarm killed those soldiers, and the winds saved who they could."

"We would deceive the Disciple, Your Grace?" The knight spoke as though such a thing was unthinkable.

"No. She chose correctly when she used the winds. We will not torment her with it and cause her doubt now that she has found a weapon against the drakes."

"Yes, Your Grace." Galter's face remained stony, but he had known the man long enough to realize he suppressed distaste at the command. The knight merely nodded but seemed unconvinced.

Rennoute saw no better alternative. If the winds could repel the drakes, the Disciple would save far more than she would slay. If news of the collateral damage made it to her ears, however, she might not use them again. She still thought like a sister and did not yet comprehend that war required choosing lesser evils over greater ones.

As it was, the fact such winds were suggested by Pencheval made them odd enough. A Silver Lion mercenary defending the faith and aiding a Disciple? Granted, other companions of Disciples in The Histories were hardly of the faith themselves, but many had only served as examples of what not to do or be. Few such companions had ever set a Disciple's feet on the path to their destiny.

It was odd, but perhaps the Lion was not setting her on the path. Perhaps it was the Lord on High's will that the Lion be turned *by her* to the path. He had certainly demonstrated less and less of a Lion's thinking, particularly during the time he attempted to rescue The

Disciple from Tarsun's Market. She did that for herself in the end, but not before Athesiene's purposes were served by them both.

"Anything else?" Rennoute waited for responses from the table.

"One of the friars, a known associate of the Lion, threatened the departing townsfolk with a quarterstaff. It took the threat of scourging to make him relent. Additional reports suggest he may be breaking under the strain of goblin attacks and siege."

"Dominik." The Knight Superior shook his head. "Inform Father Victor, and tell him to assign the friar other tasks than missions of mercy amongst the townsfolk."

Dominik was the one that spoke to him after surviving Tarsun's Market. Despite questioning a decision to evict the Lion from the valley, he had no history of causing trouble–only one of finding himself in it through no fault of his own. He was not someone of whom an example should be made, and Rennoute meant to ensure it remained so.

"Yes, Your Grace."

"You may go. Return to your tasks with all haste, as chaos precedes the battle to come. It must not be here when the horde finally arrives."

***

"Athesiene's mercy, what did I do?"

Nan paced back and forth before the dais in the castle's chapel. She had filled the entire courtyard with storm winds to stop that blighted swarm, but was that the right thing to do? What had she done to those below?

"Disciple?" The knight guarding the door sounded as he always did, impassive and disturbingly unaffected by the carnage from last night.

"The winds, brother. I sent the winds to the courtyard. I couldn't see any other way..."

"They stopped that swarm from killing anything or anyone else, Disciple. Your judgment in that matter was correct."

"Correct? It was desperate and rash action. What if the power had done harm?"

"It did not," the knight reassured her. "Inconvenience was a small price to pay. Many more would have died had you done nothing."

"Many more? How many slain?"

"Fewer than would have died had you not acted, Disciple."

Nan resumed her pacing. Why was the knight talking in circles, and what was he not telling her? It was something about the power they all wanted her to use, but what? As Pencheval suggested, nothing flew in a storm, but should she have used it sooner? Why did she not do so from the roof instead of wasting precious moments descending?

Because she knew nothing of the swarm until it acted, and only knew it attacked those in the courtyard when she saw it through an embrasure. Too much wind? Perhaps it was enough, only too late. Perhaps the harm done by the delay was what they did not want her to know.

Those in the castle were still treating her like something to be protected and not a part of the struggle. It frustrated her but contradicted nothing she had read. The Histories suggested that the temple did that with all of their novice Disciples. In the past, followers of their faith did what they could to ensure those like herself lived to accomplish whatever plans Athesiene had for them.

And Pencheval? He was still Pencheval, as much as he had changed. Buried under the darkness inflicted on him by his circumstances and the Silver Lions but still there. The only one among them all with whom she could have a sensible conversation. He wanted to save her, but that was only because he remembered his days as a boy in Terris Lyn.

With everyone else, one would think she was the Lord on High Himself. How did one remain informed or plan with such people? She was not a holy relic to be stored in a reliquary!

Nan huffed. "Can you tell me more of the Knight Superior's plans?" And perhaps treat her like she was human!

"Nothing has changed of which I am aware, Disciple. If you mean to aid us against the drakes tonight, you should gather your strength. The goblins have every reason to attack if they believe their malice did enough harm."

Nan nodded thoughtfully, but then resumed pacing. Gather her strength? It was always there, like an ocean of might behind far too flimsy a barrier to prevent it from gushing forth.

That meant the Lord on High still found her worthy. She hoped He was correct and could live up to what was now expected of her. Should she lose control of herself, or decide poorly on using the power He granted, those she meant to protect would suffer.

***

"You thought this was council-worthy, you sniveling dungstain?"

The Stonemaster sat back on his bone chair and listened to the Bloodmoon Speaker encourage an excess of caution in Leth. Jux had confronted Beastwarper while the chieftain studied a bat-lizard, likely obsessing over it as he had done with the books in Tarsun's Market. It was obvious that the spat would make its way back to Leth, but that was unavoidable and wholly by design.

Beastwarper had gone to their pens with the warlord's blessing to find some way to gain a rider, or any information at all, about the bat-lizards. It made things tense between the horde and the Skyfang, but that was something the Stonemaster was willing to risk. The was nothing else for it but to send Beastwarper, as the bat-lizards would not reveal their secrets of their own volition.

"We require our own space for the riders, Speaker. It is not too much to ask." Leth seemed reluctant to answer the Bloodmoon Speaker sternly, which made him like anyone else possessing intact sense.

"Did Beastwarper harm a bat-lizard?"

"No, but–"

"Then cease to speak of it." The warlord glared at Leth from his bone chair. "Bloodmoon speaks truly. Other things are more worth our time, like your next attacks on the mountain-castle. Two days you have not flown against it except to deliver the Bloodseekers, which by now have done all they can do. Time for you to resume the Snow Clan's destruction."

"We kept the humans from escaping," Leth protested. "They know they cannot flee now."

"Which makes a good fight certain, but not victory," the Bloodmoon Speaker grumbled.

"Enough!" The Stonemaster bared his teeth. "You will gain much from me for the work of one season. We have done much for you which was not agreed. Considering the Bloodseekers' work means we'll have to raid southward for enough to last through winter, you *will* keep to your end of our bargain."

"This is–"

"And without complaint!" The Stonemaster snapped up from his chair. Rabble near the council scattered. "One of us examined a bat-lizard too closely. They are bat-lizards, what did you expect? Will mere looks cause them harm? If so, then you should depart at once and make your excuses to your chieftain for returning empty handed!"

The Bloodmoon Speaker appeared ready to laugh at the display, but Beastwarper wisely kept his words to himself. The Allspeaker seemed to believe all would come to an end soon, but his excess of caution always made him believe it thus.

"If not, you will resume your attacks and aid us in this battle as you said you would. The Snow Clan has rock throwing things, and they are next to burn. They are big piles of wood and easy to spot."

"We need our space." The half-hearted protest made him seem more like an unruly pup whimpering over discipline.

"You still retain your space. One visit by a council member doesn't change that. Now deal with the matter at hand and don't forget your end of our bargain again."

Speaker Leth stood and shuffled away towards his riders. The warlord momentarily considered the wisdom of asserting himself that way against the Skyfang, but Leth's response hardly threatened reprisals. If anything, the more tenuously loyal Bloodmoon Speaker appreciated such displays of domination, and he would see their absence as a sign of weakness. It was not the way the Stonemaster had originally intended to sidestep Beastwarper's examination of the pens, but it would do.

"Next matter at hand."

The warlord knew there would be one. The horde never lacked for problems.

***

Pencheval stopped in the door to the infirmary as a sister rushed by him with a bucket of water and bandages. Every bed held a soldier, and in many of the spaces between them, another of the injured laid on a blanket or bare stone. Some groaned and others seemed as pale as ghosts.

Every so often a sister would pray to the Lord on High, and the white light of Athesiene's grace dawned from her hands. Its touch ended bleeding and sealed wounds. One sister used it on the telltale black and green of a wound that would otherwise require an amputation, and he watched the gangrenous blight recede to nothingness. He took stock of the nearest soldier and grimaced.

A single bite left its mark as an angry red bump, and the unfortunate man bore several he could see. Bandages speckled with fresh blood and smelling of poultices wrapped both arms and his skull, one wrap draping over an eye. Dozens of tiny holes rent the clothing he still wore where the horrid swarm was undeterred by cloth.

Pencheval searched the room and found Scout Howe unconscious on a rough wooden table. He wore bandages on his arms and chest, and a sister treated a fever with a damp cloth. Nothing on him spoke of infection or gangrene, but he bore a ghastly pallor.

It was some of the worst work he had seen from the goblins. What would have happened if the swarm attack went unmet by the storm winds? Nan had stopped what she could, but they inflicted horrendous damage before the gale brought an end to them.

"Are you injured?" one of the clergy, weariness apparent in his voice, called to Pencheval from across the room.

"No. Concerned for a friend."

"Then I ask that you leave. We can spare no pause in the current severity."

Pencheval nodded and departed, unwilling to remain between Howe and his healers. He picked through the hallway, which doubled now as a place to sleep and storage, and listened as two sets of boots walked his way.

"Why're you complaining? You're still alive, right?" The owner of the voice was a soldier, who looked at his feet so he would not trip over the mess.

"Aye, but couldn't the Disciple have just made the flies scatter without wind?"

"Maybe that's just what we got?"

"Just what we got, huh?" The soldier grew angry. "Storm brains Wallace with a rock, and all you can say is 'that's just what we got'? It ain't a miracle when it makes you dig a grave."

The soldier and his companion stopped when they saw Pencheval. One of them carried two pails of water and the other held a bundle of shredded cloth. It was torn into strips ideal for bandaging.

"Something a matter, Lion?" The one with the pails waited impatiently for an answer. He was the one aggrieved by the winds.

Pencheval's first thought was to threaten him. If the soldiers grew angry at Nan, some of them might take the opportunity to indulge their wrath. They had access to the castle and possibly the chapel where she spent most of her time. If nothing else, snarling at him would turn their anger towards a target more capable of dealing with them, namely himself.

He clenched his fist, and then loosened it. No, that was not the answer with a goblin horde approaching the castle. The man watched one of his friends die, and beating or killing him would do nothing beyond causing needless strife.

"No. Just worried about a friend."

"Be glad you still got one." The two passed by him and turned into the infirmary, announcing more water and bandages as they entered. One of the healers gave them directions and then all inside was haste again.

Pencheval reflected on his response. A year ago, in the same position, he would have terrorized the man just on principle. Then, he believed fear was all the common folk understood, and he would have granted that soldier much understanding of why he would keep his grumbling about Nan to himself.

Now, Pencheval had seen more of those not trying to rob, use, or kill him and thought before acting. Yes, if the soldier became a real threat and the knight guarding Nan did not deal with him, he would. But unlike a year ago, he refused to assume the worst. Neither grief nor anger at cruel circumstances were malice, and as long as no harm came of them, there was no reason to make a bad situation worse.

***

“What did you learn, Beastwarper?”

The Stonemaster remained near his bone chair and kept his tones low. Despite the noise all around, privacy was always a concern in the horde. It was never safe to assume his high status as its master rendered all around him deaf, even if the rabble avoided the council areas shielded by hides and wicker.

“The bat-lizards are glorious creatures, Chief of Chieftains.”

“And?” That was all? He had risked a visit and returned only to remark upon the obvious?

“Unfortunately, the reaction of the Skyfang suggests they need not ride their mounts to wield them against us. Even on the ground, it would be a disaster to attack them.”

“Fiend’s breath.” The frustrated Stonemaster gave grudging admiration to the Skyfang. They sent a disposable, if charismatic, know-nothing to be their speaker, but the rest knew their duties very well. Nor would small numbers hinder them since they had the bat-lizards. They could kill any threats on the ground if they were few, and escape any attempt by the horde to mass and swarm them.

“Not that attacking them would make sense before the battle to take the mountain-castle, Chief of Chieftains. We still need their help, and treachery would at the very least cause flight.”

“On that we agree,” the Stonemaster answered. “We take them after the battle, when the fight has inflicted losses and fatigue upon them. Sad that so many bat-lizards must then be slain to do it, but that is how it is.”

“No, take them after their part in the battle but when many are still in the air,” Beastwarper countered. “Those that see the treachery will flee, and fewer will remain on the ground to overwhelm.”

“Or they retaliate,” the Stonemaster countered, glancing askance at Beastwarper. “After the battle, not during.”

“There is time yet to determine when to attack, Chief of Chieftains, but what of the resources? It will surely take us both.”

“I will give them a space for pens near or on stones,” the Stonemaster offered. “My power can aid us then.”

“My Bonestrippers can slay the bat-lizards if they are divided, but they will also kill many riders. Yet if they are split, I have enough to overwhelm them.”

“I will give it more thought. Until then, return to your clan as though none of this was ever said.”

“Obviously.” Beastwarper almost sounded insulted by the inference that he could not scheme.

The Stonemaster cared little about offending him. The warped chieftain’s obsession over books cost him many humans. He would prevent the same from happening with the bat-lizards by granting less leeway. Yes, he would keep a firm hand in this, for if anything could steer the capturing of this greatest of secrets, it would be his own overwhelming superiority.

***

The Beastwarper Chieftain limped across the vast field of the horde with his guard, drawing occasional glances from the various clan camp guards as he passed. The horde acted as one under the Stonemaster, but the clans trusted one another no more than they ever did. Each clan camped only with its own and gave themselves more than enough space to grant a wide berth to the curving paths between them. A few glances gave him an estimate of how many clans remained, and which had taken the brunt of the revolt in human town.

His encampment was on the opposite side of the horde from the bat-lizards, for neither he nor the Stonemaster would risk an accidental clash between his Bonestrippers and the Skyfang. At least, he would not risk them yet. In the battle, he would array them on the flanks of the horde to protect it, as he had done to take the human town. They were worthless against cliff-walls, and that deficiency would keep them safe as the others accepted the worst of the losses. They were rabble, and such was their purpose aside from labor.

What concerned him now was the bat-lizards. Yes, capturing a rider was the only way to gain their secrets, but that feat required him to prevent their escape to the skies. His mind conceived and discarded approaches to ensure that as he struggled to cross the field on his staff, growing more frustrated as he went. His thinking grew more radical until he finally conceded his most brutal and costly of methods alone would suffice in that work.

A guard at the perimeter of his clan's encampment recognized him and bowed.

"Have the shamans attend to me."

"Yes, my chieftain." The guard rushed to obey.

Beastwarper leaned on his staff, catching his breath, and regretted not having someone bear him over the distance. He waited until the three shamans he brought with him approached, escorted by the guard.

"My chieftain," the oldest of them spoke.

"How many toss vials do we have?"

"Only two, my chieftain." The shaman swallowed hard. "We left most of the Deepglow at our clan-home. There is not enough to fill more."

"Fill and seal them both, then bring them to me. Keep this to yourselves, and act as though the Deepglow pot remains filled thereafter."

"Yes, my chieftain." The shamans reluctantly departed to obey. It was always so. No one enjoyed the task of filling toss vials, for any mistake could be fatal or disfiguring. Dangerous, but also useful in sorting the incompetents from true Beastwarper shamans.

The expenditure of Deepglow this time was a necessity. To remove a rider from a bat-lizard would require its death. A toss vial was the only thing he had that was lethal enough against such a beast, aside from the less predictable Bonestripper attack.

The clay pots sealed with twine and sap would fit beneath his clothing and smell faintly of trees. The long leather cords attached to them meant the pots could be tossed in the same manner as a slinger threw a stone, and the impact would break it and splash the target with Deepglow. The thought of wearing both of them until after they captured a Skyfang rider left him nervous, but the toss vials were harmless unless they leaked.

He hoped he would only need the one but was perfectly willing to use them both. Death by lethal warping was an awful thing to do to such a magnificent creature as a tame bat-lizard, but knowledge often came at a heavy price. The knowledge of taming bat-lizards was easily worth a few of their deaths.

Eight

"Your Grace, this tolerance of the Silver Lion's influence upon our Disciple is highly irregular!"

The Knight Superior suppressed the urge to berate sense into Father Victor. The indignant priest was second only to himself as ranking clergy in the Emerald Refuge. He was in the castle tending to his duties the day Rennoute arrived as the appointed Knight Superior and had not ceased since. He stood now with the aid of a staff, curly white hair circling an otherwise bald pate just above the ears and protesting through a white beard that nearly hid his mouth.

He was diligent, strict, and fit to ensure the clergy kept the temple's traditions within the valley. He was also stuck in his ways and far too bureaucratic for the current circumstances. To even suggest the Lion and the Disciple should be parted was madness considering how effective they were together. Yet there he stood, incensed by the lack of decorum, because a goblin horde and their drakes did not sufficiently weigh to tolerate the *irregular*.

"She is not our Disciple, Victor. She is *the* Disciple, and it is within her purview to keep what company she wills. The Lord on High has already found her worthy, and that includes her judgement."

"And will He continue to find her worthy should she begin to reflect the judgement of the Lion and his guild, Your Grace? What He grants, He can also withdraw, and the Disciples are ever under His watchful eyes."

Rennoute steepled his fingertips and rapped them together. It was an annoyingly salient point that their current circumstances simply did not give him the leeway to consider. That, and Pencheval's deeds thus far contradicted any assertion that he was nothing more than another mercenary.

"This Lion speeds her recovery from her time with the goblins, and may be only one of two reasons she returned from them at all. What would you have me do?"

"Keep them parted, Your Grace. The temple has its own ways to guide the Disciples. We have used them for centuries, and it is right and proper that we attend to them ourselves."

"Proper adherence to temple law would have her sent immediately to the capital for training, which we cannot do for the horde," Rennoute replied. "Furthermore, the storm winds that defeated the swarm were the idea of the Lion. She has the power, and he the years as a wandering mercenary champion slaying enemies alone or with few others. Their reunion may well have been the Lord on High's purpose for the Lion."

"I agree with Your Grace. The Lord on High did have a purpose for that Lion, but he served it when he helped rescue the Disciple." Victor wheezed and then coughed into a balled fist placed to his mouth. "We owe him gratitude but nothing more. If we allow him any more leeway, he may also become the thing that costs us a Disciple."

"Your loyalty to the faith does you credit, Victor, but my decision in this matter stands. Do not hinder the Lion or the Disciple. They may be the difference between saving this valley or its fall."

"Yes, Your Grace. The Lord on High grant you wisdom."

"You may go." Rennoute let the inference in that last statement pass as Victor hobbled away on his staff. The priest could be hidebound on his own time. The temple had charged the Knight Superior with protecting the valley, and that would require the sorts of decisions many here would find controversial. Only time would tell if he truly did lack wisdom.

***

Pencheval gazed into the night, seeking drakes and hoping the goblins found no cause to send them again. It was a vain hope and he knew it. The click and screech of the horde found its way over the walls in the castle's quieter moments, and that meant they still advanced. If their warlord retained half the sense it had already demonstrated, it would use the drakes to destroy anything threatening its forces as much as it could.

Nan stood beside him and fidgeted nervously, muttering under her breath. The two knights guarding her waited more stoically. They were well familiar with the dullness of watches, even those like this which were all but guaranteed to end in fear.

"Could the goblins not come and be done with this?" Nan toyed with the hem of her robe's cuffs.

"Would that it was so, Nan," Pencheval answered without turning to her. He maintained his Clearsight charm and stared off into the night. The skies resolved in shades of gray, and nothing that hinted of drakes appeared before him. They flew too swiftly to allow for complacency, however, and could be upon them before he noticed if he gave in to distraction.

"Respectfully, Disciple, fight the battle when it arrives. This will not serve you well." The knight's tone was gentle, and Nan stopped for a moment.

"Will not serve me well? How does one face a sky full of drakes well?"

"We will get through this, Nan. There are only three again tonight." Pencheval squinted. Three specks appeared at the limits of his vision and grew larger, and the way they moved betrayed what they were all too quickly.

"Three," Nan half-whispered to herself. "Only three..."

"Only three, and protection is within easy reach." Pencheval felt his guts churn from helpless frustration.

As harsh as his guild could be, it never allowed the *guilden* to do battle on their own without outstanding gear, rigorous training, and years of experience in apprenticeship. When he took contracts that required him to defeat great beasts alone, he prevailed because he learned under the tutelage of a master and became a veteran of real battles.

Her circumstances were a combination of pressure, power, and inexperience. She commanded forces in a magnitude none of them could comprehend and knew one slip might end in regret. No one here was qualified to train her in wielding such might, and the only real tutors under which she might study resided in the capital. He wished it could be different, but there was nothing he could do to help her against the drakes save moral support. Until the fight moved to the ground, he was little more than a scout and an advisor.

"Any hint of their plans?" The knight readied his shield.

"None yet. They still fly straight at us." Pencheval watched them grow all too swiftly as they approached from the east.

"Winds...more winds..."

"Nan, you can summon the winds. Do as you did before." Pencheval hoped he sounded reassuring. "I will estimate their direction, and you put the winds over the soldiers in their path. It might deter them."

"Might?"

Pencheval cursed to himself. What choice of words did one find inspiring? He heard many from his drill instructors that infuriated him into action or success, but inspiration was not something that came easily to him.

"The Lord on High protects us, Disciple, as He did with you in Tarsun's Market," the knight assured her. "Bring His will to the goblins."

The words seemed to hearten Nan, and Pencheval was relieved.

"They're banking right." The Lion pointed to the far walls of the castle. "They're aiming for either the top of the walls or the towers. There's nothing else over there to hit."

"They won't enjoy what awaits them."

Pencheval smiled at Nan's renewed spirit as she raised her hands and concentrated. In the distance above the southern walls, banners flapped wildly as soldiers looked up at the growing whistle and howl. They were all warned that Nan would use the winds again which averted panic, but he could see sergeants berating soldiers made skittish by the roar above their heads.

The drakes fell into the same pattern as before. A leader flew in a direction and the others followed, leaving many lengths between them, and turned to put the eastern walls along their path. Pencheval waited and ignored his doubts. They would all discover if the winds were sufficient to the task soon.

***

Wingleader Jux was not much interested in excuses or failures now.

A chastened Leth came to him the day before this flight. He informed the Wingleader with uncharacteristic brevity that the Stonemaster requested the destruction of the human rock throwing things. His illustrious leader looked like he was between the wrath of two chieftains and barely mumbled a description of what he was to hit.

When this flight was done, it was time to consider contingencies. The Speaker was too terrified to disobey his chieftain, which was as it should be. He was also increasingly overmatched by the ground-bound Stonemaster, which was not remotely as it should be. Theirs was the clan with the bat-lizards, and they were the masters. The chieftain should have put him in charge and left the idiot Leth at the clan-home, but that decision was out of Jux's hands.

A wide turn that began when he first saw the mountain-castle leveled out in line with one of the cliff-wall's rounder sections. A collection of timbers that bore a semblance to the Stonemaster's rock throwing things stood atop it. It was easy enough to swoop past while his bat-lizard spat flame at it, followed by the other two.

Jux quelled his frustration to focus on his target. Thinking past a task involving bat-lizards was potentially fatal, as there was always much to consider while flying one. Deal with the rock thrower first, then with the Speaker.

The howl of the winds near the cliff-walls temporarily gave him pause. This night had been still up until now, and yet the human clan symbols on poles fluttered violently. Still, there were no clouds, and no lightning or thunder threatened in the skies. It was merely a strong breeze and insufficient reason to withdraw.

Jux slapped the reins of his mount, which accelerated rapidly enough to push him back into his seat. A little more, and it would be close enough to set the rock throwing thing ablaze. The wind whistled around his ears, and as he tensed to command his mount to fire, he realized the din grew too loud too quickly.

Before he could reconsider, a raging storm smacked him across the face and set his bat-lizard to panicked flapping. It fought to remain aloft, screeching, only to be buffeted wildly over its intended target. It knocked him about but denied him passage, pinning him to his place in the skies.

One group of humans next to a large bow made of timbers pulled back its rope and put a spear in it. Their enforcer yelled at them and pointed at him. They turned their great wooden thing to face him and made the end drop so the spear tilted upwards.

Jux reined and screamed at his mount, voice drowned out by the roar all around him. His eyes bugged in panic as wings flapped thunderously on either side of him in vain. The Snow Clan had him in the perfect place to skewer him.

***

"It's snared by the wind!"

Pencheval smiled wolfishly as the goblin rider and its drake struggled, all but helpless as a ballista crew brought their weapon to bear. But why had the others not flown into the winds, or around them? He subdued his growing excitement and willed a Clearsight charm to grant him sight through darkness again. If they were not following their leader blindly, where were they?

He searched the skies and found one circling wide around the town and castle. It evaded the winds but arced back towards them, so it had something in mind besides retreat. He could not find the last one until it swooped up from below the eastern wall and grasped the battlements with both claws. With one powerful flap, it vaulted over the edge and onto the crew of the ballista. It snatched one in its jaws and shook him like a hound with a ragdoll before biting him in two.

A short lunge slammed it into the siege engine, and the drake snapped and twisted its body to send the weapon flying. The shattered pile of wood fell into the courtyard and screams rang from below. A roar preceded a glob of flame that sent soldiers diving before the drake's rider reined it over the edge. It soared beneath the height of the keep, gaining speed as the leathery flaps echoed from the stone. It cleared the northern walls by no more than half its length, and the soldiers manning it ducked and scrambled as it rushed past.

"Lion, where is the third drake?" Both knights stood ready with shields raised, and Pencheval resumed his search. A roar exposed the final drake as it spat flame at a trebuchet. The burning glob struck it squarely and its crew fled the rapidly growing inferno.

"Beware, it–" Pencheval snatched Nan and pulled her away from the edge of the keep's roof as the drake rushed past them. He caught a glimpse of trailing feet and fully extended wings, each twice as long as he was tall. The pass startled both knights, and the winds holding the captured drake ceased to harry it long enough for it to dive away from the castle. Pencheval released Nan to seek them again.

"Athesiene's mercy!" The flustered Nan put her hand over her chest.

Pencheval ignored Nan's vexation as he sought out the drakes and found them regrouping as they fled. They flew straight towards Tarsun's Market and the horde, unwilling to test the winds again. Despite that small victory, they had still done too much.

The glob of flame one spat on the trebuchet left it in a conflagration. Soldiers rushed along the walls with buckets, but they were too far from the wells to make any difference. The siege engine was a total loss and would have to burn itself to ashes before the flames died.

Another glob only hit the top of the eastern wall and sputtered for lack of fuel. Soldiers kept their distance and covered their faces with cloaks or arms. He remembered the acrid stench of the Drake's Lure and suspected that real drake's flame was at least as bad.

Though Nan left one goblin rider in a stalemate, its companions had the audacity to rescue it from a ballista crew. If the one that flew by the keep did so deliberately, it might have been to see if anything changed when it startled them. In all, they realized the threat of the siege engines and acted to destroy them. Worse still, they may have deduced that Nan was the source of the magic that almost saw one of them slain.

"Where are they? Lion!" One of the knights turned back for an answer.

"They have departed," Pencheval answered, snarling at the skies in the distance. Why could the goblins simply not remain primitive thieves and raiders? Black Archer take them and their rotten drakes!

***

Wingleader Jux reined to slow his mount at the edge of the horde. He felt his bat-lizard tilt backward as its wings beat, then lean forward into a glide towards the pens where the Skyfang camped. He breathed deeply and felt the hammer blows of his heart subside to normal. When he finally felt the landing jar him, he was strangely grateful.

Winds? What manner of strange weather appeared at the mountain-castle tonight? Certainly shamans could create such things, but not so powerful they could batter a bat-lizard into helplessness! That storm kept him suspended above the humans so long they nearly killed him!

Thankfully, his two hand-picked riders dealt with the Snow Clan as he would expect them to do. It was why he chose them. They were skilled, never gave in to an excess of caution, and aided him when he needed it. They landed shortly after he did, and dismounted to lead their bat-lizards by the reins.

They both approached him. "Are you injured, wingleader?"

"No." Jux stretched and tilted his head back until he felt his neck crack. He had suffered little more than some bruising from his straps. "You two did well."

"The wind freed you when I flew past the humans on the tallest peak in the mountain-castle, wingleader. One of them was the dark human from the Silver Lion Clan, who pulled one in red away from me. It seemed too wealthy to be rabble."

"It protected a shaman, and a strong one," Jux concluded. "You guessed correctly. If it was the one that escaped from the horde, we have a new problem. Its power had grown since it threw thunder and lightning at Bryx. As long as it lives it can attack us in the skies."

"What then do we do, wingleader?"

"Get rid of the shaman." That was a task easier said than done. Not only did the shaman have the power to make storms, but it would likely be of interest to both the Stonemaster and the lame chieftain of the Beastwarper Clan. That meant convincing Leth of its necessity, and that pompous fool seemed more inclined to do as the council wished than the Skyfang.

Jux wondered why the Stonemaster so eagerly accepted Leth's bargain. Permanent rights for temporary efforts? Those were generally the sorts of terms the Skyfang inflicted on rabble clans too weak to resist, not hordes. In the face of this shaman's newfound might, the battle for the mountain-castle seemed like too much risk for the gain. Even if the horde's master meant to keep his end of the bargain, they would more than earn it.

***

Dominik saw the light of dawn break over the castle walls and felt his heart sink. Another day, another tragedy. Last night, one of the drakes pushed a ballista from the walls and killed several of the soldiers and townsfolk. This morning, an undertaker walked past him, followed by an obese and balding underling leaning forward as he pulled a hand cart. They made their way towards the ruined shelters and wooden scrap that remained of the ballista's fall.

Soldiers in white tabards, gambesons, and kettle hats ordered townsfolk away from the wreckage. The ballista had landed upside down on a tent, its last intact wheel turning by inches as laborers moved to dismantle it. One of the people it killed was still beneath it, and the body would not make its final destination to the graveyard until they chopped and cut the heavy wooden wreckage into more manageable pieces.

"Why did this happen. Why?" A weeping woman on the ground looked up at him as he passed. "Why won't the Disciple stop this?"

"Because she's a bloody witch!" The interruption came from a man the next tent down, who took a deep swig of something that was clearly not water. "She don't want to stop it!"

Dominik fumed at the accusation but continued on his purpose. Father Victor saw it fit to assign him other tasks, and as he did so personally, the friar was certain they were more important. The priest also informed him that he was not to interact with the townsfolk absent permission. Given the statement of that gibbering fool, he was perfectly happy to comply. Whatever was important enough to be personally commanded by Father Victor was likely beyond the ken of such an ingrate anyhow.

He knew little of the battle, and what he did know came from snippets he overheard. The Disciple summoned winds against the drakes, and those winds snared one of them. Some said it threw the drakes back to the horde and others that it only distracted the soldiers, making it simpler for the beasts to do their worst. That portrayal of the Disciple's work bordered on blasphemy.

Did they believe Disciples grew on trees? They were so exceptional and noteworthy, entire books of The Histories were dedicated to each of their lives. They should be grateful one was sent to them in this time of need. Clearly it had been foreseen by the Lord on High, or there would be no Disciple!

Why was Athesiene's hand in this not obvious? His will and His will alone ensured Pencheval survived his defiance of the Knight Superior when he refused to leave the Disciple to her fate. In retrospect, it was obvious to the friar that was the case all along. The Lion lived, succeeded in his quest, then reaped a fortune of respect because it was His will!

So then why did this happen? If the Disciple possessed the power to stop this, why did she not? If she lacked the power to stop this, would the Lord on High protect them? Was it all a test of some sort?

For a brief moment, he wondered if he would only learn the answer as the goblin horde overran the castle. No, that was ridiculous and unworthy. If Athesiene meant to abandon them, there would be no Disciple.

***

"How could this have happened? I had it caught, and then..." Nan breathed deeply and exhaled audibly. "Use the winds, catch the drake, then the others..."

"We acted and they reacted, Nan." Pencheval tried to sound reassuring. "The outcome wasn't perfect, but they could have inflicted far worse had you done naught."

"Had I done naught? As opposed to the nothing I did do?"

"You have given them additional cause for doubt," Pencheval said. "We proved we can counterattack once more. When last we did this they ceased to bedevil us for a time, and this is twice we have proven dangerous to them. We will determine another counter."

"A counter for the drakes? Can you even hear yourself speak?" Nan scratched nervously at the back of her neck. "You want me to smite drakes from the skies and you speak of it as though we were planning a vegetable garden. A counter to drakes, indeed!"

"You are the Disciple," the knight guarding the chapel added, and Pencheval swallowed the urge to assault him on the spot.

She had suffered enough strain without this 'Disciple' business, and Pencheval wished he was capable of stopping the drakes himself. Battling monsters and miscreants was his chosen vocation, not hers, and he clenched his jaw at the realization he could not find another way. The need was so dire she was even denied the time to recover from her capture by the horde, or to come to terms with being the center of attention for Lerrisaine's dominant temple.

"Yes, so blessed am I that I carry that mountain on my shoulders!" Nan screamed the last word, and enough of her power leaked to shake the walls, pews, and windows. Pencheval gritted his teeth and stepped back into a defensive stance from habit. The startled knight took one complete step backwards.

"I'm sorry." Nan's frustration melted into a bowed head and downcast eyes. "Please, leave me for a time. I will make the effort to try again this evening."

"Disc–"

"We'll be right outside." Pencheval glared at the knight, who returned the gaze with the look of someone ready to duel the Lion for affronting him. He backed towards the door and angrily gestured for him to follow, hoping it would divert the knight's attention before his single-minded idiocy led to both their deaths.

Once the door shut, the bodyguard all but threw his sword belt to him. "If you mean to do battle with me, you need only name the time and place you wish to die."

"Is your head full of broken rocks?" Pencheval pointed towards the door. "There is another person behind that door. Not a Disciple. Not Athesiene. Not all your hopes and dreams made flesh. Only one who doesn't know war as we do and is suffering for it."

"She is the–"

"She is Nan!" Pencheval hissed a whisper in the hopes the conversation would remain on their side of the thick wooden door. "Nan. Formerly Sister Nan, who taught schoolgirls in Tarsun's Market, all of whom are likely dead now. Prior to that, a nice lady in a little barony called Terris Lyn. She didn't suddenly cross some line into ultimate holiness and become your all-saving Disciple even if the Lord on High granted her power. She is overwhelmed, so open your damn eyes and help me aid her before she is undone!"

"Tread. Carefully."

The knight glared at him and Pencheval met his gaze without flinching. Of course he could not see it. Years in his monastery had blinded him to anything but the wonder of it all. Dominik was the same way, and aside from those that now saw her as a witch, there was no one else to assist her through this but him. He was the only person in the whole castle who saw what was actually there.

He refused to surrender to the feeling that this problem would overwhelm him. He knew what it was like to attain mastery in forces he previously found unimaginable and become a warrior beyond his wildest childhood dreams. It had to be enough to see her through this. Otherwise, he would watch helplessly as the Lord on High's blessings did what captivity to the goblin horde could not: send her to her doom.

Nine

"What do you know of this storm-bringer shaman?"

The Stonemaster did not expect Jux to ask a question. Nor did his Speaker, who started in surprise when his Wingleader spoke. It bordered on impertinence, and in any other circumstances he would have Jux taught respect with a whip. In this instance, he would leave that to Leth. The Skyfang offered more than enough to tolerate a small irritation.

"It is likely the same one that threw thunder and lightning at your rider," the Beastwarper Chieftain answered. The Stonemaster sat back on his throne and allowed the conversation to continue.

"I gathered that much. Why did you not warn us of the wind?"

"It never used wind before. It created the curse of endless sleep and thunder, not wind." Beastwarper scratched his head. "Are its powers growing? How could it earn the favor of its gods so quickly?"

"It makes no difference," the Bloodmoon Speaker snapped. "Stop trying to think it to death. If this human offends the Skyfang, burn it to ashes."

"That human knows how to read," Beastwarper countered, glaring at Jux. "Its knowledge is mine once the mountain-castle falls. Do no such thing."

"It stands between you and that victory." Jux scowled back at Beastwarper. The Stonemaster's eyes narrowed. This wingleader had best learn his place again, and soon. "Bloodmoon has the right of it. This shaman must die. We can do little until it is gone."

The Stonemaster rapped his fingers on the bone armrest of his chair and regretted not asserting himself sooner. The shaman left Beastwarper and the Skyfang at odds and they could not both be placated. Though Jux forgot his place, he was also absolutely necessary in the fight against the Snow Clan.

The fact he put this forth himself meant he was also at odds with his own speaker. He had not seen Leth as fit to speak in any of this conversation, and the sniveling puddle of goat's piss quietly fumed at the usurpation of his place. Was that why Jux had come in person to deal with the council and tread the ragged edge of disobedience to his betters? If it really was dissention in the ranks of the Skyfang, it was a gift from the Fiend. However, as amusing and useful as Leth's discomfiture was, it would not lead to victory over the Snow Clan.

"The mountain-castle must fall before anything in it is ours," the Stonemaster decided. "I forbid nothing against that shaman. Burn the rock throwing things and take any action you deem fit against any humans that try to stop you."

"Yes, Chief of Chieftains." Jux gave the warlord a quick nod, and the Stonemaster noticed him glance at Leth in disgust.

"You may go."

The wingleader departed without comment. Leth remained shocked by the whole matter, and the Stonemaster feared for his head-piece if he tugged at it so forcibly again.

"Time enough for shamans when the battle is won," the Stonemaster continued. "If we find none here we will search to the south. That was where the humans fled before the Skyfang stopped them."

"How many of them will live outside of the mountain-castle?" Beastwarper leaned on his staff to rise.

"The weaker ones will." Bloodmoon bared his teeth at Beastwarper. "Find them instead, because you lost control of the last one. If your former shaman has only grown stronger, it will tell you nothing before it brings the wrath of its god to us all."

"My wingleader has made this plain enough," Speaker Leth stated. After all that had transpired, he sounded as someone simply trying to remain relevant. "There are many humans, and surely one far weaker than that storm-bringing shaman that can also 'read.'"

"It is only a skill that could change the path of goblins for all time. Why should losing it worry me?" Beastwarper directed his annoyance at Leth and carefully avoided the Stonemaster's eyes.

It pleased the warlord greatly. The council disputed everyone but himself, and Leth was all but marginalized aside from taking orders. It was a sign that he remained in power. Certainly more so than when he was in the human's empty town, struggling to forge his horde anew.

At this rate, his victory over the Snow Clan's mountain-castle would secure both his greatness and his rule.

***

Pencheval rubbed his eyes, grumbling as the insistent knocking on the door to his chambers refused to cease of its own accord. He reluctantly rose from his bed, brushed a few blades of straw from his trousers, and stumbled over to the bolt. The light glowing from under the door seemed far too bright to be the last rays of dusk.

Someone rapped on the door with a staff or cudgel as though they meant to deliver some matter of great import. But if it was soldiers, why did they not say so? They announced their presence plainly if they meant to order his compliance.

"Give it a rest! I'm coming." Pencheval pulled the bolt and cracked the door to find Friar Dominik standing on the other side.

"Friar?"

"They are after her, Lion."

"Who is after who?" Pencheval fumbled for his shirt and found it after the third try.

"They're after the Disciple. The fools that call her a witch."

Pencheval's eyes shot open and the last of his slumber departed violently. Someone breached the castle to attack Nan? Her bodyguard could likely stop them but best he went anyway. If it was one of the soldiers, the knight may well not suspect the danger until it was too late.

"Who are they and where did you see them?" Pencheval threw on his shirt and hastily snatched his sword belt from a peg on the wall. "Did you warn anyone else?"

"Why? Her knight sees me as a nuisance and nothing more." Dominik frowned. "The soldiers are too busy threatening me with scourging to stop them. Blind knaves, the lot of them. None of them can see."

"None of them can see?" Pencheval spread his palms expectantly. "Can see what?"

"That Nan is truly a Disciple! Are you not listening?" The agitated friar slammed one end of his quarterstaff to the floor. "Do you not know how rare it is for the Lord on High to find someone worthy? The last Disciple died before I was born! And the blighted townsfolk want to burn her *as a witch!*"

Pencheval gritted his teeth. Yes, there was an emergency, and it stood before him. The bags under Dominik's bloodshot eyes spoke of a want of sleep and great strain. He, like the rest of the castle, had to endure the nightly terror of drake attacks and the knowledge that there was no way to flee them. He, like few others at the castle, understood what the sound of the approaching horde truly meant and what the goblins could inflict. He had heard it once before, like Pencheval, and only just escaped it. He could not, however, endure much more.

The Lion had rescued him from capture, only so he could watch the town that was to shelter him fall from inside its walls. A forced march saw him safely to the castle, where he was caught between Pencheval and the Knight Superior's confrontation in the street. Now, in a place that should have easily repelled the goblin horde, he was again cornered. The goblins fielded the most impossible of forces against the castle–their drake riders–and the presence of the Disciple overwhelmed him. His good fortune had saved his life time and again, but not his spirits.

He did need aid, and it was good the friar came to him first. If Dominik's misfortunes led him to paranoia, he might very well attempt to kill someone he perceived as a witch-hunting heretic. With the castle under the grip of martial rule, that would end with the friar swinging by his neck from a noose.

"Did you tell this to anyone else?"

"No one else would listen. All they tell me is to stay away from the folk."

Pencheval paused for a moment, then quickly smiled in a way he hoped disguised his shock. Someone else did already know about it and merely ordered the friar away from potential trouble. If he was here unburdening himself on Pencheval, that was an insufficient remedy.

"Here's what I want you to do. Remain in this room and get some sleep while I attend to the matter."

"This is dire, Lion. Don't treat this task with your past indifference."

Pencheval jumped on one foot as he put his boot on the other. "Once I leave, bolt the door behind me and keep it shut until I return. Do you understand?"

"Lion?"

"I'll attend to it now!" The annoyed mercenary leaned up against a wall to slip on his other boot. When he finally left the room he motioned for Dominik to enter. "Go inside. Close the door. Keep it shut and bolted."

Dominik nodded, and he heard the bolt slide into place after the sullen friar did as he was told. Pencheval pulled one hand down over his face and hoped the castle still had ale in stock. After he went to the infirmary and procured something for Dominik's mental well-being, he would certainly need libations for his own.

***

Disciple. It was just a word.

Nan knelt before the altar in the chapel and clasped her hands together, breathing deeply to calm herself. Just a word. Merely a title. A title that felt needle-sharp on her ears every time someone spoke it.

It was a description of a great weight. The hopes of many on the castle rested on her now because of that one word. It was the grant of power by her god, for good and ill. As a moment's loss of temper demonstrated, it was a power that could never be left to chance or the guidance of her weaker moments.

Disciple. It was the change in everything and everyone she had once known. Alfried, the sergeant who aided her in the fight to flee Tarsun's Market, feared her now. Pencheval, the only person in the castle who still thought of her as Nan, stumbled through his attempts to aid her. This Scout Howe who accompanied Pencheval in his rescue attempt was likely as unsettled as the rest of the soldiers. Friar Dominik, who meant her well, was overwhelmed by it.

And the rest? Father Victor, who pronounced this new title and burden upon her in lofty tones after a brief hearing of her tale? The townsfolk who trampled the innocent when fleeing the goblins? The snarling malcontents who accused her of witchcraft? She felt her ears burn as she thought of what they were and only stopped when the shake and rumble of the floor shocked her into catching herself.

"Disciple?" The knight guarding the chapel spoke calmly. Perhaps his newfound evenness had something to do with his conversation with Pencheval on the other side of the door. Possibly, but it had not sounded that friendly.

"My apologies, brother. I am well."

"Yes, Disciple."

Disciple. No, she would not flinch from that word again. It was a burden and a blessing. It was the means by which she escaped her captivity and contended with the drakes. As she would hear it for the rest of her life, she silently resolved not to hear it again as anything but what it was. Momentous or not, it was naught but an appellation, like the title of sister she wore before.

An appellation of great consequence, but still nothing more than a word.

***

Pencheval greeted dusk with a yawn he tried to suppress. A knight with him on the roof of the keep responded with an icy stare. The Lion agreed with him and shook his head to clear his wits. No, this was certainly not the time for fatigue. He needed to be ready now.

At least Dominik still believed in the other clergy, or Pencheval would have had to force the draught from one of the infirmary's sisters down his throat. After ensuring the friar would not get himself executed, he found sleep in a storeroom on a pile of bags until one of the steward's servants woke him for dinner. By then he could see the light fading through a window and stumbled to his feet to prepare for the watch. The improvised arrangements left him less than pleased.

Yet it was the drake's attrition that wore on him most. It ground at his nerves, and this night he could hear the screech and click of the approaching horde. The drakes alone were misery enough, tearing one piece after another from the defenses as all attempts to thwart them failed. When accompanied by the cacophony of the horde, the morale of the defenders would truly suffer.

He was once confident that the Shield of Athesiene and all of its forces could stop them. He spent most of the summer trying to provoke this, and then the drakes upended that strategy outright. Stopping the horde was far less certain if the troops feared to take up arms because of what flew above them. That, and they would keenly feel the absence of every trebuchet burned by the riders when the horde attacked.

"Pencheval." Nan sounded subdued, and the Lion worried that this took its toll on her worst of all.

"You can do this, Nan. We caught one last night." He smiled at her and hoped it was encouraging. "Tonight, when you catch one with the storm, drive it into the ground or against a wall."

"Into what ground? I can barely see the ground within the walls."

"Crush it against the walls, Disciple. Only avoid the soldiers if it pleases you."

"We will find a way," Pencheval added quickly, hoping to change the subject. Could the knights refrain from suggesting she would wantonly slay soldiers? How did they think that would affect someone who not a few months ago chose capture over abandoning the temple's wounded?

"Do any yet come?"

Pencheval willed himself sight. The darkness resolved into a landscape in grays, closer features dwindling to collections of indistinct shapes and finally outlines of treetops in the distance. Thus far the skies were clear, but they always seemed so before the drakes appeared.

"Not yet, but we'll deal with them when they do."

"I can do this." Nan mumbled the words to herself in the manner of a person trying to rise to the impossible.

"You can, and you will." Pencheval put one hand on her shoulder. "And we won't allow you to come to harm."

"I am grateful." Nan sounded calmed as Pencheval gazed out into the horizon, willed himself sight once again, and saw two small shapes in the sky approaching.

"They come. Only two drakes tonight."

"An odd choice," one of the knights commented. "We have taken some of the heart from them. Now the Disciple can take the rest."

"I can do this." Nan sounded more sure of herself but far from what Pencheval would have preferred.

"I'll tell you their path, and you storm them from the skies," Pencheval reminded her. "With one fewer to consider, we will succeed tonight."

Pencheval hoped he was correct. The temple's forces needed a victory and Nan needed to believe her gifts from the Lord on High were not granted in vain. Anything less would be a catastrophe.

***

Dok the Unerring focused his attention on the rapidly approaching mountain-castle. Its tallest peak rose high above the cliff-walls surrounding it and even the caves nearby. Jux said his target was located there, and a fleck of red made its presence all too clear. He leered when he saw the human. That shaman was considerate to distinguish itself so.

The one rider with him was less of an assistant than a distraction. His task was to ensure the shaman believed the attack would come from elsewhere before he burned it alive. Slaying that shaman was their one and only goal tonight, but the Snow Clan would not realize that until it was too late.

Unlike most of his companions, he had learned the secrets of reining a bat-lizard in just the right way, and could aim its fire with subtle precision. He was the only rider in Jux's Wing that could accurately and repeatedly strike a target as small as another goblin while flying at his mount's greatest speed. It was a skill that earned him much favor, and he relished the thought of demonstrating it again tonight.

It would take that manner of aim to slay the human. A big metal bowl on stones covered much of the top peak. If he turned their attention too soon, they would have a strong place to take shelter, and the tallest peak lacked enough space to land and root them from under it. The height made finding his target simple, but the bowl allowed him, at most, one successful surprise attack.

His companion whipped the reins of his mount, and he allowed himself to fall behind. He needed to give the other rider time to fly ahead and get the shaman's attention. Once the human tried to summon a storm to stop him, he would blindside and burn it. By the time the Snow Clan realized the magnitude of their loss, both he and his companion would be halfway to the horde with the news.

There would be no shaman to threaten them or anyone else in the Skyfang Clan after tonight.

***

Pencheval watched one drake rise and bank northward. The other dropped lower until it disappeared behind the towers and walls.

"What are you doing?" Pencheval's eyes narrowed. The riders split up this time. One circled high, likely to attack the castle from the north on his left. The other meant to remain unknown. Did they intend to attack different targets at once, and thus reduce their chances of getting caught in the winds?

"Lion?" one of the knights prodded for answers.

"They flew in different directions. One comes from the north." Pencheval pointed to his left. "The other disappeared."

"Disappeared?"

"It flew too low to see."

"They divided and you lost one of them?" He jabbed his finger at the hatch. "We get the Disciple into the keep. Now."

"But what of the soldiers?" Nan sounded as though the knight suggested braining puppies. "I can't abandon them to the drakes!"

"Disciple, an unknown drake is–"

Pencheval heard a shriek and the crackle of flame as a drake flashed by beneath them. Another of the trebuchets burned with a fire so intense it reduced beams to ash while he watched. Soldiers scattered and rushed for water.

"Enough! Find them!"

Pencheval willed himself sight and scanned the horizon. One drake banked towards Tarsun's Market as it circled for another attack, and the other was still nowhere to be found. He cursed to himself. The knight's caution was far from unwarranted. He, too, did not want to learn where the other drake was only once he, or worse still Nan, burned alive.

A roar startled him and he snapped his attention towards the castle walls. Soldiers ducked as a drake broke its concealment over the barbican and hurled upwards towards the top of the keep. He felt his heart in his throat when he realized it was already preceded by a glowing ball of flame.

One of the knights put himself between the flame and Nan. He braced his shield, and the ball struck it with the sound of hurled mud, splashing to the stones and hammering the knight from his feet. Pencheval smelled the acrid stench of drake's flame as it reduced the knight's shield to orange-limned scrap and burned through his breastplate.

The knight screamed and writhed as the flame melted through his armor, and then him. Nan shrieked. The other knight pulled her towards the hatch, and Pencheval took his axe from its wrappings. The weapon hummed and growled its instability as he hunted the skies for the attacker.

"Pencheval?" Nan turned back to him.

"Get off the roof! I'm right behind you."

Nan hesitated, and the knight appeared ready to pick her up and throw her down the hatch.

"We're the target, Nan! Flee swiftly while it circles!"

***

Annoying. Frustrating and annoying.

Dok could not understand it. Was that warrior in the steel skin simply in the wrong place at the wrong time? It was not in the way when he commanded his bat-lizard to burn, and the attack would have landed perfectly but for that human's miserable luck. Perhaps the shaman's god found the warriors more expendable and intervened. No one ever expected to be attacked from below by a bat-lizard.

It was annoying, and unfortunately, it was enough. The other warrior in the steel skin hurried to get the shaman into the mountain-castle, which would take it out of his reach. But what of the dark one? It uncovered an axe and remained on the peak.

What did that fool think he would do with an axe against a bat-lizard? He was not riding a goat! Still, if it wanted to be such an easy target, who was he to find fault? Perhaps the Fiend had blessed him with stupid enemies. Perhaps like the Bloodmoon Clan it wanted glory in a kill. Whatever it was, it was far too good an opportunity to overlook.

He glanced backwards as he circled. The warrior in the steel skin struggled to get the shaman down into the peak. Perhaps their powerful shaman was also an old shaman, which meant he might have the chance to slay it again. He reined his mount to turn as hard as he could bear, and felt it push him back into the chair until he could hardly breathe. If he had another chance, he had best take it. The wingleader was not one to disappoint.

***

Pencheval scanned the skies and suppressed the urge to scream at Nan. The drakes were still after her, and if either attacked she might die, along with all hope of defeating them. Yes, watching a knight burn to death was a horrid thing, but that did not change the circumstances.

Naught was ever easy with goblins. Not only had they accurately assessed the source of the winds, they took advantage of the fact only one pair of eyes in the castle could see through darkness. It was impossible to track two drakes attacking independently. The one that remained hidden was robbed of its intended victim only by the sacrifice of a knight.

"Go quickly!" He searched furiously and in vain for the rider that struck at Nan. The other straightened out of a turn and barreled towards the keep.

He heard the squeaks of armor as the knight took to the ladder. He was commanded to protect Nan and not fight beside Pencheval, which was fine by the Lion. He intended take the ladder himself soon enough, if only because he did not want to wield the snarling axe for any longer than needed.

As the last of the shadows disappeared from the light flickering through the hatch, a roar on the opposite side of the beacon startled him into place. A flap and a crash threatened to flip it, splashing ash into his face and the air around him. He choked and heard the sharp grating of steel over stone as the huge iron bowl slid towards him. He involuntarily scurried backwards until he felt no stone beneath his heel, twirled his arms to catch his balance, and gasped as the beacon usurped every place upon which he might have stood.

***

Dok was grateful his companion performed his task of distraction well. It helped him end the dark human warrior tonight. He had failed to burn the shaman, and nothing less would placate the wingleader.

Had the Fiend cursed his luck? Not only had the shaman escaped in the time it took him to turn, but the cough and splutter of his mount told him it would not spit flame again for a time. All that remained was the big metal bowl on top of the mountain-castle's highest peak. As he suspected, those that placed it there relied upon its weight to keep it stationary, and that had sufficed until it the claws of his bat-lizard struck it.

The human never screamed as Dok reined and goaded his mount to push. Had he crushed it outright then? He continued until the bowl tilted away from him, and he smelled the ashes and char as it poured over the other side. No human warrior, and still no scream. Perhaps the initial hit had killed it, but it was better to be excessively successful than sorry.

He let his mount pause and catch its breath. It leaned with its front claws on the bowl's base and rested near the edge, with plenty of room to take flight again. He could spare a few moments but no more. The humans may not be able to reach him, but too long and their archers would take their chances.

Still nothing from the Silver Lion Clan warrior. Surely it was dead, as anticlimactic as it was. He reached down to pat his mount, slapped his heels against its back, and enjoyed the sound of powerful wingbeats as it rose up and forward. Time to go and inform Jux of mixed results.

As his bat-lizard ascended, he saw its head turn and tilt downward, as though it tried to see something beneath it. Dok saw nothing but a blizzard of ashes and a form moving too quickly to distinguish. He heard a snarl to his right, and his mount screeched as though grievously injured.

The bat-lizard crashed into the bowl as a blur within it fled to one side. He realized he had far too much of a view to his right; something had sheared the right wing from his mount. It roared as it slid towards the edge, desperately clawing and grasping in vain for purchase on the ashes, metal, and stone.

Dok screamed as the top of the peak ended and nothing remained between him and the fall except air. His mount screeched in pain as they plummeted, and the stone roof atop one of the human caves rushed up to meet them.

***

Pencheval wheezed and coughed, ignoring the crash of the falling drake and the cheers of the soldiers. He could taste and smell nothing but the ashes in the beacon but was grateful to be alive. No directions to go but into the beacon or over the edge, and he was perfectly happy about his choice.

Did that goblin get cocky? How could you not be overconfident if you were riding a drake? It missed him utterly, but the lack of a scream should have given him away. He would not have assumed a kill short of a seeing a corpse himself. Still, goblins were fallible, and two successful sneak attacks in a row likely contributed to its belief that the battle went its way. At least burying the axe in the ashes had silenced it, or its snarling would have made a ruin of the whole ruse.

The beacon laid wedged between its foundation and the battlements. It slid enough to crack the mortar between the stones, and he could not tell if the tilted masonry would keep the giant brazier on the roof for much longer. A small pool of blood formed around the joint of the wing he had sliced from the drake, and as if in triumph, the axe roared and snarled before calming to a ragged hum.

"Lord on High be praised." Pencheval chuckled and coughed, tasting ashes in his mouth. If he was praising Athesiene, he had been here too long.

By the time he caught his breath, he realized the other drake had not even tried to attack him. Perhaps it had fled, and perhaps it had done all it could do and merely returned to the horde. The drakes had suffered losses but their attrition continued regardless. Something burned at the far periphery of the castle walls, and with his luck it was another trebuchet. Another small victory too quickly come and gone.

He hoped the hatch remained unobstructed by the beacon. Heavy as it was, even his magic would not enable him to move it, but that could wait. He slid down to sit against its former foundation, coughing and slapping the filth from his clothing. Nan was within the keep and safe. Taking a moment to rest would harm no one.

***

Howe snapped up from his bed as he heard a horrific crash and did not know where he was.

He squinted at the half-resolved shapes around him as he slowly took stock of himself and the room. So many bandages wrapped his arms and chest they all but clothed him. He felt the dull itch under his dressings and smelled of poultice and soap. Was he on a bed? No, it felt too wooden. Perhaps a sheet over a table? His vision returned, and he realized he was on something in the middle of a room. The infirmary. Too many bandages for a barracks.

What put him here? Was it...? Yes. An angry swarm of death that chewed through leather, gambeson, and clothing alike. That torch had provoked their wrath. Something the goblins sent, and he hoped they had no more.

The shapes on the other beds left him uncertain of either Pencheval's presence or absence. He hoped the Lion was still able to fight. There was not much of a chance against the drakes, but he would be vital to any effort to attain victory over them. Howe had seen that mercenary overcome far too much to believe otherwise.

As for the commotion in the distance? Someone else could deal with it. Howe groaned as he leaned back on his pillow and sighed. An aching back and bug bites were no way to spend a night.

***

"What is that?"

Nan lifted her head and considered the muffled sound she heard was not real. Shouting in the distance? But why? Did the weight of her losses ring as ghosts in her ears? So many people screaming, and she could do nothing. All the power she possessed and that damnable drake killed the one standing next to her.

That poor knight. And Pencheval? If he had survived the attack, it was by little more than a narrow miss of snapping teeth. They had done so much for her and she could do nothing in return.

Why did she leave them? She had power. Too much power to control, but not enough to save them. One more bitter defeat to regret. She could still hear the screams...

"It sounds like a disturbance in the courtyard, Disciple. Please return to your chambers."

"Disturbance. Mourning?"

"I do not believe so, Disciple. More like unrest."

"Unrest. Why–"

"Disciple, please retire for the night. If the troops must pacify a mob, we have lost order until they succeed."

"A mob? Why is there a mob? Your brother died fighting for them. We all nearly died..." Nan felt the weight on her shoulders grow and her steps felt heavy. "This isn't...it can't be."

"Disciple?"

"It can't be...it won't be!"

Enough! Did they think they could smite drakes from the sky in her stead? That defending them against such enemies was a mere stroll through wildflowers in the spring? Greedy, selfish vermin! Like those in Tarsun's Market who trampled the innocent in their haste to save their own lives!

No, she would not leave the soldiers to deal with it. She would deal with it, and when she was finished, none of the folk would ever countenance strife again. She realized she had clenched her fists as the knight before her took one step back. Fear?

"Disciple, please get some rest. We need you come the morrow."

"You need me now!" The words were not merely amplified; they reverberated with such force the nearby walls rumbled from the power. Her bodyguard slammed his hands over his ears and staggered backwards. She felt the power roil, and it did not subside.

That meant the Lord on High had reached the limits of His tolerance, too. Why should He not? His faithful suffered and died to defend the common folk, and they repaid Him with scorn? They would learn respect!

***

Pencheval only just staggered into the great hall from the keep's stairs when he heard it. Someone shouted with enough force to shake the castle. The angry voices from outside that he thought to leave to the soldiers suddenly went silent. He heard a curse from the other side of a door, and a shield hanging on a wall next to him rattled in place.

He only knew one person with that much power and the state of mind to shout with it. The fall of that knight had left Nan at the end of her wits. With the power Athesiene granted her, she was a lethal threat to anyone who crossed her and especially to herself.

It was Spellkeeper Arthier who explained it during one of his lectures. Silver Lions were only granted enough of the liquid metal potion to perform small but useful magicks. This restriction frustrated Pencheval at the time but made it impossible for them to kill themselves when they willed magic during the strain of battle. They could cause themselves pain, muscle stiffness, and a reddened glyph in the palm so sore their fingers could not move until it healed, but not death.

That was vital, because the kind of might a mage could summon would kill them if they lost control of it. Despite their nigh universal arrogance and smug superiority, their talent to gather and wield such magic did not render them immune to it. The spellkeeper knew this first hand, for as the guild's most accomplished mageslayer, he had defeated no less than half a dozen of them by disrupting their concentration at a critical moment. The resulting catastrophic spell failures left them roasted to little more than ash or horrifically crippled.

That could happen to Nan if she raged enough to shake the castle. He gritted his teeth and stood upright. His work this night was far from done. It made no difference that he had just crawled through a beacon full of ashes to avoid death at the claws of a drake. Visor down and guard up. More was required from him, and he refused to shirk it.

Ten

"How. Dare. You!"

Nan's words boomed from the walls surrounding the courtyard. The mob that once pressed against the locked shields of the army recoiled in fright. Though the torches remained lit, all was aglow as though in the light of day, and she heard the crackle of flames below her though nothing near her burned. It could be nothing less than the presence of the Lord on High, and they would renew their respect for Him soon.

"Ingrates!" A ferocious vibration accompanied her voice and caused ripples in the air. "The soldiers fight to defend you, and you attack them? The Knight Superior lets you shelter in the Shield of Athesiene, and this is how you repay him?"

The lines of the mob and spearmen continued to part, and she gave it no more thought. It simply meant she had their attention. Those that were not fleeing stood petrified by...something. Good. They could stand silent and listen.

"A knight died last night to protect you, you verminous filth! The brave give their lives for you, and for what? So you could be angry they couldn't do more?"

The very air around her seemed to roar, and it thundered from the stones. Two radiant orange lights at waist level followed her, and she glanced down to discover both of her arms aflame from the elbows to her hands. She moved her fingers and realized they were still there, but the flames burned so fiercely she could see nothing beneath them.

"Disperse! Return to your encampment now!"

A voice from behind her gave the order, and it boomed from the walls as hers did. Male, and it sounded familiar. Despite the hints of exhaustion, it had a note of ferocity she found all too familiar. The Knight Superior? No.

The mob required no more urging and fled from her sight. She turned to determine the source of the order and saw an ash-stained warrior in a battered black tabard take a step back. Pencheval? He did survive last night! But why was he here?

***

Pencheval knew Nan had power, but he never expected to see her in this aspect.

Nan snapped around to meet him with bared teeth, eyes burning as though a furnace lit them from behind. Their glow bathed half of her face in a sinister orange and left the rest in deep shadows. Both of her arms burned from the elbow down so intensely he could feel the heat from ten paces, and he couldn't bear to stand any closer to her than he already did.

He hastily reviewed his spellcraft after a brazen burst like a massive horn rose in a deafening crescendo and then faded to nothingness in a succession of staccato bursts. It was a sign of instability, like the snarling of his axe. When such sounds thundered, the mage was on the verge of a catastrophic disruption.

Was that the case now? Though Nan's arms burned it did not seem as though she was in pain or panic. Perhaps the Lord on High's gifts behaved differently than the mage's craft. Perhaps she walked the knife's edge of a catastrophe even as he stood there wondering what to do next.

"Nan." He fought to make his tone of voice sound as normal as possible.

"Pencheval." Nan sounded relieved to see him, though the sheer power of her voice left the air rippling. It was as though the magic would tear through the very substance of what was to reveal the nothingness beneath. "You're alive. I shouldn't have left you there..."

"All is well, Nan. Another drake is slain."

"Not before it killed a knight," Nan growled. "And then that mob? Sniveling, ungrateful rabble!"

Pencheval speculated on the dispersed townsfolk. The Disciple failed to deliver their miracle, and they gained what little victory they won tonight when it crashed through the roof of the castle. They rose up out of desperation and panic, and he surprised himself by giving them the benefit of the doubt.

The shock was in hearing himself in Nan. That had been him, once. After the betrayal in Terris Lyn and his time in the slums of the capital, it was the sum total of what he ever believed of the common folk. Sniveling rabble. Betrayals only awaiting their opportunity to happen. Everything he ever thought he had before merely an illusion as the ugly truth made itself all too clear. His cynicism guided all of his actions until it, too, was finally revealed as a lie for no less a reason than Nan.

"Some few of them are worth our help."

"Which ones would those be? Those that fear me though I risk everything for them, or the ones who want to burn me as a witch?" Nan pointed to where the mob once was. Her arm crackled as it traced a burning arc through the air, and those soldiers near where she pointed scattered.

"Some few. Look at me."

Nan snapped back around. Loose straw and debris near her caught flame, and the hem of her robe was limned with it.

"I do not jest. In all the time I have contested this place with the goblins, I never fought to save the valley or the kingdom. But a few of the people here were worth my help. I can count them on the fingers of one hand, but it makes no difference. Small as it may be in the scheme of things, it is a worthy purpose."

The glow in Nan's eyes faded, and a slow, undulating ripple of power replaced the ferocious bursts from before.

"Purpose, Nan. It was something I lacked for far too long. You helped me realize I could have one again, and now you must find your own."

"I am weary of this destiny."

"Forget destiny. Forget the mob, and the drakes, and those who cannot see you as anything but the Disciple. Somewhere, you have a belief, or a friend, or a cause for which you will fight. You had it once in Tarsun's Market when you remained behind so you could aid the wounded. All may have changed since then, but you can find your purpose anew."

"Purpose? It is all madness." This time, she spoke without thundering, and the flames along her arms crackled and sizzled until they burned to nothingness. Not so much as a mote of soot stained her intact hands and robe.

"It is there. Start with one thing." Pencheval smiled in a way he hoped was friendly. "Otherwise, some annoying senior sister from Tarsun's Market might hound you incessantly."

Nan chuckled and then sniffled. "Better than a grouch of a Lion, I suppose."

Pencheval snorted, and then realized he had nervously clenched his fists the whole time. His strain drained away in the banter.

"Wasn't it noontime a few moments ago?" Nan looked up as though confused by the last of the stars slowly giving way to the colors of morning.

"No," Pencheval assured her. "You've not been here half an hour. Please get some rest now, and think on what I've said."

Pencheval turned back towards the keep to find the castellan and Knight Superior watching. Some straggler huffed his way down the stairs behind them, and he did not care who it was.

"Your Grace."

"Go to my study, Lion. My brothers will attend to the Disciple now."

"Yes, Your Grace." The soldiers with them parted as Nan passed, preceded by a knight. Pencheval followed her to reach the keep's stairs.

He chuckled to himself as he passed terrified and awestruck spearmen. Of course this was not over yet, and it was almost nostalgic.

There were days during the six fortnights his guild spent determining his worth for apprenticeship where he drilled in the early hours of morning because he never went to bed the night before. All that was absent was a drill instructor yelling in his ears about how pathetic and worthless he was.

He climbed the stairs to the keep and passed an old priest wheezing on one of the landings. The man shot him a dirty look as he walked by, and he merely shook his head. One drake dead, Nan saved, and some clerical ass hating him merely because he wore the Lion's tabard? It could not be a more perfect morning.

***

Jux frowned as a single bat-lizard glided to the ground near the pens of the Skyfang. No other flew near it, or even trailed in the distance from the mountain-castle. One more bat-lizard slain.

The agitated wingleader watched the rider dismount. He was too tall to be Dok. So not only had he accepted another loss, but the Snow Clan robbed him of his assassin. Jux strode out to meet the diversion rider as he walked his mount back to its pen.

"Wingleader." The rider swallow hard.

"Explain."

"Dok attacked the shaman as you commanded," the rider blurted. "He killed one of the warriors with the shiny metal skin instead. The shaman escaped into the mountain-castle."

Jux bared his teeth. "Escaped?"

"Yes, wingleader."

"So if he failed to kill the shaman, and he was in flight, how did the Snow Clan bring him from the skies?"

"Dok tried to crush the one warrior that remained with the big metal bowl on the tallest peak. He failed. As he tried to fly again, it removed one of his bat-lizard's wings, and he fell to his death."

"Penn Cheval and that Fiend-forsaken axe!"

He had discounted the tales of that Silver Lion Clan specialist until now. No human could possibly be that fell, especially if the Skyfang attacked from beyond its reach. Yet the same ground-bound idiot killed two bat-lizards that should never have died!

How many more times did these fools have to offer it chances to kill them before they realized it could? Did he have to explain even the simplest things to them again? The Skyfang fought their battles on wing! Yet some few of them ignored the obvious and insisted on believing the Snow Clan were just another mob of rabble. That misjudgment cost two of them their lives, and more importantly, cost the Skyfang two bat-lizards.

"Tend to your mount, rider." Jux motioned for him to continue and stepped aside as the rider eagerly obeyed.

This attack was a failure, and the humans took more than they lost. Leth would learn of it soon, assuming the idiot stopped mewling at the feet of the warlord long enough to hear the news. What would the Speaker do in response when their first loss left him near panic? What would the Stonemaster do to take advantage of his Speaker's distress? Jux felt caught between a hardened enemy and the warlord and considered what to do about them both.

***

"You summoned me, Your Grace?"

Rennoute glanced up from behind his desk at the Silver Lion standing before him. He was not as the first time they met. No more than a few months ago, Pencheval's professional demeanor masked his barely concealed contempt for those around him, and he lacked more than the necessary courtesies to speak with nobility. His gear was used but in good condition, and he wore the black and gray of the Silver Lions as one who does so because it is commanded of them.

This one was different. The sleepless nights left him ragged, and his once immaculate tabard endured only through coarse stitching and a stubborn refusal to fray entirely to rags. Though he wore his sword belt now, he recently came to favor an axe he took from a goblin champion. Rennoute was well versed in the lack of utility a sword held against drakes, and understood his choice.

"I once again owe you my gratitude in your aid with the Disciple," Rennoute began. "Your resolve saved her and much of the castle."

"Thank you, Your Grace."

No more undertones of contempt or irritation. No callous disregard as was reported from Tarsun's Market when the Lion merely wished to depart upon news of the horde. He stood here now a changed man and proof of Athesiene's word. Anyone who sincerely wished to rise and start anew could do so, and with the aid of the temple many had. The priests and clergy put it in simpler words so the masses could understand, but despite smacking of mere dogma it was true. They could find the light in the darkness.

"Was she the reason you became the Hopeslayer?"

"Your Grace?"

"You knew the Disciple in the past, or so my brothers inform me. I also know she mentioned the Hope of Terris Lyn in Tarsun's Market. Was she the reason you pursued him? You do know that was unusual enough to investigate."

"How did you..."

"Just because I rule a monastic valley does not mean the temple keeps what is needful to know from me. The presence of a Silver Lion along the Gnomeroad suggested the suppression of rebellion, and the agent of the temple who sent me that information believed the king might call upon us as well. But it ended with the capture and subsequent death of the rogue that gave you your title. None of the barons had ideas above their stations, just one Lion pursuing vengeance, which I understand does not sit well with your masters."

"No, Your Grace." The corner of the Lion's eye briefly twitched at that reminder.

"So, I ask you again. Was Nan the reason you did this?"

"No, Your Grace. Nan disappeared years before I was forced to go. I avenged myself and my fallen against the Hope and believed her lost."

"Hmm." The shared history was the bond between them, then. Was that bond why a Lion was the greatest asset of a Disciple now? The Lord on High had purpose in His works, even if it was not immediately apparent. Some called His ways a mystery, but it was more as though He simply thought so far ahead no one could see it–until they did.

"Will there be anything else, Your Grace?"

"Yes, Lion. The temple is very clear about the rise of Disciples. Under normal circumstance, we would send them to train with those in the capital who can assist them along their path. We cannot do that now, so I will help her by making the obvious official."

Rennoute removed a brass medallion from his drawer and offered it to Pencheval. The Lion cocked his head at it.

"Your Grace?"

"Wear this. For now, it marks you as one of my agents," Rennoute explained. "It will keep whatever place the Lord on High has for you in this from impediment and stop clashes with any others over her station and yours."

"Your agent? Why?" Pencheval seemed utterly shocked as he hesitantly took the amulet from him.

"She cannot bear this alone, and you have most successfully aided her. I ask that you do so again, else we all fall to the goblins, and you lose both her and your life."

It would not be a popular decision, but the circumstances required it. Right now, all that stood between disaster and the Disciple was a Silver Lion. He had proven that twice now, and the Knight Superior refused to believe two such signs were mere happenstance.

Previously unthinkable as it was, the Silver Lion was who he needed, when he needed him. The hour came, and the Lord on High provided. There may even be another lesson in this somewhere, had he the time to divine it. Once this was done he could trace how these threads wove this particular tapestry at his leisure. For now, much more was required of them all, and quiet contemplation would have to wait.

***

"Who summoned you?"

The Stonemaster glowered at the parting hides as Wingleader Jux stepped through them and strode into the council. The Bloodmoon Speaker seemed bemused by it, though all the others were less pleasantly surprised. Speaker Leth snapped to his feet in indignation and did his best impersonation of a scowl.

"Jux? Do you have some explanation for this?"

"Yes," Jux told him offhandedly. "I have determined a way to improve upon the Skyfang's fortunes."

"How would that be?"

"Like this." Jux lunged out at Leth and snatched him by his shirt. The Speaker lost his balance and staggered forward as Jux drove a knife under his ribcage. The wingleader narrowed his eyes and twisted, and Leth fell to his knees.

The Stonemaster shot from his seat. The Bloodmoon Speaker snatched two metal axes from his belt, and Beastwarper reached under his rags for something he did not immediately reveal. The Allspeaker cringed next to the throne as one of his endless delusions of disaster finally came to pass.

Leth gurgled his shock before Jux threw him to the ground. He calmly cleaned the blade on Leth's clothing before giving one contemptuous look to his fallen headpiece. None of the others relaxed, and the Stonemaster suppressed the urge to call on his staff's magic.

"Wise," Jux stated as he confirmed no one intended to kill him. "Now that I have your undivided attention, Chief of Chieftains, listen."

The Stonemaster bared his teeth but did nothing more.

"Leth could not deal with you, and I grew weary of coddling him like a pup," Jux explained. "Whether or not I tell my chieftain that he died because of you or the humans is entirely in your hands. If I die here now, that is what he will hear from my riders. You will find yourself with an enemy to the north, and you have no such great shamans as the Snow Clan."

"You don't know who you've crossed," the Stonemaster snarled.

"I have a better idea of it than that fool," Jux countered, pointing at Leth. "Now it is thus. We will keep our end of the bargain and you will cease trying to steal the secrets of taming bat-lizards from us. Keep your distance from our pens, and if you mean to discuss something, come to me. I am the speaker now, and I say that this is the last warning we will grant you."

"Get out. We will summon you again soon enough."

"Yes, Chief of Chieftains." Jux thrust the knife back into his belt and parted the barrier of skins before him. "Feel free to keep the headpiece."

The Bloodmoon Speaker watched him go, and when he finally departed, laughed. "That one is my kind of speaker."

The Stonemaster was not nearly so amused. Jux lacked Leth's silver tongue but had divined their intentions and did so at a distance. He was loyal to his clan and just killed the only soft point in it. It was possible they might manipulate him, but he was far more wary of it, and had no purpose or ambitions except to do as he was commanded and then leave. He would never be a chieftain, but he would also never be a dupe.

***

"What madness is this?"

Pencheval stopped, in no mood for the indignation of the priest before him mouthing silently through a thick snowy beard. He was not cowed by it; the Lion had provoked far more extreme reactions in the past. It was merely a surprise, as this senior clergyman expressed no real contempt for him previously.

What had changed? The bronze amulet hanging around his neck. The priest recoiled from it as a fop might from the thought of dirt upon his clothing or hard labor. It was as though he could not reconcile 'Silver Lion' and the sanction of the Knight Superior in his thinking.

"What's your problem?" Pencheval made no effort to be polite.

"How did you come by that? It's not some trinket you take as a prize, varlet!"

"No, it's not. The Knight Superior explained what it meant when he gave it to me." Pencheval fought the urge to smirk. Yes, he had power now, but he always had power of the harder sort. He had spent years judiciously employing what he already possessed and saw no cause to start behaving like a smug nobleman. All this fool required was his usual refusal to yield.

"How you must enjoy the favor you have now. So very clever of you to use the drakes as an excuse to gain it."

"Do I look like a courtier? I rescued your Disciple while you were gasping for air on the keep's stairs." Pencheval jabbed a finger at him. "I rescued her at the risk of swinging from a noose when all told me to depart. And I did this only so I could jostle for position as the valley burned? What color is the sky in this waking dream of yours?"

"Because the Silver Lions give such weight to honorable behavior?" The priest scowled. "I have seen your guild before. I watched a baron pay another of you to suppress a revolt. That Lion killed every man, woman, and child in Bartleshire for no more than coin. This is the manner of character his grace has granted permission to impress upon our Disciple? Rubbish!"

"If you take issue with the Knight Superior's judgement, discuss it with him. If you take issue with my aid to the Disciple, I will render it with or without your approval. Are you fool enough to impede me?"

"No. I cannot stay this course but consider this much. You saw the power of a Disciple. Now consider that power in the hands of a butcher and think twice before you make one of her."

"Spit your venom at someone else and don't stand astride my path." Pencheval departed for his chambers without a farewell.

Ridiculous. Make a butcher of Nan? Even distraught she did little more this morning than scold a crowd. Scold, when she possessed enough power to lay all of them to waste.

And why would he change that? He was not a butcher. A mercenary, certainly, but all he killed were bandits and the great beasts threatening Lerrisaine. He put hundreds of goblins eating all substance from the Emerald Refuge to the sword. While the barons, lords, and chevlers were prancing about with one another, he and his guild secured the safety of a kingdom.

And what fabrication! A Silver Lion kill an entire village for coin? Did this fool think he knew more about Pencheval's guild than he did? Either the priest meant to deceive him by citing an 'incident' that occurred before his birth, or merely repeated one of the endless rumors and dark legends his guild attracted like bees to honey.

He felt some small nagging doubt and shook it from his mind. No time to wonder if the priest's anecdote was real. The drakes might well return this night despite their losses, and he needed rest.

***

"Gather here!"

Jux screamed the command to be heard over the horde and his riders scrambled to obey. Many of them showed fear and others merely seemed resigned to whatever wrath he would bring to bear. The Wingleader resolved not to disappoint them.

"Who are you? Did some gaggle of novices with rocks in their heads replace my wing? What curse from the Fiend Under The Mountain has rendered you so stupid that two of you have lost batlizards and your lives to a ground-bound clan? Perhaps your dams dropped you on your heads while you were pups, and only now when we battle the humans do you fail me!"

"Winglead–"

"Did I tell you to speak? Still your tongues until I tell you to speak!" Jux bared his teeth. "Listen and heed my words, for if you don't, I will whip you for your idiocy if the Snow Clan doesn't slay you first."

One of the riders near him swallowed hard.

"The mountain-castle is home to a warrior with the Bloodmoon's axe. Its name is Penn Cheval and you can identify it by its black clan shirt with the gray mountain lion on it. You will not *ever* land near it, or take any action that will force you to land near it. You fly and burn your targets as we have always done, and what you will continue to do from this point onward unless I say otherwise!"

The riders again nodded, heads bobbing up and down furiously.

"The Snow Clan and their Silver Lion Clan ally are not the stupid and weak rabble near our clan-home. The fact they are ground-bound gives them no pause at all. You will never again grant them the opportunity to kill you or our chieftain's bat-lizards! Remain swift, strike, and fade away."

The riders nodded again. Jux was perfectly satisfied with their response, as he did not wish to hear their excuses.

"Hear this above all else. There is a shaman in red at the mountain-castle, and it is the only hope they have of victory over us. It is your first target regardless of any other task. Kill it, even if you must expend all of your bat-lizard's flame in the attempt. Now what will you do?"

"Fly and burn!"

"Will any of you fools land and give the humans more of your lives?"

"No, wingleader!"

"Don't forget any of this again. Your lives and the lives of our chieftain's bat-lizards depend upon it. And now, there is much we must do to guard against the horde, for much here has also changed..."

***

Pencheval yawned and trudged towards his chambers. It was not yet the time of morning he would eat breakfast, and he had yet to sleep from the battle of the night before. Not long after he killed that drake he was forced to avert potentially catastrophic magic, received a token of the Knight Superior's sanction, and argued with a priest who was concerned his very presence would turn his precious Disciple to darkness.

He brushed more loose soot from his tabard and slapped it from the armor on his sleeves. As he took a moment to be grateful he was merely ash-stained instead of dead, he found Nan alone and staring out a window. She smiled wanly at him.

"Nan? Is all well?" Pencheval froze in an attempt to keep from agitating her, and then caught himself. His recoiling would not agitate her? He fought back the memories of the courtyard and took a less strained posture.

"No, but it is better. Lord on High show mercy, what did I nearly do?"

"Better you thought of what you did do, which was naught," Pencheval offered. "You needed to dismiss what power you summoned, and you did."

"And if I hadn't? What would have come of it?"

"It's best only to say that your power should never go that far out of control again." Pencheval knew of no more neutral a way to tell her she nearly died and took most of the courtyard with her.

"Yet more destruction and strife." Nan bowed her head. "If nothing else, becoming a Disciple has made me appreciate the smaller things."

"Smaller things?"

"Smaller things, like not being capable of yet more destruction and strife. The normalcy of life far away from capitals and goblins, even in Terris Lyn. Do you ever miss what you were before all of this?"

Pencheval found the question odd. What might his old life have been absent a vain and grasping baron and the Hope? He would be wed to Cecelia, raising their children, visiting their grandfather, and perfectly content farming.

Yet his simple and pastoral life in Terris Lyn never was. He learned the truth about the Hope and the barony at the cost of those for whom he most cared. Remembering the brighter days before his disillusionment felt much like the joy of a mouse that believed itself safe while a cat laid in wait.

"I remember much of what was before my path changed. All the memories are just...wrong."

Nan pulled her hood around her ears as she gazed out a window. The click and screech of the goblin horde seemed hollow from within the walls, but she had to endure it as a prisoner within Tarsun's Market for months. She shivered from the sound.

"Things were so much simpler there."

"Until they weren't. The entire barony was a flock of sheep celebrating the very wolves that hunted them. Our ignorance led us both to misery, and we can't do more now than follow our paths. Nor should we."

Nan sighed. "Do you know I prayed for this? I wanted this, or I thought I did. The goblins are horrid captors, and I wanted the power to free us all. To simply save the lives that bled away." She slumped her shoulders. "I should have taken more care with my wishing."

"How else would you be here now? I tried to goad the horde to its doom, and instead they allied with drakes. They revolted against their master, and still it leads them here. But for the Lord on High finding you worthy, you would be dead and so would the other survivors."

"And now everything has so much weight." Nan looked up at the sky. "No time to even watch the clouds."

Pencheval gazed through the embrasure and saw the large swirls of pink and purple against the first blue of dawn. They were unusually distinct for late summer. "At least the sky is real."

"And so are the clouds." Nan seemed thoughtful. "Not wind. Clouds."

"Nan?"

"Clouds. Will the drakes attack what they cannot see?"

Pencheval blinked twice. That was an excellent question. The drakes could soar faster than sparrows, but what happened if they could not see the trebuchets, or the walls and towers? He imagined soaring over the soldiers, looking down, and not knowing where clouds ended and the stone began. Every attack would be a blind shot or a life and death risk. Would the goblin sense of self-preservation then render the drakes harmless?

"I believe it's worth a try."

Eleven

"This will not do."

The Stonemaster spoke more to himself than the Beastwarper Chieftain, who nodded regardless. This would not do at all. Wingleader Jux was not Speaker Leth and nowhere near as easily manipulated. While it annoyed him, it also left him thoughtful.

The same situation would stymie any lesser Chief of Chieftain and leave them furious. It was one of the innumerable reasons they were in the dust of history and his greatness only increased. Helpless anger was useless and beneath such a leader as himself. He would defeat this rival, not rage over him, even if the wingleader's assassination of his speaker was a masterstroke.

"The Skyfang remain here despite their discovery, which means they expect punishment from their chieftain for failure," Beastwarper reassured him. "Even so, it will be impossible to get near them until the final battle, and Jux will be even more on guard then."

"Which is a fact that remains unchanged from what was," the Stonemaster said. "Unfortunately, he no longer takes commands from a fool."

"Something he well knew when he killed Leth, and something he meant to demonstrate to you beyond all doubt."

The Stonemaster rapped his fingers on his staff. "He will pay for that affront in time."

"There is no moving against him," Beastwarper warned. "The horde is in awe of the bat-lizards. After the revolt at the human's town, the Skyfang may be all the rope that keeps it lashed together."

The Stonemaster bared his teeth. He had heard the truth of it himself in their endless chatter. The awe over the bat-lizards replaced even the fear of Penn Cheval on most goblin tongues. While that meant the horde was not terrifying itself over the dark human warrior, it left Jux's position unassailable. Fortunately for him, those circumstances were also useful.

"That is also the answer."

"Chief of Chieftains?"

"Jux believes he has the matter well in hand after killing Leth. Make him keep believing it. If he thinks he has won, he will eventually slip."

"And how should we do this, Chief of Chieftains?"

"We do something to make his task easier," the Stonemaster explained. "Just enough to let him believe we chose, however unwillingly, to submit to this new arrangement."

"Yes, Chief of Chieftains."

***

Nan knelt before the altar in the chapel and felt for the power. As before, her reservoir of it seemed limitless. The Lord on High still found her worthy, and furthermore, granted her mercy after her fury in the courtyard.

That fury drained her of her rage and frustration, and at no more of an expense than the fright of a witch hunting mob. Her burden felt perceptibly lighter, and the power felt restrained enough not to burst forth at one errant motion or thought. For the time being she could find peace again.

The crack of the door led her to stand and turn. Had Pencheval more to discuss with her? No. Instead, Friar Dominik entered with his staff, appearing determined.

“Disciple! My sincerest apologies!”

“For what, friar?”

“For not aiding you in punishing the objects of the Lord on High’s ire, Disciple! He did send you to the courtyard early this morn?”

What had she wrought? Whatever believers divined from her slightest action is what she wrought. This one thought her near break was the commanded wrath of Athesiene. How many more would approach her about this before all was through?

“That matter is resolved, Dominik. Please concern yourself with it no longer.”

“Resolved? Why? Those who think you are a witch are still there, Disciple.”

“We will attend to them, friar,” the knight guarding her in the chapel spoke as though his word was final. If Dominik continued to press, it may well be, and for what? Disciples had said words that caused schisms and wars. She appeared ready to burn heretics this morning, and he would willingly follow.

If they had to imprison or kill him to stop him from ‘punishing’ them in her stead? It would be because of her frailties. She frowned. No, it would not, for she would not allow it. That much she learned from her time with the goblins and from Pencheval. If you had a problem, act, and if her words had weight, they could divert his course.

“Dominik, I have done all that was needful. Leave what remains to the Knight Superior and his forces. I have every confidence they have this matter well in hand.”

“What would you have me do, Disciple?”

“Keep the faith, and remember.”

“Remember what, Disciple?”

“Yourself.” Nan sat on a pew and motioned for him to sit next to her. “You do remember your past service?”

“Yes, Disciple, but of what importance is that now?”

"What importance, friar? Your work was ever important." Nan remembered her time teaching novices and fell back into familiarity. "Is charity in such supply in Lerrisaine that it is trivial?"

"No, Disciple, but–"

Nan put up one finger to silence him. "Then continue to provide it, friar. The soldiers have their place, and we have ours. After these battles, lean times come, and many will need the charity of a wandering friar. Now trouble yourself no longer with my defense. Contemplate your place in this, as I contemplate mine."

Nan bowed her head in prayer and heard Dominik do the same. Pencheval suggested she find new purpose, and at that moment she did. Though she fought with His power now, administering the Lord on High's mercy as she could gave her meaning. Once they had slain the goblins, she would put the power to its proper use and rebuild the valley with it.

The Emerald Refuge granted serenity to the broken once, and it would do so again.

***

The Knight Superior sat behind his desk and placed his head in his hands. It was one of the few moments he could relax and let his strain show, if only for a time. Despite being able to delegate some matters to the castellan and his knights, his troubles were far from resolved.

No, he could not be out there with the Disciple every night, though he wished it was otherwise. She needed the Lion, as their connection was most likely to see her through this. Furthermore, ruling the valley meant attending to future matters as well as dealing with the goblins. If they were defeated–no, when they were defeated–there was still the matter of winter. Those here would be in need of food and shelter, and arranging that before the snows blocked all commerce would be no small matter.

The village at the base of the castle burned to ashes. Earthworks seemed less likely to stop the horde by the day. The goblins killed all those unable to escape Tarsun's Market, and he took a moment to commend their souls to the Lord on High as he considered them. Even if they prevailed, that town could not be used for shelter, as the folk would see a haunted ruin and flee it. The horde had likely stripped all else in the valley bare as well, which meant all he now had was at the castle.

Food enough to get them to winter, and then it would become a white season of death. Pigeons he sent calling on favors and calling in favors returned with the same answer; they would aid him once he dispersed the goblins and no sooner. No one would risk sending trade or charity until then. Nor could they flee because the drake riders denied that option to them, so this war for the castle and the valley it controlled was literally victory or death.

It was nigh maddening. Keep the army from desertion, retain order, suppress revolts, and ensure the safety and sanity of a Disciple in grievous distress as the drake riders attacked them every night. After that, make sure the victorious did not then starve or freeze. He took a deep breath and resumed his study of the papers before him. He still had too much to do to stop now.

***

"Why are we here?"

Pencheval stood with Nan on the easternmost portion of the wall circling the courtyard and inner buildings of the castle. This spot was within easy reach of a door leading into one of the towers. The soldiers near her attempted not to notice her with varying degrees of failure, and some few were openly dismayed at her presence.

"If you mean to obscure the castle, we can't stand on the keep tonight," Pencheval explained. "The soldiers would be hidden by the clouds, but we'd either be visible targets standing above them, or buried within them and unable to see."

"It's also easier for the Disciple to escape through a door now that the beacon is knocked from its place," one of her knight bodyguards offered. "There is no protection on the roof of the keep any longer."

Pencheval suppressed his regret at that arrangement. In retrospect, the vantage afforded by the top of the keep came at the cost of being easily slain, as Nan proved unable to flee swiftly down its ladder. At the time, he thought the beacon would serve as protection, but its tilted perch against the battlements abundantly demonstrated his misjudgment.

"There is no need to wait for the drakes to appear. If you merely intend to obscure, summon the clouds now and cover the skies above us with them."

"Do you think they will come? They didn't when the last one fell." Nan almost sounded hopeful the goblins would spare them this evening.

Pencheval wished he could reassure her. Yes, a night without drake riders would be a boon of no small measure. Their ceaseless attacks slowly ground his health and spirits to dust, and his frustration grew as he failed to stop them time and time again. Yet nothing else was ever simple when it concerned goblins, and with drakes they were that much worse.

"Even if they don't, it's best to practice. Summon the clouds, and your familiarity with them will grow for the next time."

Nan turned towards the keep, paused for a moment, and then raised her arms. Above the courtyard, a small white puff of a cloud appeared, slowly billowing outwards. Tufts of fog and mist wove and tumbled into sheets of white as it expanded, casting a shadow across those below and arousing more than a few shouts.

"Grow." Nan closed her eyes in concentration as the shadow expanded, and Pencheval watched the furrowed underside of white and gray billow until it was overhead. The clouds floated so close to the tops of the towers it blanketed the few trebuchets that remained but left a sizeable gap between itself and the soldiers on the walls.

"Is it going to rain on us?" One of the archers near them looked up at it, genuinely curious as to its intent.

"Yes, the Disciple summoned a cloud to rain on us. Are you daft?" A sergeant pointed towards the east. "Get back on watch!"

"Aye, sergeant."

"Almost, Nan." Pencheval pointed upwards. "They will still be able to see too much."

"Patience," Nan said as though talking to a little boy. "I have never molded a cloud to a castle before."

***

Drim could not believe the change he saw in the mountain-castle.

It did not glow in the distance as it did when he burned the first wooden warrior home of the Snow Clan. This time, there were a few flecks of light, but clouds or fog cloaked the top of it. He had passed some few mountains with clouds clustered around the peaks, but they stood taller than most and far taller than this place.

How then had they formed? The season had not changed, and yet this fog floated over the mountain-castle like a blanket. Only its highest peak broke from atop it, and he saw the giant metal bowl Dok displaced before his death.

He squinted as he searched for a view of the humans. The clouds floated high enough to leave gaps between them and the Snow Clan warriors on the cliff-walls, but there was no diving from the skies while they were there. Yes, he could assume they floated over the stones and peaks, but how high? Guessing badly could cost him his life.

Perhaps the clouds would fade come the dawn. Perhaps this human shaman so many feared made them, and they were more than just clouds. Best to get a look at them first. One pass with the riders to see how they clung to this place, and then another to burn any target he still could.

At least they offered one advantage. However they came to be, the humans could no more see through them than they could. Tonight might see little done, but at least fewer arrows would fly.

***

"They're coming. Three of them."

Both knights took up shields. Pencheval supposed it was out of habit, but he saw no use for shields against drakes. Unless they invoked the power of the Lord on High, any flame from the drakes would end them as it had the knight on the keep. The best defense against great beasts was the one he preferred, which was to not be struck.

"Clouds. Why did I want this over wind again?" Nan seemed nervous.

"It blinds them to where exactly we are and they require no aiming."

The clouds extended ten paces farther than the edge of the battements like the awning over a porch. In the torchlight, it was little more than a blanket of grays spotted by lit patches of white. Despite the clearance between them and the clouds above, the riders would have to guess where the overhang ended and the walls began. Given goblin courage, he suspected none of them would care to risk their lives flying blind between the clouds and the walls.

He saw the drakes bank northwards into line with one another until the tower and the clouds blocked them from view. "They're turning for a pass. If the clouds shield us, they will refrain from attacking for want of targets."

"From your mouth to the Lord on High's ears, Lion." An archer's grip tensed on his bow. "Don't need any more flame."

The first leathery pop of wings against the air left the soldiers silent and looking upwards. The second confirmed rapidly thumping wingbeats as the drake regained speed. Twice more, the irregular beats passed overhead, and twice more there was no more to it.

"Effective so far." Pencheval willed his magic to grant him vision in the darkness and saw one drake bank to the east towards Tarsun's Market.

"Where are they now?"

"The one I saw turned towards the horde."

Pencheval's eyes narrowed. Yes, the clouds successfully obscured the castle from above, but rendered him just as blind as the goblins. If even he could not see with charms to enhance his sight, the temple's forces would fare worse. Their sight was wholly obscured, but the horde would be on the ground when it arrived. The clouds hindered the drakes but also hindered the army, and left any goblins below the walls unaffected.

He heard a shriek and saw a blast of orange land within the last of the town. It hit one of the few remaining buildings and set it to burning in the same swift fashion it inflicted on all combustibles. The screech of a second rider, and then a third, caused a spreading conflagration under the walls. Pencheval watched as the riders turned towards the east, finally soaring off into the distance.

"The town..."

"It can be rebuilt, Nan. We need the weapons and castle far more, and you saved them."

"Aye, it's a dull night for once, Disciple," the sergeant near them said. "Could do for more of that."

One night, Pencheval mused. Yes, one night was a small victory, but it would not last. The screech and click in the distance was still too soft to drown all speech and sanity as it had in Tarsun's Market, but it hinted at what was to come. Even muted, it suggested the cacophony he remembered all too well, and the last sounds he might have heard when they were everywhere within the town's walls.

It was a success but not a victory. Not yet.

***

"You only burned a few huts in the town the humans already abandoned. A whole mountain-castle of targets and a shaman to kill, and you have no more news than this?"

Jux watched as his riders cringed. After two deaths, they had better know that manner of fear. The chieftain punished losses if they were suffered without good cause, and he already had too much to explain. If the riders tonight had made no real progress, their explanation had best be spotless, or they would feel their lashes first.

"The mountain-castle was covered in clouds, wingleader," the enforcer he knew as Drim wailed. "We could see nothing beneath them. All we could burn was the town."

"Clouds? As in wisps around the peaks?"

"No, no, no!" Drim looked horrified. "Clouds over the mountain-castle as cold dampness in a cave. Thick and endless! Only its highest peak reached above them! They hid even the warriors on the cliff-walls."

"So if I go there, I will see them? For I will ride to behold this strange thing for myself."

Drim nodded vigorously and his riders agreed with him. Jux saw no reason to believe they lied. They were too terrified, and the answers too absurd to be anything but the truth.

It these clouds were truly there, the shaman was responsible. It meant to blind what it could not strike, and this would be an issue he would have to attend himself. If the clouds were there when he went, he would find a way to defeat them. If they were not, Drim would regret it upon his return.

***

"It was not much, Your Grace, but it was successful."

Pencheval addressed the council called by the Knight Superior after the night's stalemate. For the first time in a long while there was little destruction to report. The drakes did burn the rest of the town, but naught remained there aside from empty buildings.

"How fares the Disciple, Lion?"

The aging priest who had confronted Pencheval earlier seemed taken aback by the question. More likely, he was shocked by the fact the Knight Superior asked it of him first. None of them missed the brass medallion around his neck and Pencheval suspected more than a few of them quietly resented it.

"Creating the clouds caused her no distress, Your Grace. She is still able to aid us."

"That's all, Lion?"

"She is far from what she was in the courtyard, Your Grace, if that is your question."

"Still your tongue!" The priest all but rasped for breath after that burst of anger. "You speak of a Disciple!"

"I'm speaking of someone I truly wish didn't have to endure this," Pencheval answered evenly. "And despite the want of better guidance than me, she grows stronger."

"She is a Disciple, Lion," one of Rennoute's knights said. "The Histories say it is always thus."

"That is enough," Rennoute commanded. "What action will the horde take next? They know their drakes cannot see. If this remains true, what will they do?"

"We cannot say for certain, but their warlord is no idiot," the castellan answered. "It has burned us down to four trebuchets. The ballista crews cannot hit them in midair, and from their heights on the walls they're little more than large spear throwers against any on the ground."

"Archers?"

"Those we still retain in great numbers. We can launch burning arrows into the horde as the earthworks slow it to a crawl. The clouds cannot stop us from sending those aloft."

"The clouds alone aren't enough," Pencheval added. "This warlord tricked Tarsun's Market into believing itself surrounded. It's possible it will discover a way around them."

"What do you suggest?"

"We think of something else to use against the drakes, Your Grace. Something far more final."

"Aside from smiting them from the sky?" The castellan waited expectantly. "What would that be?"

"I...don't yet know."

"Attend to that with all haste. Time is not our ally," Rennoute decided. "Should any of you conceive of a counter or strategy, bring it to me or the Lion at once."

"Yes, Your Grace."

***

Pencheval stood in the grass before a cottage he never owned. Behind him wound a dirt road in Terris Lyn he never once travelled. Before him, Cecelia clasped both her hands to her chest in joy and smiled at him. She spoke to him as if elated, but no sound fell from her lips.

Was it a dream? It must be. Cecelia was here, as beautiful as the last time he saw her. Grass lapped at the hem of a green dress as she celebrated the new marriage that would never be. A low corset over a white blouse pressed tightly to her curves, and auburn hair fell across one bare shoulder.

He could not move or speak as Cecelia glanced back at him time and again, until she finally turned and silently spoke his name. Her smile darkened to concern, and concern wilted into sorrow. She gestured for him to join her once more, and the bright rustic scene he wished could be real faded to a jumble of color until only she remained.

"Do you not want this, my love?"

A darkened stone ceiling replaced the dream, and he realized he was half awake. Yes, he did want that. He wanted to be there now instead of in this castle more than she would ever know. No drakes, no goblins, no guild; just a life with his adoring love in some place none of them could ever reach.

He banished the thoughts from his mind and calmed himself. Rest was in short supply, and it would only get worse as the horde grew closer. Time enough for bittersweet dreams after they won, or a reunion with her at last if they did not.

***

Wingleader Jux narrowed his eyes and ignored the rush of wind in his ears.

There were clouds forming over the mountain-castle. Clouds, just as Drim said, and they told him all he needed to know. The Snow Clan humans saw them approaching and the shaman reacted. So not only had the rider's information been good, but it confirmed his suspicions about the source.

Clouds roiled and billowed in all directions, growing as quickly as he could fly to them. Even from his distance it was obvious the thing would cover all the mountain-castle by the time he arrived, if not before so. Now it was time to see the extent of it, and how it might be defeated.

He banked to his right and his riders fell into line behind him. By the time he completed enough of an arc to attack from the north, nothing of the mountain-castle was visible from the sky save its highest peak. The large metal bowl atop it laid between its former base and an edge, and no humans stood on it that he could see. He saw no reason that they would. Why stand somewhere unprotected by clouds?

He reined his mount to skim the top, and wisps of clouds tumbled and blew in his wake. There was nothing special about them; they were merely clouds but impenetrable to his sight. He could command his mount to spit flame through them, but attacking blind was wasteful.

Nothing rose from beneath him as he passed. No arrows, no screams of panic, nothing. That meant the humans were just as blinded by the clouds as he was. That smacked of a desperation move, or something to buy them time. Unfortunately, it was also effective.

So, how far down did they go? A pass along the eastern cliff-wall would tell. The cloud bank had a clear edge which only carried so far. A dive to gain speed would carry him quickly across the wall, far too swiftly to attack, and still grant him an estimate of the depth. He completed his turn and faced the mountain-castle from the south, then reined his mount to dive.

He pressed back into his chair as the wind roared in his ears, and the cloud bank swiftly rose above him. He adjusted to clear the unobscured walls and found enough space between the clouds and the warriors to target them clearly. A brief flash of red and two humans in steel skins revealed the location of the shaman and its defenders. It created its clouds from the front, and if he so chose he could take a shot at it before departing.

He was momentarily tempted, but flew instead towards the horde. That was a rash action against the shaman now that he knew how to counter it. Perhaps it did indeed put a cloud over everything in the mountain-castle. There were ways around that–free of risking a fatally bad guess while soaring through a cloud bank–and those ways were better.

Time to return and inform the council. He smiled to himself as he saw his riders pull up on his wings. The shaman had a defense, but defeating it would be almost too easy.

***

"Howe?"

Pencheval recognized the bandage-wrapped scout wincing at the end of a long table. He, and everyone else who could find space, ate whatever remained from the larders. Despite being seated, the injured Howe took care to keep from nudging into the others, as the long hall was filled past its capacity with soldiers.

One of the friars handed Howe a wooden bowl full of stew, and he fumbled for the spoon. He moved as though stiffness and pain would accompany any haste. The winds saved Howe from the swarm, but not before it did its worst upon him.

Howe found Pencheval as the mercenary picked his way through the crowd, and noticed the Knight Superior's medallion. "You're rising in the world, Lion."

"Would that this promotion came at another time. It's good to see you moving again."

"Damn goblins nearly put an end to that." Howe ate a spoonful of stew. "The bugs were bad enough. Eating nothing but broth for a few days? Much worse. And no whiskey, either."

"On the bright side, the drakes also haven't tried to kill you for a few days."

Howe chuckled. "You jest, but that is genuinely comforting. What news?"

"I slew another drake from atop the keep, and we found a way to hinder them."

Howe looked down at his food. "Knew there was more meat in the stew than usual. Thanks for that."

"Unfortunately, they also seem to know that Nan is their most formidable opponent and mean to kill her."

"Are you there with her?"

"Aye. Why would I not be on the walls with her?"

Howe took another slow bite and swallowed with visible effort. "There's the start to your troubles right there."

"What?"

"Word is the Disciple is on the wall accompanied by you and two knights. Or, because you don't think like a scout, the four of you together are only a fanfare and a crier away from openly announcing you'd like the drakes to kill you."

"We're...what?"

"Did you learn nothing from me this summer?" Howe twisted his head to stretch, wincing as he pulled himself too far in one direction. "I know it's not the way you and Her Holiness normally see the world, but this one time you need to think like a scout. You have been granted a blessing in subterfuge and you aren't using it."

"Subterfuge?"

"Dress like a soldier, Lion. Dress the Disciple like a soldier. You needn't even be that convincing, as fast as those goblins fly. Can you tell one rider from another as they flash past? You have certainly given them the benefit of marking you, and you had best cease."

Odd as Howe's advice was to him, Pencheval had long ago learned never to discount him. During the summer, when he attempted to goad the horde into an ill-considered attack, the scout had accompanied him. Not only was he a deadly shot with a bow, but he had the uncanny knack of leading them somewhere the goblins were not when they needed to disappear.

Howe demonstrated incredible skill then, and he had a point now. If Nan was a target, that red robe of hers made her far too easy to find. He frowned at the thought of wearing a quilted overcoat in the summer himself, but he could not fault Howe's suggestion.

"Presenting this to her knight should be amusing."

"Be grateful you have that medallion to help you," Howe replied. "But all jest aside, find the quartermaster at once. Take too long and all he'll have left to give you are large wooden signs painted with bullseyes to hang from your shoulders."

***

"You wished to be the Skyfang Speaker. What have you to say?"

The Stonemaster made no attempt to hide his impatience with Wingleader Jux. Two days without news as the bat-lizards flew overhead was two days too long. This one kept his plans concealed, another sign he was not that idiot Leth, but if he wanted to speak for his clan, he best well do so.

"The Snow Clan shaman has covered the mountain-castle in clouds, Chief of Chieftains."

"Clouds? And?"

"They are an irritation, but only an irritation. Its latest tricks are futile."

"Yet it still lives, which is another day of delays," the Bloodmoon Speaker grumbled. "And we sit here and eat all the food."

"How is this shaman so easy to defeat?" Beastwarper seemed genuinely curious.

"It is simple. We always attack at night, and it is always preparing something for us. I saw it make the clouds the night I flew against it. How could it do this except to assume we'll always attack at night? So we don't slay it, we attack in the day and avoid it. If it doesn't show itself, we burn the rock throwers. If it hastens to face us without preparation, we burn the shaman."

The Stonemaster nodded in grudging respect. He wondered what manner of goblin a chieftain would allow to lead a group of bat-lizards and their riders, and now saw one before him. Jux possessed cunning, ruthlessness, and loyalty. But for the fact he robbed him of that potentially useful fool Leth, he could find it in himself to admire the wingleader. This was a plan for the keeping, but with one small change.

"A sound plan, but not yet."

"Not yet, Chief of Chieftains?"

"Do you not see it? We attack the Snow Clan. The Snow Clan learns something we didn't consider and kills a bat-lizard. We do something else, then they do something else. But the power of their shaman is also their weakness."

"I don't understand, Chief of Chieftains."

"We attack with the new plan, but then they will find a new way to stop you. They learn and change for fear of their deaths. They will do so again unless we give them reason to believe the might of their shaman is now enough."

"There is no cause to wait, Chief of Chieftains. If we attack unpredictably, it will drive the humans to despair and thwart defense. All they have to use against us is that shaman, and it cannot counter if it is forced to guess when and how we'll appear."

"And they will change again," the Stonemaster insisted. "There is a place for this, but it is not now. Let them believe you struggle in vain and refuse to relinquish the night until the horde is so close our sound robs them of their wits."

"It has done this before," Beastwarper agreed. "It served this purpose well in the human town we left."

"Let us aid you," the Stonemaster offered. "When the horde has them clawing at their ears, attack at strange times. We will crush them between us, and if the shaman appears, it will die. They may then try to counter you again, but with the horde at their cliff-walls and a dead shaman, there will be nothing for them but fear."

"Vengeance comes. Finally!" The Bloodmoon Speaker boomed with laughter and Jux smiled.

"It will be as you say, Chief of Chieftains."

He saw no reason Jux would dispute this plan. Why would he be upset with the assistance of the horde? It would work, but sadly, it had one major fault.

The aggression would overwhelm the Snow Clan, but it did badly constrict the time he had to learn about the training of bat-lizards. One desire met as another slipped between his fingers. He momentarily gave thought to letting the Skyfang go if only to conquer his new clan-home. It was the human secrets he originally sought, and they were valuable enough alone.

He considered it, and then dismissed it as the whimpering of a lesser chieftain. One of his greatness limited themselves in no such way. He would have it all and take his place as the only goblin Chief of Chieftains ever to endure.

Twelve

Athesiene's mercy, could he never be free of that sound?

Dominik gritted his teeth, fighting to forget what the screech and click in the air meant for the now fallen Tarsun's Market. Before the horde breached its wall, some few of the wounded made it to the temple. After the walls fell, those few who escaped the swarm of goblins joined them, and everything around it fell to darkness. The lights extinguished one after the other, even while the soldiers were too intent on the battle to notice.

He did not know why the goblins left the temple alone until the end. Perhaps they believed it full of soldiers. Perhaps they had fallen into disarray or looting. What he did know was what had happened when they finally attacked.

It was a testament to the character and courage of the Disciple that she refused to leave the wounded. It must be why the Lord on High found her worthy. If she remained within that nightmare for months to keep the faith, she deserved what He had granted.

He could see it all starting again as the horde grew close enough to torment the besieged. Posted guards glowered their irritation and adjusted their helmets. Townsfolk scurried past, pulling hats or the hoods of cloaks tightly over their heads. One of the children near him put his hands over his ears and pestered his parents endlessly about the noise in the distance.

"Not again. Not again. Not again." A ragged man sat on a barrel, bending forward with his hands laced behind his head. He repeated the words over and over, rocking back and forth in a vain attempt to shake his misery.

"Courage, friend. It is but noise." Even the friar was unconvinced by his half-hearted attempt at comfort. It was not merely noise, though it would grow unbearable in time. It was a harbinger of something far worse; death at the claws of an endless swarming hunger.

"You weren't in that cage for months, friar. That sound don't stop and you didn't see what...and Nan, I mean the Disciple, can't stop it."

"She will find a way. The Lord on High has not abandoned His faithful."

"Aye, she did it once. But there were no drakes then."

Dominik thought back to the time he would have argued with the man, but the Disciple shepherded him past that error. She made it clear she would redress these wrongs herself, and that he should be as he always was. He did hope she would find a way. If it eluded her, there was nowhere else to flee.

***

"Who did you say recommended this again?"

It was all Pencheval could do not to shake his head at the absurdity of his circumstances. One of the castellan's quartermasters, a short and energetic man, was busily tending shelves when they arrived. He stood dumbstruck after he recognized them, and silently mouthed the request for two uniforms, complete with gambesons and tabards, for the Lion and the Disciple. He procured an assortment of items after a mad scramble through the crates and shelves, including a kettle hat Nan held by the brim as if trying to determine why she would possibly wear it.

"His name is Howe. He's one of the scouts here and the person with whom I spent several months trying to rescue you from Tarsun's Market. I can assure you from firsthand experience I've known no one better at blending into the countryside than him."

"I'm not sure I have something that will fit the Disciple. I mean, uh..." The quartermaster scratched his head and tried hard not to complete his thought.

"This is unthinkable," the knight guarding Nan protested. "The Disciple is not a common soldier and this is well outside the orthodoxy!"

"Howe is absolutely correct," Pencheval countered. "We're all targets, and there's no point in granting the drake riders ease in finding us. This is the way we will deceive them."

"As you say, so it will be. But it is highly unusual."

Pencheval felt a surge of relief and was grateful for the medallion Rennoute gave him. As the Knight Superior said, it would smooth the path for him in aiding the Disciple, and it had. There was trouble enough without the discord it prevented.

After a few more quizzical glances, Nan placed the metal-brimmed helmet on the counter before her. "Do you know what happened at Tarsun's Market?"

"What happened? When?"

"When the whole horde turned on itself. Something happened at the western wall of Tarsun's Market. Dominik said you wandered the valley for much of the summer. Do you know what that might have been?"

"I happened," Pencheval answered. "They fell into discord when I killed their champion and mocked their warlord. I meant to goad it into breaking its forces across the walls of this castle and goaded a revolt instead."

"You caused that?" Nan put her hand over her chest. "The horde fell into chaos, and our guards meant to eat us all. But if you had not acted...little by little, the goblins killed us, and absent that intervention, continued killing us until none remained. And what champion?"

"A great brute with an axe. I took its weapon after it fell and now wield it against the drakes. I still don't know how that bastard knew my name–"

"It what?"

"It knew my name. Surprised me with it and nigh kicked me back to the Shield of Athesiene."

Nan gasped. "No. The Beastwarper Chieftain?"

"What?" Pencheval's eyes widened. "You spoke with one of them?"

"More than one, but the one I may have told your name called itself the Beastwarper Chieftain. It was a lame goblin with bones growing from its shoulder, leaned to one side on a staff."

"You told one of them? *How*?"

"One goblin among them all spoke our tongue. This chieftain retained him constantly, and they asked about you. It just...slipped. They seem to fear you greatly."

"And the one with the staff and the silver plate on its chest? I believe it is their warlord."

"It visited me once," Nan replied with a frown. "It had a collaborator, and it wanted to know why we were on such friendly terms before I attacked you. That one called itself the Stonemaster, Chief of Chieftains, or some such."

"Nan, this is important. What else did you tell them?"

"As little as I could! I distracted the Beastwarper Chieftain with books, but the collaborator may have spoken more freely."

"Books?"

"The goblins don't have a written language. When I showed this Beastwarper a book, it became obsessed with creating its own, and ceased to ask of tactics and armies."

"If it pleases the Disciple, do you know anything more of the horde?" The knight was polite, but Pencheval nearly burst from the thought of this new advantage.

Knowledge of a goblin horde, of *this* goblin horde, was invaluable. He knew some wrote about them based on survivor's tales, but to actually know one from the inside? Could it provide them with knowledge that might win this war against them?

And for the rest? Yes, Nan had given them his name. Nan had likely done more than a few things to stay alive and protect as many of the survivors as she could. In her place, would he have thought to distract them with books, the least useful knowledge the goblins could possess?

There was no perfection in any of this mad war. The chaos he sparked in the horde threatened her life, even as it provided the opportunity for her to escape. It was both the best news the temple's forces received all summer, and something that may well have seen her slain. It brought goblins riding on drakes to bear against them, and a source of real knowledge about this horde and its master announcing herself in a stockroom. He was grateful that the better moments in it at least balanced against the worst and that it was not all calamity and despair.

"I will tell you what I know, of course." Nan lifted the kettle hat again. "Now, why do they make these so heavy?"

***

Jux never before rode to stall until a victory, but he was perfectly content not risking any more bat-lizards until the horde could assist him. Determining the value of this particular strategy would cause him no harm. On the contrary, if it proved useful against the humans, it would be a good one to know.

Use bat-lizards for deception? No one had ever considered it before. Most of the time, the Skyfang flew them over the lands of the nearby clans to remind them of what waited if they crossed them. They flew to train new riders, and on occasion to destroy a threat outright.

As he approached the mountain-castle, he once again saw clouds blossom above it. As the Stonemaster surmised, they attempted nothing different to oppose him. If the horde's chatter affected the humans as the warlord claimed, it would rob them of their wits when his timing finally changed. That would reduce the hazard of attacking, but what would happen after they completed their work?

The Stonemaster was perfectly happy to assist Jux for now, but the reason was obvious; the Skyfang currently served his ambitions. The same Stonemaster also had enough guile to overcome Leth. Leth knew nothing of worth to steal, but manipulating the idiot nearly let the warlord bring his own chieftain's authority to bear on him.

Perhaps he should end this outright and tell his chieftain they were betrayed. That Leth died when the Stonemaster killed him, and they would never again bargain with that Fiend-blessed rival. This one was like no other he had ever met and far above the weak clan chieftains the Skyfang ruled. How did a goblin become a shaman, a chieftain, and a Hordemaker all at once?

Curious as he was about that, it made no difference in the end. He was a threat. A genuine if ground-bound threat and like nothing in either tales or living memory. What he knew of other Hordemakers led him to believe they were merely stronger chieftains whose followers remained loyal only so long as they reaped plunder and victories.

This one had a stable horde despite losses and setbacks. He even overcame a revolt and took knowledge from the humans. This was far beyond being even a strong Chief of Chieftains. He was *more*. Entirely too much more.

The horizon tilted back and forth to the thunder of wingbeats as Jux guided his bat-lizard to attack from the north. He turned briefly to confirm his riders aligned behind him, and they did. He would make one pass and send flames through the clouds with little more than a guess of what they might strike. It would keep the Snow Clan deceived and occupy them while they awaited the horde.

Jux reined his mount into a dive. He frowned as an orange flame burst from its mouth and lanced through the clouds over the mountain-castle. This Stonemaster came closer to stealing the secrets of the Skyfang than any other he had ever met. Perhaps that was why he had agreed to hard terms. Yes, it gave the warlord the Skyfang's aid for a battle but also gave him the opportunity to learn the taming of bat-lizards. Could the Stonemaster turn even such a lopsided bargain as this to his advantage? If so, it was time to depart while their losses were light and never go near this one again.

***

"Our time grows short, Beastwarper."

The Beastwarper Chieftain nodded, hoping to fill the space while waiting for the inevitable question: How would they steal the secrets of the bat-lizards from the Skyfang? The Stonemaster wanted to know and refused to hear of anything else.

"My plan remains the same. Take one on the ground during the battle. Wait until after they have served their part in it but before they return. There are fewer to subdue that way."

It was the best scheme he could conceive, but even he found it imperfect. Yes, they would flee when it happened. They would also attack if they could. However, unless their aim from the air was particularly precise, he and the Stonemaster were likely to survive it. It was the wrath of the horde that might prove fatal, and it was by far the larger threat.

"Then nothing changes, and the best we can find between us is not enough."

"There is one other plan, Chief of Chieftains."

"Which is?" The Stonemaster glowered impatiently.

"The one you originally made," Beastwarper answered. "Take the humans and their secrets. Leave the Skyfang to the agreement. Grant them their hunting and landing privileges. Surely when they return in the future, they will come in fewer numbers far easier to overwhelm?"

Beastwarper expected indignation, possibly anger. Instead he received an almost blank look from the Stonemaster. Perhaps he, too, contemplated taking only one prize at a time? Use the Skyfang now, and take from them later once the Snow Clan was broken to submission. Patience would see all brought to them.

The Stonemaster nodded slowly. "Yes, the original plan was good."

"It was, Chief of Chieftains. It was inspired. Glorious. We will use it to take the humans now, and the secret of bat-lizards–"

"Now." The Stonemaster's eyes narrowed. "We will never see so many trained bat-lizards and their riders in one place again. Who will they send south after this? Those like Jux, who could tell us everything we need to fly our own bat-lizards? No, they will be scouts and fools like Leth and will have no reason to land near the horde. We take them during the battle or the knowledge is lost for good."

Beastwarper adjusted himself on his staff to hide his frustration. Yes, tame bat-lizards were magnificent beasts of vast potential. He dreamed of raising them and the mighty creatures warping them might create. But even a horde had its limits, particularly against potential enemies that could fly.

"Chief of Chieftains, patience is the only answer now. If the Skyfang turn on us while the horde attacks, it will mean defeat."

"Do not fall to an excess of caution. Knowledge enough to make us both legends is within our reach, but we must find a way to seize it and soon."

"Yes, Chief of Chieftains." Beastwarper bowed his head obediently so he could consider options without revealing himself as less than compliant.

Contingencies demanded his attention now. How would he escape if he was forced to depart through both the horde and the Skyfang? Most of what immediately came to mind was not pleasant, but at least it made him appear thoughtful. The Stonemaster nodded approvingly.

"You may go, Beastwarper. Consider our next actions swiftly."

"Yes, Chief of Chieftains."

***

Nan sat at the pew she had taken since she began seeking refuge in the silence of the chapel. When she had first returned, it was a blessing; a comforting, deep fleece of tranquility that shielded her from the horde's cacophony and the memories it provoked. Now, it seemed more like an endless indulgence.

It was not because she rejected the faith. She had come here for solace and found it, but now it was only the place where she kept...herself. The piety it once contained seemed drained away, removing the weight from the silence and luster from the stained glass. Yet it had not changed–she had.

It still was a place of solace and worship that no longer contained a broken sister. The weight of her burden became more bearable over time, and the power less terrifying to wield. Purpose returned to her when she rescued Dominik from his darkness, and the answer to it all suddenly seemed obvious.

"Why am I still here?" Nan mused the question aloud without realizing she had spoken.

"My apologies, Disciple. I did not hear your question."

"Why am I here, brother? Why am I still in here?"

"The Disciple came here this morning." The knight frowned with worry.

"No, brother. I know how I came to be here this morning. I merely ask myself why I remain."

"I do not understand, Disciple."

"No, you wouldn't. This is a question I must answer for myself."

"Perhaps his grace or Father Victor may aid you?"

"No, but thank you, brother."

No, the others couldn't help her, but not because they wished her ill. All of them did what they could to defeat the horde and tried to see her through her newfound power. But her successes, both in using the clouds and aiding Dominik, came when she chose to be herself. Everyone acted as though she became something else entirely, and even she thought to leave her former self behind.

They had all been wrong. It was true she had to grow stronger, but that did not demand she discard all of what she once was. She was still Nan, and the power in no way changed that.

To save the castle and the others, Athesiene's will must be brought to bear in violence. She was prepared to do that, but it was not her destiny. It could not be, for it felt as alien to her as it always had. The goblins deserved everything she inflicted upon them, but Athesiene gave her this might knowing exactly who she was. What else could He want but more of it?

Who was she? She was someone who taught children and saved others from the darkness, whatever form it took. She was the person who refused to allow the power to inflict pride and haughtiness upon her, though the Knight Superior himself treated her with deference. She was one who would never again threaten innocent people with displays of holy might, even if their fear drove them to destroy her as a witch. And in no way did she hide in little rooms when her faith was needed elsewhere.

"I am done here, brother."

"Done, Disciple?"

"Done contemplating in solitude. The people suffer and the soldiers despair. I mean to attend them now."

"I humbly submit this is unwise, Disciple. You need to gather your strength for tonight."

"You are wrong, brother. We are both called to the Lord on High's work, and my place to serve it is among the faithful, not behind the stone of castle walls."

She snapped up from her pew, pulled her robes straight, and strode towards the door. The power had distorted her perceptions, but all this time the answer awaited her in plain sight. Power or not, she was still meant to be herself, and realizing it at last left her feeling feather light.

***

"What purpose drove this?"

Pencheval scratched his head at the blackened spot staining the stones. The gelatinous remains of drake's flame not consumed as fuel left a lingering acrid stench. A dull heat rose from around it as wisps of smoke and vapor twisted in a breeze too delicate to feel.

"If only the rest of their attacks were as futile." Howe frowned as he knelt by the scorched stones. "They just spat flame through the clouds without aiming. Did they mean to rob us of spirit? They did little else."

It was as good a guess as any Pencheval had. One pass, three bursts of flame, and then departure? He was tempted to say they had lost heart over the clouds, but that was too much like good fortune for him to believe.

Attacking the center of the cloud mass would do nothing. At best, they would strike something of value only out of blind chance. Surely they knew this, and still they did it? Was it desperation? Did the frustration drive them to acts of futility? Was it something else?

It was goblins, he mused. Of course it was something else.

"Now what?" Howe rose from the ground and turned his attention to the blackened splash across the stones of the wall. One of the balls of fire struck the inner face of the northern wall, splattering those below and setting a few small fires that the townsfolk easily extinguished.

"If this is all the goblins can do against the clouds, Nan continues to summon them." They were insufficient alone, but would buy them time until he thought of something else. Until anyone thought of something else.

"The Disciple..."

"Yes, the Disciple," Pencheval grumbled. If Howe had to absolutely insist on calling her that, he would just have to suffer it.

"No, the Disciple is *here*."

Howe stood with his mouth agape as the murmurs of surprise and unease rose among the crowds. Pencheval turned to see Nan walking towards them. Though she still wore her hood she moved with more purpose than he had seen from her in some time. One of the Knight Superior's order accompanied her, white and red tabard over full plate.

"Nan?"

"Do these bear some significance, Pencheval?" Nan gestured to the blasts. "This was where the flame struck?"

"Yes, but why are you here?" Pencheval hoped he did not sound dismissive, and Howe pulled his cap from his head.

"You see, Disciple, we don't know why the drake riders attacked as they did, and, uh..."

"Thank you. Howe, is it?"

"Yes, Disciple." Howe wiped his forehead with his arm.

"If I understand correctly, you were with Pencheval through much of the summer. I'm grateful for your efforts on my behalf, and I apologize for not telling you sooner."

"Real–I mean, you're very welcome, Disciple!"

"Nan, why are you down here? We still don't know who in the crowds means you harm."

"Which has no bearing on my responsibilities, Lion. I still do the Lord on High's work, risk or no. Do you not remember?"

Yes, he remembered all too clearly. She had refused to leave the wounded in Tarsun's Market and struck him to the floor when he attempted to drag her from harm. That had been the lowest point of his retreat to the Emerald Refuge, which not so long ago was famed for its serenity.

He had left a different Nan in Tarsun's Market. The one that returned was overwhelmed, until now. Perhaps she had taken his advice and found her purpose again–a purpose that put her in the middle of potential trouble.

"You already are doing good work, Nan. You battle against these blighted drakes, and you need to rest."

Nan smiled gratefully. "No, but thank you. I did as you suggested and found my way again. It is the same path I walked for all my years here, and the one I mean to resume after we defeat the goblins. I respect your way, hero, but I will not share it."

"Must you call me that?"

"What?"

"Hero. They are lies and fables. Farces prancing about on stage until the actor playing a god descends in a wooden cloud to solve his problems. Have we both not heard enough foolish blather about heroes?"

Howe scratched his head and the knight frowned at him. Nan stood puzzled for a moment, and then smiled.

"Of course you are nothing like the Hope of Terris Lyn, Pencheval."

Of course he was not the...the remark struck him so deeply it left him speechless.

"Please, give this some thought when you can. Your deeds here will earn you adulation, and much of it will be the word 'hero.' Don't let the Hope of Terris Lyn take it from you. Just because that monster called himself one does not mean the word defined him, or defines you as him. Now please excuse me, the folk need succor."

"Good day to you, Disciple!" Howe waved excitedly, and Nan nodded back before walking past Pencheval towards the encampment.

The dumbstruck Lion straightened his tabard. Was she right? Was this particular bit of disillusionment something else inflicted on him by the Hope of Terris Lyn? Perhaps it was, and perhaps he should heal the wound that word caused him as well. There was no point in letting that vicious bastard punish him from beyond the grave.

It was worth some thought. Later. Right now, he needed rest, as the return of night on the wall always seemed to happen a little sooner than the night before.

***

Another wasted night of foolishness.

Drim sighed at the clouds floating over the mountain-castle. Jux had told him to send flame through them and then fly away. As it was the command of the wingleader, disobedience was out of the question. But the wingleader was not here, so he could grumble over how ridiculous this was.

The Snow Clan shaman created the clouds and it wore red. It may have well glowed with its own sunshine as obvious as it was. Why not simply spit flame at it and then be gone?

He briefly considered hunting the shaman, and then remembered Dok. He had been sent to hunt the shaman and never returned. Perhaps it was best if it contented itself with creating clouds instead of doing to him what it did to Dok. Or did he die by the hand of the warrior in black, who somehow managed to slay bat-lizards despite being ground-bound?

On second thought, commands were commands and best not contradicted. The clouds required burning, just as Jux said. No need to risk his life and then report that he had disobeyed, even if he did kill the shaman.

He reined his mount south and turned in a gentle arc to descend and soar over the cloud tops. The billowing mass covered all but the tallest peak of the mountain-castle, and that seemed as good as target as any. It would burn no better than any other peak, but if they were to spit burning futility at this place, it was a better target than most.

Perhaps the flame would enter one of the small holes along it and give the humans one more reason for fright.

Best of all, it threatened no thunder, lightning, or wind like the shaman. As far as Drim was concerned, that made it an ideal target. It was not as good as burning the warrior home, but still better than dying.

***

"And you say there is no reason to it?"

"No, Your Grace." Pencheval shrugged. "The drakes spat flame at the side of the keep last night. It's possible they aimed for the embrasures on the only target they could still see."

"So they meant to burn it from within?"

"It is but a guess, Your Grace. They showed no purpose at all these past nights."

"The Disciple's work appears to have the desired affect then, Lion. But what of the battle?"

"The horde has reached the outermost watchtowers, Your Grace," the castellan answered. "This was reported by several scouts that retreated from an outpost. They were briefly pursued by trollish creatures but outran them."

"How close is that?"

"Three days at most." The castellan frowned.

Rennoute tapped his fingers nervously on the table. "After their work from afar, what remains of our forces?"

"Four trebuchets and a half a dozen ballista, Your Grace," the castellan answered. "We retain the bulk of our archers and the drakebows. We also retain the Knight Superior's order, Father Victor, and enough infantry to route the horde if we can break it into disarray."

"They retain the drakes, Your Grace," Pencheval responded. "We have slain two of them, but their masters remain undaunted."

"And we win or lose the battle on those winged marauders." The castellan gritted his teeth.

"Prepare the drakebows," Rennoute commanded. "All of them are to be on the field the day of the battle and well supplied with bolts."

"We put all who could fletch or make arrowheads to the task, Your Grace. They have done so until we exhausted supply of materials." The castellan moved reports about on the table before him. "There aren't enough townsfolk for militia, but we have filled buckets of dirt for fires. I recommend we put those townsfolk who are able to that task."

"And the walls?"

"We have rocks, spearmen, and archers, Your Grace."

"Expand the infirmary into any room we have for it."

"Regretfully, Your Grace, we have much room in the stables," the castellan reported. "We have no more cavalry due to the vile magic of the goblins. Despite the fallen drake, it is mostly serviceable."

"We have no leeway to be choosy," Pencheval added.

"And the Disciple?"

"Remarkably, she had some knowledge of the horde she shared with me," the castellan answered. "She met at least two of its chieftains, and there might be some dissention in the ranks. She also confirms their warlord has power over stone."

"I've seen that firsthand," Pencheval said. "It sought me out with them in Tarsun's Market."

"Its powers are more than just tricks to awe its vermin then?" The castellan seemed unconvinced.

"Its magic is powerful. It breached the walls of Tarsun's Market by its use."

"It will find that futile here," Rennoute reassured him.

"I have battled that one before, Your Grace, and I tell you now, don't underestimate it. I should be on the wall."

"You will be, but your foremost task is to protect the Disciple," Rennoute commanded. "She does not fall, or we all do."

"Yes, Your Grace." That suited Pencheval greatly, as he was unwilling to leave her survival to someone else.

Howe's advice also served that purpose well. The drakes seemed less able to find them since they donned their newfound costumes as soldiers. But the goblins would do something to upset the current stalemate of things. Nothing in his experiences with them left him believing they would be defeated in anything resembling polite order.

***

"Are we done spitting flame into the dust, Chief of Chieftains?"

The Stonemaster smiled. Jux kept his tone even but his impatience was obvious. That meant he believed himself part of the council, or at least saw them as accomplices. It was a slip in the wingleader's vigilance even he may not have noticed, and one more thing that fell into place so beautifully.

Soon, the Stonemaster would stand in the plains beneath the mountain-castle. Shortly thereafter, he would take it as his new clan-home with the help of the bat-lizards. Once they served their purposes, he would take the Skyfang's secrets from their wingleader turned speaker, and all would belong to him.

"How much longer until we arrive?"

"Three days at our current pace, Chief of Chieftains," Bloodmoon rumbled. "The power of fifty clans of rabble and my Berserkers waits."

"The Bonestrippers will guard our flanks as before, Chief of Chieftains. They will be more than adequate to defend us."

"We have a human and five of their rock throwing things," the Allspeaker said. "We have enough rocks to use each of them ten times."

"And we have enough bat-lizards to burn those warriors and the Snow Clan's rock throwing things from the cliff-walls, Chief of Chieftains." Jux crossed his arms. "I have a plan for them, as I have told you."

"It is time for you to use it," the Stonemaster commanded. "We have toyed with the humans long enough. Finish their rock throwers. Burn their homes. And if you see them, burn their shaman and Penn Cheval."

"Yes, Chief of Chieftains." Jux gave the Stonemaster a wolfish grin.

The Stonemaster smiled back at him. Jux was ready to do his worst, and they were both eager for an end game. The wingleader simply did not suspect he would fall in it as well.

Thirteen

"Disciple, this action would not be as inspiring to the army as you intend."

"I stand watches with the soldiers, brother. I cannot remain aloof if we are to fight the horde together." Nan frowned at the knight, and he seemed unsettled by it. "I'm not a noblewoman to think them beneath me."

"You are the Disciple, but you have spent all night on watch. Surely you need rest now."

"I am the Disciple, yes, but it is long overdue that I at least greeted those on the walls."

"Yes, Disciple."

Her bodyguard answered evenly, but then none of them ever let her know if they were ever exasperated by her disagreement. He dutifully escorted her to the door to the western wall, opening the ways and ordering those in the halls to stand aside. After a winding walk up a flight of stairs, the knight finally opened a door to the sunlight she had rarely seen since her return.

The western wall was as the others, thick enough to allow a half a dozen soldiers standing side by side to pass. Most ignored the open door as they stood watch over the broken foothills to the west, an approach devoid of any place an enemy might hide or shield themselves from arrows. A handful of soldiers nearest the door did turn, and she greeted them by adjusting the uncomfortable tie of her arming cap.

How did they wear their armor for hours upon end? After only a day or two, her neck felt stiff from the helmet that seemed as an anvil on her head. The gambeson may as well have been three thick quilts over her clothing, and the beige trousers beneath it all itched. And to add to this uncomfortable mess, what was the wisdom of those blighted boots?

"Um, is that the Disciple? Why's she dressed like us?"

"Quit your gawking," a sergeant answered. "She's the Disciple and she'll wear what she likes."

Nan smiled at them both. The soldier smiled and resumed watch over the wall, and the sergeant simply nodded a greeting in return.

"I can't rightly say I expected to see you again, Disciple."

Nan turned to the sergeant who addressed her. He wore the tabard and gambeson, and a sergeant's mace dangled from a loop on his belt. He smiled, and Nan smiled with relief when she saw him.

It was Alfried, the last of the soldiers to survive captivity in Tarsun's Market. He had fought alongside her to escape in the chaos and was the only other person in their cage to think of any life other than his own. Her power might have seen them all out of that nightmare, but without his clear thinking under pressure, panic and disorder would have slain them all that day.

The word 'Disciple' sounded stranger coming from him than from anyone else. "I am the same, new title or no. How have you fared?"

"Would do better if I couldn't hear the goblins again, Disciple," he replied. Their noise drowned out most of the more distant sounds, and they both knew exactly what that meant.

"We will defeat them this time," she reassured him. "The Lord on High is with us."

"I know, Disciple. You wouldn't be here otherwise."

"I am Nan, sergeant. The same Nan you knew from Tarsun's Market."

"No, Disciple. Begging your pardon, but you're far more than that now. You've risen to a challenge no one here ever thought they would ever see, much less confront. I've never witnessed anything like it before, and I'm honored I could help you."

Nan felt tears threaten to fall. Pencheval was correct; some few of them were worth her aid, and here stood another of them. Perhaps he had not sought her out was because he, too, had been overwhelmed by the proclamation she was a Disciple. He was still no different than who he was then.

"Thank you," she barely whispered, trying to keep her voice from cracking. "I must be on my way."

"Lord on High protect you, Disciple. And be sure to drink a waterskin every hour or two. Wearing a padded jacket in the summer will leave you dry enough to faint."

"Take care, sergeant."

Nan returned to her walk down the wall, looking back once to see several soldiers awed that their sergeant had gained the attention of the Disciple. Perhaps her appearance had provided no inspiration after all, but at least she would be familiar to them. If the screech and click of the horde was this loud now, they were not far away. Causing only awe and fright in the soldiers would be a detriment to the army, and that much at least she might remedy.

***

Not good. At all.

Myrl was angry Jux chose him for the first daylight attack against the mountain-castle, but his place was not to cross the wingleader–that was a far more certain way to die. He only wondered why it was thus. One shaman, however powerful, hardly justified ceding the advantage of night to the humans.

He suppressed his fear as the mountain-castle grew swiftly larger. Despite the glowing sun behind him, it was not all poor fortune. If Jux appraised his opponents correctly, the shaman with the thunder, the wind, and the clouds was elsewhere. By the time it even knew they struck they would be done and away.

His plan of a single curving attack would see to it. Three of the things Jux described as targets stood on the thicker, rounder peaks within the cliff-walls surrounding the mountain-castle. They would attack from the north, and he would hit one farthest along his path. Each of the riders, trailing far away, would strike another behind him. Starting from a high dive, their swiftness would prevent the humans from attacking them in return.

He smacked his heels upon the top of his mount and slapped the reins. Thundering wingbeats accompanied its climb, and he smiled as he saw nothing but sky before him. Dive, burn, and retreat. One pass would see three rock-throwing things destroyed and nothing for the humans but flame.

When the mountain-castle seemed diminutive beneath him and his target was a barely defined speck of tan and gray, he reined his mount to dive. His stomach dropped and the wind rushed past his ears as his bat-lizard's wings folded closer to its body. He waited until he was within range, force pressing him against the back of his chair, and then struck its back again. His mount roared and spat the only burst of flame it would loose today. He briefly saw the black smoke and aggressively growing orange of a direct hit before hurtling past it and away.

The landscape fled beneath him as he leveled his flight and soared back towards the horde. He slowed to allow his riders to join him, and both returned in no great time. Smiling, Myrl reined his mount and left the mountain-castle dwindling into the distance behind them.

Jux had been right; the shaman was elsewhere, and now it had no idea when they would return. They finally ended this foolishness with the clouds. The Snow Clan would know fear and then defeat.

***

Nan continued her walk along the walls, greeting soldiers and assuaging their discomfiture with her as she could. All was normal until the shouts of alarm only just preceded a blur and the blossoming orange of an ignited trebuchet. It happened so quickly it hardly seemed real to her, and then all around her fell to chaos.

Soldiers jostled past them, some in panic. Alfried barked orders and disappeared into the press. The knight took her by one arm and attempted to drag her back to safety. In the confusion, two more blurs flashed over the courtyard, and conflagrations topped two more of the towers. She pulled back at the knight's hand and he snapped around at her.

"Disciple, you cannot–"

"Enough!"

Nan started at the reverberation of her own voice and caught more than a few glances for it. Pencheval's voice did this when his rage or frustration got the better of him, and for just a moment his power would slip the reins. Hers had done so for the same reason. Now was not the time for her to flee, and she was weary of hearing it.

"Yes, Disciple."

The trebuchet burned on the tower before her. Soldiers kept their distance and moved what they could from the path of the blaze, but none fought it. Something about drake's flame, she remembered. It was almost impossible to douse.

Perhaps it was time to try regardless.

Yes, her power was a great sea, but no longer almost beyond containing. She calmed herself and bade it to douse the flames. Not in a violent burst, but as a blanket of foggy mist. She willed it to appear, and a gray gloom coiled and wisped into being atop the tower.

The first of it burned away, and she willed more to appear. The fog thickened until it seemed as a thundercloud. The flame sizzled as it first blazed behind its folds, then merely glowed, and at last smoldered to intermittent flickers of light. She willed the fog to billow forth and then pour in upon itself until at last the sizzling ceased, and the glow fell to darkness.

A wave of her hand dispersed the fog to nothing, leaving only the blackened remains of what stood on the tower before. A wet damp darkened the stone of the battlements, and soldiers cheered at the subdual of the blaze. Despite the success they still lost the trebuchet, but there was precious little other cause for joy.

She again heard the horde in the distance through the kettle hat. It was close now. The chatter was of the horde going about its daily tasks, but no one on the walls knew that. To everyone else, it was just the screech and clatter of a goblin horde, harbinger of a battle. The time during her capture let her tell one goblin cacophony from another, but she found the knowledge dubious at best. It all inflicted the same madness in the end.

"We go to the eastern wall. If they intend to come now, I'll await them."

"Disciple, you will not endure this."

"I will. I must."

She heard the knight guarding her say something to a soldier, and the soldier rushed to obey. She gathered herself and trudged along the wall to circumnavigate it to the other side. It would bring her close enough to douse the other tower, and it was devoid of those execrable stairs. She found even the thought of using them again exhausting, and a straight but long walk along the walls seemed a far better thing by comparison.

***

Pencheval stopped with a spoonful of stew half-lifted to his mouth when the spearman barreled into the main hall and called for him. He let the spoon plop into the bowl and stood, taking up the bundle beside him that wrapped the goblin champion's axe. There was no way a rushed and gasping soldier brought good tidings.

"What is it?"

"Drakes have attacked us, Lion! The Disciple is going to the eastern wall!" The man leaned on his knees. "The knight guarding her told me to inform you and the Knight Superior."

"What?" Pencheval resisted the urge to pull at his hair. "No, never mind. I will meet her there. Go and tell His Grace!"

"At once!" Pencheval was momentarily surprised that a soldier would rush to obey him, and then he remembered the brass medallion around his neck. He had rank here, temporary as it was.

He broke into a run through the halls. This was a rarity. The goblins almost invariably took advantage of their vision in the dark. Yes, he knew secondhand of goblins attacking caravans during the day, but that was in large numbers and well away from the patrolled areas of Stonewall Pass. But a handful of goblins against an entire castle in broad daylight?

The damnable horde grew aggressive and unpredictable. Why now? What had changed? Did their warlord mean to burn them to ashes before arriving? No. Nan had changed, or to be more precise, their understanding of her.

They had discovered that all the castle had to wield against them was a single Disciple, and that Disciple was only out at night. The counter was to attack when they believed her gone from the walls. She was on them now, but if there was no report of fallen drakes, their plan had worked well enough.

At least the soldier found him before he only brought news of Nan's death. Her altruism would get her slain. After relentless drake attacks, she could not be in any better condition than himself. The endless grind of it wore away his vigor and his nerves. How would one unaccustomed to long night's watches fare, and what kept her on her feet?

The same measures of character and courage kept her in Tarsun's Market, even as goblins tore at the walls. They could do her credit another day. Either he convinced her to gather her strength, or the horde would find her exhausted and unready when it arrived.

After running through the halls and shoving his way past the distressed, Pencheval staggered out of a tower's door to the wall. Two trebuchets on towers before him were consumed by flame. A column of smoke rose from behind the tower from which he emerged, and he assumed another of the siege engines burned. Soldiers pointed and scrambled along the walls

The noise of the horde rang loudly now. Not so much they had to scream to hear themselves speak, but close enough to grate on nerves and morale. The goblins would be here soon, and they had enough sense to randomize their attacks in their attempt to both avoid and exhaust Nan.

He respected her stubborn refusal to quit, ill-timed as it was. Nothing of worth came to anyone without perseverance. Surrender certainly did not win battles or complete contracts. Yet these circumstances demanded something else. It was absolutely vital that he persuade Nan to depart the walls and rest. Once the entire horde attacked, it would make all the difference.

***

Jux put his hand over his eyes as he watched the bat-lizards slowing to land. All of them returned, which means his riders heeded his words about remaining swift. In daylight, when human eyes could see, doing so was more important than ever.

Three days until the horde reached the mountain-castle. It was but a speck in the distance from where they stood but could be seen from the hills and higher places. Large as it was, only one thing there could protect the Snow Clan from the bat-lizards. It could, but only if it could predict when they would come.

That was for the best. Though he could now attack as he pleased, he could only send three more raids against them. Otherwise, too few of the bat-lizards would be fresh when they arrived with the horde. There was no victory without the bat-lizards, and after his losses, he refused to give word of defeat to his chieftain. That meant he had to make his attacks count, and they would with no clouds to dismay them.

Mounts screeched as they slowed to a hover and then descended to the ground. Goblins among the rest of their horde watched in fear and awe. He wondered how many of them paid heed for other reasons and was sure some few had designs on them as he went out to meet his riders.

“Success, wingleader. We burned three more of their rock throwing things. Only one of them is left.”

“And their shaman?”

“It wasn’t there, wingleader, just as you said. But with so many attacks, will it not come?”

“Let it run itself to exhaustion trying to predict us,” Jux replied. “What will it do if it cannot prepare? Nothing.”

“Yes, wingleader.”

His rider sounded more as though he feared to dispute Jux's words than believe them. As far as he cared, they could remain intimidated. His strategy would bring victory if they followed it, and if they feared him they would.

"Wingleader." Another of his riders approached him from the pens.

"Speak."

"Several of the rabble pretend to do tasks near us, wingleader. They leave but always return. They are spying on us."

"Of course they are," Jux grumbled. The clans always kept watch for threats, especially from each other. Yet given the scheming against Leth, was that all it was? Was it merely the usual doings or something else?

For one brief moment, he had believed the Stonemaster's pragmatism overcame his ambitions. The Hordemaker could not take the mountain-castle without him. It was the reason he had accepted Jux's removal of Leth, despite a spattering of empty threats and posturing. But was it all a ruse? He hardly put it past him or his lame lunatic of a council chieftain, Beastwarper.

"What do we do about them?"

"If they do more than keep watch, feed them to the bat-lizards," Jux commanded. "Until then, do nothing."

"Yes, wingleader."

Jux reconsidered his plans. They would not stay with the horde a moment longer than it took to win the mountain-castle and secure their bargain. When this was done, he would immediately leave with his wing, then warn the chieftain on his return. The Stonemaster could chase his ambitions with the rest of the ground-bound while the Skyfang flew out of reach. Otherwise, his bat-lizards might well become part of the horde's spoils.

"Next riders to the field. Go!"

One of the riders removing the rope from his bat-lizard's neck scratched his head. "Will the shaman not be there if we go now, wingleader?"

"If it is, kill it."

"Yes, wingleader."

***

Nan bade her power to surround the remains of a siege engine with mist. Again, it swirled and sizzled until nothing remained of the flames but moisture and blackened stumps. She smiled wanly at her work and then slumped. The path atop the outer walls of the castle was lengthy, and in retrospect walking along it seemed a poorly considered idea.

"Once more along the walls then." Nan took one more deep breath and straightened her robes. Her fatigue could wait. The drakes would not.

"Would that you rest, Disciple. There is little anyone can do if they are exhausted."

"I will remain until–"

Nan stopped talking as soldiers shouted and pointed into the skies. Many cringed in fright and stepped or scrambled away from nearby flammables. More drakes came, and it was good she was here.

"At least in daylight there is enough warning." The knight's sword left its sheath and he dropped to a knee.

"Athesiene, Lord on High," he prayed. "You who bring light to the darkness and redeemer of the lost. I pray you, grant this humble servant the strength to defend Your faithful and Your works. Make me Your instrument!"

Nan gasped as bright white light illuminated the edges of his armor and shield. He rose as his sword at first twinkled, then burst into the radiance of a beacon. Soldiers shouted and cheered as the warrior dropped his visor and raised his sword over his head.

"The goblins have erred! They fight in our time, and we will know victory!"

Nan had heard of the Invocation of Service. She knew second hand that Knight-Brother Galot used it on the wall in Tarsun's Market, but she had never been next to a knight who called upon the power. The very sight of him refreshed all fatigue and inspired her to defy the horde. It also provided her an insight.

Yes, her magic could be willed into being, but perhaps it would be better to simply ask Athesiene for His assistance. If nothing else, the words would help her focus on what she wished to do. Small spells as Pencheval used were easily willed, but it made larger ones unpredictable. It was also Athesiene's might only granted to her, and speaking the request meant she could show a proper amount of gratitude for it.

"The eastern wall is through the tower, brother. We must get there now!"

"Yes, Disciple." The response boomed through the helmet, and soldiers cheered as the pair passed among them.

***

Pencheval emerged onto the eastern wall just as the knight guarding Nan rose from kneeling. He had invoked the Lord on High's power as Knight-Brother Galot had done those months ago in Tarsun's Market. The edges of his tabard and armor plates glowed with a white light as though just barely containing it. His sword was a blazing beacon, and his very presence heartened those soldiers around him.

The random drake attacks may have disrupted the defense, but they also gave the knights enough time to pray for Athesiene's favor because they could see them approaching far in the distance. He remembered how much punishment that invocation withstood in Tarsun's Market. Perhaps it would be enough against a drake.

The riders would have cause to attack him. The knight was impossible to ignore and would stand his ground now that he wielded Athesiene's might. Nan was next to him, and even if she was not recognized from the air, the splash of a drake's flame targeting her bodyguard could kill her. The pair of them practically begged to be incinerated.

He glanced towards the east where the soldiers pointed. The rapidly approaching trio of drakes arranged themselves into a long and trailing single file. Their targets were not readily apparent beyond the obvious options before him, for only a ballista remained on that section of the wall. The knight stepped before Nan and braced his shield, and that confirmed it.

"Make way!"

Would one of the drakes crash onto the knight's barrier? If it flew too close to it, there was a slim chance that the shimmer would stun it or force it to land. If it did, he would be there to punish its mistake with the axe.

He barreled through the soldiers. Perhaps between the three of them they might find some small victory, but time was not the ally of that opportunity. If the drakes beat him to the knight, they would be out of reach.

***

A glowing human? That was a rare sight. More so since it insisted on holding its ground as Bral soared towards the cliff-walls.

Was it another shaman? Of course it was; it glowed. It stood before something that looked like one of the other human warriors but protected it for some reason. Why it did this was unimportant. It could not reach him, it would be within range in mere heartbeats, and if it meant to make itself such a sweet target, he would happily burn it to ashes.

The bat-lizard rider gave thanks to the Fiend Under The Mountain and urged his mount onward. One ball of flame, and then bank to the right. The shaman's proximity to the round peak made it impossible to simply fly over it, but he had more than enough time to burn the fool and make his escape.

Bral all but leered as a roar sent a bright orange ball of flame towards the glowing human. A matter of moments showed him that it would strike true, but it splashed across a brilliant ripple instead. It shimmered from the impact of the flame, as with water after a stone fell into a pond, and left spots dancing before his eyes. His mount shrieked from the glare, and he reined hard to prevent it from hovering.

How was such a shaman trick possible? Were the ones in the shiny metal skins always this powerful? If so, why did they wait until now to summon such power? He snarled. Because in the day time, they could see them from far away and prepare.

Bral heard two more roars behind him as he banked to avoid the ground and the round peaks of the mountain-castle. The roar of flame and crackling of wood reached his ears. His riders reacted to the new shaman by changing their targets, and it was for the best. This was a matter for the wingleader, and something he would want to know. The humans could bring much to bear in the daylight which their eyes kept them from wielding at night.

He squinted, rubbed his eyes to regain his vision, and saw his riders pull up beside him. While not a complete attack, it was hardly wasted. It also ensured that this new threat did not kill another bat-lizard and send him fleeing back to the wrath of Jux.

***

Nan felt her heart pound in her chest and wondered if her eyes had deceived her.

She knew that once the knights invoked the favor of the Lord on High, He provided well for them–knew it, but never witnessed it. The drake dove at them, and all it could do was cower when its flame struck and dripped to the stones from the rippling light of the knight's shield. The impact did little more than stagger her bodyguard backwards a step.

The drake had flinched and slowed from it. Slowed enough to be shot. What caused it? Why did it stop? It very well should fear the will of Athesiene, but that was not the cause of its distress.

She snapped around as the beast flew past, but the knight only regained his footing and braced his shield against any other attacks from the sky. They came but not against him. The second burst of fire provoked billows of black smoke from the last of the trebuchets, and the third panicked soldiers as the ballista on her section of wall burst into flames.

"Nan!"

Pencheval called to her from farther down the wall, stopping well short of the blazing wooden heap that now bisected it. His chest rose and fell as one who had just run a long distance, and he leaned on a cloth bundle across his knees. He looked their way long enough to give a respectful nod to the knight, and then scanned the skies for the drakes.

The three of them grouped together as they withdrew towards what she presumed was the horde. Even now she could hear their nightmarish chittering. Memories resurfaced of the months she spent in captivity watching those around her die, helpless to do anything about it.

She resolved to deny the goblins any opportunity to capture them again.

***

"What. Other. Shaman?"

"One of the warriors in the steel skins," the enforcer called Bral insisted. "It put up its shield and stopped the bat-lizard flame with a shaman trick! Looked like a glowing pond!"

Wingleader Jux scowled at Bral and he flinched. This idiot did not have the temerity to lie to him about this, did he? Yet no excuses or blame for his riders followed the wild assertion. Those told of a failed attack, which would have meant the whip for him.

These words were more a description, spoken with the fury of someone who prayed his master believed the truth. That meant it was time to listen. If something had again changed with the humans, the Stonemaster's plan to thwart their defense by only attacking randomly in the last days had failed.

"What else?"

"The last of their rock throwing things burned, wingleader." Bral adjusted his rags away from his neck nervously. "Little remains of the wooden things the warlord wanted us to destroy but the spear-throwers."

"I will consider what to do next. Tend to your bat-lizards."

"Yes, wingleader."

Jux watched the riders as they led their mounts back to the pens. How did the Snow Clan thwart them? Despite walking as though every step was an act of deliberation, a bat-lizard borne on the wind was the most gloriously perfect thing known to the Skyfang. None had ever stopped them and few had ever downed one.

What had changed? Jux looked up at the blue sky. That had changed. They attacked in daylight to confuse one shaman, but the rest could then see the attack and react accordingly. So once again he was left to robbing the humans of their sight and their time to respond to the Skyfang with the night.

"You three! Pen your mounts. No more flights until the sun sets."

Three of the riders preparing to fly against the mountain-castle nodded acknowledgement and returned their bat-lizards to their pens. Jux was unconcerned by the delay. The powerful shaman with the thunder and wind would be a day and a half with no real rest and uncertain of the skies. However fresh the lesser shamans were, their greatest shaman would be ragged come the final battle.

Let it be there at night. Perhaps the Snow Clan would strain it until it dropped. If they did, it would be so much easier to burn.

***

"You look how we feel, Lion."

Howe stood next to Pencheval as he waited for the blaze along the walls to die. The knight's invocation had faded, and with it the burst of hope and inspiration it provided. Along this wall, a rally fell to haste as soldiers fought the flames of their siege machine. Among the rest it faded to the ubiquitous realization that despite suffering no loss of human life, the drake riders had once again done most of what they wished.

Some fell back into their tasks, and others seemed busy only so their officers would not berate them. Howe himself was slumped forward and lacked his usual roguish cheer. He shook his head slowly at the burning ballista and sighed at the last of the trebuchets.

Pencheval was not apart from the despair. Most of what he had done was aid someone else in the hopes they might succeed where he was unable to fight. It was a dreadful sensation. He had defeated the hordes' other beasts, their strongest warriors, and the worst they could muster until the time it mattered most.

The Lion forced himself to stand up straight when he caught himself slouching. This war was not yet at an end, and the knight possessed the only victory of the last fight. If anyone had noticed anything that might be useful about that, it was that remarkably perceptive Scout Howe.

"Did you see the attack on the knight?"

"Yes. He fared better than the last one. At least when the time comes, our ends will be properly illuminated."

"Take courage," Pencheval said. "Naught is done until it is done. We yet breathe."

"Lion." Howe did not speak the word in sarcasm or dismissiveness; it was said by someone who could only manage enough to acknowledge the encouragement and nothing more.

"Howe, did you see anything else, anything at all?"

"What was there to see? It spat flame, roared, and flew..." Howe scratched his head. "No. It spat flame from a dive, saw the light of the Lord on High's protection, and tilted backwards briefly. It slowed. Perhaps flinched. Was it surprise?"

"The drake wouldn't care about the glowing ripple of the knight's shield. It was far above it. What else could it be?"

"Light in the eyes? I could see the knight clearly from the other side of this wall. The goblins could have seen him clearly from Tarsun's Market."

Temporary blindness? That made more sense. The knight's sword burned brightly enough to see from two hundred paces away. His ward was also a brilliant white. If nothing else, the fact remained that drakes needed the use of their eyes.

What happened if they were made temporarily sightless in midair? The drake that flinched suggested they would do the only thing it was safe for them to do: hover until they could restore their sight. Anything else risked collision.

He had not considered blinding them before because flame gave them no pause. One even walked through a bonfire to feed on its prey. Athesiene's magic, however, created brilliance well beyond mere flame. Would it stop the drakes?

No, but it would still them for someone wielding a drakebow. The last one shot with that wieldy thing could not even walk after the venom coating its bolts took effect. If an archer shot a drake with one when it was in midair, it would suffer a swift and final journey to the ground.

"It is something, Howe. A promising something."

"One of these somethings best amount to more than something soon." Howe pulled his hat over his ears and gritted his teeth against the sound of the horde. "Our guests won't wait for us much longer."

"It will."

Howe managed a nod before resuming his watch. It was almost beyond him to look to the east, knowing what would come as well as Pencheval did. Contrary to the Lion's belief not so long ago, The Shield of Athesiene was no longer an impenetrable fortress, and the defeat of the horde here was less than certain. The drakes had seen to that, but he would see to them.

He pushed down the creeping sense of defeat as the ballista's flames receded to embers. First, reach Nan and convince her to gather her strength. Give his observations to the Knight Superior and his council, then take his own advice to rest. The drakes would return at some point, and the rare opportunities to slay them would not yield themselves to the weary.

The guards at the door to Rennoute's study snapped straight-backed when they saw him.

"I need to speak with His Grace at once."

One guard nodded and swiftly moved to announce him. Pencheval took no pleasure in his obedience. This time, the amulet around his neck guaranteed only that he would remain unobstructed in telling the Knight Superior of their circumstances.

"He will see you." The guard swung the door open for him, revealing the well-concealed worry of the Knight Superior from behind his desk.

"Your Grace." Pencheval waited for the door to close behind him.

"What news, Lion?"

"The goblin's change of strategy is taking its toll on Nan, Your Grace. She was willing to remain on the walls, but far too weary for it. If she is to fight once the horde comes, she must rest, and I have persuaded her to do so."

"And what of the drakes?"

Pencheval hesitated a moment. "We remove what we can as targets and take shelter if they come again."

"You want us to cower?" Pencheval met the glare, which was nigh as severe as it was when he faced Rennoute in the streets during the spring.

"No, I want us to stop presenting targets. If Nan isn't able to wield Athesiene's power, we can't fight the drakes. There is no reason to leave the soldiers on the walls helpless if there is naught they can do."

"Which gives the goblins the run of the castle."

"They already have it in Nan's absence, Your Grace. Aside from burning stone, what will they do if we aren't there?"

"Anything they please. This plan does not sit well with me." Rennoute rapped his fingers on his desk. "This sacrifice best improve our chances, else we all suffer the fate of Tarsun's Market."

"There is one hope, Your Grace. One of the drakes flinched at a knight. I believe it was because it was blinded by his invocation."

"Blinded?"

"Enough to startle them and make them hover," Pencheval replied. "But to do it across a whole battlefield will take far more radiance than even the beacon."

"Hence the need for the Disciple." Rennoute sighed. "I will reduce the watch only to those who can safely flee. It is only until she is ready. All will be on the walls when the horde comes, drakes or no. Do all you can to make us ready for that day."

"Yes, Your Grace."

"You may go."

Pencheval departed, no more happy about the arrangement than Rennoute. Fighting only to minimize what an enemy might destroy was a poor way to win a war. Until Nan could once again endure, however, it was all they could do.

***

Wingleader Jux soared towards the mountain-castle with his two riders and his eyes narrowed as it came closer. Now that their greatest shaman was weakened and confused, he would attend to its death personally. After the loss of Dok, taking that matter into his own hands was the only way to ensure success.

They flew well past sunset this time. Tiny flames lit the cliff-walls as before, but no clouds protected them. As they soared closer, the Snow Clan warriors filed into the small round peaks. So not only did the shaman huddle inside the Snow Clan caves in fright, but even the warriors refused to meet the Skyfang in the open any longer.

Jux leered at them. They had finally laid the mighty Snow Clan low. The humans resisted them better than most, but the damage spoke for itself. Two blackened ruins that were once warrior homes and scorched huts laid at the foot of the mountain-castle. The charred remains of rock-throwing things were testaments to their work. And now, none of the Snow Clan offered so much as their presence on the cliff-walls to stop them.

Hiding from the Skyfang was all they had left. His clan had fought other clans to starvation by making them fear to leave their own caves, and such was the way it would end here. Only the horde would do most of the work while they kept the humans terrified of the darkness above them.

Jux watched his riders fall into line behind him and reined his mount upwards. There was little left to burn but the spear-throwing things, and he chose them over the cloth huts. Any such weapons gave the humans advantages over the horde, assuming they even left their caves to meet it. They could kill and eat Snow Clan rabble after they won.

The first pass over the mountain-castle left a spear-thrower burning, and two roars behind him informed him that his riders had followed his lead. He reined up and banked to his left, stars and horizon tilting in the distance as the straps strained to keep him in his chair. The humans remained in their round peaks, and he saw no signs of any shaman.

Another pass went unanswered as he burned another spear-thrower, and his mount coughed after its last burst of flame for the night. One roar behind him, and all the spear-throwers he could see were aflame. There was nothing left to target except...the large metal bowl atop the highest peak.

It sat precariously perched between its old foundation and the edge. He remembered that Dok knocked it loose attempting to kill Penn Cheval with it. A poorly patched and exceedingly large hole in a cave's roof below showed him Dok's fate. He wished he could signal his riders to put a fireball through it, but there was no way to do that now.

One pass and it would fall, smashing an even larger opening into the cave. If nothing else, the falling beacon would terrify and demoralize the Snow Clan. Unable to see any shortcomings in this with the total lack of Snow Clan resistance, Jux reined his mount to gain speed before banking around for an attack.

Wind rushed past his ears as his mount climbed. One small adjustment put him on course, and another command sent his mount slamming into the metal bowl. He felt a shock through his bones, and the massive thing grated out of place as thundering wingbeats pushed it over the edge. The crumbling of rock preceded its descent, and a dull gong accompanied by the crash of stone alerted him to the destruction below.

Jux reined his mount toward the horde and did not look back. It could deal with rooting the shamans from their hiding places. He had done his worst, and they could exploit the new entry in the final battle. For now, it could entertain the Snow Clan while they waited to die.

***

Pencheval winced at the sound of discordant, clanging metal crashing through a roof. Helpless frustration showed on the soldiers inside the tower with him. Some gritted their teeth as others bowed their heads from the tears, and some few glared at him as the goblins did as they wished.

The tower felt that much colder. All the efforts, all the battles, and his best idea amounted to nothing more than taking shelter. He caught glimpses of the drake riders as they flew away and could imagine their laughter. Free rein against whatever they wished, and a fallen beacon to cap a night's destruction.

The courtyard door to the tower crashed open. "Fire! Bring water to the walls!"

Soldiers rushed to obey, and Pencheval almost joined them when he caught a glimpse of the drakes descending within range of his sight. Beneath them, gaps in the hills and trees hinted at the motions of a swarm in the distance. The horde was close enough to make its presence seen, and they made no attempt to conceal it.

Pencheval frowned. Other than their inability to kill Nan, they could not have arrived to better circumstances.

***

The Stonemaster surveyed the mountain-castle for himself at long last, and its size beggared belief.

Yes, his scouts and the Skyfang spoke of it repeatedly. Until now, he believed it all exaggeration. It was not as large as a real peak, but still...how could the humans build such a thing?

Its cliff-walls dwarfed those of the human town. At every turn along them, they had built a great round peak with strange flat tops circled by the unusually rough stone he had seen before. All of it was on its own hill, and within those cliff-walls stood even taller peaks and larger stone caves. There was enough room *between* the cliff-walls and the caves for whole clans and it was large enough to provide shelter to a half a dozen clans by itself! How much would it take to force the humans to give him the secrets of making mountain-castles?

It was not yet his, but no turn of events until these pleased him this much. The Skyfang burned all of their rock and spear throwing things. To his great delight, Jux reported the humans had fled the cliff-walls in the last attack. The riders flew uncontested even as they threw a great metal bowl from the tallest peak through the caves below.

He fought back the urge to let his mind tumble and fall into the belief it was already won. Yes, he was doing well, but Beastwarper's shaman and Penn Cheval yet lived, and the warriors of the Snow Clan yet lived. Jux reported at least one warrior-shaman who could summon the white light of its god as the under-chieftain in the human town once did. He very nearly lost his battle with that one, even with the power of the staff, and almost cringed at the thought of fighting any more of them.

But the spoils! The valley, the humans and their secrets, and the knowledge of taming bat-lizards would be his soon. Contemplating the accomplishment left him dizzy. No other Chief of Chieftains had ever conceived of such ambitions, and his greatness alone led him to within reach of them!

Had any other goblin been so mighty as to be one step from changing all their history? No, for no other goblin would have even seen the potential in this. This was the turning point for all goblinkind, soon to be *his* goblinkind. The knowledge to create goblin clan-homes, and then fly between them! Not a horde or a clan, but hordes and clans at his beck and call! Minions and servants without number!

Could one Chief of Chieftains be the master of them all? One could, if that one was the Stonemaster. He leaned back on his bone chair and smiled. Yes, he very well could. All he had done to get this far bore fruit, and he would soon pluck it at his whim for the remainder of his days.

Fourteen

"I have read much about goblin hordes. The inked word does not do them justice."

Pencheval stood on the top of the barbican next to the castellan and the Knight Superior, watching as the vast host of goblins swarmed and milled in the distance. The morning light made them easy to see, if hard to accept. Their numbers defied belief, as they were less an army than a sea.

At their flanks, larger creatures paced alongside them. Pencheval knew what they were, for he had faced them before. Perhaps they could serve no other purpose in a siege except to guard the flanks, and he was grateful. The ravenous beasts were hellish enough on open ground.

"How many, Lion?" Rennoute gave no sign of fear and continued to gaze out over the wall without flinching.

"Thirty to forty thousand, Your Grace. If we are fortunate."

"We have hope of neither retreat nor surrender, Your Grace," the castellan added. "They won't allow us to depart, and if what the survivors of Tarsun's Market say is true, we will slowly perish as their prisoners."

"What of our preparations?" Rennoute clasped his hands behind his back.

"I stand by my previous suggestion, Your Grace," Pencheval reminded him. "We know now that drakes hover if they can't see. Blind them, and their dismay will leave them vulnerable."

"Which may only be accomplished by the Disciple," Rennoute answered. "Anything else?"

"We still have archers, Your Grace. A thousand of them, and enough arrows to punish them dearly. If we can use them despite the drakes."

"Which for now are thankfully still."

"They won't attack us in the daylight, Your Grace. They stopped there to mass and plan." Pencheval pointed to the horde, which showed activity but not an advance. "If they remain consistent to their history, they will attack after dark."

"If I was their master, I would send the drakes to harass the troops while the bulk of them advance," the castellan said. "The earthworks will slow their mob, but they can still attack us from the air."

"Issue all drakebows. I want the archers with them on the walls and near the tower doors. They are to shoot any drakes that present them the opportunity."

"Yes, Your Grace." The castellan nodded.

"They sent vines against the walls at Tarsun's Market, Your Grace," Pencheval added. "They may do that here."

"They may try, to their disappointment," Rennoute reassured him. "We have hardened these walls against true magecraft, and the primitive works of goblins will find no purchase on them."

"If their warlord attempts to rip them down as it did in Tarsun's Market, you will need it."

"That matter is attended, but the most dire one remains. The drakes are the key to this. If they prevail, we will die. If they are slain or broken, my order will lead the counterattack against them in all the Lord on High's glory."

Pencheval remembered what that meant. Knight-Brother Galot had stood alone in Tarsun's Market and nearly defeated the warlord by himself. Before he fell, he slaughtered dozens and possibly hundreds of goblins. The Lord on High's might burned them to ashes before they could get close enough to harm him.

Only the warlord possessed enough might to defeat Galot, and its power crumbled to rubble facing him. The thirty of Rennoute's order here could inflict enough burning wrath to turn the tide. They could, if they could mount a counteroffensive for the blighted drakes.

"I will speak with Nan by the leave of Your Grace."

"Lion, you will not leave the Disciple's side for the battle save by my word alone. I need not remind you of her importance in all of this. Go to her now and plan. Though such preparations tend not to survive the first trading of blows, it is best to make them regardless."

"Yes, Your Grace."

Pencheval gave one last glance to the goblins and then hastened from the roof. He was glad the stouter walls of the castle protected him here instead of those in Tarsun's Market, but they were not enough. The drakes would come again soon, and with them came the endless numbers of the horde.

***

"I never thought to see such a place. And the Snow Clan built it?"

The Stonemaster smiled as Beastwarper echoed his sentiments in the council. "It is the greatest thing we will take from the humans. Imagine the treasures and secrets it holds."

"If we can get into it, Chief of Chieftains," Beastwarper countered with an offhand remark.

"We will," the Bloodmoon Speaker rumbled. It sounded more like a threat than assurance.

"The rock and spear throwing things are gone?"

"None of the wood things stood when last we attacked, Chief of Chieftains," Jux informed him. "Unless they built more, no rocks will fly upon the horde."

"They will still have archers," the Allspeaker observed. He seemed to be recalling memories from the attack on the human town.

"We can deal with them," Jux said, "but not quickly enough to set up our own rock-throwing things."

"It is no matter," the Stonemaster told him with a sweep of one hand. "Leave them out of this battle. They can go in the mountain-castle to help us defend it once it is ours."

"What then, Chief of Chieftains?"

"The rabble of the horde will wait on the edge of their holes and stakes," the Stonemaster commanded. "They will remain there until the bat-lizards attack. Then they will cross the field and scale the walls. Have our shamans send out vines as they did before."

"Yes, Chief of Chieftains," the Allspeaker answered, sounding less than certain.

"Once the rabble swarm the humans, the Bloodmoon will go and kill the strongest defenders. Be wary of those like the under-chieftain of the human town. If they glow with bright light they will burn you."

"And what of you, Chief of Chieftains?"

"Once the horde scales the walls, I will tear down the wood-wall entrance to this place. I have enough command of the stone to do that." He wished knew the staff could make him so powerful before the attack on the human town, but was glad he knew it now. "The horde will become like the fangs of a mountain lion and attack the Snow Clan from above and below."

"Yes, Chief of Chieftains."

"Make all ready. We attack after the sun sets."

***

Pencheval stopped in the hallway leading to the chapel. He expected to find Nan inside, but instead she stood at its closed door, speaking with the priest who had confronted him earlier. When he noticed the mercenary, he frowned and excused himself.

Pencheval snorted as he departed. The priest's contempt merely lessened the strain of an impending attack by reminding the Lion of less calamitous days. Perhaps he might live long enough to see them again.

"Pencheval?" Nan smiled at him. "Father Victor does not take kindly to you, it seems."

"He likes my medallion well enough to avoid any real trouble." Pencheval held it out, more idly than anything else. "What matter did he discuss with you?"

"He passed me on the way to the walls. He goes to wake them now."

"Wake them?"

"It is the old thing to say for empowering the wards. These walls are far stronger than those in Tarsun's Market." Nan smiled at him. "He will have to walk along all of them. Likely it will take him all day."

Pencheval was almost envious at the ease with which she answered him. Between the sound of the horde and memories of the last time they battled, his nerves remained on edge. Nan faced the same with a quiet strength and tranquility he had not seen in her before. Her softness now was from someone who had no need of harsh affectations to adorn true substance.

"You seem well, Nan."

"The Lord on High provides," Nan answered. Her voice contained a combination of resolve and inner peace.

"The goblins will come tonight. Please gather your strength while you can."

"I have strength enough for this," she replied. "And you?"

"I will end their warlord and every goblin that gets within sword's reach or die trying," he snarled. "I swear it."

"I never doubted your resolve, nor did the Lord on High. Not now, nor in Tarsun's Market."

"The Lord on...what?"

"It took no small amount of contemplation in the chapel for me to finally understand. When I remained behind to help the wounded, Athesiene wasn't merely judging my worth. He was guiding you as well."

"I, uh..."

"Do you not see what you've become? The Silver Lions gave you your might but also their darkness. You were immersed in it so long you knew not how far you fell, and it was obvious to the Lord on High that mere words could not pull you from it. He gave you a reason to remain in the valley at Tarsun's Market and continue your ascent."

"Ascent?" Pencheval shook his head in confusion.

"What do you think you were doing all this time?"

"Trying to rescue you!"

"No, that is merely where it began. Each moment of found purpose, each clumsy effort at charity, each time you remembered you were more than just a mercenary; they were all rungs on the ladder rising out of your darkened pit. You have more ahead of you, old friend, but climb you do."

"Can we speak of this later?" Pencheval was ready to pull at his hair. They could discuss the finer points of why Athesiene willed no such blighted thing another time.

"We can. Did something else bring you here?"

"Yes. Scout Howe saw the drakes flinch at blinding light. They might cease flight if they cannot see. If so, the archers with drakebows can hit them. Is it something you can do?"

"I will find a way. For now, others here need my help. The impending battle will bring uncertainty and fear to the townsfolk."

"Salve them as you wish after our victory, but not now."

"I will, for it is my way. But I thank you for your concern, Pencheval. It's good to see you return."

The flustered Lion watched Nan depart for the opposite end of the hall. He breathed deeply and focused his mind once again. Epiphanies and the saving of his soul could wait a while longer. There would be nothing left if the goblins prevailed, and he was determined not to let that happen.

There was no way the events of Tarsun's Market and what came after was the work of any higher power. It was something he repeated to himself as he sought out his chambers to make the last of his preparations. It was simply not possible. It could not be.

***

The Stonemaster kept watch from his bone chair, ready to make his will known and *felt* unless the forces around him found order and soon. Bonestrippers snorted and resisted their reins while waiting on the flanks. The rabble of the horde grouped into clumps, eyeing rival clans with suspicion and casting nervous looks towards the mountain-castle. They would require no small amount of motivation.

The last brilliant sliver of the sun set behind the Snow Clan's massive home, taking with it the light the humans so dearly needed to see. Only Penn Cheval had displayed any amount of sight greater than its cursed fellows, and it would die before the night's end. It was time to begin.

"All of you, make ready your preparations."

The Beastwarper Chieftain and Bloodmoon sent rabble to their destinations. Jux left in person after a curt nod of acknowledgement.

"Silence the horde."

A messenger scurried to obey, and slowly, the sound throughout the horde decreased until nothing remained but the growls of the Bonestrippers on the flanks. It took a longer time than it had at the town, and the Stonemaster frowned. All of the humans that had cost him that much of the horde's awe and fear would pay with their lives tonight. For now, it was time give the rabble purpose and direction. He rose and thrust his staff into the air.

"This night is the end of the Snow Clan! Tonight, we will take the last of this valley from them, and make the first true goblin clan-home!"

Chatter and cheers, but more perfunctory than sincere. Of course it was. None of them had the manner of vision to care if they had a better clan-home. Nor did any of them want to charge the mountain-castle. That would require some reassurance.

"The bat-lizards fight with us tonight! They burned the human rock-throwing things and drove the Snow Clan cringing to their caves! What will they do against the might of the whole horde? Perish!"

The rabble chittered with increasing enthusiasm. What did he need to say to them? What they wanted to hear, and what this victory offered them. In retrospect, the Stonemaster found it obvious. Rabble minds were too small for ambitions such as his to dwell within them. Keep it simple and stupid for the simple and stupid.

"Once we have killed the Snow Clan, we will take their treasures and feast on their defeated as we did before!"

No, most of the humans in the town were not meant to die that way. He refused to admit that was not his will, however, and the unbridled cheering among the horde kept his face blank. The loss of so many humans frustrated him then, but it served a purpose now.

"The mountain-castle is ours! The lands of the Snow Clan are ours! Go forth to the edge of their field of holes and stakes! It is time to take it all!"

He returned to his chair as he felt the goats roll its platform forward. The rabble poured around him, cheering and chittering as the whole mass moved towards the strange human field. Miniature hills with wooden stakes dotted it and would make crossing difficult, likely as the Snow Clan intended. There was no approach to the mountain-castle left unfortified in this way, and the Stonemaster gave the humans a grudging respect. They had used the time he spent in Tarsun's Market to prepare well. Had the Skyfang never come, attacking this place would have destroyed the horde.

As it was, there was far more certainty they could make it to the walls. These were not as rough as those in the human town, and much taller, but did not lack for holds to climb. It would also be that much easier once the shamans sent their vines to them and the horde scaled to the humans above.

When the edge of the horde reached the stakes, it ceased to move in fits and pushing until all stopped. The Stonemaster stood and waited for the return of messengers. The one sent by Bloodmoon returned first, bruised and terrified. "The Berserkers are ready, Chief of Chieftains."

Likely they were bloodthirsty, the Stonemaster mused. They wanted revenge on Penn Cheval and the return of their clan's best weapon. At least one of them had slapped the messenger for daring to bring word of anything other than a charge.

A short time later, a messenger Beastwarper sent to the flanks returned, and then the other. They spoke to him under their breath.

"The Bonestrippers are ready, Chief of Chieftains. Should the humans leave the mountain-castle to attack, we will meet them."

"The Skyfang await, Chief of Chieftains." One of Jux's riders appeared from behind the throne.

"Kill the shaman and Penn Cheval when you see them."

"Yes, Chief of Chieftains." The rider ran to relay the message to Jux, and the Stonemaster continued to watch the mountain-castle as he waited for the sound of wingbeats.

***

"They grow silent, Your Grace. When last they did this, they demanded our surrender."

Rennoute stared silently across the earthworks as darkness robbed him of viewing the horde. They would meet that demand with defiance if the horde made it again here. Galot's valor had done them all credit, may the Lord on High shelter him for all eternity, and he would do no less. He could not, for the goblins would see them all dead, surrender or no.

"From that distance, Lion? No." Rennoute shook his head. "What are they doing?"

"Listening to someone or something speak, Your Grace."

The Silver Lion standing next to him squinted through his barbute to see. Whatever unique charm gave him sight in darkness was invaluable against goblins. If his information was correct, the journeyman adept learned it early in his apprenticeship. Such creatures infested Stonewall Pass, and the various sources he consulted by pigeon confirmed he fought them there for some years.

Right now, he seemed to be wavering between an eagerness to finally be done with this and nerves. None of the others he saw near him fared any better. The drakes would attack again, and the only one who showed any true calm was the Disciple. Between contemplation, epiphanies, and the hard lessons of experience, she had found her way at last.

"My brothers and sisters in arms, hear me!" Rennoute turned to address the whole castle, and his voice carried over the stones. If the goblins fell silent, he would put the time to good use.

"Before us stands a blight upon our lands! They have reaped all before them; your friends, your families, and the serenity of our homeland. They have reduced our peace to a wasteland, and now mean to do the same to us."

Nearby, a few of the soldiers nodded.

"Yet this is not the night for fear! This is the night you will remember to your graves! This is the battle of which you will tell your grandchildren, that when duty called you to face the darkness you chose courage and stood! Every one of you who has lifted spear or bow, sword or spell, mace or pitchfork are exalted in the eyes of Lord on High! When you at last meet Him, you can tell Him what you can tell all others come the dawn and every day thereafter. You fought in the battle for this, the Shield of Athesiene, for your families, your homeland, and your faith!"

Cheers thundered from around the castle. All the soldiers he could see stood with the steeled resolve of a King's guard. The Silver Lion curled his hand in anticipation around the hilt of his sword while holding the wrappings Rennoute knew held the axe that had slain two drakes thus far. He hoped it would kill many more tonight.

"Your Grace, the drakes rise in the distance. They come."

"Time to blind them," Nan said, and Rennoute watched as clouds formed over the castle. It was not what he hoped the Disciple could use against the drake riders, but it had kept them at bay for some time and would protect the archers.

"To arms, and glory to the Lord on High!" The Knight Superior drew his sword and pointed it at the horde. "Throw them back!"

***

"Take it all!"

The horde less charged than flowed into the fields beneath the mountain-castle like a slow river, forced to twist and turn to a crawl by the obstacles before them. The booming of wings from the bat-lizards announced six of the beasts tearing across the skies towards the Snow Clan far more quickly. The Stonemaster bared his teeth. Whatever the Skyfang meant to do, they had best pull their weight.

The first to the cliff-walls smacked headlong into the Snow Clan warriors beneath the clouds and disappeared. Another did the same on the opposite side, knocking them from the heights. The next two chose to remain above the clouds and shoot a pair of brief orange glows through them. The last two banked and turned to attack from the north as the remainder emerged and followed their own paths through the air.

A small swarm of miniature lights arced from above the clouds towards the horde. The humans could put them aloft without sight, but shot fewer than he expected. The Stonemaster smiled. The bat-lizards successfully sowed disorder and panic among the Snow Clan, and the clouds proved little hindrance to them.

The nights of preparations he had the Skyfang make before attacking made themselves known by the glorious absences. No stinking, burning filth hurled down upon them from the skies. No spears flew from spear throwers. They garnered no more protection from the clouds, as their one powerful shaman should have realized by now. If it panicked, its tricks would disperse, and the horde would inflict its will on this place unhindered. It was time to set other plans into motion.

"Beastwarper."

"Yes, Chief of Chieftains?"

"Move the Bonestrippers so that they can charge the Skyfang pens. They, too, will be ours."

"Yes." Beastwarper paused for a moment longer than the Stonemaster expected. "Yes, Chief of Chieftain."

Beastwarper spoke to the messengers of his clan, and they left in all directions. The Stonemaster wondered for a moment, and then shrugged. What else would that warped, obsessive chieftain do but follow his commands? If he did something foolish and the horde suffered a defeat for it, he would lose all the knowledge within the mountain-castle that he craved. His self-interest laid in the same direction as the warlord's own, and neither disobedience nor betrayal would serve it.

Just an excess of caution on his part then, or perhaps not in excess. The Skyfang were a great prize but also a great danger. Still, so long as he had Bonestrippers and retained his nerve, he would have their knowledge, too. Beastwarper had coveted this too long for that fact to be lost on him now.

***

For a moment, Nan stopped feeding power into the clouds above the castle as soldiers on the wall next to her simply disappeared. One moment, the beat of wings, and the next, a horrific smack preceded their fall. A lone survivor standing nearest to the knights who protected her froze, realizing to his horror that the drake might have been a mere arm's length from slaying him too.

Two bright orange bursts behind her sent archers screaming as they splashed from stone buildings into the formations below. She could see the glows in the darkness behind her and fought to keep the clouds from dispersing.

"Nan, we must blind the drakes! Blind them with light!"

Light? She could no more hit them with lights than she could with wind, or with the blasts she used on the goblins in the temple of Tarsun's Market. They were too swift even if she could see them in the darkness. Clouds. Yes, clouds were the answer.

The twangs of bowstrings preceded the roar of a drake, and shrieks rose up from the ground as it tore into the archers below. Behind her, another roar descended into the courtyard. She turned in time to see the beasts rise from a small clearing of the slain lit by the burning of drake's flame. Soldiers scattered from formations and archers dropped their weapons to flee.

How did the drakes suddenly overcome the clouds? No matter. Lights. But how?

"Damn goblins picked their time," the soldier next to them cursed. "Refused to attack with the sun in their faces."

The sun. Yes! It simply was and required no aiming. But was it enough? Clouds dissipated as she thought, and she watched Pencheval snarl in frustration. No, even the sun was insufficient, but she knew what would serve and where to put it.

"I must get to the top of the barbican."

"What?" Pencheval's strange axe growled. Its wrapping laid at his feet. "You'll be exposed to the drakes, Nan. Can you not cast from here?"

"No, I must be atop it. Please, trust me now."

She watched as Pencheval took a deep breath. Yes, it was a risk. Could he believe in her after all he had seen of her struggles? He had certainly seen enough to wonder if she had mastered her powers or if they had broken her.

"We move now." The knights looked at them both as if they were mad.

"Now!" Pencheval all but tore the tower door open and ascended the stair towards the roof. She followed as fast as her breath allowed her. If this failed, the drakes may well kill her, but there was no avoiding this.

***

The bat-lizards decided that quickly.

The horde still picked its way across the field to the mountain-castle, but nothing flew from that place aside from the first volley of arrows. A mere six bat-lizards kept the humans pinned and panicked. Nor had they neglected the shaman. The clouds above the castle thinned, and then dissipated into tiny patches before disintegrating to nothingness.

Had they slain it? Perhaps. Even if they had only scared it into fleeing and remaining in one of the round peaks, it would be enough. If it was too frightened to use shaman tricks, it was as good as gone. No shaman meant the Skyfang could do as they pleased, and the rest of their riders remained at Jux's call.

He saw a bat-lizard briefly arc over the southern cliff-wall and then dive below sight on the other side. The riders had repeated that several times since the attack began. A bat-lizard descended on what he assumed were human archers, killed a few, then rose before it could be slain. It was a satisfyingly brutal tactic. The humans feared to shoot arrows when gigantic beasts kept pouncing on them from the skies in the dark.

One of the riders circled, possibly to attack one of the round peaks for reasons he could not discern. They ignored them up until now, which he guessed was the case because there was nothing there to attack. It would be by far the safest target, otherwise.

Some of the humans had gone there, then. No matter. The bat-lizards would make short work of them as well.

***

"Do what you mean to do with all haste!"

Nan watched Pencheval scan around him with an intensity bordering on panic. Whatever it was he could do with his eyes likely showed him nightmares. Drakes attacked like gigantic hawks or falcons, and wove through the air like wrathful hornets. The screams of the soldiers mixed with their roars.

She took a deep breath. Let all around her fall to chaos, the power would fly true. She looked over the castle to the space behind and above the western wall, split in her view by the keep. She narrowed her eyes, frowned in intense concentration, and imagined what she required. Not light or sun, but brilliance. The brilliance of glints on water in daylight, or the sparkle of crystal, only vastly more of it.

"Athesiene, Lord on High, bringer of light unto the darkness. This humble servant begs you to cast your gaze across this castle."

A brilliant sphere burst into being on each side of the keep, well behind the western wall. She closed her eyes against the glare and willed more power into them. Once they had grown so bright it seemed as day even behind closed eyes, she turned away and cast her gaze to the ground.

It was not as bright as day; it was far brighter. Brilliant white light lit the stones so fiercely she could clearly see their slightest detail. When the gleams struck something in the way, it cast a pitch dark shadow that hid the ground on which it fell.

Three shadows from the figures behind her suggested the knights and Pencheval shielded their eyes. In the distance, the parts of the horde under the glare placed arms and shields over faces and moved only because those behind them still advanced. They yet staggered forward, blinded and terrified, or were trampled by those behind them until they all stumbled to a halt.

Powerful wing beats and pained roars turned her attention back to the drakes. One horrified screech preceded the sound of something large impacting on stone, then crashing to the ground. Other shadows flapped their wings in midair, hovering where they were as they tried to turn away. What glimpses she had of their riders showed them desperately covering their eyes, unable to see in order to guide their mounts.

Nan smiled. She had at last defeated the goblins. They could not fly into the light, nor could the horde charge it.

***

Pencheval stumbled in the brilliance and forced himself to stop. It left him briefly sightless, and he refused to plummet over the edge because he staggered blindly to his death. He put his back to it and blinked twice, spots still dancing in his vision as he took stock of what happened.

Either dark shadows or blazing light covered all about him. The burning white from behind the western wall staggered and blinded all of the horde. So long as no soldiers were fool enough to turn to the west, they would be safe. The drakes, which thus far purchased their victories on their speed and agility, could no longer see to fly, and neither could their riders.

Four within the bounds of the castle screeched and hovered as they slowly turned to put their backs to the light. They had moments before the drakes fled to fight another time.

"Take the shot before they flee!" Pencheval willed power into his voice, and it boomed across the walls. He hoped those with the drakebows were able to act despite the brilliance.

One drake turned away, and then flinched as something struck it. It made it as far as the horde before its slowing wingbeats were not enough to keep it aloft, and it fell from the skies into the cringing masses. Another only just cleared the eastern wall above the soldiers before it did the same, dropping like a stone into the burned village below. A third failed to escape even the courtyard.

The last of them beat its wings and screeched, arcing toward the tower on which he stood. It had no intent beyond a desire to flee and crashed into the battlements. Two claws ripped at the stones for purchase, wings beating just to keep it in place. The drake squinted and its rider tried to rub sight back into its own eyes.

Pencheval willed himself speed and smiled wickedly. It would overcome its dismay in a few heartbeats, or even threaten Nan, but it did not have that long. He gripped the axe of the goblin champion with both hands and charged to strike. One blow to the top of the beast's head, and he would extend the list of drake rider fallen.

He squinted one eye against the light. At three paces, the beast still scrabbled against the battlements to keep from falling. At two, one slowed burst of its wings put it over the wall and instead of a clean shot at its head, he found himself slammed backwards.

The banded scales of its chest pushed him just out of the reach of claws flailing in air for speed. Its wings beat again, forcing his retreat to keep from being crushed or mauled beneath it. He staggered back until at last, one foot found nothing behind him but air. Time still slowed, he fell back as the drake snapped its wings once more. With only a moment to grasp at the claws and strap beneath the beast, he let his axe fall and reached forward with both hands.

The world returned to normal as he dangled by one hand from a claw and felt the drake try to pull it from him. His legs kicked wildly at air. Another hand found purchase on the strap beneath it, fingers barely wedging themselves between it and a rubbery hide. The beast roared and thundered as it clumsily attempted to remain aloft, dropping towards the shadow beneath the eastern wall. He saw the indistinct shape of a half-burned cottage below him, and chose to fall into it rather than remain clinging to a sinking drake.

Thatch and ash crashed beneath him. A beam snapped across his back as he fell through it, flipping him forward to land on his face in the dirt below. The cold sod floor slammed the air from him and left him wondering if he should have remained with the drake a while longer.

The cacophony of the horde drowned a roar and leathery wingbeats as the rider flew off into the distance. Pencheval staggered to his feet and willed himself sight. The flame eaten furniture and straw bed of a peasant's hut resolved in shades of gray, and the walls of the castle rose above the hole in the damaged roof. Two small suns burned beneath the line of the walls, and the soldiers upon them were little more than darkened silhouettes.

He was not in the courtyard. The buildings there were roofed with slate. He staggered from the hut and gazed west towards the horde. Goblins cringed, brightly lit, on the other side of the wall's shadow, unable to advance from the glare. The click and screech suggested fear, but all that kept them at bay was that onslaught of blinding light.

Pencheval ripped his sword from his scabbard and backed away, heartbeat pounding in his ears. He had survived the fall but was now between the castle and the horde. If they overcame their terror and realized the shadow of the wall protected them from the light, they would drown him in a tide of goblins.

Fifteen

"The drakes are broken! Rally the archers and set the sky aflame!"

Rennoute yelled his instructions down the wall and was amazed he could be heard over the horde. A screeching sea indeed, as one of his tomes had described them. It was as though all other sounds were rendered mute by the endless squawks of birds or the chittering of gigantic insects.

The castellan bowed and rushed to make the Knight Superior's will known. Cheering archers once again took up bows and ceased to fear the skies. Sergeants pointed and gave orders Rennoute could not hear, and soldiers obeyed them.

Perhaps Athesiene had sent His guidance to the Disciple. Perhaps she had found the answer on her own. Whatever it was, the burning lights at his back changed the whole battle. Now the army had a clear view of the advancing horde, and the goblins could hardly stagger forth into the glare. They practically stood there begging for the archers to slaughter them. Had the trebuchets remained intact he would rain their due upon them in stones and pitch.

Only one drake he could see succeeded in fleeing. It dipped into the town as though overladen, only to put air once more beneath itself as it escaped. Yet it had come from the direction of the barbican. That was where the Disciple stood!

He thought his worst fears confirmed with the overwhelming brilliance dampened so much he could bear to gaze at it. Two spheres of graying light revealed themselves and weakened as he watched. He rushed to the roof of the barbican's tower to find the Disciple screaming at the ground below. The knights with her kept watch as they tried to console her.

"Disciple! Are you injured?"

"He's down there! I can't see him!"

"Who, Disciple?"

"Pencheval! He can't have fallen now!" The Disciple searched the town below in desperation.

"Your Grace, he attacked a drake that crashed into the tower." A knight pointed to the edge. All that remained of it was jagged rock. "It struck him from the roof in its escape."

"Yet it appeared too heavy to fly, Your Grace, and there was no final cry from the Lion."

Why would the Lion do that? Perhaps he believed he defended the Disciple. Perhaps the Lion's frustration made him reckless. Eager to repay the torment of the drakes, he instead fell victim to its fear. He wished it was otherwise, but the battle was far from done, and matters remained dire.

"Disciple, please, restore the light."

"No. Not this senseless end!" She continued to search as the lights dimmed again. Instead of the wicked luminescence that set drakes to flee, it was little more than a dawn's sun.

He had asked the Lion to help him with the Disciple because of their history. What would he have done to convince her of anything? "Disciple, please restore the lights. It is all that keeps the drakes and horde at bay."

"I possess all of this might. Why did it end this way?"

"Nan. Sister." Rennoute kept his tone conciliatory. "If he did take hold of the drake, he may not yet be slain. And if he lives below, all that stands between him and the horde is the light. Please, aid him now."

The Disciple turned to him, smiled wanly, and closed her eyes. The glow over the castle brightened until it was once again too much to directly bear. Once again the horde appeared, only now at the edges of the ruined fortresses below. They had advanced in the reprieve.

Rennoute took one deep breath. What could he learn from the Lion? Exactly what he ever saw from him. The mercenary always spoke plainly, sometimes to a fault, and never hid what he was from anyone. He had been the only person here who saw the Disciple as his friend and ally Nan, and in that way relieved enough of her burden to aid her to this moment. It was always that obvious.

The awe of a new Disciple had clouded his judgement and that of everyone else in the Emerald Refuge. The Lion had said it plainly, and he was right. She was not a holy relic or a witch. She was a person still, however worthy Athesiene found her, and to treat her otherwise only made her journey to this point worse.

If they lived through this, he would make amends. For now, where were the storms of arrows? This battle yet raged!

***

The burst of light from the mountain-castle surprised Jux so badly he staggered backwards, covering his eyes. One moment, he watched in satisfaction as his riders dispatched targets and harassed warriors without leaving anything more in return than fear. The next moment, what could only be the work of their shaman unleashed this Fiend-forsaken glare. What manner of god did the Snow Clan worship?

He frowned at the irony. The humans, whose cursed eyes were to make this battle easy in the night, now rendered the goblins sightless and themselves able, at least from this approach. What had it done to his riders? They were in the middle of it!

The lights dimmed briefly enough for him to see two spheres suspended in air. The eyes of their god? And if the shaman which eluded death and his riders to this point could summon such a gaze, what would they do to defeat it? As they continued to diminish, he quelled a sense of false hope. No, the lights dimmed not because the shaman expended its power; assuming that would be disastrous. They dimmed because they had done their work.

He heard the beating of wings over the horde. A rider landed hard, bat-lizard growling in agony as it shook its head from side to side with eyes tightly shut. The rider half-fell from his seat and kept his back to the glare as he tried to rub the spots from his vision. Jux watched for any others, and no more appeared. He bared his teeth. The other five slain?

After a painfully long span, another rider in the air soared into a landing and leapt from his mount. He walked it forward to check its gait and inspected the straps of his chair. The bat-lizard favored none of its limbs nor bled from any injury, but it worried the rider regardless. Jux strode over to meet him, and he cringed and held his arms before him.

"Wingleader, it is not hurt. I swear it!"

"Why would it be hurt?" Jux's eyes narrowed as his rider shrank from his gaze.

"I saved it from that shaman trick, wingleader! It merely had to climb one of the peaks to regain its wings! It may have struck a human, but there were only four there!"

"And?" That could not be the whole story. His rider hesitated to tell him what it was, and only spoke again when he reached for the knotted rope on his belt.

"Something weighed it down and nearly pulled it to the ground! But then it flew again. Perhaps a human got caught in the straps?"

"Which. Human?"

"There were few of them on the peak, wingleader. One shorter one. It raised its hands towards the western cliff-walls. Two others near it, one charged the bat-lizard with a hammer... or–"

"An axe." Penn Cheval. Could his rider have knocked that dark warrior to its death? If so, the Bloodmoon's axe waited for them beneath the walls. If not, their axe and their revenge waited. It was the merest hope of a worthy outcome to balance out the loss of so many.

The lights of the mountain-castle returned with a vengeance, and both he and the rider averted their gaze. Perhaps the Bloodmoon might make more headway. Those lights forced the Skyfang to remain on the ground so long as they burned. If the shaman who created them could maintain them all night, the Snow Clan could send enough arrows into the rabble to break and scatter them before they even reached the cliff-walls.

"Pen your mount. No one leaves until I say otherwise."

"Yes, wingleader."

***

Those humans summoned the sun!

The Stonemaster dropped his staff and shielded his eyes with both arms at the sudden glare. Had their strongest shaman done this impossible thing? If so, the Skyfang has been far too confident about the Snow Clan's weakness. They fled to their caves the night he toppled the beacon not from fear, but so they could gather their strength.

The glare lasted but moments, and then faded to tolerable light. Perhaps the power was fickle, or perhaps they had accomplished what they wished. He watched as only two bat-lizards returned where six had flown to attack, and he concluded that they had found their weapon after all. Worse still, they found it during the main battle, and dismayed the overwhelming swarm he sent to the walls with the blinding light.

As things now stood the battle turned on this. Unless the shaman was mind-numbingly stupid, it spared its own warriors from the light. That meant the arrows would fly and strike down horde in lots with no way for them to go forward or back. That was ripe for scattering them.

It was likely, if not certain, the Skyfang would remain grounded as well, which the Stonemaster refused to accept. The blazing glare hardly freed them from their agreement, so Jux had best have an answer for it. The fact the glare lessened even as he watched made him even less inclined to sympathy.

"Beastwarper, where are the Bonestrippers now?"

The lame shaman had turned his back to the mountain-castle and cringed from the light. "They are where you have asked them to be, Chief of Chieftains."

"Be ready to send them if the Skyfang flee the horde," the Stonemaster commanded.

"Yes, Chief of Chieftains." Beastwarper whispered to his messengers, who rushed away in different directions. Two left towards the flanks and the third towards the rear.

"Three, Beastwarper?"

"The enforcers at the flanks and the spies need to know," Beastwarper answered him evenly. "What more do you command?"

"Nothing."

A goblin staggered into the council area with his arms over his eyes. It took a few moments for the Stonemaster to realize that it was Jux.

"Chief of Chieftains, we have an opportunity."

"An opportunity for you to resume flights against the Snow Clan?"

"No, Chief of Chieftains. We cannot fly into this. But one of the riders knocked a human from a peak on the eastern cliff-walls. He believes it was Penn Cheval."

"Why?" The Stonemaster wanted to believe it. His relief felt as though a Bonestripper was lifted from his shoulders at even this rumor of its demise.

"The rider said it struck an axe-wielding human from the peak. Only one human with an axe ever accompanies the shaman, and that shaman was also there. It was Penn Cheval."

It was plausible then. The collaborator, who he still retained in its cage, had said they were allied back in the town. But the shaman had told him this was no longer the case when he spoke to it in the human great cave. It meant nothing given the reports that the Skyfang saw them together. Any shaman with this kind of power certainly knew how to lie.

"Bloodmoon."

"Yes, Chief of Chieftains?" The Bloodmoon Speaker seemed little affected by the light. He had merely turned his back to it and crossed his arms.

"Your task and your revenge lie before you now. Inspire the horde to charge again, and it will help you reach Penn Cheval at the walls. At the very least, you will find its body and your Rage. When you have done this, climb the cliff-walls and kill that Fiend-forsaken shaman!"

The Bloodmoon Speaker smiled wickedly. "It will be done, Chief of Chieftains. I will attend to it personally!"

The gigantic Berserker strode off, pumping his weapons into the air and gathering the rest of his clan. They could certainly frighten a horde into charging again and not a moment too soon. He saw brief, tiny flashes of orange rain down upon patches of the horde, striking some dead and panicking others, before the glare burst back into being once again. A fickle shaman trick or not, time favored the Snow Clan now.

***

This was the way he would end?

Pencheval looked out over the horde and lowered his sword. All the fighting he had done, all the battles, the risks, and the victories, and he would die from an accident. But for one unexpected burst of panic from a drake, he would not be here at all.

He stumbled onto the road leading to the barbican and its gate. He restrained the urge to run and hammer on it in desperation. He already knew they had the other side braced and barricaded. If they had any sense at all, every reinforcement they placed behind that gate would remain until the horde either broke or laid dead before them. That assumed they could even hear him over the cacophony.

No one on the walls appeared to notice him, and he had no way to signal them aside from a Pitfire spell. Even if he used it, and they could see the illusion of a burning demon his sword would become, what would they do? Believe it was the goblins.

The horde was easily visible in the light, even as it waned. Had something happened to Nan? He saw no other fallen in the dimming light above, or in the blue glow of wards behind the seams of the castle walls. All they did was show him that there was no place among the ruins of the town he could use as a position to deny the goblins the benefit of their numbers.

The horde screeched in pain and shielded their eyes, inching forward and finding new heart as the glare faded. Two volleys of burning arrows fell into them, changing their cacophony to screams of pain and panic. The arrows blunted their resolve but did not stop them.

Could he run to another wall? He willed himself sight through darkness with a Clearsight charm and hastily searched to the north and south. The horde's line was wide enough to hit the whole eastern wall. In the distance, the goblin beasts waited on the flanks. There were more than enough of them to catch and overwhelm him if he attempted to circumnavigate the walls before any of them noticed.

There was nothing for it then. Tonight would reunite him with his father and Cecelia. All he could decide was how, and the trepidation gave way to the same refusal to yield he had felt in Tarsun's Market. No, he was not trapped between the walls and the horde. The horde was trapped between the archers and *him*. He took up his sword with both hands, roared at the top of his lungs, and charged along the road at a mob of goblins. As if in response, the glare returned in force, and he smiled at the realization that Nan had indeed survived.

Let the horde come. Let them all come. If the Black Archer meant to take his life tonight, he would damn well make that specter earn it.

***

Rennoute gazed out over the horde. It pushed against the light as though trying to struggle through a storm, not quite so threatening as before. Yet despite the turn of fortunes, his face remained impassive. Telling Nan that the light might save Pencheval was needful, as cruel as was to even hint that the Lion might still live. He should not have met the fate he did, but there was far more at stake than any single warrior, and the Disciple's place in this battle was essential to their victory.

The goblins struggled and screamed, and yet they inched forward to where the eastern wall cast its shadow. If they made it there, they could resume their charge in earnest. If the Lion was between them and the wall, may the Lord on High grant him mercy. Nothing he saw in the press below led him to believe the horde would fail to gain that much ground. The volleys of burning arrows descending upon it in swarms barely reduced its numbers.

A silvery glint caught his attention. At first he believed it part of the glare, but it flashed again. A third time, and a goblin flew through the air as though knocked backwards by some powerful force. One more flash, then another, and part of the line pressed back from a shadow attacking them furiously. Every time it moved, silver flashed again, cowing more goblins.

Argentsteel. The Lion yet lived.

"Lord on High be praised," the Knight Superior said to himself.

"Your Grace?" A knight walked up beside him and glanced over the wall.

"The Lion is alive. Athesiene's mercy, the valor...Send word to the archers on the eastern wall. Open fire on the horde and retrieve the Lion."

"Yes, Your Grace, but will we not harm him?"

"He wears drakescale armor over chain and a steel helmet. He will fare far better against errant arrows than he will against that horde. Be swift!"

"Yes, Your Grace!"

"What distress, Your Grace?" The Disciple lowered her arms and half-turned to him as the knight rushed down the stairs.

"Pencheval lives, Nan. Maintain the light, and grant us enough time to rescue him."

Rennoute watched her sniff and suppress tears. "I knew the Lord on High would not abandon him."

"No, He would not, and neither will we."

***

What possible way could that be the Lion?

Howe pulled another arrow to his check and let it fly. It struck another goblin cleanly, and he quietly thanked the Lord on High for His favor. With the glare to his back and his eyes on the horde, he had his pick of choice targets. Blinded, stumbling, and so easy to see, he had not yet missed.

The struggling drake desperate to keep itself aloft caught his attention, but so had its impact on the barbican. At the time, he believed the crash caused its agonies. But the glints in the distance spoke of one other, and there was only one way that Lion could have found his way to the ground and lived. Lucky enough to avoid his fate at the claws of a drake so he could meet another. How did that madman find so much trouble?

The sword's flashes were too brilliant to be anything but the silvery steel he remembered from the summer's festivities. Pencheval had stepped out into the light but kept his back to it. Only his very unique and precarious circumstances even gave him a chance, though he swung the blade with too much abandon to have planned it.

The goblins remained blinded, and he struck down those who found relief in his shadow. Yet the rest of that impossible line crawled and inched forward into the gleam. If they could pull themselves across no more than another twenty paces of it, the shadow under the wall would grant them enough relief to swarm him.

Howe less stroked than pulled at his goatee. The only way to escape that was up the wall. In order to facilitate that improbable feat, he would need to find a rope strong enough to bear the Lion, get his attention despite his preoccupation with the horde, and then lift him up a mere four stories with all of his armor and gear. And perhaps he would suddenly find his flask enchanted to ever flow with whiskey, which was far more likely than managing any of that.

A knight burst through the tower door and strode over to the nearest sergeant. "The Lion is below and in need of succor. Get him up here now!"

Howe shook his head and snatched up the nearest coils of rope. If the Lion lived through this, he had best do more than growl at Athesiene for it. Naught but the intervention of the divine had willed that command spoken.

***

Pencheval bared his teeth as his descending blade struck another goblin dead. The feral hound within him was unsated. Argentsteel still gleamed beneath goblin blood. The lion on his tabard was yet visible through the gore. He would not sell his life this cheaply!

Pencheval's next blow smashed a goblin shield into tinder and killed its owner. It was a tiny moment of victory before the horde forced him to step back. The goblins before him did not want to advance into his blade or the glare, but the numberless press behind them gave them no choice.

It also gave him no choice. He took another step back to once again grant himself room to swing, and the first ragged shadows of the wall appeared in the corners of his eyes. Only the light kept that line of goblins from swarming him to death, and the horde slowly depleted it.

Arrows dropped goblins and they crawled ever forward. Burning rain fell in small storms among the horde, diminutive compared to its size. The soldiers continued the struggle, yet what could they do about saving him in the end? If the Knight Superior was worth his title, that gate stayed closed.

He willed a Waymaker spell into his sword and with a thrust, sent it into the goblin before him. The power of the spell hurled it through several of its fellows and crashed them all to the ground. The push from behind trampled them.

For a moment the Lion imagined he saw the figure of a longbowman in black take careful aim at him. Pencheval smiled at it. The Black Archer would be well sated tonight and would do him the service of reuniting him with his father and Cecelia ere long. Before then, he would reap goblins until he made hills of their corpses.

***

The Stonemaster tilted the wicker shield he held just above his eyes and glowered at the horde. What was the delay? Did they not also have shields or arms with which to cover their eyes? Did they not realize that darkness awaited them just below the cliff-walls? That haste would save them from burning arrows? Of course not. That assumed the rabble were more than minimally useful.

He caught a glimpse of the Bloodmoon's Berserkers shoving their way to the fore. At least their desire for revenge kept them advancing. But would they survive without the rabble if they scaled the cliff-walls alone? Their fury, though formidable, gave that no certainty, so the horde required additional motivation.

Where sense failed, fear would prevail, and one council chieftain had beasts in blindfolds. "Beastwarper."

"Yes, Chief of Chieftains?"

"Send any Bonestrippers you are able to the rear of the horde and walk them forward. Command them to kill the rabble if they catch them. If deserters scatter to the flanks, kill them as well."

"Chief of Chieftains?"

"Use your Bonestrippers to drive. The horde. Forward!" The Stonemaster glared down at Beastwarper.

Beastwarper blinked twice, then slowly nodded his head. "Yes, Chief of Chieftains."

"Be at ease," the Stonemaster reassured him. "The rabble will die, but you will have human secrets and treasures."

"Yes, Chief of Chieftains."

Beastwarper sounded unconvinced, but at least he obeyed. The Stonemaster returned to frowning at the horde, shield once again above his brow. The reluctant chieftain's concern was unwarranted. None of his own clan stormed the walls with the rabble, and nothing less would serve either of their ambitions.

***

Something tapped Pencheval on the back as his sword stroke left a spray of blood in its wake. Had a goblin found its way behind him? No. If it had, it would have jumped on his back, and there was no weight. He resumed his focus on the horde. It was just his imagination, and at a time he could least afford it.

He grabbed a handful of a leaping goblin's face, breaking its arc with a stiffened arm and a vicious twist to its eyes and nose. He let it drop to all fours and kicked it away when it screamed. He took another step back and found himself at the line between light and shadow. Two paces before him, goblins struggled to see and stagger forward. Their troubles were at an end in a matter of steps, and so was he.

Something tapped him on the back again, and his foot snapped something beneath it. He glanced down and saw an arrow. Were the archers shooting at him? He knew they shot and felled no small number of goblins from the eastern walls. The shafts landed silently along the front line, hums drowned by the cacophony of the horde, and two struck him in the back.

A third arrow flew past his face and into the horde. Pencheval turned and snarled. Bad enough he would be overwhelmed, but to die from an arrow set to flight by his allies? He turned to see the black outline of the towers and wall, silhouettes of soldiers, and a single torch waving beneath the battlements.

Had someone noticed and signaled him? With only a pace between the goblins and the shadow that would grant them their reprieve, he sheathed his sword and ran. He willed himself speed, and wind whistled around his helmet as he matched the pace of a galloping horse. Perhaps they had noticed him, and perhaps he only wanted to believe they did. It was better to take that chance than to stand and die.

When he reached the walls, a knotted rope dangled before their soft blue glow. Was it thick enough to bear his weight? He willed strength into his arms as he leapt for it and climbed. The first two bursts of strength pulled him upwards easily. The third and fourth left his arms aching, and the next two meted out agony and threatened even his means to cling where he was. It felt as though he tried to climb with an anvil strapped to his shoulders.

The rope pulled upwards by a pace. Then another. He dangled as the soldiers lifted him and glanced below. The goblins had reached the walls and scaled, ascending far more nimbly than himself.

Halfway up the wall he risked two more bursts of strength. His efforts and those of the soldiers left him nearer the battlements than the ground, but his arms screamed with pain. A glance downward showed him a swarm of shadowy figures in the intensifying blue light of the walls. Something had triggered the wards, and they countered the goblin's work well.

Rocks fell from the trapdoors in the machicolated battlements, falling before him and onto the climbing goblins. A few struck and bounced from his drakescale armor and grit splashed from his helmet. He shouted and willed himself strength twice again.

The first pull left him within reach of the battlements and the second granted his fingers purchase on the stones. A pair of soldiers grabbed him by his arms and pulled him over. Pencheval resisted the urge to drop to the ground and gasp for breath as his heartbeat pounded through his ears. The terrified mercenary staggered to his feet and ripped his sword from its scabbard.

"Now you owe me one, Lion," Howe exclaimed, and struck the goblin cresting the battlements nearest to him with a torch. "Put that blade to use!"

Pencheval found the nearest empty spot and killed a goblin with a thrust. Of course he would join the fray. Either they defeated the horde, or they died.

***

The Stonemaster sat impassively and watched as a Bonestripper swiped several of the rabble skywards. A few of them gone to motivate the rest; hardly a consideration with so many to expend. If the crawling movements dampening the blue glow of the cliff-walls in the distance meant what he suspected, the beasts had performed their task well.

"You do realize you must command this horde after the battle, do you not?" Jux shielded his eyes. "Have you considered what to say to them once you have taken the mountain-castle?"

"I'll say I am the reason the bat-lizards flew again, which is quite true."

"Best hope the Bloodmoon kill their shaman, then. No Skyfang fly until we can see."

"Not all of you, anyway. The other half of you will remain here as a certainty that the rest of you succeed." The Stonemaster's eyes narrowed. "The Bonestrippers prowl your flanks. Keep your end of our agreement, or you'll never return to your clan-home to make excuses to your chieftain."

Jux snarled and glanced towards his pens to confirm the truth of what the Stonemaster said. What he saw left him furious but silent. His grip tightened around a knife on his belt before he thought better of it.

"Did you believe I would come within sight of my final prize and simply leave?"

Jux bared his teeth. "Beastwarper, you mad–"

"What I want is there as well, wingleader," Beastwarper replied calmly. "There is no way out of this but mine. Now consider your next actions carefully. Failure here is beyond toleration."

"I will peel your hide from you for days."

"If you try, you'll have even more deaths to explain to your chieftain," Beastwarper warned him. "I already told you. Consider your next actions carefully."

The Stonemaster dismissed them both with a wave and sat back in his bone chair, smirking. The light had blinded the Skyfang but also distracted them enough for the Bonestrippers to move into place unnoticed. It was something only one of his greatness could do: take advantage of the enemy.

Yes, he would need to tell his horde something. It should be easy, given the glow of victory after the fall of the Snow Clan's mountain-castle. If he gave them most of the humans to eat and some time to loot, any ill will caused by his more aggressive motivation would pass away as water down a stream.

This valley and everything in it belonged to him, especially the mountain-castle. The others best realize that they were not his equals and soon. They could serve and be rewarded, like Beastwarper, or be made to serve in exchange only for a lessening of pain. Those with any sense would find obeying his will best for them, one way or another.

Sixteen

The horde came first as a trickle, and then as a flood.

Pencheval kicked the head of a goblin that rose between two of the battlements and sent it to its death. Something drove them through that blazing light but he wanted for time to determine what it was. Neither he nor any of the soldiers could afford to stop fighting, even for a moment.

The goblins were not merely eager to crest the battlements; they were terrified of remaining below. Something scared them out of their reluctance to attack, and those that reached the line fought tooth and nail. This was not merely a battle, and it eclipsed even the desperation of Tarsun's Market.

His sword split a skull. He tore a goblin from a soldier's back and hurled it over the edge. Spearmen struck with spear and shield until they gasped for lack of wind, and archers waylaid their foes with daggers, hammers, or the wood of their bows.

Pencheval could smell the ash snowing down from the barbican where two knights defended Nan. Those few goblins who scaled the tower met their fate as they reached the top. Athesiene's power burned them to sparks and bones.

He gave a moment's thanks for Nan's courage. A sea of goblins crashed against the Shield of Athesiene and she kept the lights ablaze—lights which kept the drake riders at bay. But for her blinding them, the horde would meet soldiers too afraid of the skies to repel them, and pour forth in even greater numbers.

True that it lacked the power of thunder and wind, but Nan had never been one for thunder and wind. Might it have been best to let her find her own answers? Perhaps, but there was too little time for passivity. His vocation was defeating enemies, and he played what part in it he could. He wished he could defend her now, but there was nothing for it but fight where he stood.

There were goblins enough to overwhelm everyone and everything if he did anything else.

***

Nan stood near the center of the barbican's roof, feeling the power flow into the lights at her back. She hoped Pencheval had returned safely but had no news of him. She could barely see over the battlement from where she stood, and anything she learned of the battle came to her in sound.

Clashes raged on either side of her. The screech and click of the horde rang from below and nearly overpowered all else. Goblins which crested the battlements of the barbican hissed into ashes as the power of the knights burned them from the edge.

She could see nothing from her vantage but the well illuminated horde. They covered all within the plains and earthworks below, and the faded gray illumination at its borders revealed more motion beyond them. Despite the light, despite the swarms of arrows arcing down upon them, and despite the punishment they faced from the soldiers on the walls, they pushed forth. What had given them such resolve?

"What more can be done?" Nan shivered. How would anyone defeat this?

"Disciple, maintain the light!" One of the knights turned at her remark. "Blind the goblins and the drakes. We will attend to their defeat!"

She nodded and narrowed her eyes. They would defeat this, and she would help them. The Lord on High had such confidence in her He made her a Disciple. She would not flee her charges or betray His trust in her, however grim the battle seemed.

She fought back the butterflies in her stomach and the feeling of weakness in her limbs. Let the goblins press into the glare if they could. It would be the last thing that horde ever saw.

***

The Stonemaster snorted at the Allspeaker, who had turned his back to the light and shivered, overwhelmed by his excess of caution. Shivering and fearful as the battle finally turned? That was why the shaman could never forge and rule a horde. Unlike the Stonemaster, he lacked the capacity for greatness and the willingness to do what it took to achieve it.

No, this was not the time to shiver. The horde swarmed the Snow Clan warriors on the cliff-walls and the Bloodmoon would kill that shaman soon. This was a prelude to victory and the time to consider what came next.

Should he crack the wood-wall of that place now? The humans were well occupied by the horde. Perhaps he should summon the stone body that was so useful in crashing through the walls of the human town. The little burning arrows would cause him no harm while he was within it, and the loss of a few rabble as he waded through them would cause him no distress.

Yes, that was the thing that would turn the battle. He remembered the thrill of ripping through a stone cliff-wall and the hard-won victory against the human under-chieftain in their town. He would repeat those feats once the bat-lizards flew again.

In fact, they should already be on wing. Where then were they? He had amply demonstrated an upper hand to Jux not long ago, and yet no beating of wings. Since he heard no roars from the rear of the horde, Beastwarper's pets were not the culprit in their disobedience.

"You." He motioned to one of his messengers, who promptly scurried forth.

"Yes, Chief of Chieftains?"

"Tell the Skyfang to send their bat-lizards again, or I will attend to them personally."

"Y-yes, Chief of Chieftains."

The messenger cringed, reluctant to carry those words, but he departed regardless. It was possible Jux might kill the rabble for speaking them, but unlikely. That act of disrespect would result in his death and he knew it.

***

Pencheval pointed his blade at the ground, slid the goblin corpse it impaled off with one foot, and sent it over the edge with a quick kick. The display froze another goblin between the battlements with fright. The Lion took advantage of its hesitation and skewered it as well.

He wondered when their warlord would come. It attacked them at Tarsun's Market, encasing itself in a great stone construct so it could tear through the walls. He was uncertain why it had yet to do so here, and the drakes were the only answer that came to mind. Why risk itself and its ambitions when it had such minions to act on its behalf? It almost found itself facing Galot without magic and only defeated him by one desperate and fortunate blow.

Reserves rushed from the northern tower, and booted feet trampled corpses in the soldiers' haste to replace the fallen. There was no time to mourn for those the horde had slain. The goblin assault continued unabated.

He noticed something odd from below after striking another goblin from the battlements. Soldiers and knights gathered at the gate and not as reserves. Spearmen hastily formed into a shield wall and both knights dropped to a kneel. Something threatened the gate, but what?

He had little chance to survey the horde but saw nothing but wicker shields. He could hear the crunch of them underneath the walls as the goblins discarded them to climb. There were no rams, no sappers, or any siege engines at all except...

The axe. He let it slip from his grasp as he struggled not to fall to his death. Did one of them find it below? If they did, they surely knew its power more than himself. He already knew it could chop cleanly through wood with little more than the flick of a wrist. How long would it take a wielder to cleave through a gate swinging it with both hands?

Not so long it would leave the soldiers watching that gate at ease. And once it did? Goblins would swarm from above and below as they poured through unhindered, possibly led by the giant warriors and their deadly axe.

Pencheval gritted his teeth and redoubled his efforts. Had one mere moment of chance, the same moment that robbed him of the axe, handed the horde the instrument of their victory? The implication that he might be responsible for the fall of the castle, however inadvertently, was nigh more than he could bear.

***

The Stonemaster frowned at the passage of time, unable to see much in the way of progress through the glare. Surely by now the Bloodmoon Clan had reached the cliff-walls and scaled them? Perhaps their Fiend-granted strength meant they could breach the wood-wall that obstructed entry. With some good fortune, the horde may even have slain Penn Cheval by now. Whatever they did, they had best attend to matters and *soon.*

They had that shaman, Penn Cheval, and...them. He remembered the Snow Clan under-chieftain of the human town he attacked. How many more such warrior-shamans did the humans command? However many it was, they would all be here in their clan-home, for it was the strongest place to face the horde in the whole valley.

They were mighty but could not fly, and thus a matter for the bat-lizards. Why had the Skyfang not yet flown? Had that idiot Beastwarper gotten himself slain? Jux certainly made short work of his last irritation.

"Allspeaker."

The shaman clung to the canopy surrounding the warlord's bone chair, cringing at the lights and the battle, oblivious to anything else.

"Allspeaker!"

"Yes, Chief of Chieftains!" The yell jolted the nervous shaman into giving the warlord his full attention.

"I'm going to encourage the Skyfang to take flight. Should anyone ask, tell them to keep pressing forward."

"Yes, Chief of...wait. You want me to command the horde?"

"I want you to maintain control until I return," the Stonemaster explained with a deadly calm. "Don't be among those who disappoint me tonight, and do as I tell you."

"Yes, Chief of Chieftains!" The Allspeaker swallowed hard before tentatively approaching the bone chair.

At least the shaman's fear meant betrayal was beyond him, the Stonemaster mused as he strode toward the Skyfang pens. It was the Skyfang that worried him, and perhaps Beastwarper as well. Could they have been scheming together this whole time?

***

"We'll fly when the lights fall and no sooner!"

Wingleader Jux glared at the chieftain before him. Beastwarper leaned on his staff just to remain standing, weighed heavily by the growth of bone on his shoulder. The effort to stand, and the lack of bat-lizards in flight, left the lame chieftain irritated and unreasonable.

He had pulled some manner of jar from beneath his rags and dangled it like a stone from a sling at Jux's first refusal. He then informed Jux it was filled with Deepglow and that he would cease all complaint. The wingleader was not sure he believed the sinister chieftain, but he already knew Beastwarper was mad enough to collect and use the stuff. The bones on his left shoulder were likely caused by it.

The eight or so Bonestrippers too close to the pens made his precarious position all too clear. According to both Beastwarper and the Stonemaster, they were enough to slaughter a sizeable portion of his wing. The great beasts stood the height of four goblins and bore maws that could swallow humans whole, and were thus another claim he was unwilling to test.

"You made an agreement with us. It was not contingent upon ease. Now live up to your bargain."

"We will, once you darken that light! The bat-lizards won't fly into it!"

Did he not know his own bat-lizards? Certainly he did. He knew they would not fly anywhere if blinded. They only flew away from the mountain-castle at the initial onslaught of this Fiend-forsaken light because they had their tails to it. The riders on those that returned still complained of seeing dark spots dance before their eyes.

"I grow weary of standing. When I grow weary of talking, one of you will pay for it."

"Grow weary, do you? Perhaps you should grow weary of your warlord's ambitions. He spares none in his push to achieve them."

Beastwarper leered at him. "I am a council chieftain. He won't cross me for he fears my Bonestrippers."

"Until he doesn't, as he has no more fear of the Bloodmoon or my bat-lizards!"

"Why are you still here?"

Both of them turned at the angry question of the Stonemaster, who strode up to them with a scowl. "You see what we can do to you if you fail us, yet you persist?"

Jux frowned. Of course his circumstances were so insufficiently dire the Fiend saw fit to make them worse. He had chosen this spot for the pens to minimize the stone, but it still offered the warlord enough rocky outcroppings and rough ground to give his power much from which to draw. He was grateful to feel cool damp dirt beneath his feet.

"They will not fly into the light."

"Do they require additional encouragement?"

A low growl silenced the argument. One of his riders, taking advantage of the distraction, had mounted his bat-lizard and reined it towards the Stonemaster. At that distance, even a novice rider could roast the warlord alive.

"Better question, Chief of Chieftains. Do you want to burn?"

***

Nan kept her back to the light and wondered what had changed below. No goblins attempted to crest the battlements on the barbican in too long a time, and for a moment, she let herself believe that all might be well. It lasted until one of her bodyguards glanced over the edge and recoiled.

"Brother?"

"Athesiene preserve us, they've–"

The warrior quickly bit his tongue, but he did not need to finish the thought for Nan to know the truth. There was no call for goblins to climb the walls if they could pass through them. The horde had breached the gate.

If so, it was the beginning of the end. The goblins were not merely numerous. They were a great screeching current of living beings that could drown their opposition in numbers in a way she never cared to see again. All that prevented it here was the walls, and if they no longer served...

"No, this cannot be. Not again..."

Nan walked tentatively over to the edge and peered down into the courtyard. Two knights gleaming with the power of the Lord on High and a phalanx of spearmen faced down a tide of goblins. Though the power of the knights burned many to ash-stained bones, one large nightmare pressed forward undaunted. Smoke rose from its skin, but it stubbornly refused to drop as it raised an axe and struck.

The blade cut through a knight's sword as though it was straw and sheared half of his torso away. Even above the sound of the horde she thought she heard it roar. It was the axe Pencheval took from a goblin champion. The awful thing was enough to cut drake's hide, the wooden gate, and even the power of the Lord on High.

"This cannot be. It will not be!"

Nan willed power down to the ground below. Half the goblins that had breached the portal dropped into the same endless sleep she inflicted on the horde in Tarsun's Market. Terrified and frustrated by the lack of targets, Nan rushed to the other side.

"Disciple, ward the drakes!"

"Enough, and do not hinder me!"

Yes, the lights kept the drakes at bay. Yet they were slow to fade, even as she refused to maintain them. The glow dimmed to a bright summer's day as she took stock of the incoming horde and willed a burst of light in their midst.

A bright flash appeared briefly within the tide, followed by a thunderous blast and the goblins it threw into the air. She felt no lessening of the power as she unleashed it time and again. Though unable to send it farther than the gate at the edge of town, the reservoir of it never lessened as one burst after another tore holes in the endless press.

She heard the tenor of the horde change to something akin to fear. Instead of advancing, goblins pressed backwards against those behind, or tried to flee north and south from the walls entirely. The tide ceased to flow and instead tried to scatter in fear and disarray. Eddies formed in the great sea of goblins, and some few disappeared underfoot when the press overwhelmed them.

One last blast, and those attempting to funnel through the gate dispersed instead. Nan shivered from remembering what had happened at Tarsun's Market and poured power back into the western lights. They grew so bright none could again face them.

Had the horde forgotten what she could do? The sleep and the thunder would remind them of what Athesiene's will did to them in Tarsun's Market, and what it would do to them here. Let them wonder if they would be next as they shielded their eyes from the glare.

She would inflict many more reminders on them tonight.

***

"Is your perch precarious enough yet?"

The Stonemaster ignored the leering Jux and took the measure of the bat-lizard brooding at him instead. Jux and his riders stood flanked by Bonestrippers, the only creatures that could conceivably harm them, for all the worth that had to him now. He could order them to attack, but he would likely burn for it. Either that, or Jux would use it as a distraction to dispose of him as he had disposed of Leth.

Jux could, but that meant he and his wing would then be attacked by Bonestrippers, and he would find that the warlord was far superior to his former speaker. After drinking the red water the human had traded him along with the staff, he could kill goblins with his bare hands. With the staff, Jux would be a triviality, which the wingleader would learn too late. He could then use the stone to attack the bat-lizards and defeat them with the aid of Beastwarper.

The lame chieftain stood there, less confused than thoughtful. He was the only uncertainty in this. While the chances of defeating Jux favored him if he attacked with his Bonestrippers, the Skyfang threatened his life as much as the warlord's own. His ambitions, however, stood with the Stonemaster. All those human secrets lost but for the horde.

Would Beastwarper side with Jux regardless and withhold the Bonestrippers to save himself? That would change the matter considerably. And what did he have in that clay pot dangling from his grip?

"You dare defy me?"

"I won't throw my wing at a place where they cannot fly, Chief of Chieftains. You forget we aren't part of your horde."

"At best, you will return to your chieftain empty-handed if we fail here, or if we win without you."

"Better that we return empty-handed than not at all. The might of the Snow Clan's shaman is literally glaring in your face. Why would I want to fly against certain death?"

"You may care to consider you will die on the ground," Beastwarper interjected.

"Or that you, too, will burn," Jux snarled. "What good do you suppose my death will bring you? You will toss your pot of Deepglow at me, and all my riders will simply stare?"

Beastwarper hissed and bared his teeth. The Stonemaster considered his next words and noticed the light dimming around them.

He glanced over one shoulder towards the mountain-castle. The lights were no longer so brutal they scorched his eyes. A pair of bright orbs replaced them and grew dimmer as he watched.

"You know what that is, do you not? The shaman has met the horde." The Stonemaster smiled. "Vengeance for your fallen awaits. If you fly now, perhaps there will be more than scraps left for the Skyfang."

Jux narrowed his eyes at the mountain-castle. The Stonemaster gave him time to watch the lights dim. He had to want blood after all he had suffered at the hands of the Snow Clan. He had to want victory to give his chieftain when he returned to his clan-home. He would realize both were within his grasp very soon.

"A pity." Beastwarper shook his head. "That human was useful."

"There will be others. This season, we will take this valley and the mountain-castle. In the spring, we will go south for more humans. What would stop us?"

A thunderous crash echoed over the horde. For a brief moment, it drowned out even the sound of the chatter. The Stonemaster snapped around at the brief and brilliant flash of light, followed by another echoing boom. The third display made him recoil, and the fourth left him wondering how stable his position truly was.

"What would stop you, Beastwarper?" Sarcasm dripped from the Wingleader's words. "That shaman, for one. Its god has granted it power over thunder, lightning, sun, and wind. What else can it do with such favor?"

"It cannot do this and maintain the lights," the Stonemaster countered. "It could not touch the Skyfang before, and will do nothing if it is dead."

"It attacks because it is cornered. Now is your time." Beastwarper seemed unconvinced of that assertion himself.

"It attacks because it is desperate. We will be safe if it loses, which is far from certain. If it prevails, we will again fly into our own blindness and the Snow Clan will slay even more of my wing."

"There are no lights if it is harried!"

Two more thunderous crashes flashed briefly into being, each one a momentary return to daylight. The horde stopped crawling forward and fell into disarray.

"If the horde fears that shaman more than your Bonestrippers, you will be overrun," Jux told Beastwarper. "Choose wisely, for you and yours are at stake now. More meat for the butcher, and your warlord the only one to feast."

"Treasures for all and secrets for us when we prevail, Beastwarper. Human knowledge! Do not falter now that all is within our grasp."

Beastwarper gazed at something over the Stonemaster's shoulder. The Stonemaster watched as bat-lizards, Bonestrippers, and the two before him were once again lit more brightly than the sun. He noticed the slightest blades of grass or tiniest stones cast black shadows, and only too late saw the spin of the pot in Beastwarper's hand.

The clay cracked and shattered from the silver plate he wore on his chest, and its contents melted it like thin ice. He briefly saw the glowing water dribble onto his skin before unrelenting agony knifed into his bones. He convulsed and dropped to his knees, staff falling from his grip. Jux and Beastwarper watched him impassively as they both backed away.

Beastwarper said something to him, but words no longer made sense. His vision disintegrated into a red blur and all noise became one garbled, indecipherable screech.

***

"I'll content myself with your human, Chief of Chieftains. A treasure within my grasp is worth a hundred out of reach."

Beastwarper shielded his eyes from the light and bared his teeth at the mad ambition of the Stonemaster. Yes, the Snow Clan knew many things. Even as they spoke, their shaman made that abundantly clear by wielding that knowledge against the horde. How did one channel such power from their god? He would never know, for no being with such strength could be made to talk.

"Wise counsel," Jux replied. The wingleader glanced down at the warlord. "Will it kill him?"

Beastwarper watched the Stonemaster convulse, bone spikes and spurs protruding from everywhere the Deepglow splashed. He remembered the pain from his own accident as an apprentice. He had slain the idiot that spilled it on him, but removing the mistake was too agonizing to even attempt. It had been his constant companion ever since.

"So much Deepglow is invariably fatal." Beastwarper cocked his head to one side. "However, it is usually more... spectacular."

"What now?"

"I mean to take the human and the Allspeaker. They are mine. So long as all you do is leave, my Bonestrippers will allow it." Beastwarper reached within his rags and produced the other pot of Deepglow. "Take my offer and go. If you turn on me, you will die the same way the Stonemaster did."

"I want nothing more to do with any of this," Jux grumbled. "I will abide by this arrangement. But never cross my path again."

"I have more sense than ambition, unlike this fool," Beastwarper replied. "Be gone. I have enough."

"Fiend take all such hordes as this one and the blighted Snow Clan. Mastery of the skies is all we ever needed." Jux turned to his riders and commanded them. One after another they mounted their bat-lizards, rose into the sky, and flew northward. Beastwarper motioned to his riders to remain, and they reined their mounts away from the flapping of wings.

The Stonemaster laid on the ground, eyes wide in agony. All that remained of his death throes was the occasional twitch, and his staff laid beside him. Had that been the source of his powers over stone? Until he came to the valley, he treated it merely like an affectation. Then he commanded the stone without speaking and gestured with the staff ever since. It was a wise and useful deception that had ended from unforeseen circumstances, as many other such fabrications did.

Groaning from the weight of his bone encumbered shoulder, he reached down to lift it. It felt like stone, and the crouched winged figure kneeling atop it was very shiny in the light. Did it have power? Perhaps, but none he felt or comprehended save one.

It displayed to all the horde that he had taken it from the Stonemaster. That meant he would be the focus of those who would follow him, which would be few, and the far greater number of those who were loyal or wished the horde for themselves. He dropped the staff and shook his head. It told too many tales and threatened far too much chaos, and thus was a hindrance while he collected the human and Allspeaker.

Beastwarper limped back towards the bone chair as fast as he could manage. In every tale he had heard of hordes, the only successor to a warlord was chaos. His time to take what he wished and quit the field would flee as swiftly as a frightened mouse. For long enough, however, this horde belonged to the Bloodmoon. It would do them little good, but at least they would occupy each other's attention.

***

Pencheval flinched at the first blast from the ground below. It briefly and silently lit the shadows below the walls brighter than day, then exploded with the violence of a thunderclap. One burst after another ripped into the lines before the gate, and Pencheval smiled wolfishly.

Nan had changed the battle. He was grateful she was not slain, as he first believed when the lights behind him once again dimmed. The first of her works sent goblins flying, the battle all but stopped after the second, and panicked screams rose from below the walls after the third. The destruction became the center of attention on both sides, but only briefly.

As the lights rose again, Pencheval gritted his teeth and threw himself back into the fray. The bursts inflicted disarray and fear upon the horde, but not a rout. Some still climbed, if only to escape the ground below, and others crested the walls for the press of those behind them. He snapped the heel of his boot into another goblin face and kicked it to its death. This battle was over when the horde scattered to the winds and no sooner.

"They fly!"

Pencheval followed the finger of a terrified soldier to the rear of the horde and saw the drakes rise from the ground, one after another. How did they mean to attack the castle? He could hardly bear to turn either north or south for the torrents of light, much less look directly at them. Had they found a way to defeat it?

No. They rose into the sky and flew northward towards the mountains. He caught glimpses of them as he battled goblins rising over the walls and considered cresting a tower to confirm their intentions. What he saw never changed. The glare overcame the drake riders, and they flew to quit the field.

"She did it."

"Nay, Lion. It's not nearly over yet!" A sergeant smashed a goblin skull with a mace. "Keep swinging that pretty sword of yours 'til the goblins stop coming!"

"No, Nan did it. The drakes flee!"

The sergeant backhanded a leaping goblin with his shield and stared into the distance. “Lord on High be praised. It’s true.”

Pencheval raised his sword over his head. “This night is ours! Kill them all!”

“Glory to the Lord on High!”

“Lion!”

Pencheval snapped around at the call of a knight. The warrior in plate reaped his way down the wall from the barbican, smacking or slashing goblins in his path but not stopping to defend the battlements. He pulled Pencheval away from the fray when he finally reached him.

“The Knight Superior sends word! Descend to the courtyard and help defend the breach! I will relieve you here!”

A breach? The blighted goblins did find that axe! “At once!”

If the Knight Superior wished him to quit the walls and fight below, it fared badly for Rennoute’s Order. The axe was in play, and if it wreaked such havoc he had to retrieve it. It enabled the horde to strike from both the ground and the battlements, and they could still overrun the castle even as the drake riders fled.

***

Meat.

The Stonemaster mouthed the word slowly, feeling as though he had too many teeth. The motion of his jaw felt blocked by a too-small face and his chest burned. His limbs felt too long and spindly to be of any worth. He twitched and felt bones grind under his skin.

Meat. Despite the pain, his hunger left him with an all-consuming need for meat. Something swirled around in his stomach like live snakes, and the need was a palpable thing. It all but threatened him with agony if he tried to ignore it. He groaned and heard the rumbling, rasping thing that might now be his voice. What had happened to him?

Beastwarper? It had something to do with that chieftain. He flipped over to his stomach and felt something on his chest poking into the earth. He stared down and found horns of bone protruding from his skin. The melted remains of his silver chest plate laid nearby, and he remembered.

Beastwarper had done this to him. Fool and traitor! He gazed around, and empty pens remained where the bat-lizards once were. The Skyfang cut their losses, and Beastwarper could be sitting on his chair this very moment, commanding his horde, even as he laid here on his hands and knees!

He staggered to his feet. His legs felt like twigs, but despite his uncertain sense of balance, he did not fall again. He shambled over to his staff and with great pain, lifted it from the ground to lean upon it.

Whatever else, Beastwarper found it useless. Since the human that traded it to the Stonemaster gave him the only thing that let him use it, that worthless betrayer was correct.

"Chief of–" One of the rabble staring at the empty pens saw him rise and gasped.

The Stonemaster smiled when he noticed the rock behind him and before he could stop himself, willed the staff to act. A single impaling spike struck the rabble through the back, lifted him from the ground, and extended until the twitching victim was no more than an arm's length from the warlord. The Stonemaster lunged forward and sank his teeth into his meal.

He felt something erupt from his guts and punch downward into the rabble through his mouth. The sensation was euphoric. Meat! He fed until the corpse in his grip felt like old leather, desiccated and withered. He left it impaled to the stone spike, little remaining of it but skin and bones.

The sense of frailty fled his limbs, as though his muscles returned upon being fed. Reddened, blurry vision cleared to see the darkened hues of night time and the torrents of light. He stood straight backed and felt more alive than when he rose. Perhaps whatever the Beastwarper had used on him was meant to kill him, but it had failed utterly.

The Stonemaster leered, again feeling too many teeth in his mouth. This was the proof that he possessed true greatness! Whatever struck him unleashed something more–something that needed to feed in order to emerge. That something made him stronger.

He would add Beastwarper to the feast. Perhaps even one of the Bonestrippers. Such things would provide much for his transformation. Feeling that his time was short and watching the horde's attack disintegrate before him, he staggered into the light towards his bone chair. No, he was not merely a Chief of Chieftains any longer. He was the Stonemaster, Hordemaker and Prophet of the Fiend!

Seventeen

Pencheval scrambled for the barbican's entry. Dozens of soldiers rushed from it to reinforce the line on the wall, and a nearby sergeant roared orders to his men. The goblins all but flowed over the battlements and their sinister faces were everywhere.

The Lion took stock of the courtyard and recoiled. One of the large goblin brutes either scattered or struck dead anyone within its reach. When it smote a knight, it nearly struck him to his knees despite the invocation of Athesiene's might. Though it was near the barbican's exit doors in the courtyard, descending to meet it there was out of the question. If the guards had any sense, they would have barricaded the doors, and to dislodge the blockage would open both the eastern wall and Nan to an assault from below.

Pencheval gritted his teeth. How then? Down the first tower on the northern wall. Pencheval rushed into the barbican. Enemies pounded on the doors below and he heard the twangs of bowstrings as archers shot through the arrowslits. The next door put him on the opposite wall, which was cluttered with dead and reinforcements battling to hold it.

He struggled through the press, dodging soldiers and attacks. He gripped his weapon in a half sword guard to kill a goblin that was about to knife its fallen victim to death. The screech and click of the horde rang from everywhere, mixing in with screams and battle cries. Reserves massed and waited their call on the north wall, and he warded the unendurable brilliance of Nan's lights from his eyes with his left arm.

Guards started as he burst into the next tower and scrambled down the stairs. He willed himself strength to tear boxes and other barricades from the door, soldiers watching in surprise but not impeding him. Path clear at last, he pushed through into a surprised mob of goblins attempting to flank the soldiers in the courtyard.

Pencheval kicked a goblin into its fellows before taking up his sword with both hands. The half-staggered group tried to push their companion away and regain their footing as he waded into the fight, striking one dead with each swing. Limbs flew, heads split, and blood once again wet his blade as he stood within a small field of corpses twenty paces from the goblin champion with the axe.

He willed power into his voice and roared. The Lion's Roar echoed from the stones and brought the immediate attention of the brute. Several broken arrows stuck from its chest, and the burns on its skin seemed less like injuries than additional menace. It returned Pencheval's challenge by baring its teeth and lifting its weapon into guard.

"Penn Cheval!"

"Step forth and die!" Pencheval motioned for it to attack with his left hand and it obliged him by charging.

The Lion put his blade into guard and waited. To countercharge was to ask for death. The axe was preternaturally sharp, and there was every reason to believe his opponent was both heavier and far more solidly built. All the rest of them had been monsters, not the least of which was the one who originally wielded that raging and unstable weapon.

He waited until it committed to a chop and then willed his magic to grant him speed. The stroke slowed to a near parody as he stepped out of the way. Not enough time to strike back at his opponent, but the blow missed wide as the giant goblin briefly wondered why he had vanished.

Pencheval smiled. Despite its aggression, its wounds were not superficial and did drag it down. That bit of information was worth his restraint. If it was prone to mistakes, he could goad more from it easily.

Pencheval nicked its right shoulder with his sword and laughed at it. The goblin bared its teeth and shivered in rage as Pencheval resumed his guard with a leer. If it was going to err, it would do so now.

The onslaught that followed left the Lion stumbling and wishing he left the taunts to Gantillion. They had served their apprenticeship together in Stonewall Pass, and the cocksure rogue could mock someone with the patience of a saint into a fatal mistake. However, most of his opponents there were human and nothing like this beast.

The brute slashed at air as Pencheval dodged, listening to the snarls and roars of its weapon. Perhaps it was erring, but its ferocity robbed him of the opportunity he needed to kill it. He wondered if he would stumble into another brute as he dodged or feel a goblin possessing just the wrong amount of fortune for his health crack of a cudgel across the backs of his knees.

Frustrated at last, his opponent stopped swinging and lunged for him. It slapped one paw around his sword wrist but sacrificed its balance to do it. Pencheval willed himself strength and pulled it forwards. As it staggered to regain its footing, Pencheval's magic granted him might once again, and he snapped an uppercut into its face.

Sharp teeth and blood flew from its mouth, and its grip around his wrist loosened. Pencheval willed himself speed, pulled his arm free, then struck downward into the goblin's skull. The blade refused to cut the bone, but left blood streaming down its face and knocked it to its knees. The next stroke fell across the back of its neck, and its head bounced away.

The harried mercenary quickly wiped his blade on its rags and sheathed it. He took up the axe and refused to let its growl unnerve him. No, its instability made no difference. What mattered was that the goblins never again gained possession of it, and the best way to prevent that in this battle was to wield it.

He roared and charged into the melee at the breach. He could nurse his regrets for losing the axe and making this possible for the horde later. The threat was far from over, as more and more of the goblin brutes harried those within.

***

Words. Yes, they were words.

The Stonemaster lurched towards the warped form of Beastwarper, swaying from one side to the other on limbs that felt too spindly. The chieftain appeared to be threatening the Allspeaker next to the warlord's bone chair. A Bonestripper stood not far from him, accompanied by several dozen goblins herding his human. His rage rose and the strain left spots before his eyes. That fool had the gall to rob him! He would...no, he would not, because of the Bonestripper.

There was no killing Beastwarper for his treachery while it protected him. It was brutal, powerful, and enticingly substantive. Delectable. A massive haunch of meat to sate his still overwhelming craving for sustenance, and by the good graces of the Fiend, it stood on rock. Beastwarper could wait until his protection died, and then the Stonemaster would punish him. Feast on his limbs first...

He shook the thought from his head and willed power into his staff. The ground split beneath the surprised Bonestripper, and it fell waist deep into the newly formed trench. Stone closed around it and pinned it into the hole, and it roared as it tried to pull itself free. Beastwarper started at the attack, then turned and gaped as he met the gaze of the Stonemaster. The shambling warlord bared his teeth at him.

"Beast. Warper." He half spat and half growled the words, unable to form them any better.

Beastwarper recoiled. "No, this cannot be. Why are you not dead?"

"Dead? What?" The Allspeaker cringed, either too frightened or oblivious as to why Beastwarper might think his master was slain.

"He is feeding! Flee with me if you wish to live!"

"Yes!" Allspeaker broke and ran without any further urging.

Beastwarper screamed at his rabble, which did not so much retreat alongside him than lift him from the ground and carry him away. The human gave the Stonemaster one horrified look and ran after them. The last of them to scramble was the rider of the Bonestripper, who squeezed from under the coverture on its back and scurried away, screaming off into the night.

The Stonemaster glared into the distance as the opportunity to avenge himself on Beastwarper fled too quickly to catch. A panicked roar reminded him of meat. One more burst of will to the staff sent a stalagmite through the lower jaw and skull of the Bonestripper, silencing it immediately. He bolted to it and sank his teeth into its collarbone. Tendrils erupted up his throat from his guts and lanced through the thick hide.

The Stonemaster gorged. It felt as though impossible amounts of meat flowed down his throat only to disappear, and it was euphoric. He felt the sensation of reconstituting limbs, and something lifted him slowly from the ground. He swore he would execute whoever disturbed him as he shifted his grip on the staff, which felt smaller in his hand every moment that passed.

Something pushed him upwards so far he dropped to his knees to keep his jaws from slipping. It was as though the thing beneath him had changed proportions. He remembered the rabble, little more than skin and bones when he was done. Perhaps that was it.

The tendrils finally slid back down his throat, and he released the Bonestripper to catch his breath. He leaned on his staff and found it oddly diminutive. Had he snapped it? No, his hand merely covered more of it. He rose and took stock of himself and found the change to his liking.

He was not as large as one of the Bloodmoon. He was larger and felt as powerful as the Bonestripper he just consumed. The staff now was little more than a slender club in one brutish hand. His legs felt as strong as stone, and teeth no longer crowded his mouth. He stood thrice as tall as any goblin he saw, and those that gazed back at him recoiled in fear.

“I am the Stonemaster, and you will obey!” The sound of his voice cut through the chatter of the horde and reduced every goblin that heard it to mewling obedience. He narrowed his eyes. He had lost two clans but the battle could yet be won. Whatever he had become was beyond the threat of revolt!

It was not a moment too soon, as he could no longer motivate the horde with the threat of Bonestrippers. The beasts at the flanks remained, but those in the rear had since fled. The others would soon realize that their clan’s chieftain had departed and that they should do the same.

But the horde would obey him again, and without question. He could prevail this night regardless of his losses. He would have to take matters into his own hands, but was that not already inevitable? Only his greatness could salvage this; greatness he possessed even after the

Beastwarper was failed by his own idiocy and treachery. All the Deepglow had accomplished was to give the warlord true power to pair with it. What harm would the humans cause him now? What goblin in the horde would dare defy him?

He rushed towards the rear of the horde, trampling any rabble in his path that failed to make way in time. If the Skyfang and Beastwarper Clans feared the humans so much, he would take all the spoils for himself. His destiny and place in the Fiend's scheme of things was far greater than even he had realized, and everything in this valley should be his alone!

***

Pencheval sank the blade of his axe into the spine of a goblin brute a heartbeat before it struck a spearman dead. The soldier scrambled to his feet, gave the Lion a quick nod, and fell back into a shield wall. The block of soldiers pointed spears in all directions, beset on all sides by the horde pressing through the breach.

Many of the knights fought in the courtyard now, glowing with the power of their god. They were small beacons in the maelstrom, fighting to prevent the brutes from breaking their defense as the soldiers skewered the dregs of the horde. The knights stood their ground, but the brute with the axe had slain no few of the order before the Lion reclaimed the weapon.

There was no time for regret. The spearmen prevented the horde from swarming the courtyard and the goblin brutes knew it. One who made it past a knight tore a shield away from a spearman before snapping his spear and smiting him to the ground in one blow. The shield wall could not stop them, and if they succeeded in breaking through the soldiers, the horde would spill through the gate like torrents of water through a collapsing dam.

Pencheval yelled and charged. The axe roared and sheared through the parry of a goblin brute, who fell to the ground without its arms or head. The snarling weapon cut flesh and bone like butter, and the wood and stone weapons it used to try and parry fared no better against it.

He was far from alone. The knights wielded the power of their god, and unlike the larger goblins, cooperated well with each other. Where the brutes focused only on their own glory, the knights thought of the soldiers, the defense, and each other.

Nor had the crossing done the goblins any good. They squinted their eyes from passing into the glare, and all wore arrows and burns, fighting first through the defense and then through the power of the Lord on High. Injured and uncooperative, they fell one after another to the knights or Pencheval as he wielded their axe.

In painful degrees, the general melee in the courtyard surrounding the spearmen lessened into pockets of resistance, and finally into goblins vainly attempting to flee through the gate. Pencheval joined four knights and trapped them in the tunnel beneath the barbican. The knights left patterns of light and shadow along the walls as they struck goblins dead or burned them to ashes.

A sergeant barked orders behind them to rally the spearman, who held the space behind them against the stragglers still loose in the courtyard. At the other end of the breach where the gate once stood, the ragged outlines of the timbers hung from their hinges in the stone. They were merely shadows in Nan's bright light, which poured through the gaps between them.

He could see and smell the ash as the goblins who were pressed forward by the mass of the horde burned to skeletons. They could neither stop nor turn, and the passage funneled them very slowly. The defense held, for now, but in the distance something tremendous rose.

He put his axe in guard and waited. The battle was not over yet.

***

The Stonemaster assessed his circumstances and leered.

The rain of burning arrows had ceased, which meant the horde was inside the cliff-walls and upon the archers. That shaman still kept those lights in the sky, but that was only to slow the onslaught now. It could only attack the horde if it could afford to let them swarm, and if the small suns still burned it could not.

Too bad Beastwarper thought to betray him before the battle finally turned. Let him have his one human. Let the Skyfang return to their chieftain empty-handed. Should either of them visit the valley again, they would make for excellent eating.

He strode towards the rear, elated by a strange new sense of proportion. The rabble were too small. The shelters were too tiny. He roared at one of them as the scurrying bug tried to flee the field, and his own vehemence surprised him. The sense of power left him exhilarated.

"Forward to the mountain-castle! Now!" The command thundered, and the rabble scrambled to obey it.

The warlord covered his eyes with one arm and struggled to see before him. He would need some proof against that, and a wicker shield was far too flimsy. He saw a rough patch of stone with weeds struggling to find purchase between its cracks. He put one hand upon it and willed his staff to do its work.

The stone sheathed his arm to the elbow and grew into a widening circle. He let it expand until it threatened to weigh even his strength beyond endurance, then rounded off the point of growth. He lifted the bulky but substantial circle of rock above him, shielding himself from arrows and light. He strode forward ponderously, as quickly as the stone's weight would allow.

"Where are you going, idiots? To the mountain-castle, or perish!"

He struck one of the rabble with his staff when he refused to move for too long, and the blow sent him flying through the air. He crashed into the wooden stakes of the humans' strange hills and did not move again.

"Obey or die!" The goblins before him turned and pressed for the mountain-castle.

The Stonemaster smiled. Nothing here would thwart him, despite the betrayals and setbacks. They were merely the price of this greater form. Once he took his rightful place as master of this valley in the mountain-castle, he would find better clans to rule than the lot that fled.

***

That thing could not be.

Pencheval saw it over the heads of all the horde. It was well illuminated by Nan's light and towered far above the rest in the distance. Perhaps it was a troll? No. A troll would not hold a gigantic round burial stone aloft against the light. It would be mewling at Nan's power and fleeing from it.

It had something in its right hand, if it could be called a hand any longer. A stick of some sort? As it approached, something black atop it shined in the light as though made of obsidian. Could that be the warlord's staff? Could that *be the warlord*?

Pencheval reeled in shock. Was it the warlord? If so, *how* was it the warlord? Not even human mages could have changed themselves so. Yet that thing desired victory so greatly it did this to itself to attain it.

He remembered his training, when his drillmasters repeatedly warned him against underestimating what an enemy would do to prevail. In previous contracts, he had seen many of them do horrible things to bystanders or their minions to escape him. Then again, would it consider what it had become a sacrifice?

The goblins before it cringed at its very attention. Wielding that kind of awe and terror would be a boon to a goblin master seeking power. Goblins cared for little else other than themselves and would obey for naught but fear of strength. A warlord with this manner of might would command obedience as no other.

Whatever it was, the lights and arrows did not slow it. Its ponderous gait would eventually see it to the walls, and what then? Did it scale them and attack Nan? Would it breach them instead as it did in Tarsun's Market? He would get to watch from within the passage through the barbican unless he could meet it somehow.

Pencheval bared his teeth. Nothing about goblins was ever easy, but this was almost worse than the drakes. The only small mercy was that there was only one warlord, and it seemed the last of the horde's ugly surprises.

***

The Stonemaster plodded forward and watched his new body as though a spectator to it.

The shield on his left arm easily weighed as much as a score of goblins and left little more than a dull ache in his shoulder. Each footstep thumped the earth, and he could feel his feet sink into it from sheer weight. Rabble seemed as a swarm of scurrying beetles now, and so much as a glance at one would send them from his path or begging for his mercy. He would thank Beastwarper for this if he ever crossed paths with him again, and then he would execute him on principle alone. One never rewarded betrayal.

His hunger, once impossible to control, grew tamer now. Nothing roiled within him, feeling as though it would burst forth of its own volition and devour whatever he saw before him. His nose was acutely sensitive and told him he was surrounded by goblins, until the hint of another meal set his stomach to growling. His feet followed the smell of their own accord to a fallen bat-lizard half-trampled by the charge of the horde.

Its wings were splayed across the earth and its head bent to an odd angle. Its forked tongue lolled out of its mouth, and its rider had since been trampled under the press. It was dead, crushed, and fresh despite it all. He wondered if he should stop to sate his hunger with it, and one last growl from his belly made the decision final.

The Stonemaster planted his staff in the earth and lifted its head by the upper jaw. Once he saw the underside of its neck, he sank his teeth into it. The first bite tore scale and skin away, exposing meat and a drizzle of blood. The second planted his teeth, and he felt the tendrils again emerge from his guts and burrow. They thrust and returned bearing partially liquefied chunks of warm meat, and once again he felt himself change.

This time, it warped his skin. He felt it thicken, and the heat of the evening dulled as it became less able to feel. The change was more sluggish now, and his hunger sated too soon. The Deepglow had run its course.

When he could feast no longer, he rose and roared. The screech overpowered all other sound around him, and those nearest him recoiled in fear. A glance showed him a scaly hide over his limbs and chest, strong and springy to the touch. He felt powerful and...complete. It was as though something within him had finally finished its task, and he had at last achieved the greatness he always knew he possessed.

He was a power unto himself, commanding strength, fear, and the stone.

He lifted his shield to block a volley of arrows, but he had grown too large for it. Some few struck his staff arm and feet, only to bounce from him like so many warm pebbles. He laughed and leered at the castle. The humans could not stop him now, and once he robbed them of their shaman, the horde would take it all.

***

At first, Pencheval believed the warlord fell under the weight of its stone shield. It stopped, dropped to a knee, and jammed its staff into the ground. Exhaustion? Injury? Had whatever dire magic it had used upon itself granted only defeat?

No, it was worse. It lifted something from the ground and sank its teeth into it. The warlord was feasting on corpses in the middle of an attack. Had it cast its way into some brutish state of mindless hunger? He wanted it to be true, that the goblin's master succumbed to spells over which it had no understanding. For a moment, he hoped, then it rose to its feet and shrieked...like a drake.

It had changed. It was mighty before, but now he noticed the gray scales, hints of red patterns playing along them. It had not fed mindlessly but to make itself stronger. Whatever else, it had become the embodiment of its own ambition. It fed on everything around it, ally and enemy alike, to grow more powerful and cared nothing for the deaths that took.

A volley of arrows fell upon it, and the shield it lifted to ward them was too small to serve. They landed along its arms and legs as well, but its newfound scales warded them as though they were dust. After laughter and a moment's pause, it took up its staff and plodded forward again. In its grip, it seemed more a scepter now.

"Athesiene's mercy, it must not reach the walls."

Pencheval's eyes narrowed at the knight's proclamation. No, it must not, and it was just that painfully simple. He had seen this warlord turn a battle before, and that was merely when its magic gave it a great body of stone. What could the warlord do as this, besides slaughter everything within reach?

Pencheval's axe snarled in his hands, and he glanced down at it. Irregular vibrations bubbled and chipped the blood upon it. Would it be enough, along with the knights, to send this horde's master to its god?

A brilliant light preceded the crack of thunder that startled all within earshot and blasted the warlord to the ground. Goblins wailed and soldiers cheered along the walls.

"Ha! The Disciple has dispatched it for...us?"

A screeching laugh rose above the goblins' chatter as the ponderous form of their warlord crested above them unharmed. It roared at the horde in a growling parody of its tongue, and they flowed towards the walls once again. Nan's attack against it was not enough, and it was beyond the reach of the axe if they remained inside the tunnel.

"We counterattack."

"Counterattack?" All four knights look at him as though he had lost all sense. "If we go out to meet it we will drown in goblins, unless the arrows or the Disciple's might slay us first."

"No, not out into the press. Just enough to keep it from the walls. No more than thirty paces from the gate."

"And we will stop it when the Disciple could not?"

When the Disciple could not? What did that matter? Nan had done enough turning the battle against the drakes, and now they were the only ones left who could defeat the warlord. He refused to whimper at his fortunes when the means to slay it was literally within his grasp.

"This axe has slain drakes and goblin champions. It will fell that warlord." His companions seemed unconvinced, and he refused to leave their obedience to the rank granted to him by Rennoute.

"Ours is not the path of ease!" Pencheval remembered the fury of his drillmasters and embraced it. "We are not perfumed and pompous courtiers, little regarded except for flattering the king. We are warriors! This is our place, and this is our hour!

"The head of that great snake of a horde is before you. If we sunder it, we strike the will to conquer from them all! Don't despair in this when victory is at hand. Avenge your fallen, and take back your valley!"

One of the knights nodded, then turned to the spearmen behind them. "You hold this breach against the horde at all costs. They do not pass this gate!"

"Aye, milord!"

The knights put their shields before them. "Glory to the Lord on High!"

"Victory over the horde!" Pencheval grasped his axe with both hands and inched towards the gate as the power of the knights incinerated goblins before them.

***

Was that what the shaman had used in the great cave?

The Stonemaster remembered hearing its thunder across the human town he captured but was unable to act against it. He was still sorting loyalists from rebels after the horde fell to disarray. In retrospect, the circumstances that caused that revolt seemed ridiculous. He would never lose so much face again, if only because of what he had become.

The blast threw him violently to the ground. After a few moments, he realized to his delight that its wrath was unable to kill him. In fact, aside from a few spots dancing before his eyes and a ring in his ears that quickly departed, he bore no wounds at all. He rose, laughed at the walls before him, and ordered his horde to continue.

He hoped Beastwarper's shaman looked down from wherever it stood on the cliff-walls and despaired. The might of its god could do no more than knock him to the dirt. When he was done, once again, making way for his horde because only he could, he would deal with that shaman. No, he would *feast on that shaman*.

And Penn Cheval? It was here at the mountain-castle. The Skyfang had seen it, and it was another long overdue for punishment. Since the humans could not smite him with anything that would do him harm, he would finally inflict it.

The Stonemaster glanced down at his feet and noticed the horde flowing around him. They were but so many bugs compared to his greatness. He had led them this far, and despite the betrayals and desertions, he would still have this place and its humans. The Snow Clan's mountain-castle would fall before him just as their town did.

***

Pencheval breathed in deeply, held the air for a few heart-beats, then exhaled. For one moment at the end, he felt all fear depart him. He repeated the sequence again slowly, and the pounding of his heart in his ears subsided. What he had to do was needful, but no less nerve wracking for it.

In this enclosed space, the grace of Athesiene wielded by the knights would incinerate all in their path. Once out of the tunnel and away from the walls, they would have to space themselves to prevent the goblins from overrunning them all. They would succeed if they stayed near the walls and that monstrosity of a warlord was otherwise occupied.

Ensuring that was his task and one he was certain he could perform. He had slain trolls in single combat and two drakes. He knew the Silver Lion's tactics against great beasts and trained in them. But they were mere animals, and trolls were notoriously stupid. This warlord had the wits to wield magic and now had preternatural size and toughness to accompany it.

He saw it lumbering forward, ponderous now. It would never return to what it once was, but did that even bother it? The chevlers, barons and lords certainly had no compunctions about betrayal, murder, and worse to gain power or simply advantage. What would that warlord care that its former form was lost? Only that it had left its weakness behind it?

Perhaps it had, and in that loss there was enough to exploit. It was a once diminutive creature suddenly rendered powerful, but it was inexperienced in that power. If nothing else, surviving Nan's spellcraft may give it a sense of invincibility it was unhealthy to possess. Then again, it may well be effectively invincible given what they could bring to bear upon it. It was already proof against spell, flame, and arrow. If he was not enough...Pencheval gritted his teeth. He had best be enough.

He and the four knights reached the ragged remains of the gate. He stepped on and over the wooden planks as they edged towards the entrance. Behind him, he could just make out the shouting of officers and sergeants as spearmen reinforced their phalanx. There remained no direction to go but forward.

At thirty paces distance from the walls, the warlord stopped and gazed straight at him. It was easily larger than the goblin riding beasts that had attacked him over the summer as he attempted to free Nan. Irregular spikes of bone and horn jutted from its chest. Where it was not covered in a thick and wrinkled hide, banded scales like a drake's protected it.

"Penn. Cheval." The words left its mouth as a combination of a reptilian hiss and a rumbling bass. He noticed two full rows of very sharp teeth, the second just behind the first.

The stone it wielded as a shield on its left arm split. It appeared to shiver apart as the portions above and below the arm crumbled away to leave nothing more than an elongated strip. It flowed to extend past the fist and taper into a short, thick blade.

The chunks that struck the ground swirled as a puddle of debris. It knelt to put its right fist into it, and the rock flowed around it to sheathe staff and hand, merging them both into a double pick of stone. Jagged blades formed over its fist, and the warlord rose and growled.

"Lord on High be with you, Lion," a knight spoke without sarcasm.

Pencheval cracked his neck. "This ends now."

He stepped forward first and narrowed his eyes. This might be a fearsome beast, but it was not some evil god. He could beat it. He could force it to expend its magic. It might be too slow to keep pace with him, or it might reveal something of itself that he could use to kill it. Those tactics had served him well in the past, and they would do so again. The Lion fought to remain focused over panic as the warlord strode forward to meet him.

Terrified or not, he refused to quit. He would keep his life, and so would all of those whom he had befriended in his time here. This nightmare and its horde had to end, even if he was ready to vomit at the sight of it from fear. Let it do its worst; they *would* end.

***

Could Penn Cheval be that foolish?

The Stonemaster felt the prickling of teeth when he grinned too widely. The Silver Lion Clan warrior stepped forth from the cliff-walls with only four of the glowing Snow Clan in their steel skins? Did it believe the horde exhausted?

No. It wanted to kill him. The four warriors in steel skins struck down or incinerated the rabble around them with burning long knives, but Penn Cheval stood where it was and struck down rabble as it awaited him. It kept glancing at him, worried that he would arrive at some inopportune time.

Was it seeking glory as the Bloodmoon did? None of the Bloodmoon Clan fought in the battle now. If they had all died seeking glory, that lesson was apparently lost on Penn Cheval. Still, if it wanted to repeat the errors of those brutes, who was he to reject the sweet and demoralizing kill it would give him?

It would have to be him alone. Goblins split like a flow of water around a rock from behind him and did their best to avoid the glowing Snow Clan warriors and Penn Cheval. As he approached, the two gaps in the line grew closer together, revealing trampled dirt and the corpses of those who fell.

He felt a feeble prick strike and then bounce from his head. Every so often he would hear a hum before another such prick struck him and fell. He chuckled as he realized they were more arrows. Let the humans waste them on his newfound skin and despair from the futility of resisting him.

They could watch as he slaughtered and feasted on their Silver Lion Clan champion and the glowing warriors. They were the only true barrier remaining between the horde and the gap in the cliff-wall. He could see human warriors behind them with spears and shields, but they gathered within the stone tunnel under one of the circular peaks and did not yet know they stood within their own graves. The power of the staff would see to it.

***

The horde parted to remain clear of their warlord's path, and Pencheval was grateful for that small measure of good fortune. He feared he might be awash in goblins despite the knights as he tried to slay their master, but their fear of it gave both that monstrosity and himself a wide berth. Its slow approach and the slaughter the four knights inflicted on its horde left him enough space to move.

He intended to use it. While he refused to will spells into the already unstable axe he held, he could still will power into himself. If the warlord was as slow and ponderous as it appeared, speed would counter being struck and make defeating its guard easy. The preternaturally sharp axe would do the rest. He was barely waist high on this fiend, but its knees were effectively unguarded, and it was about to lose one.

Pencheval stepped forward as though aiming a chop at its guts. When it raised its right arm to strike him, he willed himself speed and changed direction. The raised stone pick fell slowly, but not usefully so, wielded as a curved dagger by the warlord. For a moment, his target seemed clear, but a strange flowing in the corner of his eye convinced him to change direction again.

Three stone blades lanced through where he would have been. The beast was too slow to counter him but could make the stone do so in its stead. He staggered while dodging under magically enhanced speed and stumbled backwards as the blades flowed back into the stone wrapped around its right arm.

The warlord turned, laughed, and rumbled in its tongue. Pencheval realized he was too far from the knights when something jumped on his back and slapped a garrote under his helmet. Surprised, the Lion flailed and choked as he tried to dig his fingers between the cord and his throat.

***

The Stonemaster chuckled. Perhaps the human remembered it was in the midst of a horde now. It may have found the fortitude to face him, but it still did not speak the goblin tongue, and his horde had only grown more obedient since he had attained his destiny. His growth into this magnificent thing could be nothing less than the will of the Fiend.

He remembered that the human was swift; swift enough to trick him into tearing a cliff-wall from under his own feet in the human town. It was too swift for his ponderous strength but not for the power of the staff. Though he was unable to punish it personally, it stumbled into the horde dodging him. There the rabble could swarm it without him, for one of the glowing humans in its steel skin advanced to meet him.

It wielded the same manner of burning big knife as the glowing under-chieftain had in the human town and struck at him with it. He caught the blow with the stone on his left arm. It was uncomfortably hot, and smoke wisped from his skin as the big knife slowly melted through the rock. He roared and punched downwards with his other fist. No, he would not burn here, and this one would meet the same fate as the other.

It raised its shield to ward the blow. An undulating white light radiated just above it at the point of inpact, rippling like the waves from a stone cast into still water. It buckled under the force, unable to press its attack. The Stonemaster leered. If one hit left it desperate to defend, what would a storm of blows do?

He struck with his left fist. The stone blade snapped on contact with the strange white light, but the Snow Clan warrior staggered. Another right sent it to one knee, and another left to its back. He raised his foot to finish it when he heard a snarl from behind him and felt something bite into the back of his thigh. He roared and snapped around to find Pencheval gasping but ready to do battle.

***

Pencheval coughed and rubbed his throat. That damnable cord around his neck felt like greeting death itself. At least the haste of that goblin to strangle him left its hands too close to his shoulders. When his fingers would not slip between the cord and his neck, he clutched one of its fists and crushed it with a burst of magically enhanced strength. The axe did the rest before it finished screeching from the pain.

When the warlord spoke, he should assume it commanded something behind him. That lesson was nearly fatal for him and the knight he only just rescued. At least the axe found its mark. It could hurt that monster and bit deeply enough to draw it back to him.

It limped slightly as it circled him. It was no more eager to keep its back to the knights than he was to keep his back to the horde. They kept their eyes on each other as they wheeled, and Pencheval heard the hum of arrows as archers on the walls felled the goblins near him.

He cleared his throat and spat, annoyed by his circumstances. The axe would do its work, but he had no room maneuver around or behind it. Its whole horde protected its back if he tried.

***

The Stonemaster glanced at his left arm. The stone around it was half-melted and its blade had snapped. If it was useless for either blocking or attacking, the dead weight could be put to better use. That axe had left him limping, and he refused to carry anything that served no purpose to him.

He pointed the arm at Penn Cheval and willed his staff to command the stone. The rock around it flowed, coiled, and then leapt like a striking snake, oversized stone jaws filled with jagged teeth. The dark warrior flowed from its path with its strange speed, and the improvised attack crumbled to rubble upon striking dirt.

A glimmer of light from his left caught his attention. One of the human warriors in the steel skins raised its burning big knife to strike at him. He flinched, and then willed power into his staff as it stepped upon a rock. The stone snapped upwards like a trap and congealed over one foot. The grasping rock broke its charge, and the Stonemaster raised his other fist to crush it.

The blow descended on its shield, and it nearly fell to one knee as the gleaming ripple repelled it. He pressed until he heard a snarl, and turned to counter the attack he already expected from Penn Cheval. The dark warrior was strong but predictably aggressive if it believed it had an opening.

He twisted just enough to catch the blow on the stone of his right fist. The Silver Lion Clan warrior's axe squealed as chips and dust flew from the impact. The warlord willed his staff to command the stone on his right arm, and it poured from his hand and leapt as a wave at Penn Cheval. It wrapped around the dark warrior, half-covering it in the flow before congealing again. It staggered under the weight and fell to the ground.

He shrieked in triumph. He had hoped to torture it, but this was far better. With that fell human helplessly pinned and his newfound size, he could crush it underfoot. What better way to defeat the spirit of the humans here than to kill their champion as though it was a worm?

First, the glowing warriors. They would not simply stand by as he did it, unless there was nothing else they could do. Best to deal with them now, as Penn Cheval would await him imprisoned whether it chose to do so or not.

***

Pencheval willed magic into his limbs and twisted himself in all directions. Every move resulted in another crack of the stone encasing him, until he could once again breathe. He drew a deep breath and coughed. Had that stone wave splashed a little higher, it would have covered his nose and mouth.

It laid upon him like a heavy blanket, forcing him to the ground. It pinned his arms in an odd pose, and left the goblin champion's axe buzzing out of reach. He willed himself another burst of strength and strained, shivering his muscles into spasms as the stone crumbled and bent all too slightly.

Why had it not finished him yet? Were the knights buying him time? It would make short work of them with its newfound size if it was the same warlord that attacked the walls in Tarsun's Market. Pencheval willed himself strength once again, enough to crack his left forearm from its bonds.

At least it was not using magecraft. Those spells were spectacularly powerful and accompanied by much ritual. Was it then an adept like himself? One who stood between those unable to use any magic at all and true mages? Its power over stone matched nothing he had ever seen from the goblins. So how did it attain such a thing?

It had found it. That was why even now, as a troll-sized goblin demigod, it refused to drop its staff. That was the source of its ability over stone, and without it? It was still a powerful foe, but it would be unable to defend itself from the axe.

He heard a scream and the irregular thumping footsteps of a staggered giant. He took a deep breath and willed himself a steady flow of strength. Pushing back the memories of the pain using such long bursts of magic would cause him, he twisted, thrashed, and pulled. Muscles felt as though they would pull from bone and joints ached to rest, but the stone cocoon cracked and crumbled until he could rise from its pieces.

He snatched up his axe and gasped. A long stalagmite impaled one of the knights and left him twitching in midair. His sword lay near him, no longer blazing with the light of Athesiene's power. One remained pinned where he had tried to rescue him, and the other two were small islands of light far on the flanks, fighting for their lives.

The warlord held its left hand to its head, stumbling around as though drunk. Had the knight done something to it? He saw no wounds on it so grievous they would stagger that beast with loss of blood.

No. Nan had tried to stop it again, likely in response to the death of the knight. The spell did not fell it, but was enough to buy him time. He gritted his teeth, yelled, and willed his magic to give him speed until he felt it begin to burn him from within. The world slowed to a crawl, including the warlord. He charged and leapt at his target.

***

Fiend-blighted wretch! The Stonemaster snapped from his daze as a dark blur struck at his right arm. It flew through the air and slashed his forearm before landing and revealing itself to be Penn Cheval. One more cut he could not afford.

The dark warrior was too swift to stop. The Stonemaster had the might, but not the speed, which had been the case in Tarsun's Market. At least this form was strong enough to endure.

He willed power into his staff and commanded it to pin Penn Cheval as he had done to one of the glowing warrior-shamans. Though he stood on stone, nothing happened. He glanced at his right hand to see what was wrong, and saw nothing beyond a stump. To his horror, he realized that his hand laid on the ground, still grasping his staff.

A dark blur charged towards him, and he raised one fist to strike it. By the time he was ready nothing more remained of his target than a gushing wound in his left leg. Penn Cheval spun in a blur of black and weathered metal, and he felt the crack across his right knee. Unable to stand, he fell with a crash onto his back.

His last thought in the hail of stings that followed was that this was the work of the Fiend. He had grown so great and mighty he had provoked the wrath of his own god. The Fiend's jealousy alone led him to this end, and what a master goblinkind would lose in him.

***

Down at last!

Pencheval restrained his sense of triumph as the warlord fell. How long would its shock last? How long would its horde hesitate? Believing he only had moments to finish his work, Pencheval hefted his axe and struck at anything he thought might be fatal. One blow slashed the groin. Another opened the guts. When he reached its chest, he savagely hacked into the ribs and heart until the warlord did not so much as twitch.

Would its horde avenge it, or had he finally struck the will from them as he had planned? Naught of it assailed him. Instead, he saw a mob of cringing, flinching goblins terrified at his gaze as the body fell flat.

He roared at the top of his lungs and let his magic flow into it. "Which of you is next? Your gods await you!"

A panicked screech arose from those closest to him and cascaded back through the horde. He understood nothing they said, but the charge fell into disarray. Goblins fled in all directions, crashing and trampling into one another as those nearer the edges or rear made a better retreat. Storms of burning arrows fell into their midst, and others near the walls dropped as though suddenly asleep.

"We have done our part, Lion." A knight joined him, dented armor clanking. "The rest we leave to the archers."

Pencheval nodded before he stretched and winced from the pain. The magic would take its toll on him soon. A few hours at most, but they would all benefit from his victory for the time being.

He never in his life expected to fight alongside the knights of Athesiene, much less in such circumstances as these. A year ago, he would have found even the thought of cooperating with them, much less avenging them, utterly ludicrous. Likely they found it almost as unthinkable to fight alongside a Silver Lion.

His grabbed his right shoulder after a stabbing pain. He could wax philosophical later. For now, it was time to defend the breach. This battle ended when he saw no more of the horde and not a moment before.

Eighteen

Pencheval squinted at the first signs of blue and the glimmers of dawn behind the eastern mountains. The sight accompanied a stillness he found hard to believe. Aside from the indistinct sounds of soldiers above him on the walls, naught remained but the cawing of crows and the first birds of dawn. The absence of the horde's cacophony seemed less than real to him, but gave him no small relief.

He enjoyed the triumph wanly. Pushing himself and his magic to its limits left him sore and barely standing. The axe that had slain the warlord was wrapped in the rags of the nearest goblin corpse, silent and stable once again. His celebration would be bed rest, and he welcomed it.

The battlefield slowly revealed itself as light crept over the mountains. The impaled knight remained, and the corpse of the warlord laid where it fell. It bore the wounds of his desperate attempt to defeat it once and for all and its dried blood painted it black.

The earthworks and battlefield were a sea of corpses. Arrows stuck from goblins and blackened circles remained where Nan blasted those as they charged. He heard one thud, and then an irregular beat of them as the soldiers tossed the bodies of goblins from the walls.

All that remained of the horde fled to the hills, and he remembered the cowardice the goblins showed him time and again. Without a warlord to lead them, they would neither reunite into such a force nor return as single clans to contest the valley with the temple. They knew what awaited them if they did, and their rout was decisive enough to guarantee their absence from the Emerald Refuge for a long time to come.

"Glory to the Lord on High. We have won." The knight beside him sounded as weary as he felt.

Pencheval smiled weakly. Yes, it was a victory. A sore and weary victory, but enough to see himself and those he meant to save to the end of this short war.

***

"Disciple?"

Nan started awake and momentarily wondered where she was. She could see the dawn clearly, and no walls surrounded her. Two of Rennoute's knights faced her, and the closer of them had removed his helmet and coif. Sweat matted his short hair, and he smiled at her.

"Brother? Where are we?"

"We stand on the barbican still, Disciple. You fell asleep shortly after the rout."

"The rout?"

"We defeated the horde, Disciple. Those who escaped our arrows scattered to the winds. They will fear even the thought of waging war upon us again. We are victorious."

Nan rubbed her eyes and felt stiffness in her legs. Asleep on her feet? She tentatively approached the edge of the battlements and gasped at the field below.

Thousands of goblin bodies carpeted the earthworks below the town. The sprawled corpse of one drake sat prominently within them, and the gigantic corpse of something she could not defeat laid too close to the walls. But it was the absence of sound that most convinced her of victory's reality.

The grating screech and click was gone. Wholly, gloriously gone. Officers yelled orders on the walls to either side. Wagon wheels squeaked and clacked across the courtyard. Soldiers gave thanks in prayer to the Lord on High. Compared to the cacophony of the horde, all was chimes and dulcet tones, and it was magnificent.

"Lord on High be praised. He has delivered us this day."

"Glory to the Lord on High, Disciple."

Nan's eyes darted over the field. "Pencheval. Where is Pencheval?"

"The Lion, Disciple? Last report was that he slew the horde's master and returned to the breach. We know no more of him."

"Can we find him now?" Nan felt her stomach drop at the uncertainty.

"Disciple, soldiers and healers aid the wounded below. They will learn much about our forces soon."

"Soldiers below?" Of course they were below. There was still much to do. Recovering from this would be at least as great a task as defeating the horde. "No, I won't leave that to the soldiers below. To the courtyard, brothers."

"Disciple, you have wielded Athesiene's might most of this battle. You should rest."

Nan smiled at the knight and shook her head. No, she should not rest. She had duties to attend. Duties and responsibilities she could properly attend now that war no longer called upon her.

She had wielded the Lord on High's power in the battle, so much so that it no longer felt like an exertion or a disaster awaiting to its chance to happen. She saw it more as a trusted ally ready to come to her aid. The days when it felt as a great reservoir of power cracking the dam that was her will, ready to overwhelm her and everything near her, seemed far into the past.

It would serve another purpose in the days to come. These people needed her help, and she could give it to them. They did all they could for her, misguided as some of it was. It was time to fulfil her role as the Disciple, and despite the fatigue, she no longer doubted that she could.

"I serve, brother, and my work is just begun."

***

Wishing he could go to his chambers and sleep for a day, Pencheval trudged from the barbican towards something atop a platform in the distance. It was the most prominent fixture in the loosely organized mess that was once the horde's little used encampment. A knight watched him leave, surprised, and he could all but feel the shock of those on the walls. No one with sense would do anything in that field of corpses but bury or burn them.

He spared both them and himself the effort of an explanation. None of them knew the inner workings of his guild. They knew its reputation as the home of brutal and deadly mercenary champions, but that told them very little. Its masters were strict and very particular on one point, and after his service to the temple during this war, they would settle for nothing less than getting it.

It was the one inflexible, unquestioned tenet of his guild: payment. They did not tolerate its absence or the failures of their adepts to garner it. As things stood now, they would find what he currently had to offer them woefully inadequate.

At first glance, the goblin encampment revealed nothing beyond their impoverishment. A swarm of tiny feet had crushed all the grass and churned it into the mud. Wicker scraps and primitive foodstuffs scattered in a way that confirmed the night's retreat. All the remained untouched was a platform, upon which sat a strange bone throne topped by a pair of elk horns.

"Can't imagine what you expect to find, Lion."

Pencheval did not turn at Howe's appearance. "Something to retain the good graces of my guild."

"The good graces of...why is that even in question? You were the straw that broke the back of a goblin horde. They fled for the hills the second you ended their master. Your heroism reflects on them, and the temple will pay them much coin in the future for what you have done here. What more would they want from you than that?"

"Payment, Howe." Pencheval ceased his searching. "They will want payment. They make no exceptions on that point. Ever. Even the king pays them for their services, if only in publicly declared patronage."

"Madness. But if such is not avoidable, the box beneath the bone chair might contain something."

"What box?"

"The one some fool goblin thought it concealed behind those bones stacked at the foot of it. Doesn't make sense to pile loose bones in front of a chair unless you're hiding something." Howe pointed at the bone throne. "Enough to fool its horde, but a sad attempt at concealment nonetheless."

"I won't doubt those hawk's eyes of yours, Howe."

"Nor should you. But you best get to your spoils soon. It doesn't take much thinking to deduce why a Lion's in the goblin camp."

Pencheval climbed the platform and took a better look. The ornate skull topping the chair was not a fabricated decoration aside from the symbol carved into its forehead. Whatever horrific beast had once owned it left nothing but the blackness of its eye sockets and a pair of spiraling, weathered horns. Skulls decorated what appeared to be the sharpened and shortened roots and branches of a carved out stump, and the pile before it hid anything that might appear to be a shelf or a box.

Howe was correct, though. The bones seemed piled, but when he tried to move one, they resisted him. He grabbed with both hands and pulled harder. Several skulls bounded down the sides, but one in particular bounced in place as the whole front of the chair pulled forwards, revealing a sizeable shelf. The relieved Lion took stock of its contents as Howe peered over his shoulder.

"There's a few baubles for your guild." Howe whistled. "Don't think his lordship will begrudge them to you."

Pencheval blinked twice, and then smiled.

The coins in the bottom were gold, but trivial. They bore the markings of several kingdoms, including some he did not recognize. Not only were their edges rough, as though painstakingly forged or filed, but they bore runes and symbols of hammers. Perhaps it was the crest of some royal house long lost?

A single, silvered helmet laid among them. Two thick and angular representations of wings decorated its sides, and its nose guard was as thick as his thumb. It was an artful but overly sturdy thing of rivets, silver, and masterful smithing, meant for a head much wider than his own. When he lifted it, its weight surprised him, for it was far heavier than either his old bascinet or his current barbute.

Beneath it, a gold medallion set with a single large ruby surrounded in diamonds wrapped around an empty bottle. It nestled within the links next to a silver belt buckle and a smattering of sapphires. Its shape seemed vaguely familiar.

He pulled it out to examine it in the light. Howe snorted.

"That empty bottle will satisfy them for sure," the scout joked. "You can just leave the rest here with me."

"No." Pencheval turned the bottle in his hands to get a closer look. The dried remains of its contents clung to the bottom in clotted strands and a blotch of red.

"Well, obviously I didn't mean it."

"No, it couldn't be that." Pencheval pulled the crystal stopper and smelled the contents; hints of a cloying sweetness, cinnamon, and the last of a sharp stench cut through his nostrils. Its owner had long since drunk the rest, but enough remained to identify it. He snarled and gripped the bottle so tightly it threatened to crack.

"Peddler! How did he get this to the goblins?"

"Peddler? What?" Howe backed away. "Could you perhaps make more sense?"

"I've crossed paths with the one who sells this." He showed Howe the empty bottle. "He used a different name each time I saw him, so we call him Peddler. He's a dangerous brewer of potions with a tongue of silver. This particular brew was something he named The Potion of Dreams, a name that made it easy to sell to fools."

"And what does this 'Potion of Dreams' do?"

"It turns men into monsters, after a fashion. It makes them preternaturally dangerous and ambitious beyond all reason. Twice before I have seen its effects, and twice before the drinkers forced me to kill them. Those under its influence make fell opponents and ideal agents of chaos."

"Then you think he sold one of these to the horde's master? Why?"

"Perhaps it had something he wanted. Perhaps he has a master that governs his actions, for he couldn't have made it to the goblins without aid. Whatever it is, I will warn the Knight Superior. If he does appear here, don't suffer either his presence or his life. The temple is now among those that owe him for his treachery."

***

Rennoute watched the flight of pigeons from the window of his study as his two pages released their messages into the air. Under any other circumstances it would have been an inappropriate and mundane task the morning after a battle. For the Knight Superior, the sounds of their cooing and the feathery flap of wings were another spoil in this war.

He had long since written the messages they carried, in the darker hours of the drake attacks, to give himself the hope that he could send them once the horde fell or scattered. They were messages of victory and the calling on promises of aid he received. He smiled as he watched every one of those words take wing to their destinations. Living to send them was a triumph second only to defeating the goblins.

Much still awaited his attention. The fallen in the field would rot soon, and the only habitable building in the valley now was next to that field of flies and crows. Perhaps the Disciple could assist him with that, but the mass graves and burials were of immediate concern. He would be driven from his own castle otherwise.

After that was a question of food, shelter, and repairs. The bowl of the steel beacon still laid where it fell through a roof from the top of his keep. They had since stripped the drake to the bones for meat, and sent its hide to a tanner, but the damage remained. There had been no opportunity to repair any of it during this short war.

And as for the Lion? When he first met Pencheval, he was a necessary evil. An abrasive mercenary from a hostile guild who for some reason found himself in the Emerald Refuge. Since then, that mercenary had proven himself a dozen times over, not the least of which for his part in rescuing the Disciple.

His presence was the work of the Lord on High, though the growling Lion would be the last to accept that. He had proven far too timely, and his knowledge of the enemy too useful, for him to be anything but Athesiene providing for His faithful. There was no need to belabor that point with him. That task he would leave to the Disciple's chronicler, should one ever seek him out so as to record his story for The Histories.

A formal scroll bearing his regards and compliments to Pencheval's guildmaster was due, if not a letter of introduction itself. Nothing he had heard of that guild led him to believe they would be kind to Pencheval if he returned empty handed. With nothing else to spare but more drake hide, it would have to be enough.

Rennoute returned to his desk and took a quill from his inkwell. First the introduction, then on to more pressing concerns. Their worries had not ended by far, but at least they were still alive to worry.

***

"Have you ever seen such a thing?"

Howe shook his head as Pencheval and he both examined the giant corpse of the goblin warlord. Pencheval was certain whatever had happened to it had something to do with Peddler's work. Something horrific always emerged when that hedge alchemist was involved, and this was no exception.

He had outdone himself with this monster. Cheeks split in its elongated face to reveal both rows of pointed teeth. He could see in its hide the bone plates of the goblin riding beasts, the scales of the drakes, and misshapen but powerful muscles. Bone horns jutted out of its chest in odd places, seeming to radiate around some central point for no real reason.

"No. Even mages avoid changing themselves so. If the words of my masters in spellcraft are true, one must cast to change, and then cast again to undo it. The risk of failing to return to their former selves is too great for even the most arrogant of mages."

"And how did it resist the Disciple?"

"Magic doesn't like to go where magic already flows, or so the rule of thumb went in the lectures. This warlord had so much of it already, it shrugged off much else. Perhaps that is why their champions also avoided incinerating as they should."

Howe spat. "Filthy blighter won't be making any more hordes, anyway."

"Truly," Pencheval agreed. "It must take a rare strength in a goblin leader to forge such a thing."

"Nothing left now but to clean up its mess and be grateful for our lives, thanks in no small part to you."

Pencheval nodded. Yes, he did have cause to celebrate. He had saved Nan and his allies here at the castle. He lived through a battle after yet another desperate gamble. And despite all odds, he had fallen into a fair bit of treasure. Perhaps he might even keep some of it, should his guild not find his recompense wanting.

He hefted the box under his arm. Stuffing rags into the hollow concealed its contents, and striking the bones from it made it far easier to carry. It was little more than a hollowed block of wood, but it would suffice long enough to get to his chambers.

Howe glanced up at the walls. "Someone's addressing the army."

Pencheval heard nothing but trusted the unusually perceptive scout. "What is it?"

"Nothing I can hear from this side, but all inside listen. Time we did as well."

The words became audible as they walked through the shattered gate of the barbican and intelligible as they exited into the courtyard.

Father Victor stood at the left hand of the Knight Superior on the southern wall, leading the assembled in prayer. Nan stood to the right of the valley's lord, head bowed, as Victor gave thanks to the Lord on High for them all. Howe bowed his head, and Pencheval stood respectfully as they finished.

Yes, the Lord on High stood with his faithful. Nan and the power of the knights in His order turned the tide. They had also prevailed because they refused defeat when it was offered time and again. So yes, it was good to give thanks where it was due, but they should not forget the parts they played.

Father Victor lifted his head and briefly stopped speaking as he noticed Pencheval, distaste evident. Nan beamed when she saw him, and Pencheval waved wearily as she did. He would have stayed for the rest of it, if only out of courtesy, but a few too many of those in the courtyard noticed of the box under his arm. Given that his guild was both famed and notorious for mercenary work, realizing what might be in it took little sense.

He nodded respectfully at the Knight Superior and strode towards the keep while Howe remained. There was no point in giving those around him time to wonder if he was too weary to defend himself. He had enough trouble with his guild as it was without suffering banditry.

***

"Is it the same as when you first arrived, Lion?"

Pencheval snorted at the question from Friar Dominik. Was it the same? Of course not, though he stood to watch the clouds pass over the castle from one of the towers. 'Seeking counsel from the clouds' the friar had called it. Now that the battle and its aftermath were days behind him, he had the time to do it again. Only now, he had fewer questions and more answers.

"Very little is the same, friar."

"That much is true, I think," Dominik replied. "You are not the Hopeslayer any longer. You are Pencheval the Hordebreaker, and guide of a Disciple. These are deeds to outshine any of the dark paths in your past."

Pencheval gave him a wry grin. Yes, he supposed they were. Something more to add to his reputation, but far from compensation for what he lost.

"And what of you, friar? Does the Disciple's presence yet overwhelm you and all others?"

"I'm almost embarrassed to look back upon that," Dominik answered sheepishly. "But to live in the time of a Disciple! To have seen one rise..."

"Nan, Dominik. Still Nan, if no longer just Nan."

"In the end, your particular view of her may have been what she most needed. Your presence here was nothing short of Athesiene's grace itself."

"I came for the respite." Pencheval shook his head. "Just my luck that it fled before the horde."

The creak of hinges announced the opening trapdoor, and a page emerged. The boy rose to his full height, searched his belt for his pouch, and produced a small roll of parchment.

"Message for you, Lion. It arrived by pigeon today."

Pencheval took the note. "My thanks."

"Well?"

"When I find a scribe, I'll know." Pencheval slipped the tie loose on a pouch.

"If you mean to improve yourself, Lion, learning to read would be your next task. Until then, I would be happy to read it for you."

Pencheval shrugged and handed him the message. "I've gotten along without it so far."

"Most cannot read, true. Yet it opens doors most never will." Dominik unrolled the message and moved it forward and back from his eyes, squinting.

"'Journeyman adept. You are summoned to declare your fifth and make your report of the Emerald Refuge before the first snows of winter. Return or we will find you. Bountymaster Guilliam.' Bountymaster Guilliam?"

"One of the guildmaster's officers," Pencheval answered. "His task is to ensure that coin always flows into the guild. It seems he has found my presence here unacceptable."

"Unaccep...what?" Dominik's eyes widened. "What is there to find unacceptable? You broke the will of a horde! Yours is the sort of heroism found only in the songs of minstrels!"

Pencheval grimaced at the suggestion he was a hero. "The guild doesn't train heroes, or so they repeatedly told me. They will once again make that plain on my return, though it should amount to little more than shouting with what news and treasure I bring them. There is no avoiding it."

"They would reprimand you for such feats of arms and courage as yours? Small wonder you came here for respite."

Pencheval took the note from the friar and stuffed it in the pouch on his belt. "My vocation has tracked me to ground again. It is high time I returned to it."

He felt his heart sink. He had found new allies and a restored sense of purpose since he arrived, as fell as the horde had been. The reunion with Nan, and her acceptance of what he had done to the Hope of Terris Lyn, took more of a burden from him than he realized he carried. It was much, and though he wished it would last he already knew otherwise. Guild membership was for life, and they did not tolerate indolent adepts.

Out with the first caravan and back to the capital then. He despised visiting that glittering cesspit, but if he was to find Peddler and placate his guild, there was no avoiding it. All roads in Lerrisaine led there sooner or later.

***

In the month it took the first caravan to arrive at the Shield of Athesiene, Pencheval finally found his respite.

After a spring and summer living under threat of goblins, boredom and common tasks seemed a luxury. He spent the days in recuperation and repair. The goblin's axe remained safely in its wrappings under the bed in his chambers, and he happily left it there. The time in the mess hall saw fewer desperate faces and more merely annoyed with their labors, grumbles replacing barely contained fear and strain.

All around him he heard sawing, hammering, and complaints of those at work as they repaired the castle. The rush to be rid of goblin corpses and the pestilence they would bring passed. It became the half-constructed frames of buildings as the town at the base of the castle also rose anew. The efforts were considerable, and certain to restore their shelter by winter.

He worried less about Nan than she did about him. She was rarely in the chapel now, though always accompanied by a bodyguard of knights. He would find her in the courtyard or the town, bolstering spirits as she could, and never once heard mention of witchcraft from either the folk or the soldiers. She had risen to the challenge of her new powers, and bore them with a mix of confidence and quiet strength.

It was almost routine when they finally arrived. A train of ten wagons, accompanied by enough warriors to dissuade bandits, clopped up to the Shield of Athesiene mid-morning. A knight walked out to meet them, making introductions and haggling with them.

It would be his time to do that soon, and he found that he would miss this place. Still, it was not home despite an old friend and new allies. It was just somewhere he had done remarkable things, not the least of which was remember there was more to him than what he thought he had to be.

Greater deeds eclipsed the empty notoriety of the Hopeslayer. In its place was a sense of purpose beyond taking contracts and garnering payment. His vocation could mean something more, and it did here.

He had stood against a horde twice to save an old friend. He found some small sense of community again with Howe and Dominik. In the past month, many glanced at him now with respect and a few with undisguised awe where once they gave him only nervous regard. All was not futile and wasted, and that was the answer he sought, even though he never knew it was the question.

Yes, it was time to say his farewells and go, as more such purpose awaited him with Peddler. One of those goodbyes was to his former self. Something far better had replaced him.

***

"The Lion requests an audience, Your Grace."

Rennoute glanced at the Disciple, who nodded and smiled. The mercenary's timing was impeccable, and perhaps he might persuade her to do something needful.

"Let him enter, soldier."

"Yes, Your Grace."

The soldier opened the door and gestured, and Pencheval strode to the desk, medallion in hand. It dangled as a pendulum in his left fist.

He noticed the Disciple and nodded. “Nan?”

“Good day, Pencheval. You should find our conversation... familiar.”

Pencheval scratched his head. “Your Grace?”

“I am right glad you have taken this moment to join us. All news says you return to the capital, and I would like for you to escort Nan to Saint Marion’s cathedral there.”

“Nan?”

“Yes.” Nan chuckled. “At least the Knight Superior uses my name again. But it changes little, Your Grace. Winter comes, and this valley is in ruins. The survivors need me here.”

“Much has changed, Disciple. The capital has word of you now, and no such thing as a risen Disciple remains secret. Accompany the Lion there. If you stay, we cannot protect you or even feed you. They can protect you, train you, and begin your chronicle in The Histories. Become what the Lord on High intended.”

“I was chosen to be who I am, Your Grace,” Nan countered. “At no point was I ever anything else, and granted this power regardless. Therefore, I will continue to be who I am, for such is His will. I won’t abandon you to starve and freeze when there is much I can do to prevent it. My service is of consequence, not my glory and protection.”

“The temple needs you, sister.”

“It does,” Nan agreed. “Right here.”

“And you, Lion? Surely you can lend some credence to what I say.”

“She spoke truly, Your Grace. This conversation is familiar to me.” Pencheval placed the bronze medallion Rennoute gave him on his desk. “I spoke similar words to her in Tarsun’s Market, to no avail. If she says she won’t go, there is no changing her mind. A whole goblin horde couldn’t do it.”

“Some things were worth more than my life, Pencheval. Surely you understand this now, or you wouldn’t have fought the horde beside us.”

Rennoute thought quietly on that point. The Disciple was correct. He remembered summoning him for that contract offer in the early spring. The Silver Lion seemed more a brigand in a tabard than a mercenary and only took the contract out of boredom.

Now, he wore every inch of the battles he had fought during his time here. The dark and too rich tabard was all but rags, and his demeanor less aloof and abrasive. True that he had availed himself of the goblin horde’s treasures, but that much concerned Rennoute little. The Lion had his own masters to appease, and he had more than earned whatever he found.

"If nothing else, Lion, your valor and daring are the stuff of legends." Rennoute reached into his desk and drew forth a sealed scroll. "However, what I know of your guild informs my belief that they will conclude differently. Give them this letter of introduction. Perhaps a new source of coin will dull any wrath they may have with you."

"That is kind of Your Grace." Pencheval took the scroll. "If you deal with them, don't do so by my example. If you wish for the aid of any other Silver Lions, they will want coin and without fail."

"Of that I have no doubt." Rennoute nodded. "And we will be wary of this 'Peddler' you described to our scout."

"If you believe nothing else I ever tell you, Your Grace, slay that one the moment you find him, or he will cause you mischief like no other."

"If he was responsible for the warlord in that horde as you suspect, I require no further persuasion on that point."

"We will meet again soon, Pencheval." Nan put her hand on his shoulder. "The Lord on High be with you. We have parted company too often through all of this, but I'm glad to have found you again."

"The next time we meet, Nan, I hope it is under better circumstances." Pencheval gave her a wry grin. "For now, I must arrange my passage on that caravan. My guild's patience is not extensive."

"You may go, Lion. It has been an honor to battle beside you."

***

Pencheval inspected his treasures one last time before two of the caravan's laborers packed their rations over it. The goblin champion's axe was wrapped in cloth and appeared as little more than a common package tied in twine. The packed the treasure of the horde's warlord within his backpack, below the gear he thought he might need, and padded it well with cloth so no one would suspect its true nature.

Bartering passage on the caravan took no time at all. He offered the services of his blade in exchange for free passage to the capital, and its pleasantly surprised master immediately accepted. Wagons still bulging with goods spoke of a merchant, and this one was perfectly happy to have a Lion dissuading bandits and brigands.

It was well into morning, and the sun long since dried the first dew Pencheval saw this season. A spattering of yellow leaves appeared on one of the trees in the distance, and an early morning chill warned him of autumn.

"What awaits you ahead, Lion?" Friar Dominik waited by the caravan but had no bags of his own. He, like Nan, intended to remain.

"At the capital? Some explanations due and the Peddler, should I be so fortunate as to find him. Naught of any real trouble, however much I hate that city. And you?"

“They need my assistance here. I have the same duties as the Disciple, and I am glad she hasn’t forgotten them now that she has ascended.”

“Nan, Dominik. Remember, she is still Nan.”

“And you remember what you learned here. You aren’t the same man I met this spring. Keep the light of the Lord on High with you now that He has shown you the way to defeat your demons.”

Pencheval snorted. “Still at it.”

“We never stop, Lion. Surely you understand this by now.”

“It will never fail to surprise me.” Pencheval held out his hand. “Fare you well, friar.”

“Common courtesy? And so quick to dismiss me when I say you have changed.” Dominik took his hand and shook it. “Should you need respite from your travails again, we are here.”

Wheels and axles squeaked as the riders took their places and a horse snorted. Those still securing the goods climbed into the wagons alongside them or sat next to the drivers. Pencheval nodded one last farewell to Dominik, then sat on a wagon next to his backpack.

“Oy! Next time you come, leave the goblins where you found them, yeah?”

Pencheval glanced up at the wall. Howe waved down at him until a sergeant told him to get back on watch. The scout stepped back from the battlements to obey.

The Lion smiled. He had friends and allies now. Friends and allies who were alive and safe from a horde because a stubborn and highly skilled warrior with an Argentsteel sword refused to accept any other outcome.

A warrior. Not an animal contemptuous of all around him. A *warrior* had defeated the threat of this Stonemaster with his skills, refusal to quit, and courage in the face of dire chances. Skills and power that remained even after he put his former contempt for the common folk aside as one more illusion inflicted on him by Terris Lyn.

Not everyone was as those people there, and he was wrong to assume all common folk were vermin on the actions of a few. Good people did exist, and he had saved some of them. Perhaps he should grant others the benefit of the doubt. If they made poor use of it and showed darker colors, he knew exactly what to do about them. He had done it professionally for years.

As for being a hero? Nan insisted that he believe that title was a compliment again. He intended to take her advice but still thought it an absurdity. Heroes? The brightly dressed, sword-flourishing speakers of rhyming couplets in stage plays and bard’s tales? They always seemed to dispatch their foes with such ease. Come the tale’s end, they would disappear back into the mists of fiction until their tales were told again. They never dealt with matters of earning their keep, injury, or mishap.

Those heroes were lies and fables. He would never be one of them and was glad of it. He had been not a hero but a lion when there was need for one, and proud of it once more.

***

"Do you know anything of this 'Peddler,' Your Grace?"

Rennoute chuckled. The Disciple would likely call him 'Your Grace' all through winter, which concerned him little. If it restored her sense of stability until spring, when she could finally be sent to the capital for instruction, so be it.

That was the lesson of the Lion and what he would tell the chronicler who would write about Nan in The Histories. Pencheval's purpose was not merely to rescue the Disciple, as Father Victor believed. His purpose was to remind all those at the castle that becoming a Disciple was its own journey–one that did not begin and end when the Lord on High found a worthy. Not seeing her as anything but his old friend Nan was how the Lion had saved her during his time here, and in recognizing this had contributed to the defeat of the horde.

"I know nothing about him, Nan." Rennoute caught himself from saying 'Disciple' and she greeted it with a relieved smile. "Yet the Silver Lions deal in all manner of contracts and clash more frequently with outlaws and the underworld than we do. He may know of things we do not in that regard, and certainly by personal experience."

"I thought I would find the light in his darkness, Your Grace. I didn't expect him to guide me in return."

"No, and I fear in exchange we will bring him to conflict with his own guild."

Nan recoiled and put her hand over her chest. "Horsefeathers! We saved him from his demons and he fought beside us against a horde. What harm could his guild see in this?"

"He is more now than when he arrived, and in that much we served the purposes of the Lord on High. Yet his guild is set in its ways and will not appreciate the man he has become. If they refuse to tolerate it...he will always be welcome here."

"Come the spring, Your Grace, I will be there. He won't want for allies, even against his guild if need be. Until then, I have responsibilities to the faithful, and the power may assist in keeping winter from taking too many."

"I am honored to have you here, sister. You, as Pencheval, will always be welcome."

"Thank you, Your Grace." Nan pulled down the hood of her robe, closed her eyes, and listened. "Blessed silence. The absence of goblins does so improve the peace."

"It does, sister. It truly does."

***

The Beastwarper Chieftain and the few hundred of the horde that accompanied him trudged through a pass in the mountains it took two days to find. No more than a dozen of the Bonestrippers walked with them. The rest had been slain or scattered at the battle of the mountain-castle in a costly escape from defeat and the Stonemaster. The chieftain shook his head because he knew where it had all gone wrong, and that he could have fled sooner and avoided this.

The human Snow Clan were the masters of that valley. The Stonemaster believed he could prevail with goblin numbers and bat-lizards, fighting them on their own terms to take what was theirs. The power of their god proved stronger than even the Skyfang, however, and they remained masters still.

It was the mountain-castle that had proved their undoing. He had only agreed to attack the humans' clan-home under the belief they had even more knowledge he could steal, as he had with the knowledge of books. The Snow Clan did indeed have knowledge, and they used it to slaughter the horde.

Now the Beastwarper Chieftain would have to rebuild his Clan with those that followed him. Once he had a new clan-home, and re-united with those who remained at the old one, he would put what knowledge he did take to use. He had yet to grasp such human secrets as 'masonry' and 'smithing,' but he had a human of his own to help him find other humans which could teach him these things.

Gaining them by invading that valley again was out of the question. If he wanted more knowledge, he would capture a few humans by stealth and take it. He could question them, for the Allspeaker had survived and traveled with him. His was the caution that might have saved them, and the guide to what should have been in the first place.

All is not lost.

The Beastwarper looked around but saw no one. The Allspeaker and a number of the rabble searched the air for the voice, either confused or cringing.

"Did you hear that?" Beastwarper pulled himself upright on his staff.

I am not there, but I see you, chieftain.

"Are you the Fiend Under The Mountain?"

No. I am knowledge. Power. Survival.

"I have heard these promises in the past. I was fool enough to believe them once. Not again."

Not promises. Reality.

The Beastwarper Chieftain staggered at what felt like a river rushing into his mind-staggered and saw the knowledge it contained. The knowledge of how to make bronze and work it into tools and weaponry. Not just the bits and pieces he thought he could build upon from the humans they had questioned, but everything. Enough to teach and practice it.

This is only a beginning. I know much, and so can you. Enough to make you the master of many clans.

"In exchange for?"

Obedience.

"We are not enough to follow another Chief of Chieftains on a fool's errand. I won't be slain leading goblins into Snow Clan lands again."

Not at all. The humans are mine alone. What I want is for you to build your own clan-home. I want you to be the chieftain of the mountains. If you will but call me your master, I will give you more knowledge. Knowledge is power. You know this to be true.

"We will find our new clan-home. Then, and no sooner, will I consider bowing to another Chief of Chieftains."

You could be the Chief of Chieftains of all goblins. Such is the worth of what I can grant you, if you will but become my servant.

"Not if I am dead." Beastwarper motioned to the followers behind him. "We build a new home, then I will consider your words."

I can be patient with you, for I will never die. But do not trifle with me. You are not the only goblin chieftain that would benefit from my wisdom. Where you refuse, another may accept, as the Stonemaster did. Then you will bow to another Chief of Chieftains when others might have groveled at your feet.

Beastwarper hissed even as he felt the inscrutable presence disappear. Was it truly the one that had given the Stonemaster his power? If it did know more than how to make this 'bronze' it had shown him, it did indeed possess the means to make another powerful. Or himself.

"Send forth scouts. Find the nearest caves where we may make a home. We have found our way."

Rather, the way had found him.

Afterwords

Thank you for reading Silver and the Stone. If you enjoyed this omnibus and want to keep up with more of my work, visit GeneHerington.com and subscribe today. All of my books and where to find them are listed there as well.

Gene Herington

www.ingramcontent.com/pod-product-compliance
Lightning Source LLC
Chambersburg PA
CBHW020345220726
48290CB00014B/1105
* 9 7 8 1 7 3 3 0 1 8 7 1 5 *